COLD HEART
&
ENTWINED

Also by Lynda La Plante

The Legacy
The Talisman
Bella Mafia
Cold Shoulder
Cold Blood
Sleeping Cruelty

Prime Suspect
Seekers
She's Out
Cold Shoulder
The Governor
The Governor II
Trial and Retribution
Trial and Retribution II
Trial and Retribution III
Trial and Retribution IV

LYNDA LA PLANTE was born in Liverpool. She trained for the stage at RADA, and work with the National Theatre and RSC led to a career as a television actress. She turned to writing – and made her breakthrough with the phenomenally successful TV series *Widows*.

She has written eight subsequent novels, *The Legacy*, *The Talisman*, *Bella Mafia*, *Entwined*, *Cold Shoulder*, *Cold Blood*, *Cold Heart* and *Sleeping Cruelty*, and her original script for the much acclaimed *Prime Suspect* won a BAFTA award, British Broadcasting award, Royal Television Society Writers award and the 1993 Edgar Allan Poe Writers award.

Lynda La Plante also received the Contribution to the Media award by Women in Film, a BAFTA award and an Emmy for the drama serial *Prime Suspect 3*, and most recently she has been made an honorary fellow of the British Film Institute.

LYNDA LA PLANTE

COLD HEART
&
ENTWINED

PAN BOOKS

Cold Heart first published 1998 by Macmillan
First published by Pan Books 1998
Entwined first published 1992 by Sidgwick and Jackson
First published by Pan Books 1993

This omnibus edition published 2004 by Pan Books
an imprint of Pan Macmillan Ltd
Pan Macmillan, 20 New Wharf Road, London N1 9RR
Basingstoke and Oxford
Associated companies throughout the world
www.panmacmillan.com

ISBN 0 330 43258 3

A CIP catalogue record for this book is available from
the British Library.

Typeset by SetSystems Ltd, Saffron Walden, Essex
Printed and bound in Great Britain by
Mackays of Chatham plc, Chatham, Kent

COLD HEART

For my beloved father

ACKNOWLEDGEMENTS

I sincerely thank Suzanne Baboneau, Arabella Stein and Philippa McEwan at Macmillan, and the real Lorraine Page whose name I borrowed. Thanks to Gill Coleridge, Esther Newberg, Peter Benedek, and especially to Hazel Orme. I'd also like to thank my team at La Plante Productions: Liz Thorburn, Vaughan Kinghan, script and book editor, Alice Asquith, researcher, Nikki Smith, Christine Harmar-Brown, and Ciara McIlvenny.

With thanks for their contribution to:

Geoffrey Smith
East Hampton Police Department
Sergeant Gilmore and Lieutenant Salcido of the Beverly Hills Police Department
Dr Ian Hill, Department of Forensic Medicine, Guy's Hospital
George W. Clarke, San Diego District Attorney's Office
Tom Rowland of Thomas Rowland Associates
Kathy Byrne of the Chicago Film Office
J. B. Smith of the New Mexico Film Commission
Kerstin Chmielewski from the Berlin Tourist Office
Sotheby's Press Office, New York

But above all my thanks go to a very admirable lady who brought me the story of her life.

THE BULLET blew off virtually his entire face. He was naked, but he appeared to be wearing swimming trunks because of the band of untanned skin which they usually covered. His arms and legs were spread open and his body floated face down. She watched with sick fascination as the blood continued to spread like the petals of a poppy, wider and wider; he was brain dead, but his heart still pumped, and continued for longer than she had calculated. Suddenly his outstretched arms jerked, his fingers clenched and unclenched, and he gave a strange guttural snorting sound, as if his throat were clogged with blood. A few seconds more, and she knew he was dead. Only then did she move away from the edge of the pool.

The bentwood sun chairs were replaced neatly, his towel folded. His sunglasses she put back in their case, and his half-smoked cigarette she left in the ashtray to smoulder and die – slowly, as he had. She wrapped her hand carefully in the edge of her floating silk chiffon wrap to remove the glass she had used, slipped it into the deep pocket of her jacket, then walked soundlessly across the velvety lawn, past the sheets of lead and lumps of rock that Harry Nathan had considered to be sculpture,

1

to enter the house through the garden doors. She took the glass from her pocket, rinsed it and replaced it in the kitchen cabinet. She was fast, meticulous, knowing every inch of the kitchen, even wiping the taps in case she had touched them inadvertently. She surveyed the immaculate kitchen, making sure nothing was left out of place, and then, still barefoot, she returned to the garden the way she had come. By now, Nathan's cigarette had burned itself out, the ash extending for a curved inch and a half in front of the butt. She made her way round the edge of the pool, not even looking at the body, which still floated face down but was now drifting almost in the centre of the deep end. She looked round furtively before picking up the weapon, a heavy Desert Eagle, still wrapped in a silk headscarf. Then she hurried towards a small shrubbery, full of topiary trees clipped into strange geometric shapes that were clearly meant to echo the sculpture. She was careful not to step on the soil but to remain on the grass verge. She fired the gun into the shrubs then quickly tossed it free of the scarf, to land just in front of the first row of plants.

A bird screeched as the sound echoed of the weapon firing, and she thought she heard someone scream in the house, but she didn't go to investigate, didn't even glance back, intent on getting out of Nathan's estate and knowing it would take her at least five minutes to reach her car, parked further down the avenue. She did not put on her shoes until she was standing beside the Mitsubishi jeep. She bleeped it open with the alarm key and gave only a brief, guarded look around to make sure she had not been seen by anyone before she got inside and inserted the key, her hands rock steady as she turned it. The engine sparked into life and she drove off. Harry

Nathan was dead and she was now a wealthy woman, about to regain everything he had taken from her and more. She would savour for ever the look in his eyes when he had seen her take out the heavy gun, seen him step back, half lifting his hands in submission, and then, as she pulled the trigger, there had been a second when she saw fear. She would relish the fear, because she believed that, without doubt, she had just committed the perfect murder.

CHAPTER 1

12 August 1997

LORRAINE PAGE of Page Investigations had not, as yet, moved into a new office, though she had already used part of her cut of the million-dollar bonus from her last case to move from the tiny apartment in Los Angeles she had shared with her former partner Rosie, who had now married Bill Rooney, the ex-police captain who also worked with them. The couple had recently departed for an extended honeymoon in Europe.

The lost feeling hadn't happened for a few days. She had been so caught up in making plans for the wedding, choosing what they would both wear, and the laughter when they forced Rooney to splash out on an expensive suit that had made the rotund man look quite handsome. Everything had been 'fun', particularly now that they had money to spend.

It was not until Rosie and Rooney had departed for their honeymoon that it really hit home: Lorraine missed them. Waving goodbye at the airport had almost brought the tears that didn't come until a few days later. She had been sitting in Rosie's old apartment, now hers, looking at the wedding photographs, and she had no one to share them with, no one to laugh and point out how funny it had been when Rooney spilt champagne on his precious new suit. There was no one who would understand the three of them standing with solemn faces and their glasses raised. Rosie's and Lorraine's had, of course, contained non-alcoholic champagne, but they had raised their glasses for a private toast to their absent friend, Nick Bartello, who had died on their last case.

The photographs, like the small apartment, held such memories, some sweet, some so very sad, but they had made Lorraine decide to buy another place. It had not been an easy decision but she couldn't stand the ghosts – it made the loneliness even worse.

Lorraine's new apartment was on the upper floor of a two-storey condominium built on an old beach-house lot right on the ocean front in Venice Beach, one of four or five blocks where the little houses were so closely packed together that there was no room for front or back yards. Walking round the kooky old bohemian neighbourhood, she found she had already fallen for its lively energy and charm, and she loved the close proximity of the beach. Lorraine didn't think of herself as 'kooky' or 'bohemian'; in fact, in her neat suit and blouse she looked slightly out of place, but the neighbourhood reminded her of when she had been married. It had been tough, trying to juggle her job as a rookie cop and bring up two young kids while her husband studied at home and worked nights in the local liquor store. Money had always been tight, but friends had not, and there had been so much love. Lorraine had money now and she wanted, needed, more friends like Rosie and Rooney. Deep down she ached for all the love she had lost.

While viewing the new apartment, she had caught a glimpse of herself in a full-length mirror. Staring at her image, from the well-cut blonde hair down to her slim ankles in low Cuban heels, the ache had suddenly surfaced, making her gasp. It didn't matter how long ago she and Mike had been divorced, how long it had been since she had seen her daughters, the pain was still raw. In the past she had obliterated it by getting drunk but she was stronger now. She could still feel the dreaded dryness in her mouth and feel herself shaking, but she forced herself to follow the real-estate agent round the rest of the apartment.

'I'll take it,' she announced. 'Just one thing, though. Do the other residents allow dogs?' She lit a cigarette. Tiger, the wolfhound/malamute crossbred canine who had belonged to poor dead Nick Bartello, was now Lorraine's responsibility, and she needed to be near an open space where she could exercise him – clearly, the beach would be perfect.

'I don't think that would be a problem. I presume—'

'Tiger,' Lorraine interjected, using her right hand to indicate with a patting motion that Tiger was about the size of a toy poodle.

'I presume he's house-trained. The landlords of the head lease do have a proviso with regard to animals.'

'Oh, yes, he's the perfect gentleman indoors, professionally trained, exceptionally obedient.' Crossing her fingers behind her back, she hoped that this would soon be true. She didn't want to risk losing the apartment: it felt right, it felt safe.

'I think I could be happy here,' she said softly, and flushed with embarrassment: it sounded stupid. But the agent smiled warmly, eager to do the deal but rather surprised that this elegant, if rather nervous, woman hadn't even asked to see the kitchen. Lorraine insisted they drive to the real-estate office to finalize the sale. She required no mortgage, and arranged a banker's draft for the full amount.

'I'd like measurements of all the rooms so I can order furniture, curtains . . .' She wafted her hand and, as she did, the agent noticed there was no wedding ring – in fact, she wore no jewellery at all. As Lorraine stood up and bent forward to pick up her purse, her silky blonde hair slid forward, revealing a jagged scar that ran from the corner of her eye, a scar that make-up couldn't hide.

Driving back to Rosie's, she recalled her assurances about Tiger. It had proved impossible, to date, to house-train or instil any kind of normal dog behaviour into him. Rooney and Rosie had both tried, but he had become a liability during the pre-wedding arrangements. He would either attack anyone who came into the house, or dis-appear for days on end, and no matter how long they all cajoled him and fed him biscuits, he point-blank refused to wear a collar. Eventually, Lorraine had booked him into a kennel for extensive schooling with a former police-dog handler. If this failed it was unanimously decided that he would be joining his old master Nick Bartello – nobody had been able to train that son-of-a-bitch either.

When she got back to the apartment, Lorraine contacted the kennels. Tiger was progressing but they suggested an extra two weeks' training. They did not elaborate and Lorraine was quite pleased – she needed time to furnish the new apartment. She decided not to take anything from Rosie's place but to start from scratch and buy everything new. At the same time she had resolved to do something about her scar, the scar that reminded her of who she had been, of what she had been. She no longer needed to force herself to look at

8

the ugliness it represented. She wanted to put her past behind her, once and for all.

Lorraine felt as if she was high – she could hardly sleep. The shopping trips to the Beverly Center to buy furnishings and fittings were like stepping back in time. She selected everything she thought she would need, from a bed, dining table and large white sofa to wine-glasses, lamps, dishes and silverware, and arranged for it all to be delivered to the apartment. She wanted everything to be ready for her release from the clinic and she didn't want to lift anything, carrying anything or move so much as a book.

The surgery was extensive. She had decided to have a full face-lift, which was done at the same time as the operations on her scar, which was deep and required skin grafts. She decided to remain at the clinic, pampering herself with beauty treatments, until the wounds had healed. She was still paying for Tiger's 'rehabilitation' and the kennels were beginning to worry that he would become a permanent fixture, but Lorraine assured them that she fully intended to take him back.

When the surgeon, who had not allowed her to look at herself, finally held up a mirror to her face, she wanted to celebrate, to kiss and hug everyone close by.

'You're a very beautiful lady, Lorraine,' the surgeon said softly, as she cocked her head from side to side, drinking in her smooth, scarless cheek, her perfect eyes, the taut skin beneath her chin. He leaned in close. 'Mind you, I can't take all the credit. You have a wonderful bone structure. I just did a little suction beneath your cheekbones, ironed out the laugh lines,' he continued, pointing out what his magic knife had done, taking pride in his work. He asked the nurses their opinion, but

Lorraine didn't hear: she felt as if she was looking into her soul and it made her gasp.

'Happy?' the surgeon asked, lifting his funny bushy eyebrows.

'I used to look like this,' she whispered, wishing Rosie could be there to see the new Lorraine.

While in the clinic, Lorraine had worked out and eaten well and, on her release, she felt fitter than ever before. She gave her entire wardrobe to charity and hit the designer shops with a vengeance. She had never spent so much, so fast. She had always had good taste but now she went for quality, and for the first time in her life she never looked at the price tag. Next she bought a brand-new Cherokee truck and a second-hand Mercedes, the car she had always dreamed of owning. It was in perfect condition, with only twenty thousand on the clock, immaculate leather upholstery, CD player and telephone. As she flicked open the make-up mirror it lit up and she sat smiling at herself, her new beautiful self, as the salesman hovered.

'Yep, this'll do nicely.'

By mid-September, she had found a comfortable office in a small three-storey complex on West Pico Boulevard. Los Angeles had its rapidly changing fashions in office buildings, as it had in pizza toppings and nail extensions, and although the building had only been erected five years ago, the gleaming mirrored exterior was already considered behind the times. But as far as Lorraine was concerned this was an advantage, as it brought the rental more within the range she felt justified in paying. There was a smart lobby and a pleasant Filipino doorman, good security and – the biggest advantage – right across the street was Rancho Park with acres of grass for Tiger to run in. She thought about him, but kept putting off calling the kennels to say she would collect him.

The air-conditioned office, tastefully decorated and filled with plain ash furniture, also boasted an en suite bathroom and kitchen, plus a reception area furnished with sofas and coffee table. 'Page Investigations' was printed in letters of gold leaf on the main entrance door by the electronic, security-coded entryphone. The letter-headed paper, cards and office equipment were chosen with meticulous care. Only the old computer hardware from her last office was retained.

Ready to begin work, Lorraine deliberated over the wording for newspaper and magazine advertisements before committing to six-month runs. She then contacted three secretarial agencies, and asked that applicants should send their CVs before she interviewed them.

By October, appointments had been scheduled with the three applicants she felt were most suited to the job. Still running high on her own adrenalin, she didn't see them all: midway through the first interview she decided to offer the job to Rob Decker, even though she had really wanted a woman.

Decker was about twenty-eight, tanned, blond and good-looking, had worked mostly for television executives, had even tried acting himself, and his account of his unsuccessful thespian attempts made her laugh. He had a top shorthand speed, understood computers, and had a deep, laid-back voice that harked back to his theatrical endeavours. He was fit, with a tight, muscular body, and was wearing an expensive fawn linen suit, pale blue shirt and suede shoes with no socks. He had a Cartier wristwatch but, thankfully, no other jewellery. He carried his CV and other details of his varied career –

knowledge of weapons and shooting skills – in a soft leather briefcase, with his karate certificates and gun licence. With her history, Lorraine would have found it difficult to acquire a licence, but it wasn't the fact that she would have a gun-toting secretary that impressed her – she just liked him.

Decker was relaxed but not too relaxed, respectful but not obsequious, and when she asked why he had applied for the job he shrugged, admitting without any embarrassment that it sounded better than working tables at a bar and that money was short. His last employer had refused to give him references which had made it difficult to get a decent job since. Lorraine was confused: she had references from his last employer in front of her on her pristine desk. Rob nodded towards the paper, and said he had typed it himself. When she asked why he had no references from his last employer, he told her that he had refused to go down on him and, equally candidly, that he was homosexual. Then he had laughed and added that she probably knew that already, and probably he had not got this job either.

'Yes, you have.' Lorraine surprised even herself. She hadn't given it as much thought as she should have.

Decker's handshake was strong and he assured her that he would not let her down.

'I hope not, Rob. This is very important to me – I want the agency to succeed more than you will ever know. Maybe when you get to know me better you'll find out why, but in the meantime, when can you start?'

'Why not right now? We need some plants in here, and I have a contact in a nursery – I get the best, half-price.'

Lorraine arranged salary and office keys, discussed hours, and then, almost as an afterthought, asked if he liked dogs. He told her another anecdote, about when he had worked in a poodle parlour, and she said that Tiger was not exactly a poodle and needed firm handling. Just before Decker left he seemed suddenly vulnerable, and Lorraine liked him for that too. She knew Rob Decker would become a good friend.

The following morning, Lorraine looked over her office. As promised, Decker had bought two ficus trees in copper buckets, a mass of pink and white impatiens in a glazed terracotta planter, and a deep square plain glass vase, which he had filled with Casablanca lilies and placed on the little table in Reception. The whole place seemed to have come alive. He had left on her desk a note of the cost of each plant and a receipt, plus watering instructions. He had also bought coffee, tea, cookies and skimmed milk, and a new percolator, which he insisted was his own, so that not only was there a sweet fragrance from the blooms but a wonderful smell of fresh coffee.

There were no calls and no work on offer, so at lunch-time Decker and Lorraine went off to buy some exhibition posters and prints from the Metropolitan Museum of Art shop, as the office walls were bare. He also talked Lorraine into stopping off to pick up an elegant uplighter to put in Reception, a swing-arm graphite lamp, a violet glass ashtray for her desk, and – having divined her sweet tooth as though by magic – a jar of jelly beans. By three o'clock their new purchases were on display. The advertising had, as yet, failed to generate any work, but she was not disheartened, she knew things would take time, and during the afternoon they had been able to get to know each other better.

Lorraine never divulged everything about her background, but Decker knew she had been a cop, and knew she had had a drink problem. In fact, he was such a good listener she felt that she had told him more than she really should have, but he was equally forthcoming about his life and his partner, with whom he had lived for eight years – Adam Elliot, late forties, a writer for films, TV or washing-powder commercials, still hoping to crack the big time before he turned fifty.

They left the office at six. Not one phone call had come in: it was Thursday, 26 October. Decker had asked Lorraine if she would like to have dinner over the weekend at his place, but despite the offer of masala chicken and chocolate pie, she had declined. She felt that perhaps she should keep a little distance between them.

Friday was just as silent, telephone-wise and job-wise, and they had talked even more, had lunch together again and discussed how they should rethink the adverts. Decker suggested they use Adam to reword them in a way that might grab a potential client. Again Lorraine refused his offer of lunch or dinner over the weekend. The initial buzz of her getting her new life together began to dry up. She didn't feel so confident any more and even her new face began to annoy her: she was so used to flicking her hair forward over her scar, but there was nothing to hide any more. She began to wonder if it had all been make-believe and that the old Lorraine still lurked ready to pull the new one down.

She wished she had accepted Decker's invitation, as she was alone the entire weekend, going over her accounts, totting up her bank balance. She was still in good shape financially as well as physically, but she had spent a lot of money on pampering herself and seeing it in black and white made her a little scared at her foolishness. Maybe she should have taken her time, but it was too late now – the money was gone. She had just over two hundred thousand dollars in her account, a lot, but at the same time she knew that, realistically, she could not keep the office and Decker running without some finances coming in: the outgoings would drain her savings. Still, any new venture needed time. But despite her forced optimism, something was eating away at her. She awoke one night with a faint voice in her head, telling her over and over she didn't deserve this new life. As if on cue, the phone rang. It was three o'clock in the morning.

'Hello,' Lorraine said suspiciously.

'Hi, blossom, how's things?'

'Rosie?'

'Yeah, guess where we are? No, I'll tell you, Vienna! My God, Lorraine, it's *unbelievable*!'

Lorraine lay back on the pillow as Rosie listed, at full volume, the restaurants and sightseeing tours. It was so nice to hear her voice, even if it was ear-splitting. She sounded so close, as if she was in the next room. 'Eh! How's life? You found a guy?'

'Nope, not yet, but I'm looking.'

'Well, you make sure you don't get one that snores!'

Lorraine smiled as Rosie continued to fill her in on the trials of sleeping with Rooney, never once pausing for breath. 'Hey, you there? Or I did I just bore you off the phone?'

'No, Rosie, I'm still here, making notes in case I meet my Mr Right.' She could feel Rosie's smile. She gave her the new address and phone numbers, and she could hear Rosie repeat them to big, bulbous-nosed Bill Rooney. Then she put Rooney on the phone and he complained about the cost of the call and then said, so softly, in a voice she would never have expected from the old, hardened cop, 'You know, Lorraine, I've got a lot to thank you for. Not just for making us a load of money, but if it wasn't for you, I'd never have met the woman who's made me happier than I ever thought possible.'

There was a long pause and Lorraine could hear his heavy breathing at the other end of the line.

'I love her so much,' he mumbled, and then repeated it, sounding almost in tears.

Rosie grabbed the phone, laughing. 'He's drunk – but he tells me that every day. Nice, huh? Hey, I better go. We'll send you postcards, bring you presents and . . . Oh, yeah, can't wait to see your new place.'

Lorraine said goodbye. It didn't matter that Rosie had shown little or no interest in what was happening in her life because right now it didn't feel too wonderful and she couldn't see anyone in her future saying they loved her. Lorraine was lonely – deeply lonely.

The following morning she went to her local AA meeting, the only social life she had. She still couldn't rid herself of the feeling of isolation: it didn't make her want to drink, but it made her think, and face the fact that she had no friends. She started thinking about her ex-husband and his family. She had not seen her two daughters for a long, long time, and though they knew where she was, they had made no contact. She often thought about going to see them, but always talked herself out of it. She didn't want to disrupt their lives any more than she knew she had already.

She was glad when Tiger's trainer, Alan Pereira, called to say that the dog training was now complete, he would bring Tiger home. Lorraine perked up, even put on some make-up, then laughed at herself. Some weekend date, the return of Tiger.

Tiger was returned, subdued, wearing a collar in rainbow colours, his coat freshly washed, and his teeth cleaned. She had not realized how big he was, or how thick and beautiful his coat. She'd also forgotten his piercing large blue eyes.

'You got one stubborn son-of-a-bitch here,' Alan said, and Tiger's blue eyes were doleful as he first sat, then went through sit, stand, stay and heel. Lorraine was even more impressed when, on the command 'Bed,' Tiger slunk to a flower-printed foam basket and lay down.

He remained quiet, head on paws, as she cooked her supper, came like a lamb and sat when she slipped on his lead to take him for his evening walk. He performed his necessary functions, returned, ate his meal and even returned to his bed. It was about twelve o'clock when Lorraine was woken up by something tugging at her sheets. She sat bolt upright to be met with Tiger's face, and to see his two massive front paws on her bed. 'Bed. Go to bed *now*.' He slunk to the door, tail between his legs, nosed it wider open and disappeared.

In the morning she woke to find the dog's prone body stretched out beside her, with just six inches between them, comatose and snoring gently. Lorraine nudged him and, still with eyes firmly shut, he gave a low growl, his jaw opening a fraction to reveal his cleaned white fangs. She thought of Rooney snoring, and smiled, but then said with great authority, 'Bed, go to your bed. *Now*.' The tail thumped, just a fraction. 'I mean it, you're pushing your luck. Step out of line, pal, and it's the big kennel in the sky, you understand me? You're only on remand, Tiger.'

17

He was motionless, eyes closed, just a flicker of his tail. 'Okay, you can stay . . . just for a few minutes, you hear me?' She lay there, feeling the huge weight of him beside her, then squinted at the bedside clock. It was six o'clock. 'You know what time it is?' she said, turning on her side. She went back to sleep and at some point between the hours of six and seven thirty, that six inches closed. When she next opened her eyes, he was sleeping nose to nose with her, one paw gently resting across her chest.

'I don't believe this . . .' But she couldn't resist rubbing his ears. Cleverly, he never opened his eyes, just gave a long, satisfied sigh.

Before they went out for a morning jog, Lorraine discovered that Tiger had chewed two of her new shot-silk cushions and destroyed his floral bed. On returning, he was not interested in dog food, but devoured her cereal, nuts and fruit with natural yogurt. He followed her into the bedroom, nosed open the shower door, and padded after her while she dressed. He remained at her heels throughout the day, sat close to her on the sofa watching TV, and no amount of loud yells made him return to the living room when she got into bed. He wasn't a fool, and instead of climbing onto the other side of the king-size bed, he lay down beside it. But he was right next to her in the morning, his breath hot on her neck.

'Hey, this has got to stop, pal,' she said, but then blew it by hugging him close, and he knew he had got her. She just could not resist his love, because that was what she felt from the giant animal – love, pure, unadulterated love – and by Monday morning they had, although she hated to admit it, already got into a routine. All his training, with the exception of allowing her to slip on his collar, had gone out of the window. Tiger had moved in on Lorraine as no man would have dared to, and he loved her with a passion. He sat in the passenger seat of the Cherokee, his nose out of the window and his ears blown back by the wind.

Decker was overwhelmed by Tiger, who growled at him, teeth bared, until Lorraine shouted at him, 'Shut up! This is friend, this is Decker.'

'Jesus Christ, Mrs Page! He's enormous. What on earth kind of breed is he?'

'Mixed, wolfhound and—'

'Donkey?'

Tiger was not too sure about Decker or the office. He made a slow tour of each room and cocked his leg on one of the ficus trees.

'You sure as hell aren't a poodle,' Decker said warily, but when the telephone rang his attention was distracted. He snatched it up – this was the first call that had come in.

'Page Investigations,' he said coolly, as a pair of ice blue eyes stared him out across the desk top. 'May I have your name? Mrs Page is on the other line right now.' Decker jotted down 'Cindy Nathan', glaring back at Tiger.

'Who is it?' Lorraine whispered, from her office doorway.

'A Cindy Nathan, just wait a second.' Lorraine watched as Decker flicked the phone onto speaker and held it for one beat, two beats as he grinned and gave her the thumbs-up sign.

'Cindy Nathan, that is N-A-T . . .' said a low voice, spelling out the surname.

'I have that, Ms Nathan,' said Decker, 'and may I ask what your enquiry is about?'

'It's not an enquiry, I want Lorraine Page – is she there or not?'

Tiger gave a lethal growl, but as Lorraine pointed at him, he shut up.

'I'm sorry, Ms Nathan, but, as I said, Mrs Page is on the other line. If you could just tell me what your enquiry is. I am Rob Decker, Mrs Page's secretary.'

'Really? Well, Rob, as soon as she gets off the other line, get her to call me. It's urgent.' She dictated a number, and hung up.

Decker swore, scribbling down the numbers.

Lorraine threw up her hands. 'Jesus Christ, did you get the number? If that was our first case you just lost it.'

He leaned back in his chair. 'You don't know who Cindy Nathan is?'

Lorraine was furious. 'No, I don't. There's a lot of people I don't know, Decker. I had a long time when I didn't recall my own name. So who is she?'

'She's Harry Nathan's wife.'

'Really, and who the fuck is he?' she snapped.

'The head of Maximedia, the movie studio, though they do a lot of other stuff too. He used to be married to Sonja Sorenson.'

Lorraine leaned on his desk. 'I never heard of her either.'

Decker rolled his eyes to the ceiling. 'Lorraine! She's big in the art world – she owned a gallery on Beverly

Drive but moved back to New York after they divorced. Harry Nathan used to do spoofy, goofball comedies – *Killer Bimbos Ate My Neckties* kind of thing, though lately it's been more like *Ate My Shorts*, if you get what I mean.' He gave her a meaningful look. 'Not exactly family entertainment, shall we say? So, you want to call her? Or would you like me to connect you, ma'am?' He jotted the number on a yellow sticker holding it up on the tip of his forefinger. Lorraine snatched the note and banged her office door closed – only to have to open it again as Tiger threw himself at it barking.

'Get out,' she yelled. Then she sat down at her desk. 'She said she wanted me to call her?' she called to Decker.

The intercom light flashed. 'Yes, Mrs Page, and she seemed a trifle hyper. Shall I get Mrs Nathan on the line for you, Mrs Page?'

'Yes!'

Cindy Nathan was in her silk Hermès sarong, barefoot, clutching the mobile phone and staring into the deep end of the swimming pool. Henry 'Harry' Nathan was floating face down in it with a thin trickle of blood still colouring the bright blue water. She heard the police sirens, saw the Hispanic servants hovering by the industrial glass-brick doors with which Harry had replaced the former french windows and leaded diamond panes.

Her phone rang.

'Cindy Nathan,' she answered flatly.

'This is Lorraine Page. You called me and . . . hello? Mrs Nathan?'

Cindy's voice was barely audible. 'Yes.'

'This is Lorraine Page, of Page Investigations.'

'Are you a detective?'

'Yes, I run an investigation company.'

'I want to hire you, because I'm just about to be arrested for my husband's murder.'

'I'm sorry, could you repeat that?'

'I didn't kill him. I didn't kill him.' Cindy stared at the body. 'I need you, please come immediately.' She reeled off an address, then hung up.

Lorraine stared at the phone, then shouted to Decker, 'She's hung up, did you get that?'

'Yep, I got it. Maybe she read the advert – probably in *Variety*.'

Lorraine replaced the receiver and walked into Reception. 'What did you say?'

'I ran an advert for you in the *Hollywood Reporter*, plus one in *Screen International*, *Variety*—'

'What?'

Decker rummaged around his desk and laid out a fax. 'I told you Elliot was good. He suggested the wording.'

'Elliot?'

'My partner, Adam, but I always call him Elliot, he always calls me Decker. I said we needed him to beef up our adverts, and . . .'

Lorraine's face had tightened. 'What?'

'They only ran yesterday, I told you. I said he was good.'

'Lemme see,' she said tightly.

'Sure, you paid for them.' Decker passed over the fax.

Lorraine read it in disbelief. It was not really an advert, more a treatment for a TV show: 'The best, the one

22

agency that caters for the people that need discretion . . .' highlighted '. . . money no object . . .' highlighted again '. . . clients too famous to name, PRIVATE INVESTIGATION means what we say – PRIVATE. If it's blackmail, stalkers, drug abuse, underage sex, call us – no case too small, too dangerous, too notorious. We issue a confidentiality contract as standard.'

Her jaw dropped as she read the list of high-profile cases with which Page Investigations was supposed to have been involved. 'My God, this is disgusting.'

'Good, though.'

'But it's a pack of lies. You can't say we worked for these people when we didn't. I've never read anything so ridiculous.'

'Maybe, but you'll never get anyone to query it – most, as you will see, are dead. We can say we acted for River Phoenix, but who's to know we didn't because he can't . . .'

Lorraine re-read the list of dead movie stars, studio producers, executives, bankers, politicians – even Jackie Onassis' name appeared. 'This is a gross distortion of facts,' she said.

'Yes, I know, but we got a result. Cindy Nathan.'

Lorraine leaned on his desk. 'You should have run this by me first. This is illegal, unethical, and we could be sued. These people may be dead, but they'll have relatives, and lawyers. Pull the adverts this morning, Decker.'

'Will do, Mrs Page.'

She turned at her door, serious. 'You never do this kind of thing again. You have to have my approval for any advert, in fact, for anything going out of this office. Is that clear? I'll call in when I know more – and give Tiger a walk if I'm not back this afternoon.'

23

'Yes, Mrs Page.'

She closed her office door as Tiger threw himself at it.

Lorraine got into the Cherokee and drove rapidly through Century City to take the short cut behind the Beverly Hilton and into Beverly Hills: she smiled, as she always did, as the signs of wealth and ostentation began to increase as steadily as the gradient of Whittier Drive. As the properties grew larger, hedges and trees grew thicker to keep out prying eyes, but behind them could be glimpsed a pick-and-mix assortment of architectural styles. The more traditional bungalows and hacienda-type dwellings rubbed shoulders with mock everything else – Dutch colonial and Cape Cod-style, art-deco, Tudor follies, steel and glass boxes that had been futur-istic thirty years ago.

Lorraine knew she must be getting closer to the Nathan property. She was now on the borders of Beverly Hills and Bel Air, and after a quick glance at Decker's directions, she drew up at the enormous bare metal gates, with Gestapo-style searchlights mounted on the posts. A man was waiting for her. 'Are you Lorraine Page?' he asked.

'Yes, I am.'

He was thin, balding and nervous. 'I am Cindy Nathan's lawyer. She has insisted I speak with you, but I want you to know that I have already contacted my own investigation advisers and all this is now in the hands of the police. They have taken Mrs Nathan in for question-ing but I'm sure she'll be released without charge as soon as the facts have been established. Right now, the position is . . . very confusing.'

Lorraine nodded. 'I'm afraid it is. You see, I don't know exactly what has happened.'

'She shot her husband. Harry Nathan is dead. The police are at the poolside now, there's forensic and paramedics and . . . I can't allow you to come inside. I have to go to Mrs Nathan.'

Lorraine smiled. 'Maybe I should come with you, as Mrs Nathan was adamant that I speak with her.'

'That is impossible. You will not be allowed to see her. As I said, this is police business now.'

'Really?'

'Yes, there's nothing you can do here. I will, of course, pay you whatever retainer was agreed, but as I said, the police are taking care of this now. So if you would let me have your fees to date.'

Lorraine hesitated. 'Do you have a card?'

'I'm sorry, yes, of course.' He passed it over. 'The police are not allowing anyone access to the premises.'

Lorraine looked at his card: Joel H. Feinstein, attorney at law. 'Fine, I'll send you my invoice – but just as a matter of interest, is Mrs Nathan being held at the Beverly Hills PD or elsewhere?'

Lorraine drove east on Santa Monica Boulevard, and turned left on Rexford into the bizarre new complex of heavy romanesque arches and colonnades that now housed the Beverly Hills police department. She knew it was unlikely that she would be allowed to see Cindy, even if she announced herself as a private investigator engaged by Mrs Nathan. She was thinking about what moves she could make when an officer she knew, who had done some private work for her on a previous case, walked up to the car parked directly in front of her: James Sharkey, still as fat as ever, still hauling his pants up over his pot belly.

'Hi, how ya doing?' She locked her car and headed towards him. For a moment he didn't recognize her, then gave her a brief nod while digging in his pockets for his car keys. When she asked about Cindy Nathan, he started to unlock his filthy, dented Pontiac. 'I need ten minutes with her,' Lorraine said quietly.

Sharkey laughed and shook his head. He was about to open the car door when Lorraine moved closer. 'You on the case?' she asked.

She knew he was, just by his attitude and the way he looked furtively around the parked cars. He jangled his keys.

'Meal break. Lady is pretty shook up – not talking straight and asking for raspberry milk-shakes . . . with chocolate topping.' Sharkey wasn't putting himself on the line, but she could take the lady her milk-shake, maybe palm the female officer, Joan, who was sitting her. Sharkey pocketed five hundred dollars and Lorraine went for the milk-shake. He had promised he'd have a word with Joan. He lied, he always had been a cheap, lying bastard, as Lorraine discovered when she had to pay another two hundred to persuade Verna to take a toilet break.

Cindy was not held in a cell but in an interview room in the basement of the station. Lorraine walked in and put down the hideous-looking drink.

Cindy was very young, so small that Lorraine towered above her, with a heart-shaped face as perfect as her superwaif figure. Even though she wore no make-up and her blonde hair was twisted into a knot and secured with what appeared to be a barbecue skewer, all of Lorraine's plastic surgery, health clinics and exercise paled beside this woman, who was so astonishingly beautiful. Added to her perfect features was a sweetness and vulnerability, whose impact was immediate. Perhaps the reason she had called in response to the advert run by Decker was that she was as innocent as she looked.

'I'm Lorraine Page,' Lorraine said calmly.

Cindy's brow puckered. 'I'm sorry, who?'

'I'm a private investigator. You called my office, we spoke earlier.'

'I didn't do it! I didn't kill him, and Mr Feinstein won't believe it.'

Lorraine sat down and took out a notebook. 'Do you want me to investigate the circumstances of your husband's death, Mrs Nathan?'

'I guess so. I mean, can they keep me here? I've told them everything I know. Is this for me?' She prodded at the froth on the milk-shake with her index finger, then licked it.

'I don't know what has been agreed, Mrs Nathan. Just tell me about what happened. Did you make a statement?'

'I can't remember. I called the police and I called Mr Feinstein and told him I found Harry in the pool. I was sleeping and . . . then I heard the gunshot. I guess that was what I heard. It wasn't all that loud, though, just a sort of dull bang.'

Lorraine was making notes but keeping half an eye on the open door. 'Then what did you do?'

'I got up and went onto the patio. I could see the pool, I saw Harry and I called out to him. He looked like he was swimming, floating but . . . well, he didn't

27

answer, so then I went back into the house, and through the sun room, and . . .' She chewed her lip. 'When I got closer, I could see the blood, an' he wasn't swimming at all, and he had no trunks on, face down.'

'Did you touch him – I mean, go into the pool?'

'Oh, no. I ran back into the house, I was hysterical, an' then I called the cops.'

'Then you called my office?'

'What?'

'After the police you called my office.'

'No, no, I never called you. I thought maybe someone had called you for me, understand? I mean, why would I call you?'

It was odd, Lorraine thought. Cindy Nathan was behaving very strangely for someone whose husband had just been murdered, especially when she was a prime suspect and about to be charged. She seemed more distracted than upset, twice unfastening her hair and retwisting it round the wooden spike, asking why there wasn't a straw for the shake.

'So you did not ask me to meet with you?'

'No, I just said so. What's going on?'

Lorraine tapped her notebook. 'Well, I don't know either, but if you want me to look into your case, if you feel you need me—'

'Do you think I should have someone? I mean, are you a lawyer?'

'No, Mrs Nathan, I'm a private investigator, as I said.' Lorraine handed the girl her card, but she hardly looked at it.

'I don't know what I should do – maybe wait for Mr Feinstein. He'll tell me what I should do. Right now I'm all confused.'

'It must be terrible for you,' Lorraine said quietly.

Cindy lifted her delicate shoulders. 'Mr Feinstein'll sort it out, I guess.'

'I hope so, and please feel free to call me if you do want me to investigate the death of your husband.'

Joan returned, crooked her finger at Lorraine then jerked her thumb, indicating for her to leave, sharpish.

Cindy didn't even look at Joan. 'Right now I'm more worried about what's going to happen to me, because I didn't do it. I never shot Harry, but a lot of his friends won't believe it.'

'Why?'

Cindy Nathan gave that little shrug of her shoulders again. ''Cos I was always threatening him. I never got around to doing anything, though.'

'Well, somebody did. You're sure it was your husband in the swimming pool?'

Joan became slightly aggressive. 'Come on, don't get me in trouble. Out now.'

Cindy Nathan's wide, cornflower-blue eyes stared at the wall. 'Yes, yes, it was him, face down. It was Harry, all right.' And two big tears rolled down her cheeks.

Lorraine went out of the building, down the curving walkway that looked more like the approach to a smart office complex than a police department. As she bleeped open the Cherokee with her alarm key, she saw Cindy Nathan's lawyer standing by a black Rolls-Royce, parked on Rexford, arguing with two uniformed police officers. So heated was their exchange that they paid Lorraine no attention as she drove past.

*

The following morning, Decker was already brewing coffee and collecting the leaves the ficus trees seemed to shed every night when Tiger bounded in, almost knocking him off his feet.

'I've got all the newspapers. Mrs Nathan was released without charge last night. She's front page in most of the tabloids.'

Lorraine glanced over them. 'Well, until I hear back from her, there's not a lot I can do. She was very . . .' She frowned. She'd been thinking about her meeting with Cindy Nathan since the early hours. 'She wasn't exactly flaky, just, I don't know, not reacting the way she should have. I mean, she didn't seem to understand . . .'

'The trouble she's in?' Decker enquired, carrying Lorraine's coffee into her office.

'Yeah, I suppose so. Maybe she was in shock. They give any more details about her?'

'They certainly do. It was her automatic, by the way, slug taken from Nathan's head.'

'What?'

'She also inherits the house and about half of Maximedia, as his widow,' Decker said.

'Well, she won't if they can make a murder rap stick to her.'

'Mmm, well, according to the *LA Times*, it looks like that's a sort of foregone conclusion.' He rummaged through the paper to find the rest of the leading article from page one. 'Apparently Cindy Nathan threatened to shoot her husband last month at Morton's restaurant. They had a big slanging match in front of a packed dining room, and they had to drag her out.'

Lorraine sipped her coffee. She was now leafing through all the various papers, in which Decker had marked the relevant stories in green felt-tipped pen. 'She said she never called us,' she remarked, lighting a cigarette.

'Well, that's ridiculous. Of course she did. And we've got it taped.'

'You taped the call?'

'All calls. I protect you at all times, ma'am.' He slipped his headphones on.

'Play it for me, would you?' Lorraine continued reading, glancing at the pictures of Cindy Nathan being assisted into the lawyer's Rolls with her hands covering her face. The press had worked fast: they also had numerous glamour shots of her – she had been in a TV soap for a few weeks, but most of the photographs were sexy poses in swimsuits and lingerie. 'Shit, she's only twenty years old,' Lorraine said, not that Cindy had looked older – it just surprised her that she was so young. At the bleep-bleep of the answerphone she looked up.

Decker was searching for Cindy's call. He eased off his headphones. 'I fucked up, I can't find that call.'

'Jesus Christ, Decker, this is important. We need that recording. Cindy Nathan said she never made the call to the office. If Cindy didn't make that call, somebody did, someone who knew Harry Nathan was dead – maybe because they had shot him, understand, sweetheart? *That call is very important.'*

Decker was flushing bright red. 'You spoke to Cindy on the phone and met her. Did you think it was the same voice? I mean, do *you* think she made the call?'

Lorraine lifted her hands in the air. 'I dunno . . . and I'm not wasting time thinking about it. Like I just said, let's move on. I'm down seven hundred dollars on this fiasco.'

Decker was dispatched to get any back issues of articles on Cindy Nathan, and Lorraine read every newspaper. Harry Nathan had been married three times and there were photographs of Kendall Nathan, his second wife, a thin, dark woman who looked to be in her late thirties, and Sonja Sorenson, the sculptress, a tall, formidably elegant woman with prematurely white hair. Lorraine clipped out the pictures and the accompanying coverage, then tossed the rest into the trash can.

The phone rang and made her jump but she waited a moment before she picked it up. 'Page Investigations,' she said brightly.

It was Decker, speaking from the car phone. 'Hi, it's me. Turn the TV on. It just came over the radio. Cindy Nathan's been arrested for the murder of her husband.'

Lorraine hurried into Reception and switched on the TV. There was Cindy Nathan, almost hidden by a battery of cameras, being hurried into the police department. Feinstein, her lawyer, his arms wide, was trying to protect his client. She looked tiny and frightened, in a simple white linen button-through dress and carrying her jacket.

Lorraine sat on the edge of the sofa with Tiger at her feet. Then she shot up, tripping over Tiger as she snatched up a tape and rammed it into the video machine. At that moment Decker returned. 'Quick! Video this, will you?' She passed him the remote control. They recorded the coverage of Cindy Nathan's arrest every time it was screened – a lot was repetitive but they learned that she came from Milwaukee and had left at fifteen after winning a beauty competition. A few modelling jobs followed, and then her short stint in the soap drama *Paradise Motel* in which she played a chambermaid, not very well.

Harry Nathan was more handsome than Lorraine had expected, a tall, lean, muscular man with dark hair, worn quite long, and a dazzling, though somehow charmless smile. The still photographs of him were glamorous, mostly taken at society functions, premières, Oscar nights, with celebrities on his arm. His associates from the studio said in interviews that Nathan would be greatly missed by all who had ever had the pleasure of working with him, and his secretary, in floods of tears, was so distraught she could hardly speak.

Lorraine continued to watch the news coverage at home. It said nothing new. There was no mention of where she was being held pending arraignment.

Nathan was a self-made millionaire and renowned art collector, who had moved from making commercials to directing zany comedy movies, which had been a big hit back in the eighties. He had then turned his attention to producing rather than directing, and had moved gradually towards cheap, adult-oriented movies on the verge of porn.

Lorraine was about to call it a night when, channel-surfing, she caught an exclusive interview with Harry Nathan's second wife, Kendall. It struck her that there had been neither comment nor reaction from the woman who had been married longest to Harry Nathan, Ms Sorenson.

Kendall Nathan whispered that she was deeply shocked by events, and also felt compassion for Cindy. She had been married to Harry Nathan for four years and knew better than anyone that he had been difficult to live with, but their divorce had been amicable, and she had continued to enjoy a deep friendship with her ex-husband. They had also remained business partners.

33

Then she gave a tremulous smile, her voice breaking. 'Harry was always an honourable man whose many friends will be devastated, as I am, by his tragic and untimely death.'

Most people would have focused on Kendall's performance as a grieving woman, but Lorraine was trying to ascertain whether it could have been Kendall who had called her agency.

The morning newspapers were full of the update on the shooting, and as there were no other job prospects Lorraine and Decker cut out all the articles and pinned them together with the previous day's.

At twelve they had a call from a Mrs Walgraf asking for an appointment with regard to her divorce.

At two o'clock another appointment was booked and, to Lorraine's astonishment, a third call came in at four. The next two days were busy.

After being held at the Cybil Brand Institute for Women in the female facility of the Los Angeles County jail, Cindy Nathan was duly arraigned on charges of murder, pleaded not guilty, and was released on bail, security set at three million dollars. No one saw her leave the courthouse, as she was taken out through a small back entrance because of the number of press waiting outside. Her lawyer read a statement on her behalf: she was innocent and begged to be left alone to mourn the loss of the husband she adored. She would give no further press statements or interviews in the lead-up to the trial as she was pregnant. Feinstein assured the press that he was confident that all charges against his client would be dismissed, and that Mrs Nathan needed rest and care.

Her pregnancy was in the early stages and the stress of her arrest had made her ill. She was now fearful, Feinstein ended, that she might lose the child for which she and her husband had prayed.

Three weeks after Cindy Nathan's release, Lorraine had traced one missing daughter, and had discovered that Mrs Walgraf's husband had obviously been preparing for his divorce for many months before his wife had become aware of his intentions.

Mrs Walgraf did not have the money to pay Lorraine, who would not press her – she felt sorry for the woman.

'Well, let's hope we get something a bit more financially rewarding next,' Decker said.

Lorraine yawned. It was almost time to leave. Tiger was stretched out on his back on the pretty cherry-coloured sofa in Reception, his legs in the air. 'He's not supposed to get up on that,' she said, irritated.

'I know, my dear, but you try and shift him!'

The phone rang and Decker snatched it up. It was the main reception downstairs. He listened, then covered the receiver. 'It's Mrs Nathan. She's downstairs. She wants to see you.'

Lorraine smiled. 'You know, I thought I'd hear from her again. Ask her to come up.'

Lorraine put on some fresh lipstick and ran a comb quickly through her hair. She was just checking her reflection when Decker tapped and opened her door. Tiger was barking and tried to get into the office between Decker's legs. 'Mrs Nathan to see you, Mrs Page. Sit!'

35

Tiger slunk off to the sofa and lay flat on it with his head on his paws.

Decker closed the office door and returned to his desk, wishing he could be privy to the conversation. He was beginning to like the job. He'd been worried during the past week as there had been little to do, but now he couldn't wait to make a quiet call to Adam Elliot to tell him who had arrived.

Cindy Nathan wore dark glasses, a short powder blue princess-line dress, low, peep-toe shoes in white patent leather, and a silver chain and padlock, fastened tightly, like a dog collar, round her neck: a gift from her loving spouse, Lorraine had no doubt. She didn't have a purse, just a small white-leather billfold.

'Please sit down. Sorry about my dog. He's supposed to be trained, but he hasn't got it quite right yet. Can I offer you tea or coffee?'

'No, nothing, thank you.' She was perched on the edge of the chair.

'How are you?'

'Oh, I'm fine, get sick in the mornings, but they say the first few months are the worst,' Cindy said. 'Do you have children?'

Lorraine nodded. 'Two daughters. They live with their father.' She said it quickly, wanting to avoid a long conversation about births and pregnancies.

'Harry's other kid didn't live – this would have been his only child. It would be terrible if it was born in prison.'

Lorraine looked at her fingers. 'Do you think that's a possibility?'

36

'That's why I'm here. I need someone on my side.'

'What about your lawyer?'

'Oh, I have a whole team of lawyers, LA's best.'

'And what do they say?'

'Oh, they seem pretty sure I did it. They don't say it, it's just how they ask me all these questions, over and over.'

'Do you know what the evidence is against you, Mrs Nathan?'

Cindy looked down at her toenails, painted electric blue. 'Well, the gun was mine.'

'Are your fingerprints on it?'

'Yes.'

'And they have the gun?'

'The police found it in the shrubbery by the pool.'

'Did you fire it, Mrs Nathan?'

'Yes.'

'But you've said you did not kill your husband.'

'Yes, but you asked if I fired it and I did,' Cindy said, with a childish sort of exactness. 'A few times, just practising. Once I fired it at Harry, but I missed and there were blanks in it anyway.'

Lorraine picked up a pen and twisted it in her fingers. 'Did you fire your gun on the day your husband was found dead?'

'No.'

'Where did you leave it the last time you used it?'

'In our bedroom, on my side of the bed, in a silver box. Harry had guns all over the house – he was paranoid about security. He had a licence, and he even had a gun in his car.'

'Could I come out to the house, Mrs Nathan?'

Cindy nodded. 'Will you say that you're going to give

37

me a massage? I don't want them to know. I don't think they would like it, you know, me hiring you, without telling them.'

'Who are you referring to, Mrs Nathan?'

'Oh, the lawyers and the staff.'

Lorraine leaned back in her chair. 'Did you love your husband, Mrs Nathan?'

'Yes.'

'As his widow, are you his main beneficiary?'

'I get the house and the stock he had in the company, and his second wife, Kendall, gets his share in the gallery on Beverly Drive, though the will says that if there should be issue of our marriage, then the kid would be the main beneficiary and I get a lot less. The most valuable stuff is the art in the house – Harry was a collector. Feinstein says it's mine as part of the contents of the house, but Kendall's got some attorney to write claiming she and Harry agreed to split it so her half wasn't his to leave. There's something about Sonja too, but Feinstein says it won't add up to more than a few mementoes. It's all very complicated . . .' Her voice trailed off.

'I'll come and see you tomorrow, all right?'

Cindy nodded, then opened her wallet. 'You gave me your card, so I got the cheque all ready. All you got to do is fill in the amount. I don't know how much you charge, but I want you to look after me, exclusive, so that will be extra, and I'll pay extra because I don't want you to tell anybody that you're working for me. If it gets out, I'll deny it, and I'll get one of my fancy lawyers to sue you. Do you have client confidentiality?'

'Of course.'

*

Decker ushered Cindy Nathan out of the office and into the elevator, while Lorraine remained at her desk, staring at the looped, childish writing. She had suggested Cindy engage her on a weekly basis, and said it would be three hundred dollars a day plus expenses.

Cindy had counted on her fingers, then leaned over to use Lorraine's felt-tipped pen. 'I'm going to pay you five thousand dollars a week, and I want you for a month to start with. Then, if everything works out all right for me, I won't need you any more.'

When Decker returned, Lorraine held up the cheque between her fingers. He took it and looked stunned.

'Shit! Twenty grand! What in God's name do you have to do for that?'

Lorraine perched on the side of the desk. 'Long time ago, one of the boys arrested this old guy for passing dud cheques. When he was questioned he shrugged his shoulders and . . . he was crazy. He'd found the cheque book in a supermarket.'

'I don't follow. What's that got to do with Cindy Nathan?'

'I think she's crazy – the elevator's certainly not quite going to the top floor. I wouldn't be surprised if that cheque bounced. On the other hand, she's a wealthy widow.'

Decker chuckled. 'Well, hell, let's bank it first thing in the morning, and if she's out to lunch we're laughing.'

Lorraine clicked her fingers to Tiger. 'Yeah, you go ahead and do that. Oh, that phone call Cindy denies making.' Decker nodded. He still felt awful about the recording.

'Cindy has quite a high-pitched voice. If she got hysterical, like she'd just shot her husband, it's likely her voice would go up a notch. Whoever made that call, if my memory serves me well, had quite a deep, almost throaty smoker's voice.' She gave him that cock-eyed, smug smile. He said nothing.

Lorraine still hovered at the doorway. 'Did Mrs Nathan come with a chauffeur?'

'I have no idea,' Decker said. As the door closed behind her he shut his eyes, tried to remember the voice. Had it been deep, throaty as she had just said? He could not remember.

According to the doorman in the main lobby, Cindy Nathan had walked into the building. He had seen no driver, and she had not left keys for the valet-parking facility. She had asked him which floor Page Investigations was on, and then used the intercom phone to the office. 'I'm sorry if I did anything wrong,' the doorman said apologetically.

'You didn't,' Lorraine replied, as she left, with Tiger straining at the leash. But she knew intuitively that something was wrong. Nothing quite added up. She felt good, though, and she was twenty thousand dollars better off. Page Investigations was up and rolling.

CHAPTER 2

L ORRAINE ARRIVED at the Nathans' mansion with her CD playing Maria Callas singing *Madame Butterfly* at full volume. The door was opened by a middle-aged Mexican maid who ushered her into the cool hallway and motioned her through an archway framed by a broad-leafed twining vine growing around two carved pine pillars. Looking up the floating stairs, Lorraine saw several modern art works. Whether they were valuable or not, she couldn't tell.

Through the archway was a shallow flight of pink polished granite steps leading down to the main living area of the house. Floor to ceiling windows gave it a lovely, light, delicate feel, and the room had been divided into a sitting space on one side and an area for formal dining on the other. There were large plain white armchairs and sofas, and one piece of 'art' furniture, a strange green and black chair with a round, stuffed base and padded back, which looked to Lorraine like a cartoon-style tea-cup or a fairground waltzer.

Cindy Nathan sat in the tea-cup, curled up like a child with a glass of orange juice cupped in her hands, rolling a clear plastic beach ball back and forth over the same six inches of floor with a tiny, tanned foot, drying the varnish on her toenails. 'Oh, hi, have you come to give me a massage?' she said brightly, getting up. Today she had her hair in Dutch-girl braids, high on her head, and had made up her eyes in a defiantly garish blue, her lips with raspberry frosting. She wore a yellow top with peasant-style embroidery and blue and yellow windowpane check pants.

Cindy's acting – as she pretended Lorraine was a masseuse – was as bad as it had been in her TV roles. She gestured for Lorraine to follow her into an adjoining room. It was a gym, very professional with weights, sit-up bars, medicine balls and leg stretchers. Close to a boxing punch-bag, in the centre of the space, was a row of different-sized gloves in bright red leather. 'I always used to call this Harry's toy cupboard. He was always in here when he was home, working out.'

'He must have been fit.'

'Yes, he was. Well, so he should have been. He spent enough time looking after his body.' She giggled, and covered her mouth. 'I reckon the reason he was so obsessive was . . .' she held up her little finger and waggled it '. . . he was kind of small. Some parts of the body you can never build up.'

Lorraine perched on one of the black leather-covered benches, irritated by the girl's innuendo. 'Did you kill him, Cindy?' she asked.

'No, I did not. I did not.'

Lorraine smiled encouragingly at her. 'Good. Now, can we talk in here or not?'

'Yes, it's safe.'

'Safe?'

'Ah . . . yes. Harry used to record stuff,' Cindy said, colouring slightly, and Lorraine had the impression that the girl had said something she hadn't meant to. 'But down here was his private place. Nobody came down here but him,' she chattered on. 'I used to have to go out to my classes – he wouldn't let me work out down here.'

'What kind of thing did Harry record?' Lorraine asked.

'Oh . . . just conversations. He taped phone calls, and there were cameras in all the rooms in the house. For security, you know, the art.'

'You knew about that, though.'

'Oh, yes, I knew.'

Again Lorraine felt that Cindy wasn't telling the full truth, and she wondered whether the presence of a pornographer, an ex-actress and a large number of cameras under the same roof had had the inevitable consequence. 'He didn't make any other sort of recordings?'

'No,' Cindy said, a shade too quickly. 'He was just paranoid, even about personal things. I mean, he hated anyone to know he'd had a face-lift, and he dyed his hair – plus he took his drugs down here.' It was a titbit thrown out to shift the conversation away from a subject Cindy clearly didn't want to discuss.

Lorraine asked, 'What drugs did he use?'

'Oh, stuff for body-building mostly. Sometimes he'd have a few lines of cocaine, but mostly it was steroids, or speed – he was a real speed freak. But he was careful. He'd never over-indulge – he always knew exactly what he was taking.'

'Did you take drugs?'

'Me?' Cindy gave a goofy grin, suddenly the little girl again, as if it were all a game. 'Oh, yeah, I'd do anything that was going, mostly cocaine. But I haven't touched anything since I knew about the baby. I've got to take care of myself. You have to when you're pregnant.'

Cindy gazed at her reflection in the mirrors, and Lorraine considered how to question her. She would like access to the tape recordings Cindy had mentioned. 'Can I just take you through the events up to your arrest?' she said.

'Sure. Do you want a drink?'

The girl's butterfly mind digressed into trivia – either she didn't realize the seriousness of her situation, or she was trying to hold on to some kind of normality. She wandered off to a small kitchen area, tucked away at one side of the gym by the showers.

'Just water for me,' Lorraine said, following her.

Cindy opened the fridge and selected a can of Diet Coke for herself. She opened a cupboard and took out a glass. Having forgotten, it seemed, Lorraine's water, she opened the can and poured out the contents.

'Where exactly were you on that morning?' Lorraine asked, sitting down on a work bench and taking out her notepad.

'I was lying on the balcony, over there.' Cindy waved her hand. 'I fell asleep.'

'Would that be at the front of the house?' Lorraine asked.

'Sort of. There's balconies all over the house, but I kind of move around with the sun, you know, so I was on that one.' She pointed to indicate which side of the house she meant.

'And the swimming pool is where exactly?'

'Behind you,' Cindy said.

'Is there access from here to the pool?'

'Of course. Behind the mirrors, they slide back.'

44

'Right. So what time were you sunbathing?'

'Oh, the usual time.' She took a slug of her Coke, draining the glass.

'Yes, but I don't know your usual routine, so if you would just take me through it.' Lorraine tried not to sound irritated.

'Okay. I get up usually about nine, sometimes earlier, sometimes a lot later, shower, then work on my tan for a couple of hours – just my body, I don't do my face.'

'Do the servants all know your routine?'

'Of course, I've been doing it since I got married – get up, shower, sunbathe, swim, get dressed for lunch.'

Cindy started doing half-hearted t'ai chi exercises in front of the mirror.

'So on the day you discovered your husband's body, you were sunbathing as usual and you fell asleep. A loud noise woke you – about what time would that have been?'

Cindy wrinkled her nose. 'Maybe eleven. I was asleep the first time, then I heard it again. At first I thought it was a car backfiring. It was just one loud bang. Then I saw all these birds flying up, from the garden by the shrubbery. You can't see the pool from the balcony, just the edge of the garden, so I called Harry, wondering if he was messing about.'

'Messing about?'

'Yeah. Sometimes he'd take pot-shots at the birds. It used to make me mad as hell, because once he killed one.'

Lorraine doodled on her pad as Cindy went into a long monologue on how she loved all of nature's creatures. Finally she interrupted, 'You know, Cindy, if you're found guilty of murdering your husband, you'll be locked up in a prison and you'll be hard pushed to hear a single tweet. Now I know it may be tedious, but I have to ask all these questions so I know exactly what I should—'

'I never killed him,' the girl said, red-faced with anger.

'I know you didn't, but you're to stand trial for it, unless—'

'I never killed him. I found him, that's all.'

'So, will you close your eyes and tell me exactly what you did, from the time the noise woke you to the moment you discovered your husband's body?'

Cindy covered her eyes with her hands. 'You mean, like creatively visualize?' Clearly this was something she was familiar with.

'Just tell me what happened.'

'After the bang, I called out his name,' Cindy began. 'When I got no reply, I picked up my towel, and my sun creams and my straw hat. I went into the bedroom and decided I'd have a swim. I didn't have anything on – I sunbathe naked – so I put my swimsuit on and got a big outdoor towel. Then I heard another bang – I was pretty sure it was a gun this time, so I put on my mules and went downstairs . . .' She withdrew her hands from her face, and her big blue eyes stared ahead. 'I went to the pool and put my towel on the chair by the table. I saw Harry's towel, his sandals, and his cigarette packet. I looked around because one cigarette was smoked down – there was a long line of ash on it.'

Cindy blinked, and Lorraine noticed that she was looking at herself in the mirrors again as she spoke.

'I was about to dive in so I went to the deep end. First thing I noticed was the water was kind of pink, and then I saw him. I called out his name – he was lying face down, arms outstretched – but I knew something bad had happened, and I started to scream. I screamed and screamed.'

'How long was it before someone came out to you?'

Cindy stared at herself and Lorraine had to repeat the question.

'I don't know, it seemed a very long time. Then Juana came out, with Jose just behind her, and she said to me, she said . . .'

For the first time since they had come into the gym Lorraine saw some emotion. 'She said to me, "Holy Mother, Mrs Nathan, what have you done?"'

Lorraine waited, watching Cindy closely. The girl's breathing had become irregular, and she was swallowing rapidly. 'Go on, Cindy. Then what happened?'

'Jose jumped into the pool, and he said, "She's shot him! She's shot him!"' She gulped air into her lungs, her chest heaving. 'They dragged him to the shallow end. I could see white bone . . . and they couldn't lift him out.' She shuddered.

Lorraine tapped her notebook. 'Go on.'

'They called the police, I guess.'

Lorraine looked up. 'But Cindy, you told me you called the police.'

Cindy blinked. 'Oh, yes, that's right. I did.'

Lorraine made a note that the call to her office had come in at just after eleven o'clock. If Cindy couldn't recall contacting the police, maybe she couldn't remember calling Lorraine either.

Cindy continued, 'I called Mr Feinstein, because the next thing the garden was full of people and someone brought me some brandy. I was still by the pool, but sitting on one of the wooden chairs, and all I could think

47

of was that he'd been sitting where I was sitting, smoking that cigarette. Then Mr Feinstein said to me, "Cindy, they want to take you into the station to ask you some questions," and that it would be best if I got dressed.' Cindy began to twist a strand of her blonde hair through her fingers. 'I got dressed, I got my purse and my sunglasses, just like I was going out shopping or something, but I didn't put any make-up on, and then they took me to the station.'

'Do you recall the name of the officer who questioned you?'

'No.'

'Did Mr Feinstein come with you?'

'No, he came on later.'

'So you had no lawyer with you?'

'No, I was on my own.'

Lorraine jotted some notes, then looked up sharply as Cindy began to cry. 'They said they found my gun, they said I did it, but I kept on saying over and over that I couldn't have done it, that I wouldn't have done something that bad even if I said I would.'

Lorraine repeated, '"Said I would"?'

'Well, I told you, I was always threatening him.' Cindy's voice steadied a little, and her chin lifted. 'I was always saying I'd kill him, because he used to get me so mad. He could be so mean to me, I'd get mad as hell. I'd scream and shout and try to hit him, but he would just laugh, and that got me even madder, but I never meant what I said. It was just I was upset.' She dissolved into real tears again – more at the memory of her anger and humiliation, Lorraine thought, than out of grief at her husband's death.

'I need a tissue,' Cindy said, sniffing, her dark blue mascara beginning to run.

Lorraine crossed to the shower area and headed for one of the toilets to get some tissue. She dragged off a length of paper and hurried back to the gym.

'I didn't do it. I wouldn't kill him, even though he got me madder than hell!' Cindy mopped her face, then blew her nose. 'I didn't kill him, did I? Please tell me I didn't do it.'

Lorraine bent down to her, in an almost motherly fashion. 'But you didn't do it, did you?'

Cindy wiped her face and blew her nose again, her voice a hoarse whisper. 'I don't know. You see, it's all blurred. I mean, I'd know, wouldn't I? I'd know if I *had* done it. That's what you got to help me with, because I'm all confused.'

Lorraine straightened up. One moment Cindy had given her a detailed description of what she had done leading up to the discovery of the body, the next she was asking if she could have been the one to pull the trigger. It didn't make sense.

'You've just told me how you found the body, Cindy, so why are you thinking now you might have killed him?'

Cindy rocked forward, head in her hands. ''Cos I can only remember going to the pool and seeing him in the water. Nothing before that. I do the same thing every day – I mean, I could be just filling in the gaps.'

'But you said you heard the gunshot?'

'Yes, I know. *I know I said that.*'

'Are you telling me now that you didn't hear it?'

'*Yes.* No, I heard it, I'm not lying to you. I heard that one, but . . .'

'But what?'

Cindy twisted the damp tissue in her fingers. 'Maybe it didn't happen when I think it happened.'

'I don't understand.'

'What if I'd done it before?'

'You'll have to help me, Cindy, I can't follow what you're saying. How do you mean before?'

'Earlier.'

Lorraine sighed. 'You mean before you went to the balcony to sunbathe?'

'No. I mean the first shot. When I was sleeping. I mean, I could have done it half asleep. Like in an altered state of consciousness – you know, the way people remember past lives, and sometimes they just act them out? I mean, I could have been a murderess or anything. Maybe I just couldn't help myself.'

Lorraine rolled her eyes as Cindy sprang to her feet, thinking that her client had been watching too many of her husband's killer-bimbo fantasies. She watched the girl dive at the punch-bag and hit it, her face a mask of anger. Lorraine let her go until she tired herself out and eventually put her arms around the punch-bag, hugging it tightly.

'Sometimes he didn't come home,' she said softly. Lorraine kept silent. 'Often he stayed out all night, and I knew about the other women. I knew he was never faithful, he always said that to me, said he could never be faithful to one woman and that I'd just have to accept that. The day before I found him, he'd been really mean to me. We argued at breakfast, and then he came down here. I came after him and he was furious, but I wouldn't go. I said to him that if he carried on this way I'd leave him, and he said he didn't care what I did and he laughed at me, kept on punching this thing, laughing and ignoring me. So I went and got the gun, and when I came back he was on that weight machine, and I went right up to him and I pointed it at his head, and I said that was the last time he was ever going to laugh at me.'

Lorraine still said nothing, but was interested to note that Cindy was calm now, her mind focused on what she was saying.

'He looked at me, then he reached out and pulled the gun over so it was almost in his mouth and he told me to fire it.'

'And?'

Cindy sighed. 'I did. I pulled the trigger, but it wasn't loaded.' She pushed away the punch-bag, which began to swing slowly. 'He got up from the bench and hit me in the stomach. I fell backwards onto the floor and he kept on coming towards me, but he stepped right over me and walked into the showers. I screamed at him that I would get him the next time. Next time the gun would be loaded.' She rubbed her belly. 'Punched me right in the baby, and it hurt so bad I was sick, but he made me get dressed and go out for dinner at Morton's, and he told everyone what I'd done, and they all laughed. He kept on fooling around at dinner with this baby zucchini as the gun, shoving it into his mouth, and everyone laughed, and I got so upset I was crying, but I wasn't going to stay and be made a fool of. So I got up and I shouted it out. I said the next time he wouldn't live to tell anybody anything because the next time I'd make sure I killed him.'

Cindy went to fetch another Diet Coke. This time she drank it from the can. 'He didn't come home. I waited and waited, and it was six o'clock in the morning when he came back. He was in his dressing room, taking his clothes off, when I went in to see him. He just told me to get out, but I wouldn't. I said he shouldn't make a fool of me in front of people like he had done, but he just kept on choosing which shirt he was going to wear, ignoring me again.'

Lorraine waited while Cindy sipped the Coke.

'I went into the bedroom to get the gun. I meant it, I was going to kill him, and I'd just figured out how to load it, but I couldn't remember where it was, or if I'd taken it from the gym. I was looking all over the room for it when he strolled in all dressed up and Jose knocked on the door.' Cindy frowned as she tried to recall the details.

'Jose said that the car needed to be serviced, and did Harry need it after his breakfast meeting at seven. Harry said he didn't. He'd had a long, hard night and he'd just sit by the pool reading scripts after his meeting. Then . . . he started laughing and he told Jose that I'd threatened to kill him again and that Jose was his witness that I was a real flake, a psychiatric case. He knows how upset I get about him saying things like that because I've had, you know, some problems.'

Lorraine shifted her weight. 'Problems?' she said gently.

'Mmmm, I have these . . . kind of bad days, you know. I get depressed, uptight about things, angry.'

'Can you go back to what you were saying about when your husband and Jose were talking in the bedroom? What happened then?'

'Oh, yeah. Well, Harry left. And I went back to bed. I'd had such a bad night I told Juana not to disturb me. I couldn't sleep, so I got up and went out on the balcony to lie in the sun, and I guess I must have gone to sleep there. I had a nightmare, me shooting Harry, like I'd threatened to do, and something woke me up – well, I think it was me woke myself up because I pulled the trigger. I fired the gun. But I'm sure it was in my dream and then I'm not sure. That's what terrifies me. Did I do it or was I dreaming?'

'How long do you think there was between the two shots, or the one shot and what might have been a car backfiring?'

'Er . . . maybe ten minutes.'

'About how long does it take to get from the balcony to the pool, Cindy?'

Cindy drew open the sliding door. 'Oh, four, maybe five minutes, but it would depend on how fast you were moving.'

Lorraine picked up her purse and followed Cindy out. 'Do you think you're going to be all right here alone?'

'If I'm not there's Jose and Juana, but they don't like me.'

'When you said I had to pretend to be a masseuse you seemed worried someone would find out that I was investigating the case.'

'I am. I don't want Jose or that bitch Juana to know. I don't want anyone knowing my business because they all believe I killed Harry, and so they won't say nice things about me in the court. But if they saw this, maybe they would change their minds.' Cindy pulled up her top. There was a nightmare bruise across her belly, a virtual imprint of a fist. 'This is nothin'. He was always knocking me around, just not my face.'

'Does anyone know he did this to you?'

'Maybe his ex-wives or his girlfriends – my mother

53

always used to say once a wife-beater always one – but they won't lift a finger for me, will they? Nor will my mother come to think of it.' Lorraine lit a cigarette. She asked Cindy for the names of the people who had been at the dinner the night before Nathan was killed, the addresses and names of girlfriends and ex-wives, business associates, anyone who would benefit from his death, anyone who had a grudge against him. Eventually she said, 'Let's leave it there for the present, Cindy,' and got up to go. 'I'll start checking some of this stuff out.'

'Sure.' Cindy shrugged. 'But I'll see you tomorrow anyway, won't I?'

'What?' Lorraine was surprised.

'Harry's funeral. The coroner's office released the body last night. I just called Forest Lawn and told them to take care of everything – they said they'd put a notice in the papers and all that stuff. I'd kind of like it if you came. I mean, my folks aren't going to be there, and I never liked his that much.'

'I'd be glad to,' Lorraine said, thinking that a chance to get a closer look at Harry Nathan's friends and relatives would be welcome. 'What time?'

'Eleven,' Cindy said. 'It's in that fake New England church they have there. Match all his phoney friends.' She gave a wry smile, but Lorraine saw the flicker of pain in her eyes. She could see too that having become Mrs Nathan III at the age of nineteen hadn't landed this isolated, mixed-up girl in any bed of roses.

'Okay,' Lorraine said. 'Just one last thing. Can I have access to some of these recordings Harry made?'

Once again it was clear that Cindy was uncomfortable, but she said, 'Oh, sure. I'll have Jose send them over.'

'Couldn't I have them now?'

'It might take a while to find them. He kept them in weird places.'

She was evidently preparing the ground for some of the tapes to become conveniently untraceable, Lorraine noted. 'Didn't the police ask for them?' she asked.

'Well, I didn't tell them about them. I figured, I pay my taxes, let them do their job!' Cindy said with another touch of defiance. But then the fight went out of her. 'Besides, they're so fucking sure it's me that they aren't going to bother listening to ten million hours of Harry talking about all the ginseng he stuck up his ass.'

'I see,' Lorraine said evenly. 'Well, *I*'d be interested to hear about it, if you could send over any tapes you have. See you tomorrow.'

By the time Lorraine returned to the office, she felt drained and Decker looked at her with his head on one side. 'Go well, did it?'

Lorraine tossed her purse down. 'You try interviewing Cindy Nathan. The porch light's on, but there's nobody home. She's not sure that she didn't do it, because she dreamed that she'd just pulled the trigger when she heard a gunshot, or as she told me repeatedly, it might have been a car backfiring!'

'What's your gut feeling?'

Lorraine leaned back in her chair. 'I don't think she did it, but I'd better find something fast to prove that she didn't because, pushed by any decent prosecutor, she'll admit that she did. She's that dumb.'

'Why would someone like Harry Nathan marry such a flake?'

Lorraine sipped her coffee. 'Because she's twenty and

he was a fifty-year-old guy dyeing his hair and having face-lifts, and she's got a body like a fourteen-year-old Venus, and an angel's face. He also had quite a line-up of women as well as Cindy, plus remained friendly with his ex-wife, who still, by the way, runs his art gallery. I'd say Cindy was the classic babe armpiece for a man with a small dick.'

'Oh, he had one of those, did he?' Decker said, camp.

'According to Little Miss Bimbo he did, but she's having his baby. Not that he seemed all that interested – almost punched it through her backbone. I saw the bruise.'

'So,' Decker said, leaning on the doorframe, 'what's the next move?'

'I think she's hiding something about tapes Nathan made at the house – phone conversations, security videos. She didn't tell the police and she kind of let it slip to me, but she said she'd send the tapes over. We'll just have to wait and see what we get.'

Cindy Nathan brought the boxes upstairs from the gym herself and stacked them in the hall. She had listened to some of the conversations again and again, just to hear his voice, but they had agreed a code and stuck to it and there was nothing to make Harry or anyone else suspicious: even the police could have listened to them, if they'd found them. She dialled a cab company, said she wanted some items delivered, and sat down to wait for the driver to come. It would have been easier, of course, to send Jose, but she was sick of Harry's housekeepers knowing all her comings and goings, the pair of them always watching her. They had been surprised when she

56

had given them the rest of the day off, but within half an hour they had been on their way to Juana's sister.

When the cab driver showed up, Cindy gave him the boxes of tapes with Lorraine's address and twenty-five dollars. Good riddance, she thought. Mrs Page was welcome to listen to all the rambling rubbish Harry recorded. There was nothing to find.

The videos, though, they were something else – but where the fuck were they? Harry had kept all the recordings together in the safe under the floor in his dressing room but the videotapes, both the ones from the security cameras and the . . . the other ones, were gone. Cindy tried to tell herself that if she couldn't find them, nobody else was likely to, but the possibility that they might be circulating somewhere out there tormented her.

It was more likely that the tapes had never left the house, she told herself. Harry had just moved them again, the mistrustful, suspicious-minded bastard. She set off for the stairs to have another look in the gym, where there was certainly no visible hiding place for the substantial stack of videos. She deduced he must have had a new cavity let into the floor or the wall.

The noise of Cindy's tapping on what she considered various likely spots on the walls masked the sound of the doors opening to the pool area. At first she didn't notice the man's presence, and for over a minute he watched her in silence before he spoke.

'Cindy,' he said, his voice curiously cold and flat.

She froze.

'Cindy,' he said again.

'Jesus, Raymond, you gave me such a fucking scare! Don't ever do that to me again! How did you get in here?'

In front of her was a tall man with thinning silver-grey hair, and an extraordinarily handsome face. When he began to speak, it became clear that behind the distinguished façade was a vapid, unstable personality. There was only one thing Raymond Vallance could ever have been, and that is what he was: an actor.

'Through the pool doors. I still have the key to this fairy bower, Rapunzel, remember?' He had the mannered and over-emphasized diction of the lifelong performer, and shook the key at Cindy before he put it back in his pocket.

'Well, long time, no see,' Cindy said, trying to ignore his apparent *froideur* and assuming a coquettish air as she moved across to him. She made to slide her arms round his waist, but Vallance stepped away immediately. Close to, she could see that he was grey in the face, haggard, as though he hadn't slept in days, and his clothes were creased and dirty. Not that that was necessarily anything new with Raymond, she thought, but he was clearly in no mood for fun and games.

'Cindy,' he said, 'we have to be very careful now, you know that.'

'For Chrissakes, Raymond. Harry's being pickled in brine at Forest Lawn right this minute!' Cindy cried. 'We don't have to hide anything.'

'Don't talk that way about him, you tacky little piece of trash,' Vallance snapped, and Cindy recoiled from the cold anger in his voice. For a moment she had the impression that he was genuinely in the grip of strong emotion, almost as though he were fighting back tears – but if Raymond was so crazy about Harry, what had he been doing fucking the ass off Harry's wife every time his back was turned?

'Raymond, I haven't seen you in weeks. I'm, like, totally strung out and I'm *pregnant*, Raymond. Doesn't that mean anything to you?' she began, her voice trembling.

'Not particularly,' Vallance said, in the same odd, cold tone she had never heard from him before. 'Other people's children have never interested me much.'

'Raymond—' Cindy wailed.

Vallance cut her short. 'I came here to ask you only two things, Cindy,' he said. 'First, what happened to the tapes?'

'I don't know,' she said, her eyes sliding away from his.

'Did the police take them?'

'I can't find them – I mean the videos. They were in the safe and now they're gone. I took the tapes from the phone out and—'

He interrupted her again. 'And where are they?'

Cindy squirmed. 'I . . . put 'em somewhere safe.'

'Cindy,' Vallance said, grabbing the girl by her upper arms, 'tell me where the fucking tapes are right now or I'll break your arm.' He shook her hard, and she saw a darkness in his eyes she had not seen before. It chilled her to the bone.

'I – I hired a PI to, like, look after us,' Cindy stammered, beginning to cry. 'I gave them to her. I had to, Raymond, it would've looked worse if I hadn't, and I checked 'em all.'

Vallance thrust her violently away from him. She stumbled in the high, unwieldy shoes and fell backwards onto the floor. 'You sent those tapes to a private investigator?' he said, now white with rage. 'Tell me her name.'

'Page,' Cindy sobbed. 'Lorraine Page. On . . . West Pico.'

'Well, I'll take care of that,' he said. He stood looking at the girl's huddled body on the floor, listening to her cry. He turned to go, but then bent down beside her.

'Cindy?' His voice was oddly gentle. 'Just one last thing I need to know, Cindy.' She lifted her head and wiped her eyes with the back of her hand, smearing the blue eye-shadow in streaks across her face.

'You killed Harry, didn't you, Cindy?'

She sensed danger immediately and tried to roll away from him, but in one movement Vallance caught her by the hip, turned her onto her back and sat astride her. 'Did you kill him, Cindy?' he asked, as though they were exchanging pleasantries at a party.

'Raymond,' she wept, almost hysterical, 'you're hurting me! You'll hurt the baby!'

'Answer me, Cindy,' Vallance demanded, and banged her head hard on the floor. 'Did you kill him or not?'

'I didn't! I swear it! I swear it on my kid's life, Raymond – it's Harry's kid.' She did not know what prompted her to add the last words, but she felt the high tension in Vallance's body slacken.

'Well,' he said, releasing her and giving her a look almost of disgust, 'maybe it is.'

He rocked back onto his heels with a peculiarly graceful movement, and got to his feet, looking down at her as dispassionately as though she were a drunk he had to step over in the street. 'See you at Forest Lawn,' he said, and was gone.

Decker's phone rang. It was the doorman: there had been a delivery, in three cardboard boxes. He'd bring them up.

60

The boxes were stiff-sided packing cases, thickly Sellotaped across the opening flaps, and numbered one to three. Decker and Lorraine ripped open case one.

'Harry Nathan's private recordings of phone calls and anyone who called at the house,' Lorraine said.

'Dear God, this'll take weeks to plough through.' Decker looked over the rows and rows of tapes, marked with dates.

Lorraine pointed to case three. 'Start with the most recent and work backwards. See you tomorrow after I've held Cindy's hand at Forest Lawn.' She bent down and clipped on Tiger's lead. The big dog immediately began to drag her towards the door.

Decker checked his watch – almost six fifteen. He packed twenty of the tapes for the last three months into his car tape case, stuck it in his gym bag and decided that he would start playing them as he drove home.

Raymond Vallance sat in the downstairs lobby of Lorraine's building and observed Decker carefully through the iridescent blue lenses of his last season's Calvin Klein sunglasses. He had been just in time to see three packing cases go in, and one lady, a big dog and now quite a cute little fag come out. No boxes.

He gave the doorman a pleasant smile, folded his newspaper and walked out onto the street. He leaned back against the wall, as Decker went to the entrance to the motor court, and took a slim leather address book from an inside pocket.

No numbers were ever deleted from Raymond Vallance's little black book: you never knew when you might want to look up an old friend, perhaps for a favour or, even better, suggest something that might be mutually beneficial. Not that this party was a friend exactly, but he had been useful to both Harry and himself on a number of occasions in the past with respect to little matters of entertainment – company or chemicals. But this was more serious. He dialled the number and the young man picked up almost at once.

'Yo, bro,' Vallance began in the slangy sing-song voice and Brooklyn accent he adopted when talking to black people. 'You busy tonight? Got a little job for you . . .'

CHAPTER 3

N EXT DAY when Decker walked into the building he noticed that the door to Page Investigations was a fraction open and assumed that Lorraine must have called in on her way to the funeral. He extended his hand to open the door further and his nostrils burned with the smell of acid. Decker stepped back and kicked it open instead.

The packing cases remained where he had stacked them on the floor, but the cardboard was sodden, and the tapes still smouldered as the acid destroyed even their plastic surrounds. Not one was salvageable – yet nothing else seemed to have been disturbed. He entered Lorraine's office with trepidation – had she disturbed the intruder?

The desk drawers were open and a few papers littered the floor. At first sight nothing else seemed to have been damaged except for a photograph of Lorraine, which lay behind the desk, acid eating into the face, burning and twisting the features grotesquely.

'Jesus,' he said quietly, and picked up the phone, about to call the police department, then hesitated. Even after working for Lorraine for such a short time, he knew that she would want any decision to involve the police to be hers alone. Instead he dialled Reception and asked casually if there had been any security problems during the night. The doorman assured him that there had not. Decker hung up and dialled Lorraine's mobile number. He swore as an electronic voice advised him that the phone was switched off.

Lorraine drove past the fountains and through the gates of Forest Lawn. She had never been to the exclusive cemetery before and found herself in what looked like a cross between the park of an eccentric nobleman and an outdoor department store of death. All tastes were clearly catered for, she observed, as she passed birdhouses, replicas of classical temples and 'dignified' churches. It had an air of frivolity and consumerism rather than reverence or repose.

The Nathan funeral was clearly taking place in the 'Bostonian' church, from which a long line of parked cars tailed back. As Lorraine got closer, she observed a number of people standing about outside. Most were pretending not to notice that they were being photographed by a little knot of journalists, but some were unashamedly smiling and posing. She tried not to stare at the wannabe actresses who had been unable to resist the chance to wear the shortest of short skirts, evening sandals, nipple-skimming necklines and elaborate hats.

The men had mostly confined themselves to dark jackets and ties, but Lorraine noted one with a straggling ponytail in a black Nehru jacket over dirty black jeans and Birkenstock sandals – a sort of ageing rock star ensemble completed by little round John Lennon sunglasses. As he turned his head to speak to the older woman beside him, his resemblance in profile to Harry Nathan was striking. They must be the family, Lorraine thought, an impression confirmed when she saw that Kendall Nathan was standing in front of the pair making exaggerated expressions of sympathy and grief.

She, too, was dressed like a Christmas tree, in a fussy black evening dress with chiffon yoke and sleeves, and dowdy pleated skirt. Apart from Lorraine, Harry Nathan's mother, in a conventional dress and coat in black wool crêpe, was the only person whose appearance had been influenced by the sombreness of the occasion. She also seemed to be the only person genuinely distressed by Harry Nathan's death.

Lorraine turned to watch as a limousine drew up, followed by an ordinary taxi-cab. The cab disgorged its occupants first, the middle-aged Mexican woman who had let Lorraine into the Nathan house and a Hispanic man, evidently her husband, who made their way straight into the church, ignored by everyone. As soon as the staff were out of the way, the limousine door opened to reveal Cindy Nathan in a long black sleeveless dress – Empire line to accommodate her undetectable pregnancy – and black velvet platform boots. Her blonde hair was elaborately dressed into a plaited coronet on top of her head, her wrists laden with pearl and jet. A silver snake bracelet encircled one of her slim upper arms, perfectly matching the black cobra tattooed around the other. She looked like a young pagan goddess, and all the nearby long lenses were immediately trained on her.

The girl stood motionless in front of the crowd. No one approached or spoke to her – in fact, Nathan's family and Kendall looked away pointedly. My God, she must have been crying all night, Lorraine thought, as she observed the deep shadows around Cindy's eyes. But as she got near enough to the girl to smile and greet her, she realized that the effect was deliberate: Cindy's startling blue eyes and full, flower-like mouth had both been expertly made up in fashionable metallic pink.

Cindy did not speak, but gave Lorraine a strange, controlled smile, like that of a beautiful alien, and carefully arranged a black lace mantilla over her head. With a gesture bizarrely reminiscent of a wedding, she took Lorraine's arm and the crowd parted in front of them as they made their way into the church, leaving a wake of exquisite lily scent and audible hisses of outrage.

'Fuck 'em,' Cindy said, under her breath, as they reached the porch. Her lovely face remained immobile as she spoke. 'Fuck the whole damn lot of them.'

They made their way up the aisle towards the front pew, and the clergyman approached, rearranging his amazed stare into an expression of sympathy. Lorraine also noticed a tall, grey-haired man give the young widow an icy glance and immediately move way.

'Who was that?' Lorraine asked, when they had sat down.

'Raymond Vallance,' Cindy said coolly, staring straight ahead at the enormous wreath on her husband's coffin.

The rest of the mourners began to file in, the Nathan family occupying the front pew on the other side of the church from Cindy.

Once everyone was settled, the minister announced a hymn, which no one bothered to sing. Most of those present were more interested in craning their necks to see who else was there. They were eventually brought back to the purpose of the gathering by the clergyman's invitation to remember Harry in silence for a few minutes while they listened to one of his favourite songs, a rendition of 'Light My Fire', arranged as elaborately as an oratorio and played like a dirge on an electronic organ.

Then the minister paid tribute to Nathan's personal charm, energy and talent. As he moved on to talk about his civic virtues and unstinting support for many good causes, Lorraine was conscious of a stir at the back of the church. She turned to see a tall woman with strangely white hair, elegant as a borzoi, who had walked in alone. She came slowly up to the front of the church, her high heels clicking on the stone floor, and sat down with great dignity in the front pew, some six feet away from Cindy. She inclined her head, smiled slightly at the girl, and Lorraine caught a glimpse of a pair of remote, unnerving eyes.

She immediately recognized Sonja Sorenson, the first Mrs Nathan, and tried to study the older woman unobtrusively. She was about fifty, Lorraine guessed, and although her immaculately cut, jaw-length hair was white, her lashes and brows were still dark. Her clothes were formal and elegant, a military-style black wool suit worn with black gloves, hose and shoes, and no visible jewellery. She stared straight ahead, ignoring the congregation's scrutiny.

When the service ended, Vallance, Nathan's brother and four other men advanced to lift the coffin and carry it out. The congregation filed after them, to form a group around the grave. Lorraine dropped back to let Cindy and Sonja stand at the front, noticing that, the minute they got outside, the older woman had put on a pair of dark glasses. Kendall, determined not to be outdone, elbowed her way up to stand between Nathan's other two wives, clutching a single white rose. She beckoned to Mrs Nathan senior to follow her, but the old lady shook her head as though in distaste.

The minister read in a sonorous voice from scripture while the pall-bearers pushed the coffin carefully into the space in the wall and stepped back. As soon as the reading was over, Kendall moved forward to thrust her flower into the tomb, wailing theatrically, then stepped back as though challenging the other women to cap her performance. Sonja did not move, but Lorraine froze as Cindy took a step forward, calmly removed her wedding ring and laid it on the end of the coffin. There was an audible gasp as people wondered how to interpret the gesture: did Cindy mean that her heart was buried in the grave with Harry, or that she wanted her last remaining tie to her husband to be severed in the most public way?

The tomb door was closed and people turned away. Lorraine scanned the crowd for Raymond Vallance and saw that he was in surprisingly heated conversation with Jose and Juana. He was certainly making a point of keeping his distance from Cindy, Lorraine thought, to whom he had not addressed a word. But as his exchange with the two Mexicans came to an end and they drifted away, she saw him glance in the girl's direction. Sonja, she noted, was still beside the tomb.

Cindy was looking bored by whatever the minister was saying to her and Kendall, and Lorraine decided to rescue her. 'Cindy, I wonder if I could speak to you for a second,' she said, with a smile. 'Sorry to interrupt, but I'm just going.'

Cindy left Kendall with the clergyman. 'You and me both,' she said. 'Jesus – I can't stand to listen to Kendall saying she hasn't eaten a thing since he died when all I can think about is how soon I can get a tuna melt. It's the baby,' she said, and Lorraine saw her eyes lock momentarily with Raymond Vallance's. 'It makes you crave weird things.' Lorraine wondered whether it was just food she was talking about, but the girl said nothing more.

Lorraine breezed into the office just before lunchtime to find Decker showing out two men in overalls. Half the beige carpet had been taken up in the reception area.

Decker's expression was uncharacteristically grim. 'Lorraine,' he said, 'there's been a . . . problem. Sit down for a moment. Somebody broke in and sprayed fucking acid over the tapes.' He decided not to tell her about the photograph yet.

'I see,' Lorraine said, pushing her hand through her hair. 'Well, that's interesting. Cindy said no one else knew about them.'

'Well, maybe she changed her mind about letting you listen to them,' Decker said.

'Maybe,' Lorraine said, meditatively. 'I can't quite imagine her going to these lengths, though.'

'Perhaps she has some more . . . extreme friends,' Decker suggested. 'Who was she with at the funeral?'

'Nobody. Though she was breaking her neck not to be seen looking at Mr Ageing Romeo himself, Raymond Vallance. Pouting and glowering on both sides, though – sexual tension you could cut with a knife.'

'Raymond Vallance?' Decker pulled a face. 'I thought he was already planted out there. He must be about two hundred – the oldest living really terrible actor.'

'Looks every day of it,' Lorraine said. 'Though perhaps the shock of losing his close friend Mr Nathan was affecting his looks. He and the mother were the only people to shed a tear.'

'Actually,' Decker began, serious now, 'something else happened in the break-in.' He picked up the photograph. 'They did this.' Lorraine's face remained expressionless as she registered the damage. 'It looks like a get-the-fuck-off-this-case message, wouldn't you say?'

Lorraine shrugged. 'Maybe.'

'Maybe something else. Maybe somebody who knows you,' Decker went on. 'It's a really creepy thing to do, Lorraine. I knew you wouldn't want me to call the police until you got back, but I really think you should. I mean, it's like a threat.'

'Well, thanks for the concern, Decker, but there's no way I want the police knowing about either me or the tapes or that Cindy sent them here. I wish we'd got to listen to them, though. There must have been something on them that somebody didn't want us to find.'

'Well, we still have some . . .' Decker said. 'I took twenty home last night. But there's nothing on any of the ones I've listened to so far.'

'Sit down, boy wonder, I'll make you some coffee – you deserve it.' She smiled broadly. Clearly, as far as Lorraine was concerned, the subject of any personal danger was closed.

But the knowledge that Cindy Nathan had lied to her burned at the back of Lorraine's mind, and as soon as the office was back in shape she called her, only to be informed by Jose that Mrs Nathan was lying down after the stress of the funeral and could not come to the phone. He suggested she call again the following day.

Decker assembled the tapes in date order as far as he could, but some had only a number. 'How do we want to start – backwards, or at the beginning?' he asked.

Lorraine pursed her lips. 'In whatever order we can. We'll list any names mentioned, anything that may be useful. There's nothing else to do, apart from searching Harry Nathan's garden, and we'll have to do that at night.'

'Wouldn't it be easier in daylight?'

'Of course, but we'd be seen doing it. The police won't be there at night.'

'How do you know?'

'I was a cop, Decker, just take my word for it.' She pressed Play and sat on the cherry-coloured sofa, Tiger's perch. She could smell him on it.

'Hi, how you doing?' The voice was warm, easy-going, with a nice smoker's edge. It was Harry Nathan.

Lorraine leaned forward to catch the low volume. Decker turned up the sound.

'I've been better. I didn't get the fucking part.'

'I'm sorry, I thought it was in the bag.'

'So did I, pal, so did I, but they said they felt they needed a name. I said, "I have one," and this kid, no more than twenty years old, says to me, "I meant a name anyone under forty has heard of." I wanted to say, "Go fuck yourself," but what can you do? They need a fucking name to sell toothpaste nowadays. That's what I hate about this industry, no respect.'

'Mm, yeah. So, you on for tonight?'

'I guess so. I'm going down to Hollywood Spa this afternoon.'

'You spend more time in the sauna than you do in your own home.'

Their conversation droned on but, to Lorraine's irritation, Nathan never once used the caller's name.

The rest of the tape consisted of equally boring calls, as Nathan arranged his day between his masseur, his personal trainer and his yoga guru, and had a long discussion with someone about colonic irrigation. Four further tapes were just as mind-numbingly dull, but Nathan's personality was emerging clearly: he seemed to have little interest in work as every call was of a personal nature, ranging from haircuts to manicures and massage – even an eyelash tint.

'Jesus, is this guy for real?' Decker asked.

'You're listening to him, darlin',' Lorraine answered, as bored as Decker.

Decker inserted another tape and leaned back, doodling on his pad as the tape whirred and scratched before the connection was made.

'Hi, it's Raymond.'

Lorraine and Decker looked at each other – it was the sauna and steam-bath caller, Mr Raymond Vallance.

'Listen, I've just met this chick – she's beautiful. I was having lunch and she was at the next table, man. She is *stunning*. She has a body you'd cream yourself over, and she's got this blonde hair, like, man, it's down to her waist, and she's got to be five eight, maybe even taller. She's cover-of-*Vogue* class, so I won't be coming over.'

'What's her name?'

'Trudie. And she was giving me the real come-on. I mean, man, I could *feel* her looking at me. I'm seeing her tonight.'

They continued discussing the nubile blonde, their conversation more like that of two teenage boys than

72

middle-aged men. That Nathan even bothered to record the entire tedious conversation was extraordinary. Decker saw that Lorraine was fast asleep, so he rewound the tape, put on some fresh coffee and inserted the next one. He would wake her if anything of interest came up. He listened to more of Nathan's grooming arrangements and more of Vallance's lectures about diet. Then a female voice, enquiring nervously if Mr Nathan wanted to see the dailies, to which Nathan replied that he wanted them sent over, that he would look at them in the evening. No date or time was stated, but Decker listed the call: it suggested that Nathan did occasionally do some work and that some movie was being shot. The next call made him listen intently.

'Harry? It's me, and I'm pissed – you got a fucking nerve. You don't like the dailies, well, fuck you. If you could spare a second to come on the set you'd know we got a fucking brain-dead male lead. I warned you the script sucked, but this is puerile shit and I'm walking.'

Nathan's angry voice retorted that he didn't give a shit if he walked or not, and there was an angry alter- cation between the two men that resulted in Nathan screaming that the man could sue him, but as he was broke he'd never get a cent.

Lorraine woke with a start.

'Listen to this. Seems Nathan wasn't the rich man we think he was.'

Decker replayed the tape.

'You're a piece of shit, Harry.'

'Yeah, so tell me somethin' new.'

'I'm telling you straight, an' no amount of fucking blackmail and threats will make me stay on this garbage.'

Nathan laughed. 'You threatening me?'

'No, but you do whatever your dirt-bag mentality wants. I am through making second-rate porno shit.'

From then on, the tape was all business, one call after another from the studio as the film was halted. The director had walked and the cast and crew were threatening to quit unless they got paid. Then came a series of calls made by Nathan as he replaced the director, raised further finances to cover the production costs, and another when he suggested that certain incriminating photographs of Julian Cole be released to the gutter press, to teach the son-of-a-bitch a lesson – that nobody messed with Harry Nathan. The astonishing thing throughout the flurry of calls was how relaxed and easy Nathan sounded as he cajoled and bullied everyone he spoke to. Last on the tape came a pitiful call from Julian Cole, the director who had walked off the set, begging Nathan not to release the photos.

'Listen, my friend, you owed me a favour. You quit on me and caused a lot of aggravation. I warned you . . .' Nathan said airily.

There was a deep intake of breath on the line and then the weeping man hissed, 'You bastard! I'll make you sorry.'

'Try it. Many have before, Jules, but they've always failed. Screwing under-age kids'll make headlines. You're finished. You'll never get a gig in this town again.'

The tape ended and Lorraine looked at Decker. 'You ever heard of this Julian Cole?'

Decker nodded. 'He made some movie about a whale and a mermaid – Oscar nomination years ago – but I think he's got one hell of a habit. Disappeared, or his later movies did.'

Lorraine got up and stretched her arms above her head. 'Maybe he could be a suspect – maybe half the callers we just listened to could be. Seems a lot of people wanted Harry Nathan dead.'

Decker agreed. 'What a sleaze-bag. I'll run a check on all the callers we got.'

'Mm, yes, but first run a check on Nathan's finances – let's see how broke he was. Something tells me he's the kind of man that has stashes of cash but won't touch a cent of his own money if he can blackmail, or whatever else, to make some other poor schmuck pay up.'

Decker rewound the tape and reached for the next. By tape five they had Raymond again, still talking about his latest nubile love. The calls were as tedious as the rest, until the last one on the tape when Nathan suggested that, as Raymond's career was going nowhere, he should do a small favour for him.

'You must be joking, I haven't reached that level.'

Nathan laughed. 'I'm talking private tapes, man.'

'What?'

'You heard me.'

'I don't follow, Harry,' Raymond said, fear audible in his voice.

'Yes, you do. You know about my wires, my little personal kicks.'

'Jesus Christ, are you serious?'

''Fraid so. I need money, and . . .'

'But you wouldn't, I mean . . . They're just between you and me.'

'They were. But, like I said, I need cash. I got a studio to run, a movie about to go down, which will cost me, so—'

'I can't – you know, I can't.'

75

There was a long pause.

'Harry? You still there?'

'Yeah, man.'

'Don't do this to me.'

'Then you do somethin' for me.'

'I can't. Jesus Christ, I can't. I've got my career to think of.'

Nathan sighed, and his voice changed. 'What career, Raymond? You are dead meat in this town – both you and your career, if you get my meaning.'

'I thought you were my friend,' came the plaintive response.

'Raymondo, nobody is my friend when I'm tight for cash, and right now I'm tight. So, friendship apart, I need you to star in *Likely Ladies*. And I'll release my private films if you don't agree to wave your flaccid dick around in it. Now, you got that?'

'If I refuse?'

'Then I just release the private videos.'

The call cut off, and Lorraine looked at Decker. 'My God, all those calls we listened to – he was just waitin' to pounce.'

Decker nodded. 'We got another suspect, right?'

Lorraine reached for the next tape. 'Yes, sir, we do. And now it's understandable.'

'What is?'

'The acid bath. Any one of the callers we just listed wouldn't want these tapes released, and Raymond Vallance is moving up the list.'

Decker looked at his notes. A lot of people wanted, or might have wanted, Harry Nathan dead and for good reason: blackmail.

The next tape was disappointing, but just before it ended, Decker and Lorraine pricked up their ears.

'Cindy, it's me.' It was Vallance's voice.

'Oh, hi. Harry's not at home.'

'Oh, really?' There was an artificial brightness in Vallance's voice. 'When would be a good time to call?'

'Oh – I'd say if you were to call . . . Harry, between three and four, that would be a good time.' As usual, Cindy's acting wasn't up to much, and she suddenly dropped back into more natural tones. 'Though I'm real sick. I think I got flu.'

'It's important.'

'But I'm feeling real sick.'

'I have to call *Harry*, Cindy.'

'Well, OK. Between three and four. I'll tell him you called,' Cindy said, in the arch voice of the chambermaid in *Paradise Motel*.

Vallance hung up, and Lorraine made a note, looking at Decker. 'Bit of a code going on there, wouldn't you say?'

'Mm, let's play it again.'

They did so, and came to the conclusion that Raymond Vallance and Cindy Nathan were using a code to arrange meetings of their own. The last tape they played recorded Nathan talking about the reshoot of his film, with Raymond Vallance now as the 'star attraction'. Finances were in place, and the film could continue shooting. At the end of the tape Nathan laughed. 'I'm out of the shit,' he said to an unknown caller, 'and I have pre-sales that'll keep me out of it. We're back on schedule.'

'I sincerely hope so, Harry,' said a low, clipped male voice.

Lorraine rewound the tape. 'That's his lawyer, Feinstein. I recognize his voice,' she said.

'Shall I put him on this ever-growing list?' Decker asked, pen poised.

'No, lawyers don't get involved in the dirt. They just get their clients out of it.'

Decker held up the last tape. 'Ready for one more?' He inserted it and pressed Play.

'Harry, this is Kendall.'

'Hi, honey, how you doing?'

'I'm doing fine, but we need some publicity for the gallery. How's Cindy, by the way?'

'Got flu,' Nathan replied.

'I'm really sorry.' Kendall seemed to be laughing.

'I bet you are.'

'No, I really am.' There was a slight lisp in the woman's voice.

'I'd better come over and see you.'

'I'll be expecting you.' There was an almost mocking note in the sexy voice. The phone went dead.

'Put her on the list,' Lorraine said, then looked at her notes. On paper, it still looked like a Raymond/Cindy inside job, but there was something about both ex-wives that had made her suspicious at the funeral. 'I want to see Kendall Nathan and maybe I should speak to Sonja Sorenson, too. They're the ones we know least about,' she said.

'I don't follow. Shouldn't you be seeing all these other names?'

'Right. I do want to see them, especially Raymond Vallance. Blackmailers' victims don't usually murder, but—'

'But?' Decker butted in.

'I think Harry Nathan was killed by one of his ex-wives. Question is, which one?'

Decker smiled. 'Well, darling, I've heard all the tapes, and I'd say my main suspect would be Raymond Vallance.'

Lorraine grinned back at him. 'That's because you're a man. I think Harry Nathan blackmailed or screwed everyone he ever came across. We could have endless lists of possible suspects, but he was killed – murdered – by someone close to him. Call it female intuition. It was either Cindy, Kendall or . . .'

'Sonja,' Decker interjected.

'Yes. The murder was carefully premeditated by someone who knew his routine. Nathan lived by blackmail, he got what he wanted by fear and intimidation, so he would have been wary of strangers. Therefore, whoever killed Harry Nathan had to be someone he trusted.'

The office phone rang, and Decker picked it up. 'Page Investigations,' he said curtly. Then he covered the mouthpiece. 'It's Cindy Nathan, and she sounds hysterical. You want me to put her through to your office?' he asked.

Lorraine hurried to her desk. 'Tape it,' she said, but he'd already switched the phone on to record.

'Mrs Page, it's me, Cindy Nathan. Can you come over, and hurry – you got to come over here.' She was crying.

'Cindy? Are you all right?'

Lorraine signalled to Decker, who looked over. 'You want your car brought round?'

Lorraine nodded and returned her attention to the phone. 'Cindy, I can't hear you. Tell me what's happened.'

'I was only out for ten minutes. Somebody's been here. I don't know what to do, I'm all by myself and I'm scared.'

Cindy eventually calmed down enough to explain that the house had been broken into. The housekeeper and her husband were out and Cindy had not called the police, but when Lorraine suggested that she do so, she became even more hysterical, shouting that she had to see Lorraine first.

'I'll be right over.'

It took Lorraine no more than twenty minutes to get to the house. The gates were wide open, as was the front door, and Lorraine ran from the car into the house.

'Cindy?' she called, and her voice echoed round the vast hallway. There was no reply. First she went downstairs into the basement, then made her way up the wide open-tread staircase to the first floor. 'Cindy?'

All the bedroom doors were closed, the polished wooden floor giving way to white thick-pile carpet, which bore the marks of painstaking vacuuming. On a white marble plinth against one wall a massive pre-Columbian ceramic piece was balanced precariously, as if it had been knocked or pushed to one side.

'Cindy?' Lorraine called again, but still there was no response. Lorraine hesitated, and chose a door at random. Without a sound, she turned the glass handle of one of a pair of ten-foot-high polished pine double doors, and stepped tentatively into the room.

The bedroom was a sea of white: white carpet, white walls. The only colour in the room was in the centre of the bed – where there was a dark red pool of blood.

Lorraine almost had heart failure as Jose appeared from behind her. 'What are you doing in here?'

Lorraine whipped round. 'I got a call from Cindy—'

'She's not here.'

'What's happened?'

'Who are you?'

Lorraine opened her purse and handed the man her card. He glanced at it, then looked back to the landing at his wife. 'She's a private investigator.'

The woman gave Lorraine a hard stare. 'I thought you said you came to give her a massage?'

'Cindy asked me to say that,' Lorraine said, silently cursing the girl for making her go through the silly charade. 'She wanted to consult with me in private and was . . . feeling insecure.'

There was a pause, while the housekeepers registered that they were clearly the source of Cindy's mistrust. Then Lorraine asked, 'Where is she?'

Juana came closer. 'Hospital. We had to call an ambulance.'

'What happened? Was she attacked?' Lorraine said impatiently. They looked at each other. 'For God's sake, answer me. She was hysterical when she called me and now . . .' Lorraine looked at the bed as Juana went to remove the stained cover. 'Leave that and tell me what happened.'

'Mrs Nathan started to have a miscarriage. We found her in here, and dialled 911.'

'Didn't you go with her?'

'She didn't want us to,' Juana said, pulling the coverlet from the bed and bundling it up with a look of disgust.

'I think you should leave,' said Jose.

Lorraine studied him: he was very nervous, his dark, thick-lashed eyes constantly straying to his wife's. It was obvious to Lorraine that the pair knew more than they

81

were prepared to admit about the sequence of bizarre events in the house.

'What about the police?' Lorraine said flatly. 'Mrs Nathan told me the house had been broken into.'

'What?'

Lorraine sighed. 'When she called me, she said someone had been in the house, that she'd only been out ten minutes.'

Jose shook his head. 'No, we have been here all afternoon. We only left to do some shopping earlier. Nobody has been here.'

'Are you sure?'

There was yet another furtive exchange of glances. 'Have you looked around the house?' Lorraine asked. 'Because if you haven't, I suggest you do.'

Juana crossed to the doors with her bloody bundle, calling back, 'You show her round, Jose.'

Lorraine turned back to Jose. 'Is this the master bedroom?'

'No, this is a guest suite.'

She asked to see Cindy's bedroom, and Jose indicated that it was the next room along the corridor. According to him, it was Mrs Nathan's own suite. When Lorraine asked if Cindy had slept alone or with her husband he shrugged. 'I think it depended on how Mr Nathan felt.'

There were no photographs or knick-knacks in the ice-blue bedroom, but Cindy's wardrobe made Lorraine gasp. She had never seen so many designer labels, not even in the smartest department store, row upon row of evening gowns, daywear, a whole closet of beach and casual wear, and racks of shoes. The walk-in wardrobe was more like a room, the size of her own bedroom, and from the sales tickets still attached it was obvious that many of the items had never been worn.

'Mrs Nathan likes to shop,' Jose said, with humour.

'Obviously,' Lorraine murmured, and looked around. 'She's surprisingly neat and tidy.'

Jose raised an eyebrow. 'Tell that to my wife and she'd split.' He gestured to her to follow him from the dressing room. 'My wife spends hours every day just tidying up after her.'

Lorraine looked back at the pale blue room. It felt cold, empty and unused. It was hard to imagine Cindy sleeping in there, let alone dressing and . . . 'What about her bathroom?'

Jose paused, already at the door. 'Through the mirrored wall beyond the bed.' He moved soundlessly across the thick blue carpet, passed his hand across a certain area of the mirror and the door slid back electronically to reveal yet more ice-blue, this time stained floor-to-ceiling marble. Again, the room was obsessively neat. The only thing that seemed out of place was a single toothbrush left beside one of the washbasins. Jose opened one of the cupboards underneath, took out a spray of glass polish and a cloth, cleaned carefully around the washbasin, replaced the cleaning fluid and cloth and put the toothbrush neatly into a pale blue glass holder.

He caught Lorraine watching him. 'Mr Nathan hated anything out of place. He checked every room every day.'

'You mean she couldn't even leave a toothbrush out?'

'Water stains the marble. He even used to check under the taps. He was quite obsessive about cleanliness.'

Jose ushered Lorraine back across Cindy's bedroom.

'He showered sometimes six, seven times a day, and changed his clothes as often. But he worked out a lot, and he would need clean clothes to work out in, clean clothes to change into, and then he would start the whole process again.'

Lorraine followed him across the landing. 'Must have been tough to work for him.'

'Not really, you got into his routine. This is his room – the master bedroom.'

Lorraine waited as the pine doors opened, then said softly, 'Well, I think you'll have quite a job in here, Jose. I'm sure Mr Nathan never left his room in this state.'

'Oh, my God!' Jose whispered.

The lurid orange linen had been torn from the twelve-foot-square bed and strewn over the floor. The rugs had been drawn up in places and pulled into the centre of the room, throwing a tall metal chair onto its side. A glass coffee table had been broken, as had a lighting fitting. A canvas had been dragged from the wall and the drapes on the lower windows had been torn down. A marble plinth lay on its side, and what had been a Chinese *famille rose* peach vase lay shattered in tiny fragments.

'Well, Cindy was right. Somebody *has* been here, and this must have taken quite a while,' Lorraine said, watching Jose carefully. He seemed genuinely shocked by the destruction in the huge room.

There was a dressing room similar to that of the guest suite, Lorraine noticed. Its electronic door was ajar. 'Can I go in here?' she asked, and the man nodded without speaking. At first sight, Harry Nathan's dressing room was untouched, the clothes neatly stored.

'I think I should check the entire house, Mrs Page,' Jose said, 'if you would care to come downstairs with me.' Lorraine wondered if there was some reason why he wanted her out of the room. 'Could I just see his bathroom?' she asked.

Jose pointed towards it as he surveyed the bedroom. 'I just don't see when this was done. My wife and I left the house for such a short while.'

Lorraine glanced into the bathroom, another room with the charm of a meat safe, then did a double-take. 'Oh, my God . . .'

The blood was in pools, not even dried, and there was a heap of blood-sodden towels in the centre of the otherwise spotless bathroom. Jose stepped past her, bent down to the towels, then recoiled. He leaped to the washbasin and retched. That reaction clearly wasn't faked, Lorraine noted. He had not been with Cindy when she had lost her child.

'Let's take a look round the rest of the house,' she said, already heading out, not turning back when she heard Jose vomiting. The wreckage in the bedroom made her wonder if Cindy herself had caused the damage – perhaps that was what had made her miscarry, unless she had walked in on someone else and been attacked. Lorraine was still deep in thought as she crossed the landing towards the stairs. Suddenly she paused. Had she seen all the rooms on this floor?

'What's that room?' She indicated a closed door.

'No one is allowed in there. Mr Nathan never let anyone in even to clean it.'

'Mr Nathan is dead now, so let me see in there, Jose, would you?'

'It's always locked.'

But Lorraine had turned the handle as he spoke and the door opened.

This was Nathan's office: here, at least, the walls were still intact, though covered with two-foot-square wood tiles stained red and black in an ugly checkerboard effect. There was the usual office equipment, a photocopier, fax machine, computers and telephones, and a bank of four television sets, like monitors, was recessed into the wall. Two shelves that had previously contained videotapes were now empty, the tapes removed from their cases and thrown on the floor. Lorraine saw that they were labelled with the names of Nathan's films and of TV shows he had appeared in – someone had clearly gone through them to check that the contents of the boxes matched the labels outside.

There was something in this house for which someone had been searching desperately, that much was obvious to Lorraine. The fact that the phone tapes had been destroyed suggested that it might have been a recording, but it hadn't been on any of the tapes she had listened to or, presumably, the ones that had been destroyed, or the burglar wouldn't have bothered looking any further. Nor could it have been on any of the videotapes in front of her, or they, too, would have been destroyed or removed. There was, however, a cache of tapes from the security cameras, which Cindy had mentioned but which had never been found, and these must be the object of the search.

'What did Mr Nathan do with the tapes he recorded on the security cameras?' Lorraine asked.

'He took care of all that himself,' Jose said. 'I thought he kept them in here, or just used them over and over.'

'When was all the security put in the house?'

'A couple of years ago. The same firm did some of the decorating.'

'Oh, really?' Lorraine asked casually. 'Any work on the walls or floors?'

'Wall panels. Like in here,' he said.

What a surprise, she thought, scanning the checker-board walls. 'Jose,' she said, with her sweetest smile, 'could you get me something with a flat blade – like a big knife or a chisel?' She had a good idea that she would not need any implement to open the hidden compart-ment she was sure was in the wall, but she wanted him out of the room. He nodded and disappeared.

As soon as he was gone, she began to scan the rows of large wooden tiles on the walls, then spotted a row of metal bandstand chairs in dolly-mixture colours folded flat against one of the walls. She examined the floor in front of them, which, thanks to Harry Nathan's secrecy, did not benefit from daily vacuuming. She could make out the marks where a chair's sharp metal legs had indented the thick pile – deeper than one would have expected if someone had been merely sitting on it, but not if they had stood on it, particularly a tall and heavy man . . .

She pulled out a chair, set it up with its feet on the same marks, then climbed up on it. She pressed carefully along the vertical edges of the two large wooden tiles within easy reach, and swore under her breath when they remained still. Then she tried the horizontal axis. One of the tiles gave, just a quarter of an inch. It seemed to be spring-loaded on the other side to prevent it opening too easily and to keep it flush with the rest of the wall. She had to press hard but finally a wooden door opened. Behind it were pile after pile of tapes. Lorraine pulled one out. There was no title, only a date and the name 'Cindy'.

'What are you doing?' Jose spoke suddenly behind her, and she almost fell off the chair. The man was standing in the doorway with what looked like a carving knife, Juana beside him.

Lorraine looked coolly at them. She had no idea what their intentions towards her were, but she had to try to face them out. 'I was looking for evidence relevant to my client's case, and it seems like I found it. My assistant and I are working closely with the police, and I will naturally be informing them as soon as possible. I imagine they will want to talk to you about how the house came to be torn apart today, and how this evidence came to be concealed.' She willed her voice to remain calm.

'We have nothing to do with this,' Juana said immediately, angry and defensive, and Jose shot her a warning glance. 'We were going to go to the police ourselves – tell her, Jose.'

'Be quiet,' he ordered. 'There is nothing to tell.'

The woman's eyes flashed. 'How much longer are you going to hide that man's dirt, Jose?'

'Be quiet, woman!' he repeated, but his wife stood her ground.

'He is dead. We have nothing. Tell her the truth.'

The man sighed. 'Perhaps it is better. Perhaps we should go downstairs.'

Lorraine relaxed. 'I'd certainly be more comfortable. But I'd like to take the tapes. They become Mrs Nathan's property, I believe, under the terms of Mr Nathan's will, and as I just said, she has asked me to gather any evidence relevant to her case.'

Jose looked at Juana again. 'Let her take them. I want them gone.' There was a note of resignation in her voice.

88

Lorraine scooped into her arms as many of the tapes as she could hold and climbed down from the chair. 'I'll lock these in the trunk of my car before we talk.'

Juana nodded, a look of relief crossing her face. 'I will make some tea.'

Lorraine made two journeys out to the Mercedes, doing her best to appear unconcerned, but prepared for any attempt the two servants might make to stop her. Neither approached her, though, and she could hear them talking in Spanish in the kitchen, Juana's voice much more prominent than Jose's. She locked the trunk before returning to the house.

Lorraine walked back into the hall and through to where she could hear Jose and Juana's voices. The kitchen, which had the air of an operating theatre, was in monochrome black and white, and the table was set with crockery of almost transparent white porcelain in a variety of deliberately irregular shapes. 'Mr Nathan certainly seemed to like the minimalist look,' Lorraine said.

'Mr Nathan was a criminal,' Juana said, tight-lipped. 'He was a thief.' Jose said nothing: his wife had clearly convinced him that their interests no longer lay in loyalty to their former employer.

She poured Lorraine a cup of slightly perfumed tea, and pushed a plate of home-made crinkle cookies towards her.

'What makes you say that?' Lorraine said, as she bit into a cookie, but before the woman could answer, the telephone rang.

Jose picked it up. 'No, Mrs Nathan, I have no authority . . .' he said mechanically.

Lorraine looked up at the mention of her client's

name. 'Can I speak to her?' she asked, but the man shook his head.

'It is not Cindy,' Juana said. 'It is Kendall. She has been calling every day since Mr Nathan died. Cindy won't let her in the house.'

Jose continued to say yes and no to a clearly pushy caller, and told her that Cindy had suffered a miscarriage and been taken to Cedars-Sinai.

When he hung up, Lorraine asked, 'What did she want?'

'What she always wants. She says there's some property here of hers. Mr Feinstein has given instructions that she is not to be allowed to remove anything – I think it's some of the paintings.'

Or maybe some tapes, Lorraine thought, wondering when Harry Nathan's interest in home movies had started.

'What were you about to say, Juana, about Mr Nathan's having stolen something?' she asked.

Juana looked at Jose, indicating that he should speak. He pulled at his tie. 'Mr Nathan owed us a lot of money, Mrs Page. Our life savings, plus back salary. We were only here because we wanted to get paid. Six, seven years ago, he said he would invest it for us.'

Juana folded her arms. 'For the first few years we didn't question it. He said he had invested it for us and even paid us dividends, so it seemed our money had doubled, then trebled and then . . .' She went on to describe how when Nathan had married Kendall, they had wanted to leave. 'She was an evil woman, but when we went to him and asked for our money, told him we couldn't stay, he . . . he told us that he'd had some bad news about his stocks and shares. He said he hadn't been able to tell us because he was so upset about it – that he had lost everything as well.'

'But that obviously wasn't true,' Lorraine said, jerking her head towards the rest of the house.

'He said the house was remortgaged and he made us all these promises about selling his art collection. We stayed on here because we had no place else to go and no money to go anywhere with. At least by being here we could see if he did make any money and then we'd get paid. He promised us we would. He owed everybody he ever met,' Jose said flatly. 'Now we just hope that we'll get something if his estate is sold.'

'Does Cindy know about this?'

Juana shook her head. 'That silly child knows nothing, and he'd made her so crazy anyway. We think he was going to leave her, find a woman with money, probably.'

'Do you think she killed him?'

There was another exchange of looks, and then Juana sighed. 'Yes, we do. She threatened it more than once.'

'You were here in the house, though, weren't you, the morning Mr Nathan was shot?'

'Yes, but I was working in the laundry, and Jose was out back near the garages. We didn't hear anything at all, not until Mrs Nathan started screaming.'

Jose went on to describe how he and Juana had tried to get Nathan's body out of the pool, but it was so heavy they couldn't lift it.

'What was Cindy doing then?'

Jose thought for a moment. 'She was sitting by the pool, and I shouted at her to help us. She just kept saying over and over that she didn't do it – no, what she said was she didn't *think* that she had done it. That's a strange thing to say, isn't it?'

'But you think that she did?'

'Yes, I do,' said Juana.

'She had reasons,' Jose agreed. 'I think she knew he was going to kick her out. They did nothing but argue, and she was drinking heavily, and—'

'Tell her,' Juana said. 'Tell her everything.'

Jose looked shifty, and wouldn't meet Lorraine's eyes. Then he said, 'She was having an affair with Raymond Vallance, Mr Nathan's closest friend.'

Juana looked at Jose as if she expected him to say more: when he remained silent she spoke up herself. 'And *he* has offered us money – to keep our mouths shut and give him the tapes.' Juana met Lorraine's eyes squarely. 'I would have taken his money with pleasure, but we did not know where the tapes were.'

'Did you tell him that yesterday at the funeral?' Lorraine asked.

'I have told him many times.' She noted that Juana did not confirm what her conversation with Vallance had been about.

'Did you know what was on the tapes?'

'I can guess. Mr Nathan used to take drugs and party in the basement on the weekends. He would tell us to take time off. When we went in to clean, you could smell the . . . sex in the air.'

'Do you think Raymond Vallance could have been here this afternoon?' Lorraine asked.

'He has a key,' Jose put in. 'She gave it to him.'

'I see. Well, thank you both very much. If you think of anything else that might be important, I'd appreciate it if you'd call me – here's my card.' She placed it on the kitchen table. 'I'll go see Cindy tonight.'

'What about the jeep?' Juana said hesitantly to her husband.

He shrugged.

'What was that?' Lorraine asked.

Jose chewed his lip. 'Well, it's probably nothing, but I saw it very early, parked down the road. It was odd – most residents around here never park on the street, there's no need.'

Juana added, 'But it wasn't there when you looked later. Tell Mrs Page, tell her whose car you thought it was.'

'It was the same colour, maybe even the same type, as the jeep Mrs Kendall Nathan drives,' Jose said.

Lorraine could hardly contain herself. She asked when Jose had seen it and when he thought it had been driven away. He was unsure of the exact time, only that it had been there early that morning and had gone after the murder.

'You won't tell her what we've said, will you?' Jose said nervously.

'No, of course not. Whatever we have discussed remains private,' Lorraine lied, setting off down the steps. 'Goodnight.'

The couple stood in the doorway for a moment until the security lights came on, then closed the front door. Lorraine waited until she thought they must be back in the kitchen, then hurried across the lawn, stepped into the shrubbery and, under cover of the thick bushes, began to examine the ground. She got down on her hands and knees and inched her way on all fours, scratched by the bushes, feeling in front of her. She searched for ten minutes until the security lights went out and she could no longer see anything. She decided to come back the following day and continue. She was still kneeling, as she turned to make her way out of the shrubbery, when she felt something digging into her knee. When she looked down, the object glinted faintly. She picked it up: a large, snub-nosed bullet. She'd found it. At least Cindy Nathan had been telling the truth about one thing: that two gunshots had been fired the morning of the murder.

CHAPTER 4

LATER, LORRAINE realized that the discovery of the bullet might mean nothing, because Nathan had been known to shoot at birds. It was quite possible that there would be a number of bullets in the grounds. But if this one fitted the murder weapon, Cindy had told the truth. The question still remained as to whether or not Cindy had fired the gun.

Lorraine showered, changed, and put some disinfectant on the scratches that covered her arms and legs, and the two on her face. Tiger had been disgruntled – he'd been left alone most of the day – but Lorraine had fed and walked him now. He had perked up when she decided he could ride with her to the hospital. It was after ten by the time she turned off San Vincente Boulevard and drove between the imposing towers of Cedars-Sinai Medical Centre, lit up like a liner at night. She went to the emergency rooms to enquire about Cindy Nathan, and was told that Cindy had been admitted to a medical ward on the eighth floor.

When Lorraine asked at the nurses' station if she could see Mrs Nathan, they refused. Cindy had been sedated and was not allowed visitors. 'If you would like to leave your number, Mrs Page, I will tell her you came to see her when she wakes,' the night nurse said authoritatively, a challenging look in her eyes. The unit was frequently used by celebrities and their families, and it was clear that the staff were well versed in keeping unwanted attention away from them. Lorraine checked her watch, thought about waiting around, but decided to go home. She had a lot of new developments to get on top of, and she was tired.

'What time can I see her in the morning?'

'That will depend on the doctor and the patient. She's in a private room with a phone, so I'm sure she'll call you if she wants to. Now, if you will excuse me . . .' and the nurse set off down the corridor.

Two clerical staff were behind their desks at the administration station, and Lorraine moved closer. 'Excuse me, do you know if Mrs Cindy Nathan has had any visitors since she was admitted?'

One woman, with permed hair, looked over her half-moon glasses, apparently irritated to be distracted from her copy of the *National Enquirer*. 'Are you a relative?'

'No, I spoke to you earlier.'

'I'm sorry, we're not allowed to give any personal details to anyone not related to the patient.'

'What if I said I was her sister?'

'But you just said you weren't related,' the woman snapped.

Lorraine threw up her hands. 'I'm a close friend, and she's just miscarried her baby. At a time like this she'll need a lot of comfort and, above all, the support of her friends, right? And I would like to contact—'

'No visitors,' the perm said.

'Thank you for your co-operation,' Lorraine replied sarcastically, and walked out. She was, she thought, probably the only person who did care about poor little Cindy, for she felt genuinely sorry for her, but at the same time, she was relieved to be going home again.

Back at the car, Tiger had eaten his leather lead, and Lorraine was so absorbed in scolding him that she didn't see the two-toned Mitsubishi jeep pull into a space just a short distance away. She was still berating Tiger as a woman got out, carrying grapes and a bunch of flowers. But Kendall Nathan had seen Lorraine and stood in the shadows, keeping well out of view, watching her drive out.

Kendall did not get such short shrift from the receptionist: as she had the same surname as Cindy, the perm presumed she was a relative and allowed her to talk to the night nurse monitoring Cindy. She was told that Cindy was still sleeping, and, although not critically ill, in a deeply depressed state. Kendall was about to leave her gifts and go, when the nurse offered to check if Cindy was awake.

She showed Kendall into the plush private room, with its dimmed lights, controlled atmosphere and television mounted on a bracket on the wall. Kendall leaned over and smiled: Cindy was awake, but very drowsy.

'I came as soon as I heard. I talked to Jose and he told me – I'm so sorry.'

Slowly Cindy turned away her face. 'I bet you are,' she whispered, so softly as to be barely audible.

Kendall turned and smiled sweetly at the nurse. 'I'll just sit with her for a few moments.'

The nurse hesitated, but Kendall looked hard at her, and she nodded. 'I'll check on the other patients and come back, but you mustn't stay long.'

'Thank you so much,' Kendall said softly. As soon as

the door closed the sickening smile froze on her mouth. She moved to stand at the end of the bed, unhooked the notes attached to the foot and flicked through them before she spoke.

'How are you, darling? I was so sorry to hear you lost the baby.' She put the clipboard back. 'You must really regret the abortions now.'

Cindy glared at her. 'I never had any abortions.'

'Oh,' Kendall smiled, 'it must be a mistake. I'll tell the nurse to alter this "previous pregnancies" thing on my way out.'

Cindy said nothing.

'I didn't even think it was true, the baby,' Kendall continued. 'Whose was it?'

Cindy closed her eyes.

'It wasn't likely to be Harry's, you little whore. You screwed anything in pants.'

Cindy opened her eyes again. 'You mean like you did to get yourself pregnant? That was why he married you, wasn't it?'

Kendall's eyes slanted like a snake's as she cocked her head to one side. 'If you hadn't shot him he'd have kicked you out, and you know it.'

'The way he kicked you out?'

'You're a poisonous little bitch, aren't you?'

'Takes one to know one.'

'My, my, that was quite a fast retort – unusual for you. That chemical garbage you stuff yourself with usually makes you totally fucking off the wall. But I'm sorry, really I am. It won't be quite so heart-rending now, will it? "Pregnant wife on trial for her husband's murder" would have been quite a sexy angle.'

'Go away. Leave me alone.'

Kendall pursed her lips. 'Was it Harry's?'

'Yes. And that must have really pissed you off.'

Kendall recomposed her features into what she hoped was a pleasant smile. 'Look, Cindy, that's all water under the bridge. I'm sorry for . . . teasing you – I guess I'm just jealous, you know, about you and the baby and all.' She gave a sigh, as though of sorrow at the realization of her own human weakness, and her expression grew still more saccharine-sweet. 'Let's you and me not fight,' she went on. 'I mean, we've both suffered such a terrible loss and we're both in the same boat about a lot of things – Harry, and the will, and . . . well, you know there's just a few little videotapes out at the house I think both of us would rather not watch with our moms.'

'What?' Cindy said weakly. 'Harry . . . did stuff with you too?'

'Harry did stuff with the Koi carp and the juice extractor, darling.' Kendall's voice was more businesslike now. 'Did you get the key to the office?'

'No. But somebody else did. Somebody broke in – there were tapes all over the floor, but just his movies and stuff, they didn't take any. I can't find the private ones. I looked all over.'

'They must be still at the house, and Feinstein's in charge now while you're lying here, Cindy. You don't want him finding them and sitting around whacking off to them, now do you?'

'I guess not.'

'Well, then, call Jose and Juana and tell them to let me in to collect them. I won't take anything else.'

'Like fuck you won't, Kendall.' Even Cindy was not

99

too dumb to be taken in by that ploy. 'I know you'd walk out with a couple of Jackson de Koonings, or whatever they are, tucked in your tights.'

'Cindy, I don't intend to discuss this with you at this time,' Kendall said prissily. 'You got my attorney's letter and you know that the collection of art works at the house, which Harry and I built up, was jointly owned. My paintings do not form part of the contents of the house, and I can prove it because I paid the insurance premiums – which shows Harry acknowledged before he died that I had a proprietary interest. And what the fuck would you do with a lot of Jackson *Pollocks*?'

'Sell them, Kendall, same as you. And I have news for you. If you're banking on that premium business to set up your case, you're in a whole lot of trouble because he never paid the insurance. I just found that out.'

'What?' Kendall said, her expression reverting to its former undisguised anger and greed. 'How do you know?'

'I found the letters telling him that the policy had expired, last chance to renew kind of thing. He never paid a penny in insurance in the last two years.'

Kendall was speechless with rage and shock. 'But I gave him about two million fucking dollars in that time. What did he do with it?'

'The usual things, I guess,' Cindy said succinctly. 'His dick or his nose. And I have something else to tell you—'

'What?' Kendall snapped.

'I'm kind of tired now, Kendall,' Cindy said, with a yawn. 'Maybe I'll tell you some other time.'

Kendall jolted the bed. 'You straighten out with me right now, Cindy, or I'll slap your face!'

Cindy struggled to sit up. 'You lay one finger on me and I'll scream the place down. I just lost my fucking baby, for Chrissakes.'

Kendall returned with an effort to sweet-reason mode. 'Look, Cindy, we're just playing into the lawyers' hands by fighting each other. If there's some other problems with the art, I think you should tell me. Otherwise it will just go to Feinstein and he'll make ten billion dollars while we get zip.'

Cindy could never stand up to a more aggressive person for long. 'Well,' she said, sinking back on her pillows, 'you know that Chinese vase? The family of roses or whatever? In his bedroom? It fell off its perch.'

'*You broke it?*'

'Not on purpose, but . . . how old did you say it was? Only, for something so old, how come it's got a sticker inside?'

Cindy enjoying seeing Kendall froth at the mouth. 'Yeah, a sticker with a dealer's name on it, right inside the thing. Some company called Classic something or other.'

'Classic Reproductions,' Kendall said, between gritted teeth.

'Oh, that's it.' Cindy faked surprise with all her *Paradise Motel* skill. 'I knew you'd have heard of them.'

Kendall picked up her purse. 'Look, there's no point in us talking any more now, I have to go. I'll check things out with the insurance brokers tomorrow and call you.'

As the other woman turned away Cindy said, 'I didn't kill him, Kendall. I don't think I did, an' that's the truth. I even thought that maybe . . .'

'Maybe what?' Kendall was heading for the door.

'Maybe you did. Where were you when he got shot?'

'I was at home.'

'Oh, yeah?' Cindy said quietly. 'Got a witness, have you?' She turned back to her pillow and closed her eyes. Before Kendall could reply the nurse walked in, hurried to Cindy's bedside, and turned in surprise at the sound of the door slamming shut.

Cindy gave a weak smile. 'If Mrs Nathan comes again tell her I'm too tired to see her – she drains my energy centres. Can you get me something to help me sleep?'

'I'll check with the doctor. Oh, you had another visitor, a Mrs Lorraine Page. She left her card.' The nurse handed it to Cindy and went to see about sedation.

Kendall Nathan sat in her jeep, gripping the steering wheel. She was sure Cindy was lying about the vase, but the only way to be certain was to go to the house and see for herself. She knew Harry was a thief and a con-man, but would he have conned her, too, after all she had done for him? She had a terrible, sinking feeling that he just might have.

Half an hour later she was still shaking as she sipped hot water and lemon juice, and paced the black Astroturf with which she had carpeted her bedroom; the building's beautifully preserved thirties exterior had not deterred Kendall from filling her apartment with screamingly modern design as near to the décor of the Nathan house as she could afford. The sight of all these things now, which had previously given her such satisfaction, filled her with fury as the possibility of Harry Nathan's treachery sank in.

She wanted to scream, wanted to get back into the

jeep and get over to the Nathans' house, but she knew she had to be calm. If the *famille rose* vase was a fake, what had happened to the original, worth three quarters of a million dollars? She had to find out without betraying how important it was to her. And it *was* important: the vase represented part of an art collection worth twenty million dollars, half of which she knew was hers. Eventually she slumped onto her bed, and nausea swept over her.

Lorraine was in her bathrobe, eating chicken with spinach and walnut salad. She had just settled down in front of the video recorder to play some of Harry Nathan's tapes when the phone rang. She looked at the clock – it was almost eleven, and she wondered who was calling so late.

'Lorraine? It's me, Cindy Nathan.'

'Oh, hello. I came by the hospital earlier – how are you?'

'I'm okay. They give me somethin' for the pain, but it's the one in my heart that hurts more. I lost my baby.'

'Yes, I know, I'm so sorry.'

'So am I, and I would have liked to talk to you.'

'I'll come by tomorrow – I need to talk to you too.'

'There's a reason I called, but I don't want to talk about it over the phone. It's just I know something about, well, I think I know somebody with a motive for shooting Harry. I think it might be Kendall.'

Lorraine reached for her cigarette pack. 'Can you just answer me one thing? You know the telephone tapes, the ones you sent over to my office? Who else did you tell that you were sending them to me?'

103

'I didn't tell anyone else – well, not exactly. You see, there's a locked room, Harry's office, and I couldn't find the key. It's one of those plastic card things, you know – some hotels use them. I couldn't find it, an' I didn't know how to get into the room.'

'Did Jose and Juana know?'

'Hell, no. I wouldn't tell those two nothin'. I called Harry's wife, Sonja, and she said she didn't even know there was a locked room. Well, she wouldn't have, she hadn't been living there for a long time, so then I called Kendall.'

'Did you mention the telephone recordings to either of them?'

'Yes, well, maybe I did, I can't remember.'

Lorraine wondered if this was true, or whether the girl was trying to throw suspicion on the other two wives – she had seemed certain before that nobody else knew about the tapes. 'I'm sorry, I got to go now. I'm too tired to talk. They give me something to help me sleep.'

'Well, I'll come by in the morning. You sure only Mr Nathan's ex-wives knew about the tapes?'

'Yeah. I didn't tell anyone else. G'night now.'

The phone went dead. Lorraine moved back to her new white sofa, which Tiger was now occupying. 'Get off.' He gave a low growl. 'Hey, man, cut that out. You've moved in on the office and don't try it here. Get off.' He got up and padded into the bedroom. 'Not on the bed either, Tiger,' but he had already disappeared.

She pressed Play on the remote control and settled back, only noticing as she lifted the fork to eat her supper that the chicken leg had been removed. She was about to go after Tiger when the tape started, a shot clearly set up in Nathan's bedroom. Cindy was spreadeagled naked and face down on the bed, and Nathan was working her over.

Lorraine felt sick as she watched three more videos, two showing explicit sex acts with Cindy, one with Kendall, each more violent and degrading than the last. Cindy was made to beg on all fours, while Nathan beat her with a thonged leather strap. He was into S and M in a big way, screwing her so violently, every muscle straining, that the sweat dripped from his body and matted his dark hair. He had tied Kendall over the back of a chair in a way that enabled him, with a jerk of the rope, to splay her legs wide apart, then insert a selection of objects, animal, mineral and vegetable, into various orifices, while some unknown female friend shrieked in the background with hyena-like laughter.

Worse was to come. Threesomes featuring not only Cindy but other very young girls were next on the tape, then a sickening sequence starring Raymond Vallance. In this session, Nathan sat watching, grinning and jerking off as the girls strapped on black, studded dildoes and forced Vallance down on all fours. Lorraine couldn't watch another minute of it and went to bed. What she had seen might provide Cindy with a provocation defence, or at least a position from which to bargain down the charge, but it also gave both her and Kendall Nathan a motive and a half: both women had been subjected to the grossest abuse.

Tiger lay sprawled across one side of the bed and didn't move an inch when Lorraine got under the duvet. He sighed with contentment when he realized that she wasn't going to push him off.

It was the first time in her life that Lorraine had owned a dog, and she understood now what it meant to have something that asked nothing from her but a half-share of her bed. Tiger had the love she found so difficult to give elsewhere, but he could not fill the void inside her – and it was a void. Lorraine was more lonely than she had ever been, and although she was financially secure, it frightened her to think about her future. Only Tiger heard her fears, and only he saw the vulnerable side of Lorraine that she showed to no one else – so in need of love, and so afraid she would never find it.

Decker had swept up the nightly shower of ficus leaves, had placed a fresh vase of lilies in Reception, and a jug of coffee was percolating. He had already sorted the office mail, mostly bills and circulars, when Lorraine arrived at eight thirty.

'Morning. Another lovely sunny day,' he said brightly, watching Tiger set off in search of a blue rubber boxing glove Decker had bought him, which he adored chewing and flinging about. 'He seems fit and well.'

'Yeah, so he should. He had a good two miles' walk this morning, ate half my supper last night *and* demolished his own.' She threw her hands up. 'Shit! What is happening to me? He's a goddamned dog! He's taking up too much of my life!' The boxing glove was hurled across the room, and Lorraine laughed.

'You know, Mrs Page, you have a wonderful laugh,' Decker said.

'Yeah, just not a lot to laugh about. You want to come in with the coffee and I'll give you an update, before I go to see Cindy. She's in hospital.'

'What's the matter with her?'

'Get the coffee and I'll tell you.'

The curtains had been pulled back from the windows that formed one whole wall of Cindy Nathan's hospital room, giving her a beautiful view of the early-morning haze clearing from the Hollywood Hills. In daylight, the room looked even more like a luxury hotel to Lorraine, and the breakfast on the tray table could certainly have come straight from room service.

Cindy was sitting up, a bed-jacket draped round her shoulders, eating orange and date muffins and fruit compote.

Lorraine drew a chair close to the bed. 'Right, tell me about Kendall Nathan.'

'She's a vicious bitch for a start-off. She claims she owns half of Harry's art collection, so I don't get it along with the house.'

'Has Feinstein told you the value of the estate?' Lorraine asked.

'Well, there's not nearly as much money in the company as anyone thought – Harry hadn't made a film that did any business since *Mutant Au-Pairs*, so the art's likely to be the big thing.' Lorraine waited, noting that the girl seemed much recovered and even quite cheerful. 'Means I don't have as much of a motive, do I?' she said cheerfully. 'Assuming I knew he was pretty broke, which I didn't, of course.' Cindy was a prosecuting attorney's wet dream.

Lorraine waited as she carried on with her breakfast, pouring some juice and drinking it thirstily before she lay back on the pillows.

107

'Harry was a con merchant, and anythin' he could steal he did. He used everybody – that's how he got his kicks, right?'

Lorraine remembered the videos – he had got his kicks in a lot of other ways as well.

'The gallery was real expensive – I mean, it's on Beverly Drive, right? Clients got a lot of money, and they paid through the nose. But I think he and Kendall were up to something crooked.'

Lorraine sat back. 'Go on.'

'Well, all those paintings at the house, they had to be insured. Lot of dough for the premiums, which is why we got such high security – all the stuff in there is the real thing, unlike what those other poor schmucks have got. Harry got the lot – that's including pre-Columbian stuff, and there's a Giaca—' She hesitated. 'A Giacaroni and stuff like that. You with me?'

'Yes.'

'Okay. Now, Kendall was paying Harry the money for the insurance premiums, which she says is because they had agreed that half the art was hers – like, in her dreams.' Cindy licked up the wheatgerm still adhering to the rim of the juice glass with a practised flick of her tongue. 'Still with me?'

'Yes.' Lorraine sighed – it wasn't too taxing to keep up with Cindy's thought process.

'She asked me to find the insurance certificates. I didn't know then it was for some scheme that she and her lawyer have cooked up to show she owns the stuff, so I got 'em out. But the only ones I could find were out of date, which means he hadn't been paying the cover. So ask yourself why.'

'Perhaps you'd tell me.'

'Well, look at the security at the house. The place is jam-full of lasers – you move one of them things off the wall and it's the full orchestra, you know what I mean?' Lorraine nodded.

'Well, I checked the dates when he stopped paying the insurance – it was when he got all the security in and started taping all the phone calls. I only checked because I knocked this vase off its stand. This is some Chinese rose vase supposed to be worth three quarters of a million dollars.'

Lorraine smiled encouragingly.

'It fell off the plinth, an' I got real worried. I thought the fucking alarms would start screaming, but nothing happened. It just broke.'

'Yes, I saw it.' Lorraine was wondering where all this was leading.

'Broke into lots of pieces,' Cindy said.

'I noticed. Go on.'

Cindy held up her hand. 'One: no alarms. Two: I find a sticker inside it, a modern sticker like a price thing – the vase had this long, thin neck so that normally you would never see inside. There was a name scrawled on it – Classic Reproductions. I dunno who they are, but what's their name doing inside some piece of porcelain that's supposed to be a billion years old?'

'It's a fake.'

'Right. Which brings me to Kendall Nathan.'

Lorraine waited while Cindy licked her lips.

'She thinks she owns half the so-called art stuff, and she thinks it's all legit, but if it's not it means Harry sold the real art on, took the money and didn't tell her. Now if she found that out, it's one hell of a motive to kill somebody, wouldn't you say? It's called being fucked over twice. He ditched her for me, then ripped off all her money. She was paying him to cover the insurance and he took that as well. You see what I mean, Lorraine?'

'Do the police know this?'

'Hell, no. I only just worked it out myself when the vase fell off its perch. I started to put it all together and then—'

'Then?'

'I lost my baby.'

Lorraine's mind worked furiously. Having seen the videos, and learned that Cindy and Raymond Vallance had been having an affair under Nathan's nose, the possibility that either Cindy or her lover had shot him seemed, as Decker had said, the obvious conclusion. She wondered if Cindy was dragging out all these ideas about art in an effort to throw her off the scent. She said, 'Cindy, I won't press you if you're feeling low, but when you called me, you said somebody was at the house. I saw the rooms were wrecked.'

Cindy nodded. 'I thought I saw someone, like a young black guy, going down the stairs to the gym. Then I went upstairs and saw the place had been trashed. It really freaked me out.'

Another convenient mystery burglar, Lorraine thought sceptically, but it wasn't out of the question that the same person who had destroyed the tapes in her office could have broken into the Nathan house. 'You didn't mention that when you called me.'

Cindy plucked a tissue from the box at her bedside. 'Didn't I? I guess I wasn't that together – I mean, it was just before . . .' She gestured weakly at her belly. She blew her nose, then turned her gaze back to Lorraine. 'I know things look bad, but I swear I think somebody's framing me, because I'm sure now I didn't kill Harry, I know I didn't.' Cindy lay back again, and put her hand over her eyes.

'Cindy, there's a couple of things I need to ask you about,' Lorraine said quietly.

'Sure,' Cindy said, blinking back tears.

'I found some videotapes, hidden in a wall in Harry's office.' There was a pause: Cindy wouldn't look at her. 'I'm sure you know the ones I'm talking about. I think your lawyers should see them, plus—'

'No way,' Cindy said, crumpling the tissue in her hand. 'I won't allow anyone to see them, especially not those fuckin' lawyers. I hate 'em.'

'But you were subjected to extreme violence and a lot of sexual abuse.'

'Yeah, I sure as hell was.' Lorraine watched the girl pluck at the tissue. 'Me and God knows how many more.'

'Like Kendall Nathan and Raymond Vallance, for example,' Lorraine said casually. 'Jose and Juana seem to think that you and Mr Vallance were . . . close. Is that true?'

Cindy said nothing for ten, twenty seconds, then, 'Yeah, we had a thing. Lasted all of five minutes and then he pissed on me too. It's like I have a sign round my neck, which only guys like him and Harry can see, that says, "Fuck Me and Dump Me" – oh, and "Beat Up on Me While You're There."' She began to cry in earnest.

Lorraine was surprised that Cindy had admitted the affair so readily – it made things look even blacker against her. Vallance had a key to the house, and he could easily have been responsible for the damage, particularly since there was no sign of forced entry, but Cindy seemed determined to cast suspicion elsewhere, first by the sudden mention of an unknown black youth – and now she was back to Nathan's ex-wife.

'What's gonna happen to me, Lorraine?' she wept. 'I know it looks like I had more reason than anyone to kill him, but I swear I didn't do it. It's Kendall Nathan who's pulling all the strings here, I just know it. She has no alibi for the time Harry was shot, and if the art thing's true, she's got a motive as well.'

'I'll go to the gallery just as soon as I can and see if I can talk to her,' Lorraine said soothingly, reaching out to give Cindy's hand a squeeze. 'Did the hospital have anyone photograph your bruises, by the way?'

Cindy nodded.

'Well, when you next see your lawyers, at least mention it to them, and also that Nathan had been violent to you on many previous occasions. I take it you haven't told the police any of this?'

'No, nothin'. A cop, a real bastard, asked me a lot of questions, but I told him nothin'.'

'You don't recall his name, by any chance?'

'Yeah, Sharkey.'

So he was still on the case. Lorraine walked to the door. 'I'll be in touch. You try to get some rest, and call me when you're discharged. Do you know how long you'll be here?'

'Depends on the doctor – could be out later today.'

Just as Lorraine opened the door, Cindy spoke again. 'I did love him at the beginning. I was only eighteen, he was so nice and he made me all these promises, about being in one of his movies. But they were as fucking sick as he was – he was just making porn.' She pulled herself up on her elbows to look Lorraine in the eye. 'You think I killed him now, don't you?'

Lorraine met the girl's gaze before she replied, 'No, Cindy, I don't believe I do. Take care now.'

She went out and closed the door quietly after her. She had made no mention of the bullet she had found, or Jose's revelation about the parked jeep that could have been Kendall's. She didn't want to raise Cindy's hopes, because unless Lorraine could clear her name, Cindy Nathan would have to stand trial for the murder of her husband.

As soon as Lorraine got back to the office she asked Decker to check out Jose's story about the jeep. 'Find out if anyone else saw it there. Talk to any residents close to where he said it was parked.'

'Anything else?'

'Yeah, can you get me any newspaper coverage of fine art auctions or galleries selling top quality paintings?'

'Sure.'

'Maybe come on as a buyer. Don't act up the investigator.'

'As if I would,' he said, with a camp flick of the wrist.

Lorraine grinned at him. 'Get out of here – go on.'

'On my way,' and he left with a prancing swagger.

Lorraine began to thumb through notes of her last interview with Cindy, in which she had underlined the name of Detective Sharkey.

Jim Sharkey, the officer she had worked with on her first case in Pasadena. She was sure she'd be able to get some inside info on the police inquiry – if she paid for it.

She called the police department, asked for Sharkey. It was a while before he came to the phone.

'Sharkey,' he said abruptly.

'Lorraine Page,' she replied politely.

'Yeah, they said.'

She could tell he was smoking as she could hear him inhale, then hiss the smoke out from his lungs. 'Can we meet?'

'Not right now, I'm busy.'

'So am I – but I think we should meet. I may have some information for you in regard to the Nathan inquiry,' she said, still keeping her voice over-polite, almost coaxing. 'What about lunch? I'd prefer to discuss it away from the station.'

'Like I said, I'm busy.' His voice sounded tense and irritated. 'Mrs Page, if you have anything relevant to my present investigation, then you should come in and talk to my lieutenant.'

'I'd prefer to discuss it with you. Surely you don't want me to spell it out.'

'Spell what out, Mrs Page?'

'Oh, come on. Stop playing games with me. You know I'm working for Cindy Nathan, I know you're on the case. Now, if you don't want to meet, then you can go fuck yourself. If, on the other hand, you want to have a cup of coffee with me, I'll be at the Silver Spoon, corner of Santa Monica and Havenhurst, about two.' She put the phone down. Detective Jim Sharkey had been given a lot of backhanders by Rooney, and now he was coming on all pompous and squeaky clean. It infuriated her, as she knew just how much money Rooney had palmed the man in return for access to police files for the last murder case she had worked on.

114

The phone rang and, still angry, she snatched it up to hear the bleeps of a payphone. 'Mrs Page?' It was Sharkey again.

'Speaking.'

'Don't ring the fuckin' office – I got the Captain at my fucking elbow listening in on every word you said.'

'All I said was I wanted a meet.'

'Yeah, yeah. I'm gonna give you my mobile number. You want me in future you call that, not the station, and I'll see you at two at the Silver Spoon.' He dictated the number and hung up. Lorraine checked the time. Still only eleven – she would have time to see Kendall Nathan first.

CHAPTER 5

LORRAINE WALKED up Beverly Drive, looking for Kendall Nathan's gallery. Although the location was a notch below the premier sites on Rodeo Drive, the smell of wealth and luxurious living was everywhere in the air. Lorraine passed store after store selling designer clothing, shoes and leather goods.

The neighbourhood was also full of art-related retailing – jewellery and antique stores, and Gallery One was next door to a shop selling antique Oriental kelims. The gallery itself had a plain white store-front, with its name in hammered metal letters, and large, plain plate-glass windows behind which were displayed a sculpture and a couple of star attractions from the latest exhibit.

Lorraine walked a hundred yards down the block and turned up the back alley between Beverly Drive and Canon to have a quiet look at the back of the premises before Kendall Nathan was aware of her presence. The parking area belonging to the gallery had been walled off behind high wooden gates. There was, however, a gap of about half an inch between gate and post, and, squinting through it, Lorraine could make out the paintwork of a parked vehicle: it was cream and black, the same colours as the jeep Jose had seen parked near the house on the day Nathan died. As she stepped back, she noticed a young black guy walking towards her up the alley. He was looking right at her, almost as though he thought he knew her, but he dropped his eyes as soon as she met them and passed her without a word.

Lorraine walked back to the front of the gallery and in at the door, triggering an entry buzzer. She stood in the centre of the large, light, virtually square room. The ceiling had rows of spotlights positioned to show off the paintings, hung strategically around the walls. The canvases were mostly unframed, and one wall displayed the works of only one artist, landscapes in bright acrylics. On another wall were oblong canvases, all of block colours, deep crimson, dark blue, black and walnut, all with an identical white and silver flash of lightning in the right-hand corner.

The only furniture was a desk made of what seemed to be aluminium, with riveted legs, and an uncomfortable-looking chair to match. There was a leather visitors' book – open – a Mont Blanc pen and a leather-bound blotter, all neatly laid out next to a telephone.

'Can I help you?'

Lorraine turned, and for a moment her eyes were unable to distinguish anyone: the cross-beams of the spotlights made it difficult to see after coming in from daylight. She couldn't work out where the voice had come from.

'Or would you prefer to be left alone?'

Lorraine smiled, her hand shading her eyes. 'No, not at all. I wanted to speak to Mrs Kendall Nathan.'

'You already are.'

Kendall Nathan was wearing a simple black almost ankle-length cotton dress with a scoop neckline and long sleeves. Her right wrist was covered in gold bangles, and she wore a gilt chain-link belt, and a large amethyst ring on her third finger. She held out long, thin fingers, which were bony to the touch, but her grip was strong.

'Lorraine Page.' They shook hands.

'Did someone recommend that you . . . ?'

'No, I'm not here with regard to your paintings.' She laughed lightly, feeling slightly embarrassed, partly because as Kendall was standing in the shadow she couldn't see her face clearly. Kendall Nathan walked back into the main gallery and Lorraine went after her.

'I'm afraid you won't find much to interest you here in that case,' Kendall said mockingly, moving lightly round the desk like a dancer. Now Lorraine could see Harry Nathan's second wife well. She was different from how Lorraine had remembered her at the funeral. There was something simpering in her manner, and the narrowness of her body was accentuated by one of the longest faces Lorraine had ever seen.

Kendall had a wild mop of frizzy, curly hair down to her shoulders, hennaed a reddish colour, which made her olive skin tones slightly yellow. Her eyes were dark, almost black, sly and hooded, and although large, were set too close together on either side of a long, pointed, Aztec-looking nose. Her small mouth was tight and thin-lipped and, even in repose, bore the hint of a snarl.

She smiled. 'What can I do for you, Mrs Page? I'm rather busy.' Kendall obviously did not recognize Lorraine from the funeral: she had been far too concerned with her own performance to take note of who had attended. She eased into her uncomfortable chair and crossed her legs.

Lorraine looked down – even the woman's feet, in

118

leather sandals, were long and thin. Lorraine perched on the edge of the desk. This annoyed Kendall, who recoiled, angling her body away.

'I'm working for Mrs Nathan.'

The eyes flicked up, then down.

'Mrs Cindy Nathan,' Lorraine explained. She had noticed that the woman didn't like hearing the words 'Mrs Nathan' unless they referred to herself. 'Mrs Nathan, as you are aware, was arrested for the murder of her husband, your ex-husband.'

'Yes, I knew that,' Kendall said briskly. 'Are you a lawyer?'

'No,' Lorraine said. 'I'm a private investigator.' She took out her card and handed it to the other woman, who looked carefully at it, then set it down on the desk.

'Well, I'm so sorry, I really can't help you,' Kendall said, with a quick, false smile.

'You haven't really heard what I'd like to discuss,' Lorraine pointed out.

Kendall pushed up her sleeve and looked at her Rolex. 'I have an appointment shortly, Mrs Page. This will have to be brief.'

'Would you mind telling me where you were on the morning Mr Nathan was shot?' Lorraine asked. 'Cindy says you told her you were at home.'

'I was at home,' Kendall said, her eyes scanning Lorraine as she wondered what else Cindy had told her.

'Was anyone with you?'

'No – not unless you count my cats. I had nothing whatsoever to do with Harry's death, though, so if that's what you're getting at, I'm afraid you're wasting your time.'

'Though I understand you do benefit under Harry

Nathan's will,' Lorraine went on casually. 'He retained an interest in the gallery, which now passes to you, is that right?'

'Cindy gets a damn sight more than anyone else,' Kendall said, and Lorraine could hear the bitterness in her voice. 'And Sonja Nathan gets something too – you'll be treating her as a suspect too, of course?' she sneered.

'Do you think she should be treated as one?' Lorraine asked, almost matching Kendall's sarcastic tone.

'Why not? East Hampton's not that great a distance. Maybe she flew in for the day from New York, killed Harry, then flew home.'

Here we go again, Lorraine thought. Wife three says it was wife two, and wife two says it was wife one. Presumably Sonja would say Harry's mother had killed him. Still, Sonja Nathan had remained something of a shadowy figure so far, and Lorraine was interested to hear more about her. She made a mental note to check out her address in East Hampton.

'You and Sonja didn't get along?'

Kendall gave a light, brittle laugh. 'Well, considering Harry left her for me, we weren't best friends. But before Harry and I married we were . . . business associates.' This was clearly an edited version of events, and Lorraine made another mental note to check out the facts. 'I know Sonja quite well. She is not a normal person, I would say, an unbalanced woman, and cold at the core. She never got over Harry's leaving her for me – never. Of everyone around Harry, the two people I would say most capable of murder are Sonja and Harry's good friend Raymond Vallance.'

'Really?' Lorraine said, sceptical as ever of information

so readily volunteered, and attempts to throw suspicion on others. 'So you don't think Cindy killed him?'

Kendall shrugged. 'I don't know.'

'How did you and Harry get along after you were divorced?'

Kendall's eyes hardened like stones. 'We had a mutually beneficial relationship. We were business partners in this gallery, and I relied a great deal on Harry's knowledge and judgement of art.' She paused, as though flicking channels on a television, to give Lorraine a quick flash of the downcast, heartbroken friend, then clicked smartly back to business. 'We also collected together privately, and it was agreed between us that what we bought should be jointly owned. We decided to keep it at Harry's house so that we wouldn't have to install a lot of security at two locations, but I paid the insurance premiums. Half the collection is therefore mine,' she declared, as though speaking from the Supreme Court. 'And that, Mrs Page, is not any kind of an advantage I have derived under Harry's will. It was my property, whether he was living or dead. In fact it is to my detriment that Harry died when he did, before we had . . . clarified the arrangements about the collection.'

Arrangements Kendall Nathan had probably made up the moment her ex-husband was dead, Lorraine thought. 'I see,' she said, with a bright, fake smile of her own. 'Well, let's leave that one for the lawyers to fight out. I was really wondering about your personal relationship with Harry.'

'Our relations were cordial,' Kendall said curtly.

'Did you see one another socially, as well as in a business capacity?'

121

'We had lunch or dinner from time to time. Sometimes we went to art markets or sales. We did not travel together. We did not continue a marital-type relationship, if that's what you're trying to suggest.'

'Oh, no, of course not,' Lorraine said, with another false smile. 'But while we're on that subject, Harry used to record, well, a lot of things that happened at the house, didn't he?'

'Cindy mentioned there were telephone recordings,' Kendall said guardedly.

'I believe he also recorded some . . . fairly private activities, while you were married.'

In an instant Kendall knew that Lorraine had seen the tapes, and rose nervously from her desk. She walked a few paces towards the window and looked out into the street. 'Harry liked to go to the edge – a lot of film people do. I was very young at the time' – Lorraine stifled a smile: Kendall Nathan had married Harry in her mid-thirties, and must now be at least forty – 'and I went along with some things which, of course, I wouldn't have any involvement with now. Harry did make some tapes,' she admitted. 'I assume Cindy has told you about them too.'

'We've discussed them.' Lorraine was deliberately evasive.

'Mrs Page, I won't waste your time or mine,' Kendall continued, cutting straight to the chase. 'I realize you've seen these tapes and I'm concerned about what is going to happen to them now. You haven't shown them to any of your associates?' Her dark eyes bored into Lorraine's.

'Of course not,' Lorraine said, and saw the light of calculation enter Kendall's eyes.

'I'd be prepared to compensate you, naturally, if some

of those tapes happened to go missing,' Kendall said, moving back to her desk and apparently studying some notes on her phone pad.

'I'm sorry, but any evidence relevant to the case will have to be passed on to the police,' Lorraine responded. 'The tapes aren't mine to dispose of, and they may form an important part of Cindy Nathan's defence.'

'I see.' Kendall Nathan gave Lorraine a look that would have cut sheet steel.

'What are your relations with Cindy like?' Lorraine said, as much to change the subject as anything else.

Kendall shrugged. 'Our paths crossed, obviously, but I'd call her just an acquaintance, and one I wouldn't go out of my way to see.'

'So you don't like her?'

'I didn't say that. I have no feelings with regard to her.' That was a lie: Kendall was clearly as burned at being left by Nathan as she claimed Sonja had been.

'Well, thank you for your time,' Lorraine said, and smiled. Kendall nodded, already starting to move to the archway. 'Oh, just one thing,' Lorraine went on, 'I know you said you were at home the morning Mr Nathan was shot. What time did you leave?'

'To come to work, just after ten.'

'I don't suppose you made a telephone call to my office that morning?'

'I'm sorry?'

'I asked if you called my agency, Mrs Nathan,' Lorraine repeated. 'I received a phone call on the morning of the shooting – in fact it must have been made shortly after the gun was fired.'

'Why do you ask? Did whoever it was say it was me?' Kendall came towards Lorraine, her eyes sharp and her voice rising. It suddenly sounded less modulated, almost coarse.

'No, the caller identified herself as Cindy Nathan, but Cindy says she didn't make the call.'

'Well, it certainly wasn't me. What did this person say?'

'Oh, that she needed help, just shot her husband. It didn't sound like Cindy's voice.' She smiled at Kendall. 'To be honest, I didn't think it sounded like yours – until just now. I thought there might be some similarity, but if you're sure you didn't make the call . . .'

'I have never met you or spoken to you before in my life,' Kendall said, a considerably less polished Mid-Western accent now noticeable in her voice. 'I never called you, but I'll give you some advice. Don't believe a word that dumb bitch tells you. She's a liar. And don't get sucked in by the big baby blue eyes and the tears. She can turn them on at will. I know, believe me, I know.' She paused and made an effort to regain her poise. 'Now if you'll excuse me, I have things to do.'

Lorraine started to walk to the door, then stopped. 'Can I just ask you what kind of car you drive?'

Kendall looked penetratingly at Lorraine. 'Why do you ask?'

'Just to eliminate things, you know.'

'I drive a 1996 Mitsubishi jeep. It's convenient for carrying paintings. It's two-tone and has about twenty-five thousand on the clock. Is there anything else?'

Lorraine opened the gallery door. 'No, not at the present. I appreciate your talking to me, and I'm sorry to have taken up so much of your time. Would you mind if I came back if I need to talk to you again?'

Kendall looked at her calculatingly. 'No, I don't suppose so, but call first.' She went back to her desk, opened a drawer and took out a business card. 'I'll give you my home number as well.' She used her Mont Blanc, bending over the desk.

'Mrs Nathan?' A young man walked in through a small rear door, not seeing Lorraine. 'I've unloaded all the canvases – you still want me?'

Lorraine looked into the rear of the shop. She could not see him clearly, but she was almost certain it was the same black youth who had walked past her out back.

'Give me a couple minutes,' Kendall snapped, but the man remained where he was. 'I've got a workshop outside in my yard – I make up the frames and things like that. You have to have a rapid turnover in a gallery to keep the public interested.'

Again Kendall turned and this time told the man to get out. He disappeared. 'He doesn't have the right attitude for customers.'

'Do you sell mostly to passing trade?' Lorraine asked.

'A few come in, but it's mostly by appointment.'

'How does that work?' Lorraine asked pleasantly.

Kendall's condescending manner earlier was now firmly re-established. 'We have a client list and I send out an invitation every time I have a new artist I want to promote. I also work with a few designers – you know, wall hangings and textiles and so on.' She smiled with sly eyes, showing a chipped tooth. Lorraine's mind was racing: why was the woman suddenly being so friendly? Had it been the reference to the phone call? Oddly enough, Lorraine preferred her cool and snide. This smiling, over-helpful act made her suspicious.

'I won't hold you up any longer,' she said. 'Thanks again.'

The meter was almost up. Lorraine bleeped the car open, got in and sat a moment. Kendall had said she hadn't made the call, but had been at home with no alibi when it was made. She was clearly jealous of Cindy Nathan, and had continued to have a close relationship with her ex-husband. To some extent she benefited from his death, and, most importantly, she had made no secret about driving a two-tone Mitsubishi jeep, as described by Nathan's housekeepers. She also employed a young black guy. Maybe Cindy hadn't made up the man she said she had seen at the house. Kendall also knew about the phone tapes, and had admitted that she wanted to recover the videos. Someone had broken into Lorraine's office and poured acid over the phone tapes and, according to Cindy, only two other people had known that they were there. Harry Nathan's ex-wives.

Lorraine slipped on her safety-belt and started the engine. She glanced behind her, indicated and pulled out into the street. As she drove, she squinted at the petrol gauge and saw that the tank was nearly empty. She pulled in at the old Union 76 gas station on Little Santa Monica, a remarkable piece of classic sixties construction, like the wingspan of a great bird. She asked the attendant to fill up the car and check the oil, while she went in to buy a pack of cigarettes. She went to the ladies' and returned to find that the station attendant had raised the bonnet of her Mercedes.

'How much?' she said.

The man turned towards her. 'How much you worth?'

126

He crooked his finger and motioned her closer. 'I only noticed because the top of my pen dropped into the engine when I was unscrewing the oil cap. Have a look at this. Your brake cable's been sliced almost through. Dunno how long it'd have been before . . .' He made a screeching noise and walloped the side of the car. 'You got no brakes, lady, an' this'll have to go up on the ramp because it ain't safe to drive the length of the street.'

'How long do you think they've been like this?'

He pulled a face, sticking out his bulldog jaw. 'Well, I wouldn't know, it's a clean cut – like, it's not wear and tear, and you would have known about that, honey, believe me. So, maybe recent. You got any enemies? I'd give the cops a call if I was you – this is fuckin' dangerous.'

Lorraine straightened up. 'Can you fix them?'

'Sure.'

She sat on a low wall beside the garage as the man set to work. She lit a cigarette, her hand shaking. How long had they been cut? *When* were they cut? Most importantly, who the hell had done it? Kendall Nathan? The woman had had no chance to get at the car, had been with her continuously. The black man? But Kendall had had no opportunity to tell him to do anything. Lorraine found herself smoking cigarettes down to the filter and lighting the next from the butt.

What had she unwittingly uncovered? There had to be a reason for someone to be prepared to kill her, or at the very least to want her to have a life-threatening accident.

The car wasn't going to be ready for some considerable time, so she called a cab and went to the office, where she filled in Decker about her car.

'Did you call the police?'

Lorraine shut her eyes, then hit the desk. She'd forgotten to meet Jim Sharkey. 'Shit, I gotta go. I arranged to meet the cop on the Nathan case. I'll get a cab.'

Jim Sharkey looked at his watch. He'd had two cappuccinos and had had breakfast again in lieu of lunch. Now he was getting sick of sitting outside on a hard chair on the patio waiting for Lorraine – the Silver Spoon was one of the few places left in LA where smoking was still allowed, but plush surroundings weren't their strong suit. He was just about to walk out when a cab pulled up, Lorraine got out and walked towards the diner. She was a great looker, Mrs Lorraine Page, he thought, as she eased her body between the tables – nice easy strides, tight figure, long legs . . . He was getting hard as his eyes travelled up from her crotch to her bosom – not as big as he went for, but they looked a nice handful, firm.

'Hi, sorry I'm late.'

He shook her hand, half lifting his butt from the seat as she slid into the chair opposite. 'You want a cup of coffee?'

'Diet Coke – hot out there today.'

Sharkey signalled to the waiter and ordered two Cokes, then looked back at Lorraine. She removed her dark glasses and tossed her head back. He noticed how well cut and silky her hair was – nice, like a shampoo ad. 'Looking in good shape,' he said.

'Thanks. Wish I could say the same for you.'

He laughed. 'How's old Bill?'

'He's on honeymoon.'

'What?'

'Yeah, I don't know if you remember Rosie, used to work with me. Sort of curly hair, cute face. They married after his wife died.'

The waiter brought their Cokes, and Sharkey dipped his straw in. 'Dunno why I asked for this, I hate the stuff, but I'm not drinking.'

'Makes two of us.'

Sharkey looked at her face. He could see no signs of the dissipation, the rough ride she'd been on with the drink and drugs, just a few lines at the corners of her eyes and mouth. Lorraine was aware that he was scrutinizing her, but chose to ignore it, looking instead at the other tables under the awning, with their Formica tops and plain, functional crockery. If the place was basic, at least everything looked well-maintained and clean.

Sharkey took her matches and lit her cigarette. 'We got a new lieutenant, name of Burton, heading up the detective division – he's a real son-of-a-bitch.'

Lorraine exhaled, turning her head away so the smoke didn't blow in Sharkey's face.

'Burton, Jake Burton – you know him?'

'Nope, but then I've been out of the force a long time.'

Sharkey nodded – he knew all about it, but he said nothing.

'You want to start, or shall I?' she asked.

He shifted in his seat. 'Look, I came here because I wanted to get things straight. With this guy Burton looking over our shoulders, the days when we could trade off are gone, understand me? He's got fuckin' eyes in the back of his head.'

'Does he know you're meeting with me?'

'No, no way. Shit, I think I'll have a beer.' He signalled for a waiter and ordered a lager, Mexican light.

'Well, if he doesn't know you're here who's gonna tell him? And maybe I've got something. We could just toss a few things round.'

Sharkey sucked his teeth. 'You were hired by Cindy Nathan, right?'

Lorraine sat back as the waiter brought the beer. Sharkey waved away the glass, preferring to drink it from the bottle.

'Will you start, or shall I?' she said again softly.

He sighed, and shrugged his big shoulders. 'Well, I might as well. I mean, we've got her sewn up – the gun was hers, her fingerprints were on it, and when she was brought into the station she virtually admitted it. We got enough witnesses to sink the fucking *Titanic* who say she threatened to shoot him, plus, as far as we can make out, she's the main beneficiary of his estate – he's got quite an art collection.' Sharkey took a swig of beer and set the bottle down on the table. 'Though from what I can make out, there's not all that much in the way of liquid assets. Way I hear it, this so-called production company cum studio may go bust, which would soak up the cash from the collection.' Sharkey cocked his head to one side. 'But maybe she didn't know that.'

'Ah, but you do,' Lorraine said.

'Yeah, we checked him out. He's got a share in a gallery run by an ex-wife, but lately he'd been living from hand to mouth.'

'Blackmailing anyone he could,' Lorraine added, watching Sharkey. He didn't react.

'Yeah, we figured that one. He was a real sleazeball, but we don't have a suspect in that area.'

'You sure about that?'

Sharkey took another gulp of beer. 'Not sure of anything but the little lady. She pulled the trigger, maybe not for his money – maybe she knew he didn't have any – but she shot him. We've got a few statements from Mr Nathan's ever-loving friends that he knocked her around and that she cheated on him. These Hollywood types screw anything that moves, and Nathan certainly did his share – you see any of his movies?' Lorraine shook her head. 'Soft porn, and apparently he always roadtested his leading ladies – mind you, so would I if I had the chance.'

Lorraine's smile didn't reach her eyes. She wondered how much she should tell him, and how much he was holding back.

'You know she was pregnant?'

He nodded. 'We also know the child may not have been his – she was screwing Raymond Vallance. *He* was interviewed, shitting himself, not about the shooting – he's got an alibi, apparently—' Lorraine registered that piece of information with interest ' – but about it getting out, you know, harming his career. Someone should tell him he's been on the skids for the past ten years. The only way he's ever going to see his name in the papers again is to be up on a fucking charge.'

Lorraine gave another chilly smile. 'You know Harry Nathan made a lot of tapes? His phone calls, and people coming to the house, plus a few . . . adult material movies with Vallance and his ex-wives.'

'Oh, sure,' Sharkey lied. This was news to him. 'We're checking it out.'

'Well, some of the recordings have come my way, and I'll be sending them over – don't want to lose my PI licence for obstructing the course of justice.' She paused a moment. 'What I'm thinking is maybe someone didn't like the idea of being filmed,' she went on. 'Maybe didn't like it so much they pulled the trigger – and Cindy Nathan didn't.'

Sharkey sighed, then leaned forward. 'Look, he was garbage, but he'd been garbage for a long time. Sure he hit on everyone for money – he was a con man, he conned anyone and anything he could, it was a way of life. Once he stopped directing, he sure as hell couldn't produce a movie. He used them to score the chicks, maybe made a few bucks at the same time but he had a big lifestyle, so he hit on his friends, even his house-keepers – their wages haven't been paid for months. But nothing we've dug up, and no one we've interviewed, has changed my department's opinion. We think his wife, in a fit of jealous rage – and she could apparently throw quite a performance in that area – had had enough. She took her own gun, a weapon he had given to her and shown her how to use, and she waited until he was in the pool and popped him. Like I said, she's virtually admitted it.'

'What about his ex-wife?'

'Kendall Nathan?' he asked, and drained the last of the beer. 'She's been questioned, and she doesn't have a motive.'

Lorraine reached for another cigarette. 'She inherits half of the gallery, where I visited her today – and somebody sliced through my brake cable right after-wards.'

'Oh, yeah?' He didn't seem interested.

'Yeah. She also knew about the tapes in my office, and someone broke in and poured acid over them.'

He stared at her, waiting for more.

'I *don't* think Cindy killed him. I think somebody's fitting her up for it – maybe one of the people he was blackmailing, I dunno, and . . .' Should she tell him about the second bullet? The parked jeep? He wasn't giving her much in return.

'And?' he urged her.

'That's about it.'

'You reported the damage to your car?' He was checking his watch. 'If someone slashed my brake cable, I'd be worried. Did you report it?' he asked again.

'No, no, I didn't.' Lorraine frowned.

'Are you going to?'

'No. Guess I'll just be careful where I park.'

'You got any idea who it might have been?'

'No, absolutely none,' Lorraine said, and Sharkey checked his watch again. 'I gotta go. Sorry I couldn't be more help. If you come up with anything, you know my mobile number.'

'I'll pay the cheque,' she said, opening her purse. She took out three hundred-dollar bills and folded them. 'You settle up for me, will you?'

'Sure,' he said, as he raked the bills across the table. 'You string out your PI job, sweetheart. I would if I was in your shoes – you've got a while before the trial. Get what you can, and if anything else happens, I'd report it. You lived quite a life, didn't you? So I'd think about who might want to fuck with your car.'

Lorraine stood up. 'Thanks for the advice.'

He watched her walk out, pause at the edge of the terrace and slip on a pair of dark glasses. He wondered how much she was getting paid by Cindy Nathan, and how he'd slip in the video and phone recordings to the new lieutenant. They hadn't had a sniff of that but he'd look into it now.

It was just after three when Lorraine collected her car and drove back to the garage under the office, making sure to ask the valet to park her car close to his booth. She felt hot and tired, and the meeting with Sharkey had given her nothing new. She couldn't stop thinking about who had wanted to harm her. She wasn't frightened, exactly, just uneasy, and by the time she got into her office she was in a foul mood.

'Cops have Cindy Nathan down for it, don't even appear to be looking elsewhere,' she told Decker. He was elbow-deep in all the data they had got together so far on Cindy's case. She walked towards her own office, ignoring the thump of Tiger's tail. 'Book me a flight tomorrow for East Hampton, New York State. I want to see Sonja Nathan.' She kicked her door shut and sat down at her desk, where her mood become blacker.

Five minutes later, Decker tapped on the door. 'I've got you a flight at eight a.m. with American Airlines. Manhattan International limos will collect you and drive you to East Hampton, and you're booked into the Maidstone Arms. I have no idea what Sonja Nathan's address is – do you want me to call Cindy and check? Be a pity to go all that way and find out she may not be there.'

Lorraine muttered something, and Decker moved closer. 'Excuse me?'

'Ask Cindy Nathan for the phone number, and leave me alone – I've got a headache.'

'Fine, and when you are, so to speak, in the air, do

you want me to look after Tiger? I'm not supposed to have pets in the house, but for one night I don't see that'll be a problem.'

'Yeah, thank you,' Lorraine answered gruffly.

He shut the door quietly.

Lieutenant Jake Burton, new head of the detective division in the Beverly Hills Police Department, stood with his back to the room, noticing that the room still smelt of paint. His office had been freshly decorated, and was now as immaculate as the man himself. Burton stood six feet two with a tight, muscular body, and blond hair cut close to his head in an expensive salon style that flattered his chiselled face. His slight tan made his light blue eyes appear even bluer, and his teeth even more brilliantly white. His nickname in the Army had been 'Rake', but now that he was in the police force, and had moved up the ranks with ruthless determination, he didn't like nicknames any more. He knew that his subordinates thought he was a cold bastard, and in some ways he was, but he had been shipped in to clean up rumours of officers taking bribes and kickbacks, and it was a job he intended to do to the best of his ability.

Burton was originally from Texas, but he had travelled widely and his roots were now detectable only as a faint burr in his voice. It was in the army that he'd qualified as an attorney – he was prepared to thank Uncle Sam for that, but not for shipping him out to Vietnam with one of the last units dispatched. He had been there only two months before the conflict ended, but those two months lived on in his mind, and had marked him deeply. He never talked about it, or referred to himself as a veteran simply because he didn't think of himself as a one, having spent so little time in Vietnam and taken so little part in the war. It had been a nightmare experience which he buried deep inside, and on his return, he had left the army and enrolled in police academy. He was then only twenty-three, but older than most other recruits, and used that to his advantage. Before he had even graduated from the academy, he was earmarked as an officer to watch. He had been married for a short while and his wife, a secretary, had claimed in her divorce petition that, in fact, he was married to his job. He still was in many ways, although he was hitting the mid-forties. He had some private life now but it was mostly fraternizing with other officers, playing squash or tennis, for Burton was as obsessive about his physical fitness as he was about his job.

He had done such good work in Santa Barbara, cleaning up the department and weeding out officers who were found to be taking bribes, that he had become known for his ability and, above all, for his unimpeachable integrity. Jake Burton was as straight as they made 'em, and when the opportunity arose to move to LA, to a job with enhanced status, he had readily accepted it.

He had, at the time, been involved with a divorcée and the time had seemed right to move on from her too. Recently, he had been dating a girl from the legal department, a well-groomed, pretty brunette with intelligent brown eyes, but somehow he couldn't bring himself to make a commitment.

At the knock on his door Burton's attention snapped back to the present. 'Come in,' he said sharply, straightening the row of brand new, sharpened pencils on his pristine desk.

'You wanted to see me, Lieutenant?'

Burton nodded and opened a file of reports on the Cindy Nathan case. 'Sit down.' He gestured to a hard-backed chair in front of his desk. 'What's this about tapes?'

Sharkey cleared his throat. 'I got a tip-off. Apparently Nathan recorded everything but bowel movements.'

'And this is the first we've heard of it?'

Sharkey nodded. 'He filmed everyone coming in and out of the house on security cameras, and also some porno stuff with the wives, but I doubt if the tapes will tell us anything we don't already know. I mean, everybody in LA knew Cindy Nathan was a fucking whore.'

'Really?' Burton said coldly. 'You had access to these tapes?'

'No, sir.'

'So did this informant – whoever tipped you off – have access to them?'

'Cindy Nathan sent them to her.'

Burton turned the pages of the report, then tapped it with his index finger.

'Why would Cindy Nathan send the tapes to this informant?'

Sharkey squirmed in his seat. 'Well, she's a private dick, hired by Mrs Nathan.'

'Really?' Burton said softly. 'So how did this interaction come about?'

'Well, she called me . . .'

'Yes. And?' Burton waited for a reply, tapping his desk with one of the needle-sharp pencils. He neither liked nor trusted Sharkey.

'She wanted information – you know, do a trade.'

Burton waited, his eyes on Sharkey. 'A trade in what, exactly, Detective?'

'Well, you know, what I'd got – et cetera, et cetera.'

'Did you tell her anything relevant to the investigation?'

'Hell, no, nothing like that.'

'Did she pay you?'

'Of course not. Didn't give her nothing.' Sharkey grinned.

'I sincerely hope not. So what is the lady's name?'

'She used to be a cop.'

'So did most PIs. What's her name, Detective?'

Sharkey sucked in his breath. 'Lorraine Page.'

Burton opened the file again, and appeared to be devoting his full attention to it as he said quietly, 'So, tell me about this lady, this Lorraine Page.'

CHAPTER 6

CINDY NATHAN had always known something like this would happen: now that it had she found herself strangely calm, as though the fate she had always known was walking just behind her had finally taken her hand.

'Take off your clothes,' the man said, and she slowly unbuttoned the white shirt and took it off.

She began to unfasten the zip of the tight aqua jeans, then stopped. 'Will I take off my shoes?' she asked docilely, as though speaking to the nurse at school.

'Everything.' She sat on the edge of the bed and unbuckled her high ankle-strap sandals, then pulled off her jeans with her underwear still inside. She was naked now except for a choker of tiny black glass beads, strung into a fine pattern like a broad strip of lace. He did not look at her: the female body held no mystery for him.

'Now go into the bathroom,' he said. 'Take that thing off from round your neck.'

At eight fifteen that evening, Juana cooked supper at the Nathan house and pressed the number for Cindy's bedroom on the intercom. There was no answer. Juana was a little annoyed and wondered if Cindy wanted to eat in her room instead of at the dining table, where the meal had been laid. She dialled Cindy again just after eight twenty, and still received no reply from the room, although the girl had specifically ordered what she wanted to eat – a grilled swordfish steak, salad of fennel and watercress dressed with lime juice, and no wine or fruit, just a glass of sparkling water.

Juana prepared a tray and rang again at eight thirty, but still no one picked up. She wondered if Cindy could be taking a shower, waited a few minutes more, then asked Jose to go up to Cindy's room and check that she was all right. Jose went upstairs, tapped on the bedroom door and listened outside. He could hear music playing quite loudly, but there was no answer from Cindy. He tried the door, only to find it locked. Perplexed, he returned to the kitchen and he and Juana ate their own supper. At nine fifteen Jose went to Cindy's room again. This time he banged loudly on the door, and then, with Juana at his side, used his pass key to enter the room.

The room was empty, and the clothes Cindy had been wearing were strewn across the bed, her shoes discarded beside it. Jose went towards the closed bathroom door, tapped, and waited a moment. He could hear the shower running, and turned to Juana. 'She's taking a shower. I told you not to worry.'

Juana pursed her lips, put the tray down on a bedside table and closed the doors to the balcony, through which the curtains were billowing in the wind. Jose had already left the room. Juana crossed back to the bathroom and listened again: the water was still running. She knocked and called that she had left Cindy's supper tray on the

140

bed, relocked the bedroom door and went back downstairs.

Lorraine arrived home after driving up to Santa Monica to walk Tiger on the promenade, a pretty stretch of parkland on the bluffs above the beach, just as darkness was falling at about six o'clock. She immediately checked her answerphone, to find only one message from Decker, giving Sonja Nathan's home number, which Lorraine took down. After a shower, she fixed herself some agnolotti and salad, cooked up some meat and vegetables for Tiger, and was just about to make the call to Sonja Nathan when Tiger let rip with a deep bark, then growled as footsteps became audible on the walkway up to the apartment.

Lorraine went to the window and looked down into the road. She saw the Chevvy, parked directly underneath. She didn't recognize the car and looked quickly at her watch. Just after ten. After the incident with the brakes, she was immediately tense, and Tiger was ready to pounce.

The door buzzed, and Lorraine hesitated before she picked up the entryphone. 'Who is it?'

'Lieutenant Burton, LAPD.' The voice was neither friendly nor familiar.

Lorraine looked out of her window and could see Burton standing back from the front door on the steps. He was holding his ID card up for her to see, so she pressed the door-release button and told Tiger to sit. The dog still wasn't convinced and she had to hold his collar in one hand as she opened the door to the apartment.

'Hi – can you just say hello to my dog?'

Burton smiled. 'Sure. Hi . . . Do I put out my hand or what?'

'Just stay where you are, let him have a sniff. He'll be okay soon.'

As Burton leaned forward Tiger growled deep in his throat.

'Good boy . . . good boy.'

Lorraine slowly released her hold on the dog's collar and he relaxed. 'Sorry about that. Come in.'

'No, I'm sorry, I should have called first, but . . . you want another look at my ID?'

She smiled. 'No, that's okay.'

Lorraine tried to think what the hell had brought Burton to her apartment, while smiling and offering him coffee or tea, both of which he refused.

'I suppose you're wondering why I'm here?'

'You could say that.' She sat down opposite in an easy chair. Burton was not the kind of man she found attractive – she had always preferred men with darker colouring – but she was impressed by him. He seemed quite a cool guy, though the hair was too short, and judging from the pressed pants, polished shoes and so on, he was anally retentive. She laughed at her analysis.

'Did I miss something?' he asked.

'I'm sorry. It's just you being here all spick and span, and at the same time my mind is wondering what the fuck it is you want?'

He laughed – a pleasant laugh – and she also noted he had nice, even teeth.

'You had a meeting with one of my officers.'

'Yes, Jim Sharkey.'

'Yes,' he repeated softly. 'Jim Sharkey.' Nothing Sharkey had said had given him any indication about how Lorraine Page looked. Nor had anything he had read about her. He had not expected to be bowled over by her looks.

'So, you're running that division now, are you?' she enquired. He liked the way she tilted her head when she spoke, her silky blonde hair falling forward over one side of her face.

'Yes, I hope you don't mind my calling. It's not official – just wanted to touch base.'

'Really?' she said, with a half-smile, then again offered him something to drink. This time he accepted a glass of iced water. He had strong hands with long, tapering fingers, which brushed hers for a second as he took the glass from her.

Burton drew out a hard-backed chair from the little dining nook, and brought it over to the coffee table, although there was a more comfortable chair and the sofa. He twisted the chair round and sat astride it, leaning his arms along the back.

'You want to trade information,' he said, looking at her directly. He leaned over, picked up his glass, and sipped from it, then replaced it carefully. 'As I said before, this is unofficial, but I'm new in town – new to the station. I like to get a handle on some of my officers, especially if they're taking backhanders, and I know most of them are. I'm on what you might call a clean-up campaign.'

Lorraine cocked her head to one side, and waited.

'Did you offer any payment to Detective Sharkey?'

'No, I paid for his cappuccino, that's all.'

He stared at her. It was his turn to wait, and there was a long pause. 'I see. Have you traded information with Detective Sharkey before?'

'No. I did some work on a case with a former partner who was an old buddy of Sharkey's, Bill Rooney – Captain Rooney. I think they sank a few beers together and discussed the investigation. It was the disappearance of—'

'Yes, I read the file. Girl was found murdered in New Orleans, wasn't she?' He half smiled. 'You got a bonus, so I heard, a big one.'

'Yes, I did. Not that I think it's any business of yours, but it's what I used to open up my office.'

'Did Sharkey get a cut of your bonus?'

'No, he did not. It was split between myself and my partners.'

Burton drained his glass, and held the blue goblet loosely in his hands. 'You working for Cindy Nathan?' he asked casually.

'Yes.'

'You mentioned a number of things to Detective Sharkey – some tapes, telephone and video . . .'

Lorraine stood up. 'Yes, I did, but he said you knew about them, or the investigating officers did.'

'Then he lied. It was the first we'd heard of them. You want to tell me about them?'

Lorraine was getting edgy. Burton had got up and was wandering around the room. It unnerved her, as if he was mentally sizing up both her and her apartment. 'It seems Nathan recorded all incoming calls, and had video monitors set up all over the house.'

'So what did you glean from these tapes?' he asked,

bending to look at a photograph of her father in police uniform.

'That Nathan was both vain and paranoid,' Lorraine replied. 'Most of the tapes were of him making beauty appointments. None that I had the opportunity to listen to were of much interest, and some were destroyed.' She had his full attention now. 'Someone broke into my office and poured acid over them.'

'Did you tell Sharkey this?'

'No.'

'And the videos?'

'Well, they're a little different. They are explicit recordings of Nathan's sexual exploits with his last two wives.'

Burton folded his arms. 'Is that why you wanted to see Sharkey? Trade off these videos?'

'No, though I offered them. A good defence attorney will also use them – Cindy took a lot of abuse.'

'Enough to make her kill him?'

'No, not necessarily. I know the evidence against her is pretty incriminating – maybe too incriminating – but I don't think she did it.'

'You mean she could have been set up?'

'Possibly.'

He sat on the arm of the sofa. 'By whom?'

'I don't know, it's just a theory.'

'And you are obviously being paid a good retainer to find out?'

'Again, I don't think that's any of your business. I'm doing my job, that's all.'

'Apart from the tapes and the videos, do you have anything that would cast suspicion on someone else?'

It was Lorraine's turn to pace the apartment. Should she tell him about her suspicions of Kendall Nathan, the parked jeep? She played for time, tidying a stack of magazines on the coffee table.

'You had a problem with your car?' he said. 'Sharkey told me.'

She straightened. 'Yes, brake cable had been cut, sliced in two.'

'But you didn't report it?'

'No.'

'Do you think someone was warning you off?'

'I'd say it might have been a bit more than a warning – if I'd been going at any speed and had to stop I might have been killed.' She swung round to face him. 'And this unofficial visit is beginning to get to me. Do you think I'm withholding evidence or something? Why would I? Christ, I'm hired to get my client off a murder rap. Surely anything I come up with I'd feed back to—'

'I'd like to see the tapes.'

'Fine, send someone round to my office and you can have them.'

'What else have you got?'

She glared at him, and he looked back at her with laser-like intensity.

'You don't believe Cindy Nathan killed her husband. Is it just a gut feeling, or do you have other evidence that might implicate someone else?'

Lorraine thought for a moment, then said, 'Okay, there was a jeep parked across from the Nathans' house, unidentified so far, seen by the housekeeper. He was sure it didn't belong to anyone in the neighbourhood, two-tone Mitsubishi, driven away shortly after the shooting. Kendall Nathan owns a jeep that matches that description. Kendall Nathan was also one of only two people who knew that the tapes which were destroyed at my office were in there.' Burton remained impassive. 'Cindy Nathan thinks she heard possibly two shots – the first she presumed was a car backfiring, so she didn't pay any attention to it, and the second made her get up and walk round to the pool area. That's when she found her husband.'

'He was shot only once.'

'Yes, but . . .' Lorraine decided against saying anything about the bullet she had found. 'There was also a phone call,' she went on. 'Someone called me right after Nathan was shot, said she was Cindy Nathan, but Cindy subsequently said it wasn't her. Now that I've met her, I don't think the voice was hers either. It could have been Kendall's but she denied it.'

'But Kendall Nathan doesn't have much of a motive, right? She gets half an art gallery, but Cindy's the one who stood to inherit the house and the stock and everything.'

Burton had surprised Lorraine – division heads didn't usually spend much time poring over reports and, in her experience, few had been sufficiently involved with an individual case to discuss motive. But, then, she had never had an unofficial home visit from anyone that high up either.

'Maybe the motive isn't financial,' she said. Burton gave her that penetrating look again. 'Nathan's finances, as far as I can gather, are not as healthy as one would expect – Cindy Nathan is not coming into a fortune. I'd say she might even find herself in debt after she's paid off all Nathan's creditors, so I'm in two minds about money being in the picture at all.'

Burton hesitated before replying. 'Maybe you're right, but even if it's not money, Cindy Nathan is still in the frame. You've said he abused her – maybe she'd taken enough. She'd threatened publicly to kill him and, according to the reports I've read, she was pretty confused when she was arrested, not saying categorically that she didn't kill him, but that she didn't *think* she did, that she couldn't have. Then she said, "Could I?"'

Lorraine sat down on the sofa. 'Yeah, I know, but she found the body. She was presumably in a state of shock.'

'Perhaps you don't know the results of the medical examination, after she was brought into the station?'

'She was pregnant. Yes, I do know, and she lost the child – in fact she's only just been released from hospital.'

'I wasn't referring to her pregnancy. Cindy Nathan is or was a cocaine addict. According to the report, your client was high as a kite on the morning of the shooting.' He looked at his watch, then extended his hand. 'Thank you very much for seeing me, Mrs Page.'

She shook his outstretched hand, trying not to show her astonishment that Cindy Nathan had been doped up when she had first spoken to her.

'I'll have someone collect the tape footage from you first thing in the morning,' he said coolly.

She walked beside him to the front door. He stood head and shoulders above her, and she was close enough to smell his aftershave, fresh, lemony, discreet. He took her by surprise again when he opened the screen door and said softly, 'You don't look anything like your photograph.'

She looked up into his face. 'My photograph?'

'Mug-shot. I read up on you, Mrs Page.'

'Did you?' she said coldly.

He held open the screen door with the toe of his shoe. 'But, then, that sort of photograph is never very flattering, is it?'

'No, and it was a long time ago.'

He nodded thoughtfully. 'Yes, I congratulate you. It takes a lot of personal courage to beat alcoholism – beat the demons, so to speak.' Lorraine made no reply. He had read the reports of her drunkenness and her arrest for vagrancy, no doubt he even knew she had prostituted herself, but she felt sickened above all that he knew what she had done – knew why she had been cold-shouldered out of the force. It made her flush.

'What happened to your scar?'

Lorraine jerked back her head as Burton reached out to touch her cheek with one finger. 'I had it fixed.'

'You mind if I say something to you, not as an officer, but as a friend?'

She took two steps back, avoiding his eyes.

'You haven't reported the break-in at your office, that someone tampered with the brake cable on your car. You had a tough climb out of the gutter, Mrs Page. Perhaps someone from your past, nothing to do with Cindy Nathan, is carrying a grudge. I'd take a little more care.'

'Thanks for the advice.'

'Take it, Mrs Page, and if you need to speak to me at any time, please call.' He took out his wallet, adroitly produced his card and a pen, and wrote down another number for her. 'That's my extension and my home number.' He put his wallet and pen back in his jacket, and held out the card.

Lorraine took it without looking at him, and walked back into the apartment as he let himself out and closed the door behind him. She watched from the window as he went towards his car; she knew she should have told him her suspicions of a possible art fraud, which Cindy had outlined, but he had thrown her by admitting he had seen her report sheet. She continued to watch as he drove off down the street.

He had made her feel jaded somehow – his cleanness and freshness, and his neat handwriting on the card in her hand. Plus Cindy Nathan had tested positive for drugs. That put a whole new light on their meetings, and Lorraine was angry that she had not noticed, or even suspected it from the girl's odd chatter, her chronic inability to concentrate, and failure to connect with what was happening around her. Suddenly, Lorraine doubted her judgement completely, and began to think that Cindy Nathan was probably guilty, after all. The depression deepened until she sat down, her head in her hands, feeling wretched, inadequate, unable to stop the tears.

Something else, too, had crept up on her unawares – though she hated to admit it even to herself. She had been attracted to Mr Neat and Clean, and the real pain was knowing that no one or, at least, no decent man would take a second look at her, and that anyone who knew about her past would give her a very wide berth. She was almost thirty-nine years old, and she felt older. The plastic surgery only covered the cracks; it was what was inside that counted. And Lorraine was alone, with only Tiger for company, and it was the idea of a future on her own that made her weep even more despairingly.

Tiger raised his head as she sobbed, then padded across and climbed onto the sofa beside her. She put one arm around his shoulders to draw his head close.

*

It was almost ten o'clock when Juana turned on the bath taps and discovered there was no hot water. She called to her husband, who was still downstairs, asking if he had turned off the water. He didn't hear her, so she made her way along the landing, then froze as she heard the sound of water running. She was outside Cindy Nathan's bedroom – and there was no way that the girl could still be taking a shower.

'Get up here, Jose. *Hurry*, HURRY!'

Juana and Jose went together into Cindy's bedroom. Sure enough, the shower was still running, and sounded louder than normal. Suddenly both were afraid.

'Go into the bathroom,' Juana whispered.

Jose turned the handle, calling to Cindy as he pushed open the door, one inch, then two – then let it swing wide open.

'Mrs Nathan?' he said.

The water was still running and the shower screens were so steamed up that Jose could not make out whether Cindy was inside or not. He edged further into the bathroom, calling Cindy's name, seeing towels and a delicate necklace lying on the tiles. He eased back the sliding doors, which had been drawn around the bath, and gasped. Cindy was naked, kneeling in a position of prayer, a cord wound round her throat and attached by its other end to the shower jet. Her head had slumped forward, and her wet hair covered her face.

'Oh, my God,' he whispered.

'What is it?' asked Juana.

Jose didn't want his wife to see what he had seen, so he turned quickly and pushed her out of the bedroom.

Cindy Nathan was dead. Her eyes were open and her dead gaze stared down at the bottom of the bath, as water continued to spray over her kneeling body and swirl into the drain.

Kendall Nathan sat on her orange sofa in front of the TV set with a tray on her lap. She'd made her usual salad and had just poured herself a glass of white Californian Chardonnay. When the phone rang she was irritated. She had worked late at the gallery and was so tired she was in two minds as to whether to pick it up, but the ringing persisted. When she answered, she couldn't make out what the caller was saying, and had to ask repeatedly who it was.

Jose sounded terrified, his voice breaking as he half sobbed how he had found Cindy.

Kendall almost dropped the phone, and had to breathe deeply to steady herself before speaking. 'Calm down. Tell me again – is she dead?'

'*Yes*, in the shower. What do we do? What do we do?'

Kendall closed her eyes, her mouth bone dry, but her mind racing. 'Have you called anyone else?'

'No, no, we don't know what to do,' Jose said. He had tried to call Lorraine at the office but her answerphone was on, and he didn't have her home number. He had also thought about contacting Sonja, but by this time Juana was hysterical, pointing out that Sonja couldn't do anything from East Hampton. They were afraid to call the police, afraid of any blame being attached to them. Kendall had been their last panic-stricken decision – she would know at least what they should do. They could explain to her that they could not be held responsible.

Kendall calmed them, forcing herself to take deep breaths so that her voice was controlled. 'I'll come right over. Just stay calm and I'll be there as soon as I can. Don't do anything until I get there, do you understand? Don't make any more calls,' Kendall repeated, not wanting to find Feinstein in occupation by the time she got to the house. 'Wait for me to get there.' This time, she was determined to get into the house before anyone else did – and get at least one of her paintings out.

She replaced the receiver with shaking hands, and took a few moments to compose herself before she grabbed her coat, car keys and purse and ran from the house. It took her no more than fifteen minutes to get to the Nathans', where she screeched up to the garage compound and slammed on the brakes.

Jose was standing, pale-faced, at the front door.

'Where is she?' Kendall snapped.

'Bedroom. I found her in the shower,' he said, as Kendall ran past him towards the staircase.

A tearful Juana was sitting on a stair and looked up, wiping her eyes on a sodden tissue. 'There's a note.' She sniffed.

Kendall looked down at the woman, then continued up the stairs and along the landing towards the master suite, Jose behind her.

'No – she's in her own room,' he said, and Kendall bit her lip before continuing more slowly along the landing. Cindy's bedroom door was slightly ajar. She took a deep breath and walked in. Jose was about to follow her, but she turned round. 'Leave me for a minute, please.' Jose stepped back and the bedroom door closed.

Juana appeared, still clutching the tissue. 'Did you show her the note?'

'I left it on the dressing table.'

Kendall picked up the single sheet of scented pink notepaper, across which Cindy's childish writing sprawled: 'I can't live like this. It's all over. By the time you read this I will be dead – Cindy.'

Kendall sighed and set down the note on the zigzag, nursery style blue and white wood unit that Cindy had used as a dressing table, then turned towards the bathroom.

She leaned over Cindy's body, bending down first to try to find a pulse at the wrist, then reached out as though to turn up the face, but recoiled: Cindy's eyes bulged and her tongue protruded, her face swollen and discoloured. Kendall shut the shower door and walked out.

She stood in the centre of the room, breathing deeply to steady her nerves. She looked at the note again: very Cindy. But that was all finished with now, in the past. She shifted her gaze to her future, hanging in front of her in the form of a large Andrew Wyeth canvas on the wall . . .

Jose heard a single cry and looked at his wife. He was about to go into the bedroom when the door opened. Kendall almost pushed him out of her way as she hurried towards the master suite, stopping halfway along the passage to stare at another painting. She was breathing hard, and cried out again before she pushed open the doors to the master suite.

'Go downstairs both of you, just go downstairs.' She slammed the door after her.

Jose looked at his wife in confusion. 'Do as she says, Jose.'

'But shouldn't we call someone? She's dead in there,' he said, pointing to Cindy's bedroom. Suddenly there was a crash, and they heard a scream, as Kendall hurtled out of her ex-husband's bedroom, her face flushed and her eyes wild.

'Who else has been in this house? You'd better tell me, Jose. I want to know who has been in this fucking house, do you hear me?'

Jose was halfway down the stairs, but looked up to see Kendall leaning over the banisters.

'Who has been here? *Tell me.*'

Juana answered from the bottom of the staircase. 'No one, Mrs Nathan. I swear to you, no one but the police and Cindy.'

'Has Feinstein been here? Any of his people?' Kendall sprang down the stairs to stand, trembling with fury, in front of Jose and gave the man a sudden shove. 'I want to know – *tell me who has been here!*'

Jose lost his footing, stumbled and clung to the rail. 'No one, Mrs Nathan, I swear to you.'

Kendall held her head between her hands, repeating, 'Oh, my God, oh, my God, *no* . . . NO!'

Juana and Jose watched as Kendall ran from room to room like a woman possessed, screaming and shouting incoherently. She smashed ornaments, knocked a piece of sculpture to the ground, dragged two canvases from the walls. The couple were so scared they ran to the kitchen and shut the door. They stood listening to

Kendall's shouts and screams, and the thumps and crashes as she continued moving through the house. Then there was silence, but at least ten minutes passed before she walked in.

'Call the police – call whoever you want, but you'd better call somebody and tell them about Cindy.' Kendall made towards the back door.

'Aren't you staying, Mrs Nathan?'

Kendall opened the back door without even turning around. 'No, I hope she rots in hell.'

The door slammed shut after her, and they heard the jeep rev up outside and roar into the road. Jose crossed to the telephone, and Juana looked at him, all distress gone from her face and her features set.

'Who's going to pay us what we're due now?'

CHAPTER 7

LORRAINE KNEW something was up as soon as she saw Decker's face.

'Cindy Nathan died last night.'

'How?' she asked, without emotion.

'Found hanged in the shower. Looks like suicide – she left a note and, according to the guy at the house, the police aren't treating it as murder, for the present at least.'

'Jose called here?'

'Yeah, about half an hour ago – phone was ringing as I walked in.'

'What else did he say?'

Decker ran a hand through his hair. 'Odd, really – I don't think he knew why he'd called here. Said his wife suggested it. They both want to talk to you. I said you'd call when you got in.'

Lorraine pursed her lips. 'I think I'll do one better – I'll go and see them. But first get me Jim Sharkey on the phone, would you?' She changed her mind. 'No. Ask if Lieutenant Burton will speak to me.'

As she closed her door, Decker knew immediately, from her lack of reaction to Cindy's death, that something was troubling her. Her mood was abnormally flat, and she had deep circles beneath her eyes.

Lorraine was thinking rapidly. Why had Cindy committed suicide, if, in fact, she had? The girl hadn't shown any signs of considering suicide, even just after her arrest when she had been under most strain, but perhaps alone, day after day at the house, the prospect of the trial had overwhelmed her. If she had killed her husband, maybe suicide had seemed like the easy way out or, at least, preferable to prison. But what about Kendall Nathan? Could she be involved in some illegal activity to do with the art market, and had killed Cindy, or had her killed, because she had found out? That seemed too far-fetched to be true, but there were the art works, which Kendall had so insistently declared were hers. Could Kendall have imagined that she would stand a better chance of claiming them, if Cindy was dead? She must have known that she would not inherit anything in Cindy's place, and the collection would now most likely be shipped off to Milwaukee – Lorraine could not stifle a smile at the prospect of millions of dollars' worth of modern art hanging on the walls at Cindy's parents' five and dime. Unless she had left it to someone else? Lorraine wrote herself an immediate memo to do three things: find out the exact terms of Harry Nathan's will, if Cindy had made any provision in respect of her property, and to check out where Kendall Nathan had been when Cindy Nathan died.

Decker walked in, put some fresh coffee and bagels down on her desk, then tilted his head to one side. 'You seem kind of low.'

'Well, maybe I am. Let's face it, we just lost a big client.'

'That's all, is it?'

She snapped, 'Yes, that's all, and stop looking at me

like I got two heads. Some days you don't feel so bright, and this just happened to be one of them. You call Lieutenant Burton?'

He told her that Burton's line was busy, and he would call back. 'Anything else you want me to do?'

She tried to think straight. 'What about Sonja Nathan?' She made another mental note to find out what Sonja got out of the estate.

'I cancelled the flight – since we don't have a client, there's no point in wasting either her time or your money going out there. You want me to do anything else?'

'Not right now. Oh, yeah, pack the tapes up and send them to Lieutenant Burton. The PD wants them.'

'They're welcome to them, I'll do it straight away. Did you walk Tiger?'

'YES. Now get out and leave me alone.'

Lorraine sipped the coffee: Decker could really get on her nerves. The intercom light blinked.

'Lieutenant Burton, line two,' Decker said briskly, and Lorraine picked up the phone.

'Mrs Page?' Burton enquired.

'Yes, speaking.' She assumed her most businesslike tones. 'I've asked for the Nathan tapes to be sent over to you, though I understand that may be unnecessary now.'

'Word travels fast,' he said softly.

'She was my client,' Lorraine said icily.

'So what can I do for you?'

'Excuse me?'

'I'm returning your call, Mrs Page.'

'Oh, I just wondered if you could tell me any details. I understand there are no suspicious circumstances – is that so?'

He paused a second before answering. 'It looks that way, but until I've read all the reports I can't say.'

'Have they done the autopsy?'

'Presumably.'

'Not giving away much, are you?'

'As I said, Mrs Page, until I have seen the reports, I can't discuss the incident.'

'You mind if I call you again in a couple of days?'

'I should have all the facts by then.'

Lorraine felt ill at ease. It was as if they had never met: he seemed cool and offhand. 'Well, thank you for returning my call,' she said lamely.

'Not at all. Goodbye.' He replaced the receiver immediately, leaving her listening to a dull buzz.

'Prick,' she muttered, and pressed the intercom. 'Can I have some fresh coffee?'

'By all means.' Two minutes later Decker walked in with the coffee pot.

He topped up her cup and she gave his sleeve a tug. 'Bad morning, sorry.'

He perched on the desk. 'You want to talk about it?'

'Not really. It's just some days, or nights, there doesn't seem much point. You know, I keep seeing that long tunnel and the future looks kind of dark, and . . .' He swirled the coffee pot, waiting for her to go on. 'Well, I sometimes wonder what the hell I'm going to do with my life – or the rest of it. I was fine when I was planning the office and the apartment, and I've got this place up and rolling. We may not be exactly snowed under with work, but I've got more money in the bank than I ever had . . .' She sipped the coffee, and looked through the open door at Tiger stretched out comatose on the sofa.

'And I got my boy out there. I mean, I've got a lot to be grateful for.'

'But you're not happy?'

She had to turn away from him because she wanted to cry. 'I should be, I know that.'

Decker knew intuitively not to say anything. She was slowly, and for the first time, opening up to him, and he valued that, because he liked her, and seeing this vulnerable side of her made him like her even more.

'I'm not complaining,' she said, fishing in her pocket for a cigarette. Decker still said nothing as she found her lighter, lit up, and inhaled deeply. She repeated, so softly he could scarcely hear her, 'I'm not complaining.' Then she swallowed and tried a small smile. 'Gonna give these up.' She was looking at the filter tip, the smile hard to hold.

'That'll be good – well, better for your health, and mine,' he said, passing her the ashtray.

'Yeah, well, who cares about my health?'

'I do,' he said, easing off the desk.

'Thank you. But apart from you, you think anyone will ever care about me? I'm so lonely, Deck, and sometimes I guess I'm frightened that this is all there's ever going to be for me.'

'Everyone needs to be loved,' he said quietly.

She nodded, still looking away. 'They sure do, and I had so much love, Deck, and I threw it all away. It's just that, having known it, I want some more but sometimes I don't think I have the right. You know what I mean?'

He put down the coffee pot, and moved round the desk. 'Come here.'

She shifted, not wanting him close, but he lifted her

from the chair to stand in front of him, then wrapped her in his arms. She resisted, straining away from him, but he held her tightly until she relaxed. He stroked her hair, soothing her, then patted her back as a mother would her child.

The phone rang – Jose calling from the Nathans' house – and this time Lorraine took the call. She agreed to come and see him straight away. She kissed the top of Decker's head as she left, and he could see that her mood was 100 per cent better than when she had arrived.

Lorraine drove up the gravel drive to see that curtains had been drawn behind the garden doors and the sliding timber screens on the upper floor were closed.

She had to wait a few moments before Juana came to the door, looking tired and drawn. 'Thank you for coming.'

Lorraine stepped into the cool, darkened hallway as Jose walked towards her from the kitchen. He smiled sadly. 'We just thought she was taking a shower. Juana even prepared her supper tray.'

They all walked into the kitchen and Lorraine and Jose pulled up tall metal stools to the glass counter. Lorraine said little while Jose told her how they had found Cindy.

'So, she gave no indication that she was depressed?'

Juana shook her head. 'No, she worked out in the gym for a while, then she came in here and said she wanted a light supper.'

'Nothing happened that might have upset her? Any phone calls, any visitors?'

'No, we would have heard, but the phone never rang and nobody came.'

'Did you see the note?'

Jose nodded, and Juana broke down in tears when Lorraine asked what it had said. 'Oh, just that she could not go on, that she did not want to live. I know this sounds very bad, but it was the first time I ever felt sorry for her, when I saw her . . . in the shower. She seemed so young, so small, so . . . defenceless. She looked as if she was praying.'

'Could I see the room?' Lorraine asked, and they agreed to take her upstairs. As they walked from the hall to the staircase, Lorraine registered the shattered ceramics, and the pictures that had been pulled down. One had even been slashed, while others hung at drunken angles on the walls.

The room was in shadow, the blinds pulled down, and everything had been left as Juana and Jose had found it: it didn't even seem as if the police had been there. Lorraine noticed that another painting had been taken down from the wall and left on the floor, but remained silent.

She went into the bathroom where she noted the discarded towels and the necklace still lying on the floor, then turned back to the bedroom. Cindy's shoes were still by the bed, and Lorraine crossed to the dressing table where cosmetic jars had been left open, and tissues stained with make-up remover were scattered about.

'The note was left here?' she asked.

'Just there.' Juana pointed.

Lorraine examined the dressing table more closely. 'What was it written on? Just a scrap of paper, or was it like a letter?'

163

'It was on her own notepaper.'

Lorraine looked round the room. 'Where does she keep it?'

Juana opened one drawer then another, then scratched her head. 'I think downstairs in the study. I don't recall seeing anything in here.'

Lorraine asked if they had seen Cindy's purse. Jose duly searched the room, and found it half under a chair, partly hidden by the ruched frill. He picked it up and handed it to Lorraine.

'I'm surprised the police didn't find this,' she said softly, opening it. She tipped the contents out onto the bed. 'Did the police take the paintings down? It looks like they made a lot of mess,' she said casually.

'No, no, they didn't touch anything. Well, not that I could see,' said Jose.

Lorraine glanced up and caught the look that passed between the two servants.

'They didn't do that,' Jose said eventually.

'Who did?' Lorraine asked, and knew again that the Mexican couple were wondering whether to give or withhold some piece of information.

'It was Kendall Nathan. Jose . . . We panicked, he called her.'

'Kendall was here last night?' Lorraine asked immediately.

'Yes.'

'She was at home when you called her? What time was that?'

'I don't know – late. I was going to take a bath before I went to bed. That's how I noticed – the water was cold,' Juana said.

'It was after ten o'clock,' Jose volunteered.

'But when was the last time you saw Cindy alive?' Lorraine asked.

'About six, I think, when she came out of the gym. The shower was running when we took her tray up at eight thirty.'

But since she was found dead in the shower, that didn't necessarily mean she had been alive at that time, Lorraine thought, then said aloud, 'What did Kendall do when she got here?'

'She was here for about an hour, and she was – she acted kind of crazy. We could hear her up here, breaking things, but we didn't know what to do,' Jose said.

What had all that been about? Lorraine wondered. Had Kendall been trying to mask her own guilt by staging a performance of grief and shock so memorable that the housekeepers would be sure to mention it to the police and, if necessary, testify to it? Had she already been at the Nathan house once that evening – or known that someone else had and that Cindy was dead before the Mexican couple told her?

'Did you tell the police this?'

'We told no one, only you. We didn't know what to do,' Jose said again.

'What happened to the note?' Lorraine asked, examining the contents of Cindy's purse as she spoke. 'Did the police take it?'

'They must have,' said Juana. 'It was gone when they left.'

Lorraine was concentrating on the contents of Cindy's purse. There were a couple of sales receipts, a compact, lipstick, a few loose tissues and a wallet. The wallet contained two thousand dollars in notes and some loose change, a driving licence, parking tickets, more clothing store receipts, and a bunch of receipts from a jewellery store, but for payments made by the shop. There was also a small silver pocket book with a pen. Lorraine opened it and flicked through lists of things to buy and appointments for massage, beauty and hairdressing, all written in childish, looped script, which Lorraine studied closely. She looked at the date on her watch: the hairdressing appointment had been for that morning. Odd that Cindy had arranged to see people over the next few days if she had been thinking of committing suicide but, Lorraine thought, it was always possible that she had taken her own life as a result of an unexpected mood swing – the girl had admitted she had had psychiatric problems.

'The suicide note – I don't suppose you noticed what it was written with? Ink, ballpoint?' Kendall Nathan's Mont Blanc pen was in Lorraine's mind.

'In ink, I think,' Juana said, looking to her husband for confirmation, but Jose shrugged. Lorraine replaced the items in the purse, noting that the pen attached to the pocket book was a tiny silver ballpoint, and put it back where they had found it.

Juana said tentatively, 'There is something else we would like to talk with you about.'

Lorraine nodded pleasantly and followed Juana downstairs, but she was wondering whether she could persuade Burton's office to let her see the note. In the kitchen, Jose and Juana asked her if she knew what would happen to them. They wanted her to talk to Mr Feinstein on their behalf, to see if she could get him to release the monies owed to them.

'I'll do what I can,' she said, and Juana clasped her

hand gratefully. When they reached the front door, Lorraine paused. 'Cindy Nathan had two thousand dollars in her purse, plus she wrote cheques to me on her own account. Didn't you ever think of asking her for money?'

'She said that it was nothing to do with her, and she was already selling her jewellery. That's what she told me,' Jose answered.

'Well, I'll get back to you as soon as I can.'

Lorraine was itching to contact Burton. Once outside in the car, she dialled his number but hung up almost immediately it began to ring. She didn't want to look as though she was chasing him like a teenager – yet she needed to see Cindy's note, and she knew that he was the person through whom to gain access to it. Somehow it seemed less frightening just to go to his office, say she was passing. After all, it was true, she convinced herself. Driving back east on Santa Monica, she was only a stone's throw away.

She walked coolly into Reception at the police department, produced her card and told the clerk that she was there to see Jake Burton. Annoyingly, the man insisted on calling upstairs, and suddenly the idea of just turning up didn't seem like such a good one. But, to her relief, Burton must have agreed to see her, as the desk clerk gave her directions to go on up.

She made herself rap smartly on the door: there was no answer. She raised her fist to knock again and almost hit Burton in the collar-bone as he opened it suddenly.

'Oh, hi,' she said, her voice a good octave higher than it normally was, which made her sound, she thought, about nineteen.

'Well, hello, Mrs Page,' Burton said expressionlessly. 'I wasn't expecting to hear from you again quite so soon. Won't you come in?' He opened the door wide.

She was uncertain, as yet, if she was welcome and found herself talking too fast. 'I was just up at the Nathan house, and I was just wondering whether I could have a quick look at the note Cindy left?'

'If you just swung by my office, you mean?'

Lorraine found herself blushing furiously: it was as though he really did think she was inventing excuses to see him. 'Well, since this would be unofficial, I can't ask you to send it to me Federal Express,' she said, making her voice as cool as she could.

'You know I'm not in favour of this "unofficial" traffic in information between PIs and police,' he said, his manner still betraying no warmth. 'Plus, who's paying you to do this? Your client's got no more worries now, has she?'

'She paid me a lot of money up front,' Lorraine said stiffly. 'Look, you remember what I said about Kendall Nathan? It turns out she was at the house last night. I just think it's a hell of a coincidence, and I want to know if Cindy really wrote that note, that's all.'

'Well,' he said, 'I really don't know whether I can justify spending the department's time in gratifying the wishes of . . .' he smiled for the first time and she realized he was teasing her '. . . curious bystanders. I have to account to the city for every cent.'

'Don't be so tight-assed! I pay my taxes,' Lorraine said, suddenly sure she could get away with it, and laughing. 'Besides, I gave you the tapes.'

'So, we could do a little trade, you mean?' He smiled

again with a hint of mischief – or was she imagining a little flirtatiousness?

'Well . . .' she began.

'Okay,' he said. 'One-time-only offer.' He picked up the phone and asked someone to bring in the file on Cindy Nathan. As soon as the man had left he extracted from it a sealed plastic wallet containing half a sheet of pink writing paper. 'If you'd come an hour later this would have gone to forensic,' he said. 'Don't take it out of the plastic.'

'Gee,' Lorraine said with mock-innocence, 'you mean I can't paddle my pretty little fingers all over it? I was a cop, you know.'

'Sorry,' he said, smiling again. 'There's a sample of Cindy's handwriting behind it that we got from her attorney. Obviously we'll get an expert opinion but they look pretty similar to me.'

So they did: the childishly unformed letters and the unclosed As and Os were almost identical. But it was only a couple of lines long – Kendall was plenty smart enough to imitate that much of someone else's hand-writing, Lorraine reckoned, and the words were written in ink. It was interesting that the note was addressed to no one, but said, 'by the time you read this, I will be dead', as though Cindy had had a particular reader in mind. Lorraine also noticed that, though the handwriting sprawled all over the page, the gap between the two lines Cindy had written was larger than the gap between the first one and the top of the page.

'I think this has been cut from a longer letter,' she said. 'Look at the top.' Burton leaned closer, and Lor-raine was conscious that he cast an almost imperceptible appraising glance over her, taking advantage of her concentration on the paper to do so. When minutely examined, it was clear that the top edge of the paper was not completely straight. 'It's been cut with a pair of scissors,' she said. 'You can see the blades were long enough to cut the whole thing in one go.'

'Jesus, you might be right,' Burton said, and Lorraine realized he was embarrassed that his own officers had failed to notice it. 'Forensic would have picked it up, of course.'

'I'm sure they would,' Lorraine said graciously – in any case, it was true.

'Kind of makes your theory about the other Mrs Nathan a little more credible – though I don't suppose she killed both of them.'

'Wouldn't surprise me,' Lorraine said. 'She's that kind of a girl.'

She was now certain that the killer was Kendall Nathan, and found the desire to see the woman again, to take the investigation on just one more stage, almost uncontrollable. It was true that there was no reason to do so now that Cindy was dead, but loyalty to her former client, the pathos of her death, so wasteful, sordid, at only twenty years old, made Lorraine feel that she could at least spare half an hour to ask Kendall where she had been the previous night. She promised herself that she would do nothing more, that if anything made her suspicious, she would hand it straight over to Burton. After all, if Cindy had been murdered, it was his job to find out who had done it.

'I won't take up any more of your time,' she said. 'I'm sorry for bursting in on you like that.'

'It's been a pleasure – and very instructive,' he said

with a genuine smile, and she felt his eyes flick over her again.

'Well,' Lorraine said, knowing she sounded ridiculous, but forcing herself to carry on, 'you know where my office is on West Pico. Stop by any time.'

'I might just do that,' he said, still looking at her.

Oh, yeah, she thought, sure you will. 'Well, I'd better get going.' She set off down the stairs.

Gallery One was virtually on her way back to the office, she told herself, getting into her car – and she would only be inside for five minutes. She turned left into Beverly Drive, and as she pulled up outside she could see Kendall Nathan sitting at her desk, talking to the young black man.

Both of them looked round as soon as the door buzzer sounded, and Lorraine noticed at once how exhausted and haggard Kendall looked – like someone, in fact, who hadn't slept all night.

'What are you doing here?' she said immediately, with no attempt at politeness.

'I wondered if you'd heard Cindy Nathan was dead,' Lorraine said. The pair in front of her were looking intently at her, Kendall's strange eyes darker than ever, it seemed, clouded with pain.

'Yes, I heard,' Kendall said curtly. 'That terminates your involvement in other people's affairs, I think.'

'Were you here last night, Mrs Nathan?' Lorraine asked, not so much expecting an answer as wanting to observe Kendall's reaction to the question.

'What is this?' Kendall snapped. Her nerves seemed at breaking point. 'You have no business whatsoever to come around harassing me, insinuating—'

'So you weren't here last night?' Lorraine cut in,

171

noting how quick Kendall was to think she was being accused.

'Yes, as it happens, I was,' Kendall retorted angrily. 'And Eric was with me. We left at nine thirty, and I went home – all of which Eric will confirm.' She looked pointedly at him.

'That's right,' he said. 'We were both here.' Much weight you could give to *his* assertions, Lorraine thought cynically. If he didn't back up his employer he would lose his job. He was still staring at her, she thought, with anger, almost hate in his eyes. Had he done Kendall's dirty work for her?

'I see. I'm sorry to have troubled you.' She turned on her heel.

'See you don't come around here again, Mrs Page,' Kendall called after her. 'If you do, you'll have reason to regret it.'

Lorraine turned round and looked the other woman directly in the eye. 'Was that a threat, Mrs Nathan?'

'Just a warning,' Kendall said. 'Now get off my property and stay off.'

'Glad to,' Lorraine said. 'Good afternoon, Mrs Nathan.' She walked out, not bothering to close the door behind her, leaving the buzzer whining loudly.

She was excited as she drove to her office, eager to discuss the new developments with Decker. She roared up to the building, and handed her keys to the valet parking attendant, who now had strict instructions always to keep his eye on her Mercedes.

He drove it into the underground motor court, and pulled up next to an immaculate, gleaming Rolls Corniche. He hadn't recognized Raymond Vallance, and had only realized who the owner of the Rolls was when he'd parked the car and seen the name on some mail on the front seat. He would have liked to sneak a look at the letters, but he'd been summoned by Reception on his mobile, so hadn't had time. As he locked Lorraine's car, he leaned towards the Corniche again, thinking how amazing it was that people left such personal things in their cars and tossed the keys to valet parking boys, unaware that they always had a good sniff around. He knew of some cases where guys had been paid nice regular sums for information – not that he would ever stoop to that, but some folks were so dumb they deserved to be ripped off. House keys attached to their car keys was an open invitation for a quick impression to be taken, making access to their homes as easy as taking candy from a baby – even more so if you got a couple of hours clear when they were dining out. He wouldn't co-operate in *that* kind of crooked deal, but he allowed himself a good snoop around, and often found a few dollars tucked down the back of expensive limo seats. He never thought that was stealing – that was just getting lucky.

Raymond Vallance's mail wasn't that interesting, and the Corniche wasn't his. It belonged to some woman. The parking attendant smiled as he saw that Mr Vallance also had a nasty letter from his bank. His financial situation was even shakier than the attendant's. He put the letter back in the envelope, had a good feel around the seats and opened the glove compartment, whistling as he saw it was jammed with parking tickets and CDs. There was a powder compact too, with lipstick attached, a pair of sunglasses, and a number of pieces of folded pink writing paper. He looked around to see if anyone was watching, and opened out the top sheet. It was a note, childish handwriting in brown ink, from some woman, by the looks of it, rambling on about how no one understood her or cared about her. God, he thought, glancing quickly over the pages of appeals and complaints. He got enough of that at home. He refolded the pieces of paper, stuffed them back among the other contents of the glove compartment, and had another quick feel behind the seats before he was satisfied that there was nothing of interest, not even a few coins. So much for the movie star. He wouldn't waste his time asking Vallance for an autograph.

CHAPTER 8

LORRAINE BURST into the office, and Decker got up immediately. 'You have a . . .' he said quietly, nodding towards the other side of the room.

Raymond Vallance turned from the window, removing his Gucci shades. Well, Lorraine thought, look who it is.

'Mrs Page? Raymond Vallance.'

He stowed the glasses in a pocket and held out his hand. Lorraine crossed the room and shook it: it was limp, clammy, unpleasant to the touch. He was taller than she would have expected, at least six foot one, and he was certainly making a serious effort to charm, but Lorraine thought she detected a touch of strain behind the ingratiating manner.

'I'm sorry, I should have made an appointment – if this is not convenient . . .'

'No, no, please come into my office.' She gestured to him to go ahead then turned back to Decker. 'What does he want?' she whispered.

'I don't know, but he's been waiting half an hour.'

Lorraine followed Vallance into her office and closed the door. 'Sorry to keep you waiting.' She smiled, as she moved round her desk and sat down. 'Do you mind if I smoke?' she said, already taking a cigarette out of a pack.

Vallance's hand reached her lighter a moment before hers did, and struck a flame. He stared hypnotically at her with his wide-set, ice-blue eyes, a half smile playing on his slightly feminine lips. There was also something effeminate about his hands: the long fingers were tipped with carefully shaped and buffed nails.

'Not at all,' he said, his voice overtly sexual, then clicked off the lighter and put it back on the desk, folding his hands in his lap. He was wearing a navy Armani suit, a pristine shirt in the palest powder pink, and a tie in such a severely 'tasteful' muted shade that it must have set him back two hundred dollars at least. His hair was silver-white, and much thinner than she would have expected, especially in Hollywood where most actors used weaves or spider hairpieces to disguise their hair loss. He had a broad face with a slight dimple in the chin, but his profile was superb, as he clearly knew – his nose was perfect, from both right and left sides, and his high cheekbones looked as if they were carved.

It was a wonderful face, but the man behind it was so conscious of his beauty that he seemed constantly to be turning from one side to the other to display his features to their best advantage.

'So, Mr Vallance, what can I do for you?'

'It's rather a delicate subject,' he said softly, plucking at his trouser crease, and crossing his legs.

'Best just to come straight out with it, then, isn't it?'

'Mm, yes. You, ah, may or may not know that I was a friend of Harry Nathan.'

'Yes, I am aware of that.'

'And of Cindy Nathan,' he said, his manner just a fraction too casual.

'Yes,' Lorraine said, smoking. When he flashed her

that penetrating look, she met and held it unflinchingly, his eyes slid away. She wondered if he knew that Cindy was dead, but decided she would bide her time before mentioning it.

'You were retained by Cindy to . . . investigate Harry's death, weren't you?' he went on.

'Yes, I was.'

'And I understand that you received some . . .' He coughed slightly. 'I find this very difficult.' Lorraine did not help him. She found the ageing man somehow faintly repulsive, but the opportunity to find out what he knew about Harry and Cindy was too good to miss. 'I understand that you received some videotapes from Cindy.'

'Some tapes did come into my possession, yes,' Lorraine said, deciding not to reveal that she no longer had them until he had told her just a little more.

He knew, just as Kendall had known, that she had seen them. 'I'm afraid that sort of thing is quite common in Hollywood,' he said. 'Though those tapes were, of course, recorded without my knowledge.'

Well, that was a lie, Lorraine thought, but decided to let it ride.

'I've been approached about a leading role in what will undoubtedly be one of the most important films made in this decade,' he continued pompously, and Lorraine permitted herself a sceptical lift of one eyebrow. 'Very sensitive political material. The director's name I'm sure you can guess . . .' he gave her a meaningful look '. . . and I happen to know that some of our . . . ah, friendly government agencies would just as soon I didn't get past first base. Anything negative attaching to an artist's image, and an offer can be immediately withdrawn, and, of course, they don't hesitate fabricating material if nothing genuine can be found. For those reasons, Mrs Page, I have to say that I need to recover those tapes.'

Lorraine had heard all this before. 'I'm sorry, Mr Vallance, those tapes aren't mine to dispose of.'

'I want them,' Vallance said sharply. Lorraine stubbed out her cigarette. 'Obviously, a man in my position cannot have that kind of—'

'Pornography,' she interrupted.

It was delightful: he was flushing under his tan.

'I am willing to pay you for them,' he said.

'Really?' she said, almost mockingly.

He adjusted his tie. 'They are not something I am particularly proud of.'

'I'm not surprised, but it is possible, Mr Vallance, that they may be required as evidence.'

'Evidence?' he said nervously. 'But why? I can't see why anyone would want them – they're private, were recorded without even my knowledge. In fact, I could sue.'

Listening to him, Lorraine wondered if he knew about the phone tapes, also recorded without his knowledge, and if he did, had he wanted them badly enough to hire someone to break in and pour acid over them? 'I am sure you could if they were to be offered for sale,' she said. 'I understand there's quite a black market in pornographic tapes of that kind, especially featuring – or should I say starring? – someone like yourself.'

Vallance stood up, hands clenched at his sides. 'How much do you want?'

Lorraine turned up her palms innocently. 'I can't sell them, Mr Vallance.'

He leaned forward, his face distorted with anger. 'So what do you intend doing with them, Mrs Page?'

'As I have said, they might be required as evidence, Mr Vallance, and I cannot simply hand them over to you. They are not my property in any case. They belonged to my client.'

'Cindy?' he snapped.

'Yes, Cindy Nathan,' she said firmly. Vallance turned away, his hands still clenched. 'You were involved in what I would describe as quite brutal sexual games – she was young, she was innocent . . .'

'Like fuck she was! She's a tough little whore.'

'Cindy died last night, Mr Vallance,' Lorraine said, watching him closely. 'Suicide, it seems.'

For a moment, Vallance did not react. Then he said, looking straight at her, 'I'm . . . sorry to hear that.' His eyes were curiously shuttered, and Lorraine's skin crawled. Cindy's death had not been news to him, whatever he wanted her to believe.

'You and Cindy had a close friendship, I believe,' Lorraine said.

'You could say that.' He was guarded.

'Was it your child, by the way?' Lorraine asked casually. 'The baby she lost?'

'No,' Vallance said curtly. 'It could have been any number of people's, but it was not mine – that I can be sure of.'

'Really? But I have seen you in action, Mr Vallance, so to speak.'

He turned those wide eyes on her and they were beautiful, a wonderful, dazzling blue that flashed like lightning. If only he could have brought that look, or the strength of feeling behind it, to his performances, he might perhaps have reignited his dying career.

'You didn't answer me, Mr Vallance. I have seen you in the videos that Harry Nathan made and, as far as I could tell, you . . .' She gestured eloquently with her hand. 'You were very aroused. Oh, of course, I'd forgotten.' She touched her forehead, feigning surprise at her absent-mindedness. 'There was the one where you strapped on a—'

He leaned forward, almost spat at her, 'I want those fucking tapes, you hard-nosed bitch.'

'They most certainly are fucking tapes.' Lorraine laughed, and then leaned forward. 'Perhaps you'd be happier if it really was your own hard prick, and not some plastic strap-on number. You might get a whole new career for yourself. What's the matter, Mr Vallance, can't you get a hard-on? Is that the—'

He slapped her across the face. She took the blow and paused a moment before she swung her right fist and caught him full on his perfect nose. He flopped back into the chair, one hand to his face while he fumbled with the other for a handkerchief. She watched him feeling the bridge of his nose gingerly, afraid she'd broken it, staring at the fine trickle of blood on his hand before he put the handkerchief to his face.

'I'm sorry, Mr Vallance. I only just heard about Cindy and . . .'

She looked carefully at him: his head was bowed and he was weeping, covering his face with the white cloth. Lorraine picked up the glass of water and held it out to him, but he shook his head and turned away from her. It was about three minutes before he composed himself, checked his nose again and looked at the spots of blood on the handkerchief before he put it back in his pocket. He reached for the glass of water and raised it to his lips, his hand shaking badly. He sipped carefully, then slowly replaced the glass on the desk.

'How did she do it?' he asked flatly.

'She took some cord, wrapped it round the shower head and then round her throat – only a short distance, but enough. She was kneeling, as if she was praying, according to the servants.'

He sighed, and reached for the water again, drained it and held the empty glass in his hands. 'I'm sorry. Maybe she wasn't as tough as I thought.'

'Nobody ever is,' she said, and he looked up. 'Can I ask you frankly, Mr Vallance, do you think Cindy killed Harry Nathan?'

There was a moment's silence, and Lorraine had the impression of a curtain falling at the back of the man's eyes. 'Yes,' he said finally. 'Yes, I do. She would never have been convicted, of course. Harry should have kept right away from women – he just wasn't himself with them, they made him dirty, sucked him dry. I used to tell him that he ought to regard women as liquor to an alcoholic, that they were something he would have to cut right out of his life, just accept that they brought out negative things in him, things he didn't need.'

'Harry was different then, away from female company?'

Vallance gave a strange, bitter-sweet smile. 'He was such a prince when he could cut loose from all that, the kindest, funniest, most generous guy you could meet, and so damn talented . . .' God, Lorraine thought, he sounded like some high-school girl gushing over her first beau. 'Cindy never gave a damn about Harry,' Vallance went on. 'She never gave a damn about anyone but herself. She wanted his money, and she thought . . . I guess she thought she'd got it.' His quick correction didn't escape Lorraine. Could Vallance have had anything to do with Cindy's death? Was it possible that he and Kendall had acted together?

'But, Mr Vallance, although you say you and Harry were such good friends, I have to say that I know he was blackmailing you.'

He laughed softly. 'That's what I mean. The women changed him, made him dirty, selfish. That's not the way he started out, but it was sure as hell the way he finished up. Once Harry stopped making money, I doubt if there was anyone he knew that he didn't put the squeeze on. He wouldn't think of it as blackmail, though – he would probably have been shocked if you called him a blackmailer. Conman might be a better description.'

'Did you pay him?'

He stared at a point on the wall. 'I guess so. I paid Harry in women, but he also paid me his way – sometimes my rent, phone bills or whatever. He liked me to have to ask him for hand-outs, but he could be generous.'

Lorraine waited. Vallance was digging deep inside himself, and she knew from his body language that it hurt: he seemed to have shrivelled, as if he was ageing in front of her.

'So why did you put up with it?'

His shoulders lifted. 'It didn't happen overnight, darling. Our sort of relationship goes back a long way.' Again there was a pause, and Vallance sat back, as though watching a movie playing on her office wall.

'I knew Harry before any of them – we used to share an apartment.' What a surprise, Lorraine thought. 'We used to work out together – this is before anybody worked out. Harry always kept himself in shape. We'd pick up these little girls and bring them home, and we'd both come on with the heavy romance, and they'd think they'd met these two really great guys.' Vallance almost chuckled. 'And then, after a while, of course, we'd get them in bed and give them all the I-never-met-anyone-like-you-before crap, and then as soon as we'd fucked them, Harry used to put on this crazy voice and yell, "Grand Central Station, ladies and gentlemen!"' Vallance produced an odd, caterwauling yodel like an Appalachian railway porter. '"All change!" And then, of course, I'd fuck his and he'd fuck mine. Sometimes the girls'd kick up a fuss, and Harry'd say,' Vallance's face contorted with amusement, '"A fuck is only a fuck, my dear, but a friend is a good cigar."' He laughed, slapping his thighs. 'That was when Harry started all the goofy kind of comedy he used to do later on. All that came right out of that apartment we used to have, I swear it.'

Jesus, Lorraine thought: Vallance imagined he was not only Harry Nathan's heroic friend, ideal lover, but also his muse. The reality, however, was painfully clear: Vallance couldn't get sex with Harry, so the next best thing was sex with the women who did, and preferably thirty seconds after Harry had pulled out.

'Presumably all this fun and games had to stop when Harry got married?'

'You bet it did,' Vallance said bitterly. 'What he ever saw in that fucking Swedish bitch, God knows. She was great-looking, of course, but, Christ, they all were.'

'So, you didn't see so much of Harry after that?'

'Oh, I saw him okay,' Vallance said. 'Harry was innocent, and he just assumed we'd all be friends. He started making a lot of money with his movies, but Sonja just pissed on all that too. I used to go out to the house most weekends, watch her spending Harry's money doing the place up like fucking Versailles. Then when she finished the house, she started saying how bored she was, so Harry bought her the gallery. Anyone else would have got down on their knees in gratitude, but Sonja said Harry did it to stifle her talent, to make her play shopkeeper when she wanted to be alone, to create . . .'

'But she must have had talent of some sort,' Lorraine said. 'I mean, she has quite a reputation now.'

'You can sell just about anything on the modern art market, Mrs Page, provided it's full of enough neurosis, sickness and self-possession, and Sonja Sorenson had all those things to burn.'

'So what happened? Why did they get divorced?'

'Well, Sonja was miserable. Nothing was ever right for her, and first it was Harry's fault, and then it was *my* fault,' Vallance said, and something in his voice told Lorraine that he was about to embark on another pack of lies. 'She started blaming me for everything, trying to turn Harry against me, saying I was at the house too much, saying I was just taking money off him. Sonja got more and more up her own ass, and then they couldn't have kids, and by the time they finished up she was in her forties and she looked pretty terrible.'

'She didn't look so bad at Forest Lawn,' Lorraine said, thinking of the elegant woman she had seen at the funeral.

'That's just clothes,' Vallance said dismissively, turning round to lean against the sill.

When Vallance was lying, an airy nastiness entered his voice, and Lorraine knew he was lying now. She was quite certain that his account of the Nathan marriage was as biased, distorted and selective as it was possible to get.

'So, did you encourage him to leave her?' she asked.

Vallance sat down again, brushed at his immaculate suit and adjusted his perfectly knotted tie. 'Let's just say I helped along what was going to happen anyway. Kendall was on the scene by then, and she was digging Sonja's grave from the minute she walked through the door.'

Lorraine pricked up her ears.

'So you and Kendall helped things along together?' she suggested. 'Did you get along well with Kendall?'

Vallance fell silent. He got up again and straightened one of her prints without looking at her. 'Not really. Kendall didn't get along with anyone.' He seemed disinclined to say any more. The changes in his mood were rapid: sometimes he seemed to want to talk, then something he didn't like would come up and he would sink into silence.

'But would you say she was another of those self-absorbed, selfish sort of women Harry seemed to go for?' Lorraine asked, pretending sympathy with Vallance's point of view.

'Was she ever,' Vallance said, with a scornful laugh, rising to the bait. 'Have you seen Kendall lately? All set up in her fancy art gallery, with her fancy friends and her fancy clothes and her fancy voice? Kendall was her maiden name before she married Harry. Her real first name is Darleen. Doesn't play quite so well, does it? She came to LA as just another little piece of white trash and got a job as a secretary to some decorator, and then it was an antique dealer, and the next thing Sonja – God, she was dumb – gave her a job in the gallery. I guess she thought Harry would never look twice at her – she wasn't his type and she looked like shit. Big hair and big shoulders and these terrible tacky little suits, but my, that little lady was quite some operator.'

Clearly there was no love lost between the two of them, and Lorraine rapidly revised her theory of Kendall and Vallance acting together to get rid of Nathan and Cindy. 'You mean in a business sense?' she asked, deliberately misunderstanding him.

'You could say that. Kendall has been in business since she was in diapers – the business of promoting Darleen Kendall Nathan. She acted at first like she worshipped Sonja, studied her clothes, copied the way she talked, and, of course, she changed her name just as soon as she could, said it was because Sonja used to call her by her surname, like as a pet name, when they were working together. Kendall started to play up all this great artist garbage too, and Sonja'd lost the plot anyway, by this stage – her hormones had curdled, I reckon, over this whole no-kids stuff.' He gave a sigh of irritation with these unsavoury feminine preoccupations.

'Sonja said she had to start working again so she locked herself in the studio for about a year and Kendall just waved her hankie and said bye-bye. She took over the gallery, of course, and worked her ass off there until she was running it. Gradually she took over Harry too.' Clearly this turn of events had not suited Vallance.

'Of course, Harry's mother,' Vallance continued, well into his stride now – Lorraine had been waiting for them to get to old Mrs Nathan – 'hated Sonja's guts, and she rammed Kendall down his throat. Kendall started sweet-talking the old lady, and Abigail thought she was just the sweetest girl, and so maternal. Every time Sonja went out of town, Kendall would just suggest to Harry that he invite his mother, so diplomatic.'

'How long did this go on?' Lorraine asked.

'Well, they had a thing behind Sonja's back for a long time, but Harry wouldn't leave Sonja until Kendall announced she was pregnant. He had to tell her then.'

'How did she take it?'

Vallance dug his hands into his trouser pockets. 'I don't know. She just left. All I knew was she flew to New York, and she never came back. She tried to claim some share in the gallery, but his lawyers made such a fucking production out of the whole thing that she backed down. That was the way Sonja was. If she didn't get what she wanted immediately she just walked away.'

A full two minutes passed. Then Lorraine asked, 'So he remained at the house, Sonja went to New York, and they started divorce proceedings?'

'Yes. Harry and Kendall got married and had their kid, but the kid died and Harry was losing money. He changed. He was never the same again.'

'Why did you hang on?' Lorraine asked.

'Jesus Christ . . . you want me to spell it out?'

'I guess so.'

He sighed and looked at a point above Lorraine's head, then back to her. His wide-set eyes were like a sick dog's.

'I loved him, and when he didn't need me any more I let him use me. When he ditched Kendall for Cindy, I went through it all again. He used me, just as much as he used Cindy, used everyone he ever knew. But I still loved him.'

Loved him enough not to want anyone else to have

187

him? Lorraine wondered suddenly whether Vallance could have killed Harry. In a way, he had loved Nathan longer than anyone else, had been obsessed by him and, in his own mind, been betrayed by him too.

'Anyway,' Vallance said, seeming to drag himself with an effort back into the present, 'I guess I'd better go.' Lorraine stood up to walk to the door with him, sorry for him in spite of her revulsion. He had walked in like a movie star, and was walking out so weak and jaded.

'Can I just ask you one final thing?' she said, as she opened the door and Vallance fumbled with his shades. 'Were you at home last night?'

He knew at once that she was asking him if he had an alibi for the time at which Cindy Nathan had died, and he was not so emotionally battered that he could not reply at once.

'Yes, I was,' he said. 'A number of my friends called, as it happens.'

He had put on the dark glasses now, and Lorraine could not see his eyes. 'Okay,' she said. She walked with him past Decker's desk, and showed him out. He left without a smile or a handshake, and without looking back.

Lorraine raised one eyebrow at Decker. 'Well, guess who the most beautiful man in the world wanted to shove his dick up?'

'Jesus Christ, you can be so fucking crude,' Decker said huffily.

Lorraine leaned on his desk, and grinned. 'He was in love with Harry Nathan himself.' Then she gestured towards her office. 'Come in and chat to me. I want to discuss a few things that came up this morning.'

Decker collected his notebook, and asked her whether

she was doing all this work *pro bono* or if they were going to be paid.

Lorraine sighed. 'Oh, shit, I forgot. I have to go talk to Feinstein.'

Vallance drove out of the garage, unaware that the smiling, bowing valet had given his car a thorough going-over. He was on his way now to play Prince Charming to Verna Montgomery, to get his rent money out of her. She had to be sixty years old, though she insisted she was no more than forty-four. He hadn't even bothered to rearrange the white wisps of his hair because he knew that if Nathan's videos ever got out any last shred of hope he had of resurrecting his career was gone. As he drove onto Sunset he was crying, his white hair blowing in the wind – Raymond Vallance, the most beautiful man in the world.

CHAPTER 9

ECKER GOT Lorraine an appointment with Feinstein almost immediately. His address in Century City was certainly impressive, on one of the smartest blocks of the Avenue of the Stars. The building had only recently been opened, and Lorraine had to concede that it was a truly handsome piece of modern architecture, a soaring tower of golden granite and blue glass that seemed to cut the sky.

Lorraine went up the steps and into a lobby whose sheer moneyed lustre exceeded anything she had seen, even in Los Angeles. The commissionaire directed her to the forty-third floor, and she made her way to the bank of elevators.

She emerged from the elevator car into another lobby bathed in light, streaming in through semi-transparent blinds of fine white cloth. Feinstein's receptionist was a beautiful, long-limbed girl, wearing a straight tunic dress in mint green crêpe-de-chine and a pair of transparent plastic court shoes, whose four-inch heels made her well over six feet tall. She introduced herself as Pamela, with a charming smile, and asked her if she would mind waiting a moment. Lorraine sat down in one of four low armchairs with curving black backs and white leather upholstery ranged round a table of quaking-leaf fern.

Feinstein kept Lorraine waiting only a minute, then she was shown into an enormous office carpeted in a smooth silver grey like whaleskin, full of beautifully crafted wooden furniture whose dignity and majestic scale jarred with the bald, weasel-like lawyer. He only bothered to rise a couple of inches from his chair and motioned Lorraine to a lower seat placed in front of his huge desk. She began to thank him for seeing her, but his intercom blinked and his voice rasped loudly, making her jump: she had not noticed the transparent plastic speaker plugged into his right ear or the mouthpiece at the corner of his lips.

'Just tell her I'm in conference, Pamela, and that goes for the rest of the week!' He listened to whatever Pamela said in reply, then snapped, 'I am not talking to her, Pamela!' and detached the headset. He began to shuffle files on his desk, avoiding Lorraine's eye as he asked what she wanted to see him about and reminded her that he was a busy man. He opened a drawer and took out a foot-long cigar, sniffed it before unwrapping it, then sniffed again and clipped the end.

'I'm a private investigator,' Lorraine began, and Feinstein sighed, sucking on the unlit cigar end.

'Yes, Mrs Page, I know who you are.' He patted his pockets, looking for his lighter.

'I was acting for Mrs Nathan,' she said. He ran his lips around the fat cigar and puffed it alight, the smoke forming a blue halo round his head.

'Just get to the point. I'm inundated with calls from Kendall Nathan, and so I'll tell you what I've told her – and keep on telling her. Until I've had time to assess the

Nathan estate, I can't give any personal or financial information to anyone.'

'I wanted to discuss Cindy Nathan's—'

Feinstein cut her off. 'Suicide? Well, I'm sorry, obviously. Is that why you wanted to see me? Or – don't tell me – you, like everyone else concerned with Nathan, want a pay-off? Worried you won't get your fee, is that it?'

'I wanted to ask you for some details about the art gallery, and specifically Mr Nathan's art collection,' Lorraine said, controlling her temper – she would have liked to punch the cigar down his throat.

'I'm not prepared to discuss anything with you, Mrs Page. Like I said, I'm sorry about Cindy, but it doesn't come as a shock. I mean, you threaten to do something often enough, kinda takes away the element of surprise.' He gestured in the air, one hand clutching the cigar.

'Cindy had threatened suicide before?'

Feinstein looked at his watch. 'She made it public knowledge often enough, and I got enough faxes and notes from her, threatening the same thing, to paper the walls with. She was . . .' He twisted his finger at the side of his temple.

'Would it be possible for me to see them?'

'No, it would not. If however, the police require them, that is a different matter.'

'And I suppose Harry Nathan had nothing to do with Cindy's previous suicide attempts?'

'Maybe, maybe not. I don't know the ins and outs of my clients' domestic set-ups – it's tough enough getting the business side of their lives sorted out.' He sighed. 'I know she was young, but she'd been around and, to be

192

honest, I couldn't stand the girl. Never could understand why my client put up with her hysterics, but then, once a man gets involved with these bimbos, what can you expect? Money's all they're after. I see a lot of greed in my profession. I've even got Harry's goddamned domestics calling, plus his entire family, all like vultures, all wanting to know how much. I have to protect my clients.'

'But not all your clients are murdered, I hope,' Lorraine said quietly.

Feinstein examined his manicured hands. The cigar stuck in his wet lips as he dragged heavily on it and blew a wide ring of smoke behind his head, his voice halting with false emotion. 'Harry Nathan was my client, and he was also a man I admired and respected. Whatever he did in his private life was none of my concern. If you submit your account to my assistant, I will endeavour to see that it's paid. Now, as I said, I'm a very busy man, Mrs Page, so if there's nothing else . . .'

'What will Kendall Nathan inherit now under the will?' Lorraine asked.

Feinstein started at her, his gaze studiedly blank. 'I don't see that that is any concern of yours, Mrs Page. Do I have to repeat myself about client confidentiality?'

Lorraine persisted, 'Does she get anything now that might have gone to Cindy – like the art or anything?'

Feinstein wagged his finger. 'Listen, honey, you just lost one client, so this, I presume, is a fishing trip for another. You wanna work for Kendall Nathan, go talk to her. Now, please, I'd like you to leave.'

Lorraine got up and picked up her briefcase, smoothing down her skirt. 'Is that one of the Nathan gallery paintings?' She indicated a massive canvas on the wall, and Feinstein moved round his desk, impatient to show her out. 'I notice you had one similar in Reception.'

The lawyer was now opening the office door. 'Mrs Page,' he said curtly, sweeping one hand in a mock-gallant gesture towards the door, but Lorraine had moved closer to the painting, a huge composition of brightly coloured, but somehow warlike shapes, and saw a small gold plaque on the wall underneath that named Frank Stella as the artist.

'Very impressive,' Lorraine murmured, then walked towards him. 'Are you a collector?'

Feinstein turned away from her as Pamela appeared outside the open door. 'Kendall Nathan has called again – she's on the phone now,' she said in a low voice. 'She says it's very urgent, Mr Feinstein.'

'Get rid of her, and show Mrs Page out.'

Lorraine was now close to the attorney, who reached to just below her shoulder. What little hair he had left was dyed black and slicked backwards, making his weasel's eyes, under arched – and, if Lorraine was not mistaken, plucked – brows, seem even smaller and beadier. With his silk suit and Gucci shoes, Feinstein smelt of money as strongly as of his overpowering cologne, but no amount of polish could disguise the coarseness of the personality underneath.

'Is it an original?' she asked sweetly.

'What?' He blinked.

'The painting. Did you buy it from Nathan's gallery? It's just that the real reason I came to see you was that I had a conversation with Cindy, shortly before she died, and she seemed to think that her husband, and probably his ex-wife, Kendall Nathan, were involved in some sort of art fraud.' Feinstein frowned, and looked past her to the painting as Lorraine continued in the same saccharine tone. 'But, then, as you're a collector, I'm sure you would have had any work you purchased properly authenticated.' The false sweetness of her smile matched her voice as she walked past him out into Reception.

Feinstein followed. 'Cindy Nathan told you about a fraud. What fraud?'

Lorraine paused at a canvas that covered most of one wall, and tapped the frame. 'Well, it appears that a lot of the paintings, not only in Nathan's house but also sold through the gallery, were probably only copies. This must have cost a fortune, it's a . . .' She leaned to read another small gold plaque. 'Ah, a de Kooning. I mean, I'm no connoisseur, but I know his work is sought after and commands a high price – if it's an original, that is.'

Feinstein continued to follow in Lorraine's wake, glancing at the painting as he passed it. 'What else did Mrs Nathan tell you?' he asked nervously.

Lorraine had her hand on the door to the lobby, and tilted her head to one side. 'Well, Mr Feinstein, my client Mrs Nathan may, sadly, no longer be with us, but nevertheless she is still my client, and as you have pointed out, I must continue to respect the confidentiality of her affairs. Thank you for your time, and if you should wish to see me again, please call.' She proffered one of her cards, then breezed out of the door, which swung closed behind her.

Feinstein glanced at her card, then hurried into the boardroom. There were two canvases at either end of the twenty-five-foot room, and he almost ran to the one further away, then stopped in his tracks and turned to look at the other. He had nothing like the expertise necessary to tell whether his so-called investments were genuine or not, and panic began to rise like bile in his gullet. Then he yelled at the top of his voice. 'PAMELA! PAMELA!'

The girl hurried into the room, notebook at the ready, to find Feinstein sitting at the centre of the boardroom table. 'Your next appointment is here, Mr Feinstein. Mr . . . are you all right?'

He was pulling at his collar, loosening his tie. 'I need a glass of water, an' get that guy, the art historian, the one who went with me to Harry Nathan's gallery.'

'Yes, Mr Feinstein. Do you want him to meet you there, as usual?'

'No.' His voice was harsh. 'Get him here. I want him fucking here.'

Pamela scuttled out. As Harry Nathan's lawyer, Feinstein knew not only what a mess the Nathan estate was in, but that the outstanding claims against it far exceeded its worth. The only thing Feinstein had been sure about was Nathan's private art collection, whose value had yet to be assessed, but he had been depending on it to cover the majority of the debts and, most importantly, his own fees. He was sure Harry wouldn't have pulled a fast one on him. He was his lawyer, for Chrissakes. He'd been his friend, hadn't he? But as he calculated how much he had paid for the canvases, a sinking feeling engulfed him. He had always known that Harry Nathan was a thieving, conniving, two-faced bastard. It took one to know one.

Kendall hung up the telephone, shaking with impotent rage, as Feinstein's secretary informed her yet again that her boss was in conference. She had been calling him every half an hour since she had spoken to the insurance company and disovered that Cindy had indeed been telling the truth – Nathan hadn't paid the premiums on the art collection for two years.

In an effort to calm her nerves, she'd had three brandies, but they hadn't helped. If anything they had made her feel worse. Part of her was still refusing to believe what had happened, sure there was some mistake – but it was pretty clear what the explanation was: Harry had not bothered to insure the paintings because they were worthless. As soon as she had got a closer look at them she had known that they were fakes. She and Harry had had the brilliant idea of selling valuable original paintings to various ditzy members of the film community, arranging for copies to be painted, and then, after the buyers had had their purchases authenticated, delivering the fakes. No one had noticed; no one had bothered to get the paintings checked a second time.

Now, however, it seemed that Harry had pulled the same scam on her, and switched the originals hanging at the house for a second set of copies. The reason, too, was obvious: he was cutting her out of the proceeds of the fraud and intended to keep the approximately twenty million dollars they had reckoned on netting. Harry wouldn't have done that to *her*, would he?

She was almost panting with hysteria, and her outrage rose the more she thought about it: her role in the whole thing had required months of preparation, negotiation and unremitting stress.

Kendall poured herself more brandy, forced herself to try to think logically: what if Harry Nathan hadn't been shot? It had happened only weeks before they had intended to move all the paintings. What if he had carried into effect what they had so carefully arranged, that the paintings would be moved one by one to private buyers in Europe? Harry had even been in Germany arranging the deals. Kendall's head throbbed with trying to think straight. She had paid good money for two false passports for him, covered his periods away from LA by saying he was filming, and made calls on his behalf to ensure that no one, not even Feinstein, knew where he was. Maybe Feinstein didn't know about their scam. But what had happened to the original paintings and sculptures?

She had yet another drink, calmer now, her thin face pinched as she tried to piece together the events of the last weeks, thinking about what Cindy had told her. There was no other explanation, other than that Harry had been concealing the treasures somewhere outside the house for two years. She started to shake: he had been lying to her for two years and had intended to cut her out.

'You shit,' she screamed, crying with anger now. He had known she couldn't report him to the police because she would have been charged for her part in it. He had screwed her into the ground. The fact that he was dead made no difference – he had betrayed her, as he had betrayed Sonja before her, and what a fool she had been, trusting him, a blind, trusting fool . . . just like Sonja.

As soon as she had seen Harry, she had wanted him and she had told herself at the time that it was love. But it had been something darker and more complex. All her life she had wanted to get out from under, to belong, to be on the inside, and she had known that she had the potential to do that, to lead a life that her parents in Kansas had never dreamed of. Harry Nathan was the most attractive and dynamic man Kendall had ever met:

when Sonja had hired her he had been making movies that did reasonable business, still had some respectable friends in the industry. He was charm itself when Sonja brought Kendall out to the house to introduce her, talked to her easily, naturally, as though she was his equal, and over the coming weeks she felt that he took a special interest in her – used to chat to her for a few minutes on the phone if he called the gallery to speak to his wife.

Kendall had soon come to feel that she was like Sonja – her clothes became more elegant, her movements more graceful, the inflections of her voice smoother – but also that, as she herself became more attractive, Sonja was deteriorating. She had never been as beautiful as Sonja, about that she had no illusions, but she was twelve years younger, and she was prepared to make Harry the project of her life in a way that Sonja could not. It was not difficult to get him into bed, though the whole business felt rather perfunctory, almost tawdry, the first time a quick fuck at her apartment, after which he had immediately said he had a meeting and had to go. Kendall had wondered whether perhaps there was some truth in a few remarks Sonja had made, hinting that her husband was selfish and unaccomplished in bed.

Harry had been reluctant either to tell Sonja about their affair or to contemplate leaving her. Some deep, sick, neurotic bond held them to one another, Kendall decided, particularly since Sonja said she had almost finished some major project which she planned on exhibiting. Harry seemed to have bought into all that garbage about disturbing her creativity. That was fine, Kendall reckoned, as she visited her gynaecologist for shots to enhance her fertility – she gets her baby, I get mine.

Sonja produced a remarkable piece of work: a huge construction of a series of storefronts, not unlike the block where the gallery was on Beverly Drive, in which the stones in the sidewalk, the trash cans, the merchandise in the stores seemed to be living, watching the parade of humanity with strange, childlike faces.

At the opening Kendall was quiet. She was wondering whether the quick fuck Harry had given her on just the right day two weekends ago, while Sonja was working at the studio, had done the trick.

She received confirmation of her pregnancy a week later, and served this information on Harry like a writ. She intimated, too, suitably indirectly, that if he didn't leave Sonja and marry her he would indeed receive a writ in the form of a paternity suit. Harry had no option now but to tell Sonja, as Kendall would soon start to swell, and she could see, too, that the idea of a child had worked its old magic, primitive but effective, on his vanity as a man. So that was settled. Sonja received the news as silently as a dagger slid expertly under her ribs, packed her bags and went.

While Kendall was pregnant things hadn't been too bad – the prospect of the child had interested Harry more than its mother – but after she had her daughter the marriage went downhill fast. Now that Kendall was preoccupied with the baby, clucking endlessly about the contents of bottles and diapers, she bored Harry and got on his nerves.

She was baffled by the deterioration of their relationship, as though they had fast-forwarded, somehow, through what was meant to be the honeymoon period and had settled down into the stress, irritation and distance that longer-term marriages seemed to wallow in.

Then their little girl died suddenly, inexplicably, at seventeen months old, and neither of them was ever the same again. Kendall never forgave Harry for his insensitivity to her at the funeral, spending more time with that low-life closet case Vallance than with her, and he became embittered, his humour blacker and sicker, his lifestyle tackier and more decadent by the hour. Kendall knew they were in trouble now, but when she tried to talk to her husband on the odd occasions that she saw him, he said his actions were fuelled by anger at the child's death.

It was in the weeks following the funeral that Harry had developed his interest in adult parlour games. Kendall hung on grimly, no matter what she had to go along with and how much of a blind eye she had to turn to his other playmates. She refused to become a member of the army of divorced and discarded women the city was thronged with. Vallance's revenge for Kendall's hostility had been to introduce Harry to Cindy and – after they had been married a little less than four years – Kendall knew she had lost him.

As her divorce settlement, he gave her a half share in the gallery and although she thought maybe she could have got more, she was glad to have the link of a business partnership with him, just to retain some contact. Devoid of sexuality herself, she had never been able to understand its power over others, and she was certain that the Harry–Cindy alliance would last no longer than her own marriage.

On the other hand, Kendall had always had a keen business mind, and unencumbered by the tasks of parenthood, she soon put her mind to making money again. The gallery did well enough, but she figured that to make serious money, you had to bend the rules a little. Harry had jumped at the idea of the forgeries, and if it was his money that financed the scam, it had been her brains that set it up.

Everything had gone sweetly up until now, and as Harry grew predictably disenchanted with Cindy and stories of the couple's rows and public slanging matches circulated around the city, Kendall permitted herself to fantasize that he would realize what an asset she had been to him – how transitory the delights of the flesh, how enduring the joys of bank accounts containing seven-, even eight-figure sums. Kendall had convinced herself that when the fraud came to fruition and the paintings were sold on elsewhere, Cindy would be kicked out in the cold and she would be reinstalled as Harry Nathan's wife.

All those dreams were now in ruins around her. She had nothing: he'd cleaned her out, just as he had Sonja, and he had dumped her for good, just as he had Sonja.

Kendall took another swig from the bottle, but she didn't feel drunk. Harry had used her and lied to her, but she knew him well enough to be sure he wouldn't have been able to arrange this latest deal alone – hadn't had the intelligence. He must have had someone assisting him. Vallance? Cindy was out of the question, and she wondered if Sonja could have played any part in it. She began to pace up and down the room, drinking and stumbling around over the floral parterre rugs, which were meant to make the green carpet look like a garden, a witty allusion to the black Astroturf beyond. Sonja was the obvious person: she knew more about art than either Kendall or Harry. Was it possible that she had come back into Harry's life?

Kendall wouldn't allow herself to believe it. What about Harry's brother Nick? He was an artist, he could have been behind it, and there was Harry's mother – she had a considerable interest in art and antiques.

Abigail Nathan had been so friendly when Harry and Kendall were married, so pleased that Harry had got rid of Sonja, and overjoyed about her first grandchild. But Kendall had known in her heart that Abigail cared only about her sons. In her eyes they could do no wrong, and Kendall wondered if the whole Nathan family had ganged up against her. She remembered Cindy saying that someone had broken into the house and Abigail had keys, so the family could have taken the paintings, but how could she prove it without implicating herself?

Kendall began to search her desk drawers: Harry might not have kept up the house insurance premiums, but she had always paid the insurance of the gallery personally. Now it was all she had, and she knew what she would do: torch it, and claim the insurance. At least she would come out with something, and the more she thought about it, the better she felt. It could be done easily enough – the workshop was full of inflammable spirits, canvases and wooden frames and would catch fire quickly. As it was attached to the gallery, the whole site would go up.

She hurled everything out of the desk drawers, until she found the documents: the gallery was well insured, and the stock valued at two million dollars. She checked the insurance papers, just to make sure that, in the event of fire, she was fully covered, then crammed the rest of the documents, including the mass of crazy notes she had received from Cindy Nathan, back into the drawer. Those were certainly best out of circulation – she didn't want anyone thinking she had had anything to do with that fucked-up bimbo's death.

Kendall hurried out of her apartment to her Mitsubishi jeep. She loaded the cans of white spirit she kept in her garage into the back of it, muttering drunkenly that nobody was ever going to treat her like a doormat again. She would show that bastard and his family, and she was laughing as she drove out past Lorraine Page, who had parked a few yards from her front door, and whom she did not see. She was too intent on planning her revenge. Kendall wouldn't be left penniless like Sonja, wouldn't walk away without a fight.

Lorraine adjusted her driving mirror and watched the two-toned Mitsubishi jeep career down the road. She had hoped to challenge Kendall about Jose's statement that he had seen her car on the morning of Harry Nathan's death as well as Cindy's suggestion of some fraud to do with the paintings, and her subsequent mysterious death. She tried to follow the jeep, but lost it after a few minutes. Kendall was going somewhere and fast: Lorraine wondered if Feinstein had already called her.

Lorraine returned to her office and tossed the car keys to the valet parking attendant, who gave her a wide grin. 'Hi there. Nice day. You having one?'

'Yep. How about you?'

'Could be better,' he said, getting into the Mercedes.

She rode the elevator up to her floor, headed for her office, and was about to enter when she heard voices.

Decker was serving coffee and chocolate madeleines,

which he must have rushed out and bought, to Lieutenant Jake Burton. Lorraine hesitated, then smiled. 'Hello.'

Burton stood up with a smile. 'Off duty. Wondered if I could have a few moments?'

'Sure, go into my office. I'll just get rid of my coat.'

Decker ushered Burton into Lorraine's office and closed the door behind him. 'He just called in. Been here a few minutes,' he whispered. 'Single white male his age – don't pass him up. I'd pull him.'

Lorraine made a face and walked into her office. She went behind her desk and sat down. After what Decker had just said she found it hard to look at Burton.

'Off the record, Mrs Page, I called to say thank you for sending over the videos and for your . . . other assistance, and to tell you that as yet we've had no news from the county morgue on the Cindy Nathan autopsy.'

He kept staring at her, then added, 'That's all really. Thank you.'

He walked to the door. 'Is your dog a cross between a German shepherd and . . .'

'I'm not sure – I kind of inherited him, but he's got malamute or maybe wolfhound somewhere.'

'I used to have a Dobermann,' he said. 'Miss them when they go – especially the walks. Kind of clears your head, or it did with me. Anyway, thank you again.'

He was about to open the door when Lorraine said, 'Whenever you feel like walking, just call me – he's always available.'

He gave a shy smile. 'I will. I'd like it even better if there was some company too. Anyway, I'd better make tracks. Thank you again.'

'Let me give you my home number,' she said suddenly. She wrote on one of her cards, and passed it to him.

'I'll take you up on that.'

She followed him out, and he asked where she usually walked. 'Oh, sometimes the park, but on nice evenings I drive to the promenade. He loves the beach.'

Decker was listening, but pretending to be busy. Tiger raised his head as they passed and Burton patted him, then nodded to Lorraine, and grinned at Decker. 'Nice meeting you again – goodbye.'

Lorraine watched him leave, and Decker rolled his eyes. 'My God, you are so *slow*. He was *begging* you for a date – when a guy talks about taking your dog for a walk, you know, sweetheart, it's you he wants to go walkies with.'

'Oh, shut up,' she said, returning to her office.

'So what *did* he want?'

Lorraine shrugged. 'Nothing, really, just to thank me for sending the videos over.'

'Oh, really?' Decker said, raising his eyebrows. 'He had to come and see you to do that? So he *is* after your ass.'

'Oh, for God's sake,' Lorraine said dismissively.

He laughed. 'Sweetie, trust me, you'll have to make the running. He's all male, all testosterone and incapable of coming out with the line "I suppose a fuck is out of the question", *but* he has major hot pants for you, trust me.'

'Not in a blue moon, Decker. I wouldn't trust you as far as I could throw you.'

'If you could see your face – ' he giggled ' – go take a look!'

She slammed her office door, and scurried to look at

herself in the make-up mirror she kept in a filing cabinet. She was flushed, and she did have the hots for Burton. Decker was just a sex-obsessed fag – but intuitive.

Kendall turned into the alley that ran along the back of the gallery, overlooked by barred windows and full of huge commercial garbage bins. Most businesses left their back yards open to use as a parking area, but Kendall had enclosed all the space that belonged to her to construct a workroom, and she pulled up now in front of the high iron gates she had installed. On the other side of the alley were the backs of the shops and other properties that fronted Canon Drive. One was a men's accessories shop, run by a guy called Greg Jordan. Now she saw him standing at the back door of his shop. She waved across to him, making sure he saw her, not wanting to appear furtive. 'Hi, how's business?' she called loudly.

He walked out into the alley. 'Slow. How is it with you?'

'Not so bad. Got a client coming in – 'bye now.' She waved again, and pushed open the big double gates.

Eric was in the yard, stacking a delivery of old frames they would repair in the shop. She tossed him the keys of the jeep, a little irritated that he was there: she had forgotten about him. 'Eric, there's a delivery of white spirits in the jeep – bring them in for me, will you?'

'Sure, Mrs Nathan, but we've got plenty in stock,' he said, heaving an old gilded plaster frame up to lean against the wall of the workshop.

'I know, but I don't want it cluttering up the garage.'

Eric wandered out to the alley, unobserved by Greg Jordan, now busy with a customer. 'Where do you want them?' he asked Kendall, as he carried the crate of spirit into the workshop.

'Just leave them by the door,' she said nonchalantly, bumping into the big trestle table covered with paints and pots.

'You all right, Mrs Nathan?' he asked.

'I'm fine. We do any business today?' she asked, trying to appear casual, and he said there had been just a few customers, but no sales.

'Well, I might close up early,' she said, then had to hold onto the ledge of the table as the room was spinning. 'Got a headache, actually,' she muttered, and he looked at her but said nothing. It was obvious she had been drinking.

'You want me in the morning?' he asked.

'Of course. Maybe come in a bit early as I want to shift some of these paintings into the main space.'

'I can do it now, if you want.'

'No, tomorrow will be fine. I'm going out to dinner, so I won't be here long. I'll just lock up and then I'll be leaving.'

'Okay.' He stared at her again: she was dragging some wooden frames from behind a screen.

'You sure you don't want me to stay an' help out?'

'No, just go. See you tomorrow.'

Eric hovered by the door, watching her stumble against a wall. He'd never seen her like this in the two years he'd worked there. 'You sure you're okay, Mrs Nathan?'

She turned on him angrily. 'I'm fine. Now just go, go on, get out.'

'On my way,' he said, picking up his jacket. He didn't give a shit either way – he'd never liked her or her hawk face. 'See you tomorrow,' he said, as the door shut after him.

Alone, Kendall did not move until she had heard the yard gates clang shut. Then she heaved more and more wooden frames into the centre of the room, laughing softly, knowing they would catch light fast.

Lorraine was clearing her desk, getting ready to leave for home, when the phone rang. She checked the time – five thirty. Decker buzzed her office. 'Call for you, Mrs Page, line two. Lieutenant Gorgeous. Okay if I leave?'

'Sure. See you tomorrow.' She hesitated, then switched to line two. 'Lorraine Page speaking.'

'Hi . . . er, I was just wondering . . . I'm off duty early this evening, and it's a . . . well, it's a nice night, and I was wondering . . . if you were going for a walk. Or if you were busy I could take your dog out for you.'

She smiled. 'I'm just leaving the office.'

'Oh, well, another time.'

'No, no, I meant that I'd go home, change, and I'd like . . . we could walk together.'

'Oh, yes, fine.'

She gave him her home address again – just to make sure – and they arranged to meet at seven thirty. She couldn't stop smiling. She had a date! Well, she *and* Tiger had one.

Usually, when she got home, Lorraine tore off her clothes, pulled on an old track suit and sneakers, then walked to the nearest park, ran for almost two miles and went home. Tonight she washed her hair, redid her make-up, and put on a pale blue track suit with a white T-shirt that she wore only for the gym on Saturdays – it was an expensive designer label, and she knew the colour suited her. Then she tidied the apartment, arranged some fresh flowers and sprayed air freshener, while Tiger padded after her, wondering what the hell was going on. He even dragged his lead from the hook by the door and sat there waiting, afraid that she would go out without walking him.

On the dot of seven thirty, she heard Burton's car outside. She cast a quick glance round the room and tossed a magazine onto the sofa as the entry phone buzzed.

When she let Burton in, Tiger hurled himself, barking, at the door, and Lorrane grabbed his collar and yelled at him. 'It's okay, Tiger, stop it. Good boy . . . *Tiger!*'

Burton wore an old pair of torn jeans, sneakers and a T-shirt, and concealed his shyness by making a fuss of Tiger. 'Hello there . . . Who's a good house-dog, then, eh? Hello, good boy, good boy.'

Tiger allowed Burton to ruffle his ears, then tried to squeeze between his legs to get out of the half-open door.

'*Wait!*' Lorraine yelled, but Burton grabbed his collar.

'It's all right, I've got him. He seems pretty eager to go.'

Lorraine agreed, saying that she had only just arrived home, and he was used to his routine. 'I just throw on a track suit and we run.'

Burton looked at her, flushing. 'Well, you look lovely, that colour suits you.'

'Oh, thanks. I'll get my keys.'

He clipped Tiger's lead on, and went ahead of her down the stairs to the street. He hadn't had a chance to notice how she had cleaned the apartment: all he had been looking at was her, and he liked what he saw – but, then, he had thought the same when he'd first met her.

They used her jeep to drive the short distance to Santa Monica beach. Burton drove, and Lorraine liked the way he asked if she'd like him to drive, not too pushy, easy and relaxed. She tossed him the car keys, and as he got in he pushed the seat back to accommodate the length of his legs. Tiger was stationed in the back seat, his head almost resting on Burton's shoulder. She liked the way Jake had checked the gear shift and made sure he knew where everything was before they drove off. Out of his working clothes he looked younger, and she noticed he was well built, and had strong, tanned arms. He asked if she had any special route or if he should just take her the way he knew. She said she'd leave it to him, but started to direct him down the avenue anyway. He laughed, and didn't seem to care that Tiger was drooling on his shoulder. When they stopped at lights he tilted his head to one side to run it against the big dog's muzzle, and Tiger licked his face in reply.

He was relaxed, at ease, and as he drove, Lorraine was able to sneak glances at his profile. He was, as Decker had said, a very handsome man, and seemed even more so this evening than when she had first seen him. He was not exactly drop-dead gorgeous, but he had strong features: his nose was aquiline, and he had high cheekbones, and a deep cleft in his chin. His eyes were deep-set, and although she knew they could be cold and unfriendly, now they were teasing.

He knew she was scrutinizing him, but didn't mind. He would have been a bit suspicious of someone who pushed their way into his life, and would have been sure, as he presumed she was, that the walk with the dog was just a pretext.

'So, this was unexpected,' she said.

'Don't you trust me? Do you think I have some ulterior motive?'

'Possibly,' she said lightly.

He half turned towards her, then back to concentrate on driving. 'I used to have a dog, I told you. I like . . . taking walks, and I prefer some company, not all the time, but occasionally.'

Lorraine stared out of the window. It had been so long since she had had company, and not just for walking Tiger. 'Yes, me too,' she said softly.

Kendall arranged the frames, not obviously, but stacked at the side of a long trestle table, draped a length of muslin over them and soaked it in white spirit. She poured a trail of the liquid across the bare floorboards, which were splattered with paint and spirit spilt over a period of years. She brought more finished canvases out of their slats in the storage area, again not making an obvious bonfire but resting them against the walls, leaving space for air to circulate under them to feed the flames. She worked for almost an hour, sweating with the effort, and soaking rags from the bins in yet more spirit. Then she carried out more old canvases and laid them along the walls of the short passage between the workshop and the gallery, to encourage the fire to spread into the gallery itself. She was still drunk but so intent on what she was doing that she wasn't aware of it.

At seven thirty she entered the gallery, turned on all

the lights, and opened all the doors. She made four phone calls arranging for artists to meet her the next morning, opened her desk diary and entered the appointments, plus notes of possible sales – all to create the impression that she had no financial problems and had been planning normal business for the next day. She spread more papers and anything that would catch light quickly on the floor, and started to make her way back to the workshop. Half-way there, she crossed to the big gates to look out – then swore. Heading towards her was Greg.

'Hi – that you, Kendall?' he called, and she opened the gate. 'You got any fresh coffee? It's just that I'm stock-taking, and I've run out and can't be bothered to go to the store.'

'Sure, come on in. I'm working late myself – I've just got a new artist and I'm planning the show for him, so I'm moving things around to make space.'

She kept calm, walked into the little kitchen area in the warehouse with Greg, and passed him a half-used packet of coffee.

'So, business is good, is it?' he asked.

'Yep, well, I hope it'll be even better. I am always looking for new talent. You know – eye-catching stuff.' She smiled, wanting to get rid of him, but then realized he would make a good witness, and elaborated on her new deals, even gestured towards the warehouse. 'You can see it's kind of cluttered in here, so I've got plenty to keep me busy this evening.'

'Well, I'll leave you to it. Thanks for the coffee – I'll repay you in kind tomorrow, okay?'

'Oh, it's on the house.'

He thanked her again. She smelt of alcohol, and he

was sure she was tipsy. She didn't offer him a drink, though, and he hadn't really wanted the coffee – he'd wanted a chat with Eric, from whom he scored a variety of recreational chemicals.

Kendall watched him leave, and not until he was back inside his shop did she return to the warehouse.

The beach was almost deserted, and Lorraine and Burton had walked a fair distance. Tiger was having the time of his life running after sticks, chasing stray dogs, hurling backwards and forwards, and barking and diving around them.

'He's a great dog,' Burton said, throwing a stick as far as he could.

'I never thought I'd get so attached to him, but he kind of grows on you.'

They walked side by side, and then, as if it was the most natural thing in the world, Burton caught her hand. The touch of his, warm and strong, made her heart pound, and she curled her fingers tightly around it, trying to calculate just how long it had been since someone, anyone, had taken her hand and walked with her the way they were walking now.

'So, Mrs Page, do you want to start first, or shall I?' he said casually.

'Start with what?'

'Well, I want to know about you . . . I want to know you.'

'Ah, well, that might take more than a walk on the beach, Lieutenant Burton.'

'But it's a start,' he said, and released her hand to pick up the stick Tiger had dropped at his feet. After he had thrown it again, he didn't take her hand, but rested his arm loosely around her shoulders.

'I'm forty-five years of age, and I've been married once, to my childhood sweetheart. I was nineteen and it lasted four years. I joined the army and she and I grew apart, she left me, and married another childhood friend – my best buddy, as a matter of fact, and they live very happily in Seattle, two kids . . .'

She loved his arm around her. 'I'm thirty-eight, divorced, and my ex-husband lives not far from here with my two daughters. He's married again to a very beautiful lady called Sissy. I don't have any contact with my daughters because . . .' She trailed off as Tiger arrived back, exhausted, with the gnarled stick. This time she picked it up and threw it, and he hurtled after it like a greyhound on the track after a mechanical hare. 'He'll sleep tonight,' she said. She wanted Burton's arm around her again.

'You were a cop,' he said, and slipped his arm around her again to draw her closer. 'I pulled your report sheet.'

'Yes, you told me,' she said coldly.

'I know I did. Do you mind?'

'Why should I? It's public knowledge.'

'Not quite, but I wanted to know about you.'

'Yes, well, there are some things that don't make it into reports,' she snapped.

'Hey, I'm just being honest. Don't get all uptight on me.'

'I'm not uptight, but I'm amazed you still wanted to take a walk with me. Most men would have run a mile.'

'Yeah, maybe, but everyone has a past – nobody's perfect.'

She wanted to break away from him, but didn't. She

stopped walking. 'Maybe, Lieutenant, but not everybody has a past quite as colourful as mine, or as seedy, or as dramatic or as—'

'Sad?' he suggested, gently.

She glared at him. 'What is this? Yeah, I've had my problems, and I admit to them, but I don't want anyone feeling sorry for me. What do you want from me?'

'I don't want anything, or not the way you think. I wanted you to know that I knew, that's all.'

'So?'

'It doesn't bother me what the fuck you were, or whatever you did.'

'Thank you, I'm grateful, but we are just walking my dog. I know what I did, I live with it. I know what I was and I live with that too. So take your pity and screw it.'

He grabbed hold of her. 'What's with you? Pity? You think I pity you? Jesus Christ, woman, I don't pity you. I'm out of practice with these things. All I know is I wanted to see you so badly, from the first moment I set eyes on you. I wanted to be with you, so I pulled your file from records. I'm sorry – all I wanted you to know was that.'

'Well, I want you to know that I'm not some charity case, and I'm not so desperate that I'd hide anything I've done. I killed a kid when I was drunk on duty. I was a drunk for eight years. Well, I'm sober now and I'm not prepared to be anyone's lame duck. Thanks for the walk – you can get a cab ride back.'

She marched off down the beach, stopped and yelled for Tiger, but Burton was throwing a stick in the opposite direction. She turned and yelled again for the dog, but he was already galloping away.

Burton turned to face her. 'Okay, that was your turn. You mind if I have mine now?'

'What?' she yelled back at him.

He strolled towards her, and said nothing until he was within a foot of her. 'I said, it's my turn now to fill in a few things about me.'

'You think I want to know?'

He tilted his head to one side. 'I sincerely hope so. Now where was I? Oh, yeah, forty-five, been married and divorced, joined the army at eighteen, educated by them, qualified as a lawyer and . . . of uniform, couldn't make it out, so joined the cops. This of any interest at all?'

'No – should it be?'

He came a fraction closer. 'You free for dinner?'

'No.'

'Tomorrow?' He reached out and drew her close to him.

'No.'

'I suppose a fuck is also out of the question?'

She turned away. 'Very funny.'

He moved behind her and put his arms around her, pressing her close to him. 'You sure?'

'Don't play games,' she said quietly.

'I'm not. I just don't know what I should say that'll make whatever I said before you told me to get a cab back okay. It's a hell of a long way, and my car's at your place.'

She turned in his arms, tried to break free from him, but he held her tightly. Her body was rigid, her face set, but he wouldn't release her, and gradually she let her body relax against him.

She rested her head against his shoulder, loved the

smell of him mixed with the sea air. He rubbed his chin against her fine, silky blonde hair. 'You smell so good,' he said, and she eased her face round, inch by inch until their lips met. His kiss was so sweet. Then he cupped her face in his hands. 'I've wanted to do this . . .'

He never finished as they kissed passionately, and slowly sank to their knees. He pulled her down beside him, until they lay side by side, Lorraine caught in the crook of his arm, her body pressed against his. He moaned softly, and she nestled against him: there was no need for words, no need to know anything more about each other. Lorraine was filled with rushes of emotion and couldn't talk.

Tiger bounded up and dropped the stick on Burton's chest: keeping one arm around Lorraine, he picked it up with the other hand, and held it high for a moment before he threw it towards the sea.

'You free for dinner, Mrs Page?' he asked.

'I guess so.'

He rolled over to lean on his elbow, looking down into her face. 'Then let's go eat.'

She traced his face with her hand. 'Sounds good to me.'

He bent his head, and gave her another sweet kiss. She could feel that he was aroused, and her whole body ached – a fuck was not out of the question, not at all out of the question, but he was one guy she knew not to treat like a one-night stand. This man, Jake Burton, she knew she wanted more from, more than she had believed she would ever want again. She was falling in love, but had so little confidence in herself that she couldn't accept that he was attracted to her, and just might want commitment from her too. It was too much to hope for, so she made herself play cool. 'There's a great Chinese near the apartment,' she said huskily, not able to be quite as offhand as she would have liked.

'I could handle that,' he said, then sprang to his feet and whistled for Tiger, who was further down the beach where he appeared to be digging his way to Australia. Lorraine sat up, shading her eyes against the evening sun, to watch Jake bend forward as Tiger loped towards him and clip on the lead. She liked everything she saw, and it scared her.

Kendall was ready, everything was set. She struck the match and let it drop to her feet. She expected things to happen as she had seen in movies, a thin blue tongue of flame, spreading and building steadily before bursting into an inferno, and began to panic that it wasn't catching. She didn't want the smoke alarms to go off before the fire took hold, so she bent down, fanning it with her hands, but still only a single, pale blue flame spluttered weakly. She bent down further, and used the hem of her skirt to create a draught. The flame still seemed about to go out. She leaned even further forward, struck another match to throw towards the spirit-soaked rags she had stuffed into the trash can and padded around it.

'Burn, you bastard, burn,' she muttered. She hated Harry Nathan with such venom. She would beat the bastard at his own game by claiming the insurance money – she was going to be all right. Now she was leaning further towards the fire, flapping her skirt furiously, and then the flames suddenly shot upwards so fast that she stumbled backwards and fell on her side. Her skirt was alight, and she was trying frantically to beat out the flames. Next moment she screamed in terror – her hair was on fire, and she could smell it burning. No matter how much she shook her head, or hit it, it kept burning. Her hands were still covered in white spirit – they were burning too, and then she was engulfed in flames as the alarms began to scream their warning. The fire roared forwards, spreading fast now, moving in every direction, and surrounding Kendall. She turned this way and that, screaming in terror as the flames leaped higher and higher, and the thick, dense smoke burned her eyes, blinding her.

Greg heard the alarms ringing, and looked out of his shop window, to see smoke spiralling upwards across the street, from inside the Nathan gallery's yard. He rang for the fire brigade and then took off across the alley as fast as he could, flung open the gates and burst into the yard as the fire erupted skyward, like a bomb, through the workshop roof. He could hear terrible screaming from inside, and ran to try to wrench open the workshop door, but was at first forced back by the billowing smoke. The horrific, high-pitched shrieks went on and on.

At last he got the door open, but smoke and flames obscured his vision as he shouted Kendall's name.

Suddenly she seemed to launch herself towards him, her mouth wide in terror: she was burning alive, her clothes, hair, her entire body alight.

Greg dragged her into the yard, wrapping his coat over her head in an effort to suffocate the flames, then to the gate to get them both out of the reach of the fire. The flames were now shooting out of the workshop, spreading, as she had intended, towards the gallery itself.

She was curled up beneath his jacket, which covered

her face and the top part of her body, but he could see the terrible burns to her legs. As he lifted away the coat from her, he felt a rush of hysteria – his coat was smouldering, on fire from her body, but the sight of her face made him catch his breath. Her hair was burned to the scalp, and her face was a gruesome mass of burned flesh and blisters. But she was alive, and her eyes pleaded with him. She was trying to say something, her fingers plucking at his arm. Greg didn't know what to do: his panic made him scream for her, and once he had started screaming he couldn't stop, his cries drowning her awful, low moans of agony. Behind them, the fire reached the main gallery and even though the sprinklers had come on automatically, nothing could hold it back.

Within minutes the fire engines and the ambulance had arrived. Greg watched, shaken and distraught, as the paramedics gently lifted Kendall onto the stretcher. He asked if she was alive and one of the men looked down at her and nodded. She was alive, but she had already inhaled so much smoke that he knew there was little hope of survival.

The gallery alarms were ringing, police and fire sirens wailing, and the sound of the plate-glass windows cracking and shattering made it impossible to hear what her last words were. Kendall died, painfully moving her burned lips and using the last breath in her smoke-filled lungs to whisper the word, 'Bastard.'

CHAPTER 10

THEY HAD ordered too much food by far, choosing every dish they had wanted to try but never ordered before, so that half-empty cartons of Chinese takeaway littered the kitchen counter and the coffee table. An exhausted Tiger lay flat out, his head almost resting on Burton's foot. Jake stroked his head just behind his right ear, and the dog growled contentedly, wanting more.

'You've won him over,' Lorraine said, leaning back. There was about a foot between them on the sofa, but she wanted to be closer, wanted to feel his arms around her again.

'Good, that makes life easier,' Jake said, then gestured towards the cartons. 'Will he eat the rest?'

'*Will* he?' she laughed, but fell silent as he reached for her hand.

'So?' he said softly, his fingers laced with hers.

'So,' she repeated. The gap was still between them.

'So,' he said again, then loosened his hold on her hand to turn towards her. 'Can I stay?'

Lorraine said nothing, and he began to stroke her arm, circling her slender wrist with his fingers. Then he drew her towards him until she rested against him. 'Yes,

I want you to stay,' she whispered, nestling against his shoulder. She could smell Chinese takeaway, and sand, and sea, and him, and his chin rested against the top of her head as she slipped one arm around him. He reached down and drew her leg across his lap, gently stroking her calf as he eased off her shoe. It fell onto Tiger, still at their feet, who grunted and got up sleepily to walk a few feet away before he sighed loudly and slumped down, head on his paws, watching them intently with his pale blue eyes.

Lorraine sighed as Burton massaged her leg, his hand slowly moving higher, inching up her thigh. He continued to caress her, running his hand under the high-cut leg of her silk panties to find her with his fingers and feel she was wet for him, her legs parting. He slid from the sofa and began to ease her panties down. She made no effort to stop him, wanting him to do what he was doing and more. She rested her head back against the sofa as he knelt in front of her, opening her wider, and then began to kiss first the inside of one thigh then the other, kissing closer and closer to her until he bent his head and she felt his tongue inside her. Lorraine moaned and lifted her pelvis a fraction, wanting him deeper, and he continued to lick and suck her, pulling her shirt out from the waistband of her skirt so that he could slip his hand over her ribs and under her bra to feel her breasts and her hard, aroused nipples. She came quickly, her body shuddering and her thighs tightening around his head until at last he moved upwards, dragging her underwear off her body, and taking her breasts in his mouth as she moaned with pleasure.

They kissed with passion, he lifted her from the sofa, carried her to the bedroom, kicked open the door, stumbling slightly in the darkness, and laid her on her bed. He stripped off his clothes in front of her, unself-conscious about his nakedness, and he noticed the rows of slender candles at her bedside. He asked where she kept the matches. She watched his lean, muscular body bend forward as he lit each candle in turn. She was about to undress when he turned and knelt on the bed. 'No. Let me do that.'

He allowed her to do nothing to help him as he took her clothes off, kissing her as he removed each garment, until she lay naked, smiling up at him. He held up his hand and disappeared, returned with her cigarettes and put them on the bedside table before he lay down beside her. He continued to caress her, tracing the scars on her arms with his fingers, and turning her over to see the uneven white tissue of the other scars on her back. He didn't ask about them, but kissed each one, becoming more and more aroused as he touched her until he eased himself on top and into her with a long, low moan of pleasure.

He made love to her first, a sweetness to his fucking, waiting for her to climax with him, and then they had sex, roughly, but he was an experienced lover, never losing her. There was no fear between them, and no questions asked as they whispered endearments to one another, enjoying the heated sex, their mutual lust. When Jake moved Lorraine to sit astride him, she moaned, arching her body back to bring him deeper inside her, and when she lay beside him he was able to arouse her again, until they lay curled side by side against one another, her back pressing into his chest, their legs entwined. Lorraine was tired, not wanting to speak, and eventually she felt the rhythm of Jake's breathing change.

He was asleep, one arm round her, and she felt cocooned by his presence, lulled by his steady breathing, until her own matched it and she drifted into the perfect sleep of physical exhaustion.

'Jesus Christ,' Jake murmured, fully awake as Lorraine stirred, his arm tightening around her.

Tiger had inched his way onto the bed, and Jake turned round as the massive dog pushed him slightly out of the way and rested his head on the pillow.

'I told you he liked you,' Lorraine said drowsily, falling back to sleep almost instantly. Jake wasn't so sure about Tiger's presence, as the dog's hot breath on his neck meant that his fangs, too, were close, but he was too tired to argue, and just moved closer to Lorraine. He listened to her soft rhythmic breathing as she had listened to his, and noticed that Tiger's was now audible too. He had already taken more than his share of the bed, and yet Jake somehow liked the warmth of the big dog beside him, and in fact, he was liking everything about this night – especially the woman cradled in his arms.

He woke with a start to the smell of fresh coffee and the chink of china. The duvet had been carefully tucked around him and he looked at the clock on the bedside table, then relaxed – it was only five. There was plenty of time to take a shower, get dressed and go back to his place to change into fresh clothes. He didn't look much like a division commander as he joined Lorraine in the kitchen, swathed in a sheet, and she looked up and smiled shyly, indicating the coffee. He liked the fact that she was wearing only a towel, and that her face was devoid of make-up, her cheeks rosy. He went to her and put his arms around her, kissing her neck.

'Good morning.'

He felt something thump against his bare foot, and looked down to see Tiger wagging his tail. 'Morning to you.' He scratched the dog's ear. 'Does he always sleep in your bed?'

'I'm afraid so. I've tried to kick him out, but he creeps back in during the night. He's pretty good – I mean he doesn't take up too much space, he knows which bit's his.'

She fetched cups, and cream from the fridge.

Jake washed his hands at the sink, and she was surprised to see him pick up the empty takeaway containers and put them in the trash, then collect the empty cans and all the cartons that were still half full.

'He had a feast in the night,' she said, nodding at Tiger. A few noodles were scattered on the carpet, and she picked them up before she tidied the coffee table and carried the dirty ashtray to the bin.

'You should give that up,' Jake said, as he ran water into the sink.

'Yeah, I know.' She liked standing close to him, liked him being in her tiny kitchen – liked everything about him. She slipped her arm around his waist. 'You want some toast?'

They sat at either end of the sofa, Lorraine with her legs curled under her, eating thick slices of toast with blueberry jam and drinking a mug of coffee. 'What time do you have to go to the station?' she asked.

'Nine, which means . . .' He looked at the clock. 'I'll have to leave in an hour or so, unless you want me to go now.'

'No.' She leaned towards him, and he reached out with one finger and traced her lips. Their eyes met, and she put down her mug and crawled along the sofa until she was able to rest against him. 'You feel good,' she said softly. She eased around to sit between his legs, and he passed her her coffee. As she reached up to take the cup, the sleeve of her robe fell back, revealing the scars on her arm again.

'You were in the wars at one time,' he said gently, kissing her.

'Yeah, I was.' She felt her stomach tighten, and his hand massaged the nape of her neck. 'You should know, you read my sheet.' She began to slide away from him, murmuring she wanted more coffee, but she lit a cigarette, and was angry to see her hand shaking. 'Suppose you want to know how much I charge, these days.' It came out tougher than she had meant it to sound.

'Don't be so defensive,' he said lightly, then laughed. 'Besides, the takeaway cleaned me out of cash.'

'Yeah, well, I was pretty cheap – price of a drink.'

'Stop it,' he said firmly, watching her fall apart in front of him, her hands shaking as she sucked at her cigarette, her whole body tense with anger.

'You started it,' she snapped, and he raised his arms.

'All I said was—'

She stood in front of him, shoving her arm under his nose, showing him the old scars and cigarette burns. 'You missed these.'

He reached out and gripped her wrists tightly. 'No, I didn't. Like I said, I read your sheet, I know all about your self-mutilation, kind of goes with drugs, booze and . . .'

Lorraine tried to twist free of him, but he got to his feet, refusing to let go of her, then suddenly pinched her cheek, staring into her face. 'Your mug-shot's not up to date – where's the scar on your cheek, Mrs Page?'

Now she wrestled free of him and glared. 'I told you – plastic surgery. Gimme time and I'll get round to all the others. Now, why don't you get out of here and leave me alone?'

'Why don't you simmer down?'

She walked towards the bedroom. 'I've got things to do. You know the way out.'

He moved fast enough to reach the bedroom door before her, and dragged her inside, pushing her down on the bed.

'What's this? Gonna try some rough stuff on me now, are you? That on my report sheet, is it?'

He slapped her face, and she took it, laughing at him. He stepped back. 'I'm sorry . . . sorry.'

'Don't be, I'm used to it, I can take it. Come on, you want it again, take it.'

She opened the towel, lying naked in front of him, and he bent forward. For a moment she thought he was going to punch her, but instead he pulled the sheet from under her, so that she rolled sideways, then wrapped her inside it. Her arms were trapped and he held her so that she couldn't move. 'Don't do this, Lorraine . . .'

'Give me one good reason.' She pushed her face close to his, and then the look of hurt in his eyes made her anger evaporate. She couldn't keep up the act, and she rested against him again, a low sob shaking her body.

'Sssh,' he said softly, rocking her in his arms.

'I'm sorry, I didn't mean what I said. I'm sorry, it's just . . . It's just . . .' She couldn't continue.

'Just what?' he asked, after a long pause.

'Just that I am scared.'

'Not of me?'

She shook her head, then bit her lip and nodded. 'Yeah. I am scared of you, or of what you make me feel.'

'What's that?'

She sighed. 'Oh, please, don't do this.'

'Okay. What if I tell you that I am . . . I'm only interested in this woman I've got in my arms right now. I don't give a fuck about her past, what she did or didn't do. I'm not dumb enough to think it won't come up, or that we won't have to talk about it, but for no other reason than I want to know you, all of you, the good, the bad . . .'

'And the ugly,' Lorraine said, her eyes filled with tears.

'Sure, yeah, all of it. Anything to do with you I want to know about.'

She didn't know what to say to him, she just felt like weeping.

'You're supposed to say that you want to know everything there is to know about me,' he said, feeling her begin to relax in his arms.

They made love again, then showered together. Afterwards Lorraine made fresh coffee while Jake scrambled some eggs, and they ate breakfast again side by side on the sofa.

'Will you get the autopsy report on Cindy Nathan today?' she asked, trying to sound nonchalant.

Jake slipped on his jacket. 'Yes, well, it was supposed to come in today.' He crossed to her and leaned on the alcove. 'I think we might have a little talk to Mrs Kendall Nathan this morning too.'

Lorraine nodded. 'Yeah,' she said, pretending a keen interest. 'I'd check her out.' She looked at the clock. 'I should get dressed.' There was an awkward pause, while

Jake hesitated a moment, then walked to the door. She didn't want him to go, but if he had no intention of seeing her again, she didn't want him to stay either. 'I'll see you,' she said, hurrying towards her bedroom.

'Okay. 'Bye, Tiger, look after her for me.' He opened the door, and was half-way through it when he turned round. 'I'll be off at about four – you want to take in a movie?'

She felt like a kid, knew she was blushing. 'Yep, I'd like that.'

'Okay, I'll call you at your office. Are you going in today?'

'Yes. I've got a few odds and ends to sort out.'

'You're not still working on the Nathan case?'

'Well, not really – there isn't a case to work on.'

He grinned. 'You'll be touting for work.'

'Yes.'

'Okay, see you later.' He went out, and she stayed in the bedroom doorway, listening to his footsteps going down the stairs. She crossed to the window and looked out, wanting to see him walking to his car, wanting just to watch him as he unlocked it. He turned, as if he knew she was there, and smiled up at her, stood for a few moments, just looking, before he got in and drove away.

'Right, Tiger, soon as I'm dressed we go walkies,' she said, and couldn't keep the smile off her face.

Lorraine was singing as she walked into the office. Decker was sitting at his desk as she breezed past him with a loud 'Good morning.'

'It's better than you think,' he said, picking up his notebook.

'You can say that again, it's a . . .' She was about to say something silly, but instead burst out laughing.

'My, my, you got out of bed the right side.'

'I did, I most certainly did.' She sat in her chair and swung from side to side as he put a memo in front of her. 'Mr Feinstein . . . urgent, three messages on the answerphone. I called him back, but he insisted that he could only speak directly to you, and would you call him as soon as you got in.'

'Maybe they've got the autopsy results,' she said, dialling Feinstein's number.

'I doubt it. Two of the calls came in last night, and one at eight this morning.'

Decker went into his section to get coffee for Lorraine, and some bagels with cream cheese, which he had also bought. As he came back with them, Lorraine was tapping her desk with a pen. 'He won't discuss it on the phone, wants me to go round to his office. When I asked if it had anything to do with Cindy Nathan's death, he said it was an entirely different matter.'

'You want breakfast before you go?'

'No, thanks, I had scrambled eggs.' She was already collecting her purse and running a comb through her hair.

'You're looking very . . . relaxed,' Decker said, cocking his head appraisingly to one side.

'I am, and I might take off early this afternoon. Can you book me a hairdressing appointment and a manicure?'

'Got a date?' he asked jokingly.

'Yes, as a matter of fact, I have.'

'Ohhh.' Decker scuttled after her. 'So I was right!' Lorraine bit her lip and giggled, more feminine, girlish even, than he had ever seen her.

Lorraine was half out of the door. 'You just might be,' she tossed over her shoulder, and then she was gone.

Decker chucked her bagel to Tiger, who caught it and wolfed it down in two gulps. 'She got laid last night, didn't she?' he asked the dog, whose jaws chomped in reply. 'Well, well, well . . . I thought he was a pretty hot number myself.'

Clearly today was not one of Feinstein's good days. He was dishevelled, his tie askew, and he was sweating as he paced up and down the sea of carpet. 'I've had another art expert in, just to make sure, and he confirmed it. They *are* fakes, every single fucking one of them.'

'I'm sorry,' Lorraine said lamely, glancing behind him at a large painting on the wall. A letter-opener, made from the top ten inches of a narwhal tusk, protruded from the middle of it, stabbed through the canvas.

'Not as sorry as I am. Have you any idea how much money I've lost? My life savings were in those fucking paintings.' His voice cracked, and he almost broke down. Then a fit of rage seized him as with a sudden sweep of his arm he dashed pens, blotter, designer candy-dispenser and executive toys off his heroically proportioned desk. 'That shit Harry Nathan, that two-faced bastard! When I think of everything I did for that son-of-a-bitch, I'm telling you, if he was to walk in right now I'd shoot him – I'd kill the bastard.'

'What does Harry Nathan have to do with all this?' Lorraine asked, as Feinstein seized the letter opener from the canvas and slashed at it, using all his strength in an effort to rip the thing apart.

'I bought all my art through the Nathan gallery.

These are fakes, right? So somebody, somewhere, has *my paintings*, and Harry Nathan has *my money* stashed somewhere, because I've been through every fucking bank account he had and the cheque I gave him never showed up in any of them!'

Feinstein began to hurl pages of bank statements across to her. So much for client confidentiality – as soon as he was personally affected, all he cared about was himself. 'You trace those paintings, you trace his fucking secret accounts – I'm talking about millions, *millions.*'

Lorraine watched as Feinstein threw more files across the room, and waited until at last he sat down in his throne-like swivel chair. 'I will need to ask you some particulars, Mr Feinstein, and we will also have to discuss my fees.'

'I'll pay you whatever you want – just get me my paintings. *My wife will divorce me!*' He sank his head in his hands.

'I'll need to take some notes,' she said, opening her briefcase and taking out her pad.

Feinstein flicked a switch on his intercom, which had been flashing on and off since Lorraine had arrived. 'No calls, Pamela – period.' He flicked the switch off again, and patted his pockets for his cigar case. He found it, chose one, and ripped off the wrapper. 'Fucking start with Harry Nathan.' He snapped on a lighter.

'That might be a little difficult,' Lorraine said, smiling.

'You think this is funny, Mrs Page? I'm down two and half million and it's fucking destroying me.' He huffed and puffed at his cigar, then bit off the end and spat it across the room. 'Find out anything you can on Nathan's bank accounts. I can tell you some aliases I know Harry used – I want them checked out.'

'So Harry Nathan actually sold you the paintings?' Lorraine enquired innocently.

Feinstein looked at her, then at the ceiling. 'Who the fuck did you think sold me them? Sure, Kendall Nathan handled it, arranged delivery and stuff. Check her out – she wouldn't take a leak without his permission. The two of them pulled this off together and I want the slimy bitch fucking charged. I bought them through the gallery, right? I had them authenticated there, and Kendall – or somebody who worked for her – hung them for me here. So start with her.'

'Did Kendall benefit significantly under Harry Nathan's will?' Lorraine asked, knowing it wasn't strictly relevant to the art fraud but unable to resist the temptation to take advantage of Feinstein's temporarily uncontrolled state to try to find out what he had refused to tell her before.

'Well, she got the other half of the gallery,' Feinstein answered. 'Little pay-off for services rendered, by the looks of things.'

'But what about the art collection at the house?' Lorraine went on. 'Does that come to Kendall now that Cindy's dead?'

Feinstein was off on another tack. 'The police asked me for a specimen of her handwriting. I could have given them ten fucking specimens of suicide notes if they had wanted them, but they didn't ask. Cindy was always threatenin' to kill herself. She used to write letters to practically anyone she knew about how fucking miserable she was with Harry. What the fuck she thought I was going to do about it is beyond me.'

Lorraine felt another pang of grief for the tormented girl, calling out for help to everyone around her, only to meet with indifference and rejection. But it was interesting that she had apparently written letters mentioning suicide to quite a number of people. Lorraine couldn't see Feinstein killing her himself, but the idea of him perhaps selling a letter that might help in getting rid of Cindy didn't seem beyond the bounds of credibility. Or if Cindy had written to Harry's lawyer for advice on her emotional problems with him, it was not impossible that she had written to one or both of his ex-wives . . .

'Does Cindy's death benefit Kendall?' she asked again, casually.

'No way. That's not the way it works.' Feinstein had got more of a grip on himself now, had become the lawyer again. 'Anything Cindy owned when she died will form part of her own estate.'

'Will that go to her parents? They're out in Milwaukee somewhere, aren't they?'

'They may well be, but as far as Cindy was concerned they could stay and rot there. I have the last will and testament of Mrs Cindy Nancy Robyn Nathan right here in the office, and her family are not mentioned at all.'

Feinstein leaned back in his chair, sensing Lorraine's acute interest in what he was saying. He permitted himself a leisurely pause and a further pull on his cigar. 'She left everything to the House of Nirvana Spiritual Center, some fucking bunch of freaks. ' God, Lorraine thought, that was unexpected. 'Fortunately,' Feinstein said, with a self-satisfied smile, 'the tax-saving clause prevents them getting more than her pantyhose. They won't get a cent of Harry's estate.'

'What do you mean?' Lorraine said. 'Cindy didn't tell me anything about the Nathans' tax affairs.'

'It's a pretty standard thing on a large estate that will

235

attract a lot of taxes, particularly when the beneficiaries are all relatively young and in good shape. All of Harry Nathan's beneficiaries had to survive him by sixty days before the various gifts to them took effect. Otherwise, in the situation we have here, for example, we would be paying tax once on the estate when it passed to Cindy, then again virtually immediately when it passed to her heirs.'

The intercom buzzed again, and Feinstein screamed into it, 'Pamela, I said no calls – I MEAN NO CALLS.'

'Since Cindy didn't live for sixty days, it doesn't go to her heirs,' Lorraine said. 'So who gets it?'

'The residuary legatee,' Feinstein said.

'Who is?' Lorraine said, wanting to slap him. Lawyers: what a fucking pompous self-important bunch of creeps, she thought. Feinstein got up, turned aside to relight the thick cigar, then turned back to her as he drew on it, surrounding himself in a swirl of blue smoke.

'Sonja Nathan.'

'Sonja?' Lorraine said. 'She'll do a bit better now than the couple of keepsakes Cindy said she was going to get.'

'That would indeed have been pretty much the position if Cindy hadn't died,' Feinstein went on, in professorial mode. 'Nathan's big assets were the house, his holding in Maximedia, his art collection and his half of the art gallery. There were no substantial cash assets at all – or, at least, not in any accounts I knew about.' His eyes narrowed with rage at this reminder of Harry Nathan's perfidy. 'The will disposed of all of those to Cindy and Kendall, and Sonja would have got anything else not specifically mentioned. He had a substantial film library, for example, at his office, which would have gone to her.'

Lorraine's mind was racing: she had largely discounted the possibility of Sonja Nathan's involvement in her husband's death, but this certainly gave her a motive. True, she had had to kill two people to collect under Harry's will, but if she had been prepared to kill once, why not twice? She had certainly been expert in covering her tracks – maybe used a professional hitman – as Lorraine had found nothing to connect Sonja with either of the two deaths. However, none of that was Feinstein's business, and she tried to disguise what she was thinking by changing the subject to more mundane matters.

'By the way, I promised Jose and Juana I would mention this matter of the savings Nathan took off them and their back salary. It looks like they should contact Sonja,' she said, but the phone on the desk blinked again, and this time Feinstein, still on his feet, marched to the door and yanked it open.

'Pamela, what the fuck are you doing out there?' he shouted.

Lorraine heard whispers passing between Feinstein and his secretary before the attorney walked out, leaving the door ajar. He returned almost immediately. 'She's dead.'

Lorraine stood up.

'Kendall Nathan's dead.'

Burton looked up from reading the file on Lorraine Page to see Jim Sharkey outside the office door.

'Is it the autopsy on Cindy Nathan?' Burton asked.

Sharkey came in with some photographs and put them down on the lieutenant's desk. 'These are morgue shots. Hard to tell who it is, but it's Kendall Nathan. Last night. Initial view is she was trying to torch the gallery and it backfired. Her hair caught light and . . .'

'Dear God,' Burton said, looking at the charred form. If Kendall had killed Cindy as, he had to admit, Lorraine had largely convinced him was likely, and possibly Nathan too, she had certainly got her just deserts.

'Yeah, pretty horrific way to die. Place went up like a bonfire – lot of white spirit, plus all the canvases, the wooden frames . . . No one could do anything.' Sharkey went on to tell Burton that there was an eyewitness, the owner of a shop that shared a back alley with the gallery workshop, who had seen Kendall enter the building and had raised the alarm when he saw the smoke.

Burton's phone rang, and he picked it up; the receptionist told him that a Mrs Page was on the line. He asked the girl to take a message as he was in a meeting. He replaced the phone. 'What about Cindy Nathan?' he asked again.

Sharkey shrugged. It was still only nine thirty and nothing had come in as yet. Burton rocked back in his chair, and told Sharkey to see what he could do to hurry things up, while his eyes moved back involuntarily to the grotesque photographs of Kendall Nathan's corpse. Well, he figured, there was no more potent motive force to set off a chain of destruction than the cocktail of greed, hatred and lust that had seemed to surround Harry Nathan. Either Cindy or Kendall had killed Nathan, Kendall had killed Cindy, and now Kendall, too, was dead. The nest of vipers had consumed itself, and he was glad to close the Nathan case for good. The evidence could go back to the family now, he thought, recalling the hours of sickening videotapes he had made sure that no one but himself saw, and made a mental note to call

Feinstein to find out who was now the legal owner of Harry Nathan's estate.

Decker jumped as Lorraine banged into the office. 'Do I have a lot to tell you, darling,' she said, tossing a rustling deli bag full of wrapped packages onto his desk. 'Did you eat?'

'No,' he said. 'I was waiting for you. God, I'm hungry. What did Feinstein want?' He went into the kitchen for plates.

When he came back, she said, 'Cindy was right about the art scam. Feinstein bought over two million dollars' worth of paintings from Harry Nathan and Kendall and they've turned out to be fakes. He wants us to try to trace either the original paintings or the proceeds of sale.' Lorraine opened a tub of artichoke salad and scooped some into her mouth before continuing. 'Cindy also wrote stuff about killing herself to Feinstein and a whole bunch of other people – which fits in with what I thought about the note. I had Kendall pretty much down for having killed her, but – you won't believe this – Kendall Nathan died too last night.'

'Ding dong, the witch is dead,' Decker said ironically, arranging bread, bresaola and salad on a serving platter. 'What happened to her?'

'The gallery caught fire and she went up in smoke. That's all Feinstein's assistant knew.' Lorraine tore off another hunk of bread, assembled herself a rapid sandwich and began to eat.

'I'm sure Lieutenant Burton will be able to let you have a few more details,' Decker said, with mock innocence, and Lorraine flushed scarlet. 'Remember to ask him when he's scrambling eggs for you – I mean, next time he calls.'

'Did he call?' Lorraine asked, giving up the pretence that her association with Burton was purely professional.

'Nope, not yet. You want me to call him?'

Lorraine nodded, then changed her mind. 'No, I'll call him later. Anyway, two things. Feinstein figures that he bought the real thing from Nathan's gallery, as he got it properly authenticated there, but what was packed and delivered were fakes. Cindy told me she thought Kendall and Harry were pulling something like that, but to tell you the truth, I didn't believe her.' Lorraine shook her head. 'Poor kid. Nobody took her seriously her whole life.'

'It's not your fault she died,' Decker said gently. 'Don't beat yourself up about it.'

'Yeah, I know – part of the job,' Lorraine said with a wintry smile. 'But she told me she'd found out that some of the art at the house was fake too. Some Chinese porcelain she thought was antique was apparently knocked out by some company called Classic Reproductions. Check them out for a start.' She finished her sandwich as Decker made notes of what she had said.

'I also think we need to trace a guy who worked for Kendall Nathan, a sort of gofer who brought the paintings round and hung them for Feinstein,' she continued. 'He's a young kid – Feinstein couldn't recall his name, but I remember seeing someone when I was at the gallery so chase him up too.'

'Will do,' Decker said, making another note.

'These are pretty spectacular pieces that have gone missing, so we contact galleries in the US and in Europe and all the big art auction houses. They're all signed

240

works by well-known modern painters, and all had price tags from three hundred thousand dollars to over two million. Poor old Feinstein really got stung.'

'I'll make some enquiries in London,' Decker said, writing furiously. 'I think they have a register of hot art works you can have searched.' He was going to enjoy doing the legwork on this case, he reckoned, schmoozing through galleries, and looking up art-world friends.

Lorraine dug into her briefcase and brought out some loose pages. 'These are the names of the people Kendall employed. Feinstein paid the wages so the list should be legit – just three people. He said they were hired to remodel frames, do repairs and so on, but they might also have been painting the fakes, so check them out. There's also a list of regular buyers – get each of them to give you the name of their art adviser. It may mean a lot of people have been stung.'

Decker nodded, excited.

'Clever bastards,' Lorraine mused, leaning forward. 'You can see by the list – all movie people. They rarely sold to a dealer or old money, because they'd recognize a fake so fast. Most of the people they sold to were just rich trash and wouldn't know if they'd bought a Lichtenstein or a fried egg. They hung up what they'd bought, put up the gold plaque to say what it was, while the original stayed with Nathan's gallery. He and Kendall were pulling the scam together.'

'And a very lucrative one,' Decker remarked.

Lorraine nodded. She frowned, and leaned back in her chair. 'You know . . . everything Cindy Nathan said is starting to make sense. I mean about the high-tech security at Nathan's – I'd say he kept the originals on his own walls.' Lorraine leafed through the pile of pages of

241

information from Feinstein. 'There's also sculpture, ceramics, and some statues that were worth over a million dollars.'

Decker waited, pen poised, as Lorraine thumbed through the pages. 'According to Cindy, Nathan hadn't paid the insurance for the contents at the house for quite a while. Why do you think that was?'

'It's certainly a weird thing to do,' Decker said meditatively. 'Particularly since he wasn't lax about security.'

'That's what I thought. He was paranoid about it, monitored every phone call, every visitor,' Lorraine said. 'Supposing what he was worried about wasn't the paintings being ripped off out of the house, but certain people getting *into* it – like the people who thought they had the same painting hanging in the guest bath at home? I bet he was careful never to sell to anyone too close to his own social circle.'

'That's certainly one explanation,' Decker said. 'But what about Kendall getting in and trashing the stuff?'

'I've been trying to figure that one out since the housekeepers told me about it. The only thing I can think is that she discovered then that those paintings weren't the ones she and Nathan had bought.'

'What do you mean – he'd sold them again?' Decker interjected.

'Wouldn't surprise me. I reckon Nathan got two sets of fakes painted. Then he switched the originals again to cut Kendall out.'

'He was doing a double whammy?'

'Right. And Kendall found out when she went to the house the night Cindy Nathan killed herself.'

'But why the hell would she set light to the gallery?'

Decker asked. 'That was her own stock – she must have known that was genuine, at least.'

'She's going to have lost a fucking fortune on the scam – I'd say she torched it for the insurance. Which is why Feinstein wants me to look for secret banks accounts. If Nathan sold half of those paintings he's got to have millions stashed somewhere.'

'I'll start calling round and see if any of them have turned up.' Decker dangled the last piece of bresaola above his mouth and finished it with an elegant snap.

'Let me tell you the second thing first,' Lorraine said. 'Feinstein told me the exact terms of Harry Nathan's will.' And she explained how Sonja Nathan now stood to inherit not only Cindy's share of Harry Nathan's estate, but also Kendall's.

'Just so long as she lives another . . .' Decker glanced at the calendar '. . . four days. East Hampton next stop, right?'

'Yes, get me another flight. I doubt if Sonja has anything to do with it as she's been out of the picture a long time . . .' She smiled at the pun. 'But I'd like to talk to her, and besides, Mr Feinstein is paying us top dollar, so we can afford it. All fraud cases take a long time to check out too, so we don't take on anything else – well, not for a while.'

Decker rubbed two fingers together. 'Do I get a rise?'

Lorraine shooed him with her hand. 'Oh, get out of here. But if you come up with something, yes, we'll split if fifty-fifty because I'll need you to do a lot of legwork.'

'Thank you.' He bowed out, eager to make a start.

Lorraine glanced at her phone, then checked the time. It was after two, and Jake had not returned her call.

Suddenly, she felt the depression descend. It was odd, she thought, she'd got a new and interesting investigation, but a date for the movies was more important.

She spent the rest of the afternoon sifting through Feinstein's papers. When it got to four o'clock and Jake still hadn't called, she rang and cancelled her hair appointment. Much as she wanted to, she couldn't pick up the phone to Jake himself, and hard as she tried to concentrate on work, she kept thinking about him until she had convinced herself he would never call again.

It was almost six when Decker returned. 'So far none of the well-known galleries have seen any of the paintings listed, and none have been sold recently at auction. Next I'll try England, the art-loss register, and then the rest of Europe – and you've missed your hairdresser.'

Lorraine attempted nonchalance. 'This is more important. Now get out, leave me alone.'

'He didn't call, huh?' he said, hovering at the door.

'No, Deck, he didn't call. So I'll take Tiger out, and if you need me, I'll be at home. Okay?'

'Okay – but if you need me, I'm around.'

'Thanks.' She turned away from him. 'I really liked him, Deck, but I couldn't keep my big mouth shut. I just had to tell him about my past – well, some of it . . .'

Decker leaned on her desk. 'Listen, if he's put off you because of that he's not worth the effort, period. It's what you are now that counts, and I'm telling you, you're lovely.' He watched her fetch Tiger's lead and leave the office, while he stayed on to make his overseas calls to a list of major galleries that might have sold art works worth over a quarter of a million dollars. The paintings listed didn't seem to appear on anyone's records, and the case intrigued him more and more.

Burton was still in his office, wading through investigation reports and trial files. The autopsy report on Cindy Nathan wasn't passed to him until after five. The cause of death was suffocation by hanging, but she had also tested positive for alcohol and drugs. It was impossible to tell whether she had hanged herself voluntarily or whether someone else had done it.

By the time Burton called Lorraine's office, the answerphone was picking up calls. Her mobile was switched off and when he tried to call her at home he got another recording. He decided not to leave a message but to go round to the apartment on the off-chance she was there, and he continued to work, clearing his desk. Just as he was finishing, the file on Lorraine caught his eye again. He drew it towards him and leafed through it, rereading everything he had read that morning, then pushed it away. There was something that connected with the Nathan case, something that he had read or been told, that hung like a warning, but he just couldn't put the pieces together. All he knew was that it had a direct connection to Lorraine.

Lorraine sat on her sofa. She'd made herself an elaborate salad of goat's cheese and marinated vegetables, but seemed to have no appetite. She'd walked Tiger, fed him, done everything to occupy herself, even played her answerphone messages twice in case she had somehow rewound the first time and missed his call. But there was no call, and no amount of staring at the machine would make a message appear. He hadn't called, he wasn't going to call, and she had been dumb to think he ever would call. She thought back to what he had said as he had left that morning: she wasn't kidding herself, he had asked her if she wanted to see a movie – he must just have decided to skip it. She could easily call him tomorrow, it hadn't been a firm date, just a casual suggestion, but by the time it got to nine o'clock, she felt worse than depressed, telling herself that no decent guy would want to start anything with her – she wasn't worth it. She should never have thought he would want to see her again, so she took the phone off the hook, to stop herself staring at it.

It was almost nine thirty when Tiger began to bark frantically. Lorraine, wrapped in a bathrobe, yelled at him to shut up, sure he had only heard the neighbours below, but then the entryphone buzzed. 'I tried to call you at the office, and here . . .' Jake's voice said.

'Oh, yeah, sorry. I've been really busy.'

'Is it okay if I come in?'

She pressed the button to release the street door. 'Sure.'

He seemed embarrassed when she opened the door to the apartment, and paid more attention to Tiger than to her, while she wished she'd kept the appointment with the hairdresser and hadn't taken off her make-up.

'Have you eaten?'

'Yeah, I got a hamburger at the station, but I wouldn't mind a cup of coffee.'

Lorraine busied herself with the percolator, while Jake continued to mess around with Tiger. Then, suddenly, he was close and his arms slipped around her. 'I missed you,' he said quietly, and she turned towards him, putting out a hand to touch his face, feeling that he needed a shave.

'You did?' she said softly.

'Yeah, all day.'

She heard a voice inside her head telling her to say it, admit that she had missed him too, but she broke away to fetch the cups and take the cream from the fridge. 'I'd given up on you,' she said flippantly, setting out a tray.

'I'm sorry.' He ruffled his hair.

'Well, you say something about a movie, and then when you didn't return my call . . .' She reached for the cookies, and realized as she turned to him that she was holding the jar tightly. 'I did call you. Some secretary said you were in a meeting.'

'I was. I'm sorry – it was crazy all day. But when I called you back, there was just the answerphone.'

'Hell, you don't have to explain anything, I'm not interrogating you. It was just . . .' She couldn't keep up the pretence. Her voice sounded strangled. 'I didn't think you wanted to see me again, not after, you know . . .'

He took the jar away from her, and held her close. She clung to him, feeling his heart beating. 'You are wrenching feelings from me that I never thought I would have again, and I'm scared, so scared . . .'

He kissed the top of her head and the nape of her neck, then opened the palm of her hand and kissed that too, holding it to his lips. He wanted to say there and then that he loved her, but somehow the words just wouldn't come. Instead he heard himself asking her if it would be all right if he had a shower.

247

'Only if you stay the night,' she said, wanting to say something more loving, but she was as tongue-tied as he was.

It was not until he was beside her, lying on her bed with just a towel wrapped around his waist and a cup of coffee in his hand that they began to relax with each other. Neither said that they felt totally at ease with one another, that they loved the way their bodies fitted together when Lorraine slipped into Jake's arms and curled up beside him. They didn't need words, and she was unprepared for what he said when he spoke.

'Will you marry me?'

She didn't think twice, but agreed without hesitation. Then they were stunned by the enormity of what they had just agreed, and there was a pause before they laughed. Lorraine covered her face with her hands.

'Oh, my God, I should at least have hesitated a moment.' She rolled away from him, in disbelief at what had just happened.

'No,' he said, drawing her closer, as if she belonged with him.

'But it might take a bit of getting used to,' she whispered.

CHAPTER 11

LORRAINE MADE breakfast while Jake showered. Just setting two places felt good. She had lain awake beside him for a long time, replaying over and over in her mind the moment he had asked if she would marry him, half afraid she had dreamed it.

'Hi,' he said, as he came into the kitchen buttoning up his shirt and rubbing his chin. 'You've got one hell of a blunt razor in there.'

They were at ease with each other, and Jake ate yoghurt and cereal, poured coffee for them both, and even put his dirty dishes in the sink. He made no mention, though, of having asked her to marry him.

'Somebody house-trained you,' she said, watching him squirt washing-up liquid into the sink.

Tiger took up his position at the front door, waiting for his morning walk, and Jake offered to take him out while Lorraine showered. It was as if he had known her for months, not just days, and his presence didn't seem intrusive, just got better and better every moment he was with her.

Jake might have been well-trained in the dish-washing department, but he had left the shower steamed up, sopping towels and puddles on the floor and wet footprints on her carpet. Lorraine liked even that because it stopped him being too perfect. She remembered her ex-husband Mike, and the arguments they had had over his bathroom habits: she could never understand how he could take a shower and leave wet footprints everywhere but on the bath mat – and here she was liking it that the new man in her life was behaving in the same way. The new man in her life! She stared at her reflection in the mirror. In just two days her life had changed course, and from feeling depressed and alone, she knew now that a future was waiting for her.

Lorraine finished dressing, made the bed, vacuumed the living room and even plumped up the soft cushions, a small smile playing on her lips as she did the chores at top speed. She wished Rosie could see her now – she wouldn't believe it! Being loved, even if just for two days, had made her domesticated! Lorraine crossed to the window to see if Jake and Tiger were on their way back, and seeing them both coming up the street below, she opened the window and called down. Jake looked up and waved, while Tiger almost pulled him off his feet. He unclipped the dog's lead, still looking up at Lorraine. 'I'm going to be late, I'll call you.'

She was disappointed – she had wanted him to see how she had cleaned the house. Then suddenly she felt stupid, and a dark spiral of emotions started rushing through her mind. Why hadn't he mentioned their marriage? Why hadn't he come back to kiss her goodbye? Would she see him again? Tiger scratched at the front door, and Lorraine let him in. He went straight to his bowl, and began to gobble his food noisily. 'Hey, you! I just washed that floor!'

It was while she was driving into the office, accelerating along Rose Avenue, that she began to run through the case. The light at Walgrave and Rose was broken, blinking a steady red that permitted one car at a time to cross the intersection. Seeing the line of vehicles jammed bumper to bumper, Lorraine looked at the memos she'd scrawled to herself. Why *had* Harry Nathan been killed? Somehow she didn't think it was to stop the porn tapes being released – if someone was desperate enough to kill him for that reason, they would have ensured that they knew where the tapes were. But if that were the case, the suspects were Cindy, Kendall and Raymond Vallance, with Kendall and Vallance having the most to lose by the tapes becoming public. However, Lorraine thought, Nathan's involvement in a multi-million-dollar art fraud seemed a much more likely motive for his murder. It was almost impossible that he had been killed by one of the victims of the scam – or of his other blackmailing activities: the tight security at the house would have kept strangers out. No. Nathan had been killed by someone who knew him well, which meant his wives or his friends. Yet again Kendall seemed the most likely killer – especially since what was probably her jeep had been seen near Nathan's house on the day he died. Against that, though, she had given a convincing appearance of not having known that she had been ripped off in the scam until weeks later when Cindy died. The phone tapes indicated that she had been on warm terms with her ex-husband.

At last it was Lorraine's turn to cross the intersection and she speeded up along Airport and Centinela to make up the lost time, but the ten-minute delay meant that she hit another major jam on Pico Boulevard. Lorraine turned back to her notes, and considered other reasons why anyone might have wanted Harry Nathan dead.

Assuming that no one else had had any inkling that the paintings weren't genuine, Nathan had been perceived as a rich man; perhaps he, and the women, had been killed for his money by the person who would eventually inherit it – Sonja Nathan. Lorraine had never established who had made the telephone call to her office on the morning of Nathan's murder, which lent a shred of support to that hypothesis. It had certainly been a woman, she thought – though perhaps Raymond Vallance could have imitated a woman's voice.

The traffic was at a dead stop. Lorraine tapped her teeth with her pen, and continued to think about Sonja Nathan. If she was primarily motivated by financial greed, why had she let Nathan rip her off so spectacularly after their divorce? She had surrendered the gallery she had built up, her only means of earning a living – and which a court would almost certainly have awarded to her – because, Vallance had said, she was too proud to soil her hands. But soiling one's hands with petty squabbles over money might be a very different matter to Sonja Nathan from soiling them with an enemy's blood.

The impatient driver behind blasted Lorraine with his horn. She indicated in the mirror that there was nothing she could do, and glanced back at her notes, where she had written the words paintings, new partner. Had it been Nathan's own idea to sell the paintings without Kendall's knowledge, or had he been working with someone else? Someone who had decided to cut him permanently out of the picture – and out of the proceeds of the sale – just as ruthlessly as he had cut out his second ex-wife?

Lorraine ignored another toot from the driver behind her, and went back to her notes. Any new accomplice in the fraud would still have to be someone in Nathan's circle of intimates, or they could not have got past the security – or known that Nathan would have to be killed outside, away from the recording devices in the house. That brought her back to Vallance and Sonja again: Sonja was the one with the specialist knowledge of the art world but Vallance was the one most desperate about the porn tapes . . .

Lorraine felt that she was going round in circles, but at last the traffic began to move. She put away her notes.

When she got to the office Decker was at his desk, calling galleries and auction houses. 'I still haven't turned up any gallery selling the paintings on the list, but there's hundreds of 'em,' he said.

Lorraine told him to concentrate next on private dealers: they were more likely to have buyers who did not necessarily want their purchases made public. She also asked him to check out known buyers from Japan and the former Soviet republics, especially the latter, who had a lot of illegal dollars to spend, and not to forget the buyers on record as having purchased art works from Kendall Nathan's gallery.

'I'm compiling a list from the papers Feinstein gave you, but it'd be better if I could get access to the gallery books,' Decker said.

'I doubt if sales like this went into any official ledger, but there might be a record of them at the Nathan house.'

'Good thinking – you want me to go there?'

'No, I'm going to go out there myself and try to get Feinstein's art expert to confirm whether those paintings are real or fakes before we go any further,' Lorraine said. 'I'll call Jose now.' She dialled the Nathan house, and

Jose said she could come straight over – he and Juana would be there, and they wanted to speak to her in any case: they had been given a formal letter from Feinstein terminating their employment. 'We have to leave the property by the end of this week,' he said angrily. They still had not been paid any back salary. Next call was to Feinstein. When she told him that she thought Nathan had been keeping the original canvases at his own house, he agreed readily to call the man who had authenticated the paintings for him. Within two minutes he was back on the line and said that Wendell Dulane would join her at Nathan's house in half an hour.

'Okay, Decker, I'll be out until lunchtime, possibly,' Lorraine said, picking up her purse.

'Don't you even want a cup of coffee, dear?' he said in his best mom voice.

'We had breakfast.' She couldn't resist using the plural, and Decker laughed.

Jose opened the door when Lorraine arrived at Harry Nathan's house, but she said she would wait outside in the sun for Dulane to show up. Within a few minutes someone buzzed at the gate and a low-slung sports car drew up on the gravel. An elegant individual, dressed in a green linen suit, got out and introduced himself as Wendell Dulane.

She and Jose showed him where the paintings were hung, both on the ground floor and upstairs.

'I've seen a number of these pictures before – one or two on Joel Feinstein's behalf,' Dulane said at once. 'If they aren't the originals, they aren't crassly detectable fakes.'

'We were hoping you could tell us the difference,' Lorraine said. 'They all look the same to me.'

The man nodded. 'Certainly. I'll call you when I'm through.'

Jose was evidently itching to talk to her about the letter he had received from Feinstein, and sure enough, when he ushered Lorraine into the kitchen, a small pile of correspondence had been set out on a black and white laminated table.

Juana came across to greet her. 'Mrs Page, I'm so glad you have come. Did Jose tell you we have been told to leave?'

'Have you been able to find any other employment?' Lorraine asked, sitting down at the table to read Feinstein's note and his brief apology for being unable to settle any outstanding accounts until the Nathan estate was in order.

Jose shrugged, and Juana pulled out a chair. 'We have no references. We asked Mr Feinstein to provide some for us, but he doesn't mention it in his letter and it is difficult to get decent employment here in LA without them. We have a few things we are looking into, but nothing definite. We were wondering if you could help us.'

'I would if I could,' Lorraine said. She didn't know many people who could afford live-in help, but there were always movie people needing housekeepers.

'But not without good references. We have worked for Mr Nathan for so many years ... .'

Lorraine knew what they wanted, and didn't mind their rather obvious way around asking her for it directly. She said that she could give them some kind of reference and would speak to Feinstein again about their back salary and proper references. And then she had an idea. 'Perhaps Sonja Nathan could give you a reference,' she suggested, and saw a look pass between the couple.

'We have written to her,' Juana said, looking at her husband.

'She hired you, didn't she?' Lorraine said, fishing for more information about Harry Nathan's enigmatic first wife. 'Was she easy to work for?'

'Very easy,' Juana said. 'She was a lady. The rest were whores.' There was a fierce look in her eyes, and a note of finality in her voice. Lorraine glanced at Jose.

'Harry Nathan robbed her,' he said slowly, 'as he robbed us.'

A polite cough sounded behind her. Dulane had appeared in the doorway, Lorraine got up and motioned him into the hall where they could speak more privately.

'It's bad news, I'm afraid,' he said. 'They're fakes, all right – carefully executed, but I don't think there can be any doubt. Just as well, I suppose, considering the damage some of them have sustained. Tell Feinstein I'll call him later. Nice meeting you, Mrs Page,' he said.

As Jose appeared to show Dulane to the door, something suddenly occurred to Lorraine. She walked back into the kitchen and asked Juana if the police had taken Nathan's diary. 'They took a lot of things from here. He had personal things like that in his briefcase, and they took that away, but there was an appointment book – it was stacked with the magazines.'

Lorraine followed her out to the main living area and across the large light room to a glass-topped table on which a number of upmarket glossies were spread out. Juana moved them aside, brought out a leather appointments book and handed it to Lorraine. She riffled through it: there were weeks without anything written in at all, then a few scrawled appointments. 'Can I make a few notes?' she asked, and Juana nodded, then withdrew. Lorraine took out her notebook and jotted down any name she came across – there was none she had heard mentioned before, and she wondered if they were art dealers, which Decker could check out. She turned page after mostly blank page. Some had a single line drawn through them and, she almost missed it, just the single letter S printed right at the top. The Ss were more frequent in the weeks leading up to the murder, but there was never more than one in a week. Lorraine noted each date, and wondered if the letter stood for 'Sale'. Or could it refer to the first Mrs Nathan?

Juana returned with a sandwich of smoked chicken and salad leaves, in sun-dried tomato bread, neatly laid out on a tray with a napkin and some iced water. 'Juana, if I run through some dates with you, can you see if you can recall them for any reason? Visitors, or even Kendall Nathan being here?'

Lorraine listed date after date but Juana shook her head, so Lorraine asked her to send in Jose. He, too, was unable to recall anything specific regarding the dates. 'How about two days *before* the murder? Can you remember anyone coming here?'

Jose shook his head, but then he came closer and asked for more dates. 'You remember somebody?' Lorraine asked.

'No, but I think . . . I am sure most of the dates are . . . wait. Let me talk to Juana.' He hurried out and a minute later returned with her. This time Juana carried a small cardboard-backed diary, and Lorraine read the dates again.

'Ah! I may be wrong, but most of the dates you want to know about are our days off. They weren't usually on the same day every week, Mr Nathan would just tell us we could have the day off.'

Nathan must have made sure that his domestics were not in the house so they wouldn't know who came or went, what paintings were exchanged or hung or, most importantly, who was taking items away.

'Did you ever notice anything unusual going on with the paintings?' Lorraine asked.

Juana raised her hands in an uncomprehending gesture. 'They were changed so many times. Mr Nathan was always asking if anyone had been to the house, if anyone had seen them – he acted like he never wanted anyone to see them.'

'Was there anyone in particular who used to come to look at the paintings?'

The couple looked at Lorraine. 'No one in particular.'

'Did Kendall Nathan still come to the house after the divorce?'

'Many times,' Juana answered. 'She used to bring paintings out here and say where they were to be hung. Sometimes the new ones looked identical to the old ones.'

'Did anyone ever come with her to help hang the paintings?'

Lorraine waited as they thought about it. 'Sometimes she had a black kid who was her odd-job man. They were big canvases, and she couldn't carry them in and out of the house on her own.'

Lorraine pushed back her chair and stood up. 'During the last few days or weeks before Harry Nathan was shot, did anyone come and take away paintings? Or replace paintings?'

Jose said, 'Yes, once, but we didn't see him – it was our afternoon off. Mr Nathan said it was a man from the insurance company checking on them.'

'Where was Cindy when this went on?'

'I don't remember, she never paid any attention to the paintings.'

'Can you give me the date the insurance broker was here?'

'It was a Monday, a week or two before the murder. I remember because Mr Nathan gave me three thousand dollars for household expenses, and to pay the gardener. I remember the day, too, because later in the evening, we had just served dinner and he called us into the dining room. He poured us glasses of champagne, said he was going to be a father, that Cindy was pregnant, just a few days, but pregnant.'

'I see,' Lorraine said. 'Well, thank you for all your information. I'd better get myself back to my office.' She got up to go, having deliberately held back the question she most wanted to ask until last.

'I don't suppose Sonja ever came here after she and Harry Nathan split up?' she asked casually, as the couple walked out into the hall with her.

'Sonja, never,' Juana said, without hesitation, her eyes meeting Lorraine's. 'She never came here again.'

Decker was just hanging up the phone when Lorraine arrived at the office, and seemed very upbeat. 'I just got an address from the welfare department for the kid who worked for Kendall Nathan,' he said. 'The one on Feinstein's payroll was out of date.'

'Well, check him out,' Lorraine said. 'Feinstein's art guy said all the paintings at the house are fakes.'

'I'll get over to his home right now.'

'Ask him if he ever met Sonja Nathan,' Lorraine added. 'Did you fix me up a flight to New York?'

'I'll get on to it as soon as I get back,' he said.

Almost as soon as Decker had closed the door the phone rang and she picked it up: 'Page Investigations.'

'Hi! It's me.' It was Jake. She pushed away her notes and leaned back in her chair.

'I was wondering if you'd like dinner at my place tonight.'

'Yes.' She laughed, and said she knew she was supposed to play hard to get, but . . .

'Pick you up from your office at about six thirty?' he suggested.

'Yep. Oh, just one thing – the Cindy Nathan autopsy. Did it come in?'

Jake told her the results. Then Lorraine said, 'I don't think the note was genuine. Or, at least, she didn't write it that day.'

'Well, it's possible she wrote it on a piece of paper she cut in two herself, for some reason,' Burton replied. 'I'm not going to push an investigation unless another suspect emerges besides Kendall Nathan.'

Lorraine said nothing, having decided not to mention her suspicions that either Raymond Vallance or Sonja Nathan might have some connection to Cindy's death until after she had seen Sonja.

Burton went on, 'The forensic team are still sifting through the debris of the gallery workroom, but they seem to think Kendall died accidentally, possibly while trying to start a fire. Wouldn't surprise me if she was trying to burn the place down for the insurance – the business was in debt, and she couldn't afford to renew the lease.'

'Anyone else involved?' Lorraine asked, and Burton said that, according to the witness, Kendall had been alone.

'When did you know about her death?' she asked.

He had been told the previous day. Lorraine wanted to ask him why he hadn't mentioned it, but she didn't because she wanted to avoid any awkwardness between them. At the same time she thought perhaps he should have told her, and, as if reading her mind, he said, 'I was going to tell you about it last night, but . . . I got a little sidetracked, if you remember.' He laughed, in a low, intimate fashion, then had to cut short the call as there was another waiting. He reminded her that he would pick her up later, then hung up.

The light on the answerphone was blinking. Feinstein wanted Lorraine to come over to his office at her earliest convenience.

Lorraine sighed. Now that the attorney was paying her, she had no choice but to do as he asked, and by just before four she was in his reception in Century City.

Dulane had informed Feinstein that further fake copies of his paintings had been found at Harry Nathan's house, and Feinstein demanded to know what the hell was going on.

'Well,' Lorraine said, 'it looks like Nathan did to Kendall what she did to you and swapped the paintings again.'

'Jesus,' Feinstein swore. 'Crooked fucking bastard.

261

Where the fuck are the paintings now?' He glared at Lorraine as though she must know the answer.

'It looks to me like they've either been sold on to other buyers, probably outside the US, or he had another partner who's got them stashed somewhere,' she said.

'Find them,' Feinstein said, rubbing his eye sockets wearily. 'Just fucking find them.'

'Right now my assistant is checking out the man who worked for Kendall Nathan,' Lorraine said smoothly, 'and when I have his report, I will give you a further update. We're still checking out auction-houses, galleries and other possible outlets for the paintings.' Feinstein pursed his lips. 'You know, Mr Feinstein,' Lorraine went on, 'you could report this to the police. You have been used in a serious fraud.'

'No,' he snapped.

'May I ask why not?'

Feinstein pinched the bridge of his nose, then leaned back in his chair. 'One, I do not wish to appear like a total asshole and, believe me, if the media get a hold of this, you think anyone is going to want me to represent them? The schmuck that didn't even know when he was being ripped off? I have my reputation to think of and . . .' he spread his hands on his desk '. . . like I said, sometimes clients, like Nathan, do certain deals in cash . . .'

'Did you benefit from cash payments, Mr Feinstein?' Lorraine enquired.

Feinstein half sighed, half hissed his reply. 'Not cash, exactly. I thought I made that clear.'

'Not quite. If you weren't paid in cash, how were you paid?'

Feinstein steepled the fingers of his sweaty hands. 'An

early de Kooning like the one I bought costs maybe a few thousand dollars more than I paid. It was a good deal – one for the future if you understand me, not to be sold on until a few years had gone by. It wasn't hot, just an exceptional deal – in lieu of fees, you understand.'

'I see,' Lorraine said, loathing the man, who continued to play with his fingers.

'So this stays a private investigation. You find who stitched me up, then I'll deal with it my way. That's what you're hired to do so no more talk about reporting the fakes to the cops. Is that clear?'

'Absolutely, if that's what you want.'

He stood up, and began to move round his desk.

'Did you also handle Sonja Nathan's business?' Lorraine asked.

Feinstein turned. 'No, I didn't. I was introduced to Nathan by Raymond Vallance, the movie star. Most of my clients are in the industry, which is another reason why I need confidentiality.'

Lorraine headed for the door, then turned back to him. 'Do you know if Sonja Nathan and her husband were still in contact after they divorced?'

Feinstein blinked hard. 'One of my partners handled the settlement. I met her during the meetings – they both had to be here.'

'And Sonja Nathan is now the main beneficiary of the estate, correct?'

Feinstein nodded. 'Yes – considering the other two wives conveniently dropped dead.'

'Now that we know the art at the house isn't genuine, what sort of sum would Harry Nathan's heir be expecting to receive?'

Feinstein stuffed his hands into his pockets. 'I don't

know. The house is worth about three million, the corporate stock not a lot in the present climate, and the gallery nothing – Harry and Kendall didn't own the freehold on the site.'

'And if his secret bank accounts are traced, would whatever money is in them also belong to Sonja Nathan?'

'I will certainly be instituting a claim to trace the value of my property into those funds,' Feinstein said, with emphasis, 'but I can't say what anyone else ripped off by Harry Nathan will be doing. Basically if nobody else claims it, it's hers.'

It was five thirty by the time Lorraine got back to the office. She had expected Decker to be there, but he hadn't even called. She cleared up some correspondence, tidied the office, took the garbage down to the incinerator, and had almost got everything in order when the doorman called to say someone was in reception to see her.

It was Jake – wearing a casual sweater, old cord trousers and sneakers. 'Hi. Maybe thought we'd do the walk before we went to my place – you all set?'

Tiger hurled himself at his friend, tail like a windmill, then pranced around barking.

Lorraine made a last-minute check before they left. Her car stayed in the garage, as Burton had the roof down on his rather beaten-up Suzuki jeep. 'This is for going to the beach,' he said, excusing the state of the jeep, but Lorraine liked it, and so did Tiger. He had jumped in and sat on the back seat before Burton had the door half open. Lorraine patted his head, remembering Tiger's previous owner – as perhaps the big dog was too. All that seemed a long, long time ago, and she thought about her old partners, Rose and Rooney, wondering how they were, and when they would be returning from their honeymoon.

Jake looked sideways at her, then reached over and took her hand. 'You're miles away,' he said.

She squeezed his hand. 'Yes – I was just thinking about a couple of friends of mine I want you to meet. They're on their honeymoon.'

He released her hand, and suddenly she wished she hadn't said honeymoon, because the word made her think about the proposal he'd made to her. He'd made no further mention of it, and she didn't want him to think she was trying to drop hints or remind him of it, so she started talking about Rosie and Rooney instead. She wasn't aware of where they were going, just chatted about how she had first met Rosie and that Bill Rooney had once been her boss when she was a cop. Jake listened, but seemed to be paying more attention to the road as he drove out towards Pacific Palisades. Tiger stuck his head out of the window, his ears blowing upright, then rested his head on Jake's shoulder. The atmosphere was relaxed and easy, and Lorraine began to unwind from the day. She stopped thinking about Harry Nathan, Kendall, Cindy, and the repellent Feinstein, and by the time they were walking beside the ocean, and Jake took her hand in his, all she could think about was the man she was with, and how good it felt to be with him again.

'So, you're back from wherever you've been,' he said softly.

'Sorry, sometimes it takes me a while to relax.' She moved closer to him, and he put his arm around her shoulder.

'I understand – I was a bit wound up myself.'

'Had a bad day?' she asked.

'Hell no – I was nervous about seeing you, worried you might have changed your mind.' They stopped and faced each other. 'I meant what I said last night, Lorraine. It may have been jumping the gun a bit – we hardly know each other, and I'm not . . . I mean, I don't want to hold you to anything said in the heat of the moment, but if you want to just let things run as they are, then that's okay by me.'

The pain in her stomach almost made Lorraine gasp. 'Do you mean *you* want to . . . er . . . you know, let things run?' She could hardly speak with nervousness.

He cupped her face in his hands and kissed her, then looked into her upturned face. 'Thing is, I feel like I've been hit by a truck. It was tough working today because I kept on wanting to call you, just to hear your voice. I can't hide my feelings, maybe because I've never felt this way before, so if I'm behaving like a kid, then you'll just have to wait for me to calm down. I want to go to bed with you right now, I want to wake up beside you, and not just one night here or there, *I want you.*'

She felt a small twinge of guilt because he hadn't been on her mind all day – in many of her thoughts, maybe, but not all of them. But being with him now, she forgot everything else. The words came out as naturally as breathing, three words she never thought she would say to anyone again. 'I love you.'

He closed his eyes and whispered, 'Oh, thank God.'

CHAPTER 12

DECKER HAD checked out the Museum of Contemporary Art and driven from one gallery to another, sitting in the back rooms discussing auctions and buyers. He'd asked everyone about Kendall Nathan's gallery, and had prowled Rodeo, Beverly, Melrose Place and sections of La Cienega looking for other exclusive galleries that relied on private clients. He had palmed money to porters at auction houses and, dressed in his best gear, exploiting his good looks and acting experience to the full, he had posed as a buyer or a dealer.

He took one real dealer to lunch at the Ivy, and by four o'clock he was exhausted, but he felt he now knew conclusively that none of Harry Nathan's pieces had been on the market during the past two years. He had records of sales past, or forthcoming; catalogues from European auctions and a thick stack of literature from the English art houses, Sotheby's and Christie's, from both their London and New York centres of business.

He decided now to talk to the kid who had worked for Kendall. He was a little wary as he followed Washington Boulevard into east Los Angeles, more than aware that he was crossing the divide into gangland territory.

Signs of poverty became visible in the form of discount marts and Spanish-language churches, bars appeared on every building's doors and windows, and gang signatures, often half obliterated by rivals then resprayed, were noticeable among the graffiti on walls and metal shop shutters.

He made sure the doors to his car were locked as he drove, and that he knew exactly where he was going, not wanting to look lost or vulnerable as he turned south on La Brea to hit Adams Boulevard. Decker slowed down as he turned into a smaller side-street of mainly single-storey bungalows, little more than flat-roofed boxes in dingy white or ochre shades, with here or there a pantiled porch, canopy or new garage as the residents attempted to improve their homes or give them some individual character. Most of the tiny front yards were clean and neat, and only a few had old furniture and other junk piled around the back door or resting against the walls. Bars and chain-link fences were, however, everywhere and Decker reckoned astutely that the parents who lived there were probably solid enough citizens but were losing their authority over the kids, grown and half-grown, who were running with gangs.

Decker found he had overshot his target, and stopped and reversed. Number 5467 was a small two-storey frame house, one of the less run-down properties, with roses and elephant's ear fern on each side of the door and the drive clear enough for him to park in. He locked his car and looked around before heading towards the porch, carrying his portable phone.

The front door had thick safety glass, made opaque with strips of masking tape on the inside. Decker knocked and waited, then rapped a little harder. He knew someone was at home because he could hear the sound of a blaring television.

'Who is it?' a distant voice called.

Decker knocked again, then called out that he was from the art gallery. He listened while the volume of the television was lowered. 'I'm coming,' said a hoarse female voice.

It was a few minutes more before the woman inched the door open on the chain.

'Good afternoon, I'm here about Kendall Nathan's gallery, and I wondered if I could speak to . . . your son, would it be? Eric? Mr Lee Judd?'

'He's my son,' came the asthmatic reply.

'Is he home?' Decker enquired.

'No, he ain't here.'

'I just want to ask him a few questions. I'm from the insurance company, and as Mr Lee Judd was employed by Mrs Nathan . . .'

'She got burned real bad,' Mrs Lee Judd said, but made no effort to open the door. 'My boy's real cut up about it. He got no job now. That's what he's doing, looking for work.'

'Could I just speak to you?'

'You *are* speakin' to me. I ain't opening this door for nobody, I don't know nothin'.'

Decker gave up in frustration and headed back towards his car. He was about to unlock it when he looked back at the house. The curtains moved on one of the downstairs windows. The figure behind them was that of a young man. Decker hurried back towards the door and pounded on it. 'Mr Lee Judd, I know you're in there, I just saw you at the window. Please, I'm not the police, this is just an insurance enquiry. Can you just open the door for a few minutes? Hello?'

There was no sound at all now, not even the television. Decker waited, then whipped round as he heard the sounds of running feet in the next-door yard. The young man had run out the back of the house, leaped over the fence and headed into the street.

Decker started to run after him, then returned to his car. The man had set off at high speed along the sidewalk, but he kept him in sight. Decker backed out into the road and followed him: his bright red windcheater and sneakers made him easy to spot, and although he was moving fast, he didn't duck into any of the driveways but headed for Adams Boulevard.

Decker still had Lee Judd in his sights as he stopped at traffic-lights. He saw the boy cross the main drag and turn into an alley about twenty yards up ahead on the left, between a dance rehearsal studio, exhibiting all the thinly cheerful signs of an attempt at urban renewal, and a boarded-up building, which still bore the ominous smoke stains of the riots. As soon as the lights changed, he pulled over and indicated left, turned into the alley and slowed down. It ran along the back of the other stores that fronted the boulevard – a liquor store, an exotic-looking hair-and-beauty salon and a Mexican music outlet. Piles of garbage overflowed from huge battered plastic bins, and a number of abandoned-looking vehicles and a couple of narrow passages led to any number of places for the youth to hide. Decker slowed to walking pace, but he knew he had lost him.

The alley ran straight through to a side street off Adams, so Decker had to drive on through. He was swinging out of the alley, preparing to head back the way he had come, when out of the corner of his eye he saw Lee Judd again. He was walking now, shoulders hunched and head bent low, keeping close to the façade of run-down shops. Decker had to drive on: the traffic was so heavy that there was no way he could stop quickly.

He was just dialling the office to see if Lorraine was there when he noticed a green pick-up truck career out of a side street, and slot into the traffic close behind him as he turned onto La Brea. He accelerated, but the pick-up came even closer, almost hitting his bumper. He accelerated again, tossing the phone onto the passenger seat. He was about to put his foot down when the pick-up rammed him so hard that his car spun through a hundred and eighty degrees, almost into the path of an oncoming vehicle. The driver screamed and blasted the horn as Decker righted the car and now hit the gas pedal hard. His heart was thumping. These guys behind were trying to run him off the road, and his mind raced as he tried to remember when the next set of traffic lights came up. He checked that his door was locked, and overtook a car in front, but the truck did the same, its cabin so high above its customized, extended wheel-base that Decker couldn't get a clear look at the driver. All he knew for certain was that this was for real, and he started to sweat with fear, wondering whether he should take a side turning. He decided against it, hoping he would have more opportunity to outrun the truck when they had passed under the Santa Monica freeway. He hoped and prayed that there were no signals ahead, because he would be forced to jump the lights or stop.

The truck edged out to his right, and Decker was sweating freely. His hands clutched the wheel and his back arched with fear, then terror, as the truck swiped his car from the side. He screeched over to the kerb but managed to turn out of the tail spin. Now, his accelerator pressed flat to the floor, he screamed forward, burning rubber, the needle of the speedometer moving higher and higher. He was nudging eighty, with the truck still close on his tail. Suddenly up ahead were the traffic lights on Washington, at yellow turning to red. There was no way Decker could pull up in time. He gritted his teeth, accelerated harder, and crossed the traffic lights at eighty-five miles per hour.

The garbage truck had only just moved out from the left-turn lane at the intersection as Decker's car shot the lights. It was impossible to avoid collision. Decker's car left the ground and somersaulted in the air before landing on its crushed bonnet in the centre of the junction. The pick-up truck did a U-turn, and disappeared as the garbage collectors ran to Decker's crushed, smouldering car. Blood smothered the windscreen, but they could see Decker's lifeless body still strapped into his safety belt, hanging upside down as glossy art brochures tumbled around it.

Jake's condominium was in a quiet street near Pico, within ten minutes' drive of the police department, a late seventies Cape-Cod-style construction with a lot of shingled-wood facings, gables and white-painted wood on the exterior. It was simple, neat and orderly inside. A small kitchen led off the dining room, which in turn led off an equally compact lounge. There was one bedroom with bathroom en suite, and the entire apartment was carpeted in a drab grey, with featureless furnishing and bland landscape prints on the walls.

'It's rented,' he said apologetically.

'I should hope so. It's – well, a bit characterless,' Lorraine said.

'Yeah, I guess it is, but I never intended staying here. At least not permanently.'

Tiger sniffed around the room, and lay down on a white rug in front of a fireplace containing a gas fire burning round fake logs.

Burton went into the kitchen: he'd already bought the groceries, which were still in their bags on the kitchen table. 'You watch TV, or whatever, and I'll cook.' Jake began to unpack the food and set out the things he would need, and Lorraine noticed a number of small deli items – exotic mushrooms, purple basil and an hors d'oeuvre of ready-cooked stone crab, which Jake had clearly picked up to impress her.

'You want me to set the table or anything?' Lorraine asked.

'Nope, I'll do it. It's just crab, steak and salad,' he said, opening one cupboard after the next as he searched for plates and bowls.

Lorraine opened her briefcase and called the office on her mobile to replay her messages, but there were none. She called her apartment next, but there were no messages there either. She looked at her watch. After eight o'clock. She took out her notebook and looked for Decker's home number, only to find she hadn't brought it with her. 'It's odd he hasn't checked in,' Lorraine said, crossing to the kitchen. Oil was burning in a pan, and a bluish pall of smoke spiralled to the air-conditioner.

'Oil's a bit hot,' she remarked, and Jake whipped round to take the pan off. He had assembled the salad and was now rubbing garlic over the steaks.

'He usually calls in, or leaves a message for me at home.' Lorraine picked up a carrot and munched it.

'Who you talking about?' Jake asked.

'Decker – he's been out all day, checking art galleries.' Lorraine reached for another carrot, as the steaks sizzled and spat in the pan. 'I don't have his home number with me, or I'd call.'

'Is he in the directory?' He pointed with a fork to a side table. Lorraine walked over to it. Then she frowned – she couldn't remember Decker's boyfriend's name, so she looked up Decker. She knew the phone wouldn't be in his name and shut the book. 'I'll do it later when I get home.'

Jake carried out glasses, wine and a corkscrew, and set them down on the table with a clatter. He opened the wine, filled a glass and drank, then dived back into the kitchen. A few moments later he reappeared. 'I got some of that alcohol-free lager for you. It's on the side table.'

He leaped back into the kitchen, and she could hear him cursing. Then there was a hissing sound as he immersed the burning pan in water.

'Do you want me to make a dressing?' Lorraine asked, carrying the bottle of lager into the kitchen.

'No, I'm almost ready. I made it earlier.' He was pouring a sachet of raspberry vinegar dressing over the salad.

'I need a bottle opener,' she said, crossing to one of the drawers. Burton passed her, carrying the platter of crab, the steaks on their plates and balancing the bowl of salad on his arm.

'Okay, it's ready.'

Lorraine brought the bottle-opener to the table and sat in the place Burton indicated. Tiger lifted his head, sniffed and inched over to sit beside her, knowing he might be in line for a titbit.

Decker was dead on arrival at the emergency room of Midway Hospital. Adam Elliot, his boyfriend, was contacted at nine thirty-five, and drove straight to the hospital, unable to take in that Decker was dead.

By the time he was led to the chapel area to identify the body, he was in a state of such distress that he had to be assisted into an ante-room. Decker, who rarely exceeded the speed limit, Decker who always nagged him about wearing his safety belt and warned him never to take risks, who said that life wasn't worth an extra twenty miles an hour, had been killed outright travelling at eighty-five miles an hour in a built-up area of downtown Los Angeles. It didn't make sense. Nothing made sense. The loss of his beloved partner was more than he could comprehend.

Lorraine sat watching a movie, her feet resting on Jake's knees and Tiger at their feet. Jake had consumed his bottle of wine, and Tiger the charred steaks, though at least the crab and the salad had been delicious.

'I got another job today,' Lorraine said. 'It's sort of connected to the Nathan case.'

'How come?' He stroked her legs.

'Well, apparently Nathan sold original paintings, then switched them when they were hung.' She explained the

275

complex scam she believed Nathan had pulled, and that his attorney, her new client, had been one of its victims.

'How much were they worth?' Jake asked, draining his glass.

'That depends. I'm still trying to get to the bottom of it all, but Feinstein's down maybe two million.'

'And do you think this fake stuff had something to do with Nathan's murder?'

'I don't know. To be honest, all I do know is that somebody, somewhere, has a cache of art work worth a mint – or else the mint. Maybe that was the motive for killing him, but with Cindy and Kendall both dead, it'll be hard to find out. Another odd thing is that there was a survivorship clause in the will, some tax-saving scam, Feinstein says, which meant that both Cindy and Kendall had to survive Nathan by sixty days before the gifts to them took effect. Since neither of them made it, every-thing, or whatever is left of Nathan's estate minus the art, goes to his first wife, Sonja Nathan. The house will be the main asset, as any cash Nathan got from the fraud he had stashed in secret accounts.'

'How will you go about tracing hidden bank accounts?' Jake asked, and Lorraine grinned and pushed him. 'No, I'm serious,' he said. 'How do you do that? If different names have been used, how do you trace them to Nathan?'

'Well, you start with his papers,' Lorraine said, tilting her head to one side. 'Nobody ever has anything *that* well hidden – there's always some kind of documentation somewhere. Then you look into travel, abroad or other-wise, and start checking – you know, do you know this man, et cetera. It's a long, slow process.'

'So it'll be a nice cash cow for you?' he said.

She nodded. 'It'll also mean a lot of painstaking enquiries.' Lorraine's face clouded as she thought about Decker. 'Maybe I should call home, see if he's left a message.'

Burton poured the dregs of the wine bottle into his glass and studied it for a moment. 'Have you ever thought about . . .' He stopped, and sipped the wine.

Lorraine had the phone in her hand. 'Thought about what?'

'Well, I know you have two daughters.'

She replaced the phone. 'Yes, Julia and Sally.'

He leaned against the back of the sofa, looking at her. 'You want any more kids?'

'What?'

He turned away. 'I'd like a family. I just wondered if you . . .'

'With you?'

'No, with Burt Lancaster. Who the hell do you think?'

She crossed to him and slipped her arms around his shoulders. 'You're serious about us getting married?'

'Okay, I have to admit that when I said it, I kinda had heart failure. I'd not even thought about it and it must have sounded crazy. But I've had time to think and maybe why I did say it was because I was feeling like a kid on acid! That was the way you made me feel. Now I'm calmer, I've had time to think and I wouldn't change that moment for the world. I know it's what I want, so, if you want me to ask you again, I will. You want me to ask you again?' He took her hand and drew her down to sit beside him, and she nestled into his arms, curling her legs onto the sofa.

'It's all moving so fast. Don't get me wrong – I like it this way, but . . .' She closed her eyes, and he rested his chin against her head. 'First we have to find a nice place, move in, get settled, but . . .'

'You okay?' Jake whispered.

Lorraine couldn't stop the tears from streaming down her face.

'I'm sorry if what I said upset you but we do need to talk about our future.'

She couldn't speak. The tears kept on coming, and every time she tried to say something she felt as if her throat was being squeezed.

'Maybe I've moved things on too fast. It's just that, now I've found you, I don't want to waste any time. But you can tell me to put the breaks on. All you've got to do is tell me, but we have to talk, Lorraine.'

She broke away, wiping her cheek with the back of her hand, and her words came out in spluttering gasps as her chest heaved. 'I want to talk to you too, I want—' She started to sob, and he made no effort to stop her, as if he knew she had to let her feelings out before she could calm down. She gasped for breath, determined to get it out, to tell him that she wanted his child more than anything else in the world. The thought of carrying Jake's baby made her heart swell. She would be a part of him, have a future with him and be protected by him. Knowing for sure that he really loved her, that what had seemed too good to be true was not fantasy but reality, made the terrible darkness she lived with roll away. She felt as if a burden had been lifted from her soul, and that she was forgiven, cleansed. 'I want your child . . . I never want to lose you, I love you.'

They embraced, broke away from each other, laughed, kissed and kissed again. For the first time in years, she was truly happy, and it was a blissful state, a feeling she had believed she would never be allowed to know or enjoy. Leaning back against him, curled beside him, she whispered, 'I am so happy . . .'

Lorraine left at seven, having stayed the night with Burton, and as she walked Tiger in the early morning, the smile never left her lips. She went home, fed the dog, showered and changed for the office. Just as she was leaving she noticed the light on her answerphone blinking. She pressed the button, but could hardly make out what the caller was saying. He was sobbing. She knew, though, that something terrible had happened. As the message continued, and it became clear what it was, she had to sit down.

Lorraine drove to Decker's home in Ashcroft Avenue as though on automatic pilot. The neat bungalow was in a row of equally well-kept small houses, and was painted a smart navy blue with the windows, doors and eaves picked out in white. Lorraine parked on San Vincente, fed the meter, and walked, in a mechanical, non-aware state, up the hand-laid brick steps to the house. The door opened. 'Come in.' Adam Elliot was wearing a terrycloth robe, and his face was ashen, his eyes red from weeping. Lorraine said nothing as he led her down the hallway, every inch of wall space filled with paintings, prints, photographs and pieces of tribal and primitive art, which, she guessed, had been picked up on travels abroad. She could feel the woven coir matting beneath her shoes, and noticed that it was strangely dark. All the blinds and shutters in the house were drawn.

The kitchen was a blaze of colour, or would have been in normal light, as tangerine paint had been added

279

in a vibrant drag effect over yellow walls. Well-tended ferns of all sizes and shapes and a little lemon tree were displayed in polished copper planters, which Lorraine recognized with a pang as the same as the one Decker had bought for the office. She sat at a table and Elliot poured her coffee. Her hand shook as she lifted the china cup to her lips. He sat opposite, lighting a cigarette, then looked at the stub. 'I gave up two years ago but I've smoked two packs since last night.'

The coffee tasted bitter, but stirred Lorraine into life. 'How did it happen?'

There was a long pause, then Elliot explained what had happened. 'I'm so sorry,' she said quietly.

There was another terrible pause. Elliot made no effort to check the tears that ran down the dark stubble on his face. 'I loved him so much.' The words were barely audible. 'I just don't see how I can go on without him.'

Lorraine stayed for almost an hour with Decker's lover, saying little, but listening to him and looking at the photo albums he showed her of how they had met and their life together. She remained calm, saying what she hoped were the right things, but Adam wasn't really listening – he just needed to talk. He said the same things over and over again. Eventually he gave her three plastic carrier bags of things he had taken from the car, including Decker's notebook and the catalogues of paintings.

She sat in her car, still in a state of shock, then drove to her office. Everything seemed unnaturally clear and bright – the doorman, the bell-boy, the décor in the lobby, the elevator. It was as if she was seeing everything for the first time, as if she had never been there before. She placed the plastic bags Adam had given her on

Decker's desk and walked into her own office, shut the door and hung up her jacket.

It was deathly quiet, and there was no smell of fresh coffee. Lorraine bowed her head.

'Oh, Deck, I'm going to miss you so much.'

The coroner determined that death had been accidental, a conclusion consistent with the medical evidence. The speedometer of Decker's car had remained stuck at the speed he had been doing – eighty-five miles per hour. The body was cremated at Forest Lawn, and the ashes placed in a niche after a short ceremony attended by many of Decker's relatives and friends. Lorraine stood at the back of the crowd, not knowing anyone, and she, too, wept.

On the way home she bought herself a bunch of exuberant red gladioli to remember Decker, and sat with Tiger, finding him a comfort. She knew the dog would miss Decker too – the walks, and the special dinners concocted from leftovers that Decker had brought to the office. It never even occurred to Lorraine that Decker's death might have been connected to her or to the line of enquiry he was working on when he died.

In the early afternoon, Jake called to ask about the funeral, and to check that Lorraine was all right. They arranged to meet after eight as he had a lot of work to catch up on. She took Tiger for a walk, but it was still only four thirty when she returned. She tidied the sitting room and arranged her flowers but time seemed to stand still. She turned on the TV but was restless and couldn't concentrate. She began to think over the Feinstein case. She started a list of relevant facts – the art fraud, the secret bank accounts, then wrote 'Sonja Nathan', and underlined the name.

Sonja Nathan was now the main beneficiary under Harry Nathan's will: should Lorraine still make the trip to see her?

Without her notes and files, Lorraine tried to recall all the intricacies of the case. No one else had been charged with Nathan's murder and the police investigation was closed. What if someone had engineered everything so things would end up that way? Could Raymond Vallance have been that clever? How could he have planned to get access to the large sums of money Feinstein was sure Nathan had to have stashed somewhere? She wrote down his name on the list. Before she could make any real progress on suspects, though, she had to trace Nathan's missing haul. Then she could work backwards.

The entryphone buzzer made her heart pound, but Tiger barked furiously, then wagged his tail. It was Jake, and just seeing him put the investigation into the background.

'Hi, I'm sorry. I'm later than I said. There's been a double homicide over at Burbank.' He looked tired, and Lorraine took his jacket from him, told him to sit on the sofa and put his feet up. 'This bastard broke into an apartment, held the woman hostage, demanded details of the safe and their cash cards, then beat the hell out of her when she said she couldn't remember. Then her husband came home with their daughter, and he shot them both at point blank range.' He scratched his head, and gave a helpless gesture. 'Kid was only fifteen years old. I mean, how the hell do you live with that, seeing

282

it? And there was nothing in the safe, just papers – her husband never kept any valuables at the house.' He sighed and leaned back on the cushions. 'Sorry to lay it on you, but . . . it hasn't been a good day.'

'That's okay. You want me to get some wine? I can run down to the liquor store. Or maybe some whisky. What do you feel like?'

He reached out for her, and drew her close. 'I feel like lying next to my woman.'

She kissed him, and told him to take a shower, then get into bed. He looked at her, and traced her face with his hand. 'I'd like that . . .'

By the time she joined him in the bedroom he was fast asleep. He was naked, vulnerable, hadn't even pulled the duvet over himself, and she loved him. The fact that he had come to her, in a way needing her, touched her deeply.

'I love you,' she whispered.

Lorraine couldn't stop thinking about Decker. She had lain awake beside Jake for a while, then slipped from the bed to return to her notes, only getting to bed after midnight. Tiger was already flat out nose to nose with Jake, and he grunted when she got into bed. Jake stirred and lifted his arm for her to snuggle close, and then went back to sleep.

She had begun to work out the next stage of the Feinstein inquiry. She would need someone to take care of Tiger for a night, as she had decided that the next day she would fly to New York, get the Jitney bus to East Hampton, and stay overnight, as Decker had suggested, at the Maidstone Arms. She would then arrange to talk to Sonja Nathan, and could be back in LA the following afternoon. There was something else she wanted to talk about with Jake, and she was going to do it first thing in the morning before she left. She was going to tell him that when this Feinstein case was finished, so was Page Investigations. Not that he had asked her to contemplate giving up her business – it was something *she* wanted. It might look like a fast U-turn on her part – one moment striving to make the agency work, the next letting go of it – but she knew she was getting her priorities right. More than anything else, she wanted to marry Jake, and to have his child. She felt that a new phase of her life had begun.

The alarm clock rang shrilly, and Jake shot up, while Tiger hurled himself off the bed, barking. Lorraine felt as if a heavy weight was pressing her head onto the pillow.

'What time is it?' she groaned.

'Seven, and I'll have to get going.' He was already stepping into the shower.

Lorraine pulled on a robe and went into the kitchen. She had a terrible headache, the kind that hung just behind the eyes, so she took two aspirin and felt them lodge firmly in her gut; now she had indigestion too, and Tiger's constant barking at the clattering of neighbours made her head worse.

She squeezed some fresh orange juice, and brought out muesli and cereal. Jake was shaved, dressed and ready to leave. He drank only the juice, saying he'd send someone out for a sandwich. He kept looking at his watch, checking his pockets for car keys and wallet, and then bent down to kiss her. 'I'll call you.'

She hurried after him. 'Is there any way you could take care of Tiger, just for today and tomorrow?'

'What?'

'I need someone to look after him, I've got to go to New York.'

He stopped at the front door, sighed and looked at his watch. 'Will you be back this evening? I can come by later and walk him and feed him.'

'Well, I'd planned on staying over.'

'Why didn't you mention this last night?'

'You were flat out. Look, forget it, I'll find someone else. No problem.'

'You sure?'

'Yes, I'm sure. Go on – you don't want to be late.'

He stared at her, then looked away with a sigh. 'No, I don't, and I can't take him to the station with me, can I? Look, I'll call you. What time will you be leaving?'

'That depends. I might not go until later. I haven't arranged my flight or anything.'

'Who are you going to see?'

'Mrs Nathan,' she said, pouring coffee and turning to him with the cup in her hand. 'There's one left, the first wife.'

He looked at his watch again and Lorraine could see him hesitate before he crossed to her. 'I love you, and I'm sorry about not taking Tiger off your hands. Next time, huh?'

'Yep, next time. Talk to you later.'

Lorraine had showered, changed and washed her hair, but her head still throbbed, and the aspirin refused to be dislodged from her gullet. When she got to the office she took some antacid and gulped down some water.

She had considered the Hispanic family in the apartment below hers – and rejected it – as a temporary home for Tiger, and she felt depressed. She had so few friends, and without Rosie and Bill Rooney around, there had only been Decker left. She started thinking that maybe there was no reason to rush off to the Hamptons – Sonja Nathan might not even be there. But when Lorraine called, someone with rather a nice deep voice said he would ask Mrs Nathan to return her call. Soon afterwards her phone rang and Sonja Nathan was on the line.

Lorraine explained that she would like to meet Sonja to discuss a few things in connection with her former husband's estate.

'Are you with the insurance companies?' Sonja asked.

Lorraine told her that she was working for Feinstein and Sonja suggested, without asking any more questions, that Lorraine had better come to the Hamptons right away as she was planning to go to Europe. 'I can be with you Thursday morning,' Lorraine said, in two days' time.

'Fine, I'll see you then, about ten o'clock. You have the address?'

'Yes, I look forward to seeing you.'

Lorraine arranged a flight for noon the next day, booked into the hotel, and was just about to sort through all the art catalogues that Decker's boyfriend had left when Tiger barked. Lorraine walked out into the reception area.

'It's me,' said a high-pitched voice.

'Tiger, sit. Who?'

'It's Rosie, for Chrissakes. Who the hell do you think it is?'

Lorraine ran to the door, shrieking, 'Rosie, *Rosie,* ROSIE!'

Rosie was plumper, but tanned and sporting a new hair-style. The frizzy curls had been 'straightened', and the colour had also been toned down and was no longer quite such a vivid red. For a moment neither could speak, they were so pleased to see each other. Lorraine had missed her one true friend, and burst into tears. Rosie already had tears streaming down her cheeks. They had climbed together out of a dark past and now Rosie had found the love she craved, found a future. She wished all that she had for Lorraine too; then her happiness would be complete.

'You look fabulous,' Lorraine said, holding her friend at arm's length. She sniffed back the tears and wiped her cheeks with the palm of her hand. 'I dunno why I'm crying.'

Rosie kissed her again. She had an array of gifts for Lorraine in carrier bags and boxes that she had dropped as soon as the door had opened.

'Any chance of some coffee? I'm dying for a cup,' Rosie said, collecting her things and stacking them on the coffee table, before she went over to a rather bemused Tiger. He sat as she rubbed his big head. He didn't like many people to fondle him but as Lorraine joined in he accepted it.

'He's changed so much, Rosie. I don't know what I'd do without him now.' Lorraine nuzzled him and he rolled over legs in the air as she scratched his belly.

'My God, he's enormous,' Rosie said. 'He looks like a different dog altogether!' Tiger's coat looked glossy and clean and as he grunted with satisfaction, he looked as if he was smiling. 'Nick'd be happy to see him like this,' she said softly.

'Yeah, Nick would be proud of him – well, most of the time.' She gave Tiger a last tickle and stood up.

'So, this is the workplace huh?' Rosie said.

Lorraine opened her arms wide. 'This is Page Investigations, Rosie.'

They went on a tour of the office. Rosie said all the right things, then watched as Lorraine opened her presents like a child – scarves, beads and hair-bands, a watch and bracelet, souvenir tea towels, baseball caps and cut glass.

Then the two women decided to have lunch together at a small local bistro, where Rosie, as usual, ate ravenously, ordering a supposedly healthy sauté of zucchini and mushrooms dripping with olive oil. Lorraine had a small portion of fettuccini. She was regaled with stories about the trip and there were six wallets of photographs, showing the honeymooners arm in arm and hand in hand in all the various countries they had visited.

Rosie insisted she see the new apartment next, so they collected Tiger, closed the office and piled into Lorraine's jeep. Rosie was impressed with it and even more so when she heard about the Mercedes. 'Well, it's your money and you could always get run over by a car tomorrow, so live for today,' but she sounded worried, or maybe a little envious.

After the tour of the apartment, where Rosie enthused about every curtain, every piece of furniture, they settled back to more gossip. Rosie's happiness shone in her face, and through the affectionate, funny stories she kept telling about big Bill. It made Lorraine reach over and clasp her hand. 'I'm so glad it's worked out for you two, you seem so well suited.'

Rosie folded her hands over her tummy. 'Now, you've heard all my news – you start now.'

'I'm going to get married.'

Rosie's jaw dropped and then the tears started. She hugged Lorraine and wanted to call Bill and tell him, but Lorraine said she wanted to tell him herself. He might even know her new boyfriend, Lieutenant Jake Burton. Rosie's jaw dropped still further. 'A cop?'

'A chief of detectives, Rosie!'

'Jesus. That is incredible!'

Lorraine smiled. 'Yes, it is. I guess I'm happy too. But I'm also scared to death – that it might all blow up in my face. So, please don't say anything to Bill, not yet, and . . . you mind if we change the subject?'

'Sure,' Rosie said, aching to know every single detail. But Lorraine had that set expression on her face so she asked instead what her friend was working on. She listened as Lorraine, trying not to sound too emotional, told her first about Decker. Then she moved on to her case. 'It's the Harry Nathan murder. I was hired by his wife, Cindy, but she committed suicide.' Lorraine explained briefly how Cindy had contacted her, then lit a cigarette, inhaled deeply and her mood changed. Rosie could feel her tension but she said nothing, just waited, like in the old days. She had learned never to push for information from Lorraine – she'd tell you what she wanted you to know and nothing more.

Lorraine took another deep drag of the cigarette, letting the smoke drift from her mouth. 'You ever heard of a movie star called Raymond Vallance?'

'Yeah, you know me and movies. He used to be fantastic-looking. Is he involved in your investigation?'

They both jumped when the entryphone buzzed and it took Lorraine a while to drag Tiger away from the front door. Standing on the step was a sheepish Bill Rooney, holding a faded bunch of flowers.

'Hi, how you doing, eh?' he said, and squeezed Lorraine so hard against his expansive chest that she gasped for breath.

Lorraine gave him a tour of the apartment while Rosie made a fresh pot of coffee. Rooney nodded and congratulated Lorraine on her taste but she knew he must have had a few drinks because he muttered to himself as he followed her from room to room, telling her that now he liked putting his feet up and watching football on the TV and the best part was Rosie bringing him his dinner on a tray. 'I've done enough travelling, for a while,' he said, and then nudged Lorraine like a naughty schoolboy. 'Don't repeat that. God knows where she's planning on going next, but me, I've gone soft. TV, football, a home-cooked meal and fast asleep by eleven. Lovely!'

Lorraine found it sad that he seemed to need to repeat himself. He had got even fatter and his bulk made the wide four-seater sofa in the lounge seem small. He seemed ill at ease, knowing that Rosie was annoyed with him for intruding on her evening.

Rosie had the coffee ready and waiting now. She'd even found some biscuits and laid them out on a silver plate – solid silver, she had noticed. As she poured the coffee, there was a strange, uneasy silence that continued until Rosie banged down the coffee pot and nudged Rooney. 'Before you barged in and interrupted us, Lorraine was just telling me about this case she's working on. Do you remember a movie star called Raymond Vallance?'

'No,' Rooney said, selecting a biscuit.

'Tell him, Lorraine,' Rosie said, settling back on the sofa beside her husband. The pair sat riveted as Lorraine filled them in on the case. She was concise but made sure she left nothing out – except the threats on her life. She didn't want to worry her friends. When the silence fell again, it was like old times. Rooney was leaning back, eyes closed, but not sleeping even though it was way past eleven. He was 'thinking', and so was Rosie, twisting a strand of hair round and round in her fingers.

'Well, you got all the facts, almost.' Lorraine looked at Rooney, wanting him to give her the answer she couldn't put her finger on. His eyes opened, but he shook his head, pulled himself onto his feet and stuffed his hands into his pockets.

Rosie broke the silence. 'I think it's Vallance. He, out of everyone, had the most to lose, am I right? Do you think it's him, Bill?' Rosie was excited, her cheeks flushed: from what Lorraine had told them, everything pointed to the actor.

Rooney still said nothing. Lorraine was fascinated because he had suddenly become his old self: Rooney the cop. He was acting the way he used to, not wanting to give away too much, not wanting to make a mistake by jumping the gun, staring at the wall, not meeting Lorraine's eyes. Finally, his hands digging deeper into his pockets, the loose change jangling as he turned a coin in his fingers, he said, 'I think there's a hidden agenda. Christ only knows what it is, but there's something. It may even be staring you in the face, sweetheart.'

'Is that it?' Rosie blurted out.

Rooney's eyes now met Lorraine's, a steady rather unnerving gaze. He touched her hand. 'I'll call you, all right? Let me sleep on this.' Then he caught Rosie's hand. 'We should go, darlin', it's late.' There was a firmness in his voice and Rosie didn't argue. They said their goodbyes, waving from the car, blowing kisses to Lorraine by the open window, watching them drive away. She didn't wave, she just stood, arms folded.

Rosie took a sidelong look at her husband. She had been about to tell him about the new man in Lorraine's life when he swerved to the side of the road and pulled on the handbrake like his life depended on it.

'What happened? I didn't see anything,' Rosie said, looking back to the road.

'I just needed to think,' he said in a gruff voice that made him sound like a stranger. He had known Lorraine for a long, long time. He knew her heartbreak and had witnessed her pain. He had been disgusted by her spiral into the gutter and would never have believed she would climb back, just as he would have laughed if someone had said he would end up not only working alongside her, but admiring and loving her.

'I know her, Rosie, God help me for saying this, but I have known her when she was not worth the shit on my shoe. I have seen her humiliated and heartbroken. She's been beaten within an inch of her life and I've picked her up out of stinking, garbage-strewn gutters.'

'Is all this going someplace?' Rosie asked, staring out of the car window rather than looking at her husband. He was unapproachable, made her feel uneasy, and she almost cringed back from him when he hit the steering wheel with the flat of his hand, hit it so hard the car rocked.

'Yes, it's fucking going somewhere, for Chrissakes. I just needed to work it through, to think about it, because she was fucking hiding something. She wasn't telling us the truth.'

'Why would she lie?' Rosie said, easing round to look at him.

'I know her so well, Rosie.' He ran his finger round his collar: he was sweating.

'Yeah, you said, and so do I. We both know her pretty well, I'd say.' She rolled down the window, feeling hot herself.

'Rosie, I have never seen fear in that woman's face, no matter what she has been through, not once, not ever. I saw it tonight. She tried to hide it but I know she's in trouble and I'm afraid for her.'

CHAPTER 13

NEXT MORNING, Lorraine leaped back into action: her flight was at noon, and Rosie's visit had taken up virtually all of the previous day. Jake had called and said that as he happened to be off duty, he would like to see her and drive her to the airport, and that today he could take Tiger for her.

Lorraine had packed an overnight bag, changed and tidied the apartment, and was now becoming impatient, afraid she would miss her plane. He was late, only arriving at ten thirty. In the car, she gave him instructions about Tiger, plus Rosie and Bill's telephone number in case the dog was in the way, or she had to stay longer in the Hamptons than she expected. 'You think you might?' he asked, as they hurried through the terminal building.

'No, but you never know, just covering all the options,' Lorraine said. It had crossed her mind that the legacy to Sonja Nathan would not take effect until midnight the following night, and she wondered whether the next forty-eight hours might be more eventful than she was anticipating – but there was no point in worrying him. She handed over her ticket to a stewardess, who said that the flight was already boarding and she should go straight to the gate.

Jake kissed her, and Tiger almost choked himself on his lead as he tried to follow her into the departure lounge. Lorraine walked away, but then had an urge to turn back, so strong she couldn't resist it. Jake was still standing there, and Tiger still straining at his lead. Jake waved, mouthed that he loved her, and their eyes locked. She wanted to run back to him, stay with him, but she forced a smile and hurried out of sight.

The duration of the flight was only five hours, but with the time difference between the west coast and the east, they wouldn't arrive until almost eight thirty in the evening. Lorraine had been in such a hurry she hadn't brought any books or magazines, so she read the in-flight journal over dinner, and slept for the rest of the flight. After the plane had landed and she had retrieved her bag, she caught a taxi to Queens and waited for the last Jitney bus to the Hamptons.

It was right on time at nine fifty, and the driver smiled pleasantly as he stowed her bag in the hold, then helped her up the steps into the cool, air-conditioned interior. She chose one of the wide, comfortable seats midway up the aisle, next to the tinted windows – this was no ordinary bus, and the occupants were not ordinary people, either arty or glamorous: one woman even climbed on board with two Pekinese and a chauffeur.

Lorraine looked out of the window for a while, but then closed her eyes, not sleeping, just wrapped in daydreams about Jake, still hardly able to believe it was all true. He did love her – she had seen it at the airport. In some way if he had turned and walked away before she had said her last goodbye, it would have been a bad omen, but he had waited, and the last thing she remembered was his smile, and that he had said he loved her.

Rosie was grimly washing a mass of arugula in the little farm-style kitchen of the apartment Rooney had shared with his first wife, putting together a big salad. She and Bill had both half-heartedly decided to diet.

'I hate this job,' Rooney moaned, emptying the dishwasher.

'So does everybody,' Rosie answered.

'Anyway,' he said, clattering the plates into the glass-fronted dresser, 'Jim Sharkey couldn't believe his ears. He kept on saying I had to have it wrong, it couldn't be Burton. Are you sure you got the name right?'

'How many Lieutenant Jake Burtons are there, for Chrissakes?' Rosie said, tossing the salad.

'They don't like him,' Rooney said, stacking more dishes.

'You mean Jim Sharkey doesn't,' Rosie said.

'No, Jim said the boys don't like him, said he's a real bastard. Everyone knows there's a bit of a trade that goes on with information – you know, a backhander here and there. Everybody knows that. We even dish dough out of our own pockets to some informers. I've done it, we've all done it, but he's watching them like a hawk.'

Rosie started to set the table. 'Well, that Jim Sharkey certainly had his hand out when we worked with him, didn't he? You remember, when we needed the lists of statements taken in connection with the Anna-Louise Caley murder. And he got a four-course dinner, beer, wine, and five hundred dollars on top of it.'

Rooney took the plastic cutlery basket out of the machine and banged the knives and forks into the dresser drawer. 'All I said was they think he's a tight ass.'

'You shouldn't have been asking questions, I never told you to do that. I said find out what he looks like. That's not the same as rapping with Jim Sharkey, is it?'

Rooney slammed the cupboard door shut, replaced the basket and closed the dishwasher.

'So, what does he look like?' she asked, hands on hips.

'I dunno. I never saw him, did I?'

Rosie pushed past Rooney to the fridge.

'Young? Old? Good-looking? Short? Tall? What kind of cop were you?'

Rooney slapped her behind. 'He's about fifty-five, five feet seven with a paunch, red face and bulbous nose, but . . . a lot of women think he's sexy.'

Rosie laughed at his description of himself, kissed his plump cheek, and they settled to their meal.

The Jitney bus made its way through Southampton, then Bridgehampton, with few passengers getting off and none getting on. The street-lights were turned on, and the little towns looked like some magical place that time had passed by, with old-world shops selling antiques and pine furniture on every corner, along with street markets and traders offering logs for sale.

They eventually arrived at East Hampton, and the bus drew up outside the Palm Hotel. Lorraine waited as the driver fetched her bag, and pointed out the Maidstone Arms Hotel, which was just across the street.

By the time she had unpacked and taken a shower it

was after one o'clock in the morning, and even though she felt hungry, she decided to go straight to bed.

Next morning, breakfast was served in the dining room, and Lorraine, dressed in a smart tan skirt, cream silk blouse, oyster tights and court shoes with a low Cuban heel, came down and sat in one of the Queen Anne chairs. She ordered scrambled eggs, brown toast and coffee, which was served promptly by an attractive blonde girl, who also presented Lorraine with the *New York Times*. When she had finished, Lorraine took a brisk walk along the main street. The shops were all elegant, and what prices she could see were expensive. Sight-seeing over, she returned to the hotel and ordered a taxi to take her to Sonja Nathan's address in an area known as the Springs. The same pretty blonde girl who had served breakfast was now acting as a receptionist. She handed Lorraine a street map and said she would order the taxi straight away.

Lorraine returned to her room, and put in a call to Jake. He wasn't at home, but when she called his office, she was told that he hadn't got in yet, so she went downstairs to wait for her cab. She watched some of the rather elderly guests coming down for late breakfast, everyone apparently talking about the weather – it had, as Lorraine heard a number of people say, turned into a lovely clear day.

'Mrs Page,' the blonde girl called, 'your taxi is here.'

Lorraine went out of Reception and turned down a narrow path that led into the car park, expecting a yellow cab but finding a gleaming limo. 'Mrs Page?' the driver enquired, doffing his cap.

Lorraine nodded, and gave Sonja Nathan's address. 'Is it far?' she asked.

'No, ma'am, nothing's too far round here. Be there in ten minutes.' They drove on in silence for four or five. 'Turned out a real nice day,' the driver said, smiling at Lorraine via the driving mirror. 'You from New York?'

'California.'

He spent the rest of the drive listing which movie star had bought which local residence, and was very proud to have driven Barbara Streisand, Paul Simon and Faye Dunaway. Suddenly he screeched to a halt, peered at a narrow gateway, marked with only a red mailbox, checked the number, then reversed about two hundred yards, stopped again, reversed again and turned into a narrow dirt-track drive.

'This is it,' he said, now concentrating on his driving, as the track was narrow, overhung with high hedges and brambles. He made his way slowly past yellow notices nailed to the trees stating NO SHOOTING and TRESPASSERS WILL BE PROSECUTED. The tall fir trees became more dense, and now there were big red notices: DRIVE SLOW – DEER. The driveway began to curve to the right, and there was yet another notice: TURTLES CROSSING.

They were crawling along now and Lorraine was finding the drive, which, she calculated, was at least two miles long, spookier by the minute.

'Does all this land belong to Mrs Nathan?'

'I guess so, but it's protected round here. This is an animal sanctuary.' He swerved to avoid a lump of rock. Suddenly the wilderness began to appear more cultivated, and the drive widened into a tree-lined circle. Lorraine got out of the car to see a huge outdoor swimming pool, surrounded by a fence built of thick timber slabs, its margins ablaze with brilliantly coloured flowers.

The sun beat down, giving a clean dry heat, completely different from the fug of LA. She paid the driver, who asked if she would be needing him later. She said she would call.

The shingled, wood-frame house looked small, vulnerable and unoccupied, with both garage doors shut. Lorraine looked again at the garden and knew, by the flourishing, sweet-scented borders and beautiful conifers, that the garden was lovingly cared for. She tilted her head to the sun, her eyes still closed, then opened them rapidly as she thought she heard someone call. She listened, but hearing nothing more, she set off up the front steps, whose shallow treads were made of slabs of wood like stone.

The screen door was shut, as was the inner door. The bell did not work, so she tapped and waited, then knocked a little louder. The gravel crunched at the side of the house, and Lorraine turned sharply to see a tall, suntanned man with pepper and salt hair, who seemed almost as shocked to see Lorraine as she was to see him. 'I'm looking for Mrs Nathan,' she said.

'Ah! She's out in the studio. Wait a second, this'll rouse her. It's at the back of the house.' He disappeared, and Lorraine heard what sounded like a ship's bell being rung.

'She'll be right with you.'

Lorraine smiled.

'When she starts working, she's in a world of her own. We're meant to be going to a deer meeting in town tonight if I can drag her away.'

The main door of the house opened, and the tall

woman Lorraine had seen at the funeral appeared, raising one of her hands, deeply tanned with long, strong fingers and blunt-cut nails, to pull her strange white hair loose from a band which held it scraped back. She was less glamorously dressed today, in an old pair of chino pants and a deep blue linen shirt, but her intense, slightly cool presence was just as arresting.

'Mrs Page?'

'Yes, I'm sorry if I disturbed you. Were you working?'

'Oh, that's okay. I was just packing something,' Sonja Nathan said, with a taut smile.

Lorraine walked up the steps and extended her hand. 'It's very nice to meet you properly. Thank you for agreeing to see me and, by the way, it's Lorraine.'

'It's a pleasure,' the older woman said, with the same quick smile, no more than a social reflex. Her eyes, Lorraine saw at close quarters, were grey-green and her gaze had a curious quality of restless abstraction, like a sea, Lorraine thought, a cold northern sea. She noticed, too, that Sonja Nathan did not invite her to call her by her first name, though perhaps that was down to pre-occupation rather than hauteur.

'Do come in,' Sonja Nathan said, standing back to usher Lorraine into the house.

As she walked inside Lorraine gasped: nothing could have prepared her for the view. The house had floor-to-ceiling windows on all four sides, like complete walls of glass, and outside, drawing her in like a glorious living painting, was a vista of the most breathtaking seascape. 'A woman from LA came here a few days ago. She called it awesome. Tiresome word, but it does describe it.'

Sonja led Lorraine down a flight of stairs and into a spacious kitchen with a wood and brick fireplace. The

301

view seemed less spectacular from here than it did from upstairs, but still drew attention.

'Now, what would you like to drink?' Sonja said, opening the fridge.

'Anything cool, really – water, juice, Coke.'

Sonja produced a can of Coke, a tall glass and ice from the dispenser. She poured some coffee from a percolator for herself, not seeming to notice that it looked cold, tarry and unappetizing.

'You're working for Mr Feinstein, did you say?' Sonja said, moving towards the doors. 'Let's sit outside.' Lorraine followed her out onto the veranda. 'I must say, I never much cared for Feinstein,' she continued.

'Well, I imagine he'll be becoming something of a fixture in your life for the next few months at least – the estate is complex, he says.'

Sonja Nathan immediately detected Lorraine's attempt to work the conversation round to her having inherited all her ex-husband's property, and clearly was not disposed to play ball. 'So it is. What exactly did Feinstein tell you to ask me?'

'Oh, he didn't send me here, exactly. He's retained me to investigate an art fraud, which it seems Harry and Kendall were pulling.' Sonja Nathan did not react, but the restless movements of her green eyes stopped, and her gaze became opaque. 'It seems they sold genuine canvases then delivered fakes. Feinstein got stung – as did a lot of other people who haven't tumbled to it yet.'

'That is an extraordinarily audacious piece of dishonesty,' Sonja said. 'They might be found out at any time if the owner had the painting valued or sold it again, or if someone who could tell wheat from chaff just happened to come to the house.'

'I was wondering, Mrs Nathan, whether you might have fallen into that category,' Lorraine said. 'Did you go to Harry Nathan's house recently? I don't suppose you noticed anything about the paintings at any time? If I were to give you a list of the paintings, would you tell me if you ever recall seeing them at the house?'

Lorraine went back inside to find her briefcase, which she had left in the hallway. She took a quick look around the room as she picked it up: there were a number of large canvases, some carvings, wonderful pottery and antique tables. Nothing matched, but as an ensemble they worked well.

When she returned to Sonja she gave her the list, which Sonja glanced at and handed back. 'I never went there,' she said evenly. 'I haven't set foot in the house since I left LA seven years ago.'

'Do you ever go back to LA?' Lorraine asked.

'Oh, yes,' Sonja said lightly. 'I still have friends there. And the city, of course, was important to me at one time.' She got up, looking out over the woods and water.

'I've seen pictures of the work you did there – it's very powerful,' Lorraine said. 'Have you been back recently except for Harry's funeral?'

Sonja looked her straight in the eye. 'I haven't been there other than then for a year, and I wasn't in LA the day Harry was killed, if that's what you mean.' There was a moment's pause, and Lorraine felt that it was almost as if the other woman were defying her to prove anything different.

'Feinstein is concerned only to make good his own losses, but it affects you too, of course,' Lorraine went on, resisting the other woman's efforts to close the subject. 'I mean financially. Harry Nathan apparently pulled the same scam twice. He had the originals in the house, then switched them again, we think to cut out Kendall. The original art at the house was Nathan's major asset. If we can't recover it, the value of the estate, which I believe now comes to you, is greatly reduced.'

Sonja shrugged, pushing back with her arms to propel herself off the rails of the verandah. 'I never expected to inherit a penny of Harry's and I couldn't care less if I don't.'

'Sonja.' A deep voice spoke suddenly from inside the kitchen, and Lorraine thought she detected in it a note of warning. The man she had met earlier came out to them; he had clearly heard every word of what Sonja had just said.

'I'm going to take the kayak out for an hour,' he went on. 'I'll be back in time for lunch.'

'Fine,' Sonja said, glancing at him only briefly. 'You be careful now, Arthur dear.'

Lorraine watched the couple with interest as Arthur spoke again, apparently casually. 'You too, sweetheart.' She did not meet his eye. 'Goodbye, Mrs Page. I imagine you may be gone by the time I get back.' He spoke courteously, but both Lorraine and Sonja understood his message. Lorraine was conscious of a certain relaxation in the other woman once they heard him leave the house.

'Does Arthur . . . have a problem with Harry's having left you so much money?' Lorraine asked, with bold naturalness, assuming an intimacy with Sonja she knew didn't exist. She was surprised when Sonja answered equally directly.

'He has a problem with Harry. It's just jealousy, I guess, that I shared so much of my life with Harry, that we were something to one another that Arthur and I cannot be. It's just the way life is. One can't go back. Can I get you another drink?'

Sonja had picked up the empty glass before Lorraine had time to say anything and disappeared into the kitchen with her own untouched coffee: it was clear she wanted an excuse to absent herself for a few moments. Lorraine would have liked a closer look at the rest of the house, while Sonja clattered with the ice-dispenser in the kitchen, but it was the studio she most wanted to see, and now that she had mentioned the art fraud, she could hardly ask to see it without as good as announcing to Sonja that she suspected her. But did she suspect her? The woman didn't seem interested enough in money to commit such a crime – but, on the other hand, there was something about her that made one feel that death was near her.

However, by the time she came back with a tray, Sonja had readjusted her manner.

'How well did you know Raymond Vallance?' Lorraine ventured.

Sonja snorted with laughter as she handed Lorraine another tall glass of Coke. 'Raymond Vallance was an albatross round Harry's neck.' For all her amusement, there was venom in her voice. 'He destroyed any talent Harry might have had, convincing him that all those disgusting frat-party movies he made were worth a good goddamn. Any merit there was in that whole period of Harry's career he drew from me. That's where my own creativity went – he sucked it out of me and put it into his own work.'

'I'm sure,' Lorraine agreed. Vallance and Sonja were

like a pair of bookends, she thought, perfectly matched in their unshakeable belief that the other had been Nathan's evil genius and they themselves the true muse.

'Raymond never forgave Harry for marrying me, needing me more than he needed him,' Sonja went on, well into her stride now in ripping the ageing matinée idol apart. 'He hated both of us, in a way, though he tried to get me into bed, of course. I thought, talk about obvious, darling, if you can't be with the one you love, love the one *he*'s with.'

Lorraine smiled: Sonja was no slouch in the bitching department. She said, 'He had something similar going with Cindy, it seems.'

'Doesn't surprise me,' Sonja said. 'Poor kid – I never met her except at the funeral, though, of course, I saw pictures.'

'I don't suppose she ever wrote to you,' Lorraine asked casually.

Sonja looked at her with interest. 'Yes, she did – pages and pages. I knew why she wrote – she was embarrassed about calling, never thought she was entitled to five minutes of anybody's time. Sometimes I wish I'd given her a little more ... I don't know, time, assistance.' There was real sadness and self-blame in Sonja's voice.

'You never felt jealous of Cindy?' Lorraine asked gently.

'Not really,' Sonja said. 'Harry wasn't the same person I had known by the time he married her. Vallance and ... and Kendall had carved him up between them by the time Cindy got him. He was no longer a man ... but, then, Kendall was never a person at all.'

'What do you mean?' Lorraine had now dropped all pretence of confining her questions to the art fraud: she was trying to find out who murdered Harry Nathan, and wondered whether the killer might be sitting right in front of her.

'Kendall was similar to Harry in a way. There was something central missing from both of them,' Sonja said, with some deliberation. Lorraine had the impression she was delivering verdicts she had considered for years. 'Kendall, however, was full of insecurity, or she was to start with, whereas I don't think Harry ever had a self-critical thought in his life. Kendall came into our lives when our relationship was hitting a transition. Harry had been eating me to keep himself alive and fuel his work for years. Perhaps if we had had children it would have been different, but ... I let him do it. I suppose it took me quite a while to grow up.' Sonja gave another wry smile. 'Then I wanted to live my own life and create for myself, and Harry would have had to find some reason to be with me other than what ... he could consume of me. Obviously that was difficult for him. Harry never liked to do anything that was difficult.'

Sonja had got up again, part of her seeming barely conscious of Lorraine, though another part of her, Lorraine somehow knew, had been waiting for years for an anonymous listener – a confessor. 'I don't really think Kendall set out to destroy our marriage. She loved me first, if you like. She had nothing, was nothing, knew how to be nothing when I met her.' She was staring out to sea, as though hypnotized, her gaze drawn to the horizon like a compass needle to the north. A moment later, though, her voice seemed more normal as she went on. 'As I said earlier, to try to repeat the past is a sort of death.'

'But Harry must have loved you, even at the end,'

Lorraine said, conscious that she was perhaps pushing the other woman into deep water. 'You were the constant in his life.'

Sonja shook her head. 'Vallance was the constant. I realize that now. He was there before me and he was there after me.'

'But Harry left Vallance nothing in the will. He must have wanted to recognize something in leaving the entire property to you.'

'It comes to me only by default,' Sonja said. 'Neither he nor I could ever have predicted that both Kendall and Cindy would drop dead.' She turned round. 'And, of course, who knows? I might drop dead. I have another day to go, don't I?' There was a strange, hunted look in the back of her cat's eyes that chilled Lorraine, as if she were waiting for an executioner to arrive, for an axe to fall.

Lorraine realized that she had been sitting very still, barely blinking. She made herself move now, swirling the ice in her glass as though to chase away ghosts with the sound. 'I think that's correct – but you're most unlikely to die.'

'Well,' Sonja said, and again Lorraine had the sense that she was listening to the expression of thoughts that had been considered and rearranged many times, 'there is life and life. Or, rather, there is life and there is existence without dignity, which one betrays oneself to endure. I used to think that there was some kind of other dignity in endurance, but it is better to be dead than betrayed, I think now.' She had been talking rapidly and fell silent just as suddenly, then turned back to the sea again.

308

'Who do you think killed Harry Nathan?' Lorraine found herself asking, without really meaning to do so, as though it were the only chance she would ever have.

'Harry Nathan killed himself,' Sonja said, her voice low, resonant, beautiful. 'He became a thing that someone would destroy.'

The screen door banged at the front of the house, and Sonja started and looked round. 'Arthur,' she said, with a smile. 'He doesn't trust me alone for too long.'

No wonder, Lorraine thought, glancing at her watch. He hadn't been gone long and Sonja was already circling round the subjects of killing and death.

Sonja walked back into the kitchen and called upstairs, 'We're down here, Arthur.'

Did she want to warn him that she wasn't alone? Lorraine wondered.

The big man lost no time in joining them and Lorraine saw his eyes go immediately to Sonja, as though trying to gauge her mood. 'Mrs Page, how nice you're still here,' he said, with a polite smile. 'I hope you don't mind if I join you.'

'Not at all,' she said. He sat down beside her and Sonja disappeared inside, murmuring that she would bring out some wine. 'Do you work out here?' she asked, pretending to be making small-talk but, in fact, trying to place the man, as he well knew.

'Yes,' he said. 'I do, on and off.'

'Are you a writer?' She knew she sounded pushy now but she didn't care: it was the only way she could do her job.

'No,' he said slowly. 'I'm a painter.'

Well, that was interesting, Lorraine thought.

'I don't suppose I'm allowed to see any of your work,' she said, with a fake, girlish laugh she suspected didn't fool him for a minute.

'I'm sorry, I've just packed virtually all of what I have out here for a show,' he said evenly, as Sonja came back with glasses and a bottle. What a surprise, Lorraine thought, but decided to have one last try at getting into the studio.

'I'd love to see any of your work before I go, Mrs Nathan,' she said, 'Though, of course, I know all artists are very private.'

'I'm afraid even I wasn't allowed to see the last thing Sonja did,' Arthur said. 'She kept me right out of the studio for a month. Fortunately I have another room at the top of the house.'

'Do you work mainly to commissions, or speculatively?' Lorraine asked Sonja.

'I rarely work to commission – or, at least, not to an exact commission,' Sonja answered, carefully opening the bottle. 'This last piece is to open a series of shows – a women's thing, in the new gallery in Berlin. They indicated a few months ago that they would appreciate it if I had something new, but it was up to me what it was.'

'And what will you do next?' Lorraine said, conscious that she sounded like some vapid celebrity interviewer. 'Do you have any plans, or will you just wait and see what comes?'

'I have stopped working,' Sonja said, in an odd, unnatural tone. 'That part of my life is over.' Suddenly she gave a light, sweet laugh. 'It went on far too long.'

'I'll drive you back into town, Mrs Page,' Arthur said quickly. 'I think you said you had to go.'

'Arthur!' Sonja said, now laughing as though she

hadn't a care in the world. 'That's not very hospitable –
I've just opened the wine.'

'No, I really must be getting back – and, in any case,
I'm sorry, I don't drink,' Lorraine said, getting up.
'Thank you so much for your time – and it's been
wonderful to meet you.'

'Goodbye,' Sonja said simply, with a slow, almost
childlike smile.

Arthur led Lorraine out to an old Blazer jeep, and
began to make determined small-talk as they drove the
few miles into town.

'Will you be returning to New York tomorrow or
staying over?' he said, as they pulled into the Maidstone
Arms car park.

'I haven't decided,' Lorraine said. 'I may stay another
night.'

'It's just that if you were thinking of seeing Sonja
again, we do have to pack to go to Europe and Sonja
needs to prepare for Berlin – she's expected to make a
speech and she needs to concentrate on that.' It was
more than apparent that he was trying to deter Lorraine
from making any further visits.

'She's a very unusual woman,' Lorraine said, unable
to resist the temptation to fish just a little.

'She certainly is,' Arthur said carefully, pulling up.
'I'm sorry if I seemed rude, hustling you away, Mrs Page,
but the truth is, Sonja is not quite . . . herself at the
moment. You know that she and Harry parted on bad
terms, and she pretends that his death didn't touch her –
but, of course, that's not true. She has been very shaken.
She cared deeply about him, and, God knows, sometimes
I think he was the only man she ever loved.'

Lorraine was surprised at this personal and clearly

311

heartfelt revelation. She realized that Arthur did not dislike her, he was merely trying to protect Sonja.

'For that reason she is blocked in her work and she imagines she will never work again. As her work is everything to Sonja, she is in a low state of mind at the moment. So, please, if I can ask you a favour, she needs to avoid strain. Going over all this stuff about Harry is just about the most painful thing there is for her. If you've asked her everything you need to know I'd be grateful if you'd just leave her be.'

'I don't think there's anything else,' Lorraine said, preparing to get out of the jeep. 'Goodbye – it's been nice meeting you.' She smiled and waved as she watched him drive out, wondering what exactly he and Sonja Nathan had to hide.

Sonja was still sitting at the table when he returned. 'I'm tired. I think I'll go and lie down for a while.'

He looked at her, saying nothing, though he hated the hours Sonja spent locked alone in her room. Then he reached over and touched her face lovingly. 'If you should see Mrs Page again, don't talk too much.'

'I won't,' she said, tilting her head like a little girl making a promise, suddenly seeming young, vulnerable.

'I love you,' he said softly, and she smiled. He adored the way she smiled, and it always made his heart lift, even though he knew that though she was with him and was caring and loving towards him, he was not her true love. Arthur envied Harry Nathan even though he was dead, envied that he had shared Sonja's youth, that the mere mention of his name made Sonja's face fill with darkness and grief.

'You know, I think I'm too tired to go to the deer meeting tonight,' she said. 'I don't really feel like going into town.' Arthur's heart sank: sometimes Sonja would not leave the house for weeks, withdrawing into her private shadowlands in a way that frightened and excluded him. He had been counting on the deer, a cause she cared about, to get her into town: social interactions with neighbours would do her good. 'You go, though,' she said, with a smile, already moving towards the stairs. 'One of us should.'

Arthur knew, too, what that meant: she wanted to be alone, and if he didn't leave the house she would go and range about alone outside, or take the car and drive. She was gone increasingly often, sometimes disappearing for a couple of days at a time.

'Sonja,' he called after her, 'did you say you'd finished packing your thing for Berlin? If you have I'll call the freight company – the paintings are ready to go.'

'Yes,' she said, with a smile. 'Take it.'

She disappeared from sight and he heard the door of her bedroom close.

She stood at her windows, which overlooked the bay, where she watched the sun rise each morning. Another bedroom had windows that captured the sunsets and the moon's rising: to see the beginning and end of the day made each day special, each one different. She tried to convince herself that that ought to be enough for her – just to enjoy the beauty of the seasons, to drift along with the current of time instead of trying to hold it back.

Certainly she had no intention of taking any more steps to reverse the physical signs of ageing, and booking into the clinic had been an act of folly induced by Harry's leaving her for Kendall. She had fought the impulse to recapture physical youth for some time but finally she had chosen a surgeon and clinic with care, had known exactly what she needed doing. She had wanted a complete face-lift but with a small implant in her chin, and her nose lifted.

The clinic had been discreet, but Sonja was confident anyway that no one knew she was there because, under heavy bandages and dark glasses, she had been unrecognizable. However, the name of one patient had stuck in her memory. She had discovered that the woman was a private investigator and although she never spoke to her, she had heard a good deal of a conversation the woman had had with someone else. When she had come across the advert in *Variety* for Page Investigations, she had been amused by the coincidence.

She reached for the silver-backed mirror to check her profile. She was fifty-two years old and should be content to spend her time surrounded by this beautiful calm. She should be glad that the compulsion to work fifteen or sixteen hours a day was now gone, that the long torment was over. Odd that she had never realized she would miss it so much. She would go down to the studio later in the day and see if perhaps she couldn't do something about that.

CHAPTER 14

LORRAINE WALKED back into the hotel, cold despite the warm sunlight, after the encounter with Sonja Nathan. She had been chilled by the woman and her obsession with the past. If it was a kind of death to be unable to move on from one stage of life to another then Sonja Nathan herself was dying by inches.

The woman had seemed on the verge of confessing to Harry Nathan's murder, but it was obvious, as Arthur had said, that she was also on the verge of a clinical mental illness, her talk moving in and out of reality and symbolic meanings. It was clear Sonja had hated Nathan, had seen herself as a moral guardian, saving him from his own worst self – embodied in Raymond Vallance – and that after he had left her she had considered him to be on an inexorable slide into the pit. Whether she had taken the pitchfork and pushed him in was another matter.

What about the paintings scam? Arthur was a painter, but that didn't mean anything – half the population of the Hamptons claimed to be artists of one sort or another. Sonja had seemed to have so genuine an aversion to Harry Nathan that somehow Lorraine could not see her coolly masterminding a fraud with him.

The dark world of poisonous emotion, betrayal and killing, the wrecks of lives, the semblances and fragments of people left drifting afterwards hung around Lorraine like a foul smell, and she was glad to sit in the conservatory and remind herself that there was a world elsewhere. Suddenly she could not wait to be out of the Hamptons, back home among people who loved and cared about her, with Jake and Tiger in her own apartment, and out of this whole dirty business for good. Rosie and Rooney had got it right, she thought, take the money, get out and get a life, and she had an overwhelming impulse to call Jake and say she was coming home. She would tell Feinstein his paintings were untraceable: neither work nor money was going to run her life.

Lorraine was walking across the lobby towards the stairs when she heard a voice she recognized at once, a professionally trained and pitched voice. 'My companion finds the room inadequate and we would like to move to a suite,' he was saying.

It was Raymond Vallance, looking old and eccentric in a crumpled, not entirely clean white suit, black polo-neck sweater and black Chelsea boots. He caught sight of her at once. 'Why, I see some of my friends from LA are here already – good to see you, Lorraine,' he called across the lobby, and began to advance on her. 'How're things at Fox?' The manager sidled smartly away, murmuring that he would see what he could do.

'I wouldn't know,' Lorraine said stonily. 'Why don't you call and ask?'

'Sorry about that, Lorraine.' His intrusive use of her first name irritated her and he had been drinking. He seemed madder, closer to the edge. 'Fucking bell-boys. No idea of service.'

'No, none,' Lorraine agreed, her mind racing and her previous suspicions about Sonja tumbling down like a house of cards. Vallance's presence here was virtually an admission of guilt, she thought. It could not be a coincidence that he had suddenly showed up in the Hamptons, of all places, on the last night that Sonja Nathan had to remain alive to inherit Harry Nathan's estate. Lorraine was certain that he was warped enough to want to prevent Sonja from receiving it. He had been, as Sonja had said, the constant in Harry Nathan's life, the one who had loved him most. Harry Nathan had been his life. He, Lorraine was now certain, had been Harry Nathan's death, and the death of the two women who had displaced him in Nathan's life. He had nothing more to live for – but, of course, there was one woman left . . .

'What brings you out here?' Vallance went on. There was a note of malice under the smarm. 'Not that I can't guess.'

'Well, I'm sure you guessed right.' Somehow she didn't want to mention Sonja to him. 'Excuse me, I'm just about to check out.'

'Sonja still out in the Springs?' Vallance went on, ignoring her. 'Thought I might pay her a call.' He rambled on drunkenly.

He was about to descend into maudlin reminiscence, and Lorraine cut him short. 'Well, I happen to know Mrs Nathan isn't home this evening,' she said, wondering if Vallance was deliberately playing dumb in telling her he planned to see Sonja if, in fact, he intended to kill her. Or did he just want someone to know he was going to be with Sonja? Could he imagine that she might harm him? 'She and the gentleman she lives with have an engagement here in town.' She turned on her heel before he could say another word and walked rapidly upstairs. So much for calling Jake and flying home: everyone had stood aside and watched Cindy die; she was going to call Sonja Nathan and tell her to call the cops if she saw Raymond Vallance.

The sense that the final act of the drama that had centred on Harry Nathan was about to be played out, and the acrid scent of danger, cut through her.

The phone rang endlessly but at last Lorraine heard Sonja's voice.

'Mrs Nathan, it's Lorraine Page,' she began, suddenly feeling silly.

'Hello, Mrs Page, did you forget something?' Sonja said. Her voice was normal, friendly.

'Well, no. I ran into Raymond Vallance here in the hotel. He said something about coming out to see you and I thought I'd let you know. He was pretty drunk . . .' Lorraine realized she was babbling and made an effort to speak more slowly. 'I just got the idea he was planning to bother you in some way.'

Sonja laughed. 'What more can he do to me? I'd say he's done his worst by now.'

'Mrs Nathan, I know this sounds foolish,' Lorraine persisted, 'but I really feel Raymond Vallance may have some idea of harming you. He seems to feel a personal grievance towards you.'

'Tell me something new,' Sonja said, but her voice was more serious now. 'He doesn't change. I'm bigger than Vallance – I always was, that was why Harry chose me. If Raymond wants to come round, he can.'

'Well, I just thought I'd let you know. It wouldn't hurt to have the number for the police next to the phone.'

'Don't worry, Mrs Page,' Sonja said, 'we have a gun in the house. Many thanks for your concern.' She rang off.

Well, Lorraine thought, she had done her best. If Sonja shot Vallance, good riddance – perhaps she'd get a call in the morning from another of Harry Nathan's wives facing a murder rap.

She could not face hearing the disappointment in Jake's voice when she told him that she had decided to stay another night, so called Rosie instead.

'Hi, darlin'.' Rosie's familiar voice, warm as a hug. 'Where are you?'

'Still in the Hamptons. I figured I might stay another night.'

'What for?' Rosie asked. 'Didn't you get to see Sonja Nathan?'

'There's something going on. Raymond Vallance just showed up out of nowhere.'

'Well,' Rosie sniffed, 'you must be the only woman who'd hang around to see Raymond Vallance these days. Bill's been looking in on the office and he says someone's been calling and calling and hanging up after the machine kicks in. I bet it's Jake – just wants to hear your voice.'

Lorraine felt a pang of conscience – but what difference could twenty-four hours make? She'd tell Jake as soon as she got back that she was winding up the office for good, that he would be her top priority from now on. 'I'll be back as soon as I can,' she said. 'And then I'm getting right out of this business. I'll be home baking cupcakes and we'll have coffee and watch the shopping channel every day.'

'Dream on!' Rosie said, and there was sadness under the laugh that she hardly understood, as though she knew she was listening to a vision that could never become real.

'I don't suppose you'd take Tiger for tonight, would you?' Lorraine asked.

'You mean would I call Jake and tell him you're not coming back today?' Rosie said, with a sigh. 'I guess so. I don't know why I do these things, Lorraine. It must be love.'

'Thanks, Rosie – I'll see you soon.'

Sonja Nathan stood at her windows, looking out over the bay. So Vallance was in town, she thought: So what? She had the gun and nothing frightened her now: she would not be frightened to rid the world of a piece of vermin, and if he killed her, he would only have outrun her own desires by a couple of hours. She felt tranquil now, as though all things were running steadily towards their appointed conclusion, feeling her own movements acquire the languorous grace of a clock that is steadily running down.

She saw the delivery van draw up outside, and a boy get out with a cardboard box in his arms. Arthur wouldn't hear him in the studio, so she set off downstairs to let him in. 'This is for you, Mrs Nathan,' he said, handing her the form to sign. She glanced at the column marked 'consignor', and saw the letters LAPD printed in it. The police department, she thought. Some clerical officer had telephoned her about evidence gathered in connection with Harry's death, which was now being returned to the family. 'Thanks,' she said, handing the form back. 'Just put it here in the hall.'

'Mrs Nathan isn't home this evening.' The words she had spoken to Vallance echoed in Lorraine's head. The temptation to go back and see if she could get a look round the studio was irresistible.

She strolled out into the street, and walked into a suitably arty-looking café, where the poster for the deer protection meeting was prominently displayed: it was at seven. That left her with the afternoon on her hands, and she walked down to the bookstore. She had originally intended to pick up some light reading, but something prompted her to ask the owner if he had anything on modern sculpture, in particular Sonja Nathan's career.

'You mean Sonja Sorenson,' he said. 'She works under her maiden name.' He produced a book devoted to three contemporary sculptresses, offering a fairly full treatment of Sonja's work, which Lorraine bought. She walked back to the hotel, flicking through it. Sonja had had two major shows since *City of Angels*, after she and Nathan had split up. The first was called *In Perpetuity*, and was a group of immensely tall structures, part-pillar, part-woman, part-tree, a cycle of strange modern caryatids in a soft, bright, reddish wood. The positions of all the figures were almost identical, but the art of the piece was in some subtlety of their overall lines and expressions: somehow one knew that the earlier figures were struggling to break free from the wood, the later ones yearning to blend back into it. Only one central figure was at rest, her face so simultaneously blank of meaning yet flooded with peace that Lorraine could not take her eyes from her: this had been Sonja's most successful show: she had then produced nothing for some time. Her latest work was a similar group, entitled *The Fall* but this time of male figures, at least eighteen or twenty, the first ten or twelve almost unchanging, but the latter ones dwindling in size and displaying a rapid degeneration into coarse, priapic, ape-like creatures. The piece was cruder and darker than its two predecessors, and you did not have to look far to see the narrative of Sonja's marriage to Nathan: it was eloquent with pain and contempt and made Lorraine speculate about what Harry Nathan had been like to inspire such intensity of feeling in the people around him. She wondered too whether, looking at the two pieces together, she could trace Sonja's attempts to liberate herself from her past and her marriage. Could she have been so tormented by him that she would contemplate killing him? Lorraine found herself wondering what Sonja's latest work would reveal, and was now even more determined to go out to Sonja Nathan's house.

It was half past six when Lorraine walked down to Reception and decided that she would sit in a coffee shop with a view of the entrance to the town hall and make sure that both Sonja and Arthur went into the meeting before she set out for the Springs.

People began to file in after about a quarter to seven. A few minutes later she saw the Blazer pull up and Arthur get out – alone. Lorraine almost groaned aloud with frustration.

Just as he walked up to the doors of the hall, Lorraine saw a couple approach him – a tall, heavy, blowsy-looking blonde woman and Raymond Vallance. They stopped and exchanged a few words with Arthur, who seemed barely inclined to give them the time of day, then continued to walk towards the hotel.

Was it Lorraine's imagination, or had Vallance suddenly quickened his own and his companion's pace? Was he now rushing back to the hotel to dump his companion and get out to the Springs? Lorraine decided she wasn't taking any chances. She flagged down a passing cab.

Sonja Nathan's house was in darkness, but all the lights were on in the studio on the far side of the garden. Approaching the studio, Lorraine stepped out of the shafts of light streaming from the windows and walked up in shadow to look inside. There were various packing materials on the floor, and it was clear that whatever work Sonja Nathan had completed was now gone. The interior was almost bare except for a row of cupboards built along one wall and a long wooden table, at which Sonja sat, staring into space, a handgun lying in front of her.

Jesus, Lorraine thought, what was the woman doing? Waiting for Vallance seemed the most likely explanation, the man who had blighted her marriage and had, if Lorraine's suspicions were correct, killed the man she had loved. The minutes passed and Sonja did not move a muscle. Something in her unnatural rigidity made Lorraine suddenly certain that Sonja Nathan intended to kill herself.

She moved noiselessly along the wall, pressed her back against the wood next to the door frame and extended her arm to its full length to rap on the door.

'Mrs Nathan,' she called, 'it's Lorraine Page.'

There was no reply.

'Mrs Nathan?' she called again. 'Can I come in for just a moment?'

Silence.

'Can I speak to you please? It's important,' she tried again, and was rewarded with the sound of the woman getting up and coming to the door. Lorraine heard a bolt being drawn, then the handle turned slowly and the door opened.

'I'm working, Mrs Page,' Sonja Nathan said. She looked deathly.

'I'm sorry. I saw Arthur on his own in town and I wondered if you were all right,' she said. It was more or less the truth, and the frank expression of concern seemed to touch Sonja.

'That's kind of you,' she said. Her eyes were turned towards Lorraine, but seemed not to see her.

'Can I come in for a minute?' Lorraine asked again.

'All right,' Sonja said. 'Just for a minute. There really are things I have to do.'

She stepped back from the door and Lorraine followed her inside. She had not bothered to conceal the gun, which lay untouched on the table.

'You see,' she said, her manner lightening, as though some oppressive third presence had left the room as soon as Lorraine had walked into it, 'if Mr Vallance comes calling, he'll find us well prepared. I've already seen a good deal of him today, as it happens.'

Lorraine raised an eyebrow quizzically. 'Did he come out here?'

'No. I received a package today from the LAPD. Videotapes of Harry's. Have you seen them?'

Lorraine nodded.

'Well, Vallance got what was coming to him. He fed all that in Harry and got bitten himself. If he walks through that door I ought to just shoot him cold,' Sonja said casually, crossing to one of the long cupboards. 'He's a destroyer.' She took out a bottle of vodka and an antique stemmed glass. She poured herself a drink.

'What were you working on?' Lorraine asked.

'Oh, nothing. What I'm always working on,' Sonja said, knocking back half of the vodka.

Lorraine sensed that she had been about to say something else, but had stopped herself. 'Well, that can't be true,' she said. 'You've produced a well-regarded body of work, haven't you?'

'A well-regarded body of work,' Sonja repeated, almost mimicking Lorraine. 'Much fucking good it does me.' She drained the rest of the glass. 'People don't live on "regard". Or on the past.' She was silent for a moment, then began to speak again, her manner now almost academically impersonal. 'What's the point of the past, do you think?'

'I don't know,' Lorraine said, 'I often wonder.'

'Well, I can tell you,' Sonja went on, bitter again. 'It's to flavour the present. In some people's lives the memory of the past is constantly present, like a sweetness, but for others it's like a poison or a mould. No matter how far you think you've got away from something, it's still always there – in every word you speak, everything you

325

are. Every piece of work you do.' She gestured around her at the empty room.

'Are you talking about Harry?'

'Of course,' Sonja said, pouring herself another drink. 'All I ever do is talk about Harry.' She paused again. 'I can't seem to stop. I loved him, you know. Perhaps I didn't realize how much.'

'Until he died?' Lorraine said gently.

'Until he died.' Sonja fell silent. 'Something in me died too.' She looked up at Lorraine, her strange eyes bright and still, and Lorraine felt again the presence of something behind them, as though death itself were looking out.

The atmosphere was unbearable, and Lorraine felt she had to talk, to make some connection with the other woman. 'That's how I started drinking. Someone I loved died.'

'Your husband?' Sonja asked.

'No,' Lorraine said. 'He was my partner at work. I used to be a cop.' She felt a strange intimacy with Sonja, so that it didn't matter what she said. Lorraine began to talk about her own life, remembering her police training and how she had been taught to talk people back from the edge, to make them feel connected. She found that she wanted to tell it all, wanted someone to understand. She could not stop herself, as though a dam had been breached. But then, mid-flow, her voice suddenly tailed off. 'God knows why I'm telling you all this.'

'I'm sure he does,' Sonja said, taking another slug of vodka with a smile. 'Why don't you just spit it all out? You tell me your ghost stories, and then I'll tell you mine.' Life seemed to flow back into her with the current of sympathy, and she swung her feet up on the table with a lop-sided smile. 'We've got a while.'

A while till when? Lorraine was sure that it was no coincidence that Sonja Nathan had been ready to blow her brains out the day before she would become the legal owner of all of Harry Nathan's property. Did she want to show she didn't care about money – or was it something she felt she had no right to accept? She smiled to see how Sonja's problems were distracting her from her own.

Lorraine could feel the past surging up inside her again, and she had to get up and walk around. Sonja said nothing, and it was because she didn't speak, either to encourage or discourage anything, that Lorraine's pent-up emotions were able to find release. 'Drinking became my life – I refused point-blank to believe I had a problem, but I was on a downward slope.'

Lorraine put her hands over her face and started to weep. Sonja sat motionless. 'I'm sorry, I don't know what's got into me.'

'Same thing that's got into me,' Sonja said simply, swinging her legs down. She walked over to Lorraine and touched her shoulder lightly. Lorraine knew that the touch had been something Sonja felt she ought to do rather than an instinctive response: she was not a caring woman. 'Except my drug is my work. Was my work. I won't do any more now.'

'I'm sure that's not true,' Lorraine said, wiping her eyes. 'All artists get blocked from time to time.'

'Art!' Sonja said. 'It's all just fucking pain and damage. Harry damaged me. I didn't know how much.'

Until he died, Lorraine mentally filled in.

'He made me like himself – dirty, commercial, tacky,' she went on, describing a mirror image of the process Vallance had attributed to her, and Lorraine wondered what she was talking about: no one could call her own austere and disturbing work commercial, but it was clear that Sonja's standards were not those of other people. 'He made me feel things, do things, I never wanted to feel or do, filled me up with bitterness and hate. I did my best to . . . exorcize them. But I didn't succeed. They possessed me, diminished me.' She was talking slowly and deliberately. 'They caused me to lose my work. Which he gave me too. Which is myself.'

What the hell did she mean? She was raving, everything she said was a riddle.

'But you said you were working here tonight?' Lorraine said.

'On myself,' Sonja said, and the peculiar resonance was back in her voice.

'With a gun?' Lorraine asked.

'Smoothest tool of all,' Sonja said, still not looking at Lorraine, and a smile spread across her face, as though she was looking at an unseen watcher. Then she turned. 'I'm sorry,' she said, 'I sound like Raymond Vallance. I think about death a lot. Liquor makes me maudlin. But you can stop babysitting now.' She poured herself more vodka and gave Lorraine a meaningful look. 'I'll never die drunk – in case people say I didn't have the guts to do it sober.'

'I used to think that,' Lorraine said, 'that I should have died. My husband left me too, you know.' She knew somehow that, despite what Sonja had just said, she had to keep talking.

'Did you get divorced?' Sonja asked.

'Yes, I did, and he got custody of the children. Rightly so – I wasn't capable of looking after myself, never mind the kids.' She lit a cigarette, no longer feeling like weeping, no longer feeling anything except the awful, cold guilt that she would carry to her grave.

'Everyone who loves has a right to be loved, Lorraine,' Sonja said. 'Whatever happened in your past can't change that.'

The sigh was long and deep, and Sonja noticed that Lorraine's hand was shaking as she flicked the ash from her cigarette. 'You want to bet?'

'Try me,' Sonja said softly.

'OK. I was on duty, a few months after my partner had died. I had been drinking heavily. We'd been called out to what they thought was going to be a drug bust to act as backup because they said the kids were tooled up. There were four kids and they split up and ran. One ran past my patrol car, so I got out, chased him and cornered him in an alley. I gave him three warnings to stop or I would shoot. He didn't stop, and I fired all six rounds. I couldn't stop squeezing the trigger, even when he went down.'

She let the smoke drift from her pursed lips, then turned to look at Sonja. 'He wasn't armed. It was a Walkman he had in his hand, and he had earphones in so he couldn't hear me. He was just a kid, and I killed him because I was drunk. If I'd been sober I would have fired a body shot.'

'That's hard to live with,' Sonja said quietly. She seemed to be watching Lorraine with particular intensity.

Lorraine stiffened as she heard a sound outside. 'Do you hear something?' she asked.

'Yes, I do,' Sonja said evenly as she picked up the gun

and cocked it. God, Lorraine thought, gooseflesh breaking out all over her body: she had meant what she had said about Vallance. Now they could both hear someone's footsteps right outside the door, which still stood an inch ajar. Sonja turned round slowly, noiselessly, until the gun was aimed chest high at the door panels. After a moment they heard a knock.

'Who is it?' Sonja said. Her voice was sweet and pure as a bell, as though a longed-for visitor had finally called, and Lorraine saw the beatific calm of the central figure of her wood of women appear on her face.

'It's me, Sonja,' a voice called. A man stepped into view. Arthur.

'Jesus,' he said in surprise, finding himself looking down the barrel of a gun. 'What the hell's going on here?'

'I'm sorry, Arthur,' Sonja said, lowering the gun. 'I'm afraid Mrs Page got me rattled. Apparently Raymond's been in town making threats.'

'Not to me he hasn't,' Arthur said. 'I saw him a couple of hours ago and he was sweetness and light. We're all old friends now.'

Lorraine saw him scan the room as he spoke, and although his voice did not alter, she knew that he knew exactly why Sonja was holding the gun.

'I thought you were lying down,' he said. 'I was worried about you.'

'You're so sweet,' she said, and Lorraine saw the flicker of pain in Arthur's eyes at the lack of interest in her voice. He loved her, Lorraine could see. 'I'll go and lie down now.' She walked out into the night.

'Can we offer you a nightcap, Mrs Page?' Arthur asked as they followed Sonja out of the building. 'I guess

Sonja's lucky you showed up, if Vallance is roaming around out there.' She knew what he meant: if she hadn't showed up Sonja would have been dead.

'No, no, thank you,' she said quietly. 'I'll just call a cab.'

They walked out into the darkness. Lorraine could feel the urgency with which Arthur moved to catch up Sonja, to try to take her hand, knowing that he felt the same instinct she herself had experienced earlier to try to hold on to the woman. But Sonja slid away, graceful and aloof, and walked on alone.

CHAPTER 15

WHEN LORRAINE woke next morning, she was surprised to see that it was already almost nine. She had lain awake for some time after she had got back to the hotel, half expecting some call from either Arthur or Sonja, but apparently nothing had happened. She dressed and called the airline to book herself a flight to LA. All they could offer her at such short notice was a seat on an early-evening departure, so she decided to spend the afternoon in New York. She packed the few things she had brought with her and set off downstairs.

'Good morning, Carina.' She smiled at the pretty blonde girl on the desk, whose name she now knew from the plate standing in front of her.

'Good morning, Mrs Page,' said the receptionist. 'The papers are here if you'd like one to take in with you.' Lorraine picked up a *New York Times* and scanned the headlines.

'There never seems to be anything but gloom and doom in the city, does there?' she said, putting the paper down. 'I think I'll just enjoy the peace here for another day.'

That surely should have elicited any news of either a

shooting or a suicide in the locality, Lorraine thought, but Carina simply smiled again. 'Good idea,' she said. 'Save your strength for LA.'

Lorraine walked into the room where breakfast was served, and found Raymond Vallance, sitting at a table with his large lady companion. He was now wearing a tweed suit and a battered pair of brogues, and was sitting ramrod straight in the dining chair, cracking the pages of his newspaper like whipcord, wearing an expression he clearly considered aloof and patrician. He seemed almost to have absorbed a new personality, aristocratic, European from the costume, or perhaps, Lorraine thought, this was his heterosexual persona.

She walked towards their table. 'Good morning, Mr Vallance,' she said brightly. 'How're things at Fox today?'

Vallance glared at her.

'Oh, Raymond,' his companion cried, 'is this one of your Hollywood friends?'

'Mrs Page and I have met in Los Angeles,' Vallance said curtly.

'We have a lot of friends in common,' Lorraine went on smoothly. 'I saw Sonja last night, for example.'

'Oh, really?' Vallance said. 'I must try to see her today.' He looked at Lorraine with eyes like stones.

'Who is that, pumpkin?' asked the lady innocently. 'I wish you'd introduce me to more of your friends.'

'The former wife of . . . a close friend,' Vallance said. 'It's a condolence call. I'm afraid it wouldn't be appropriate for you to attend.'

'Apparently Sonja gets the whole of the estate now,' Lorraine went on, observing Vallance closely. 'The consequence of the tax-saving clause, the lawyers tell me.

The other two wives died within a survivorship period and the gifts to them never took effect. It expired last night, it seems.'

'So I suppose you and Sonja had a little celebration?' Vallance said nastily. 'Burned one of those effigies of Harry she keeps turning out, perhaps? What'll she do for art now, poor dear?'

'Well, I wouldn't say we were celebrating,' Lorraine said circumspectly.

'I really must try to call on her later,' Vallance said. 'Take my last look before she kills herself or goes up in smoke. Harry's estate doesn't seem to bring his ex-wives much luck, does it? You'll be glad to get well clear of it, I'm sure.'

Was she imagining it, or was Vallance looking at her as if he expected her to take some other meaning from his words? A coded boast about the deaths of Cindy and Kendall? A threat to Sonja – or even to herself?

'I'm still working for Harry's lawyer, actually,' she said. 'So I'll be involved for a while.'

'Well,' Vallance said, 'see you around.' He raised his newspaper again and Lorraine realized she was dismissed.

She sat down at another table and ordered breakfast, wondering whether she should bother to call Sonja and say that Vallance was still hanging around, then decided not to – she was retained to investigate the art fraud, not as minder to Harry Nathan's ex-wife, and besides, Sonja had Arthur to do that for her. Poor Arthur.

Half an hour later she was ready to check out. There was no one at the desk, so she decided to walk to the bookstore again for something to read on the bus. She was barely out of the door when she heard a car engine revving. She looked across the street to see the Blazer being wrenched backwards and forwards as the driver tried inexpertly to manoeuvre it into a parking space. Eventually, Arthur opened the door and got out, leaving the vehicle parked at an angle: it was immediately apparent that he was drunk.

Lorraine hurried across the street. 'Arthur!' she called. 'Are you OK? Did something happen?'

Arthur looked at her, his face drawn with strain, but blurred and slackened with drink too. 'Well,' he said, making an effort to talk coherently, 'not really. Nothing new.'

'Is Sonja OK?'

'She's the same as she always is.' The man's bleakness made Lorraine decide she could spare half an hour to try to sober him up.

'Give me the keys and I'll move the jeep,' she said, 'and then why don't we get a cup of coffee in the hotel? I haven't checked out yet.'

'Sure,' Arthur agreed spiritlessly. Lorraine reparked the jeep and they crossed back to the Maidstone Arms. Vallance and his companion had gone, Lorraine noticed, as they walked into the dining room, though breakfast was still being served. She ordered a pot of black coffee and a quart bottle of mineral water.

'So,' she said, when the waiter had left them, 'what happened?'

'Oh, nothing, I guess,' Arthur said, with a grimace. He took a swallow of the coffee, and seemed undisposed to say any more.

'Come on, Arthur,' Lorraine said. 'Call me naïve, but I don't have you down for someone who gets pie-eyed by ten thirty a.m. as a matter of routine. What did you do, stay up all night?'

'Pretty much,' he said.

'Celebrating Sonja's inheritance?' Lorraine probed: she had a feeling that this would hit a sore spot.

'Christ!' Arthur swore at her. 'When the fuck is she going to be free of that man? She was in a bad enough state while he was still alive, but now that he's dead she's worse.' He took another mouthful of coffee, his hands shaking.

'Drink some water,' she said quietly. 'It's better for you than that stuff.' She poured a glass for him, but Arthur did not move. 'Arthur,' she said gently, 'I could see Sonja was pretty close to the edge last night. I know you care about her but it won't do her any good if you let her drag you over too.'

'Yeah,' he said. 'She would have gone over if you hadn't been there last night. I knew that stuff about waiting with a gun for Vallance was a lot of bullshit.'

'He didn't show up, then?' Lorraine asked.

'No. I don't think he has the balls to do much of anything, though he has an ugly mouth.' He picked up the glass of water and drank. 'I didn't know she had a gun in the house,' he went on. 'She wouldn't give it to me.' He caught Lorraine's eye, and she got the message that he regarded the situation as serious.

'Did you have a fight?' she asked.

'Kind of.' He gave a low, wry laugh. 'She started watching these weird videotapes the police in California sent out to her – horrible, kinky stuff with Nathan and a bunch of other people. She kept saying how disgusting they were, how low Harry'd sunk, but she was fascinated. That's what she's like with him. That's how I ended up drinking the best part of a bottle of Bourbon and taking off.'

336

'Heavy,' Lorraine said.

'Oh, just the usual late-night special,' Arthur said. 'I can't take a hell of a lot more of this. She's been all over the place since Nathan's death.'

Lorraine was intrigued. 'What the hell was it Nathan had, to have all these people carrying on about him for twenty years? I'm sorry, but I've been picking my way through every detail of this guy's life and I still feel like I don't have a handle on what he was really like.'

'That was the key to Harry,' Arthur said. 'He was plastic. He was a chameleon. He was beautiful, of course. He could turn every woman's head walking down the street when he was young.'

'You knew him and Sonja then?' Lorraine asked.

'Oh, yeah. I'm the fucking jerk who introduced them,' Arthur said. 'I met her first – she was painting then.'

'I didn't know Sonja painted,' Lorraine said, registering that piece of information with interest.

'Well, it wasn't her real talent, but she was taught like everyone else in art school and she was competent. She was living with some rich old guy, but it was clear she was bored. I had a few dates with her – never really got past first base. I knew she was looking for some kind of intensity, that she thought I was pretty fucking boring, and I suppose I introduced her to Nathan and Vallance to show her, you know, that I wasn't that straight because I had these wild, crazy friends.'

'How did you first meet Harry Nathan?' Lorraine asked.

'We were at college together. He got kicked out. It was the hippie days, and he was an acid freak. He was trying to get a career together as a director, didn't have a dime, and I never thought he and Sonja'd get together in a million years. Sonja was a real ice princess in those days, always living with someone with old masters on the walls, and Harry was so tacky – picking up girls in bars and living on tacos.'

'Must have been the attraction of opposites.'

'Yeah, bang, as soon as they met. A lot of it was just physical, I think, but the big deal about Harry was that he was a kind of blank space on which other people could write whatever they wanted – the stuff he made as a director was exactly like that too, reflections, if you see what I mean, rather than anything genuinely his own. Even Sonja admits that she kind of hypnotized herself with her own illusion of what he was like.'

'But you love her anyway?' Lorraine said.

'Yeah,' he said. 'I love her – I'd walk on hot coals for her.' He spoke quietly and directly, looking Lorraine straight in the face, and she knew that his anger had passed and that he was telling her the simple truth. 'I waited fifteen years to get her back from that asshole Nathan, and I knew he still had part of her, maybe the deepest part, but I can wait another fifteen years to get that back too. It'll end. I know it will.'

Though it certainly didn't show any sign of ending any time soon, Lorraine thought privately. Another raft of speculation floated into her mind. Could Arthur have killed Nathan? Either because Sonja had asked him to, or out of a belief that while he was alive, Sonja would never get over her obsession with him?

'Were you still in contact with Sonja and Nathan when he bought the gallery?' she asked.

'No,' Arthur said, 'I couldn't stand to see her with him – couldn't stand to see her being fooled by him.

And I was damned if I was going to hang around like the bad fairy, having lunch with Sonja once a month and hoping Nathan'd get hit by a truck. The way fucking Vallance did.'

'Do you still see Vallance?'

'Not if I can avoid it.'

Lorraine changed tack. 'Did Sonja mention to you what I came out here to investigate?' she asked.

'Not really. She just said you were tracing some assets belonging to the estate.'

'Well, I am, in a way,' said Lorraine. 'She seems very detached about it all – I mean, she gets the house, and anything I can trace will go to her too.'

'She'll never live in that place again,' Arthur said. 'I don't think she cares much about the money either – she has other assets of her own.'

'You probably know that Harry Nathan's major asset was supposed to be his art collection,' Lorraine said, and thought that a trace of tension entered Arthur's manner.

'Oh, really?' he said. 'I hadn't given it a lot of thought.'

'Well, it turns out that the major pieces in the collection were acquired by fraud. He and Kendall Nathan sold various paintings to people with no experience of the art market, then delivered fakes. Kendall thought all the real stuff was hanging in Nathan's house, but it seems that he pulled the same move again on her. All his own collection was fake too.'

'Serves her right,' Arthur said.

'Did you meet her?' Lorraine asked.

'Just once or twice,' Arthur said coolly. 'So, you're trying to trace the paintings?'

Lorraine nodded. 'That or the profits of the sale. Nathan used a lot of aliases, and he must have had secret bank accounts.'

'Well, they could be anywhere by now,' Arthur said. 'People buy hot art work and keep it in a cellar for thirty years.'

'But the money must be somewhere,' Lorraine persisted.

'Well, he was a film producer, wasn't he? Surely the quickest way to make a lot of money disappear in LA is to pour it into some godawful movie. Nathan's career was in trouble, wasn't it?'

'Maybe I'll ask Feinstein to go through the books at Maximedia again,' Lorraine said. 'Though I'm sure he'll already have done so pretty thoroughly.'

'Or, of course, Nathan could have had other production companies.' Arthur seemed to be pushing this hypothesis, and though it was plausible enough, Lorraine wondered whether he might be trying to lead her down a blind alley – away from his beloved Sonja – and she moved back into the terrain where her true suspicions lay.

'Sonja didn't keep in touch with Harry after they divorced?' she asked carefully. 'I mean, she told me she didn't, but I wondered whether maybe she continued to see him from time to time – maybe didn't want you to know. Did you ever suspect anything like that was going on?'

'No, I didn't,' Arthur said evenly, and Lorraine was reminded of the housekeeper, Juana, that an unshakeable loyalty stood between her and the truth. He had already said that Sonja periodically took off, that often he did

340

not know where she was or where she had been. 'If you're looking to trace off-record contacts of Nathan's in the art world, I'd start with his brother,' he went on.

'I saw a guy with a ponytail at the funeral, looked like Nathan. Was that him?'

'Yes, there were only the two of them, Harry and Nick. The mother had a weird relationship with them both.'

'Is Nick a dealer?' Lorraine asked.

'No,' Arthur said. 'He's a painter.'

That was interesting. Lorraine had felt she was getting nowhere with the case, but this sounded like the missing puzzle piece she had been searching for. She could have kicked herself for not investigating Nathan's family earlier – it was extraordinary how often what you were looking for was right under your nose. 'Was he any good?' she asked.

Arthur looked out of the window. 'Not bad – erratic, spoiled, a hysteric. Nick was very like Harry, you know, always in search of himself, and it showed in a sporadic, slapdash quality in his work. He was reasonably talented, but he would get into deep depressions. He wanted fame and fortune, but then he would switch styles to accommodate a buyer. He had a number of faithful collectors, but a few thousand dollars here and there couldn't keep him and the woman he always had in tow – can't recall her name.'

'Do you know where I can find him?' she said.

'Nope – he took off with the woman to Santa Fe. I don't think he and Kendall got on – she was jealous of everyone close to Harry, you know, kind of eased them out one by one.'

'Who do *you* think killed Harry Nathan?' Lorraine asked. She figured it was worth asking everyone who had known him. It couldn't do any harm.

Arthur turned away. 'I should have.'

'But you didn't, did you?'

'No,' he said simply.

A waiter suddenly appeared to tell Lorraine that there was a call for her. She excused herself to go and take it, knowing that the thread of the conversation had now been broken, and that she had lost Arthur.

The call was from Feinstein. Lorraine told him curtly that she now had a lead on the forger and would be following it up.

When she returned to the dining room, Arthur was on his feet. 'I have to go,' he said. 'I must get back to her. Thanks – it was nice talking to you, and I hope you have a good trip back.'

Lorraine went up to her room to collect her bag, leaving her door slightly open. Outside she heard the voice of Raymond Vallance's ladyfriend, and listened carefully.

'Did you book a table?' She must be talking about lunch: it was after twelve o'clock now, Lorraine realized.

'Sure.' That was Vallance.

'You certainly took your goddamned time. I've been sitting up here in this hideous fucking place.' She seemed very much in charge – no wonder, since presumably she was picking up the bill. 'I wanna eat and then check out. I want to stay at the America Hotel in Sag Harbor. Book us in there.'

'This is one of the best hotels in East Hampton, for God's sake. I know the people here, and there's nothing

wrong with the room, but if that's what you want . . .'
Vallance sounded bored.

'Yes, it is, and as I'm paying, there won't be any
argument, will there? Now let's go down and eat.'

'Do you mind if I just freshen up?' Vallance snapped.

'Fine, I'll see you in the dining room.'

Lorraine inched towards her door as the door to the
next room banged shut and the large blonde woman
walked past. Lorraine hesitated: should she talk to Vallance about Nathan's brother? Then she heard his voice
again: he was clearly talking on the phone.

'Sonja? Don't hang up.' His voice was cajoling. 'Just
hear me out. I'd really like for us to meet, just for old
times' sake. I mean, Harry's dead now, and that hurts
both of us. I know he'd hate to think of us being this
way with one another.' His voice was syrupy, nauseating.
'Can't we just call it all quits now he's gone? I'd just like
to see you for a few minutes.' There was a pause, during
which Vallance presumably listened to Sonja's response.
'Sure, sure – let me give you my mobile number.' He
dictated a number, then a moment later, Lorraine heard
his voice rise in surprise. 'Sonja?' She had hung up.

Lorraine felt the familiar quickening of her pulse, an
impulse to shadow Vallance and go after him if he went
after Sonja, the old thrill of the chase. She knew, though,
that she would have to put it aside: it was not what she
was paid to do, and Sonja and Arthur would find any
further contact from her an intrusion. Besides, she would
have to start resisting the urge to seek, to follow, to
know, if she intended taking up a career as a cupcake
baker and maybe . . . Well, maybe something else.

She smiled, thinking of Jake, and the home and family

she hoped they would have together: her place was back in LA. But now she was still working for Feinstein, and she had every intention of winding up the case professionally. At least it looked like coming to an end – it seemed too much of a coincidence that Nathan's brother happened to be a starving artist who perhaps wouldn't be averse to making a little money on the wrong side of the law. Arthur had had no idea how to find him, but it was worthwhile asking Vallance what he knew.

After a few more minutes she heard his door open and stepped out of her room. 'Mr Vallance?' she called. 'I thought I heard your voice.'

He stared at her, locking his door. 'Well, well, Mrs Page.'

'Could I have ten minutes of your time, Mr Vallance?'

'No, it's not convenient. I'm meeting a producer for lunch.'

'Well, can't you call down and tell them you'll be there in ten minutes? It won't take any longer.'

He glared at her, his Cupid's-bow lips pursed into a thin line of anger. 'I don't think I like your attitude, Mrs Page. Just who the hell do you think you are? I don't have to talk to you, you're not with the police, and I know the case has been closed. You have no right to question me.' He started to walk away.

'Apparently Harry Nathan had millions salted away in a secret bank account, and his lawyer has retained me to try to trace it,' Lorraine called after him. 'If you could help me in any way, I am sure that he would come to some arrangement.'

That stopped Vallance in his tracks. Lorraine leaned against the door frame, watching him thinking about what she had just said. 'I can't see how I can help you.'

'Well, why don't we just sit down for a few minutes and see? You never know, Mr Vallance, there might be something, and if there is, Mr Feinstein will be generous.'

'Ten minutes,' he agreed.

Vallance followed Lorraine into her room and she shut the door behind them. He didn't sit down, but wandered around the room, clicking keys.

'Have you any idea where Harry Nathan's brother Nick is?' she asked.

'God, no. Last I heard he went to some hippie commune in Santa Fe.'

Lorraine tapped her notebook. 'How good a painter was he?'

'I have no idea. Sonja bought some of his work, I think.'

'Do you know anything else about him – or about the rest of the family?'

'Nick was totally unstable, and Harry behaved pretty bizarrely when he and Nick were together, screaming and giggling like ten-year-olds.' Once again, Lorraine heard an unmistakable note of jealousy. 'The mother doted on both of them, wanted them to stay little kids for ever, but the father was different – he couldn't come to terms with Nick. He was a striking man, the father . . .' Vallance paused, and laid a languid finger against his brow. 'But I was never that interested in Harry's family.'

'Just him,' Lorraine said softly, and Vallance turned, a glint in the famous wide-set eyes.

'He was the only one who was worth it.'

'I'm investigating a possible art fraud Harry and Kendall seem to have been pulling out of the gallery—'

'You mean Kendall was pulling,' Vallance cut in.

'Harry would never have thought up anything like that on his own, but she was as crooked as they come.'

'What do you know about the gallery?'

Vallance turned his mouth down and lifted his shoulders. 'I went once or twice, more, I suppose, to show my face for them when they had an exhibition. Artists need press like everyone else, and I'd bring in as many faces as I could, but I didn't have the finances to buy anything from them.'

Lorraine opened her notebook and began to read out the names of some well-known film stars, part of the list of people who had bought paintings she now knew to be fakes. She flicked a glance at Vallance as he nodded at name after name. 'So you introduced buyers too?'

'Yes.'

'Were you paid a commission for doing it?'

'Yes.'

'Do you know any of these other names?' Lorraine mentioned producers, bankers and other professionals who had been approached by Feinstein with the suggestion that they have their paintings revalued. Vallance nodded only occasionally, and she ticked each name he acknowledged, but his contacts had mostly been the show-business buyers.

'Do you know who Nathan's contacts would have been in the banking world, for example?'

'No, that was Kendall's department. She made sure she knew anyone who might have the cash to cough up for her art.'

'How about any contacts in Europe?'

He twisted his keys. 'She made it her business to know foreign buyers. She was a real nose to the grindstone, in the early days I think because she could see Harry more by making the gallery her life. But she was a hustler by nature.'

'Did he ever mention any banking facilities he used, either here or in Europe?'

'No.'

'But he did travel abroad a lot. Did you go with him?'

'No, but during the past year he went away a lot. Just a week here or there, though he'd never take Cindy. Maybe Kendall went – I've no idea. But you're not much of an investigator if you haven't checked his passport – surely that'll tell you where he was sliding off to.'

'It doesn't. As he used so many aliases to open the bank accounts we've traced so far, we can only presume he also had a number of passports in different names.'

'Well, that's quite possible. Harry had picked up a few unsavoury friends along the way – I kept my distance from them.'

'Can you think of anyone in the art world who might have been working with him in the last few months before he died? Not Kendall, someone else.'

'No, I can't.'

'Thank you very much,' Lorraine said.

It was a moment before Vallance realized that she was saying the ten minutes were up. His jaw slackened. 'Oh – was that of any use?'

'Maybe. If you could give me an address where I could contact you, I'll let you know if I make headway.'

He swung his keys round a finger. 'I'm between residences at the moment.'

'What about your agent?'

The keys swivelled faster. 'Let's say I'm between agents too. Why don't I contact you, say in a couple of weeks? Just to see how you're progressing.'

Lorraine passed him her card, and he slipped it into his pocket without looking at it and walked out. Lorraine called Feinstein, who hadn't arrived at his office. She spoke to his secretary, listing what she would need on her return. 'One, can you find a recent address for Nathan's brother, Nick, plus his mother. Two, see if any passports have been issued in any of the other names Nathan used. There may be more than one. Three, will you run by Mr Feinstein that if I were to get assistance from someone, which led to either the money or the art works being recovered, it would help if I could hint at a few bucks going their way, okay?'

'Yes, Mrs Page. I will pass on those messages to Mr Feinstein as soon as he comes in,' the exquisite Pamela answered.

'Thank you.' Lorraine hung up, then went down to Reception to check out. It was now almost lunchtime. She realized she would now have to catch the three-fifteen Jitney, and might as well get lunch in East Hampton before she left. Somehow she couldn't face eating in the hotel with Vallance and his friend, so left her bag at Reception and walked out to a small seafood place down the street. She installed herself in a corner booth with the doom-laden *New York Times* and a platter of shrimp and crab, thinking of the dinner Jake had cooked for her at his apartment. It would be Thanksgiving soon, she thought. She would have him, Rosie and Rooney round for dinner at her apartment – she had never had more to be thankful for as this had turned out to be the best year of her life.

She got up, paid her bill, tossed the unread paper into a trash can and walked back to the hotel, her thoughts

348

drifting again to the future and to images of where she and Jake would live. Her place was too small, though she loved being near the ocean, and neither of them was crazy about his apartment. They must have a proper engagement party too, she thought, suddenly wanting to do things right, to feel the warmth of tradition and ritual around her, wondering if maybe Mike and Sissy and the girls would come. She thought about her daughters every day, and it had never been lack of feeling that had kept her away from them for so long. She had been so afraid that the craziness and chaos that surrounded her would somehow enter their lives. She focused again on the idea of introducing Jake to them. She wanted him to meet them, and for them to see their mother happy and relaxed, supported and loved.

Lorraine turned into the Maidstone's driveway. A paramedics van, lights flashing, was parked in the hotel car park, with two patrol cars and a pale blue Rolls-Royce Corniche. She continued into the hotel reception, but halfway across the lobby she was stopped by an officer, who asked if she was a guest, and only allowed her to go and collect her overnight bag when she confirmed that she was. Then she saw the pretty receptionist weeping hysterically, being comforted by the barman. The blowsy blonde woman, whom she had seen earlier with Vallance, was sitting in one of the Queen Anne chairs. She screamed, sobbed and hyperventilated, and wailed the same words again and again. 'Why? Oh, dear God, why?'

Lorraine looked around more carefully. The police were keeping everyone from going upstairs, and preventing non-residents from entering the hotel. She was just about to ask one of the officers what had happened, when she overheard the pretty girl say, 'I just can't believe it, he was talking to me earlier. I got his autograph for my mother, and I served him lunch, and . . .'

Lorraine was about to go over to her, when the manager appeared. 'I'm so sorry about this, Mrs Page.'

'What happened?' she asked.

The manager's fingers were shaking as he touched his collar. 'Mr Vallance . . . Raymond Vallance committed suicide.'

Lorraine looked upstairs, and the manager clasped her elbow, lowering his voice. 'No, it didn't happen in the hotel, but in that poor woman's car.'

Lorraine glanced at Vallance's companion, whose thickly applied make-up had now smeared over her face. 'How did he do it?' she asked quietly.

'He shot himself,' the manager answered.

He had shown no suicidal intentions when she had seen him earlier. It seemed too much to believe that he had killed himself, particularly as he had been talking of going to see a woman who had said she would shoot him. Lorraine had seen Vallance just before he went downstairs, and the waitress said she had served him lunch. How could Sonja have driven into town, caused Vallance to get up from the lunch table and go and sit in someone else's car so that she could shoot him, unobserved by anyone – and then drive back to the Springs? Hadn't Arthur said he was going straight back to the house? She would have to call them and make some more enquiries in the hotel too, Lorraine thought, but she was determined not to get too far drawn into the Nathan murder again. She was going back to Jake and LA that evening. But she had time, she figured. She'd just have to catch the later bus.

CHAPTER 16

S ONJA WAS sitting quietly, looking out over the
bay, the telephone still on her lap, when she heard
a car draw up outside. Arthur, she thought, with
a pang of conscience. She would have to apologize to
him for the scenes of the night before. He did his best,
but he only irritated her with his childish insistence that
the world was really good and beautiful, that things
could change. It was like talking to a six-year-old, she
thought, and, anyway, it was pointless for anyone to talk
to her when she got into a dark state. She was the only
one who could deliver herself from it. But it was gone
now, she had acted to discharge it: she would teach
Vallance a lesson he would never forget. She felt as
peaceful as the sheet of blue water in front of her, if a
little tired . . .

To her surprise she heard someone knock loudly on
the front door. Arthur must have forgotten his keys – it
was possible, in view of the frame of mind in which he
had left the house. Glancing out of the window on her
way to the door, however, she saw not the jeep but a
police car. Her limbs weakened and trembled and her
throat constricted.

Outside was Officer Vern Muller, an old friend: she

had known him since she moved to the Hamptons, seven years ago.

'Mrs Nathan,' he said, 'I have some bad news for you, I'm afraid.' His expression was grim. Oh, God, she thought, not Arthur . . . 'Can I come in?' Muller asked.

'Certainly,' she said, standing back to let the thick-set policeman walk past her into the hall. She followed him, her stomach turning over. Arthur, oh, Arthur, she cried silently, images of his lifeless, mangled body, mingling with those of Nathan's dead body. Everything she touched she killed, she thought.

'Do you want a drink?' she said to the policeman as they reached the kitchen, wanting to put off the moment when he told her and a new phase of her life really had begun.

'No – but maybe have one yourself,' Muller said. He waited, saying nothing, while she poured herself out a measure of whisky and sat down.

'Mrs Nathan, I have something to tell you which I didn't want you to hear on the news,' he began. 'I just heard it myself from the station and I came right up. Raymond Vallance is dead. He shot himself in town. I know you were friends for many years.'

'*Vallance* is dead?' Sonja repeated.

She knew she sounded stupid and the police officer gave her a strange look.

'Yes, Raymond Vallance. He was staying at the Maidstone Arms with some woman, and . . . they're not exactly sure what happened. He just walked outside and shot himself.'

Relief raced through Sonja like a rip-tide: she felt

giddy with happiness and had to fight to keep it from blossoming in her face.

'When was this?' she managed to ask, a second realization dawning, hard on the heels of the first.

'Just minutes ago. I heard it as I was driving past the gate and I thought I'd turn in.'

God, she thought. When she had called Vallance to tell him that, if he was so keen on reliving old times, he should be delighted to hear that she intended releasing the real record of those old times – Harry Nathan's videotapes – to the press, she had not anticipated what he would do. Had he killed himself out of shame at the prospect of his own humiliation being made public, or of Harry Nathan being seen at last for what he was? She would not have been surprised if it was the latter, and it gave her a certain, almost aesthetic, pleasure to think that the sick hero-worship that had dominated Vallance's life had finally killed him.

'You're sure you don't want a drink?' she said. She didn't feel a flicker of remorse at Vallance's death but she did her best to seem saddened and shaken by what Muller had just told her. He detected, though, that the news was less of a blow to her than he had thought it would be.

'Well,' he said, 'perhaps just a small one.'

The whole thing was perfect, Sonja thought, as she got out a glass for him. She knew that both Arthur, and possibly Lorraine Page, might suspect that she had had something to do with Vallance's death – and she had a perfect alibi, a large, solid, unimpeachable policeman sitting right here in her kitchen within minutes of it.

'He was more my ex-husband's friend than mine,'

Sonja said – she needed to offer some explanation for her lack of distress at Vallance's death. 'I hadn't seen him since my divorce.'

'Yeah, I was sorry to hear about . . . your ex-husband.' Muller took the glass, looking at her, Sonja thought, just a touch too intently. Surely he could not connect her with a murder on the other side of the country. 'It was all over the papers and everything. I guess Vallance will be too – he was a pretty big star at one time.'

'At one time,' Sonja repeated. 'Poor Raymond, he hadn't worked in anything you could take seriously for years.'

'The boys are wondering whether that might have been why he shot himself – he'd been bragging all over the hotel that he had some big movie or something coming up, and apparently he got some call or other while he was eating, got up to take it, then walked out back and . . . Goodbye, cruel world.'

'He must have lost the deal, I imagine,' Sonja said, lying effortlessly, a skill she was not proud of but had had all her life.

'You can't think of anyone around here could have called him?' Muller asked.

'I'm sorry,' Sonja said, 'I can't help you. I haven't had any contact with that whole world in years.'

'Well,' Muller said, draining his glass, 'I'd better not keep you.'

'I'm sorry if I seemed a little . . . strange when you came in,' Sonja said with a charming smile. 'It's just that Arthur and I had a slight disagreement last night and I just got the idea that something might have happened to him.'

'Arthur!' the officer said, with a laugh. 'He's asleep in

the jeep a mile up the road. I drove past him, but I didn't have the heart to wake him up.'

The hotel was full of a mixture of shock and excitement, as people sat at tables or in the bar, discussing Raymond Vallance's career as though they had known him, waiting for the press to arrive and, Lorraine thought, secretly as thrilled as children to be caught up in events that would make news. The *East Hampton Star* had already sent a reporter, and people were talking eagerly to him. Police officers were interviewing staff in one of the conference rooms, and Reception was presently unattended. It was the manager himself who appeared and signalled to Lorraine as she stood at the door of the bar. 'Mrs Page, there's a call for you.' Lorraine was surprised, and followed him to the desk. 'You can take it here if you like. I almost said you'd checked out, but then I saw you.'

'Thank you.' She took the phone, and he backed away politely, leaving her alone. 'Lorraine Page,' she said into the receiver.

'Feinstein here.' Her heart sank. 'I got your messages,' he continued. 'You know I tried to call you earlier?' He didn't wait for an answer. 'I've located three passports – we've sent copies to your office. The brother's a bit of a fruitcake, so I've put in a call to Abigail Nathan, the mother, and she'll be calling me back. Now, about this other thing, if you get any information about missing funds or the paintings themselves, by all means agree to some payment, but discuss it with me first. Any further developments?' he demanded.

Lorraine held the phone cupped to her shoulder, as

she sat on the edge of the desk and took out her cigarettes. 'Yes, Raymond Vallance showed up here, then shot himself.'

'Good God, not at Sonja's?' Feinstein said, stunned.

'No, in the car park of this hotel.'

'I can't say I'm sorry – I never liked the man.' Feinstein was silent for a moment, then asked if Lorraine had seen Sonja. She said she had.

'How is she?' the lawyer asked.

Lorraine drew an ashtray across the desk. 'Weird. On the edge.'

'Well, she made it to the finishing tape at least. She's got the estate in her pocket now. Did you talk to her about the paintings?'

'She says she doesn't know anything about them. I don't think she gives much of a damn about the whole thing – it's her money missing as much as yours, but she just doesn't seem to care.'

'Yeah, well, if she doesn't, I do. Haven't you come up with anything else?' Feinstein pressed.

'Well, there's one other thing you might check out – the accounts of the film studio, in case that soaked the money up.'

'Jesus Christ, don't mention them. I've never seen anything like it. The company wasn't really my department – I handled Harry's personal affairs – but there was a corporate accountant, total fucking crook,' Feinstein said loftily, as though his own integrity was beyond question. 'Plus a show-business lawyer that Nathan used sometimes. We've got an auditor in. It's a mess, but I'll look into it. Did Sonja tip you off to this other movie scenario?'

'No, the guy she lives with suggested it.'

'You don't think the two of them are covering their own tracks?'

'I don't know,' said Lorraine thoughtfully. 'I just don't know.'

'How long are you planning on staying out there?' Feinstein asked, in the-meter's-running fashion.

'I'm coming back tonight,' Lorraine said, hoping that would make him happy, and thinking again of Jake. 'I just think this Vallance thing's suspicious. Everyone connected to Harry Nathan seems to drop dead. I thought I might just call Sonja again.'

'Well, quit thinking and fucking do it,' Feinstein said. 'I've got to go.'

When Arthur returned to the house there was no sign of Sonja. His head ached as the hangover kicked in. He felt tired and disoriented, and had woken in a panic, full of the compulsion to rush back to Sonja's side, make sure she was still there, still okay. Things couldn't go on this way, he thought. Either there had to be more to their relationship than this babysitting, as she called it, or it would have to end.

Both kitchen and sitting room were empty, though he noticed that the videos had vanished.

'Sonja?' he called, as he walked upstairs.

Her voice floated back. 'I'm in the bath.' That was odd, he thought. She didn't normally bathe during the day, but then, last night had hardly been a normal night.

'May I come in?' he said. The atmosphere was warm and fragrant with the citrus scent of one of Sonja's bath essences. He could tell, even before he looked at her, that her mood had lifted. She lay in the pale green water, her long limbs floating, her hair, face and neck all smothered in a layer of some rich turquoise treatment cream. She looked wonderful, he thought, like some richly decorated Egyptian idol.

She smiled at him. 'I'm sorry about last night.' Her eyes were more cat-like than ever, heavy with an expression of deep contentment. God, he thought, she didn't need him: she had positively restored herself in his absence, seemed happier than she had in weeks. 'Where did you go?' she said.

'Into town. I met Mrs Page. She kind of sobered me up. She's leaving this afternoon.'

Sonja disappeared under the water for a moment, then sat up and began to rinse the blue cream from her hair and skin. 'I hope you didn't say too much to her.'

'No more than you did yesterday, I think,' Arthur said, with a touch of irritation.

'Oh, Arthur, let's not start again,' she said, standing up in the bath to squeeze the water out of her hair. 'She has no idea that she and I've ever met before.' She swathed herself in a thick white towel and walked into the bedroom. There was some part of Sonja that he could not reach. He had no idea why one day she would be energetic and warm, the next cold and inert. Certainly he had no idea what was responsible for this sunniness, but he decided to postpone the conversation he had meant to have with her about Nathan. How many times had he decided that? he thought wryly.

The phone rang, and Sonja pulled a face, so Arthur crossed the room and picked it up.

'I'm not in,' she said, selected a comb and headed back to the bathroom.

'Speaking. Who is this?' Arthur said, gesturing to Sonja to stay in the room. 'Ah, you didn't catch the bus then . . . She's in the bath – do you want me to pass on a message?' Sonja tucked the towel more tightly around herself. 'I'm all ears.' He sat on the bed, then stood bolt upright. *What?* Sonja moved closer, but Arthur's attention was focused on the call. 'My God, I can't believe it.' He listened for quite a while, then thanked Lorraine for calling, and replaced the phone.

'Raymond Vallance shot himself. He's dead.' He turned to face her. 'Did you hear what I said?'

Sonja started to comb her hair. 'Yes,' she said, 'I know. Vern Muller stopped by earlier and told me.'

'Why didn't you say anything?'

'I was going to but you started in on me so quickly about talking to Mrs Page. Is that why she's still here? Vallance, I mean.'

'I dunno, I suppose so. I think she wanted to speak to you, but she didn't push it.'

'Well,' Sonja said, 'she's not the police. She has no power to make anybody answer questions.' That seemed an odd thing to say, Arthur thought, almost as though Sonja were hiding something . . . He rubbed his head, which was throbbing.

Sonja knelt on the bed close behind him and ran her arms around him, her skin still damp from the bath. 'Does your head hurt?' Her voice was gentle, almost seductive.

'Yes.'

Sonja kissed his neck, then rolled off the bed. 'I'll get you some aspirin.'

He tried to catch her arm, but missed. 'Vallance didn't come out here, did he?' he called after her. She was halfway out of the room and, again, he had the impression that she was avoiding any discussion of Vallance's death.

'No,' she said, over her shoulder.

Arthur got up and followed her out of the door. 'Sonja,' he said, 'stop a minute.'

'Arthur, I'm soaking wet. I'll just get this and come right back.'

'Sonja, were you here all morning?'

'Of course I was,' she said, looking him full in the eye. Arthur said nothing. 'You can ask Muller,' Sonja continued. 'He was here within five minutes of Vallance's death. He called to tell me personally.'

'Sonja,' Arthur said, 'Mrs Page said something about Vallance getting some call at the dining table in the Maidstone Arms, just before he died. I don't suppose he called here, did he?'

He could see her hesitate between a lie and the truth.

'Well, yes, he did, but I wouldn't speak to him.'

'What did he say?'

Sonja shrugged. 'Just that he wanted to see me, said he wanted to talk about old times.'

'Is that all?'

'Yes,' Sonja said, her eyes flashing. 'That's all. Now stop the investigation, Sherlock. I'll go and put some coffee on and if your head still aches . . .'

'Yeah, aspirin urgently required.' He leaned back across the bed, feeling almost sick with the pain. Raymond Vallance was dead: he still couldn't believe it – he'd seen the man only that morning. The news shocked him, and he had hardly known Vallance – but Sonja had hardly reacted at all and she had known him for years.

He sat up, with a sense of foreboding: what if she had called Vallance? What could she have said that would have made him shoot himself?

Lorraine hung up and eased out from behind the desk. She glanced quickly round the reception area, and could see the manager deep in conversation with the journalist. Shielding with her body what she was doing, she began to flick through the accounts, looking for Vallance's name, noting that all outgoing calls appeared on the bills. She leaned closer to turn over the pages, but there was nothing under the name Vallance. Lorraine straightened up and was about to go when a computer screen caught her eye. She walked over to it. The cursor was blinking on account ledgers. She entered her own name, and her check-out time, outgoing phone calls and other items on her bill came up on room 5. She moved to room 6, and saw that it had been booked, not in Vallance's name but in that of Margaretta Forwood. The date of arrival and an intended length of stay of two days had been entered, but a cancellation typed in subsequently, with the booking fee, luncheon, wine and phone calls in a column opposite. There were four calls to LA, one to Chicago, and two local numbers, one of which she recognized immediately. Sonja Nathan's.

She heard footsteps behind her, and turned, reaching for her cigarette pack from the desk. 'Thank you so much, Mr Fischer,' she said, glancing at his name-badge. 'I'm sorry to leave my bags for so long and if it's inconvenient I'll . . .'

'Not at all. Do you know how long you'll be here, just in case anyone else should call for you?'

361

Lorraine said that she was now intending to take the six o'clock bus into New York.

'I hope you enjoyed your stay with us.'

'I did, very much. It's been a pretty terrible day for you, though, hasn't it?'

'Yes, dreadful. It's tragic, just terrible.'

'How is his companion?' Lorraine asked, assuming a look of sincere concern.

The man sucked in his breath. 'Well, the poor woman is distraught – he didn't leave a note. They had just decided not to stay over. Mrs Forwood had gone to the bar and their cases were being brought down. Mr Vallance walked past me, and I think he smiled – I know I acknowledged him, because I recall seeing him coming down the stairs. He didn't appear to be in a hurry, very casual, and he left the hotel.'

'How long after that was the body found?'

He blinked rapidly. 'I can't be too sure, not long. Mrs Forwood was just leaving, and next minute we heard this screaming.'

'You didn't hear any gunshot?'

'No, nothing. Everything's pretty confused – the shock, I suppose – but I ran out to the car park. She was hysterical, couldn't speak, just screamed and screamed, and then I saw him. The gun was in his hand, but he was sitting upright.'

He was interrupted by the telephone and excused himself to take the call. Lorraine waited, but another phone rang, and then another, lights blinking on the board. She walked out, hearing him refuse to comment on the day's events.

Lorraine made her way into the bar. The crowd had thinned, and a stool was vacant at the far side. She ordered a Coke and lit another cigarette, discreetly eavesdropping on conversations which all centred on the suicide of Raymond Vallance.

Carina, the pretty blonde, now came on duty. She no longer seemed upset, if anything rather enjoying the notoriety of having served Vallance and his lady-friend their luncheon. 'He was so charming. I was asking for an autograph for my mother – she had been such a fan of his – and he was so obliging.' Lorraine stubbed out her cigarette, unable to repress a small smile: poor Vallance – the last thing he would have wanted to hear from an attractive young girl was that she wanted an autograph for her mother. The girl went on, 'They'd finished eating and were just having a Madeira when he left the table and said he had to call his agent. He was here for a big movie – that's what he told us, wasn't it?' The barman nodded, polishing a cham-pagne flute. 'It was going to be shot here, that's what he said.'

'Well, *he* certainly got shot,' said a man with bushy eyebrows, and there were a few guffaws, but even more murmurs of disapproval at the joke, and he apologized. Lorraine wished he would be quiet, as she was trying to hear the rest of what Carina had to say, but the girl was called out into Reception.

Lorraine followed and saw her go into the office. The phone was ringing constantly and the manager was clearly at his wit's end. He covered the receiver and told Carina to get someone to help him. Carina nodded, and turned back, almost bumping into Lorraine.

'Are you all right?' Lorraine asked, with a show of concern. 'It must have been dreadful for you. You found him, didn't you?'

The girl was clearly happy to talk. 'No, I didn't, but I served him lunch.'

Lorraine waited while she was told the entire story about how Carina had asked for his autograph for her mother. 'Did he have any calls?'

'Yes. He got up from the table either to go and call someone, or I think there was a call for him.' She sighed, and tears welled up in her wide blue eyes.

Lorraine gave a brittle smile. 'But at least your mother has his autograph, and it'll be of considerable interest now – the last one he ever gave!'

Carina blinked, aware of the sarcasm, then hurried into the bar.

Lorraine decided to screw subtlety, and went into the manager's office. 'Sorry to bother you again.'

Fischer looked up, one phone in his hand, a second off the hook in front of him. 'I'm sorry, Mrs Page, but I really am very busy. If you need—'

She interrupted, 'I do need something – I want to know who called Mr Vallance. If you don't have the name, then I would like to see the number.'

He gaped, then flushed. 'I'm sorry, that's private information.'

'I know, and I'm a private investigator.' She took out her wallet, and showed her ID.

'I'm sorry, but I've been instructed by the police not to divulge any information or discuss the incident with anyone.' Lorraine took out her wallet, and the man stood up, flushing a still deeper pink. 'Please don't even consider offering me money.'

She slipped her wallet back into her purse. Since the direct approach hadn't worked, she tried another. 'I'm sorry, I didn't mean to insult you. I'm conducting an investigation into the murder of Harry Nathan. Raymond Vallance was his closest friend. I have to report back to LA this evening, and until I have the coroner's report, I have to consider the possibility that Mr Vallance was also murdered.'

The manager's flush drained, leaving his face chalk white.

'I don't want anyone to know what I'm investigating. I have full co-operation from the East Hampton police, and I'm sure you will assist me.'

He opened a drawer and took out a sheet of computer printout.

He looked down at Mrs Forwood's account, and said that some local calls had been made when Mr Vallance arrived and some to Los Angeles during the early part of the morning. The last call, though, had been on Vallance's mobile, and the hotel had no way of knowing who or where it came from.

'So, Mr Vallance left the dining room because a call came through?'

'Yes, on the mobile. We don't allow them in the dining room so he had checked it at the desk. He was speaking to someone on the phone when he went upstairs to his room.' Lorraine watched while the man went to the computer, and typed the commands for a printout of the Forwood account.

'Has Mrs Forwood left?' Lorraine asked, as the machine printed.

Fischer turned back to her, folding the sheet. 'Yes, she ordered a helicopter to take her to New York. We're arranging for her car to be returned, after the police get through with it.'

'Did they also remove Mr Vallance's luggage? You

said you were arranging to take it to the car, so it wasn't in the car already?'

His mouth opened a fraction, and he frowned. 'Well, it must be still here, unless . . .' He walked across the room to a large double-doored cupboard, opened it and looked inside. 'It's still here.'

He took out an old-fashioned pigskin case and matching briefcase. 'I'd better contact the police. I think the confusion may have been caused by Mrs Forwood because she took hers with her.'

'Could I see it?' Lorraine asked, stepping forward. Fischer tried to open the case, but it was locked. He set it down and took the briefcase to his desk: Lorraine saw that it fastened with a zipper, had flat, beaten metal handles and two outside pockets – in one of which was a mobile telephone.

'Could I see that?' She already had her hand out. The manager hesitated, then passed her the phone. She pressed the green power button, then Recall. The telephone bleeped, and Lorraine began to scroll through the digits logged in the memory.

'Should you be doing that?' Fischer asked nervously.

'It's all right, I'm not using it to make a call, just checking something.'

She took out her notebook and jotted down number after number – none she recognized – then tried to bring up the last number dialled, but got a blank screen and a bleep. She noted the make and serial number of the phone, then turned it off. 'Thank you.' She handed it back, and the man put it back where he had taken it from.

'Perhaps there's a note inside the briefcase,' he said.

He was now very uneasy, but Lorraine moved quickly

to unzip the case. Like the locked suitcase, the briefcase was old and worn, but had been expensive. It opened into two halves and Vallance's name had been mono-grammed on one corner. The compartments on one side contained writing paper and envelopes, some letters held together with a rubber band, a paperback novel, a manicure set, some hotel toiletries, and a Cartier pen. On the other side were three scripts, some flattering publicity photographs of Vallance, some postcards of India and, tucked deep inside, a worn manilla envelope.

Lorraine removed the old movie stills, and another photograph of Harry Nathan and Vallance together, arms around one another, smiling into the camera. A third person had been crudely cut out of the photo, but Lorraine could see the edge of a woman's dress and a picture hat: he had been unable to cut the section off completely because the woman's arm was resting on Nathan's shoulder. Lorraine recognized the strong hand and close-trimmed nails as Sonja Nathan's.

There was another larger, plain envelope, and Lor-raine opened it to reveal several sheets of expensive, flimsy paper in a feminine pink, which she recognized at once. Her pulse speeded up as she took them out and unfolded them carefully. The bottom of the first sheet of paper was missing – it had been cut in two after the words 'Dear Raymond' and the date, some six months previously, scrawled in ink in Cindy Nathan's childish script. Lorraine flipped open the manicure set, knowing what she would find: a small pair of round-tipped scissors, the blades less than an inch long, with which Vallance had cut one of the desperate letters in half to fake a suicide note.

Poor Cindy, Lorraine thought. Her hunch had been

right. The girl hadn't committed suicide: the last of the parade of men who had entered her life, first to desire, then to abuse her, had destroyed her. Not that it mattered now: there could be no doubt as to Vallance's guilt, and now he was dead himself. That he had murdered Cindy made it more likely that he had killed Harry Nathan too. Perhaps she had the solution to the Nathan case right there in her hands, and she could leave the affair now with a clear conscience, do her best to find Feinstein's art, and go back to her own life.

But *why* had Vallance killed Cindy? Lorraine thought back to the morning he had come to her office, the night after Cindy died, with a wafer-thin veneer of normality concealing a state of considerable emotional turmoil. He had talked compulsively about Nathan and the past and, as she replayed the conversation in her mind, virtually the first words out of his mouth had been hatred and condemnation of the women around Nathan. He had raved about how they had cheapened and damaged his idol, and how he believed Cindy had been responsible for her husband's death, though she would never have been convicted of his murder. The motive that seemed most likely was a desire on Vallance's part to exact vengeance for Nathan on the woman who killed him, which made it most unlikely that Vallance had shot Nathan himself, unless he had completely lost his mind. But having spoken to him shortly before his death, Lorraine knew that that wasn't so. So who *had* killed Nathan? Would Kendall have killed him to prevent the porn tapes becoming public? Or could it somehow have been Sonja? Lorraine found it hard to believe that it was pure coincidence that Vallance shot himself in the Hamptons, within a few miles of Sonja Nathan's house, shortly after calling her . . .

Lorraine replaced everything as she had found it, and zipped up the case. She wanted to get out and was already planning a diversion to Santa Fe. She said to the manager, 'Don't let me prevent you any longer from attending to business, and thank you very much for your help. I'd pass these on to the police.' Then she hurried out to avoid any further conversation. She had found nothing relating to paintings or secret bank accounts, and no reason why Vallance had shot himself.

Lorraine sat down at a vacant table in the sun lounge and ordered a Coke and a prosciutto sandwich. She looked over the list of phone numbers she had taken down from Vallance's mobile, then circled one. She was sure the code was for Santa Fe. She was so immersed in her own thoughts that she jumped when Fischer slid down beside her, and told her in conspiratorial tones that the police were sending someone to collect Mr Vallance's luggage. She felt the man's breath on her face as he whispered that he had not mentioned that she had opened it.

'Good, and perhaps you'd better not mention that I was asking questions either – you know, there's always competition between the police in different counties.'

'Oh – well, yes, if you say so.'

'Is this a Santa Fe code?' she asked, repeating the number.

'I believe so, but I can check it out for you.'

'You could go one better and call the number for me. I'd like to know who it's registered to.' She gave him a cool smile, and he glided away. Lorraine finished her

Coke and sandwich, then walked out to Reception to collect her luggage.

A uniformed police officer was standing at the desk talking to Carina, who was handing over Vallance's cases, and Lorraine made out the same words that had been on everyone's lips all day – terrible, tragedy, unexpected – and Sonja Nathan's name.

'Of course, she'd known him more than twenty years,' she heard the officer say. 'She looked like she'd seen a ghost when I gave her the news.'

'Excuse me,' Lorraine said, glancing around quickly to make sure that Fischer was not nearby – she did not want him to see her talking to the officer and deduce that she was not, as she had said, working in association with the local police. 'Did you say you had to break the news of Raymond Vallance's death to Mrs Nathan?'

'Yes, ma'am,' Muller said, viewing her with interest.

'I know Mrs Nathan, I visited with her yesterday, and I wondered if perhaps I should call her. Was she very distressed?' Lorraine said, concern in her voice.

'Well, she was shaken,' Muller said. 'I knew she would be.'

'That's the difference between a city like LA and a place like this,' Lorraine gushed, trying to get him to say more. 'There's no way a city police department would ever have time to go and break the news of a friend's death personally to someone.'

'Well,' Muller said, 'it isn't usually part of the service here either. It's just that I was driving right past her gates when I got the news.'

'Goodness, how awful,' Lorraine went on, hoping he would not guess that she was fishing. 'So you had to tell her just a few minutes after he died?'

'Just about,' Muller said, eyeing Lorraine closely. 'You a friend of hers?'

'Not a close friend,' Lorraine said, keen now not to talk to him for too long. 'I know some connections of hers in Los Angeles and, since I was in the area, I gave her a call. I'm leaving now, actually – I'm just waiting to pick up my bags.'

She caught sight of Fischer coming towards her from the other side of the lobby with her case, and moved off to intercept him before he reached the desk. She gave Muller a final sweet smile, which she hoped convinced him that she was just an innocent visitor.

'The number – I'm sorry I didn't get back to you quicker, but the phones are still going crazy. It was Santa Fe, and the subscriber is Mr Nicholas Nathan.'

'Thank you for your help,' she said. And despite his previous strictures, she slipped a hundred-dollar bill into his hand. He watched her leave, then turned to Vern Muller who had joined him.

'Who is that lady?' Muller asked him curiously.

'Mrs Page?' Fischer replied. 'She's a private investigator working on the Harry Nathan murder inquiry. She said she was working with the police in LA and had full co-operation from you.'

'Oh, yeah?' the officer said. 'If she has, it's the first I've heard of it. She looks more like a newspaper reporter to me.'

'Well, she's gone now, whoever she is,' Fischer said. 'Let's get on with it.'

Sonja tucked the comforter round Arthur: he was fast asleep and snoring. Sometimes he looked like a scruffy

371

kid, and she felt such a touching warmth towards him. He took such care of her, and she loved him for it, had not realized how much until today. She moved quietly around the room, then went to a closet to select the clothes she wanted to pack and get out her case. She heard a car drawing up in the driveway and went into the other bedroom to look out to the front of the house. Vern Muller had sweat stains under the armpits of his blue uniform shirt, and was hitching up his navy police-issue trousers over his paunch. He tossed his hat into the rear seat, then looked at the house. Sonja saw him stop to admire her beloved garden before he set off up the path. She went downstairs and had the door open before he could wake Arthur by knocking or ringing the bell. 'Hi, Mrs Nathan. Sorry to bother you again,' he said, walking up the steps.

'Not at all, Vern,' Sonja said. 'Come on in.'

'I won't, Mrs Nathan, if you don't mind,' the police officer went on. 'I just stopped by to ask you if you know a lady named Lorraine Page.'

'Well, yes, I do,' Sonja said carefully. 'She called out here yesterday. She's a PI working for my late husband's lawyer in connection with the estate.'

'That's the story she told Fischer in the hotel, but when I spoke to her she said she was just a friend,' Muller went on. 'She told him and me another couple of things that weren't true, and she seemed pretty interested in this stuff about Raymond Vallance too – asked me if you were shocked and so on.' Sonja kept her face impassive. 'Wouldn't surprise me if she was some journalist come out here to dig dirt, or if you saw your name plastered with his across the papers,' the police officer concluded.

If that was all Lorraine was interested in, that was fine,

Sonja thought privately. 'Thanks for warning me, Vern,' Sonja said. 'I'll be careful what I say to her if she calls again.'

'Something about that lady makes me think she's looking to cause trouble for you,' Muller said. 'Take care now.'

'You too, Vern,' Sonja said, and closed the door. She leaned back against it for a moment. Upstairs Arthur lay sleeping. For the first time she had begun to believe that things were changing, that the dead hand of the past was losing its grip on her and a new life waiting to begin. There was only one person who could possibly stand in her way now – and that person was Lorraine Page.

Lorraine stared out of the window. There had been an accident, and the traffic tailed back for miles on both sides. They had been stationary for fifteen minutes, and the driver had got out to try to see what was going on. 'Nothing anyone can do,' he said, climbing back up. 'They're waiting for the recovery truck with a crane to drag two cars off the road, and there's a third overturned. Sorry, ladies and gentlemen.'

A collective moan went up, and Lorraine swore – she had been cutting it fine anyway, and now she doubted that she would catch the plane. The frustrating thing was that all she could do was sit and wait. She had been unable to concentrate on the book she'd bought, about art fraud through the centuries, so she opened her notebook. There were a few leads she could take further, but she was really no closer to finding either the missing money or the paintings than when she had first arrived.

She turned to a clean page. What if Nathan had

poured the money from the sale of the paintings back into his films? If that was the case, then there must be some record, but the investigation was cold. What if Nathan's brother had worked the fakes scam? He was family, would have got a slice of the money, and might even know where Harry had stashed it. She had to see him.

The bus jolted, advanced a few hundred yards, Lorraine stared out of the window. One of the vehicles going in the opposite direction was a cream Rolls-Royce, which brought Raymond Vallance to her mind.

What had made him kill himself? She turned to a fresh page in her notebook. Harry Nathan – dead, shot. Cindy Nathan – dead, probably murdered by Vallance. Kendall Nathan – dead, accidental fire? Raymond Vallance – dead, suicide. Lorraine tapped her teeth with the pen. Was it all a bit coincidental? Could Sonja have threatened him with the videotapes? What if there was no coincidence, but intent? She grimaced.

The bus moved forward another hundred yards before it stopped again, but Lorraine wasn't counting the minutes until her flight to LA. She had made up her mind that Santa Fe was her next destination.

CHAPTER 17

B Y THE time Lorraine arrived in New York it was almost eleven thirty p.m. and her flight to Los Angeles had long gone. She booked into the Park Meridian hotel and started to make some calls. She had to arrange travel to Santa Fe, first thing in the morning, and she knew she had to call Jake. As she dialled his number, part of her longed to hear his voice, but the other part, knowing what she was about to say, hoped that his answerphone would pick up.

Jake answered the phone almost immediately it rang.

'Lorraine!' he said, pure pleasure in his voice. 'Where are you? Do you want me to come pick you up?'

'Actually,' she began weakly, 'I'm still in New York.'

'New York?' he repeated, unable to mask his disappointment. 'What are you doing there?'

'Well,' she said, 'I got stuck in traffic and I missed the flight.'

'What a drag,' he said sympathetically. 'Can you get a flight in the morning?'

'Oh, sure,' Lorraine said. 'It's just that I have to make a detour, just for a day, to interview someone.'

'Where to?' he asked.

'Santa Fe. Nathan's brother is an artist out there – I

think he might have been the one forging the paintings. I'm pretty sure it was him and that'll wrap up the case – I mean, I can't just dump Feinstein, I said I'd try to trace his art . . .'

'Lorraine,' Jake said gently, 'you don't have to make excuses to me about doing your job.'

'I know, it's just that I don't want you to think I don't care about you. I'd give anything to be coming straight home.'

'I know you would,' he said. 'Don't worry about it. When will I see you?'

'Tomorrow – or at worst the day after.'

'That's okay,' he said, with a laugh. 'I waited for you for forty-five years so I figure I can manage another forty-eight hours.'

'This is going to be the last time I go away like this,' she said. 'I'm winding up the agency after this case – just as soon as I can get Feinstein off my back.'

'You don't have to do that, sweetheart,' Jake said, clearly taken aback. 'Why don't we talk about it when you get back?'

'I don't need to talk about it,' Lorraine said. 'It's my decision and I've thought about it. Bill Rooney was right – you get dirty in this business, dealing with sick people, damaged people, crooks all day. I've had enough.'

'Well,' Jake said, 'let's see if you feel the same way when you come home. It sounds as though the case still has its teeth in you for now.'

'Yeah, I know,' she said wryly. 'Don't worry, I can cut loose.'

'Sure you can,' he said, with a laugh. 'Hurry home.'

God, she thought, what had she done to deserve a guy like that? And why had she put off calling him for so long? She had assumed he would be irritated and resentful that she had been delayed, but it was clear that his only concern was to make life easier for her. There weren't many like him out there.

Next she called Rosie, who had now met Jake when he had brought Tiger around. 'You're a lucky lady – he loves you, and he was open about it, came right out with it. He said he was gonna marry you, and me and Bill never even mentioned it, I swear.'

Lorraine felt warm inside. 'He said that to you?'

'Yeah, and to Bill – like he wanted our approval. He and Bill got on like a house on fire, and you know what a prick Bill can be. Well, they acted like old buddies, and the best thing is, Jake started asking about Mike and your girls. He said he felt you should get to know them. I think he kinda wants a family . . . are you there? Hello?'

'Yes, Rosie, I'm here.'

'He also said he was missing you and you didn't call often enough.'

'Well,' Lorraine said, 'I just called him, so that's taken care of.'

'About time!' Rosie said. 'This one you don't let off the hook.'

Lorraine felt so good she laughed.

Then Rosie told Lorraine that all she wanted was for her to find the same happiness she had found, and she reckoned that, of all the people she knew, Lorraine deserved it the most. 'See, I love you, and so does Bill.'

Lorraine lay back on the bed. 'I love you, too, and I'll see you both very soon.'

'How soon is that?' Rosie asked. 'Something tells me it's slightly later than planned.'

'Well,' Lorraine said sheepishly – how well her friend

knew her! 'I got a bit of a lead on this case, so I'm going to Santa Fe – just one interview, then I'll be on my way home.'

'Lorraine!' Rosie said, exasperation in her voice. 'There's some things more important than this case and that interview, you know. You gotta take care of the rest of your life.'

'Jake'll take care of me for the rest of my life,' Lorraine said, knowing that that was what her friend wanted to hear. 'Just after this one interview, okay? I'm still working for Feinstein and I can't just drop the case.'

'Okay,' Rosie said resignedly. 'We'll take care of Tiger, and I'll stop by your place and water the plants. It's hot as hell here.'

'Can you check my fridge too? And there's a crate of dog food under the sink.'

'Okay, he sure does eat. So when will you be back?'

'Tomorrow evening, next day at worst.'

'I'll be waiting.'

'Great, see you then – and, Rosie, give that Bill Rooney a big hug from me.'

'I will. 'Bye now.' Rosie hung up.

Lorraine rolled off the bed, her spirits high. She took a shower, washed her hair and got into bed. It was just after two, and she fell into a deep, dreamless sleep.

It was only six when she woke up, but she couldn't go back to sleep. As there was still an hour before the breakfast she'd ordered would arrive, she got up and sat at the writing desk in her room. Just as she had on the bus from the Hamptons, she went over the case – her last case, she said to herself, and as it was the last, she would not rest until she'd cracked it.

Something still unexplained which irked Lorraine was the phone call, apparently from Cindy, that she had received the day Nathan died. Lorraine would have bet her bottom dollar that it was either Kendall or Sonja, and if so, one of them had known about the murder virtually at the time it was committed. Or had Cindy called one of them to ask for help, and then that person had called Lorraine? Kendall would not have given Cindy the time of day, but Sonja had seemed to feel some measure of concern for her – that had struck Lorraine as odd because she did not consider Sonja either caring or altruistic.

She was still sitting hunched over her notebook when her breakfast arrived. Half an hour later, Reception called to say her car was waiting to take her to the airport.

Sonja lay back in the luxurious, king-sized bed, her breakfast tray beside her. She had arranged a hair-dressing appointment, manicure and massage in the hotel, leaving plenty of time to prepare for the flight, and was looking forward to being back in Europe again. She always looked on the Old World, where she had grown up, as home. Harry was dead, Raymond was dead, and she had vowed that the years of pain and obsession would be buried with them. She would choose the right man now where she had chosen the wrong one before, would choose a real life now over a living death. There was just one final statement she had to make.

Arthur, smart in a navy suit with broad pinstripes, walked in from the dining area with an armful of newspapers. 'Vallance got good coverage – they're using photographs of him from back in the fifties. There's the

New York Times, LA Times, Variety . . .' He had not questioned Sonja any further about Vallance's death, fearful of disturbing the fragile equilibrium of her mood.

Sonja read the articles, then turned to the arts page in the *LA Times*. She glanced over at Arthur. 'You read this?' Arthur sat on the edge of the bed and Sonja went on, 'It's about the fiasco in Spain at the Prado – they fired some art historian who wrongly hailed some painting found in the archives as an undiscovered Goya. It was already registered as a Mariano Salvador Maella.'

Arthur picked up a piece of toast and bit into the crust. 'He was one of Goya's contemporaries, lesser known, but how the hell they could confuse his work with Goya's is beyond me.'

Sonja continued to read, then looked over at him again. 'They only had a preliminary sketch listed as Maella and registered in their records.'

'Typical,' he said, shrugging. 'But these national art galleries have so many political strings attached and are run by assholes.'

'It says that they should have bought Goya's *Marianito*.'

'Better still, they should have snapped up *Condesa de Chinchon* – it's recognized as his best work. That's in private hands, though.'

'Is it?' Sonja peered at the paper. 'They say they don't have the funds to do renovations so that they can show one of the finest art collections in the world. It's bursting at the seams with nine out of ten of its treasures buried in vaults for lack of space . . .' She smiled at him. 'Would you like to be let loose in there?' He wandered to the window without replying. 'Could you do a Goya?' she asked, turning to the fashion page.

'No. I can't do anyone that good – every brushstroke is a signature. The stuff Harry had wasn't in the same class.'

She lowered the paper. 'Are you all right? Not nervous about the deal, are you?' He kept his back to her, so she crossed to him. 'What's the matter?'

'Nothing.'

He tried to move away, but she caught his arm. 'Tell me what it is.'

'It's nothing, sweetheart. Now, if you're going to get your hair done, I should—'

'I don't need to. I can stay with you.'

'Don't be stupid. Not that you need any primping – I love you any way you look.'

She reached up and touched his cheek. 'Thank you, but it gives me confidence to look good. You know how I hate standing up on platforms, let alone giving speeches. Though this will be the last one.'

'Sonja, don't talk that way. You'll work again if you want to. Just give it time.'

'I've given all the time I intend to give to my work in this lifetime,' Sonja said, a trace of bitterness in her voice. 'That's over now. Harry killed something deep inside me, and it just won't come alive again.'

She was about to say more, but Arthur swore, almost frightening her. The tension he had been suppressing since he walked into the room now rushed to the surface in a torrent of words. 'He's dead, Sonja, for God's sake – *the man is dead*. You make everything I am, everything *we* are, second best, second rate. Whenever you bring up that son-of-a-bitch – and you do, at every opportunity—'

'I certainly don't,' Sonja said, needled. 'I don't know

what more I could have done to put him out of my life. It was just that PI asking questions about him stirred up the memories again.'

'Really? Well, I'm sick of hearing his name, and I've been patient, but I don't know how much longer I can go on living with just the leftovers. I don't want to hear about him any more. Whatever he did, whatever happened between you, is in the past, and if you want to keep it in the present, then *I'm* past, Sonja, because I can't take it. I never wanted to get involved in this paintings scam, I did it for you. I—'

'It's going to make you very rich,' Sonja snapped.

Arthur moved quickly across the room and grabbed her. 'You don't hear me, Sonja. Believe me, I know how much we'll be worth. We've had to wait for it long enough, but without you, and I mean all of you, it won't mean anything. All I want is some kind of assurance that he's not going to dominate your life from his fucking grave. I don't understand how you can keep on and on about him, keep loving such a cheap bastard.'

'You think I still love him?'

'It's obvious. You can't stop talking about the man! You go on and on about him to anyone who'll listen, even to a woman digging around for stuff that could put us in jail. If that's not love, then . . .' He raised his hands in a helpless gesture.

Sonja put her arms around him. 'I don't love him, you big fool.'

He had to prise her away from him, wanting to look into her green-grey eyes see if she was lying. They were steady, and she didn't flinch from his gaze.

'I hated him, and I have hated with such intensity I have hardly been alive. He betrayed and destroyed everything I valued, he made everything I was meaningless. He threw all I had done for him back in my face, mangled all the love and care I gave him. It was as if he held me in his bare hands and kept wringing me like a rag, until—'

Arthur interrupted, his voice soft, 'I've heard this before, Sonja. I'm not listening to you, but you should listen to me. I don't want his leftovers, I need more – and if you can't be free of him, then, for my own sanity, I have to be free of you.'

The phone rang and Arthur snatched it up, exchanged a couple of curt words with the caller, then said Sonja would be right down. 'The hair salon – you're late.'

He made as if to leave, but she held out her arms to him in entreaty. This time he did not, as he always did, cradle her to him and say it was all right.

'I'll be ready in a couple of hours,' she said, letting her arms fall back by her sides. 'I'll never mention his name again.'

He wanted to smack her, shake her, throw her across the bed. He said, 'Not enough – *that's not enough*. I don't give a shit if you talk about him, that's not what I've been trying to get across to you and you know it. Whether it's love or hate is immaterial. I'm just sick and tired of him being between us. When he was alive it was bad enough, but now he's dead . . . I sometimes wish to Christ I'd pulled the trigger.'

She gave a strange, sad smile. 'No, you didn't, but I did.'

He felt as if he'd been punched. He swallowed hard. 'Go and have your hair done.'

'I love you,' she said softly.

Arthur halted in his tracks. 'Say that again.'

She was smiling again now, but a different smile of fun and pleasure. 'I love you.' She laughed.

'No, what you said before that. After I said I wished I'd pulled the trigger. Repeat what you said.'

'I said I wished I did.'

'No, you didn't. You said, "I did."'

'Artistic licence – I needed an exit line.'

'No, your exit line was after you said you loved me. So – was it a joke?'

She closed her eyes. It was not that she was afraid to look at him, she was afraid she might lose him, that as soon as she had decided wholeheartedly to commit herself to him, he would be the one to back away. Suddenly she knew that that was more than she could bear.

'Of course it was a joke,' she said. 'I mean, if you wanted to pull the trigger, do you think I didn't?'

'Open your eyes,' he said, bending closer, and she did as he asked.

'Give me the exit line, only this time look at me.'

'I love you,' she said softly.

'You got me,' he said, his voice gruff. He had waited a long time to hear her say it, and mean it.

Lorraine ate her plastic lunch on the nine thirty flight out of Newark, eager to get the interview with Nick Nathan over and done with, and hoping the journey wouldn't be a waste of time. She landed in Albuquerque just after lunch and stepped out into the surprisingly pleasant dry air of a high altitude and to the limitless New Mexico sky: even in fall it was like walking on the bottom of an ocean of blue, which made even the mountains surrounding the desert city seem only knee-high. She carried her jacket over her arm, her briefcase in one hand and made her way through the terminal to the travel agent's. She picked up a rental car, a Buick, then, armed with road maps, pulled out of town into the landscape of grey rock, desert pine and juniper to look for signs for the I-25 to Santa Fe.

As she joined the Interstate, Lorraine noticed on the map that its first thirty miles followed the course of the Rio Grande, and she could not resist turning off the highway for a few minutes to look at the great canyon, plunging down hundreds of feet to a truly breathtaking depth. Its sheer scale produced an overwhelming sense of the measureless, almost the eternal, and Lorraine understood now why so many artists and writers had chosen to make New Mexico their home. Still, she allowed herself only a couple of minutes' delay – one middle-aged painter was all the scenery she had come to see.

Sonja came back from the beauty salon feeling glossy, gleaming and beautiful from top to toe, and she knew that part of the feeling of newness and freshness had nothing to do with the beauty treatments or the new hairdo: she felt that she and Arthur had turned the corner at last. It had been her fault, she knew, that it had taken so long, but she would make it up to him now.

When she got back Arthur was not in the suite, but there was plenty of time to dress, and she decided to wear a tailored navy suit with a crisp white shirt, dark navy stockings and matching navy court shoes. She had a Valentino navy and white check trench-style coat that she would slip around her shoulders. She had made up carefully and slightly more heavily than usual, glossing her lips in a deep pink shade she had bought downstairs to match her expertly lacquered nails, and she smiled in the mirror at her new manicure. It had been months, years, since she had taken such care of her hands, but she could have inch-long talons covered in scarlet glitter now if she wished. It had been months, too, since she had bothered to accentuate her eyes, her most striking feature, with shadow and mascara and the fine tracing of dark liner on the lids, which extended their length. When she had finished she studied her reflection carefully – a new woman, she thought, or, rather, a transformed one, risen from the ashes of the old.

She checked her soft leather document case for her passport and tickets, then snapped it shut and cast an eye over the rest of the luggage, which she had lined up by the main door of the suite. She checked that Arthur's cases were packed and ready, then searched the room to make sure nothing had been left behind. The limo would be arriving any minute, and she wondered where Arthur had got to. She hated last-minute scrambles to get to airports.

The phone rang – Reception, as she had expected, to say that their car was waiting. She told them to send up a porter for the luggage, and to take the other items the concierge was holding for her to the car. When the porter arrived with the trolley and loaded the luggage, there was still no sign of Arthur and Sonja sat at the writing desk drumming her fingers.

She didn't hear him come in, but she turned as she heard his voice. He counted the luggage, and then, as Sonja had done, reminded the porter not to forget the other things with the concierge. 'They know, I told them,' she said, then gasped. Arthur was wearing a white shirt with a Russian collar and a dark grey pinstriped suit. His hair had been trimmed and he was sporting a pair of round Armani sunglasses with steel frames. 'My, my, you've been shopping,' she said, smiling, and he posed with one hand on his hip.

'What do you think? It's too straight?'

'You look fabulous – turn around.' He did so, and Sonja clapped. 'You look so good – I really like it. My God, new shoes as well.'

Arthur looked down and removed his shades. 'Yeah, got everything from the same place, and I had a haircut and a shave at the barber's in the hotel, and . . .' He dug in his pocket and produced a small leather box, which he tossed to her. Then he looked closely at her, and took in her appearance with surprise: it had been months since he had seen her looking so elegant, so feminine, and he was almost unnerved by it. 'You look very grown-up,' he said, walking round her.

'I've had all these things for ages,' she said. 'Just never got around to wearing them.' She opened the box and gasped – it contained a solitaire diamond ring. She snapped it shut as the porter wheeled out their luggage. 'Are you crazy? I thought we'd agreed to be careful until . . . afterwards. How much did this cost?'

He pointed to the box. 'That was a legitimate hole in my legitimate earnings. Now open it again. You're supposed to look at me, all dewy-eyed, then I put it on your finger.'

'What?'

'Jesus Christ, it's an engagement ring – didn't you look at it properly?'

Sonja opened the box again and started to laugh gently. 'Engagement? Aren't we a bit old for that kind of—'

Arthur took the box from her and removed the ring. He hurled the box across the room. 'Now, gimme your hand and let me do this properly.'

The ring was a little too large for her finger, but it didn't matter – it made Sonja feel happy and warm. Arm in arm, they went to the elevators, where the porter was waiting.

Sonja twisted the ring round and round her finger, then she held up her hand to look at the stone. Arthur laughed as she examined it closely, and by the time the elevator stopped on the ground floor they were both laughing: the jewel was a fake, but an exceptionally good one. Sonja kept turning it on her finger as she watched the luggage being loaded into the trunk of the limo. Arthur's 'wardrobe' of paintings had been sent ahead on an earlier flight so that the canvases would be stretched, framed and ready for collection on their arrival in Germany, as had the new piece of work Sonja proposed to exhibit for the first time in Berlin. While she was receiving her award, Arthur would be delivering his own exhibition to the small independent gallery in Kreuzberg – a cover for negotiating the sale of a second collection, accumulated over years and valued at twenty million dollars, with the list of private buyers he and Sonja had carefully selected.

After leaving the Rio Grande flood plain, Lorraine drove through a switchback of gently rolling hills before she reached the lower slopes of La Bajaba, and began the ascent of the notoriously steep mountain. At last she reached the plateau and the centuries-old settlement of Santa Fe came into view, surrounded by the same backdrop of mountain landscape against the huge, azure sky. She drove into town, chose a small motel near the downtown area almost at random and booked a room in which to change and make phone calls.

She rang Nick Nathan's number. A woman answered and was at first wary, asking how Lorraine had got their number. She told her that Raymond Vallance had suggested she call: she was opening a gallery and needed to find work by unknown artists. Vallance had recommended Nick. The woman kept her waiting for some time before she returned to give the address and a time at which it would be convenient to call. Lorraine had two hours to kill, so she decided to check up on some of the local galleries and enquire whether any of Nathan's work was on sale.

Lorraine walked past a number of galleries in the Plaza and the surrounding streets, and even without specialist knowledge of art she could tell that some of the works displayed were as sophisticated as anything she had seen in LA. It was clear that the old town was an art snob's heaven. Everywhere, too, was the beautiful American-Indian jewellery, glowing rows of semi-precious stones surrounded by silver settings, whose traditional designs Lorraine recognized as the height of current fashion. She studied piece after piece in turquoise, lapis, amethyst, citrine, rose quartz, freshwater pearls and a dozen other stones, whose names she didn't know, before eventually buying a serpentine ring for Rosie, some lapis cuff-links for Rooney, and an elaborate necklace of five inlaid hearts suspended from a beaded choker, all in precious minerals and stones, for herself. She savoured, too, the opportunity to look for a gift for Jake. It had been so long since she had had someone special to shop for that the time flew past. Then she saw two heavy silver cuff bracelets, set with bars of turquoise and speckled leopard-skin jasper. She went into the shop and bought them both. When the assistant remarked on how beautiful they looked on her wrist, she spoke without thinking. 'They're for my daughters.'

As she waited for the bracelets to be wrapped, she repeated, 'They're for my daughters,' in her mind. She knew that what Jake had said, and Rosie had repeated to her, meant yet another step towards her future.

When she returned to the car, she checked the map, then began to concentrate on how she would question Nathan, and, most important of all, what she needed to get out of the interview.

The narrow alleyway ran between two four-storey houses with shop fronts, situated in the most rundown part of town. She headed down the alley past boxes of old garbage from both of the shops, and found a peeling door marked 48. As it was ajar, Lorraine pushed it open.

The hallway was narrow, cluttered with bits of broken furniture and a mattress was propped up against a door. A girl of about nine was sitting on the stairs, whose bare boards were dusty and well worn.

'Hi, I'm looking for someone called Nick. Do you know which floor?'

The child wiped her nose with the back of her grubby hand. 'Up, number eight,' she said, and held out her hand. Lorraine opened her purse and gave her a dollar, and the little girl ran out, squealing with pleasure.

Lorraine tidied her hair, then tapped on the door. She could hear a male voice talking and laughing, so rapped again louder, then hit the door with the flat of her hand.

A chain was removed, and the door opened an inch. 'Yes?'

'I'm Lorraine Page – I called earlier.'

'Oh, yes, one moment.' A dark-haired woman un-hooked the chain and opened the door wide, stepping back almost to hide behind it. 'Come in.'

Lorraine followed her into the apartment. The cramped hallway was dark, with coloured shawls tacked to the wall. A fishing net was draped over a doorway, and a large papier-mâché sun hung above a stripped pine door, which stood open.

Lorraine was surprised – the room was large, and very bright. The sloping ceiling and walls were painted white, while the bare floorboards had been stripped and stained, then varnished to a gleaming finish. All four windows were bare of curtains, as the room was obviously used as a studio, and the light was important. Paintings were displayed on easels, and stacks of canvases lined the walls, propped against one another.

The woman, who had still not introduced herself, moved with a lovely fluid grace from window to window, drawing down blinds for much-needed shade: the room was unbearably hot. 'We don't have air-conditioning,' she said.

Lorraine recognized her vaguely from Harry Nathan's funeral. She was pale, almost unhealthy-looking, with large brown eyes, quite a prominent nose, and a rather tight mouth with buck teeth. She was not unattractive, but there was a plainness about her, and her straight dark hair, swept away from her face with two ugly hair-grips, needed washing. She wore leather sandals and a loose-fitting print dress, which left her arms bare, and she held her hands loosely in front of her.

'Do you want some coffee?' Her voice was thin, and she kept her head inclined slightly downwards, as though she didn't want to meet Lorraine's eyes.

'Yes, please, black, no sugar – but if you have some honey . . .'

'Sure.'

She started to walk out, but stopped and performed a sort of pirouette when Lorraine asked if she was Nick's wife. 'I suppose so – I'm Alison. Please look around. He won't be long – he's just on the phone.'

As the door closed Lorraine smiled. She began to look first at the half-finished work on the easel, a portrait of a dark-haired man with finely cut features, but full, sensual lips, apparently looking through water, with flowers resting against his cheek and the lips slightly parted, as if he were gasping for air. The painting was unnerving, because Lorraine was sure the subject was Harry Nathan. She didn't like it, not that the work wasn't good, for it was, but it had a childish, almost careless quality. She turned her attention to some of the bigger canvases on the walls, all of which had a similar wash of pale colour in the background, and featured the same man from different angles and in a variety of poses – hidden by ferns, screaming and, in one, with a sports shoe carefully painted on top of his head.

Other canvases were traversed by a series of palm-prints, or featured pieces of fabric and leaves, but all appeared half-finished, as if the artist had grown bored mid-way and moved on to something else. Lorraine looked closely at a painting on the wall furthest from the door, which showed a group of tall trees with some scrawled writing superimposed on them.

She turned as Alison reappeared with a large chipped mug, and held it out to her. 'Coffee.' Lorraine took it, and the woman remained standing nearby, her head still bowed.

'Are you a painter?' Lorraine asked, with false brightness: there was a servile quality about Alison that made her skin crawl, as if she were afraid of something.

'No.'

She was tough to make conversation with.

'Have you lived here long?'

'A while.'

Alison straightened up and flexed her shoulder. She began to massage the nape of her neck, then gave a faint smile and left the room.

Lorraine could hear what they were saying in the next room.

'I'm going out now – I've got a class.'

'Okay, see you.'

She moved closer to the open door: Alison was standing in the doorway opposite and the conversation continued in audible whispers.

'Is she looking at them?'

'Yes, she was when I took her coffee in.'

'I'll give her a few minutes, then. What's her name again?'

Alison replied, but Lorraine couldn't hear what she said, nor could she see the man she presumed was Nick. A phone rang, and Alison turned to cross to the front door, but waited a minute listening. Nick said hello to the caller, and Alison left.

Lorraine finished her coffee. She was becoming irritated – the call went on and on. She set the mug down on the floor and started to detach some of the canvases from the stack – all of the same man. She moved to the next group. These were much better, stronger. She found one she liked a lot and pulled it out. It was a crude, but powerful, life-sized portrait – not, for once, of the dark man but of an Indian brave in feathered headdress. She put it to one side, planning to ask the price – it would make a nice present for Jake. She was about to move to the next group of canvases when she heard a loud shriek, sustained for some time. She ran over to the open door.

'It says *what*? Go on! How old does it say he was?'

The cries continued. Lorraine stepped into the hallway and made her way to the doorway at the end of the passage. She stood just outside the kitchen.

Nick Nathan had his back to her and was leaning against the side of a table talking on a wall-mounted phone. His dark, slightly greying hair was pulled back, as it has been at the funeral, with a rubber band. He was barefoot and wore torn, dirty jeans and a paint-stained cotton shirt, whose sleeves were rolled up to reveal muscular arms, one wrist encircled by a heavy silver bracelet, and a similar ring on the third finger of his other hand.

'*Vallance shot himself*? You're kidding me.'

He listened, then shrieked again in the same high-pitched fashion. He was almost bent double, and Lorraine realized suddenly that he was laughing. And whoever was on the other end of the line was telling him about the suicide of Raymond Vallance.

The call continued for another ten minutes. Lorraine returned to the studio, wishing there was somewhere to sit down. She lit a cigarette, and had smoked half of it when the shrieking stopped.

Finally Lorraine heard the receiver banged down. She hoped that Nick Nathan would finally come in and greet her, but then heard the clatter of dishes, and his voice calling the cat. At last the man came in like a whirlwind. 'Hi – sorry to keep you waiting. I'm Nick.'

He danced across to her, and pumped her hand up and down. His eyes had a manic look, and he was sweating profusely, his thinning hair sticking to his scalp. He darted close to her, then moved just as rapidly away, looking pointedly at the cigarette and opening a window.

'I'm sorry.' She gestured to her cigarette, but Nick shrugged.

'You want to die, it's your choice.'

He smiled suddenly, showing even white teeth, but his eyes were hunted, and he couldn't keep still, wandering around the room dragging out one canvas after another. Now that she had seen him, Lorraine wondered if the man in the paintings was himself, but he didn't have the same high cheekbones – his face was flatter and plainer than his brother's.

'I'm interested in that one,' Lorraine said, tossing the cigarette out of the window.

Nick whipped round to look at the painting she had pulled out of the stack.

'How much?' she asked, uncomfortable. She couldn't seem to get centred around Nathan – he was so off-beam that he unnerved her.

'Five thousand dollars,' he snapped, as if challenging her, but she didn't flinch.

'I'll take it,' she said calmly, and he beamed, picking the piece up to admire it himself. Then he started to drag out canvases at an alarming rate, laying them around the room. He babbled to her, asking about her gallery, if she was looking for a one-man show, or intended displaying a number of artists' work together.

'How did you find me?' he said, so intent on finding work to show to her that he didn't appear interested in her reply.

'Raymond Vallance suggested I call you,' she said, and saw him stiffen.

'He's dead,' he said, staring at her.

'I know, he committed suicide.'

She was wondering how in the hell she could start to question him – the reason she had come – but knew that she had to tread carefully. From what she had seen of his work, Nathan did not have the technical virtuosity to imitate better artists, and he seemed so mentally unstable that he would be too dangerous to have in on any scam – but she had come all this way to interview him and she intended to do so.

Lorraine took out her cheque book and started writing. 'Do you show your work mainly in Santa Fe?' she said, pretending to make conversation but paving the way for the real question she wanted to ask.

'I guess,' Nathan said. 'I've shown in California too.'

'Did you work with your brother's gallery?' Lorraine said casually.

Nick eyed her suspiciously. 'How do you know my brother had a gallery?' he asked.

'Oh, just contacts,' Lorraine said airily. 'I know a lot of people in the art world – I've come across Kendall too. It must have been very useful, having a gallery in the family, so to speak.'

Nick said nothing for a while. Then, 'I had a few pieces in there.'

'Did you ever live in Los Angeles?'

'No. I just stayed at his place a few times.'

Lorraine finished writing the cheque with a flourish and Nathan slowly relaxed. 'I hated LA,' he said. 'Full of fucking phoneys. They wouldn't know art if it walked up and bit them in the face.'

'That's a pity. I'm sure Kendall could have promoted your work.'

He sneered, 'The only person Kendall ever promoted was herself, money-grubbing bitch. My brother wanted more of my work, but she wouldn't have it.'

'Her gallery was successful, though,' Lorraine said.

'Bullshit! Filled with crap, wallpaper paintings.'

'Yes, some of those paintings look as though just about anyone could do them,' Lorraine said innocently. 'I'm sure you could do stuff in exactly the same style if you wanted to.'

'You bet I could,' Nick said. 'If I wanted to.'

'It must be a great temptation,' Lorraine said, flattering him, 'I mean, for a real artist, if money's tight, to know you could make a lot more just by imitating someone who happens to be flavour of the month.'

'Well,' he said, 'sometimes I've worked in a particular way because that was what a buyer wanted – that's the difference between working to a commission and working for yourself.'

'You haven't ever copied, say, a specific painting?' Lorraine went on.

'What? You mean an exact copy of a named work?' Nick said. 'Absolutely not – that's forgery, in case you hadn't heard.'

'But it must be quite a temptation,' Lorraine persisted.

'Not to me,' Nick said. 'I couldn't do it if I tried – it's a specific skill, and besides, my own work's too strong.'

'You don't know anyone connected with your brother who maybe . . . wouldn't have quite the same scruples?' she asked. She tore out the cheque and laid it on the table.

'Who the fuck are you?'

'Someone who's got five thousand dollars on the table for you, but I need you to answer a few questions.' He shook his head, and kept on shaking it. 'I'm a private investigator.' She flipped him her card, but he didn't take it. 'I've been hired by your brother's lawyer, Mr Feinstein. Do you know him?' Nick glared at her, his arms wrapped around his body. 'I've been hired to trace assets missing from your brother's estate.' This elicited a flicker of interest. 'Paintings.'

'What?'

She'd hooked him. 'Either there's a mountain of valuable art concealed somewhere, or there's several million dollars hidden in an undected account.' She took the list of missing paintings from her briefcase, and passed it to him. 'These are the works I'm looking for.'

He took a long time reading the list, then let the paper drop onto the table. 'I wouldn't pay a hundred bucks for any one of those assholes' pictures.'

'Maybe you wouldn't, but other people did – or at least they thought they did. Various buyers at Gallery One viewed an original, got it authenticated, but then someone copied it, and it was the copy that was hung on their walls.'

'Well,' Nick said, 'it was nothing to do with me. Nice scam, though – I wish the bastard had cut me in on it.'

Lorraine studied him. Her gut feeling was that he was telling the truth. 'You don't know of anyone Harry could have been working with?' she asked.

'Well, Kendall's a pretty obvious candidate, isn't she?' he said. 'She would have dug up her grandmother's grave if she thought there was a nickel in it.'

'She was certainly involved in setting up the initial part of the operation with Harry, but he switched the paintings again to cut her out. I was just wondering if that was all his idea, or if someone else was pulling the strings.'

'They must have been,' Nick said. 'Harry was never like that.' Unexpectedly, he started to weep uncontrollably, rubbing at his eye sockets while Lorraine watched in fascinated horror at this sudden switch of mood. The crying jag ended as suddenly as it had begun. 'Sorry,' he said. 'My brother was better-looking than me, better at everything. He was a hard act to follow, and all my life, until he died, I was kind of following . . . I still can't believe he's dead.'

'Kendall's dead, too, now, did you know?' Lorraine said.

'Yeah,' he replied. He was obviously not interested in discussing Kendall's death so Lorraine changed tack.

'What does Alison do?'

He smiled, and stretched out his arms. 'She's a dancer, but dancing's a hard world, almost as hard as painting.' Then he asked, 'You know Sonja?'

'I've met her.'

'She sent you here, didn't she?' he demanded.

'No, I told you, it was Raymond Vallance.'

He shrieked with laughter again, mouth wide open. 'That old queen! He clung to his past glories like a falling climber.'

'At least he had some to cling to,' Lorraine said quietly, but her sarcasm was lost on Nathan, who gave another loud hoot of laughter.

'He was in love with my brother, everybody was in love with him. Everybody always thought he was something special, and you know something, I did too. It wasn't until he was dead that I realized he was a loser.'

Lorraine had heard enough and Nick Nathan irritated her. The trip to Santa Fe had been largely a waste of time, but at least she knew he hadn't been responsible for the forgeries. It was interesting, too, that the family's suspicions, like her own, seemed to centre on Sonja . . .

'I have to go,' she said. 'Can you pack up the picture for me?'

He parcelled it in newspaper and handed it to her, saying that if she wanted any more of his work, all she had to do was call.

'Just for my records,' she said, 'could you tell me when you last saw your brother?'

'Must be a couple of years ago, just before he and Kendall broke up. Come to think of it, they were talking about getting some painting copied. I thought they meant onto a slide – it was one of that asshole Schnabel's.' He moved out into the corridor, heading for the stairs, and Lorraine followed.

'Was it just Harry and Kendall, or was anyone else there?'

'There was another guy – Arthur something, I don't know his last name. It was after a show Kendall had, and he and I had a kind of fight – over the Schnabel. I said it wasn't worth the hook it was hanging from and he kind of went for me. Fucking asshole.' Nick stopped on the landing to continue his tirade against Julian Schnabel, talentless bum, in his opinion, promoted by a clique of art insiders interested in lining their own pockets by inflating the prices of certain court favourites' work. 'Everything's fixed, you realize that? Art has got nothing to do with the market.' He jabbed his finger into Lorraine's chest. 'I've trailed my work round every fucking New York gallery. I send in my slides and they lose them. Then they buy a fucking piece of canvas with a wooden plank sticking out of it. That's not art.'

Lorraine stepped back to avoid Nathan's finger, and decided to risk interrupting him. 'Do you recall anything more about this Arthur?'

'Big guy, dark,' Nick said, setting off down the stairs.

'Do you know if he was a painter?' Lorraine asked, hurrying after him.

'I don't know. Bastards like Schnabel probably pay people like him to talk up their work. He hung around after the show, like he was waiting for me to go, and I thought, Fine, screw you, I'm just the guy's fucking brother, so I walked out. Then I forgot my jacket so I go back, and the three of them were out back in a kind of workroom, and Kendall and Harry were standing behind him, and he was using this big lamp, looking over the canvas, right, and . . .'

'What exactly did he say?' Lorraine asked. 'It's very important.'

'Oh, I can't remember. Kendall said something about

having a buyer and he said something about getting a copy made quickly. Maybe he's your rip-off artist.'

'Did you ever see him again?' Lorraine asked.

'No, I never went back to LA,' Nick said, then gave a boyish smile, and clapped his hands together, like a salesman who had just clinched a big deal. 'I hope you enjoy my work, and you have a real nice day. Been great meeting you, Loretta.'

Lorraine didn't correct him. 'Nice meeting you too, Nick,' she said, turning to go. Had he really just remembered this vital detail from the past, or was it a ploy on the part of Nathan's family to incriminate Sonja and her lover?

CHAPTER 18

LORRAINE RETURNED to the motel, her head aching. She called Feinstein and told him that she was beginning to find leads, and asked if her expenses could run to another trip, this time to visit Nathan's mother.

'Christ, she's in Chicago,' he demurred.

'I know, but it might tie up some loose ends.'

'Go ahead, then,' he said, and gave her Abigail Nathan's address and phone number.

Lorraine called Rosie to say she would not be coming home that afternoon, but would try for the following morning. Rosie agreed to keep Tiger for another night, and Lorraine heard Rooney in the background asking to speak to her.

'Lorraine,' he said, 'I've stopped by the office a couple of times and there's someone calling you all the time.'

'Well,' Lorraine said, 'if they're looking for my professional services you can tell them I'm about to retire.'

'It's not that,' Rooney said. 'Whoever it is hangs up the whole time – no message. Rosie and I thought it might be Jake, but you've spoken to him, haven't you?'

'Yes, I have. He's too busy for that kind of thing, anyway,' Lorraine said.

'That's what I thought. There's so many calls it's like someone's doing it deliberately, to make you realize someone's trying to get to you – it's like they think you must know who it is. I was just wondering if you've trodden on someone's tail.'

'Well, that's a possibility,' Lorraine said thoughtfully. 'How long has this been going on?'

'A few days,' Bill said.

That meant it could hardly be anything to do with Nick Nathan, which left only Sonja and Arthur, Lorraine thought, but said nothing to Rooney.

'Is there anything I can do from this end?' he asked.

'There is, Bill. In my office there are two plastic bags. They've got a lot of catalogues from art galleries, with notes from Decker. Can you go through them and find out about a painting by Julian Schnabel? It would have been in the Nathan gallery about four years ago. It's not on my list, but see if there's any record of it, and I'll call you from Chicago.'

'Okay, will do . . . and you look after yourself.'

She caught Burton at the station, and once she heard his voice she wondered what the hell she was doing planning yet another detour.

'So,' he said, 'I get three guesses, right? You're coming home late, you're coming home late, or you're coming home late?'

'Well,' she said, 'I did say it might be tomorrow.'

'I know you did,' he said, easily. 'I bought you an extra-specially non-perishable present.'

'I bought you one too,' she said. 'A timeless work of art by Nick Nathan.'

'Mine's pretty timeless too,' he said, and something in this voice told her immediately what it was.

'Oh,' she said softly. 'Do I get three guesses?'

'No,' he said. 'I don't want to spoil the surprise. Just get your ass back here fast.'

'Will do,' Lorraine said. 'I swear I'll see you tomorrow even if I pass all of Feinstein's paintings at a garage sale on the way to the airport.'

'If *that* happens,' he said, with a deep laugh, 'you can miss the plane. Otherwise, see you then.'

She was about to hang up when she remembered what Rooney had said about the messages left at the office. 'Just one thing,' she said. 'You haven't been calling my answerphone at the office for any reason? Rooney says there've been some weird calls.'

He laughed again. 'I'm flattered I'm the first person you thought of but, much as I miss you, the answer is no.'

After they hung up, she had another fifteen minutes of considerably less cordial conversation with an irate agent at the airline before she succeeded in rearranging her flight, but she was en route to Chicago by late afternoon.

Sonja and Arthur waited for their luggage in the terminal at Tegel, the airport at Berlin, having already enlisted the services of a porter with a trolley. They had arranged for a car to pick them up outside. Sonja got in and leaned back, closing her eyes. 'God, I feel nervous, now that we're actually here. I kept thinking someone was going to challenge us when we went through customs.'

'Why would they? The paintings are at the gallery now.' He took her hand and squeezed it. 'We're here, and the paintings are here, it's nearly over. Just stay calm. We've already got over the most difficult part.'

'Yes, but you've still got to do the deal.'

'Don't worry,' Arthur said. 'The buyers are lined up and waiting and they'll eat right out of my hand.'

Lorraine booked into the Chicago Hyatt, where the room was pleasant and well-furnished, and called Abigail Nathan at once. Her voice sounded young, and when Lorraine explained that she was working for Mr Feinstein in connection with her son's estate, she immediately said she was free that evening or Lorraine could call the following morning. It was already after ten and Lorraine asked if she could come at nine the next day.

She planned an early night to be refreshed and ready for Mrs Nathan, so she showered, booked an alarm call for six and went straight to bed.

Rooney let himself into Lorraine's office and crossed to check the answerphone: the light was flashing, and the new message indicator was displaying the figure twenty-two. He replayed the messages to discover that only one was legitimate, from Feinstein. On the remainder the phone had been put down. The caller's attempts to alarm Lorraine had, however, intensified, and there were ominous silences, sometimes heavy breathing, and, on the last, what sounded like six blasts of gunfire. This was clearly intended as a threat, and Rooney was certain that the caller believed their identity was known to Lorraine.

He picked up the plastic bags he had come to collect, turned off the lights and left the building.

Back home, Rosie was cooking up a storm, trying out a new recipe for pork tenderloin with a complicated pink sauce, and was red-faced and flustered. 'I don't know what I've done with this sauce – I put enough cornstarch in it to hang wallpaper, but it's not thickening like it should,' she said, waving a wooden spoon.

'Whatever you serve up, honey, will be fine by me.'

He went to get a beer, and they jostled each other for space in the small, but well-equipped kitchen. 'Go on, go sit down. Table's already set,' Rosie said, pushing Rooney away gently.

He plodded out with his beer, then turned back to her. 'Usual creepy messages on her answerphone,' he said.

'Probably Jake.' She laughed.

'Yeah, probably,' he said. He was on the point of telling her about the gunshots, but decided to wait until after dinner, not wanting to spoil the meal she had taken such trouble with: Rosie worried enough about Lorraine as it was. Almost as soon as they had finished eating, however, Rosie's former AA sponsor called and asked if she would help him out at a meeting where he needed someone to sponsor a young girl.

'Do you mind, Bill?' she said. 'I know I said I'd stay home this evening, but if someone had been too busy to sponsor me, I never would have quit drinking.'

'And you would never have been working for Lorraine and I would never have met you.' Bill smiled. He knew that Rosie had a genuine desire to put something back into the organization that had changed her life. 'Go on out – I'll go through this stuff of Lorraine's.' She dropped a kiss on top of his head, got her coat and hurried off, with a promise not to be too late.

Left alone, Rooney spread out the catalogues and thumbed through them, looking for the painting

Lorraine had mentioned. He found no record of it. He flicked through Decker's notes of dates and times for each gallery he had visited, saddened by the task – the boy had been so organized, such a good find for the agency, and it was dreadful that he had died in such a terrible way, so young and, as his voluminous notes testified, so eager to prove himself. Rooney kept on flicking backwards and forwards, matching catalogues to Decker's notes on the galleries, then saw something that made his blood run cold.

In Decker's neat handwriting was a name and address – Eric Lee Judd, employee at Nathan's art gallery. Rooney sat back and drank some beer. He couldn't be mistaken. He knew it had been a long time, but it was a name he would never forget. When she had been drunk on duty, Lorraine Page had shot a teenager. The boy's name had been Tommy Lee Judd.

Rooney put in a call to Jim Sharkey's home, but he was out on a case so he left a message asking him to call. It was after nine and he wondered if it was too late – bad district to go calling on anyone late in the daytime, never mind at night, but he mulled it over, and drained his beer. To hell with it, he thought, why not? His adrenalin buzzled like old times – it was too much of a coincidence, and he wondered if he had just solved the mystery of Lorraine's unidentified caller.

Half an hour later, Rooney was heading towards the eastern suburbs of LA, having packed a shooter – he wasn't taking any chances. Like Decker before him, he had a hard time making out the numbers of the houses on the side-street near Adams and, like Decker too, he passed the Lee Judd bungalow and had to reverse back to it down the street. Lights blazed, so he knew someone was at home. He got out, took a good look around, locked the car and walked up the drive to the front door. He rapped hard and waited several minutes before knocking again. This time he saw the outline of a figure shuffling towards the door through the dirty glass.

'Who is it?'

'Bill Rooney. Mrs Lee Judd? Is that you? I'm Bill Rooney – used to be Captain Rooney, you remember me?'

The front-door chain was eased off, and she peered through, fear on her big moon face.

'It ain't bad news? Please, God, you ain't come with bad news?'

'No, Mrs Lee Judd, no bad news, not this time, but I need to talk to you.'

The door opened, and the woman looked up with frightened hazel eyes. Her dyed blonde hair showed two inches of dark root growth, and mulberry lipstick ran in rivulets round her flaccid lips. She was grotesquely overweight and her body gave off the distinctive stale smell of sweat. 'You ain't lying to me, are you?'

'No, ma'am, I'm not lying, but I need to talk to you.'

Rooney stared at the photograph. The boy was wearing the jacket with the yellow stripe down the back, his face half turned towards the camera. Unlike the other children in the photograph, Tommy took after his mother and was pale-skinned, while all his brothers and sisters had the dark colouring of their father, Joshua Lee Judd.

'Tommy's been gone a long time now,' she said sadly.

'Yes, a long time, Mrs Lee Judd, but never forgotten.'

She shook her head. 'You don't forget a boy you've

given birth to, no matter what he done, or what they say he done. He was my youngest, you know?'

'I know. Can I sit down?' he asked.

'Sure, you want something to drink?'

'No, nothing.'

She eased her bulk into a worn armchair, and Rooney sat opposite her.

'So, how have you been keeping?'

'My legs give out on me – knees all swelled up – and they say my heart's beatin' too hard or something, but I'm near sixty.'

There was a terrible tiredness about her, which made her seem much older.

'How's your family?' Rooney asked kindly.

She sucked her teeth. 'Joshua upped and left with some little girlfriend of his daughter's – may the good Lord forgive him, for I sure don't. I had six mouths to feed, and all he could think of was having his way with an eighteen-year-old. Some husband, some father.'

'I'm sorry.'

She shrugged her shoulders. 'Saved me from gettin' beat on regular, and good riddance, but sometimes he could be a real sweet-hearted man – it was just the liquor turned him mean. I've heard he's straightened out, got himself a regular job – not that he sends me no money – and got himself another couple of kids too, so I don't press for payments. I know it's takin' from the mouths of his new family, and you always got to put them first.'

'You're a good mother.'

'Yes, sir, when the good Lord takes me, he'll know that. It's all I was put on this earth for, 'cos God knows I ain't been good for much of anything but rearing kids.

Losing my little Tommy hurt me bad. When they die young, they stay young.'

'How's all his brothers doing?'

She took a wheezy breath. 'I got one working for a real estate outfit, suit an' all, another in a bakery, another in prison, and I got one . . . He was going bad, but he straightened out real good. He had a job uptown.'

'Doing what?'

'Odd jobs. For an art gallery – hanging paintings, sweeping up, cleaning. It was permanent, but the pay wasn't good, so he's looking elsewhere right now.'

'Was it the Nathan gallery?'

'Yes, sir, but a lot of bad things happened. There was a fire and she – the lady that owned it – was killed in it, so he was out of a job. Since then he's been looking hard.'

'That'd be Eric?'

'Yes, Eric, my oldest. I know he was in trouble a few times, but I swear to you, he's a good boy now.'

'He live at home with you?'

'Sometimes. He got his old room, but he comes and goes. He sees I don't go short, though. Why you come here? On account of my Eric?' She leaned forward. 'What you want here in my house?'

'I'm not sure – just an answer to a few things. Did you ever meet with a guy, maybe asking questions about the gallery?'

'No, sir.'

'You sure about that? Only I have some notes he made and, according to them, he paid a visit to you. It'd be a while back now.'

'No, sir, I had no one visit me.'

411

'How about someone calling to see Eric?'

'No, sir, no one has been here, I'd swear to that on the Holy Bible.'

'Is Eric around now? Could I see him?'

'No, he's out right now.'

Rooney was sweating – the cluttered room was stifling hot, even though only the screen door was closed. There was no breeze from the yard, and no air-conditioning.

'Does Eric drive?'

'Sure he drives. He needed a clean licence for his work at the gallery, and Mrs Nathan, she provided a van for him to deliver an' collect. He was workin' there quite a while.'

'Did you ever go to the gallery?'

'Who me? No, sir, I don't get to go no place, not with my condition.'

'Did you ever meet Mrs Nathan?'

'No, Lord have mercy on her, I never did. I'm praying my boy gets work soon – see, with her gone, who's gonna give him a reference? An' he worked a long time for that gallery.'

Rooney turned to the bank of family photographs, dominated by the large one of the dead Tommy.

'Which is Eric?'

She smiled and pointed. 'The sharp-lookin' one. He always was a fancy dresser.'

Rooney stared at the picture of Eric, gold chains round his neck, leaning against a wall and smiling to reveal a gold-capped tooth. Rooney had seen a few other photographs of Eric – in police files. 'So he's been straight since he got out?'

The big woman pursed her lips, then took a folded cloth from her pocket and dabbed her face and neck. She

412

was sweating profusely. 'That is all behind him, mister. He swore on his brother's grave he would get out of that bad crowd he was mixin' with. It wasn't easy, believe me. You get into one o' those gangs round here and they don't let you out.'

'No drugs any more?' Rooney asked quietly.

'No, sir. Like I said, he swore on his brother's grave, day he came out of the pen. He went straight to the graveside and he got down on his knees, in front of me and his brothers and sisters, and he said he would stay clean. That was more'n seven years ago.'

'You sure now, Mrs Lee Judd? I mean he's unemployed right now, and, like you said, he comes and goes, so how can you be sure?'

She banged the side of her chair. 'One brother, one son dead is enough. He wouldn't do that to me.'

'Does he blame himself for Tommy?'

She dabbed her neck, then looked at him directly. 'There was one person to blame. We knew it, and you cops knew it too, but she never come to justice. She never come to court, she got away with murder, an' *no, no,* my boy don't blame himself. It was that bitch cop.'

'You recall her name?' Rooney asked.

'No, sir, I do not.'

'Does Eric know who she was?'

'I can't answer for what Eric knows.'

'So he blames her too, does he?'

She clenched the arms of her chair. 'You tellin' me he ain't got the right to blame her? She fired into that boy, kept on shooting. He was nothin' to do with what was going on, he was just an innocent boy, and she shot him down like a dog.'

413

'But he was there, wasn't he? Looked like he was being used by Eric as a runner.'

'Eric says it was a lie to get that woman off.'

'But there were traces of cocaine found.'

'No, sir, don't you tell me lies. They'd have had that poor child shooting up to serve their purposes, but he was innocent, and Eric swore on the Bible he was not using him. An' if you come here today to try an' rake up dirt for some reason, then you get out of my house, you hearin' me?'

Rooney stood up. Mrs Lee Judd was panting with anger, and he patted her shoulder. 'Now, don't you go gettin' all upset.'

'Why you come here? What do you want?'

Rooney hesitated, then looked at the big framed photograph of Tommy Lee Judd. 'Just making enquiries, Mrs Lee Judd, an' if you tell me Eric's a reformed character, then . . .'

She dragged herself up to stand in front of him, shoving her face forward. 'Like I said to you, Eric stood over that grave, an' I won't hear no bad things about him – he's a good son.'

'Well, I sincerely hope so, and more than that I hope he's not runnin' with the gangs again, because if he is I'll be right on his neck an' fast. I think your boy is looking for trouble, big trouble, so you warn him to stay in line. Warn him to back off – and quit making nuisance phone calls.'

Rooney got up. He had wanted to unnerve the woman, even though he wasn't sure that it had been Eric Lee Judd calling Lorraine. It was just that old second sense, plus the fact that Eric might have seen her visit the gallery.

'I'll see myself out. Just tell that boy of yours I was round, okay?'

She wouldn't let him go by himself, but shuffled after him, down the dark, dingy hallway. She wasn't going to let him wander around her house like those snooping cops were inclined to do – she wanted this fat man out, and the door bolted behind him.

Rooney heard the bolts being slammed across the front door, then the chain, and he knew she was watching him through the broken stained-glass window. He went straight to his car, and drove out of her drive.

He parked about a hundred yards away down the street and made sure all his doors were locked. He wondered how long it would be before Mrs Lee Judd contacted her son and told him about the visit – his old cop's nose knew she'd be trying, because one look around that cramped, dilapidated house had revealed a new TV set and video, fridge-freezer and washing-machine. They stuck out like a sore thumb beside the rest of the furniture, and were obvious signs of ready cash, signs of a kid handing over fistfuls of dollars to his mama.

Rooney sighed, and lit a cigarette: Lorraine had got off lightly from the Lee Judd episode. She was never called to court, as by the time of Eric Lee Judd's trial she was long out of the force, hell-bent on drinking herself to death. There had been a major cover-up – he knew that better than anyone, as he'd been responsible for most of it – but the boy was not the innocent his mother had tried to make out. They had found traces of cocaine on his hands and inside his jacket pockets, that black jacket with the yellow stripe down the back that little Tommy had coveted because it had belonged to his brother Eric. They had also taken statements from two other kids they'd picked up, who had said that Tommy was running for his big brother, who was dealing to some of the clubs, mostly cocaine and ecstasy. Six months after the trial, Eric Lee Judd had been arrested in another bust, and this time he had served three years.

Rooney smoked the cigarette down to the butt, and lit up another. Maybe he was putting two and two together and making five, but the whole thing was just too much of a coincidence. Maybe Eric had sworn to go straight on his kid brother's grave, but he might also have sworn some kind of revenge.

As soon as Rooney had gone, Mrs Lee Judd heaved her bulk up the worn stairs, one step at a time. She had a bed made up for herself downstairs, and hardly ever went up to the bedrooms – when any of the family stayed her daughters cleaned up there, and Eric changed his own sheets. She was frightened, not wanting to believe what Rooney had hinted at, just like she didn't want to believe that Eric had been up to no good since he lost his job at the gallery. She'd confronted him with it when he brought home the new TV set for her birthday, and he'd flown into a rage, saying that he'd spent all his hard-earned savings to make her happy, but he could never make up to her for Tommy. She always put Tommy first, just like she'd done when they were kids, and now he was dead he still got more love and attention than she ever gave to her surviving son. She had wept, and then he had put his arms around her, crying too, saying that all he ever wanted was to make up to her for what happened to Tommy.

She was crying now, as she heaved herself up stair after stair, because deep down in her weary heart, she knew that Tommy would have done anything for Eric. Little Tommy always followed Eric around like he was some kind of hero, had started to strut about the streets in his bomber jacket, and she had been worried he was getting into trouble, with his big brother leading him by the hand.

The bedroom was untidy, dirty, with old beer cans and bottles lying everywhere, and ashtrays piled high with cigarette butts. The wardrobe door was open, revealing rows of suits and shoes, and she rifled through the dresser drawers. They were full of shirts and T-shirts, some stuffed back dirty, likewise a drawer full of underwear. On the top of the dresser was a picture of Tommy, held in his brother's arms when he was no more than four or five, and she picked it up, kissed it, said a silent prayer for forgiveness for searching her son's room like a thief. As she put the photograph back on the dresser, she saw a smaller top drawer, open just a fraction, and slid it open. Inside was a tangle of jewellery – watches, bracelets, rings and heavy gold pendants with thick twisted-gold chains. There were also rolls of dollars, secured with rubber bands. She eased the top drawer closed then searched the others, finding two guns, knives and more rolls of banknotes. Her bosom heaved as she drew a deep breath, standing in the untidy room with her swollen feet planted wide apart to maintain her balance. Then, helping herself along the wall, she moved out and down the stairs, one by one.

Her breath rattled in her chest as she returned to the living room, picked up the phone and dialled a telephone number written on a pad beside the phone – Kelly, Eric's current girlfriend, whose number he had left in case of emergencies. There had been a lot of numbers over the years, always thoughtfully tucked by the phone. 'Kelly, honey, this is Eric's mama – he with you?'

She could hear loud music thudding in the background, heard Kelly shouting for Eric, who came quickly to the phone, his voice full of concern. 'Mama? You sick?'

'Yes, boy, I am. You come right home now.' She put the phone down before he could say any more, then eased her bulk into the sagging armchair. She picked up her walking stick from the side of the chair, raised it high, and brought it down on the new TV set, smashing it repeatedly against the casing, then thrusting it with all her might into the screen. The glass cracked, and still she kept on thrashing, as if she was thrashing Eric, the way she had when they told her about Tommy. She had beaten the hell out of him then, and now she attacked the fruit of his crimes with the same violence.

The pain shot down her left arm like a red-hot iron passing through her veins, piercing her again and again. The stick dropped from her hand as her body jerked in spasms of excruciating agony, and the last thing her frightened eyes saw was the picture of her dead son, Tommy Lee Judd, shot six times by a woman detective she'd heard was a drunk.

Rooney lit a third cigarette, inhaling deeply. He'd been outside in the car a good fifteen minutes. He could be wrong, he knew, she'd said the other kids were all in good jobs, and maybe they'd bought all the fancy new domestic appliances. He leaned forward to turn on the ignition, deciding he'd call it quits for the night, and check it out in the morning.

Not five minutes after Rooney had driven off a new black-on-black Cherokee jeep with black-tinted windows screeched to a halt in Mrs Lee Judd's drive. Eric, high on crack cocaine, ran from it and tried his keys, knocking when he found the bolts still fastened inside. He raced round to the back door, and kicked the screen door aside to see his mama lying face down, close to the fireplace, with her right hand outstretched. Just a few inches from her fingers was the framed picture of Tommy, the glass smashed to smithereens. In the last moments of her life she had tried to hold him – a last-born child is often the favourite, and Tommy had been hers.

Eric stood rooted to the spot, his head feeling as though it was on fire. He knew she was dead, that her big heart had burst in her chest, as blood oozed from her nose and mouth, and he didn't need to feel for a pulse. Slowly he stepped over her, and bent to retrieve the broken picture. He removed the jagged pieces of glass, and set it back on the shelf, his hand shaking. He felt it was some kind of omen, a message from the grave, and one that he would obey. The bitch cop would pay for what she had done. He'd make her pay.

Rooney let himself in, and was attacked by Tiger, though the dog was clearly more motivated by affection than any desire to guard the household. Rosie had already gone to bed, and Rooney undressed, cleaned his teeth, and got into bed beside her. She turned over and propped her head on her elbow.

'You know, you were making the floor shake. You

men are all alike, creeping round the bed, then sitting on it to take off your shoes.'

'I was trying not to wake you,' he grumbled.

'Well, you didn't succeed – first bang on the front door did it. You were gone a long time.' She stared at him, but his eyes were closed. 'Want to talk about it?' she asked.

He lifted one big arm up to let her snuggle in beside him, then drew her closer. 'I may be wrong, and I hope to God I am, but I think Lorraine may have a problem. You know the kid she shot? In a drug raid?'

'Yeah, I know about him.'

Rooney sighed. 'Well, he's got a brother, and this brother worked for the Nathan gallery, sort of handy-man-cum-driver-cum-delivery. Kid's been out of work since the gallery went up in smoke – and I just feel uneasy about it. Could be him making the phone calls. I kind of gave his mother a bit of a warning to back off just in case I'm right, that he's gonna try and take some kind of revenge on Lorraine.'

'You really think so?'

'Yep. There were another twenty-odd calls on her answerphone and one had what sounded like gunfire, six shots. She pumped the same amount into Tommy Lee Judd.'

'What you going to do?'

He sighed again. 'I'll talk to Burton, maybe see if he can sort it out, or run a check on the guy.'

Rosie lay on her back, staring at the ceiling. 'How did you find all this out?'

Rooney yawned. 'From the catalogues and stuff in that fag Decker's bag. His notes gave the Lee Judd address so I called round, talked to his mother.'

Suddenly Rooney sat up, and tossed the bedclothes aside. 'That accident, the crash that guy was in – it was on the intersection just a mile up La Brea from the Lee Judds' place.' He stomped out of the room, and Rosie grabbed a robe and followed him. He was banging around the kitchen looking for tea bags. Rosie reached up and took them out of a tin.

'It's another fucking coincidence, isn't it? He puts in his notebook that he's going to see Eric Lee Judd, the guy's mother said nobody ever came, but she could be lying, so what if Decker had come up with something, and . . .'

'But there was no other vehicle involved, apart from the garbage truck he drove into. It was an accident – he jumped the lights,' Rosie said, getting the teapot and setting a tray with cups, milk and a tin of cookies. She carried the tray into the bedroom, and poured tea for them both, but Rooney seemed disinclined to discuss Lorraine any more. 'Nothing we can do tonight,' he said. 'Maybe just keep this to ourselves – no need to get her all worried. Let me see if I can sort it out.'

Rosie sipped her tea, agreeing with him. She knew he was worried, as she was herself, but as he had said, there was nothing they could do that evening. By the time she put the tray on one side, turned off the bedside lamp, and settled back on the pillow, she thought Bill was asleep. But his hand reached out for hers and held it tightly. 'Nothing's going to happen to Lorraine, trust me.'

Lorraine went to the hotel gym for a workout, then returned to her room to dress and pack before going downstairs for breakfast and to settle her bill. At eight twenty, she took her luggage and asked the doorman to call her a cab. By ten to nine, she was drawing up outside Abigail Nathan's house in Norwood Park, an area northwest of the city centre. She was surprised that the house didn't match her expectations. It was in a nice white-collar area but it was small, an unattractive, square building. The lawns in the street had no fences and the properties abutted directly onto one another, divided only by garage drives and dinky, crazy-paved paths to the front doors. Mrs Nathan's drive was covered in leaves and rubbish, which looked as if it had been there for some time.

Lorraine stepped onto the veranda, which also needed sweeping. The lamp on the porch was broken, but antique. Lorraine rang the doorbell and waited. She could hear soft music playing. She rang again and a woman's voice called out that she was coming.

Mrs Nathan was wearing a satin floral print robe, which reached to her bare, mottled calves, and a pair of very old and worn pointed Moroccan leather slippers. She looked older than she had seemed at the funeral, but perhaps the deterioration in her appearance was due to grief. She put out a tiny hand, with thin fingers and arthritic knuckles. 'Hello. You must be Mrs Page.'

'Yes, thank you for seeing me, Mrs Nathan.'

Mrs Nathan ushered her straight into the drawing room, as there was no hallway. 'Sit down.' She indicated a satin-covered Victorian sofa, with curving sides and ugly, heavy legs. 'I won't be a moment.' She disappeared into the kitchen.

Lorraine looked around the room: there was a huge chandelier of fine Italian glass, and the place was crammed with antiques, ornaments and trinkets. A collection of hundreds of tiny glass animals and Victorian children's toys stood in several glass-fronted cabinets. Dust was thick on all the ornaments and furniture, and newspapers, empty envelopes and circulars were littered around the room – a complete contrast to her elder son's obsessive neatness. Lorraine wondered if the house had always been so neglected, or if Mrs Nathan had simply let everything go after her son had died.

She returned with a carved wooden tray, two chipped china cups and mismatched saucers. As there was no space on any of the tables, she set the tray down on a footstool, and asked how Lorraine took her coffee. 'Black, please, no sugar,' Lorraine answered. 'Have you lived here long?'

'Forty years,' the old lady answered. 'I meant to move when my husband died, but I brought my boys up here and you can't put memories like that in a packing crate.'

She carried her own cup to the big armchair, kicking aside the newspapers that covered the floor around it, and settled herself, like a small, rotund Buddha, her feet resting on an embroidered footstool in front of her. 'Also, of course, I can't bear the thought of having to pack up all these treasures – I'm a collector, as you see. I don't collect anything that isn't of intrinsic value, of course, I've never seen the point.'

'You have some lovely things,' Lorraine said.

'It's a sort of pastime for me, since I've travelled so much, all round the world so many times,' Abigail Nathan continued, seeming to want to make sure that Lorraine realized that she had been a rich woman and accustomed to deference. 'My boys came with me when they were young, and that's where they got their education. Artistic talent can't flourish, I've always thought, without the soil of culture,' she concluded grandiosely. 'I knew from the time the boys were babies that they would create.'

Lorraine made an effort to keep her face impassive as Mrs Nathan talked as though her elder son's vulgar movies and her younger son's daubs ranked as great art. 'You mentioned that you were working for poor Harry's laywer – did you ever meet my son?' Abigail Nathan went on.

'No, but I met Nick – in fact, I bought one of his canvases,' Lorraine said, hoping that she would be pleased.

'You'll be able to sell it for ten times what you paid in a couple of years,' Mrs Nathan said with complete confidence. 'I have high hopes that Nicky's work will be recognized. Ever since he was a small boy, painting has been his life.'

'Do you mind if I ask you some questions?' Lorraine said.

'Please do. I'm obviously interested – my son must have left a considerable amount of money. I haven't been told how the estate is to be divided, and when I telephoned Mr Feinstein, he said that woman' – clearly, as Raymond Vallance had said, there had been no love lost between Abigail and Sonja – 'has the house at least. I feel certain that there must be some mistake. Harry would not have forgotten his brother, of course. They simply adored each other. The boys always got along so well.'

Lorraine eased the cup and cracked saucer onto a table crowded with knick-knacks. 'It is indeed a considerable sum of money, Mrs Nathan, and there seems to be no trace of it in any of your son's known accounts. That means that it's likely he had banking facilities elsewhere – perhaps here in Chicago, I thought, or perhaps in other names?'

'I don't know anything about that. My son never discussed either money or business with me,' Abigail Nathan said, as though mentioning subjects unfit for ladies' ears.

'Did he visit here frequently?' Lorraine asked.

'He came when he could,' the old lady said. 'He had a busy life in Los Angeles, though he wrote me regularly and, of course, I used to visit with him, when he was married to Kendall.'

Lorraine seized the opportunity to embark on another line of questioning. 'Mrs Nathan, the primary assets missing from your son's estate are some valuable modern paintings. It seems that there may have been certain . . . irregular dealings on the art market.' She knew better than to accuse Harry Nathan directly of fraud to his mother. 'Which Kendall may initially have instigated.'

'Well, I find that simply impossible to believe,' Mrs Nathan responded, with a haughty sniff. 'I count myself a pretty fair judge of character, and Kendall was the only decent woman my son was ever involved with.'

'Can you think of anyone else involved in the art market whom Harry might have been working with?'

'I certainly can,' Abigail Nathan said with emphasis, then hesitated as though trying to bring herself to utter an indecent word. 'That wretched woman who wrecked my son's life. Sonja, whatever she calls herself now. I can tell you that if there was any kind of irregularity going on, that woman was behind it. She is a person without moral sense or scruple of any kind.'

'I have recently interviewed Sonja Nathan,' Lorraine said, keeping her voice expressionless. 'She denies having any sort of contact with Harry since they got divorced. The separation was not amicable, I understand.'

'No wonder.' Mrs Nathan snorted. 'Sonja couldn't stand the fact that Harry finally realized that he should have married a nice, sweet, normal, natural girl.' God knows how he ended up with Kendall in that case, Lorraine thought privately, but the older woman was in full flow. 'Sonja was a completely unnatural woman from the day and hour Harry met her, and she simply got worse with age. I blessed the day Harry got that woman out of his life, and it broke my heart when he started seeing her again.'

'What makes you think he *was* seeing her again?'

'He used to telephone her from here,' Abigail Nathan said, and Lorraine felt her pulse quicken. At last: someone had stated that Harry and Sonja Nathan had indeed remained in contact, but whether it was an indulgent mother's attempt to cover up her son's wrongdoing and incriminate a woman she disliked remained to be seen. 'It was the only time Harry ever lied to me. That woman had a hold over him of a kind I've never seen.'

'What sort of untruth do you mean?' Lorraine asked.

'He said he was talking to some business associate, fixing up meetings, but I knew it was her.'

'How did you *know* it was her?' Lorraine asked.

'Because I called the phone company and got a record of the long-distance calls made on my line,' Mrs Nathan said, giving Lorraine an arch look.

'I don't suppose you still have these records anywhere in the house,' Lorraine asked, glancing around the room – it looked as though nothing had been thrown out in a decade, and it struck her suddenly that if Nathan had been in regular correspondence with his mother, those letters, too, were in all probability nearby.

'I might have,' Mrs Nathan said, looking carefully at Lorraine, as though her appearance might yield some clue as to whether or not she could be trusted.

'Mrs Nathan, if Sonja is responsible for a substantial fraud and perhaps a more serious crime,' Lorraine said, meeting Mrs Nathan's eyes with what she hoped was a frank, honest gaze, 'then I will naturally be handing over the matter to the police.'

'I told the police that I suspected that woman was mixed up in my son's death and they pretty much told me to go home to my patty-pans. Just an old lady with a bee in her bonnet. They didn't have to say it, but that's what they were thinking.'

No doubt they were, Lorraine thought, and the fact that Harry Nathan had called his ex-wife a few times must have seemed innocent enough. But in the context of so many other circumstances that seemed to point to Sonja, and in particular the flat denials Lorraine had received from both Sonja and Arthur that there had been any contact between her and Harry after they divorced, it was important evidence. Though Nathan could, of course, have been calling to speak to Arthur – the two men had known one another for years, and it was possible that Arthur was helping Nathan with his forgery scam without Sonja's knowledge. Lorraine realized she had never asked Arthur if *he* had had any contact with Harry Nathan. But that had seemed unlikely – Harry Nathan had to be the last person with whom Arthur would secretly have been best buddies.

'I'm afraid that the police often take such allegations

427

lightly when they're made by a member of the public,' she said, 'but they might be more inclined to take it seriously against a background of other evidence coming from a . . . more professional source.'

'You mean from you,' Abigail Nathan said bluntly.

'Yes, I do.'

There was silence for a few moments while the old lady weighed up the pros and cons of trusting Lorraine. 'Well,' she said at last, 'I could go and look upstairs, if you have time to wait.'

'I'm in no hurry,' Lorraine said. 'Or I could come and help you, if you'd like.'

'That won't be necessary,' said Abigail Nathan. 'You wait right here. You can look around my collection.'

She got up, and Lorraine heard her slow footsteps climbing the stairs. Look around the collection was exactly what she would do, and particularly the collection of papers in the ginger jar. She waited until she heard the woman's footsteps overhead, tipped it out and flicked through the contents – Abigail Nathan had kept all sorts of junk, matchbooks, photographs, dinner menus and letters, but the most recent was from a woman friend, dated 1994.

There were papers all over the house, and Lorraine decided to investigate further. She opened the door to the next room noiselessly and found herself in a den full of trinkets and toys, bursting out of cupboards and balanced on a number of little spindle-legged tables. Looking round the room, her eye was caught by a most unusual display of carved red wooden devils, no more than a few inches high, with hideous faces and cloven hoofs, holding a pack of miniature playing cards. Lorraine bent down to look closer, genuinely interested, and saw, tucked into the corner of the cabinet, an airmail envelope with a German stamp. She eased it out, recognizing Harry Nathan's large, untidy handwriting. The postmark was a few months old.

'Mrs Page?' Abigail Nathan called. 'Are you down there?'

Scarcely thinking what she was doing, Lorraine reached under her jacket and slipped the letter into the back of the waistband of her skirt, then walked smartly out to see the old lady making her way downstairs.

'Yes, I'm here, Mrs Nathan. I just went to the bathroom.'

'I see. I have what you wanted here – I never throw anything away.'

She held out two sheets of paper. Lorraine's hand almost trembled as she took them. 'Thank you, Mrs Nathan,' she said. 'May I take these back to LA?'

'You take them wherever you like,' Abigail Nathan replied, 'if it'll help to get justice for my son.'

Lorraine placed the sheets of paper in her briefcase, and said, 'I'd better be on my way now, I'm afraid. Can I call a cab?'

'Certainly,' Mrs Nathan said graciously, waving her hand towards the filthy kitchen as though ushering Lorraine into a palace. 'Phone's through there.'

Lorraine found a card for a cab company pinned next to the phone and made a quick call. 'It'll just be a few minutes,' she said, hanging up. 'One last thing, Mrs Nathan. I don't suppose you know anything about a man named Arthur? I don't know his last name, but Harry knew him as a young man and he's living with Sonja now in the Hamptons.'

'You mean Arthur Donnelly. He and Harry were in

college together. He was a painter, he said, but I knew he'd never get anywhere. Masterly technique, of course, but simply nothing of his own to say. I told him he ought to count his blessings and join the family firm.' She laughed at the recollection.

'What was that, Mrs Nathan?' Lorraine asked curiously.

'Oh, an outfit in the antique trade. All reproduction.'

Another piece of the puzzle slotted into place, Lorraine thought, recalling the sticker Cindy had found inside the fake antique jar. It looked like Arthur had indeed taken Mrs Nathan's advice.

The doorbell rang and Lorraine picked up her briefcase. She thanked Mrs Nathan profusely.

'So glad to have been of assistance – if I have – and if you hear anything you will contact me, won't you?'

Once the cab was clear of Abigail Nathan's house, Lorraine reached carefully under her jacket and extracted the envelope. She took out a single sheet of folded airmail notepaper, with no address, simply the salutation 'Dearest, sweetest Cherub-face'. The first few lines expressed hopes that she was sticking to a diet, using her exercise bike and not, underlined, eating too many cookies. He went on to say that he was abroad for just a few days, and from Germany he would be going on to Switzerland, but then underlined was, 'No one must know, that also means do not' underlined 'tell even Nicky.' He said he would explain on his return. He went on to say that within a few months he would be megarich, that he was on to something that would set him up for the rest of his life. The writing was slapdash, and looked as if it had been scrawled in a hurry: some was in cursive script, the rest in capital letters.

Lorraine replaced the note in the envelope and slipped it into her case. There had been no record of this trip to Germany and, most importantly, to Switzerland on Nathan's official passport. This must be a clear lead to the secret bank accounts. She suddenly sat up. Germany! Sonja Nathan had said what? There was an exhibition of her work being shown in Berlin. Sonja was there now, and Lorraine did not doubt that it was in connection with the art fraud that she and Arthur had evidently been running with Nathan.

The net was closing, and Lorraine felt an almost ungovernable impulse to follow Sonja to Europe and run her to earth. She would have to act immediately – but the thought of telling Jake that she had to make just this one trip, follow this one lead, pushing his patience and understanding yet again was too much for her. She knew that next time he saw her, he wanted to give her a ring and make their engagement public. Suddenly she wanted nothing more than to see him, Rosie, Rooney, Tiger. She had been away too long.

CHAPTER 19

S ONJA STOOD in one of the airy, vaulted halls of the Hamburger Bahnhof in Berlin, the former railway station that had been stunningly restored as an art gallery. All the pieces she had executed during the past seven years were placed around her. People stood sipping drinks in front of them, but even more were gathered before her latest work, a huge rectangular structure draped in a black cloth, which was to be unveiled later in the evening. She scanned the unmistakably prosperous but vapid-looking crowd as she waited for Arthur to come back with her drink, and reflected that art snobs were the same all over the world.

Arthur returned with a glass of champagne for her just as she observed the two organizers of the exhibition bearing down on her. 'Arthur, I think I'm about to be carried off.'

He knew that she wanted him to go and, glancing at his watch, saw that it was almost time for him to pick up the car that would take him to Kreuzberg.

'Well,' he said, 'I'm afraid I have to run. Good luck, Sonja.'

Outside, the car was waiting, and Arthur switched his mind to the negotiations, which had been complex, though on the surface not illegal – none of the paintings he was about to sell were known to be stolen, none had been reported as such. By the time that happened he and Sonja would be long gone, and if the Japanese buyer he had lined up took the bulk, he wouldn't care. In Japan if a buyer of a painting could prove ownership for two consecutive years, the work became irrecoverably his or hers, and could be shown with impunity. This evening's sale had taken years of planning, years of secret meetings and hours of his time forging the artists' work. It was his own work now that he was thinking about: if this deal came off he would have the rest of his life to paint in luxury. If it went wrong, then he might spend it in prison. Either way, he mused, he'd be able to paint.

Because California time was two hours behind Chicago, it was only mid-afternoon when Lorraine got back to LA. She went straight to her office, eager to check Decker's research, but it wasn't until she was there that she remembered Rooney had it. She dialled Feinstein's number. To her irritation, he was in court, so she left a message. Next she called Rosie and Rooney, and left a message asking Rooney to bring Decker's carrier bags to her apartment as soon as he could.

At that moment Rosie and Rooney were with Jake Burton in his office. He had listened intently to everything Rooney had to say about Eric Lee Judd.

He had warmed immediately to the couple, knowing how highly Lorraine regarded them. 'Did she mention

433

anything to either of you about her brake cables being cut and that someone broke into her office?'

They shook their heads.

'Well, whoever it was did some damage – didn't steal anything but made their presence known by using acid to destroy some tapes.' He shrugged. 'Could be whoever it was had been hired by one of the suspects and discovered something else in the office.'

'Like what?' Rooney interjected, leaning forward.

'That it was someone from her past who knew her, had a grudge against her,' Burton said.

Rooney looked to Rosie. 'I said there was some kind of hidden agenda, didn't I?'

Rosie was chewing her lip. She felt very uneasy. 'Do you think Lorraine knows?' she asked Burton.

'No, I don't, but she must be told. Have you any idea when she'll be back from Chicago?'

Rosie tried to recall exactly what Lorraine had said when they had last spoken. 'I'm sure she said she'd be back in LA this evening.' She looked up as Burton eased from his chair. He cracked his knuckles. He was obviously worried.

'Is she in danger?' Rosie asked.

'Not for the moment but, all the same, I want you to go back to your apartment in case she makes contact. In the meantime, I'll check out this Eric Lee Judd, maybe get someone to monitor what he's up to.' Burton put an arm around Rooney. 'I appreciate all you're doing for Lorraine, but don't worry, I won't let any harm come to her.'

Rooney coughed and stuck out his hand, which Burton clasped. 'I wasn't sure about you, not at first, but . . . we also appreciate everything you've done for our girl. She's very special.'

'Yes, I know,' Burton said softly.

As he closed the door behind the Rooneys he stood in the centre of the room. He could feel an ominous tug in the pit of his belly because just the thought of any harm coming to Lorraine made him realize again how much he loved her and wanted to protect her.

It was almost six when Lorraine was dropped outside her apartment, paid off the cab, and checked all her luggage and parcels. She had quite a few, plus the painting from Nick Nathan, so her hands were full as she opened the street door and climbed the stairs. The apartment door was ajar, and she smiled, sure that Rosie was inside. She called her friend's name as she pushed open the door with her case. 'Rosie? Are you here? Rosie?'

She put down the briefcase containing the phone records Abigail Nathan had given her, her overnight bag and painting, and turned to close the door. She didn't see or even hear her assailant, as the blow to the right side of her head had such force it lifted her off the ground. She tried to roll away, curling her body against the blows that continued to thud into her. One slammed into the small of her back and it felt as if her kidneys were exploding. She straightened out with a scream of agony, but the blows kept on coming, no matter which way she tried to fend them off. She couldn't tell if she was being kicked or punched. The pain was so vivid it was as if she was on fire. She couldn't cry out, she had no strength, and the last blow to the side of her head rendered her unconscious. Lorraine had not even glimpsed her attacker, who now, out of some reflex instinct for robbery, rapidly searched through her overnight bag. He found nothing of value, and as the briefcase was locked, he took it, throwing it into the back of his car before he drove off.

She lay motionless, face down, her battered body twisted like a broken doll, blood forming a dark pool around her head.

Sonja waited for the applause to subside as she stood on the small podium at the front of the gallery. 'Ladies and gentlemen,' she said, 'first of all I would like to thank the board of this exciting new treasure house of contemporary art,' she turned to smile at the two women behind her, 'for the honour they have done me in asking me to open the series of shows dedicated to living women working in sculpture. This will, however, be an occasion of endings as well as beginnings,' she went on, 'because as well as inaugurating a chapter in the work of this great new gallery, this evening will mark the end of my career.' She delivered the words in clear, ringing tones, knowing that they would take everyone present by surprise. 'My work has been my tyrant, my torturer, and it has come close to being my murderer,' she went on. 'It did not exorcize and transform the dark parts of myself, it fed and magnified them, and it has left me to live with the result, which is what I, and the man who has been brave – or foolish – enough to make a commitment to me, now intend to do.'

Somehow it was the mention of Arthur, of her private life, that turned the murmuring and head-shaking to hissing and booing: Sonja looked at the audience with the gaze of a heretic, hearing the crackle of her reputation burning around her.

Rosie was first up the steps. She knew something was wrong: Tiger was barking and yelping frantically, running from the open front door to the apartment and back inside. Rosie called Lorraine's name, but when she made it to the top of the steps she started to scream.

Lorraine lay slumped by the side of the front door, her face unrecognizable. Her shirt and shoulders were soaked in blood, which had sprayed up the walls and splashed over the door, and formed a puddle beside her head. Rooney pushed her out of the way and knelt down beside Lorraine, feeling for the pulse on her neck, then her wrist, shouting instructions to his wife to call the emergency services. He could feel only a faint throbbing, so faint that at first he had thought Lorraine was dead. 'She's alive – get me blankets, hurry. Are they on their way?'

Rosie was weeping, nodding, running into the bedroom. Rooney had to knock Tiger out of the way as he tried to get to Lorraine, then growled at him. He had to shout to Rosie to get the dog out of the room.

Rosie rode with Lorraine in the ambulance to the nearest hospital, St John's in Santa Monica, and Rooney followed behind in his car. He felt icy cold, shaken to the core, and he doubted that Lorraine would survive.

Jake had to sit down, his whole body shaking. It was some time before he could speak. 'How bad is it?'

Rooney wanted to weep, but gritted his teeth. 'She's hurt real bad. She's in a coma and they've taken her into Intensive Care.' He swallowed as the tears welled up. 'It's bad, Jake, real bad. They don't think she's gonna make it.'

'I'll be with you in ten, fifteen minutes depending on the traffic.'

Jake let the phone drop back onto the cradle. His body felt stiff and his mind blank. He was unable to take in what Rooney had said. He made himself go over the call again, then picked up his coat like a robot, and walked out. She was not going to die, he told himself. She was going to be all right.

Rosie handed Rooney a cup of coffee from the machine and sat close, resting against him. 'She's going to be all right, isn't she?'

'Yes.' He sipped the lukewarm excuse for coffee. 'She's as strong as an ox. She's gonna be okay.' But his words sounded hollow. Rosie's tears trickled down her face. They had been waiting for news, any news, for fifteen minutes.

Jake walked in, his features drawn and frightened. 'How is she?'

Rooney stood up, offering his hand. 'We don't know – they told us to wait here.'

'You want to tell me what happened?'

'We don't know. We got to her apartment and found her. At first I didn't think she was alive – she'd taken one hell of a beating. He used a baseball bat, left it by the door.'

'Who did you call?'

'Local guys, Pacific Area Homicide. They were on the spot within minutes, so were the paramedics. They brought her into Accident and Emergency to get her blood matched for a transfusion, and did some X-rays.'

Jake sat down and clasped his hands. 'You get a name? Someone I can talk to?'

Rooney wiped his face with his hand. 'Yeah, officer said his name was Larry Morgan.'

'I'll go call him.'

Jake was gone for several minutes. When he came back there was an almost pleading expression on his face – begging for news, good news, but there had been none. He sat down beside Rooney. 'They've taken the baseball bat for finger-printing, and they also got some bloody shoe-prints, some kind of sneaker. It looks like he broke in and was lying in wait – they found some screwed-up cans of Coke by the bed, as if he'd been waiting for her in the bedroom.'

Rosie said, 'I was there yesterday. I watered the plants, and there were no Coke cans then. I'd have seen them, put them in the trash can.'

There was an awful silence, as all three sat staring straight ahead.

'I've put out a warrant for this Lee Judd guy's arrest,' Jake said softly.

'Good,' Rooney said.

'You think it was him?' Jake asked, frowning.

'We'll soon find out. They get prints off the Coke cans?'

'Too early yet – it'll take a couple of days.' Jake got up, then sat down again.

Rosie took out a tissue and blew her nose. She had been crying off and on ever since she found Lorraine. No sooner did she get a grip on herself than the tears poured down her cheeks again.

Rooney lit a cigarette, ignoring a prominent 'No Smoking' sign. He leaned forward with his elbows resting on his knees, inhaling deeply and hissing out the smoke. He could think of nothing more to say to Jake, could think only about the lady he had grown to love and admire so much, sure that this couldn't be the end: life couldn't be that cruel.

Jake sat straight-backed, gripping the arm of the grey airport-style armchair, still in shock, still unable to believe that he might lose the woman he felt it had taken him his whole life to find.

The three sat in silence, but all with the same hope, that Lorraine would live. They were each wrapped in their own thoughts and memories of her, knowing there was nothing they could do but wait. That was the worst part of it all – the awful waiting, and the helplessness.

'Perhaps I'm addressing myself particularly to other women artists,' Sonja said. She had to raise her voice to be heard over the critical rumblings from the crowd gathered around the podium. 'The relationship of art to life is a complex one, on which wiser commentators and greater artists than myself have expended a considerable amount of thought. Whatever else is true of art, it is true that its practice changes the nature of one's relations with other people – and I think it deprives those relations of precisely the qualities of equality and repicrocity which women, in particular, cherish as ideal. For those reasons I think some women artists are not kept out of art by hostile conspiracies, but choose to remove themselves from it – as I now choose myself.'

The room erupted into chaos: Sonja's face had returned to mask-like impassivity, and she stood motionless on the podium, as people continued to shout, jeer, and hurl incoherent questions at her.

As she turned to descend the steps, the crowd parted with ill grace to allow her to pass. She made her way to where her latest work was waiting to be unveiled. Taking a deep breath, she turned back to face the crowd.

'Ladies and gentlemen,' Sonja said, 'I consider art to be a sort of second-hand synthesis and simulacrum of other more truly destructive arts, acts in real life, of which the artist is also the author.' She finished quickly before the reaction to her words set in. 'That is certainly the case with this piece, my last, entitled *Quietus Est*, which I present to you now.'

She pulled the cloth off the sculpture, to reveal a huge glass tank full of reddish water. People crowded closer to observe the figure of a man floating inside it, the head hideously damaged and the face as though exploded.

Two more hours had passed, and Rooney and Rosie were still waiting in the small seating area outside Intensive Care, from which no amount of new carpet or pot plants could remove the atmosphere of anxiety and tension. Jake had gone to Reception to make some calls, and looked expectantly at them when he returned, but Rooney shook his head. No one had walked out of the unit, and the double doors had remained firmly closed.

'They just arrested Eric Lee Judd – holding him overnight for questioning,' Jake said. 'What do you think is going on in there?' He glanced at the doors.

Rooney lifted his shoulders with a sigh. 'Means she's still alive. That's all I can think.'

They all turned as the doors banged open and a small army of green-clad doctors and nurses appeared, removing their masks as they walked past. They looked exhausted. One youngish man lagged behind the others as he took off his mask. 'How is she?' Rooney blurted out.

'Are you relations?'

'Yes,' Rooney lied.

As the doctor slid off his green cap he seemed less young. 'I'm Dr Hudson – I've been heading the team. You mind if I sit down? It's been a long night.'

He sat, holding the cap loosely in his hands while his mask dangled round his neck.

'I might as well give it to you straight. She's in a very deep coma. She has a base-of-skull fracture and her right ear-drum is perforated, which means that she's losing fluid from the brain through the ear.' He rubbed his scalp, then took a deep breath. 'She is on a ventilator. Her ribs have been fractured, and have punctured the lungs, so both air and blood are escaping into the chest cavity. We've had a tough fight in there, as tests have also shown her kidneys are malfunctioning. The right cheekbone and right side of the jaw have been shattered, and there is also serious damage to the right eye.'

Rooney's heart was pounding. 'Is she going to live?'

Dr Hudson twisted his cap. 'She is critically ill and, as I said, in a very deep coma. We have a long way to go. We'll just take each day as it comes, and see whether she regains consciousness when the sedation is reduced. The main work we've been able to do this evening was to insert drains in the chest wall to clear air and blood from her lungs. We have to stabilize her breathing before we can carry out any other procedures.'

'Can we see her?' Rosie asked.

'You can see her through the viewing window outside the IC unit, but I'm afraid you will not be allowed inside.' He stood up. 'I'll ask one of the nurses to come and take you through. It may be quite a while.'

'We'll wait,' Jake said.

Hudson kept on turning his cap in his hands. 'I'm sorry it's not better news. Mrs Page is a very sick lady.'

He hated these sessions, trying to give hope, when in reality there was very little. In Mrs Page's case, it was already more than a probability that she had severe brain damage.

It was midnight before Sonja got back to the hotel to find Arthur waiting for her, a glass of whisky in his hand. 'How did it go?' he asked.

'Well,' she said, 'you won't believe it but it was one of the most bizarre evenings of my life. I announced that I was retiring and I couldn't resist telling them that art had all but wrecked my life and that I was getting out because I was sick of it and that I wanted a life with you.'

'You said that?' Arthur was incredulous.

'More or less. They went wild. But then I showed them the new piece and they went wild again – they loved it. I think I just had the most successful show of my life.'

'Sonja,' Arthur said evenly, 'I haven't asked you this before, but what is your new piece?'

Sonja looked away. 'I'm sorry, Arthur,' she said, 'I had to do it to get rid of him.'

'Sonja,' Arthur said again, 'just tell me. I'll see it in the papers tomorrow.'

She said nothing for a moment, then looked him steadily in the face. 'It's Harry,' she said. 'It's Harry in the swimming pool. The way they found him dead.'

He knew then that Sonja had killed her ex-husband. For a moment he thought of asking her the question directly, but he knew there was no need to do so: they both knew the truth. Perhaps he, too, had become as detached, as amoral, as she was, for he found he was indifferent to Nathan's physical life or death: the invisible hold he had had over Sonja for so long was all that concerned him.

'So,' he said, 'they loved it?'

'They were practically jamming commissions into my coat pockets.'

'So what's the next project?' Arthur said, with a sudden bitterness. 'Son of Harry?' Sonja flinched, and he knew his words had hurt her enormously, but he carried on. 'Or should I say ghost of Harry?' He was almost shouting at her now. 'How long is this going to go on? We talk about it again and again, but nothing ever changes. Your heart belongs to Harry, winter, spring and fall.'

It was the crudest and most painful speech anyone had ever made to Sonja, and it was only with an intense effort of self-control that she prevented herself from weeping. 'On the contrary,' she said, standing very still and upright, 'I will not be working again, no matter what commissions are offered to me. I meant what I said – it is finished.'

Arthur saw a tremor run through her and he knew that, no matter what Sonja said about wanting to give up her work, it was a sacrifice, and one that cost her dearly . . . Or maybe now that she had destroyed the man who had inspired and obsessed her, her art had simply left her as a bird takes flight from a tree. An abyss of doubt suddenly opened in front of him as he looked at the ring he had put on Sonja's finger and wondered what bargain he had made, what it was to which he had pledged himself. A murderess? A woman who was finally prepared to commit herself to him, to make sacrifices for his happiness? Or just an empty shell? One never could know the secrets of another soul, he thought, and suddenly he knew that he did not care what she was or what she had done: what he felt for her lay deeper than any question, any answer, any doubt.

'I'm sorry,' he said, moving close to her and putting his arms around her. 'Perhaps I'm the one can't stop talking about him now.'

'It's all right,' she said, her voice oddly thick. 'It really is finished now.'

There was silence for a moment, and then she broke away. 'How was your evening?' she said with a smile, her tone normal. 'Are we in the clear, or on the run?'

He smiled back at her. 'The former, it seems. It went even better than we hoped – the money will be transferred into the Swiss account by nine tomorrow.'

'How much?' she asked.

'Twenty million dollars.'

Sonja inhaled deeply, then let out her breath slowly. 'My God, I don't believe it.'

'You'd better, it's taken long enough but ... we did it.'

He crossed to the mini-bar and she watched him take out a half-bottle of champagne. 'I think we should drink a toast.' He opened it and handed her a foaming glass. 'To Harry Nathan,' he said, and saw her eyes widen in shock.

'Arthur ...'

'No,' he said. 'Lay the ghost. To the man who made possible both our successes this evening. Harry Nathan, RIP.'

'RIP,' Sonja echoed. 'I never want to say his name again.'

'Well, then, that's a second toast,' he said. 'To us.'

She raised her half-empty glass, and he saw that she closed her eyes as she drained it, as though holding her nose to jump into a new and strange sea.

'To us.'

Lorraine's head was swathed in bandages to just above her eyes, and her face was grossly bruised and discoloured. Drips for fluid, plasma and blood fed into her arm, while others had been inserted in her mouth. Her arm was encircled with a blood-pressure cuff, and she was connected to a cardiac monitor. The rhythmic hiss of the ventilator, pumping air into Lorraine's lungs, and the dreadful bubbling noise of her breathing were the only sounds. A probe-like clip to measure the levels of oxygen in her blood was attached to her finger, and she lay perfectly still, unaware, in some limbo between life and death.

'Oh, God,' whispered Rosie, her hands pressed against the glass partition.

'There's nothing we can do here,' Jake said quietly.

'Come on, Rosie, let's go home,' Rooney said, taking his wife's arm.

'No,' she whimpered.

'We'll come back tomorrow, and we've got to take care of Tiger.'

They left, unable to speak. Seeing Lorraine so isolated, so vulnerable, so distant from them, frightened them. Having seen with their own eyes the terrible punishment she had taken, it was hard to believe she could ever be the same Lorraine again.

'She's a fighter,' Rosie said hopefully, as she got in beside Rooney and slammed the car door shut.

'This is one fight she might not win, Rosie. We got to face up to that.'

Rosie wouldn't look at him. She clenched her fists. 'Well, maybe I know her better than you, Bill, and I'm telling you she's as strong as an ox. She'll beat this, I know it.'

'I hope so, darlin'. I sincerely hope so.'

Lorraine was closely monitored through the night: she remained in a deep coma, her pulse low. She showed no sign of movement in any of her limbs, and as yet they had been unable to establish the extent of the brain damage she had sustained. When the surgeons and staff reconvened the following morning, it was suggested that

Lorraine's close relatives be told to be ready to come. There had been no progress; if anything she had regressed, and there was little hope of recovery.

Rosie had stayed with Tiger at Lorraine's apartment. She packed nightdresses and toiletries ready to take to Lorraine as soon as she was allowed to have visitors, but she knew when Rooney called at eight thirty in the morning, it was bad news. At nine o'clock she and Rooney called Lorraine's ex-husband to inform him of the situation. Mike Page was shocked, asked which hospital Lorraine was in, and if he would be allowed to visit. Rooney suggested he call the hospital himself, saying only that he had been asked to inform Lorraine's immediate family and that she remained on the critical list.

Mike replaced the receiver, shaken. Although he had not seen or spoken to his ex-wife in over two years, he was still affected emotionally by the news of what had happened to her. He immediately saw in his mind the Lorraine with whom he had fallen in love, the Lorraine who had worked day and night to allow him to gain his law degree, the Lorraine who had given birth to his two beautiful daughters. All memory of the violent drunkard, the pain-racked woman he had been forced to divorce for his own survival, was gone.

Sissy, his wife, walked into his study with the morning's mail. 'You're going to be late, darling, and the girls are waiting for you to take them to school.' She stopped, and took a good look at him. 'What's happened?'

He took a deep breath. 'It's Lorraine, she's . . .'

'Is she dead?' Sissy asked.

'No – on the critical list. It didn't sound very hopeful. Not that they'd tell me much over the phone.'

'I'm sorry,' she said, putting her arms around him.

'I'll go and see her this afternoon.' He hesitated. 'Do you think I should take the girls with me?' Sissy shrugged her shoulders, and began to tidy his desk. He took her hand. 'Just stop that. I mean, she is their mother.'

'Well, she hasn't been one for a long time, Mike, and they're so settled. I just don't want them upset. The last time she visited – the only time – Sally was in a terrible state, and Julia . . . Look, it's not up to me, but I'd think twice about it. Maybe see her first and then decide.'

'Okay, I'll go straight to the hospital after lunch.'

'What happened?'

'I don't know. As I said, they weren't too forthcoming over the phone. They just said the outlook wasn't good.'

'Was she drinking again?'

'I don't know, Sissy. I'll find out, and I'll call you.'

As he left, Sissy could hear the girls, waiting outside by the car, calling him to hurry up. She crossed to the window and watched them drive away, then went back to his desk, covered with family photographs – their son, away at camp, and the two girls. No one could believe they weren't Sissy's daughters: they were as blonde as she was, both tall for their age, both pretty, but so like their mother, Lorraine . . . It made Sissy feel sad just thinking about what Lorraine had lost, their growing up, their first prizes at school, their first tennis matches, their first time swimming without water-wings, the trill of their voices calling, 'Mommy,' because they both now called Sissy by that name – had done so from almost the start of her relationship with Mike.

She picked up one photograph after another – herself with the girls, Mike with them, the family all linking arms on a forest trail when they had been on a camper trip. Lorraine had never been any part of the girls' lives, and now she had appeared again. Sissy was fearful of what it would do to them, and to Mike especially. She knew Sally and Julia would have to be told and, if Lorraine was as ill as Mike had implied, they should at least have the opportunity to get to know her before it was too late. Sissy had no idea that it was already too late: that Lorraine was dying.

'I found these,' Rosie said, producing two gift-wrapped packages, one marked 'Julia', the other marked 'Sally'.

'She must have bought them for her daughters. Maybe she was planning what Jake suggested, getting in contact with them again.' Rooney sniffed, and turned away. 'Maybe we should call him, give him an update.'

'Yes, we should,' Rosie said sadly, then forced a smile. 'She's going to pull through this, Bill, I know it. Do you feel it too?'

He didn't say anything – he couldn't, because deep down he didn't believe what Rosie had said.

'We'll take that goddamned dog with us then, shall we?' he said.

Rosie's face puckered, and she went into the bedroom. Tiger lay stretched full-length on his mistress's bed, with her nightgown, dragged from beneath her pillow, in his mouth. He didn't know what was going on, but when

Rosie tried to get him off the bed he flatly refused to move, and when she tried to take the nightgown out of his mouth he gave a low growl.

Rooney and Rosie left Lorraine's apartment, dragging Tiger by his lead. Neither had been able to prise open his jaws to remove the nightdress, and it trailed on the floor, clamped in his teeth. They packed the car with everything they thought Lorraine might need, and then drove off. Rosie turned to look back at the apartment.

'Don't look back, darlin', it's unlucky,' he said quietly, and suddenly Rosie had a terrible premonition that Lorraine would never come home. She started to cry, and he patted her knee, near to tears himself, but the sight of Tiger's grizzled head on the back seat, still with Lorraine's nightdress between his jaws, touched him more than anything else. It was as if some sixth sense had told the dog, too, that Lorraine wasn't coming back.

Feinstein was told what had happened later that morning – Burton had called him after he had checked Lorraine's answerphone and collected her mail. He'd even watered her plants before he'd locked up and returned to the station.

By now they had questioned Eric Lee Judd, who maintained that he had been with four friends the entire evening, and was adamant that he didn't even know Lorraine Page or where she lived. The four friends were contacted and each verified Eric Lee Judd's alibi. Without further evidence, he would be released.

No prints were found on the baseball bat, none on

the crushed Coke cans. Whoever had attacked her was a professional, Burton knew, and had been careful to avoid leaving any trace detectable by the forensic lab. The bloodstains on Lorraine's clothes were found to contain no other blood group but her own. However, the bloody footprints taken from the carpet, and from the vinyl flooring by the stairs at the entrance to the apartment, were size nine, and showed the clear outline of a sneaker sole. Eric Lee Judd allowed the police to take samples of all his footwear. Nothing matched.

By twelve fifteen that morning there was no evidence against him and Eric Lee Judd was released from the police station. He was cocky and self-assured, warning officers that if they continued to harass him he'd take legal action.

Detective Jim Sharkey had been the main interrogator, and he had stared with loathing at the boy, then shaken his finger. 'You tread very carefully, Mr Lee Judd, because I am going to be right here.' He tapped the young man's shoulder. 'You put a foot out of line and . . .'

Eric Lee Judd glared back. 'What'll you do, mister? Get some drunk cop to fire six rounds into my back? That what you'll do, huh? Then cover it up, so they get away with it? Fuck you.'

'One foot out of line and I'll fuck you, son – just remember that. Now get out of my sight.'

Eric Lee Judd whistled as he strolled down the corridor. He stopped in his tracks when Lieutenant Burton stepped out of his office and their eyes met.

Lee Judd had no notion of who the tall, fair-haired man was – all he knew was that his eyes were like lasers, and those eyes watched his every move as he passed and bored into his back as he continued along the corridor. He turned back, a little afraid now but unable to resist another look, then kicked open the double swing doors leading into the last corridor before he made it to the street. He began to run then, run like his kid brother had all those years before. But that was settled now: the bitch had paid the price, and he had got clean away with it.

'How is she?' Sharkey asked Burton, who was still standing as if frozen.

'No news yet. No news.' He lowered his head, then gave Sharkey a small, bleak smile. 'Thanks for asking.'

Burton turned on his heel and returned to his office, closing the door quietly, leaving Sharkey alone outside. Sharkey went to the incident room: work would continue as usual – nothing ever stopped at the police department, not even when the life of someone many of the officers knew hung in the balance.

Burton's door opened again, and he snapped out Sharkey's name. The officer whipped round. 'In my office, Detective Sharkey, in fifteen minutes. I want you to go over some files I've taken from Lorraine Page's office. It's the Nathan case.'

Burton's door slammed shut with an ominous bang, and Sharkey sighed and muttered as he continued up the corridor, wondering what that damned woman might have found that he hadn't, and sure that he was going to be bawled out. Old Rooney had always maintained she was one of the best. He didn't notice that he was already thinking of Lorraine in the past tense – as if she was already dead.

CHAPTER 20

MIKE PAGE met Jake Burton in the hospital reception area: neither knew enough about the other to be embarrassed, nor were they there to find out about their respective places in Lorraine's life and affections. They shook hands and went to the small hospital coffee shop, stood in line to order their coffee, and didn't speak until they sat down at a small corner table.

Mike pulled at his collar with nerves. 'I haven't been allowed to see her yet. The head honcho was in the unit, said maybe in half an hour.' He sipped his coffee and coughed. 'They told me there had been no improvement – did they say that to you?'

Jake nodded. He had seen Mike arrive and had introduced himself: Mike had been a little confused to begin with, presuming he was there in his police capacity, but then Jake had quietly told him that he and Lorraine had planned to be married.

'Do we know what happened to her?' Mike asked.

'All we know is, she was attacked on entering her apartment. We had a suspect in custody, but we released him – no evidence.'

'Does anyone know why it happened? I mean, I know

she must have met some unsavoury types, but was she investigating something or . . . Was she still not drinking?'

Jake stirred his coffee. 'She was on a case, but as yet I haven't found any connection to her death. We're still checking it out. She was not drinking.'

'So this suspect – was he found there?'

'No.'

Jake was still deeply shocked and unsure how much he should tell Mike. He was unsure about everything but his own despair.

'Who was the suspect?' Mike enquired.

'He had a possible connection to an incident that happened a long time ago.'

'Like what?'

Jake looked away. 'He was the elder brother of the boy Lorraine shot.'

'Oh, Jesus, God . . .' Mike bowed his head. There was a lengthy pause during which neither man could say anything, each immersed in his own thoughts, until Mike looked at his watch. 'Time to go to the unit.'

Jake pushed back his chair. Then, as he stood up, he asked if Mike minded him saying something personal. 'Sure, say anything you want,' Mike said apprehensively.

'Bring her daughters to see her. Just before this happened she and I talked. I know she wanted to be reunited with them and . . .'

'I don't know if it's such a good idea. They haven't had any communication with her for a long time, and it would be unsettling for them.'

'She's their mother,' Jake said quietly, and Mike flushed.

'I'll think about it – I'd like to see her first. Been nice

meeting you, and I'm very sorry. Maybe she'll pull through. She always was a fighter, and she's taken a lot of punishment in her life.'

Jake walked past him, teeth gritted. 'Nice meeting you.'

Mike was ill-prepared for Lorraine's appearance. He focused on her hands, resting on top of the linen. They were white, with an almost bluish tinge.

He sat in a chair beside her and just said he was there, then slowly inched his hand over the sheet to touch hers. There was no response, so he withdrew it, and stayed for another few minutes without saying anything, just remembering. 'I'll bring the girls to see you,' he whispered. Again, there was no reaction, and he left the unit quietly. He asked to speak to whoever could give him most information about Lorraine's condition. What he heard was not good: there had been no improvement since Lorraine had been brought in; she remained in a deep coma, unable to breathe unaided; her pulse rate remained low; they were concerned about her kidneys and had a dialysis machine standing by.

Jake Burton came twice and also sat with Lorraine, talking and talking to her, willing her to react, but there was no response. He returned to the station, where Jim Sharkey and two other detectives were scrutinizing her files and notes, first with regard to the murder inquiry, then poring over the art scam, of which they had not previously been notified. When Burton returned they discussed it with him and he suggested that perhaps they should interview Feinstein. If their first suspicions regarding Eric Lee Judd had proved unfounded, perhaps Lorraine's attacker could be connected to the art fraud.

Feinstein was irate. He did not wish to bring charges as he was dealing with a client's private affairs, and if he did not wish to press any formal charges then the police had no right to do so. He also knew, without a shadow of a doubt, that none of the other police who had been stung by Nathan would want their names associated with a police inquiry.

Sharkey tried to change Feinstein's mind: what if the murder of Harry Nathan was connected to the art fraud? Maybe *he* was content to let whoever was behind the scam walk away scot-free, but perhaps someone else had cared enough about it to shoot Nathan? Feinstein almost wet himself, but refused to pursue any further enquiries in relation to the fraud. Sharkey asked if the money could be traced. But Feinstein refused to be drawn. How could he know what a dead man did or did not do? Yet again he insisted that he did not wish to pursue the fraud.

Sharkey stared at him with distaste, then rose slowly to his feet, buttoning his jacket. 'Thanks for your time,' he said curtly.

'So that's it, is it?' Feinstein hovered at the side of his desk.

'Might be for you, Mr Feinstein, sir, but we will still be investigating the art scam's possible connection to the murder of Harry Nathan.'

'But I refuse to press charges,' Feinstein said, his voice rising an octave.

'That is your prerogative, sir, but whether you like it

or not it's a police matter and it will therefore be treated as an ongoing investigation.'

'But everybody connected is fucking dead!' Feinstein screeched.

Sharkey was at the door, his back to the room. 'Yeah, I'd say that was a pretty good reason not to try to sweep it all under the carpet. Maybe you won't have to give evidence. There again, you just might not be able to get out of it. Have a nice day.'

Feinstein slumped into his leather swivel chair, took a deep breath and turned slowly towards the large empty space on the wall that had once been occupied by one of Harry Nathan's fakes. The faint dust line indicated the painting's proportions and the spotlight fitted to show it off was still trained on the blank wall. He didn't scream the words as he usually did, but almost spat them with venomous hatred: 'God damn you, Harry Nathan, you bastard!'

Burton rocked in his chair, drumming his fingers, his mouth down-turned. Feinstein's refusal to co-operate infuriated him.

'Any news?' Sharkey asked. Burton shook his head. 'Holding her own, is she?' he persisted, then saw that Burton could hardly answer.

'Not quite . . . but we're hoping. Okay, thanks for the extra work, I appreciate it.'

Sharkey and the two other detectives walked out to the nearest bar.

'That Feinstein is a prick,' one detective said, as Sharkey carried the beer to their table.

'Yeah – what kind of guy can be stung outa that much dough an' not want to do something about it?'

'Not just him. How many others got stung? Mind-blowing. I mean, if some shit diddled me outa a hundred bucks, I'd have to go after him. Wouldn't you, Jim?'

'Yep, but that's the difference between you and me and the likes of Feinstein and his rich clients. They got more fucking money than they know what to fucking do with, and he'll more'n likely make it up off their bills. So if they don't miss it, fuck 'em. They'll hopefully be made to look like real assholes by the press. I'd like to see them get a hell of a lot more, but you know how long these fuckin' fraud cases take to unravel. Not like somebody got away with murder . . .' He didn't finish the sentence, but took a deep gulp of his beer.

'You know some son-of-a-bitch just might,' said one, a thin film of beer froth on his upper lip.

Sharkey turned his head. 'What?'

'Well, they got nobody for Lorraine Page's beatin' and word is she's not gonna make it.'

Sharkey drained his beer in one, and banged down the glass.

One of the men had known her from the old days, when she had partnered Lubrinski, and he grinned. 'But she ain't dead yet, an' that lady's one hell of a fighter. Did I ever tell you about that story, with this guy, he's dead now . . . Yeah, Jack Lubrinski. Well, they go to this bar right, downtown someplace . . .'

They continued telling anecdotes about Lorraine and Lubrinski, and, as often happens, the good memories obliterated the bad. It was like some kind of wake. No one spoke of the shooting of Tommy Lee Judd, and

Lorraine Page's decline into alcoholism and drug addiction. They were remembering her as a good cop, the one that took the hassle and never made a complaint.

Three days later, to the amazement of everyone, Lorraine was still hanging on to life. She remained in a coma, still on the critical list, and the specialists testing her brain were noncommittal.

Reports of Lorraine's condition were relayed to Rosie and Rooney, and they were heartened to hear that she was still battling for life, but they knew that even if she did pull out of the coma, there was a strong possibility of permanent brain damage, causing severe physical incapacity.

'Is she paralysed?' Rooney asked.

'We're unable to do tests to ascertain the degree of paralysis with coma patients,' Hudson told him. 'As the sedation wears off and time passes, all we can do is wait and see if motor function returns.'

Day four, and still she clung on, the medical team reporting a slow improvement in her breathing.

Mike Page visited every other day, while Burton, Rosie and Rooney came daily. On day six Mike brought his and Lorraine's daughters. Rosie had been told they would be there and she brought the gifts Lorraine had bought for the girls in Santa Fe. They clung to their father as they were led into the unit.

The girls sat in awed silence. The bandaged woman in front of them was a stranger, and they didn't know what to say to her. When Mike encouraged Sally to touch her mother's hand she wouldn't, whispering that she was too frightened.

The doctors and all the staff were kind and thoughtful, suggesting to the girls that although their mother could not respond, they should talk to her to let her hear their voices. The girls looked at each other. Hearing this woman called their mother felt wrong, and Julia began to cry, saying she wanted to go home.

Two weeks passed slowly and the number of tubes attached to Lorraine's body gradually diminished. More tests to determine brain damage had been done, but she remained in a coma. The healing process of the external damage had been rapid though: she no longer looked like a monster for the terrible bruising to her face was fading and the bandages were removed.

The girls came regularly now, and the more they got used to seeing her, the more freely they chatted about ordinary, girlish things. They never called her Mom, but Sally often touched her hand, and Julia stroked her mother's pale arm. Both girls wore the bracelets she had chosen for them.

Rosie and Rooney divided their visiting time between them, and talked and talked, never giving up hope of a response. Jake came before and after work, spending hours sitting beside her, planning their wedding. He brought the ring he had bought for her, and asked her if he could put it on her wedding finger.

Christmas was now a week away, and Lorraine was still in a coma, her eyes closed, as if she was sleeping. The ventilator tube had been moved from her mouth to pass through a tracheotomy incision in her neck, and there was hope, hope that none had believed possible. She remained in the intensive care unit, as she still needed to be monitored round the clock. She was dressed now in her own nightclothes, and Rosie combed her hair and cared for her. She read magazines and books to Lorraine, played music tapes, and when she was through, Rooney took over. He talked for hours, all about his old work, and found it quite therapeutic to chat to Lorraine, asking her if she recalled this or that case.

Jake would take over from him, and sat holding her hand, willing her to acknowledge him. He brought fresh bouquets every other day, unable to bear the sight of flowers wilting, always insisting that fresh ones replaced them. Like Rooney, he talked about his work, discussing things with her as if she was replying. When it got to week eight, everyone was tired – and angry that Lorraine was still a prisoner in some alien world. She looked almost like herself – and yet she wasn't there. Rosie had brought in a small artificial Christmas tree and had decorated it with baubles and ribbons. Small gifts for the nurses were arranged beneath it, all bearing tags: 'Happy Christmas, with love from Lorraine.'

The first time she heard his voice was at the moment he had put the ring on her finger. She had started talking to him, saying how happy she was, and asking him why he didn't reply to her questions. It was frightening that she could hear them talking to her but they couldn't hear her.

The visits were the worst, when they seemed to ignore what she was saying, talking at her, not to her, not hearing when she called their names. Then she listened intently, and realized that the high-pitched chattering voices she had been hearing day after day belonged to her daughters, talking about what they wanted for Christmas. She wanted to cry with happiness that they were there with her – but *why* couldn't they hear what she was saying? She could hear Mike, and told him how pleased she was that he had brought the girls, asked him if he had met Jake. She asked so many questions, and sometimes she laughed at what they were saying, especially old Bill Rooney, forever droning on about some case he knew he should have beaten, then complaining that Tiger had chewed up his best sweater. Her visitors came and went, not hearing her answers, her voice, and when it was night she wept, because it felt as if she would never see them again, and she couldn't understand what had happened, or where she was. She started to be strict with herself, telling herself to pull herself together, that she had to straighten out. Crying every night was not doing any good: it was just using up all her energy, and she had to start thinking about other things. She forced her brain to be active, even though it hurt to think – yet she had to do something.

Lorraine felt as if she was gritting her teeth with determination, that if she could just get through the pain barrier her mind had erected, then she was sure she would be able to see again, see her loved ones. She told herself that she was having a nightmare, that she'd wake up soon, but that she had to make herself do it by retaining a mental connection with her active, waking self and her life, and convince herself that she would soon be coming back to them.

Worst of all were those silent night hours when all she heard was the clatter of things around her, the alien whispers, sounds that reminded her of a hospital, and her mind drifted back to the last time she had been in a hospital, when she'd had the plastic surgery on her cheek to get rid of the scar in an expensive private establishment. She made herself visualize the place, taking herself on a tour of her room, the corridors, the television lounge, the day room, the other patients.

Lorraine had had no visitors then – no one had even known she was undergoing surgery – so she spent many hours alone in the sunny, comfortable TV lounge, not that she had ever had much interest in television but this was the only room in which patients were allowed to smoke, and she had passed the time by watching the others, playing detective as to their real ages and backgrounds.

Most were women between forty and sixty, and some had already had so much surgery that at first sight they looked much younger, but there was always some incongruity between their faces, uniformly taut, tanned, slightly android-looking, and the way they dressed, moved or, most noticeably, spoke, that betrayed their real age. There were other dead giveaways too: the slight slackening of skin tone on the under surface of the arm that no amount of exercise could firm, plus, of course, the hands and feet. There were a couple of veritable Zsa Zsa Gabor lookalikes, dyed blonde hair piled up, stretched and lifted faces that could have passed for mid-forties, but with the liver-spotted hands, thickened knuckles and prominent tendons of old age. Only a lucky few seemed to escape *that* tell-tale sign of time's passing. There had been a woman in a wheelchair, wearing dark glasses and still bandaged so that virtually none of her face could be seen. Lorraine had assumed, from the few visible strands of white hair, that she must be in her sixties or seventies, but she had noticed that the woman's large, fine, restless hands were those of someone much younger, conveying an unusual impression of simultaneous flexibility and strength. She remembered noting how short the nails were cut, and had thought at the time that the woman must use her hands – perhaps as a musician or, at her age, a music teacher – which would explain how they had escaped shrivelling into an old lady's claws. Now she knew that the woman was no musician, no teacher, and no old lady: it had been Sonja Nathan, she would have taken an oath on it.

The woman had kept herself to herself, only coming into the TV lounge once and taking no part in any of the casual conversations that were going on around her. Lorraine had thought, though, that she had seemed to pay attention when she herself had revealed to a chatty lady who worked for a real estate company that she was a private detective – they had commented quietly that they seemed to be in a minority here of working women: most of their fellow patients were pampered wives. When Lorraine had said she might be looking to rent a new office shortly, the woman had insisted on knowing Lorraine's full name and the name of her company, Lorraine remembered, and she remembered, too, how she had thought of trying to draw the bandaged woman into their conversation, but some separateness and aloofness in her demeanour had deterred her from doing so. It was that indefinable *froideur*, as much as anything in Sonja Nathan's physical appearance, that now made Lorraine certain it had been her.

Sonja Nathan had left the clinic knowing exactly who Lorraine was and, weeks later, had been able to recall those details.

Sonja had said that she had not been in Los Angeles

at all for the previous year. That was a lie, and Lorraine was positive now that Sonja had also lied when she had said she had not made the call to Lorraine's office on the morning of the murder. Lorraine already had documentary evidence – presumably lying in her apartment, she thought, in her briefcase – that Sonja and Harry Nathan were in contact after their divorce. Now she had the last piece of the jigsaw: proof that Sonja Nathan had been in LA the day her ex-husband was killed. She was sure now that if she ever got out of this goddamn hospital and was able to get voice experts to analyse the recording Decker had made of the call which had to be somewhere on that tape, they could identify some feature of Sonja's mid-Atlantic, faintly European accent. That would be the final link and would put the woman behind bars.

It was painful to drag up each memory, worse than any headache she had ever known. The pain was excruciating, but Lorraine wouldn't, couldn't stop. Now everything had fallen into place, and Lorraine understood Sonja's odd concern about Cindy, her saying that she wished she had given her more time – 'or assistance'. Sonja's lack of interest in the fact that so much money was missing from the estate had also seemed strange – but not, Lorraine thought wryly, when one knew that the assets had been taken *before* the bizarre sequence of events that had left Sonja, ironically, Harry Nathan's legitimate heir.

Sonja Nathan knew the house, the gardens, and more than likely her ex-husband's routine – or she could readily have arranged to meet him in advance. Sonja was clearly capable of premeditation, as she must deliberately have hired a jeep identical to Kendall's to conceal her comings and goings at Nathan's house – perhaps she had even hoped to incriminate Kendall, Lorraine thought, and she had managed to take every nickel of the woman's money through the art fraud. Even if Kendall's death really had been accidental, Sonja bore some indirect responsibility, as it had been after realizing that she had lost her stake in the paintings that Kendall had been tempted to try to burn down the gallery for the insurance. That must have given Sonja considerable satisfaction, Lorraine thought, for, as Arthur had said, she was all too human – or inhuman – under the cool, superior façade, and had clearly hated Kendall as intensely as she had ever loved Nathan.

As for the paintings, Lorraine now knew that Harry Nathan had been to Germany, to make preparations for the sale of the real works of art, and she was sure, too, that once she got out of here and could get to Berlin, she could find out exactly how Sonja and Arthur, the expert copier, had stepped into Nathan's shoes and netted the proceeds of sale.

Lorraine's head throbbed, but she carried on, piecing the jigsaw together. All the dead faces floated in front of her – Harry Nathan, Cindy, Kendall, Vallance – faded, and then became clearer, but her concentration was wavering like a guttering torch. It was on Vallance's death that she tried to shed the last of its light. Lorraine knew now how Sonja had killed him – or made him kill himself – by threatening to release the porn videos, the murder weapon Jake Burton had innocently sent her. Sonja could not, of course, be made to bear legal responsibility for that murder, or for Cindy's death, for which she was also morally responsible: Vallance had strangled his former mistress, believing mistakenly that she, not Sonja, had killed the man he had idolized and

467

lusted after all his life. Christ, Lorraine thought, that this should be the woman to whom she had poured out her own most private griefs to turn Sonja's mind from suicide – but once she got out of here . . . The faces blurred and parts of the conversations she was trying to recall began to crackle and echo in Lorraine's brain. The pain grew worse and worse: she was losing her grip, unable to think any more. She screamed in agony, as if a red-hot iron were forging up from her spine, blinding her, exhausting her, and she couldn't take it any more.

Rooney went pale. Even though he was outside Intensive Care, on his way to see Lorraine, he knew something had happened. Nurses and doctors, running as if for their own lives, entered the unit, and the curtains were drawn across the viewing window. Lorraine was shielded from his sight, and the last thing he saw as they clustered around her was the heart monitor, bleeping loudly.

A little later, Jake Burton walked up the corridor with fresh flowers, and Rooney turned to him. 'Something's happened, I don't know what, but they shut the curtains and there's got to be eight of them round her. I don't know for sure, but I think it's her heart.'

Sonja had had one white wedding, and she had decided that this time she would get married in deep red, a rich colour more suitable for both a Swiss wedding in winter, she thought, and for a mature bride. The close-fitting crimson suit, with rich brown fur collar and cuffs, accentuated her tall, slim figure, while she had bought a frighteningly expensive hussar's cap in the same fur, which she was now wondering whether or not to wear.

She put it on, took it off, fluffed out her hair, then crossed to the far side of the room across the expanse of pale green carpet: she and Arthur had booked the Grace Kelly Suite in the best hotel in Geneva, with private sitting and dining rooms and a marvellous view of the lake. She walked towards her reflection in the long cheval mirror, studying it intently.

'Too much fur?' she asked, as Arthur appeared. 'I don't know whether or not to wear the hat.'

He was wearing a smart suit, with a rose in the buttonhole, and a matching waistcoat, and was knotting his tie. 'Put it on and let me see,' he said.

Sonja did as he asked and turned to face him: she looked beautiful, he thought, but she was different now, and it wasn't just the unfamiliar new costume. For all these years he had yearned to possess her without Harry Nathan, but now that Nathan's shadow had gone, she was not the same woman, less driven, less intense, as though someone had dropped the end of a rope she had pulled against for years, sometimes seeming younger, sometimes older. Was she free now, he wondered, or adrift?

She had always been able to read his moods, almost his thoughts, and it was as though she sensed his scrutiny. 'You're sure you want to do this?' she said quietly. 'You know you can still back out.'

'I don't want to back out,' he said. You could never tell with love, he thought, whether it would last or fade, stay constant or change. You just had to trust and step in. 'Wear the hat.'

Sonja looked at herself again in the mirror, then turned. 'Shall we go?' she said, her expression grave.

Arthur tossed something towards her. 'Here – this time it's not a fake.' She caught the ring box in both hands, knowing that the price of the jewel didn't matter now: all the money had been transferred to Switzerland, and they would decide later how to move it back to the United States if and when they needed it.

He watched her take the ring from the box, admire it, then hold it out. 'You put it on.'

He took it and held her hand, slipping it onto her wedding finger. Then he bent down to kiss her.

'Well, we did it,' he said softly, then smiled. 'And we got away with it. Was it worth the wait?'

'Yes, yes, it was.' She was not looking at him. 'Believe me, it was worth it.'

She turned away to catch another glimpse of herself as Arthur checked the time. They should go down to Reception, the limo would be waiting. Arthur crossed to the doors: as a small surprise, he had ordered some deep red roses as a bridal bouquet.

'Give me two minutes . . . I'll join you,' she called.

He held the door half open.

'Two minutes. See you down there.'

She waited for him to leave, adjusted her hat, needing a moment alone to look in her room of memories one last time before she turned the key. She remembered crossing the lawn, seeing Harry towelling himself dry after his swim. She had not decided then that that would be the day she killed him – a day she had been thinking about for a long time, and neither of them had known then that everything Harry Nathan did that day he was doing for the last time. It was when she had seen the gun on the table, one of Nathan's own guns, and had known that there would be no difficulty in disposing of a weapon, that she had felt she had received the signal to put the plan into action, had known that there would never be a better chance.

Harry had tossed aside his towel, not bothering to cover his nakedness in front of her, vain as ever of his body. Sonja had taken a handkerchief out of her pocket. He had paid no attention when she picked up the gun, turning it in her hand and covering it with the cloth. It felt cold and heavy – like her heart. She had raised it first to his chest, then a little higher, and he had smiled, told her to be careful as it was loaded. Then his face had slowly drained of colour as she aimed it at his neck, then tilted the barrel to his face.

'I've wanted to kill you for a long time, Harry, and until now I never thought I could. But you know something, Harry, I can.'

He had backed away, terror visible in his face, as his eyes widened in fear. Then she had pulled the trigger, and he stumbled two steps forward, then toppled into the pool. She had stood there, watching the petals of blood unfold from his head, as he floated face down, arms outstretched, the image that had never left her, and that she had felt driven to replicate, partly as a triumphal shout, a final exorcism – and partly as a confession that no one had heard.

She had then picked up her shoes, and walked back across the gardens, returning to the rented Mitsubishi jeep – Harry had agreed she should get one as close to Kendall's as possible just in case anyone saw her driving in and out of the house for their meetings and to remove the paintings. Suddenly she knew how fortunate that

471

was. Sonja could not have cared less if the phoney, odious Kendall ended up paying the penalty for Harry Nathan's death.

No one else could possibly be incriminated, she had thought – but Cindy had been her one mistake. She had thought Nathan had told her on the phone, when they arranged the meeting, that he and Cindy had had a fight and she had left. It was only when she had heard the girl's scream after the killing that she had realized that she must have misunderstood. He must have said that Cindy had threatened to go, or was about to. Poor Cindy, she had thought. She had had no desire to see the pathetic, abused girl stand trial, and it must have been fate that had ensured she had not only met a local private investigator a few weeks previously but had remembered the woman's name. She had stopped the jeep at once, had got the number from Information, then called Lorraine Page's office from a public phone.

Her plane trip back to New York was, as always, booked in a different name, and she had carried the paintings like posters in rolls of cardboard. She was never stopped or questioned.

By the time she had returned to the Hamptons, the news had broken that Harry Nathan had been murdered and Cindy Nathan arrested. Next day, it had transpired that things were worse than Sonja had thought: the gun she had used had been Cindy's.

After that she had just sat back and watched the aftermath. Now there was no one left to hate, no one left to blame. She had told the world of her guilt, but no one had noticed, and it was over at last, she thought. *Quietus est*.

*

472

Rosie was out of breath as she joined Burton and Rooney – she'd rushed to the hospital as soon as she had heard.

'What happened? Is she all right?'

Rooney sat her down. 'There've been complications. Her breathing has deteriorated, and her temperature's started rising. She's holding her own, but now they're worrying that her heart's been under too much strain.'

Jake took Rosie's hand. 'Mike's on his way in, and the girls. It's just a matter of time now.'

'No, no, I don't believe it – she was getting better. They said her breathing wouldn't stabilize – well, it did. She'll get over this relapse – it's just a kind of a relapse, right? Look, I know her, I know her, and . . .' Rosie's face crumpled but she kept on talking about how she and Lorraine had first met – how ill Lorraine had been, how she was so thin and weak that no one would have ever believed she could recover, quit her alcohol addiction . . .

'It's part of the problem, Rosie, sweetheart. Her body took so much punishment for so long, it's just tired out.' Rosie started to sob and Rooney gripped her hand tightly. 'Now you listen to me, her daughters are coming in, and we don't want them upset and scared. Just pull yourself together – there's been enough tears, and you don't want Lorraine to see you crying.'

'She can't see me, she's in a coma,' Rosie said, wiping her nose.

'I know, but nobody knows if that means she can't hear. So dry your eyes, and go freshen up.'

Rosie went to the powder room, and Rooney felt exhausted. He had no tears left to cry, and he looked at the quiet, composed Jake. 'You okay?'

Jake was far from okay, but he nodded, and Rooney

sighed heavily. 'You know, maybe it's for the best. I mean, it's likely she's got brain damage, and I wouldn't want to see her all crumpled up, unable to do anything for herself. I know she wouldn't want that either.'

Both men stood up as Dr Hudson came out of the unit and gestured to them to sit down. He asked if Lorraine's daughters were coming in to see her, and Jake said they were on their way.

'You want it straight?' he said, pulling at the collar of his white coat. They both nodded. 'I've always been level with you, and I've got to admit I didn't think we'd be able to hold her for this long, but this recent development . . . Her organs are just giving way, and I am afraid there's nothing more we can do. It really is a matter of hours. She's in no pain, but her heart is now in trouble, and what with that and the cumulative malfunction of her kidneys and lungs . . .'

'How long?' Jake said quietly.

'I doubt if she'll last the night. I'm very, very sorry.'

Jake stood up and looked at Rooney. 'I'd like some time alone with her, before her daughters arrive.' He turned his gaze to the doctor. 'Can I go in?'

The doctor nodded: the staff were already making Lorraine look more presentable by removing some of the drips and machines from the room, which was already screened off from the rest of the unit to give more privacy. 'The nurse will come out in a minute, but I'll be here if you need me. Just tell the duty nurse, or Reception to buzz me.' The doctor hovered for a moment, then walked away from the tiny overheated anteroom with a grave nod.

Five minutes later, when Rosie had returned, a nurse

came out. She smiled cheerfully and held the door ajar. 'You can see her now. Thank you for all the gifts.'

'They were from Lorraine,' Rosie said firmly. The nurse moved away, and Rosie saw as she went in that the little Christmas tree had been taken down.

Sonja and Arthur exchanged their vows in a quiet ceremony, with only one other person as a witness, a clerk from the mayor's office, a small, balding man who had obviously performed this function on innumerable occasions. He gave them an encouraging smile, signed the register with a flourish, and wished them every happiness in their future life. They walked out arm in arm, Sonja's bouquet of roses matching Arthur's buttonhole.

'Holy shit, they gone an' put my nightdress on back to front,' Lorraine said, then angrily told Burton that one of the nurses should be fired as she had a rough bedside manner. He drew up a chair and sat close to the bed.

'I have to say you must have shares in a florist!' Lorraine joked. 'I mean, this is getting to be ridiculous. When I get out of here, I'm taking that bunch with me, the lilies – I always liked lilies, it's the smell. I've been meaning to ask you, though it's a bit embarrassing, do I smell? I know they clean me up, but that fucking nurse, the one with the frizzy hair, I don't think she's a pro. She almost had me out of the bed earlier you know, whipping out the fucking tubes as if she was playing an organ.' He touched her hand, and let one finger trace the dark bruises where the needles and drips had been attached. 'I know – they think they're digging for gold trying to find a vein.' She laughed, then frowned.

'I worry about wearing this ring – I don't know if you can trust these nurses. I remember when my dad was in hospital, you couldn't leave fifty bucks. Mind you, he wasn't in a private ward like this. Thank Christ I blew so much on a private medical plan.'

He gently traced her fingers, touching each nail. 'I love you, will never forget you, and with this ring I thee wed. You are the wife I always wanted and never believed I'd find, but we did find each other, didn't we? If just for a short while.'

'Yeah, we sure did, and you know I've never been the romantic kind, but . . . remember the beach? The first time you came walking with me and Tiger – I knew I was in love with you then. Actually I knew when you knocked on the door. Did I tell you that? You have a way of holding your head, on one side, and when you're going to say something romantic, you get these two red dots in your cheeks. You've got them now . . .'

'Remember the first time we walked on the beach?'

'Yes, I just said that. But it was even better later with all that takeaway food – my God, we ordered every single thing off the menu. You know I truthfully never thought I'd have someone love me.'

'I love you.'

'I love you, too, with all my heart, and . . . Hey, where you going? Don't go yet, I want to kiss you. Don't go, let me kiss you.'

Jake got to the door, stopped, turned back. He found it almost unbearable to see Lorraine propped up, but with her eyes closed, just as if she was sleeping. He returned to the bed and gently kissed her lips, then rested his head against hers and touched her cheeks. For the first time her flesh felt cold.

'I don't call that a kiss, and listen, we have to talk before you go. Listen to me, it's very important. I cracked the Nathan case. Sonja Nathan killed him, I'm sure of it. I know I've got nothing but circumstantial evidence, but you've got to get my briefcase and get some phone company records out of it, and contact the clinic where I had my scar fixed. I'm sure she was there. You've got to get the tape recording Decker made of that call that was made to my office too – the one Cindy never made. He couldn't find it, but it's just got to be there somewhere. It was Sonja. Why don't you listen to me? Where are you going?'

Jake leaned out into the corridor. 'Bill, you want to come in? I'll just take five minutes, go to the john.'

Rooney came in, sweating as usual, wanting to take off his jacket, but not sure that he should.

'Sit down, Billy, before he gets back. We got to talk – he doesn't seem to take me seriously, but I think I cracked the Nathan case. I'll need help, and there could be big bucks in it if we can recover the stolen art work. It's worth millions and I have a damned good idea where it is. Germany. I also know Sonja Nathan killed her husband.'

'Rosie's with me, she won't be a minute.'

'Okay. Let me get this sorted out before she comes in. First you have to check out Nathan's fake passports, there's a letter in my purse he sent to his mother from Germany. I think – in fact, I'm sure – Sonja Nathan was

477

working with her ex-husband on this art fraud scam. It's big money, Bill, not a few hundred thousand dollars, but millions.'

He looked at her, lying so still, eyes closed as if she was sleeping.

'You look beautiful, darlin',' he said softly.

'Oh, quit with the flattery. Listen to what I'm saying. We trace those paintings, we'll all be in for a few bucks to retire on, Billy. I'm out after this case, and all I want to do is crack it – you know the way I am. Now, I need you first to contact Feinstein, then get my briefcase out of the apartment, Bill. Then you and Rosie do another trip to Europe. I want this case cleared before I quit, know what I mean? I get married to Jake and . . . You like him, don't you? He's an okay guy, isn't he? And I'm going to tell you something. I was so scared, Bill – you know, I didn't think I had any right to love or be loved. He loves me, Billy.'

'We're taking care of Tiger,' Rooney said, trying to think of something to say, then told her how the dog had already destroyed their new sofa.

Lorraine laughed, that big, bellowing laugh of hers. 'Hey, Bill, did you ever tell Rosie about that guy, remember him? With the lottery ticket? God, that was funny.'

Rosie came in, smiled at Bill, and drew up a chair.

'Hey, Rosie, did Billy ever tell you about Chester Brackenshaw? When we were working together. Well, this guy Chester was a real pain in the butt, always going on about what he would or wouldn't do when he won the lottery, and he was a real practical joker, wasn't he, Bill? Anyways . . .'

'She looks beautiful,' Rosie said.

'Thank you, but my nightdress is on back to front. Anyway, Chester goes every Friday to this club, an' me and the guys work this scam out – like I said, he was a real practical joker – and we get his lottery ticket numbers. It was you, wasn't it, Bill? You got 'em out of his wallet. Anyway, hasn't Bill told you this, Rosie?'

'She's got her nightdress on back to front,' Rosie said, fussing.

'I know, I know . . . but listen, he goes to the club, right? And we get the DJ in on the joke and tell him to announce the winning lottery numbers. So he stops playing records and he announces all Chester's numbers, and we all expected him to start buying drinks for the house. After we'd got him to spend his wages, we were going to let him in on the joke, but . . . he did nothing. Like, we saw him check his card, but he puts it back in his wallet, right, Bill?'

'Shall I comb her hair?' Rosie said to Bill.

'Leave it, just leave it, and listen . . . we all think he knows he's been had, and we're all waiting for him to get back at us some way, but he doesn't, but then as we're all leaving the place, he suddenly throws his car keys at his wife, Sandra – her name was Sandra, wasn't it, Bill? Yeah, "Sandra," he says, "take the car, it's yours, and you can have the house. I hate your guts and I've been screwing your sister for two years, but I've won the lottery, so fuck you!"' She roared with laughter, seeing all the guys lined up behind Chester trying to make him shut up.

Lorraine fell silent then as Sissy, Mike's wife, appeared in the doorway. 'Mike's coming, he's in court,' Sissy said, ushering in the girls. Just hearing her daughters made Lorraine feel so emotional she couldn't joke any more.

The two girls took Rooney and Rosie's chairs, side by side, and she was so proud of them.

'Come on in, Sissy, don't be embarrassed, I'm not. In fact, I'd like to say something to you. It's ... well, it's thank you. You've taken such care of my girls, and I want you to know I don't resent you. I did, but I don't now. In fact, I'd like to kiss you.'

Sissy leaned over the bed and kissed Lorraine's cheek. 'I'll be outside if you need me,' she said to the girls, then left them alone with Lorraine.

Julia was the first to reach out to the still, cold hand. 'I'm wearing the bracelet you got for me.' She hesitated and then said softly, 'Thank you, Mom.'

'Oh, now, don't you cry – I don't want to see you crying,' Lorraine said, but then was so close to tears herself she couldn't continue.

Julia turned to Sally: 'Say thank you to Mommy, Sally, go on.'

Sally gently touched Lorraine's fingers. 'Thank you, Mommy.'

Lorraine burst into tears: she had never believed she would hear them call her that again. She told them how proud she was, that she knew Julia was a great tennis player and Sally was a gold medallist at her college for swimming. 'One day, maybe you'll understand – I wasn't really me for such a long time, but all the times I wasn't with you, all the times I should have been there, I never stopped loving you both with all my heart. I want you to have a good and happy future, and I know you've got a good father ... because I loved him too. Hey, Mike, I was just talkin' about you.'

Mike came and stood between his daughters, then took Lorraine's hand and kissed it.

'Say goodbye to your mom.'

Both girls whispered goodbye, and Lorraine was upset that they were crying – she didn't want them to cry. She watched them leaving the room, and called after them, called each daughter by name, and they turned and looked at her.

'I love you, babies. I love you.'

She wanted Jake again, needed him, in fact wanted him to be there more than Mike or the girls. She felt so light, as if she were floating, and she wanted him to hold on to her. She had the eerie feeling she was going somewhere, and she called out his name.

He stood in the doorway, and she sighed with relief. For a few moments she had thought he had gone, but he came to her side. 'I'm here, darling, I'm here,' he said softly, and she began to relax, knowing he was holding her hand.

'I want you to know, I don't care how long it takes, but I'll get him. We even had him in custody, but we had nothing to hold him on – there were no prints on the baseball bat, nothing.'

She was confused for a while, not understanding what he was talking about, but then he said the name. Eric Lee Judd. Where had she heard that name before? Then she remembered the alley and the moment she had shouted at the boy to stop. She remembered it all now, all the years she had tried to bury the guilt with drink and wanted to pay for what she had done: now she knew that at long last she was paying the ultimate price.

She knew then that it was over, and the last thing she heard, and would ever hear as she floated free of pain was Jake's voice, filled with love, the love that had given her a happiness she felt she had no right to enjoy, and that now absolved her of guilt and gave her final release. She began to float, way above the bed, and the pain stopped. It was such a relief when the awful pain in her head stopped, and she felt at peace. Hearing him say that he loved her had freed her soul: it was the best way to go.

Lorraine had left life surrounded by people who loved her dearly, and reunited with her daughters. But she would never be able to tell anyone the solution to her last case.

None of her private analysis of the murder had been discussed with anyone, none of her notes made on her travels had been read by anyone. Lorraine's last case appeared to have died with her – the only time a case had not ended in success. Sonja Nathan had not only got away with murder, but with a massive fraud that netted her twenty million dollars.

Lorraine had been at rest for six months when a battered briefcase, its lock forced, was found by a garbage sifter. Lennie Hockum made his living scavenging in garbage dumps, salvaging anything he could recycle and sell on. It often surprised him just how much some of the junk he collected was worth. The briefcase was leather with a suede lining and he was sure he could fix the locks, or make them look good enough for a local garage sale.

Lennie did not inspect the contents of the briefcase thoroughly until he was back at his trailer. There was nothing of immediate value, not even a pen, but there were hotel receipts, sales stubs from various stores and a few business cards in the name of Lorraine Page Investigations. There was also a thick notebook with scrawled writing covering almost every page. Lennie skim-read it, flicking the pages over with his gnarled thumb. Some pages had lists of names with some underlined, but nothing made much sense to him. But he had the woman's card, he had her address. Maybe he could make a few more bucks if he returned the case to its rightful owner.

Lennie took the case to Lorraine's office, but he was disappointed when the valet told him the office was closed and had been taken over by another company. He held up the case, asking if the valet knew where he could find the woman.

It was almost a month before Jake Burton was contacted and the briefcase brought into his office. He sat staring at it, then slowly ran his hands along the top. It smelt of mildew and leather polish. Inside there were water stains and the suede had green mould at the edges. The thick notebook seemed fatter due to the damp and some of the pages were stuck together, but he recognized Lorraine's handwriting. Burton read every page, made copious notes as he went along. Then he had to wait a further week before the Nathans' housekeepers were traced. He used favours to gain access to their personal finances, but it was evident that they had improved considerably lately: they had purchased a small but quite expensive condo, just off the Ventura highway. They also owned a new Pathfinder and appeared not to be employed.

Using Lorraine's notes, and with Sharkey as backup, Burton questioned and requestioned Juana and Jose, putting pressure on them to give details of their income. They insisted that they had simply been paid their back salary from the Nathan estate, but when they were informed that it would take only a phone call to verify their statement they began to waver. When they were taken to the station for the interview and questioned separately the cracks began to show. Juana broke first, sobbing hysterically and insisting it was money they were owed, that they had had no choice and had been forced to agree or they would not have been given what was rightfully theirs.

'I am sure you *were* owed a lot of money, but as you were not paid out of the Nathan estate, who did pay you?' Burton asked. He repeated, 'Who paid for the apartment, the car? Please answer the question. Who is financing you?'

Jose was the one to admit that it was Sonja Nathan and, like his wife, he started to weep. They had promised Mrs Nathan they would use the money to return to Mexico, but had changed their minds. He kept insisting they had done nothing wrong except lie to Mrs Nathan about moving back to Mexico . . .

Distressed, Juana revealed that Sonja Nathan had always been kind to them, had promised always to take care of them. 'She was only keeping her promise. She was a good woman . . .'

Burton kept up the pressure. He was calm, encouraging, and yet relentless. 'So, on the morning of the murder, you have stated that you saw no one and that you did not hear anything, but were drawn towards the swimming pool when you heard Cindy Nathan screaming. Do you still maintain that to be the truth?'

Sharkey waited as the couple sat, heads bowed. The room so silent you could hear the desk clock ticking.

After an interminable silence Burton softly asked again: 'Did you see anyone else on that morning?'

No reply.

'Did anyone you know arrange to be at the house on that morning?'

No reply.

Sharkey shifted his weight, looking from Juana to Jose as they sat, their hands clasped tightly in front of them. He then looked at Burton, who was staring at a large silver-framed photograph on the desk. Sharkey couldn't see the front, but he knew it was a photograph of Lorraine.

Burton continued, in the same calm, almost disinterested voice, 'Did you see anyone in the grounds of the house on the morning Harry Nathan was murdered?'

'Yes.'

It was hardly audible. Sharkey had to lean forward to hear it.

Juana reached over to hold her husband's hand. 'Tell him. Tell him. I don't want to lie any more.'

Jose clung to his wife's hand and took a deep breath, but refused to look up and meet Burton's eyes.

'Sonja Nathan.'

Sharkey's jaw dropped. Burton sat down. 'Thank you, that will be all for now. I suggest you get legal representation before we question you again. You may take one of the tapes we have used to record this interview. Thank you for your co-operation.'

Sharkey ushered the couple out and into the corridor. As he looked back into the room, Burton was sifting through a notebook, head bowed.

'Pick up Sonja Nathan?' Sharkey asked.

'Yes.'

'She almost got away with it,' Sharkey said, closing the door.

Burton sighed, running his hand over Lorraine's closed notebook, then laying his palm flat against it. He looked sadly at the photograph on his desk. Her face smiled back. It was a photograph he had taken on the beach: she had been so happy, so full of life, her head tilted back, her arms lifted towards the camera, as if about to break into laughter. He knew she had been happy – it shone out of her like the sun that glinted on her silky blonde hair.

'Well,' he said softly, 'you got your man and you'll be pleased to know you got your killer too.'

ENTWINED

La Plante dedicates *Entwined* to a wonderful mentor, a woman she worked closely with for many years, who died shortly after the editorials for *Entwined* were completed. Jeanne F. Bernkopf was a constant encouragement, a source of inspiration who will be sadly missed, a consummate professional whose advice and dedicated work will never be forgotten. Goodbye, dear Jeanne F. Bernkopf, and thank you.

AUTHOR'S NOTE

Of the estimated three thousand twins – most of them young children – who passed through Mengele's experimental laboratories at Auschwitz between 1943 and 1944, less than two hundred were known to have survived. Their survival rate had been less than ten per cent. Theirs was the untold story of the Holocaust.

CHAPTER 1

HYLDA DIEKMANN moved silently across the sitting room of the exclusive hotel suite and paused to check her appearance in one of the floor-to-ceiling gilt mirrors. Her dress had seen better times – but, then, so had the hotel. It was not back to its original splendour, but it heralded the changing times. East Berlin was free; that nightmare Wall had come down.

Hylda stood by the sashed windows. She could see, way below in the street, the hotel porters in their new red and gold uniforms. She had not been told who booked the suite, and she waited with excitement. An adjoining smaller suite had also been reserved; there would be no other guests to disturb the penthouse occupants.

From the windows Hylda saw a black Mercedes limousine glide to the entrance and a tall man in a fur-collared coat step from the front passenger seat. He gestured to the porters for the luggage to be removed from the boot of the car as a second car drew up behind them carrying more luggage. A blonde woman, wearing a bright red coat, was assisted out of the rear of the Mercedes. She turned to speak to the fur-collared gentleman as a second woman, wearing a dark coat and hat, hurried from the second car. All three conferred, before

1

bending to the remaining passenger, still seated in the Mercedes. Before Hylda could see who was about to leave the car, the double doors to the suite opened.

An array of matching fawn leather cases and trunks was wheeled in on a cart. Hylda directed the porter towards the master bedroom, then turned to see a second cart containing more leather travel bags. The suite was suddenly filled with movement: the porters removed the cases and placed them on luggage racks; champagne was brought in by a flustered waiter with a large silver ice bucket and tall fluted glasses, iced and ready for use, followed by a young waiter with caviar, finely chopped onions and egg whites, arranged on a scalloped crystal dish.

In swept the assistant manager, his face red from the rush up the stairs. He moved a champagne glass one inch, waved frantically for the porters to leave, then snapped instructions to the waiters. He came over to Hylda and told her that he was not sure if her services would be required: the Baroness appeared to have her own lady's maid.

Hylda could hear voices in the corridor speaking in French; the manager's stilted, heavy-accented replies were in English. 'You will be assured of the utmost privacy . . . please, this way.'

Baron Louis Maréchal, his fur-collared coat now hanging loosely on his shoulders, swept in. He was an exceptionally handsome man, grey-white wings at the side of his temples, his thick hair combed back from his high forehead. He wore a grey pin-striped suit and an oyster-grey tie with a diamond pin. The heavy gold ring on his left hand gleamed as he gestured to the suite.

The Baron turned as the woman in the red coat,

2

carrying a square leather vanity case, was ushered in. The Baron again gestured to the rooms, as the manager directed them to the bedrooms. They remained at the doorway, turning to the corridor as a rather plain, drab young woman entered. She, too, carried a square leather vanity case, but paid no attention to the room, looking back down the corridor.

'Madame . . . please.'

Baroness Maréchal paused at the open doorway. It seemed as if everyone held their breath in anticipation of her approval. She was very tall and so slim that her black mink stole appeared to weigh her down. Her gloved hands rested on the fur. She wore large dark black-rimmed glasses that hid most of her face. Her black hair was cut short, almost boyishly. She gave the impression of feather lightness, as if at any moment she would faint, or fall, or float. She moved like a dancer, quick light steps as she walked into the suite.

She let her wrap drop, and the young woman was at her side to retrieve it. The Baroness turned, almost spinning, and her voice was husky as she exclaimed: 'Champagne! Chandelier! Flowers! Caviar! Louis – it is divine!' She was everywhere in a rush of energy, touching and admiring, running like a girl to the bedroom suite, throwing wide the doors. As if by magic she brought the sun into the room . . . and yet her face, her eyes, her expression remained hidden.

Hylda blushed as the tall willowy figure rushed to her side. She was introduced to the Baroness Vebekka Maréchal, and there was a lovely gurgling laugh as the Baroness repeated: 'Lady's maid, lady's maid! My lady's maid – but how divine! Do I have you all to myself, Hylda? I do? Well, isn't that lovely! Louis! My very own lady's maid. I

3

love this hotel – this hotel is the most divine hotel. Close your eyes, Louis, we have travelled back in time!' Hylda saw the look that passed between the Baroness's own maid and the woman in the red coat.

The room, as if by unspoken command from the Baron, had emptied. The Baroness didn't appear to notice as she continued in her light, dancer's steps from one side of the room to the next. Hylda asked the Baron if she was to unpack the Baroness's clothes. He turned, smiling, clicking his heels. 'Yes, Hylda, immediately.' The Baron spoke German quite well. He introduced Hylda to Anne Maria, the young woman, and then to the woman in red, Dr Helen Masters, a family friend, who would be using the adjoining suite.

Hylda's head was spinning – she felt so unsure of herself – but then the Baroness was at her side, cupping her chin in her hands. Her height meant that she had to look down into Hylda's startled face. 'Hylda, do you speak English? You do? Good. Then, Hylda, we shall be able to talk to each other. I don't speak German, I apologize, Hylda. Hylda, we shall become good friends.'

The Baroness jumped as her mink stole was slipped around her shoulders but the Baron gripped his wife's elbow, whispered something to her, and guided her out of the room. Hylda looked over the stacked trunks and was about to open one when Anne Maria returned. She pointed to three cases and asked for them to be taken to her quarters. Hylda nodded, and attempted her English. 'I hope to be of good service, if you need for me to do special, you ask me, yes? You are the Baroness's maid, yes?'

Anne Maria paused at the doorway. 'No, I am not the

4

Baroness's maid. I am . . .' She hesitated, but said no more, closing the door behind her.

Hylda opened the first of the Baroness's standing trunks and began to put away the garments in the wardrobe. One trunk contained silk lingerie, the delicate silks and fine embroidery reminiscent of bygone days, many embroidered with the letter V. In all the trunks not one item appeared ever to have been worn; even the rows of shoes looked new and each pair had a small handwritten note tucked inside, giving details of the matching handbag and scarf, the colours all co-ordinated: muted soft fawns, palest oyster pinks and blues. Hylda read one designer label after another.

The large leather vanity case which the woman in red had carried was placed at the side of the bed. Hylda carried it into the maid's room, and could not resist a peep inside. It was not, as she had expected, filled with jewels or make-up, but with bottles and bottles of pills.

Just then, the doors burst open. The Baroness hurried in and called out for Anne Maria to come to the bedroom. Hylda tapped on the bedroom door and the Baroness wheeled round to face her, startled. 'Hylda! I can't remember if I carried my jewel-box in with me. It's a square, dark blue leather box.'

Hylda looked around the room; she could not recall seeing it. The Baroness rushed to the dressing-table. A vanity case, smaller than the one Hylda had placed in Anne Maria's room, was stashed on a shelf beneath the mirrored top. The Baroness hugged it tightly. Hylda watched the Baroness take small silver-framed photographs from it and place them on her bedside table. She then gestured for Hylda to come to her side. 'My children, my two daughters, Sasha, Sophia, and my sons . . .'

Hylda studied the photographs of the smiling children, no more than toddlers . . .

The Baroness's hands fluttered constantly, touching her mouth, her hair . . . She was sure she had lost her make-up, her hair brushes. She began to rifle through the unpacked clothes, throwing garments to the floor. 'My make-up box, where is my make-up box?'

Anne Maria walked in and said rather sharply that there was no vanity case downstairs. The Baroness said she had found it but now she was looking for the navy-blue box, her make-up box. Hylda stood silently as if she were part of the furnishings: she was confused about the vanity cases, or boxes, or indeed how many there were.

'The photographs . . . you've unpacked the box, Baroness!'

The Baroness retorted that she had found her children, but now she could not find the other case. She was on her hands and knees, looking beneath the bed, when the Baron walked into the room, carrying yet another square case, placing it on the bed.

'I think, dearest, you should rest, it's been a long journey. Hylda, please run a bath for the Baroness.' He turned to his wife. 'Darling, do you want your jewels put into the hotel safe?'

'*No!* I want them with me!' She held tightly to the jewel-box. He raised his hands.

'All right, all right, but take care of them.' He turned to Hylda, his face set with anger. 'Run her bath – she needs to rest!'

*

The bath was filled with oils and perfumes and the towels were warming on the heated rails. Hylda tested the water. The Baroness, wrapped in a white towelling robe and still wearing her glasses, was singing at the top of her voice as she let the robe drop. She was skeleton-thin, her body white-skinned – the body of a young girl. She handed Hylda her dark glasses, and then stepped into the bath. 'Hylda, will you order some hot chocolate and biscuits – chocolate biscuits.'

The Baroness was not as young as Hylda had at first thought. The tell-tale signs of age showed beneath her chin, the skin a little loose, and around her mouth were fine lines, as also around her eyes, big dark amber eyes, very bright. Like a child she submerged herself in the soapy water, blowing at the bubbles; then she lay back and let the water cover her face, her dark hair fanning out. Hylda heard the soft low voice whispering . . . 'I am drowning . . . drowning . . .'

Unsure if she had heard correctly Hylda moved closer, but then stepped back as the Baroness submerged her head deeper. She was transfixed, as first the Baroness's hands broke the surface of the water like a ballet dancer's, then her back arched, the nipples of her small breasts lifted, and lastly her face emerged, cheeks puffed out. Like a child at play she spurted a stream of water from her mouth.

Hylda gave a light, nervous laugh, but the Baroness seemed unaware of her presence. As she slowly submerged herself again, Hylda left the bathroom and didn't hear the low gurgled voice, distorted by the water, as the Baroness repeated again, 'Drowning . . . help me.'

*

The Baron was sipping a cocktail in the sitting room with Dr Masters. From the bedroom, Hylda could hear their voices, mingled with soft laughter. She busied herself putting away the array of cosmetics, perfumes and powders. The Baroness had tried on and discarded a number of shoes; she was still barefoot and the black crêpe gown she had chosen to wear to dinner was trailing the floor.

Hylda saw her cross to the wardrobe, then move back to the dressing-table. She repeated the movement twice but took nothing from the wardrobe, nor did she look at herself in the mirror. Then the Baroness quickened her pace and arched her back, her hands in front of her as if pushing something away. She caught Hylda's reflection in her dressing-table mirror, saw that she was being watched, and didn't like it: her lips pulled back over her teeth and her body arched again, like a cat's. Hylda was mesmerized.

The moment was broken as the Baron entered, took one look at his wife, ordered Hylda from the room and called out for Anne Maria, at the same time gripping his wife's wrists. Anne Maria entered the bedroom with the case of pills and slammed the door behind her. Hylda heard screams of terror mixed with a stream of abuse in French and English. Then there was silence.

When the Baron left the bedroom, he found Hylda still waiting. 'My wife is very sick, she is in Berlin to get treatment. I would be grateful if you did not repeat what you have seen tonight.'

Hylda nodded, murmured that she was going home, but added, 'I will be here in the morning.'

'I think not, Anne Maria will take care of her needs.'

*

Helen Masters hurried into the bedroom and found him looking at the toothmarks in his hand, his head bowed. 'She bit me, like a dog! An animal.'

'She's quiet now . . . Do you want a brandy?'

He shook his head. 'I've seen this coming on all day. She gets excited, a rush of energy and then she explodes with this terrible rage, always against – it's against me.'

'I know, Louis. Here, drink this.'

He ignored her. 'It's as if she hates me, hates her children . . . She attacked Sasha. Sasha! I think she's going to kill someone – me probably!'

Helen stood by the mantelpiece, running her fingers along the cold marble carving. She felt uneasy, she had never spent time alone with the Baron, except for brief meetings when he came to collect Vebekka from her office. It had been her decision to travel to Berlin with them, taking two weeks' holiday break to do so, and now she realized how deeply she was becoming involved. She had suggested that they consult Dr Franks, her mentor and former teacher, because Vebekka was clearly beyond her help; this evening more than substantiated that. 'I have not seen her this bad, but that is all the more reason to take her to Dr Franks.'

She looked at the Baron, whose face was taut with anger. She chose her next words carefully. 'Dr Franks will have to ask you a lot of personal questions – he'll need to probe into the background of her illness, which means your background, your marriage.'

Louis sprang to his feet. 'Illness! Everyone she has been to has cloaked her madness with a name. Well? What do you think, now you've seen her in the midst of one of her furies?'

9

Helen coughed. 'She is obviously very distressed tonight—'

'Distressed? You tell me she has been like this with you?' he snapped.

'No, but I was aware the journey might upset her, and her behaviour was not unexpected. Now, if you'll excuse me, I'll go to my room.'

Louis gave a small disarming bow. 'I'm sorry, you must be tired, forgive me. Will you dine with me?'

Helen paused by the door, and half turned. 'You have nothing to be sorry for, I understand this must be a very emotional time for you.'

He gave a wonderful smile, all his previous anger melted, as if the trouble had not occurred. 'Can I order dinner?'

'Thank you, but no, I'll just have a sandwich in my room. Goodnight.'

He did not press the issue further. 'Goodnight, Helen.' As she left, he noticed that she had very shapely legs. He picked up his brandy glass, rolled the liquid around the bowl before taking a sip, then pursed his lips, reprimanding himself for allowing his mind to wonder what the neat Dr Masters would look like with her oh-so-neat chignon loosened to her shoulders.

Vebekka was unaware of whether it was day or night but she knew it had happened again, though she was beyond remembering what she had done, what she had said or who she had hurt this time. The strange room, with its ceiling so far away . . . Why did they not understand? How many strange rooms had she been brought to over the years? She stared at the ornate chandelier above the

10

bed, and wondered if, half hoped that, it would fall and crush her to death. Why had she agreed to come to this place? Why had she insisted they stay in East Berlin? *Had* she insisted? She could not remember. She could not remember why Louis had brought her to Berlin.

The tranquillizers made her thirsty; she slipped out of bed and stood by the adjoining room's partly open door. Louis was sleeping, one arm crooked over his face, the other spread across the empty space next to him. She had often watched him sleeping, sometimes for hours, fascinated by the contours of his handsome face. Vebekka moved silently around the bed, sniffing, closer and closer to him. She was close enough to touch him, wanted to lie in the crook of his arm, wanted to slip her hand into his, but she could see the dark red bruises, the toothmarks, and she crept out, knowing she had subjected him to yet more violence. She wanted to weep, but she had wept too many times for too many years. She knew she had alienated him – and even her children. It was a terrible thing to see the fear in their eyes if she laughed too loudly, called out too sharply; no matter what assurance she gave, the fear hung in the air. And, lately, she had no longer known when she was well. She could no longer fight it. It was just a matter of time before she was swallowed by the darkness.

The streets were empty but as she stared at the curtained window, someone called out down below, a disembodied voice, and made the panic swamp her. It was coming, it was beginning.

'Oh, please, dear God, no.'

She tried to draw back the dark green curtain, but her hand pulled away. Something was crawling inside the curtain, she didn't want it to open. Her heart began to beat rapidly and she couldn't catch her breath. She was suffocating. She whispered, for someone, anyone, to help her, she didn't want the curtain to open.

She felt her hands tighten, the nails cut into her palm. Her right hand clenched into a fist and she began to make heavy downward punches. Deep, dark, blazing flashes burned across her eyes, and a red rage took hold. Now both hands clenched together in hammer blows. She knew she had to stop, had to turn the rage onto herself. The blows would not stop, could not stop. She picked up a heavy marble ashtray, began banging it against the table until it cracked and shattered, but the blood-red blaze was still there, still blinding her.

Anne Maria had heard the muffled sounds, the breaking glass, and quickly checking the Baroness's room, found the bed empty. Panicked, she ran into the adjoining bathroom where she found Vebekka, naked, curled up by the toilet. She had slashed her arm with a razor. The tiles and floor were covered with blood. She was weeping, saying over and over she wanted to leave Berlin. As Anne Maria touched her, she struggled and kicked out viciously. She wanted to be taken home, she wanted to die. Her voice rose to a screech as she cried out that it was here, it had come for her, it was here, it was taking over, and they should let her die.

Anne Maria woke Helen Masters, and the two women sedated Vebekka and together carried her to her bed. The struggle had exhausted her, and at last she seemed calm. They waited until she fell into a deep sleep.

It was a sleep of nightmare dreams, unknown terrors, a terror no one could understand. As the darkness swamped her, she was powerless to tell them to stop the demons, the devils in white coats who worked on her brain when she slept. She fought against the induced sleep, but she was helpless.

Anne Maria had left, and Helen Masters sat by Vebekka's bedside, her head throbbing; she inched open the shutters to get some fresh air, staring down into the dark street below. She was startled when the Baron opened the adjoining door and looked in. He was still half asleep, his hair unruly. 'What happened?'

She flushed, drawing her dressing-gown closer. 'Rather a lot, but she's quiet now. I'll stay with her.'

He crossed to the bed and leaned over Vebekka, gently brushed her hair from her brow and rested his hand against her cheek. 'My poor baby.' He saw her wrist was bandaged, lifted her hand, kissing the palm, and then tucked it beneath the duvet. As he returned to his bedroom, he said to Helen, 'I am glad you are here.' The door closed silently behind him, and Helen concentrated on her patient, sleeping deeply, her face, in repose, like an innocent child's.

At 10.30 a.m. Hylda was ushered into the suite. The Baron was dressed and taking a late breakfast in the restaurant with Dr Masters. Anne Maria whispered to Hylda that the Baroness had specifically asked for her lady's maid to assist her dressing, but that Hylda must make no mention of what had occurred the previous evening. The Baroness had been taken ill during the night, but she was calm now. 'Don't worry, she won't do anything, she's sedated, she may not even remember she asked for you.'

Hylda entered the bedroom, smiled and murmured, 'Good morning.' The Baroness's hair and make-up were immaculate, and she had painted her nails a dark crimson. Her eyes were expressionless, her voice low, husky. 'I apologize if I caused you any embarrassment yesterday.' She pushed her breakfast tray away. The glass of fresh orange juice was untouched, there was an almost full cup of black coffee. The bread, however, had been carefully rolled into balls: small grey pellets surrounded her place setting.

While Hylda helped the Baroness to dress, not a word was spoken. She spent a long time deciding what she would wear, touching the clothes, holding them against herself. She chain-smoked, taking no more than two or three puffs of the gold-tipped cigarettes before she stubbed them out. She carefully placed into a small black clutch bag a gold cigarette case, a lighter, a handkerchief and a gold compact. Nothing else, no wallet or cards.

The Baroness had tried on three hats before she was satisfied. She flipped open the jewel-box, her hand shaking badly as it hovered over the array. She removed an ornate brooch of a tiger's head and then seemed upset and let it fall back into the velvet-lined box before she withdrew an exquisite sapphire and diamond bluebird clip. She held it to the light, smiling, whispering to herself, oblivious to Hylda.

The Baroness sat patiently by the drawing-room window and smoked while she waited for the Baron to come for her. She had eventually pinned the bluebird to the side of her hat; the bird's exquisite wings glittered as if about to take flight.

Hylda remained in the bedroom, but could see the Baroness clearly from the open doors. Anne Maria was watching from her own room, the door ajar. The seated, immaculate woman appeared unaware of their presence. Both saw the Baron come in and take his wife's arm, watched her withdraw from him and his head bend to whisper to her that she must come. Finally she gave way to his quiet persistence.

Before leaving the apartment, the Baroness gave the sweetest of smiles to Hylda, then put on her dark glasses and bowed her head. But not before Hylda had seen the fear in the beautiful eyes.

After they had left, Hylda looked over the breakfast table. 'The Baroness did not eat anything,' she said with motherly concern.

Anne Maria nodded to the small balls of bread. 'She always does that, or hides food in her pocket.'

'She seemed very frightened.'

'She's always frightened, frightened of doctors, frightened of anyone in a white coat.' Anne Maria gave a soft smile. 'They are going to hypnotize her – she's always refused before.'

Hylda placed the blood-stained towels into a laundry bag. 'Have you worked for Baron Maréchal long?' she asked Anne Maria.

'Five years, I think I'm number thirteen . . . unlucky. Not many stay long: when she's nice, she's very very nice and those times, well, obviously I am not needed, but when she's bad, she's – she can be very dangerous. I was told not to tell you, but you should know, especially since she has taken quite a liking to you. Don't trust her, these violent moods seem to come on without reason, she just goes crazy, and she'll go for you like an animal, so be prepared.'

Hylda pursed her lips and continued to tidy the room.

15

Anne Maria drew the curtains back from the window. 'I used to like her, she was the kindest, sweetest woman I had ever met. I also felt deeply sorry for her.' She turned to Hylda. 'She was exceptionally kind to me and my little daughter.' She let the curtains fall back. 'But she can be so hurtful, say such terrible things, things you cannot forget, or forgive. She is evil, and she is very strong. So be warned, when she turns, get out. Just run away from her – all the others did . . . but I need the money.' She sipped the orange juice, looking at the small pellets of bread.

'They brought her to Berlin to see some specialist. I doubt it'll help. We've been visiting doctors for years, but there's little that can be done with schizophrenia, apart from controlling it, and she won't take her pills. I've waited and watched her, sure she's swallowed them but then I find . . . she holds them under her tongue, you see, so I am not to be blamed, what happened last night was not my fault, she must have spat out the pills, and I get the blame.'

The Mercedes moved slowly through a group of jeering students. It was almost time for the yearly celebrations to begin marking the fall of the Wall. The students gathered by a café set up in an old barracks, the ominous sentry box, now swathed in ribbons. They shouted abuse, their shorn heads and leather jackets, their boots and jeers directed towards the sleek car. Their raised voices frightened Vebekka. She sat between Dr Masters and the Baron, her hands clasping and unclasping in her fine black leather gloves.

The Baron took a hand and held it tightly. 'It'll be all right, no one is going to hurt you.'

When she replied, her husky voice was almost inaudible. 'It's close, Louis, it's so close I can feel it. You should take me away from this place, please, I've never felt it so close to me before, I'm so scared.'

Helen Masters looked at the Baron, and then turned to stare out of the window. It took her by surprise: Vebekka's small gloved hand reaching for hers, holding on tightly. They both held a hand, as if she were a child, and they could both feel her body shaking.

CHAPTER 2

D R FRANKS'S waiting room was comfortable, with deep sofas and coffee tables. The receptionist and secretary were kind and friendly, offering coffee or tea, trying to make the patients feel relaxed and at ease.

Franks had been told that the Baroness had a deep distrust of anyone wearing a white coat, so he strolled into the reception room in a sweater and shirt, his hands stuffed into his old cord trousers. He was sixty-nine years old. His craggy face and gnarled hands belied his sharp-eyed nature; he was a man who could smile warmly, but his eyes would bore into you.

The Baron shook the doctor's hand and Helen kissed him warmly. Without waiting to be introduced, Dr Franks moved to the sofa and sat beside Vebekka. He took her hand and kissed it. 'Baroness, there is nothing to be afraid of. I will spend most of my time today with your husband. You will chat with my nurse and my assistant . . . Maybe tomorrow you and I will spend some time together. Would you like coffee? Or tea?'

Vebekka kept her head down and withdrew her hand; she said nothing.

'Helen, will you stay here, or do you want to sit in on the sessions?' asked Franks.

18

Helen bent her head to try to meet Vebekka's eyes. 'Would you like me to stay with you? Vebekka?'

The Baroness looked up, and her wide amber eyes met Dr Franks's. 'I will stay here. I am quite capable of being left on my own, thank you, doctor.'

Dr Franks noticed the way she recoiled from Helen, as if she did not want her touch. He gestured towards Maja, his assistant, to indicate she should stay with his patient, but Vebekka paid no attention. Nor did she see Maja switch on a tape-recorder; she was too busy reaching forward to the coffee table as Dr Franks, the Baron and Helen Masters left the room.

A child's worn storybook lay on the table for younger patients; Vebekka slipped it beneath her coat. Maja pretended she saw nothing. She sat opposite Vebekka, as the elegant woman slowly began to inch the child's book into her handbag.

Maja waited patiently, watching as Vebekka looked around the room. Their conversation would be recorded so that Dr Franks could listen to it before he began a formal session with his patient.

'Will they be a long time?' the Baroness asked.

Maja smiled. 'Knowing Dr Franks, the answer is yes.'

The lovely throaty giggle took Maja by surprise. 'Oh, my husband won't like that, I'm supposed to be the crazy one.' Maja laughed, and Vebekka reached over and tapped her knee. 'I've forgotten your name!'

'Everything you can tell me will be of interest and importance.'

The Baron sat opposite Dr Franks, asked if he might smoke, and lit a cigar without waiting for a reply. Helen

19

Masters had drawn up a chair, not too close to the doctor.

'Tell me everything you know of your wife's childhood, her relationship to her parents and family, how many brothers and sisters, etc. I see from the files there is very little recorded on her background.'

The Baron shrugged his shoulders. 'I know very little. I met Vebekka in Paris, 1961, when she was twenty-two years old. We married two years later, but the year I met her, her mother died, and then in 1972 her father died. I never met either of them. They were originally from Canada, then emigrated to Philadelphia when Vebekka was still quite young. She is an only child, and I have never met any relative – she has said there is no one. All I know is that her parents were wealthy, and that on her father's death Vebekka was left a considerable amount of money. When I have questioned her about her childhood she has always said it was unexceptional, but very happy. She speaks fondly of her parents.'

Franks seemed to doodle on a notepad. 'So your wife is not French by birth?'

'No, Canadian, but she has always spoken fluent French. Doctor, I have questioned my wife over the years to determine if any other member of her family suffered a similar illness. After all, I have four children . . .'

'Has she made any mention of mental illness in her family?'

The Baron's lips tightened. 'No. She is adamant about that. She can recall no member of her immediate family ever being ill.'

'Does she speak about her family?'

The Baron hesitated, only a moment, then shook his head. 'No, she has never really discussed that part of her

20

life with me. In fact when I offered to accompany her to her father's funeral, she refused. Perhaps I should mention that my own family were very much against my marriage. I was the heir, an only son, my family felt Vebekka was not a suitable match, I was only twenty-three years old myself.'

'Do you know if there is any possible way we can contact anyone who knew your wife in America?'

The Baron flicked his cigar ash. 'I know of no one, but if you think it is important, I can try to trace someone.'

'It is, believe me, of the utmost importance. I would appreciate your trying to find any documents, medical or scholastic, schools, friends, anyone who knew your wife in her early childhood.'

The Baron nodded his agreement, and the doctor leaned back in his chair. 'So you met your wife in Paris . . .' He gestured for the Baron to continue.

'She was an in-house model for Dior. I was at a function with my mother. We met, I asked if Vebekka would dine with me, and she accepted. We were married two years later as I have said, my first son was born ten months after that, 1964 – he is twenty-seven – my second son was born eighteen months later and my first daughter after another eighteen months. My fourth child, Sasha, is only twelve years old.'

The doctor swivelled in his chair. 'Is your wife, or was she, a good mother?'

The Baron nodded, again flicking his cigar ash. 'Excellent, very loving but firm. They adored her. They are all well adjusted, normal children. However, of late her behaviour has greatly disturbed them.' The Baron stared into space and then looked down at his hands. 'My younger daughter has suffered the most. Perhaps it was unwise for us to have her. Vebekka's breakdowns had begun before Sasha was born.'

The doctor again motioned for the Baron to continue, but noted how agitated he was becoming.

'After the birth of each of my sons she was depressed and unstable, twice spending some time in a clinic.'

'So you think her illness is connected in some way to the children?' asked Dr Franks.

'No, no, I have always had nannies to oversee them – she never had any responsibility, nothing that would put pressure on her, I always made sure of that. I am in a financial position to make her life very comfortable. We have the family château outside Paris, a summer villa in Cannes and two apartments – one in London and another in New York.'

Dr Franks interrupted him. 'Explain how she behaved during pregnancy, and after the births.'

The Baron began twisting his signet ring round and round. 'She had a fear the baby would be born deformed, which became obsessive. She insisted on visiting her doctors sometimes five times a week. Midway through a pregnancy the fear of producing a malformed child made her even consider an abortion even though her doctors insisted her pregnancy was normal. After the birth, after being told the baby was perfectly well, she seemed to sink into a terrible despair, a depression, not wanting to hold the baby, touch it. She seemed almost afraid of it, but then the depression would lift, and she would be exhilarated, checking the child out, inspecting every finger and toe, looking for any possible problems. I thank God there was none.'

'When, in your opinion, did you detect a severe

behaviour pattern, or breakdown as you call it, not connected to her pregnancies?'

The Baron still twisted his signet ring round his finger as he answered, 'There have been so many, but the worst breakdown occurred – it was totally unexpected, it came out of the blue – after a lengthy period when she had been so well I believed our problems were all in the past. Then she became as obsessive about having another child – we had two sons by then – as she had been about them being born with some disease. She wanted a daughter, and so, when she did recover, I gave way, partly because she had been so well and stable . . .'

Dr Franks frowned and tapped his desk with his forefinger. 'But you have two daughters, so the same pattern continued some years later when your second daughter was born, er . . . Sasha, yes?'

The Baron nodded, and then gestured with his hands, shrugging. 'Sasha was – how do you say? – not expected, and my wife's gynaecologist suggested terminating the pregnancy.' He paused, crossing his legs, and again he gave the slight shrugging gesture with his hands. 'It was unacceptable, the termination, on two counts. I am Catholic, and . . .'

Franks waited for him to continue, but the Baron seemed disinclined to embroider on the religious aspect.

'So now tell me, in your opinion, when did the problems begin that were not directly linked to the births of your children?'

The Baron sighed. 'The birth of Sasha was not as traumatic for my wife, in fact she recovered quite quickly. Sasha was doted upon, spoiled I suppose. She is the most delightful child, and the one most physically like my wife.

23

I really felt the problems were over, but they began again. This time my wife said, or felt, that someone was taking over her body.'

'So that culminated in another breakdown?'

The Baron stubbed out his cigar and clenched his hands. 'Yes. We were in Monaco for the polo season and Vebekka took the children to a circus. During one of the acts, I don't recall which one, my wife began to behave strangely, she kept on getting out of her seat, she appeared to want to get into the circus ring herself. She became abusive when she was restrained by one of the ushers – she was screaming about the clown – it was a midget or a dwarf but she was screaming at him, totally hysterical. She somehow got into the ring from her seat, physically attacked the clown, and by the time I was called she had been taken, incoherent, to a hospital and sedated. That was the first time she had actually been violent, to my knowledge. Since that time, her violence and irrational behaviour have grown. She has attacked every member of the family, including myself. Sasha is very much afraid of her.'

'Are you saying she has physically attacked her own daughter?'

'No, no, not actually gone for her, but she has destroyed Sasha's possessions.'

'I don't understand, what do you mean?'

The Baron looked to Helen, and then back to Franks. 'The child's toys, her dolls, she ... she breaks them, burns them, destroys them.'

Franks muttered, and then leaned back in his chair. 'Has she ever been self-abusive, hurt herself in any way?'

'Very often, she has tried to kill herself countless times, in fact she attempted to do so in the hotel last night. But surely you have her medical history?'

24

Dr Franks raised his bushy eyebrows. 'Of course, but I would like to hear first-hand. Please continue.' Again he noted the way the Baron looked to Helen Masters, as if for approval, or out of embarrassment, he couldn't surmise which.

'Dr Franks, this present attack has been coming on, or building, in my estimation, for weeks ... It was Helen's suggestion that with a possible attack imminent, this would be the best time for you to see her. I think Vebekka agreed because of Sasha.'

'If I decide that I can help your wife, would you agree to her staying in my clinic even though I cannot tell how long she will need to be there?'

'Dr Franks, if you can help my wife, I will agree to anything you suggest. I cannot subject my children, myself, to any more torment. I have had enough.'

The silence in the room felt ominous, as if in some way accusing, and the doctor could see a small muscle twitching at the side of the Baron's mouth. 'Do you regret marrying your wife, Baron?'

The Baron pursed his lips. 'That is an impossible question. I have four beautiful children, of course I do not regret marrying. But my sons, my daughters must know if this illness is hereditary. I need to know, that must be understandable – if my wife is to be institutionalized it will affect each and every one of us. You are my last hope, Dr Franks.'

Franks coughed. 'Tell me about the first time you noticed your wife behave in an irrational manner.'

The Baron leaned back and raised his eyes to the ceiling. 'You have all her records, doctor, is this really necessary?'

'Yes, yes, it is.'

The Baron remained silent for at least half a minute, then sighed. 'She was four months pregnant with my first son, she was very beautiful, and being pregnant even more so. She took great care of herself, she ate well, good healthy food, and seemed content and very happy, we both were. We were very much in love, exceptionally close, idyllically happy. One night I woke up, and she was not beside me. I searched for her, called out for her. I found her in the kitchen, food everywhere, eating, stuffing food into her mouth, she must have been doing it for some time because there was vomit on the floor, over the table, and . . . she was eating it, her own vomit. Her face was rigid, she was like a stranger. It was terrible.'

Franks interrupted, holding up his hand. They could hear laughter from the next room. Helen stood up, as if prepared to go into the reception area, but Franks waved his hand. 'Maja is with her – she is very adept at relaxing my patients . . . seems she has succeeded!'

Vebekka had been telling Maja, the doctor's assistant, about her days as a model: the behind-the-scenes gossip and back-biting. She was entertaining, witty, and the more she relaxed the more animated she became. She stood up to demonstrate how she had first been taught by the Madame at Dior to cat-walk: arching her back at an angle, pushing forward her hips and parading up and down the small waiting room.

'You know how many models have back trouble? I mean, can you imagine any sane person walking in this way?' She swivelled on her heel, turning to demonstrate, and then she glided to the sofa and sat. 'The gowns were spectacular, and it was amusing for us to see which celebrity bought which design. Can you imagine the fun we had, seeing those superb works of art adorning the most frumpy, the most rotund women?'

Maja was entertained – it was difficult not to be – but she also detected a strange wariness. Vebekka's eyes constantly strayed to the closed door and she would fall silent, sometimes in mid-sentence, and then quickly recover and launch into a different story. Maja did not attempt to steer her into discussing how she felt, knowing it would either come out naturally or not at all. But, as adept as she was, she was still taken by surprise when suddenly, in one quick move, Vebekka gripped her wrist.

'What are they doing in there? Why are they taking so long?'

Maja made no move to withdraw her hand.

'He's talking about me, isn't he? Of course, stupid question, stupid question.' She released her hold, and her hand went to her hair, patting it in place.

'He may not speak with you today, but he needs to know so much about you,' Maja said kindly.

'Why doesn't he ask me?'

'He will, but your husband will probably speak more freely without your presence.'

Vebekka nodded. 'Yes, yes, that's true, poor Louis. I am all right though, now. This is a waste of time, you know.'

Maja looked at her watch. They had been there a long time. She got up and went towards a window panel between the rooms. She was going to pull up the blind to see if one of the kitchen helpers was there to make some fresh coffee but, as her hand reached for the string, she froze—

'*Don't* – please don't. I don't want to see through the window.'

Maja let her hand fall and turned to Vebekka. The Baroness was hunched in her seat, staring ahead. Before Maja could say anything, the Baron came in, alone and grey with fatigue.

'I'm to take you home, darling,' he said flatly.

Maja watched Vebekka closely, saw the relief when she learned she would not have to see the doctor. She kissed Maja warmly as she left with her husband.

Dr Franks leaned on the kitchen sink, as Maja washed up. 'Well, what do you think?'

Maja slowly turned off the water tap. 'I think she is a very disturbed woman. She is very entertaining, very sharp and witty, but I think she is also—'

'Dangerous?' he enquired with his head tilted to one side. Maja touched her wrist, remembered how strong Vebekka's grip had been, and nodded her head. 'Yes. Very.'

Dr Franks returned to his study, where Helen was still waiting. He shut the door, and stuffed his hands into his pockets. 'Maja agrees with you.' He poured Helen a glass of sherry. 'Tell me about her violence. Have you witnessed it?'

'Yes, she becomes disorientated, very angry, verbally and physically. She is quite frightening, because although she appears to lose control and has no recall of what she has said or done, I think she has, and refuses to admit to it – or is unable to admit it. For example, she knows what she did to Sasha, her daughter; she knows, but denies it.'

Franks asked Helen to elaborate on the destruction of the dolls, and listened intently as she described what the

Baron had told her Vebekka had done. Helen, chewing her lips, looked directly at Franks. 'He said he had come in in response to Sasha's screams, had found to his horror that his wife had taken every doll belonging to the child, mutilated all of them, smashed their faces in, torn off their arms. She had stacked them, one on top of the other, and set light to them. The house could have caught fire, but she just stood watching the toys burning, forcing her daughter to watch with her. Sasha was terrified, tried to run, but Vebekka held her by her hair, forcing her to see the dolls melt. The Baron quoted her as saying, "Watch the babies, Sasha, watch the baby dolls!" He had had to pull his daughter from her grip.'

Franks interrupted. 'Did she give a reason for her actions?'

Helen shook her head. 'I spoke with Sasha, asked her to tell me about the incident, but she kept repeating that her mama looked strange. Oh, yes, I remember something else. Sasha said she screamed for her father, said she called out, "Papa", and this is interesting, Vebekka was still holding the child by the hair and she said, "He is my papa, not yours, my papa. Papa loves me." I asked the Baron about this, and he said that his wife did not allow any of the children to call him Papa. When I asked her about it, she said only that she didn't like them using "Papa", and when I pressed her on why not, she had no answer.'

'The Baron said she attempted to take her own life last night. Is this true?'

Helen shrugged. 'She cut herself, self-abuse. I don't think she would have killed herself. She wants attention, screams for attention all the time. She is a great attention seeker.'

29

'What about the violence to her husband? I noticed he had a nasty bite mark on his right hand.'

Helen drained her sherry glass. 'She will attack anyone who is close to her when she is irrational. He happened to be there. I surmise that she mistrusts everyone when these periods occur – that includes her children. But I find it interesting that she did not actually attack her daughter, just her toys. Yet her daughter was close by . . .'

'What about the other children?'

Helen referred to her notes. 'Again, these attacks have occurred when they were close by her. When she was in her so-called irrational state, she would bite, kick, punch, but she has not to my knowledge taken a weapon, a knife or anything like that.'

'What does she say when she is in this condition?'

Helen flicked through her notes. 'Back in 1982 she was to be given the truth drug, sodium pentathol. I sent you the transcript.'

Franks opened his own file and leafed through.

Helen continued. 'She believes someone is taking over her mind, just as she believes that anyone in a white coat, doctor or nurse, is going to hurt her. She has a terror of injections, and refused the pentathol treatment. She was disorientated at the time, but still was able to refuse the injection just as she has refused shock treatment, and, until now, refused adamantly any form of hypnotherapy.'

'Why do you think she has changed her mind?'

'She knows she is getting more dangerous, has even told me she fears she will kill someone. I have gone as far as I know how. Can you help her? Do you think you can?'

Franks tapped her nose. 'My dear, I never give up

hope. But first things first, sweet Helen, we must eat. I am starving and there's a nice little restaurant, close by. And you can give me more details of her obsession.'

Hylda had dressed Vebekka for dinner, and was delighted by her good spirits and exuberance. Louis, however, was tired and not in good spirits. He could hear his wife on the telephone to Sasha; Vebekka's resilience was astonishing, unnerving. He could hear her telling Sasha about Berlin, their plane journey, as if they were on holiday. The call completed, she danced over to the dinner table and began lifting the silver lids from the tureens with relish. But she ate little, just sat with her chin cupped in her hands watching his every mouthful. She reached over and stroked his hand gently. 'I'm sorry for all the trouble I cause you, my darling.'

He smiled, as she poured a glass of wine for him. She was forbidden any alcohol, but he took his glass and raised it to her. In the candlelight her amber eyes were as bright as a cat's. Looking at her now made him feel deeply, horribly sad. This was the Vebekka he had fallen in love with, the young girl he had showered with gifts and flowers until she had succumbed to his charms. She had been crazy, fun-loving, mad-cap and wilful. She was still all those things, but now, the craziness, the madness was a hideous constant torment.

'What are you thinking about, Louis?'

'How beautiful you look! You remind me of when we first met.'

The next moment she was on his knee, kissing him frantically. 'I'm still your favourite baby, I haven't changed. Please, please, take me to bed, carry me into the bedroom, the way you used to, please, Louis, let's pretend this is a honeymoon.'

He lifted her from his knee. 'Eat, finish your dinner.'

She pouted, then returned to her side of the table, but she continued to pick at the food, nibbling on the French beans as she watched him. She had a glass of lemonade, and she slurped it like a child, trying to amuse him with coy, sweet smiles, smiles that had won him over so many times. But Louis wondered how long it would be before she turned on him. He could no longer tell how long the bad spells lasted, all he knew was that this sweet creature would turn, if not tonight, then a week, a month or a year later, into a vicious, violent bitch.

Her eyes narrowed, but she smiled. 'Take me home, Louis, please. I'm all right now, it's over. I know I have said this to you before, but this time I know it's over. The darkness is gone. I felt it go in the waiting room at Dr Franks's. And Sasha misses me, she needs me to be with her.'

He drained his wine glass, patted his lips with his napkin. She fetched a cigar, clipped the end for him, struck the match, like a puppy. 'Please, Louis, take me home, we can be together, a family. I am fine now, really . . .'

He grabbed her wrist and held it tightly. 'No, no, we stay here, we stay until Dr Franks has seen you. That's what we came for.' She made no attempt to free herself and he released his hold.

'Bekka, please don't do this to me, please don't. Maybe you feel fine now, but it could change – in the car, on the

32

plane. Please give it a try, if not for yourself, if not for me, do it for Sasha.'

Vebekka wrapped him in her arms. 'I would never hurt my baby, please believe me. Just say you will take me home, I don't want to stay here.'

Louis pushed her away. 'Sasha is afraid of you.'

Vebekka recoiled as if he had slapped her. 'She is not, I just talked to her on the phone. She is not afraid of me.'

Louis spun round. 'You don't even know what you do to her! You will stay here, you will go to Dr Franks. I'll make you see this through.'

She cocked her head to one side and smirked. 'Then you will leave me? Yes? That's why I'm here, you want to get rid of me. I will never divorce you, Louis, not for any of your women. I will never release you, you are mine.'

The Baron ignored her, turning towards Anne Maria's room. 'I'm going to bed, I suggest you do the same. *Anne!* Anne!'

Anne Maria appeared from her room.

'The Baroness is retiring. Will you see to her needs?'

Vebekka swiped at the dishes on the table. 'I don't want any pills. I don't want that ugly little bitch near me. I won't be locked in my room.'

The Baron looked hard at his wife. Her act was dropping already. He walked into his room and slammed the door.

Vebekka turned on Anne Maria. 'I don't need anything, especially from you. Go to your room, you plain, ugly bitch! Go on, get out of my sight! Get those short squat legs moving. You smell – in fact you *stink* – your body is putrid!'

Anne Maria began to return to her room, but paused

33

at the door to look back at the Baroness. 'At least my daughter isn't terrified of me.' She shut her door quietly.

The Baroness's bedroom was lit by one bedside light. Vebekka threw herself on to the bed, then sat up panic-stricken. Where was her jewel-box? Her make-up box? Finding them comforted her, soothed her. She carried them to the bed and spread the contents around her. Then, in a rapid mood change, she gleefully began to make up her face.

Louis's eyes were closed, but he was not asleep; he knew she was in the room. The bed moved on his right side, the covers lifted. He sighed, lifted his arm, and she nestled against him, curling round him. He slowly turned to look at her.

It took all his willpower not to push her away. Her face was painted in hideous streaks and colours, like a clown's. He tried to keep his voice steady. 'What's that all over your face, Bekka? What are you doing?'

'I'm a clown for you, don't you remember? When we were in New York that time? How we laughed at the little midget, the little clown . . .' She slid off the bed and fell to her knees, bouncing up and down, pulling at her face grotesquely. He sat up, looked at the time, then back at his wife. She jumped up on the bed, rolled on top of him, giggling and tickling him, until he held her tightly.

'It's one o'clock in the morning, I'm exhausted, this is crazy.'

She pulled her mouth down. 'In the present circumstances I don't think that is a very funny thing to say.'

He sighed. It was horribly true. It was as if she were balanced on a delicate trapeze wire; if he said the wrong word, made the wrong action, she would fall, fall from his hands, from his care, a care he hated still to feel. He could contain himself no longer; his body shook as he wept. Vebekka held him as she would her children, soothed him, quieted him. Louis had taken a mistress within months of the birth of his first son, and he had continued a similar pattern throughout his entire marriage. He told himself that he had needed to do so because of the anguish Vebekka caused him, and yet she could still make him want her like no other woman he had ever known. She whimpered now, whispered for him to forgive her, then asked again if he loved her. He could feel himself giving way, too tired to argue. She rested her head against his shoulder, her lips touching the nape of his neck, inching upwards to touch his.

Her soft feather-light touches to his cheeks, his ears, his temples, began to arouse him. 'Don't do this, Bekka, please don't . . .'

'Let me make love to you, please, Louis, I can feel that you want me.' Her hands drew his pyjama top open, pulled it from his body. She began to kiss his nipples.

'Bekka, listen to me, it's over between us. I will always take care of you, I promise you, but . . .'

She slid open the cord of his pyjamas, easing them over his buttocks, caressing, never stopping her sucking, kissing, licking until she eased herself to her knees. He moaned as she began to masturbate him. 'You see, Louis, you do want me.'

Suddenly she sprang to her feet, and smiled at him. He made an unconscious move to draw up his pants, as if to hide his erection, and she laughed a soft, low, vicious laugh. 'You'll never get rid of me.' She twisted the handle on his door, and she was gone.

He felt wretched, sick to his stomach, but he didn't follow her. Not this time.

Helen Masters had covered her head with a pillow so as not to hear them, but even after Vebekka had left Louis – she had heard the door closing – she was still unable to sleep. She got up and went into the main suite to fetch a brandy. As she eased the stopper from the brandy decanter, her heart almost stopped. There was the Baroness, like a broken doll, hideous make-up smudged over her face, curled up by the window. Her eyes were staring blindly into the darkness beyond the cold windowpane.

Helen gently touched her shoulder. 'Come to bed, you'll catch cold. Come on, Vebekka.'

Helen tucked the quilt around her, and then sat on the edge of the bed. 'Do you want a hot drink?'

Vebekka slowly turned her head, as tears streamed down her face. She whispered, 'No, nothing, thank you, Helen.' She was staring ahead, as if listening intently. 'There's something here. Can you feel it?'

'Feel what?' Helen asked.

'I don't know. I don't know, but it's here, it's taking me, Helen, it's taking me over.'

Helen felt Vebekka's brow: she was sweating. Her head felt sticky from the make-up, damp. 'Do you need Anne Maria to give you something to help you sleep?'

'No, I don't want her. Please, take me away from this place.'

'I can't . . . this is for your own good. It will all be all right, you'll see.'

The Baroness clung to Helen, her hands strong as she gripped her tightly. 'Something takes over me, Helen. I have to leave here. Please talk to Louis, tell him I must go home.'

Helen embraced Vebekka, rocked her in her arms. 'There's nothing here, try to sleep.'

Vebekka whispered, 'We have done something terrible tonight.'

Helen went rigid. Dear God, had the woman hurt Louis? She eased Vebekka from her arms, tucked her in, sat with her until she was quiet, and then ran to Louis's room. He was sleeping deeply. Make-up covered his pillows, clown's make-up, it was even on his face. She shut the door and leaned against it. The insanity was getting to each of them, dragging them all down.

Vebekka could not sleep. She could see by the bedside clock it was almost two-thirty. The dread slowly began to envelop her, the dread she was incapable of describing. A terrible weight began in her feet, trapped her legs. Like wet cement, the weight oozed slowly over and up her body. She could not call out, could not move as it trapped her arms, restricted her throat, a deadly white substance that left only her brain to fight the terror of the whiteness inching towards it. Only her willpower could keep the creeping mass away. It took all the energy she could conjure up to drive the substance back, replacing the whiteness with brilliant colours and forcing them to cut across her brain, bright flashing primal reds, greens and sky blue; like electric shocks, shaking her, swamping her with such an intense violence she became exhausted, had to give in, had to let the mass consume her. As it seeped over her nose she could no longer breathe, as it filled the sockets of her eyes she became blinded. And then it hardened: she was encased in cement and she could not move, as if she had been buried alive. Just as she felt she was dying she caught a glimpse of a girl in a white frilly dress, little white socks and black patent shoes, a child holding a doll in her arms. She was so far away, so distant. Then a white-gloved hand drew a dark curtain, hiding her, and the darkness oozed over her face and she heard the soft persuasive voice whispering for her to remember, remember the colours. The gloved hand began to draw back the heavy curtain again, inch by inch, but what lay hidden behind it filled her with such terror that she gave in to the darkness.

Hylda was the first person in the suite that morning – the first to see Vebekka. She was lying on the floor, her eyes unseeing, staring in horror, her limbs rigid, her body in a catatonic state. Spittle and vomit covered her white nightdress. Hylda called frantically, first for Anne Maria, then for the Baron and Dr Masters, who told her that she would not be needed further that day. But it was not until Hylda was on the bus heading for her apartment later on that what had occurred that morning took effect. She got off the bus a stop early in her confusion. The cool air calmed her, and she patted her face with a handkerchief, repeating over and over, 'Poor woman, poor woman.'

As she waited at the pavement edge for the next bus, she decided she would walk and prepared to cross to the opposite side of the street. Not until then did she see the brightly coloured poster pasted to a wall, about five yards to her right. Schmidt's Circus was appearing in West Berlin, the big brash poster announced. Hylda moved closer, and stared in disbelief. The central part of the poster was a massive male lion's head. Beneath the lion was the defiant face of a woman, a strong face with wild hair; a woman with wide, amber eyes that were daring, yet mocking.

THE WORLD'S MOST FAMOUS
FEMALE WILD ANIMAL TRAINER,
RUDA KELLERMAN – award-winning act
straight from Monte Carlo!

For a moment Hylda could have sworn that the woman in the poster was Baroness Vebekka Maréchal.

CHAPTER 3

RUDA KELLERMAN stepped down from her trailer. The weather was not good, the sky overcast, with rain falling lightly. She drew her raincoat collar up and tightened her belt; her black boots barely showed beneath the long trenchcoat. Ruda wore a man's old cloth cap and her long hair was braided in a plait down her back. She carried a small riding crop and was tapping it against her leg as she strode towards the Grimaldi cages, their canvas covers rolled up. There were sixteen tigers, four lionesses, five lions and one black panther. The animals were three or four to a cage, except for one lion, Mamon, who sat alone in his own vast cage, and the panther, Wanton, who had a small one to himself. Ruda had, as always, checked their arrival and unloading from the circus train. Now she was making her second inspection of the morning, noting each animal with a piercing stare of her wide cat-coloured eyes.

The tigers were very vocal now; occasionally she stopped as one or the other called to her. She pressed her face close to the bars, blowing what appeared to be a kiss. It was a welcome, a contact, a call of recognition from one animal to another. She rubbed their noses, calling their names softly, but she was never over-familiar; Ruda had always to remain the dominant figure of authority.

The purring sound was so loud it was like a rumble, but there was no purring from the smallest cage in the semicircle, Wanton's cage. Ruda called out to him, but kept at arm's distance, as he sliced his paw through the bars, his sharp claws always ready to lash out against anyone passing close. Wanton was the smallest cat, but one of the most dangerous, and Ruda glanced upward to check that the tarpaulin over the top of his cage was well battened down. Her sharp eyes checked that there was no loose rope for Wanton to leap at, possibly hurting himself. Unlike the tigers, he paid no attention to Ruda's voice as he pawed and snarled at her. She laughed at him and, in a frenzy of anger, he lashed out again and then slunk to the back of his cage.

Ruda moved on to her babies, her lionesses. The rain was heavier and she snapped orders to two of her helpers to keep the tarpaulins on all the cages until it was time to move the cats into their sheltered quarters. Hearing her voice, the lionesses pressed their massive bodies to the bars, and each one received a rub on her nose. Ruda spoke softly, calming, soothing them, knowing they would be restless for some time, that they always were when they arrived at a new site. Any new location was greeted with suspicion, and it would be at least twenty-four hours before they settled down. Now they called to each other, acknowledged Ruda and paced their cages.

Ruda ran her crop along the bars of the next to last cage, and three of her prize babies, the fully grown male lions, loped to the bars, their massive heads bent low, their paws too large to reach through the bars. These lions with their full manes never ceased to touch a chord

41

of wonder inside her; they were kings, magnificent killers, and she admired the sheer force and power of their muscular bodies. As they pressed their heads against the bars, she noted that their straw needed changing. She turned angrily to an assistant, snapping out the order to prepare the clean straw. The young man, Vernon, who had been with Ruda's team for only six months, muttered for her to give him a break, he had just arrived himself.

In two quick strides Ruda was at his side. 'Do it now! And don't answer me back!' The rise in her voice made one of the lions snarl, then all three huddled together at the rear of their cage, watching her, ears flattened, eyes sharp.

The boy backed off, and hurried towards the store trailer, where four helpers were pitchforking the new hay and sawdust. Ruda made sure every bale was checked, lest they were damp in the centre, and each sack of sawdust tested for the tell-tale smell of poison, laid down to get rid of rats from farmers' barns, which could endanger her cats. All of it was always sifted by hand until she was satisfied.

The air was filled with the sound of animals calling out, the elephants trumpeting their arrival. Horses were led from trailers to the practice ring, dogs were barking, and a group of performers were greeting each other almost as loudly as the animals.

Ruda stood looking over the bales of sawdust, prodding one bale after another with her crop. 'Keep them out of the rain, don't let any damp sawdust get into the cages. I'll be with you in a moment to open up, get everything ready for me.' Turning back to her last cage, she quickened her step. She gave a soft whistle, and then leaned by the side of the cage, whistled again and peered

42

around to the front bars. He was in solitary confinement, a state he seemed to prefer. Ruda often wondered if he misbehaved to ensure he was solo . . . and Mamon could misbehave like none of the others. But, then, even his name was unique. He had had it when Ruda purchased him. Mamon was moody, uncooperative, a bully, but he could also be playful and sweet-natured. Lions, on the whole, are family-orientated and like each other's company, but Mamon was very much a loner and he constantly tested her. Ruda liked that.

His unpredictability made him dangerous to handle, and he had been exceptionally difficult to train, but he was the sharpest, the most willing performer of all the Grimaldi cats. Mamon seemed genuinely to enjoy the crowd's adulation. As if he knew his value, he behaved at times like a real star: his tantrums, however, were a lot more lethal. He swung his head towards Ruda as soon as he heard her soft whistle, then loped slowly to the side of the cage. When Ruda whistled for the second time, he squatted down on his haunches, his nose pressed to the bars, his massive black mane protruding through the rails. As Ruda peered round to him, his jaws opened and snapped shut. 'How you doing, eh? Want to say hello to your mama? Eh?'

Mamon rolled on to his back and Ruda reached through and tickled his underbelly, but she never stopped talking to him, soothing him, always aware that even in play he could slice off her arm.

The high-pitched voice that interrupted their play was like that of a young boy reaching puberty, slightly hoarse, half low, half falsetto. 'So you got what you wanted, after all . . .'

Mamon sprang to his feet, all four hundred and ten

pounds of him, in one swift move, ready to attack. The cage rattled as he lunged at the bars. Ruda gripped the riding crop tighter. The voice was unmistakable. 'You got even taller, Ruda.'

Ruda turned and snapped, 'I wish I could say the same for you, Tommy. What piece of wood have you crawled from under?'

Tommy Kellerman gave a mirthless, twisted smile. 'You're doing all right for yourself. That's some trailer parked up front! How much does a trailer that size set you back, then?'

Ruda relaxed her grip on the riding crop, forced a smile. This was something, after all, that she had expected. She had known he would turn up one day. Ruda had to look down almost to her waist level to meet his eyes. Tommy Kellerman was very spruce: his grey suit and red shirt must have been made for him, as was his red and grey striped tie. She had seen the white trenchcoat before: he wore it as he had always done, slung round his shoulders; he also sported a leather trilby, a hat being about the only normal garment Tommy could buy outside a children's-wear department. Kellerman was a dwarf.

'That raincoat's had some wear!' She tried to sound casual, but her heart was hammering, and she gave a furtive look around to see if there was anyone she knew close by.

'We got to talk, Ruda.'

'I've got nothing to say to you, Tommy, and I'm busy right now.'

Kellerman inched his leather hat up a fraction. 'You didn't change your name. How come?'

'I paid enough to use it. Besides, I like it.'

Ruda walked a few steps to the side of the cage, out of

sight of anyone passing. She leaned against it and beckoned for him to come to her. After a moment, Kellerman joined her. He was drenched in some sweet-smelling cologne which wafted up, mixing with the smell of the cats' urine.

'Like I said, Ruda, we need to talk. I just got in from Paris – I got a room reserved in the Hotel Berlin.' He had a small leather-sided bag which he dropped by his tiny feet. Then he took a stance against the wheel of the cage, his square hands stuffed into the small pockets, his polished child's shoes and red socks scuffed with mud.

'Have you been to my trailer? Asked for me there?'

He laughed his high-pitched laugh, and shook his head. 'No, I came straight from the station. I've been following you on quite a few venues – not in your league, of course, but I keep on seeing your posters, your face, star attraction. You got what you wanted, eh?'

'What do *you* want, Tommy?' Her voice was flat and emotionless.

He looked up at her, and inched his hat further up his domed forehead, scratching his head. Then he removed the hat and ran his stubby fingers through thick curly hair flecked with grey. The last time Ruda had seen him, it had been coal black. It was the nicest thing about him, his curly hair. She noticed it was dirty now, sweaty from the hat.

'I said, what do you want, Tommy? You're not here for a job, are you? Not after what happened – they wouldn't touch you. I'm surprised you can still find circuses that'll employ you.'

Kellerman spat into the mud. 'Isn't there some place we can discuss this in comfort? It's raining, and I could do with a bite to eat . . .'

45

'I'm real busy, Tommy, it's feeding time any minute now. Maybe we can meet some place later.'

He stared up at her, and his eyes searched hers before he spoke. 'You owe me, Ruda: all I want is my fair share. I can't get work, good work. I'm broke, I've had to sell most of my props and, well, I reckon you can give me a cut.'

'Cut of what?'

'Well, there's a few ways to look at it. I'm still your legal husband, and I bet *any* dough your old man doesn't know that! Now you're rollin' in it, and you're on the number-one circuits, this must be one hell of a contract . . . and all I want is a part of it. You either get me in on the act—'

'They'd fucking eat you, Tommy, no way!'

One of the helpers passed the small alleyway between the cages. He paused. 'Excuse me, Mrs Grimaldi, but the freezers are open. You want to come over and sign for the meat?'

Ruda nodded. 'Be right with you, Mike.' She hid Tommy by standing in front of him, and remained there until Mike had gone.

'Ruda, I need money, I'm broke.'

She turned on him, snapping angrily. 'When have you not needed money, Tommy? If it moves, you'll slap a bet on it. You owed me, remember? I paid you off years ago, I owe you nothing.'

Kellerman's face twisted with anger. 'You had nothin', not even a fucking passport, I got you out of Berlin, me! I put food in your mouth, clothes on your back. Don't give me this bullshit, you owe me a lot, Ruda, and if Grimaldi was to know you was still married, he'd hit the fuckin' roof. I keep my ears to the ground, bitch. I know you took over his act, and I know he's relegated to watchin' outside the ring like a prick! And I hear he hates it, he's still screwing everythin' in a skirt, so how do you think he'd feel if he knew you never got divorced? I reckon he'd be a happy man, Ruda. Now you tell me how much you owe me. I am your husband, and I got the marriage licence to prove it. You got the divorce papers? Huh? Well?'

Ruda scraped at the ground with the toe of her boot. 'Don't mess me around, Tommy. How much do you want?'

'Well, you got two options, sweetheart. Make me a part of the act, cut me in, or ... I know what they pay top acts, so I don't think it's too much, just give me one hundred thousand dollars.'

'Are you crazy? I don't have that kind of money! Everything I earn goes into the act. I swear I don't have—'

Kellerman's short squat legs ran to the front of Mamon's cage. He pointed with his stubby finger. 'Well, sell this bastard. They're worth a lot of dough, aren't they? Or flog your trailer, I know how much that's worth, and I know Grimaldi must be set up. I need dough, I got to pay some heavy guy off, and I got no one else. What you want from me, want me to beg? Fuck you! *You owe me!*'

Ruda remained in the narrow alley between the cages. It took all her willpower to contain her anger. 'Tommy, don't stand in front of the cages, they don't like it, come round here. I'll get you as much as I can, but not dollars, not here.'

Kellerman leered back at her. 'That's not good enough, Ruda. You want me to go over and have a chat with Grimaldi? You can get the cash from the head cashier. You think I dunno how much dough you're getting paid per show – it was the talk of Paris, so don't give me any bullshit.'

Ruda reached out and drew him close. 'I'll see what I can do. I'll see what I can raise and I'll come to your hotel tonight after I fix their night feed. But only on condition you don't work here, you leave. I also want our marriage licence. Is it a deal?'

Kellerman looked at his watch, the big cheap clock face almost the entire size of his wrist. 'OK, I'll go grab a bite to eat. You get me the dough, I'll give you the licence. We got a deal, my love.'

'Then leave now, I don't want you yapping to anyone.'

Kellerman grinned. 'Eh! There's guys here that'd cut my throat if they saw me, so I'm gone ... but you'd better turn up. You got until midnight.' He scrawled on a card the hotel and phone number and tucked it into her pocket, smiling. Then he perched his hat at a jaunty angle and departed.

Ruda watched the small squat figure scuttle away, watched him leave the perimeter of the trailer park. She was rigid, her face set with anger, but she forced Kellerman to the back of her mind, she had work to do. She strode over to the meat trailer that had arrived from the city and spent some time arranging the delivery, signing for the fresh carcasses and even haggling with the butcher until she had a good deal. She signed the delivery orders, then went over to her own freezer trailer.

Mike was already sorting out the midday feed. He used a heavy-handled hatchet to slice the meat from the bone, and a carpenter's sledgehammer with a short handle to crack open the carcass. Ruda collected the large trays,

48

carefully listed and tagged for each cat: the trays were clean, the freezer trailer immaculate. Between them, she and Mike weighed the feeds, placing the trays in readiness for the cages. By now Ruda had on a rubber apron, blood over her hands and arms. Like Mike she wielded the knives and hatchets professionally.

After they had washed off the blood, Ruda said, 'You can grab a coffee, Mike, I'll do the rest. What time have they allocated the arena for us?'

He handed her a carefully worked-out rehearsal schedule showing when the main rings would be available for her to rehearse the act. Ruda looked over it, frowning. 'Have the new plinths I ordered arrived yet?'

'I think so, but until everyone's settled, I can't get to the delivery trucks. They're all parked out at the rear.'

She swore under her breath, and snapped, 'Go and check, I'll need to rehearse with them tonight. We've no time to mess around.'

Ruda fed the cats herself, as she always did – no one else was allowed to; that way she had a constant check on whether any were off their food or had tooth problems. After the feed, she helped the boys clean out, sweeping and washing down the boards. By the time she had done the last cage, the first would be dry and ready for the clean straw. Not until each one was dry, straw and sawdust covering the floors, meat trays removed, was she satisfied to leave her animals, lazily snoozing, their bellies full.

The helpers were tired, it had been a long journey, and they retired to their trailers exhausted. None of them had ever been able to keep up with Ruda; she seemed to have unending energy and stamina. She was as strong as any man, and her expectations were high: anyone not prepared to give one hundred per cent was fired on the spot.

Not until now did Ruda allow herself to concentrate on the Kellerman problem, and she was soon so engrossed in her own thoughts, desperately trying to think what she should do about her ex-husband, that she virtually moved on automatic pilot. She had been so anxious to leave him that she had never considered divorce, but she had always consoled herself that no one would ever know because when she married Grimaldi, Kellerman was in gaol. He wouldn't know, and Luis would have had no reason to suspect she wasn't divorced. Now she knew what a stupid mistake she had made. For Luis Grimaldi to find out now that they were not legally married would be very dangerous, especially since Ruda was poised to make her move and take over the act. Ruda and Grimaldi were partners, everything split fifty-fifty, but they were at loggerheads. The act alone tied Ruda to Grimaldi, the act that she had built up. Ruda was planning to draw up new contracts to alter her take to seventy per cent of the proceeds. After months of bitter quarrels, she felt she had Grimaldi ready to sign. But what if he now discovered they weren't legally married and she had no legal hold over him at all? The act was still in Grimaldi's name, every contract she signed was in his name. It didn't matter that everyone knew she had taken over – the act was still his.

Ruda dragged her boots over the iron grille outside the trailer, inched them off and stepped on to the portable steps in her stockinged feet, opening the door. Carefully she placed her boots just inside the door, and then hung up her raincoat. The trailer was spacious. Her large bedroom led off the central sitting room, her husband's was at the far end by the kitchen. Grimaldi had not travelled with the trains but had driven their trailer and hooked it up to the water system. Ruda showered and

50

washed her hair. Wrapped in a robe with a towel around her head she went into the kitchen. The coffee pot was on: she tested it with her hand – it was still warm – and poured herself a cup of thick black coffee, then sat with the mug in her hands.

The walls of the trailer were hung with framed photographs of herself, Grimaldi and the various animals and circuits. Her eyes rested on the large central picture of herself. It was the new poster, the first time Ruda was the main attraction of a circus. The fame of Schmidt's was worldwide and she was at the pinnacle of her career, her life.

The coffee tasted good, bitter, and she clicked her tongue against her teeth. Her big, strong, mannish hands were red raw, the skin hard, the nails cut square. She wore no wedding ring, no jewellery. Slowly she removed the damp towel, and her hair uncoiled in a wet dark twist. When it was scraped back from her strong, heavy-boned face, strange deep red scars were evident on her temples: they looked like burn scars, as if someone had held a red-hot poker to either side of her head. Ruda often aggravated the scars, because she had a habit, when she was thinking, of rubbing her forefinger up and down them, as if the feel of the smooth scarred skin comforted her. She began to do that now, worrying about Kellerman, what she should do – what could she do? – all the while staring at the picture of herself. In the photograph, surrounded by her lions, she looked so powerful, so invincible. This was not just her career at stake, or her partnership, it was her life. And no one was going to take it from her. No one had a right to take it away.

Ruda rinsed her mug and placed it on the draining board by the small sink. Suddenly she realized she was not alone in the trailer. She moved silently towards Luis's bedroom; a low orgasmic moan made her step back. Then she heard her husband gasping, his groan louder, louder, until he sighed deeply. Ruda remained standing by the bedroom door, wondering which of the young girls was being serviced – more often than not it was one of the eager starstruck grooms. Grimaldi earmarked these young girls virtually on arrival at the site. In his heyday he wouldn't have looked in their direction but now he fucked whoever he could still dazzle.

Ruda sat down on one of the comfortable cushioned seats and lit a cigarette. She inhaled deeply, letting the smoke drift into rings above her head. She heard a soft girlish laugh, and looked to the bedroom, wondering if they were about to start again, but the clink of glasses and the low voice of her husband asking for a refill made her think that she should move away as they could both be coming out. She half rose to her feet.

'I love you . . .' Ruda raised her eyebrow; poor little besotted tart. 'When will you tell her?'

Ruda sighed, the poor stupid little girl didn't know his wife was well aware of these affairs. She looked to the bedroom, and said to herself, 'Well? Answer her!'

'I'll discuss it tonight, after the show. She'll be too busy beforehand.' Ruda could tell by the slight slur in Luis's voice that he had been drinking.

The girl's voice rose to a whine. 'You said that days ago, you promised me. If she doesn't care about you, why wait? You promised me, Luis, you promised.'

'I'll discuss it tonight, sweetheart, I give you my word.'

Ruda decided she had heard enough. She was about to open the main door of the trailer and slam it hard, so they would know she was there, when she was stopped in her tracks.

'The baby won't wait. I want you to promise me you'll tell her tonight, ask for a divorce tonight, promise me?'

'Shit!' Ruda pursed her lips. The bloody tart was pregnant!

Grimaldi's voice grew a little louder. 'Come here, look at me, Tina, I promise you we'll talk tonight, OK? But it's feeding time now. I can't talk it over until tonight – she's gonna have to rehearse. It's not the right time.'

Ruda walked out of the trailer, her feet stuffed into her old boots. So what was another bloody Grimaldi brat? But could this one turn his head? He was over sixty. Could this one make his warped, drink-befuddled mind take some kind of responsible action? The timing could not have been worse. Jesus Christ, if Grimaldi was to discover he wasn't legally married, maybe he would, out of sheer perversity, think about marrying this tart.

Ruda's mind began to spin. Grimaldi was old, he was feeling bitter and jealous of her success, he had been relegated to nothing more than a watcher outside the ring. This child coming now could give Grimaldi some sense of power. Would this bitch of a girl give Ruda's husband the strength to confront her? With her shoulders hunched, Ruda sloshed through the mud, hands clenched into fists at her sides. The rage inside her made her whole body stiffen, and the cats picked it up. As soon as she reached the perimeter of their cages, they began to prowl, to growl, pacing up and down, heads low.

The cages had to be driven under cover. The rain was pelting down, and the big animal tent had been pitched; all the animal trailers were being moved into the covered arena, each having a delineated site within it. Ruda climbed aboard the tractor with the first caged wagon ready and Mike gave her the signal to drive it in. Ruda wheeled the tractor round, hitching and unhitching each cage, her arms straining; to her this was as much a part of the act as feeding, and she wanted to oversee every single stage. Not until all the cages were positioned and secured in their allocated space did she relax. The large heaters were on full blast to ensure that the tent and grounds were kept dry and warm. All the tarpaulins from the tops of the cages were removed, laid out flat, and rolled up in readiness for the next journey.

When she at last returned the tractor to the car park, she started checking the massive equipment trucks to make sure that all her props had arrived. Then she had to check out the show cages: each one weighed a ton, but they had to be carried and stacked. She worked along with her boys until the sweat ran down her face. Time was now pressing: she had to be ready for her rehearsal period. Each act had its specific rehearsal time, and if she was not ready she would lose hers. The new plinths and pedestals were still in their wrappers. Ruda helped the men heave them down from the truck and roll them into the practice ring, reinforced steel-framed leather-based seats or stools for the cats, ranging in height, and with reinforced interlocking frames; some were barrel-shaped, some used under the ends of the planks that connected them. Each section had to be stacked for easy access and fast erection. They ranged from three feet to forty feet high, and they were very heavy to take the weight of the cats.

She had stripped down to a T-shirt, and sweat glistened

on her face and under her armpits as she drove herself to work harder than any man. Her boots were caked in mud, her big hands covered in old leather gloves as she used wire clippers to uncover the first plinth. Standing back to view it, she swore loudly, then ripped off the second and third covers. The plinths were correct in measurement, and exceptionally well made, but she swore and cursed even louder as she pointed to the leather seat base. She had paid in advance for the plinths and pedestals to be made for her in Berlin, and had stipulated the specific colours to be used: red, green and blue. They were, as she had instructed, red, green and blue – but they were too bright, too primary, and the gold braid too yellow.

Ruda had just completed unwrapping the last one – stacking them side by side, all the covers and wires removed – and was standing, hands on hips, in a rage, when Grimaldi at last made his appearance. He stood over six feet tall, and had thick black curly hair, very black as he regularly dyed it. His once handsome face was bloated now from age and excessive drinking, his dark eyes red-rimmed, but he could still turn heads. He was wearing his high black polished boots over cords, and a Russian-styled shirt, belted at the waist. He reeked of eau-de-Cologne. Ruda smelt him before she saw him.

'We got a problem?'

Ruda snapped that indeed they had, and it was all his fault. 'All you had to do, Luis, was give the colours for the plinths and you fouled that up – look at them, they're far too bright. I'm gonna have to use the old ones when I link up the pyramid formation. *Look* at the fucking colours. I want our old ones.'

Grimaldi shrugged. 'You can't have them. I sold them

in Paris. These are OK – they'll get used to them. Give them more rehearsal time, they look fine to me. What's the panic? A few rehearsals, they'll get used to them.'

Ruda turned on him. 'It's not you in the ring with them, Luis, it's me. And I'm telling you, those colours are too fucking bright!' Her face was flushed red with fury. Luis knew, probably better than anyone else, the danger that new equipment always generated – even a different coloured shirt worn in the show could disturb the cats. They hated change of any kind. Although they accepted Ruda's old rehearsal clothes, they seemed to know instinctively if she wore a different stage costume and they could really play up. They always had to be given time to get to know the changes – and two days, Ruda knew, was not long enough.

Ruda glared at her husband. 'Get the old ones back, Luis, and get them by tonight!' she snapped.

His eyes became shifty; he hated to be spoken to in that way in front of the workers. 'I said I sold them. Just work through the act, they'll get used to them. No way can I get them back from Paris in time for the opening.'

Ruda kicked out at one of the plinths in fury. 'Just do what I ask. Jesus Christ! It was the only thing you had to do and you foul it up!'

Luis began to pick his teeth with a matchstick. 'I'll call around. What time do you rehearse?'

Ruda was walking out of the tent and shouted over her shoulder for him to check the schedule. Luis ambled across to the main noticeboard: they were not on until later that afternoon, so he joined a group of men going off to the canteen and restaurant provided for the performers.

Alone in the trailer, Ruda paced up and down like one

of her cats. She opened the safe, counted the money kept for emergencies and noted that Luis must have been dipping into it. She slammed the door. There was about fifteen thousand dollars left. She checked her own bank balance: in her private account she had fifty-two thousand dollars of hard-earned money. She rubbed her scar until it was inflamed, then began to open drawers in her dressing table, feeling under her clothes for small bundles of dollars she kept for day-to-day emergencies – like a squirrel she hid small stacks of notes in various currencies and denominations. But no matter how she searched and calculated, she did not have one hundred thousand, and the more she mentally added up the amount, the more her fury built. This was hers, every single hard-earned cent was hers, and that little bastard felt he had a right to it. Kellerman had no right to anything, least of all her money.

The cashiers said they could give Ruda an advance on her salary, but not until after lunch when they would go to the bank. They would require Grimaldi to sign the release form, but if she came back at three they would have the money in dollars as she had requested. Ruda smiled, and then shrugged, said not to bother, she'd changed her mind. She was smarting with the knowledge that she needed Grimaldi's signature for an advance on her own wages.

Ruda fixed herself a salad in the trailer, and then changed into her practice clothes. She was just about to leave when Luis returned. He shook his head, his hair soaked. 'It's really coming down, maybe going to be a storm. It's sticky, clammy weather, and the forecast isn't good.'

'Did you try to sort out the pedestals?'

Luis had totally forgotten. He nodded, and then lied that he was expecting a return call at the main box office. She watched him in moody silence as he unlocked the wooden bench seat and checked over his guns; he rarely had one when watching out for her, but it was a habit from the past when his own watchers had always been armed. He habitually checked that his rifles were intact, but never even took them out of the box.

'I'll need you in the arena. Can you get the boys ready? We're due to start in an hour.'

Luis sat on the bench, picked up the towel Ruda had used to dry her hair and rubbed his head. 'Ruda, we need to talk – maybe after rehearsal.'

Ruda was already at the trailer door. 'Which tart was it today?'

Luis laughed, tossing the sodden towel aside. 'It's been the same one for months and you know it – it's Tina, she's one of the bareback riders.'

'You'll be screwing them in their diapers soon, you old goat.'

Luis laughed again. He had a lovely rumbling laugh and it relieved her, maybe it wasn't as serious as she had thought. He said, 'See you in the ring, then! After, we can go out for dinner some place, you need a break.'

Ruda paused, still by the door. 'Maybe, but I've got a lot to do, we'll see . . .'

He gave a rueful smile. 'I'm sorry about the mix-up with the plinths. I'll get on to them and see you in the ring.'

Luis heard the door click shut after her, lifted his feet up on to the bench, his elbows behind his head, and stared at the photographs along the top of the wall. Some of them were going brown with age. They were of him in his prime, standing with his lions, smiling to the camera; there was such a powerful look to him, such youthfulness ... Slowly his eyes drifted down, as he aged from one poster to the next; it was as if his entire life was pasted up in front of him. He stared at the central poster, Ruda's face where his had always been. The side wall was filled with Ruda. He eased his feet down and stood, slowly moving to the wall, to the pictures that showed he was past it, a has-been.

He opened a bottle of Scotch, drank heavily from it, and looked at a photograph, curling up with age. The Grimaldi family, the act passing from father to son. There was the old man, the grandfather, his own father, with Luis beside him no more than ten years old. Luis's father had taught him everything he knew, just as his father had before him, three generations of big-game trainers.

Luis downed more Scotch as he stripped to get showered and changed. He bent to look at himself in the bathroom mirror, staring at the scars across his arms – warrior scars his papa used to call them – scars from breaking up the tiger fights. But there was one, a deep jagged line from the nape of his neck to his groin. His fingers traced the deep jagged line, and he started to sweat, needing the Scotch more and more as his mouth dried up. He could never go back into the ring. She had done that to him. Ruda had made him inadequate, but it had been Mamon, her favourite baby, that had almost killed him. The cold water eased the feverish sweats, and he soaped his chest. He had been mauled so many times; how often he had stepped between two massive tigers, more afraid they would hurt themselves than him, but

59

every one of those scars had been dismissed as part of the game. Only the terrible scar on his chest made the fear rise up from his belly.

Mamon had lunged at him, dragged him like a rag doll around the practice ring, toyed with him, dared Luis to dominate him, and Luis had been overcome with a terror of which he had not believed himself capable. It had frozen him. He had no memory of how he had been dragged from the arena, no memory of anything until he woke in the hospital, the wound already filling with poison, a wound that wouldn't heal, a nightmare wound that opened with pus every time he moved. The anguish and the pain had kept him in a state of fever for weeks. Nightmares had kept him afraid to sleep, because in dreams the scar opened and oozed and suffocated him. Luis Grimaldi had almost died. To be so physically incapacitated was hard enough for him to deal with, but harder still was the relentless fear. A fear that he could confess to no one. At first he had tried to hide it, making excuses – so many excuses – as to why, months after he was healed, he had still not been near his cats. It was during those months that Ruda had begun working solo with the cats. He had said that he wasn't fit enough, that he needed more time to regain his strength, but the relentless fear was still there, and Ruda knew he was afraid. Ruda had encouraged him, half-heartedly he realized now, because she didn't want him back in the ring. She wanted the act for herself and she had encouraged him to take his time.

The bottle was almost empty, and the more drunk he became the more embittered he felt. He did not consider the lengths to which Ruda had gone to salvage the act,

60

how she had worked herself to exhaustion, keeping him and his cats at their winter quarters. Luis had forgotten that he never lifted a hand to help her, never queried how she had managed to finance them. All he could recall was the way she had humiliated him.

It was all Mamon's fault, he had decided. He could not get back into training with a cat that no longer respected him. Luis had entered the arena and a cold sweat had drenched his body. He felt it as if it were yesterday, the terrible fear as Mamon's cage was drawn closer to the gate. A number of people at the winter quarters had gathered to watch: they came in admiration, to watch the famous man face his attempted killer, and they stood in silence as the cage drew closer and closer.

Mamon was motionless, his head lowered, but his eyes held Grimaldi's. Ruda, standing close to the cage, had spoken calmly, softly, asking Grimaldi when she should release the cat . . . Grimaldi drank now, gulping the liquor from the bottle as the heat of his humiliation made him shake.

Alone in the arena, he had not been able to stop his legs shaking; his breath felt tight in his chest. He looked from Mamon to Ruda, he wanted more than anything to give her the signal. But he froze. She kept watching him, her eyes like the cat's, and she was smiling. It was her smile, mocking him, knowing he was afraid, that finished him. The great Grimaldi walked out of the arena and back to their quarters. That short moment finished his career, he knew it then.

He began to cry as he remembered the way she had held him close, wrapped him in her arms. He recalled every word she had said. 'It's not the scars on your body,

Luis, but the ones inside. They are always the worst, the unseen ones. I understand more than anyone else, I understand.'

Luis had pushed her away from him, shouted that she did not understand, there was nothing wrong in his mind, and he had pulled open his shirt to display the raw ragged line of the tear. Mamon, he said, was dangerous, he was a rogue lion, he should be shot. He had then tried to get his gun, pushing Ruda out of his way. Ruda's physical strength had stunned him, she had almost lifted him off his feet with a back-hander that sent him sprawling. Standing over him, her eyes as crazy as a wild cat's, she had virtually spat out the words. 'You touch Mamon, and I swear to God I'll kill you.'

Luis had dragged himself to his feet. 'You shoot him then, it's him or me, Ruda.'

Ruda had taken his own whip, the whip Luis's grand-father had used, and, for a second, he thought she was going to use it on him. Instead, she laughed in his face. 'Watch me! Just watch me, Luis.'

From the trailer window, Luis had seen her stride to the practice arena. He heard her shrill voice instruct the old hand who had been with Grimaldi's for thirty years, heard her give the order for Mamon to be released into the arena. She had wheeled the old, well-worn and well-used plinths into the centre of the ring, and then stood waiting, hands on her hips. The massive lion moved slowly and cautiously through the makeshift barrier tunnel from his open cage. Luis inched open the window to hear her. Her voice rang out, a high-pitched call: 'Mamawww, Mamawwwww *up, yup yup* . . . Mamon . . . come on, angel . . . good boy, Mama's angel.'

Mamon swung his massive black-maned head from

side to side and then, to Luis's astonishment, reared up on to his hind legs and walked towards Ruda, his front paws swung towards her. He kept on walking towards her and then, as she called out to him, he turned, as if dancing for her. Her high-pitched voice called out something – Luis couldn't quite hear the command, a rolling 'rr' sound . . . '*Reh!* Rey, *reh . . . reh . . .*' and then Mamon jumped on to the red plinth. After steadying himself, he cautiously tested the plank, a thick wooden board balanced between the two plinths. Carefully, cautiously, front right paw patting the plank, still balancing himself as she now called: '*Huppp! Blue . . . blue . . .* Ma'angel!' The animal trod the narrow board towards the blue-based plinth. He eased himself into a sitting position, his thick tail trailing the ground as he perched. Ruda moved closer and closer to the blue plinth, until she was near enough to be within the lion's territory. Only another trainer would know that this was reasonably safe: the animal sitting on the plinth, needing all four paws to give him balance, is unlikely or unable to attack, his hindquarter overhanging due to the position of his tail. If he attacked from a seated position, he would automatically lose his balance.

Luis couldn't take his eyes off Ruda, as she moved in close and then audaciously turned – leaving her back within half a foot of the animal. She never stopped talking, whispering encouragement, as she knelt down on one knee, her head virtually beneath the massive cat's. She gave another high-pitched command, lifting her voice because she was facing away from Mamon: '*Up . . . up . . . greeee, greeee . . .*' The green-based plinth was five feet in front of her and she was encouraging the lion to leap from one pedestal to another, from the blue to the green.

Mamon lifted his front paws and balanced himself to stand on his hind legs on the pedestal. All his muscles strained as he made a flying jump, right over Ruda's head on to the green pedestal. She ran to him and gave him a titbit, rubbing his nose. She then looked to the trailer window, just a fleeting look, but there was a small, tight smile on her face. Finally she lifted both her arms, giving the final command for Mamon to head out of the arena, and bowed mockingly to the small group of onlookers, who applauded, as Luis slunk away from the trailer window.

The word spread fast that the great Luis Grimaldi had lost his nerve. They joked that his wife had taken it from him.

Now Grimaldi staggered slightly as he left the trailer. The rain had not ceased and the ground was mud. He made his way towards the rehearsal tent. The cashier who had talked with Ruda earlier that morning called out to him. He turned bleary-eyed towards her large brown umbrella. 'I can give you the advance, Mr Grimaldi, if you come over and sign for it.' Luis had not the slightest idea what she was talking about, and stumbled towards her. 'Your wife wanted an advance on her salary. If you need it, I've come back from the bank, I just require your signature.' Grimaldi mumbled incoherently, and she passed on, turning to see him slither and slide against one of the trailers. The cashier shrugged, disinterested; his drink problem was well known.

The big man mumbled to himself. Not content with taking over his act, Ruda was trying to steal his money.

He was going to face her, and nothing was going to stop him.

Ruda had made the boys dismantle and re-erect the cage arena twice. She timed them to the last second, and even bolted and heaved two of the cage walls herself. She wanted it timed down to less than two minutes. This was tough going: the arena cage was very heavy and unwieldy, the caged tunnel sections even heavier. As they dismantled it all for the third time, they moaned and muttered to each other, making sure 'Madame Grimaldi' didn't over-hear. She now checked the formation of the cages at the entrance tunnel. The cats were to be released on cue to head down the tunnel into the arena.

Mike asked if they were using the new pedestals, which were still stacked outside the ring. Ruda pursed her lips and then shook her head. 'No, I'll do that first thing in the morning when I'm fresh. Let's just run the easy routine for today, give them some exercise, and tomorrow we'll have a real crack at it . . . so for now it's the herd, then the leap, followed by the roller roll.'

She called up to the electrician. 'Can you give me a few spotlights, in the usual places, just to keep them on their toes, red, green and blue formation?'

A disembodied voice called down that it was rather her toes than his, and a few spots came on and off.

Ruda shaded her eyes, calling out to the electrician again. 'Most important one is directly after the leap, Joe. Last show it was a fraction late.'

She paced up and down, her head shaking from side to side as she relaxed her shoulders. The rehearsal would have no music, it was simply to warm up the act, get the cats used to the new location. It also kept them on their mettle after a long night's travelling and calmed their restlessness.

The cages were now lined up, ready to herd in the animals. Ruda gave a look around the ring and noticed that Luis had not turned up, but two of the boys had already placed chairs at either side of the arena, waiting to watch over the act should they be needed. They had no guns; they could, if needed, break up trouble by creating noise and yelling.

'Okay, Mike, let's go for it!' she shouted at the top of her voice to the tunnel and waiting cages some distance from the arena.

Ruda used the small trapdoor at the side of the main show cage and entered the arena, then turned back to head into the animals' entrance tunnel. When the act was live, she always entered from the tunnel, straight into the ring, as if she was one of the cats herself. She double-checked that the sections were bolted, as she headed down the tunnel, bending her head slightly as the bars joined over the top. Midway she gave Mike the signal to release the cats on the count of ten: the exact time the opening music used. She tightened her thick leather gloves, her voice hissed slightly, one . . . two . . . three . . . As she reached nine, she spun around, running back down the tunnel into the wide caged arena. She carried only her short practice stick, and wore old trousers and a shirt knotted at the waist with her old worn black-leather knee-high boots, caked with mud and excreta – they had never seen a lick of polish since Luis gave them to her.

By now the cats had been released, any second they would be heading into the arena. Ruda paced herself, gave a bow to the empty auditorium: she always practised every move she would do in front of a live audience. Arms raised, adrenaline pumping, she could feel the ground shudder as the animals charged down the tunnel. She loved this moment, as the sixteen tigers hurtled into the main ring, as if frighteningly out of control. But the cats knew exactly which was their leader and which place each had. Ruda backed to the wall of the arena and picked up a heavy double-sided weighted ladder. The cats stormed round the arena, forming a wide circle around Ruda, as she stood nonchalantly next to a small ladder plinth. They were loping, moving fast . . . The circle tightened as she yelped a command. Her second command, hardly detectable, was a lift of her right hand to the lead tiger, her eyes never off him. Roja was the number one cat, and it was he who appeared to split up the circle, breaking to his right. Now the cats gathered into two factions, grouping either side of her. A third command, again to Roja, and the animals began to weave around each other. The circle became tighter, tighter, closing in around her. She became more vocal, calling each tiger by name, high-pitched calls. Then, on a signal to Roja, the cats touched, pressing their bodies hard against one another. Ruda, her back to the small ladder, slowly eased herself up it, step by step, as they kept up their circle, like a Catherine wheel turning, turning.

Ruda reached the top rung of the three-foot ladder. There was total silence in the big arena as off-duty circus performers watched the rehearsal. Luis entered the arena, lifting the flap aside, and stood for a moment before he began slowly to thread his way through the seats. Ruda gave Roja the command: 'Down . . . Roja, down . . . ja ja ja down!'

Tigers are instinctive fighters; their close crossing of each other's body territory was dangerous, filled with snarls and teeth-baring. But one by one they began to lie down side by side, until sixteen tigers lay like a wondrous carpet. Twice, Ruda reprimanded two females for beginning a spat, banging her hand flat on the top rung of the ladder as a warning. The watchers were uneasy now, aware of how perilous a position Ruda was in – if one tiger accidentally knocked over the ladder, brushed too close, they could attack.

More and more performers had slipped in to watch. But Ruda saw nothing, no one, her attention riveted on the carpet of cats. Satisfied they were in position, she lifted both arms above her head, speaking all the time, never stopping talking to them ... Then she gave the command: '*Upo ... upahhh.*' Sixteen tigers rose up, sixteen tigers in almost perfect formation, then lowered their heads. It was a magnificent sight, as the glorious carpet of gold and black stripes lifted and rose magically into the air.

Ruda called out again, made it on to the top rung of the ladder and then flung herself forwards, face down, to lie spreadeagled across the sixteen cats, balanced on their backs. They began to move, carrying her round in a terrifying wheel. She then dropped to her feet, arms above her head in the centre of the seething mass. She flicked Roja with her stick and he broke the circle and spread wide at a run; the others followed, spreading wider, running around her as she gave a low bow. She held the bow as rehearsed for three long beats, then turned back towards the tigers. As if by no command at all, they formed two lines facing her. She yelped out an order, her voice cutting through the air, high-pitched, and up they reared to sit on their hindquarters. They clawed the air, Helga and Roja in a snarling match; Ruda quickly pushed

Helga aside and flicked her hand at Roja, stepping back. Facing them she spread her arms wide, giving a small signal to Sasha, one of her females, leading the second section of the line-up. They were ready, and she gave the command. '*Up . . . upppp.*' Now they all reared up from squatting to stand on their hind legs, their growls and swiping paws showing their dislike of the position. They were poised perfectly to attack, for tigers always attack from the front, never the rear. Shouting, she urged them back like a chorus line.

Grimaldi wanted to weep. She was spectacular, he had never attained such perfection even at the zenith of his career. Her face shone, her eyes were brilliant in the spotlight, as if the risk to her life was exhilarating. There was a radiance to her that humbled him and, drunk as he was, he bowed his head, trying to steady himself on the seat in front of him. The seats had not been battened down, and the chair was loose; it fell forwards, Luis with it, into the second row of seats. The bang was as loud as a shot.

Ruda turned and saw him and, at the same time, Sasha and Roja lost concentration, came down on to all fours. Ruda gave the command to move out, signalled for the watchers to open the trapdoor – fast. One of the boys watching for Ruda hurried to Grimaldi's side, helped him to his feet.

Ruda turned all her attention on Roja, dominated him, knowing that if he was in the tunnel the others would follow. She never took her eyes off him, as he hesitated, then wheeled round to head back down the tunnel, followed after a moment by the others. Ruda clamped the trapdoor, shouting for Mike to hold the rest of the act. She moved like lightning, but she didn't go for Grimaldi.

Instead, she strode to the boy who had helped him to his feet and grabbed him by the scruff of his neck. 'What the fuck do you think you're doing? You watch out for *me*. If this place goes up like an inferno, *you watch out for me!*' She swiped him a back-hander, so hard he fell to his knees.

Still ignoring Grimaldi, Ruda turned to the watcher on her left, and snapped for him to put the next part of the act on hold. '*Now! Do it right now*, get to Mike, tell him to keep the cages shut!' The two boys ran, leaving the drunken man standing alone, his face flushed a deep red.

Then Ruda slowly removed her thick leather gloves, and spoke to her husband, her voice kept low. 'Get out of here, Luis. Get out before I have you thrown out.'

Grimaldi held his own; swaying slightly, he glared at her.

'I'm sorry, I fell, you know I'd never—'

Ruda flicked his face with the glove. 'Get out of my sight, you drunken bum!'

Luis touched his cheek. 'I want a divorce, you hear me, bitch? I want a divorce. *I want you out of my life.*'

The show continued for those performers still hanging around. Ruda gripped her husband by his shirt and hauled him to the exit of the tent. She pushed Grimaldi out; he fell face down in the mud. She said nothing, but turned on her heels and strode back into the tent. She saw a cleaner standing with his wide long-handled broom, and told him to sweep out the drunk, and not to let him near the arena until she was through.

By the time Ruda had finished the rehearsal, got the cats back into their cages and fed, it was after six. She hoped Luis had passed out so she wouldn't have to confront him, but when she walked back into the trailer he was remarkably sober – and obviously waiting for her. A pot of steaming black coffee made the trailer windows thick with condensation. She switched on the air-conditioner without saying a word. Luis poured coffee and handed her a mug. 'I'm sorry, I should never have done that, I was drunk. I am ashamed, I'm sorry.'

Ruda threw her coat on to the heater and began to unbutton her shirt. 'You know how dangerous it was, you don't need me to tell you that, dangerous and stupid, and from you of all people.'

Grimaldi nodded glumly and held out his hand, but Ruda didn't take it. She unzipped her trousers, kicking them off. He picked them up, and fetched her shirt from where she threw it, took them to the laundry basket. She wore a silk one-piece with dark green stains under the armpits. But she didn't strip completely. After all the years they had been together, Ruda was still self-conscious about her body. She fetched an old worn robe, wrapping it around herself before she took a sip of the coffee. She uncoiled her hair, the nape of her neck still damp from the workout.

'Did you mean it, Luis? About the divorce?'

Grimaldi looked at her sheepishly and sat down, his big hands held between his knees. 'I guess so, I've been meaning to talk to you about it for a while now, but . . .'

'But what?'

'Well, why not? We don't have a marriage, we haven't ever really had one – you know that . . . and she's – Tina's going to have a baby.'

'You've got kids all over Europe, what's one more? Anyway, knowing that little tart, how could you be sure it's yours?'

Grimaldi cocked his head to one side. 'It's mine – I

may be worn out and past it, but my dick can still work. It's about the only thing that never lets me down.'

'What about the act?' She tried to keep her voice nonchalant, but she was shaking. He still wouldn't look at her. 'Luis, what about the act . . . if we divorce. We're partners, do you still want me to run the act?'

He turned to her then. 'You can do what you like with it, it's not mine anyway, but I'll still retain fifty per cent. I mean, half the animals are mine.'

Ruda felt drained. 'I see. So my money, all the money I've earned and poured into the act, everything, all the new cats that I've trained, my cats, it's all split fifty-fifty, is that right?'

Luis nodded. 'That's only fair, you had nothing when we met, everything you have is from me. I mean, if you want you can pay me what you think the act is worth, what the animals are worth, and then, do whatever you want, but you can't use my name – not any more.'

Ruda snatched the poster off the wall. 'Look at it, Luis, it's not your name, it's mine! I've not used your name for the past two years, I don't want your name!'

'Just my act! You think nobody knows? My name is still a crowd-puller, may not be on the fucking headlines, but it's the Grimaldi Cats.'

'It's not your act any more.'

Grimaldi shook his head and half smiled. 'All I want is my fair share, my cut. Anyone can take over an act. I can work in someone else.'

'You can what? *What did you say?*'

'I said I can work in someone else. If you want to take the act as it stands, then pay me – it's as simple as that.'

Grimaldi opened the trailer door. 'Where are you going?' she snapped at him.

'I'm going out, OK? And while I'm gone, Ruda, just sit down and remember, remember where you came from, what you were before you met me. Sit on what you made your living on an' *tell me how much you fucking owe me!*'

The trailer rocked as he slammed the door. She buried her head in her hands, gripping her head in a rage, wanting to rip out her hair. What did he know about pain? What could he know? Almost in confirmation she felt the burning sensation in her head. He couldn't stand up to pain, but she could. She kicked out at the trailer wall, punched out at the doors, the walls, with all her strength until she had to heave for breath. It was then that she shouted, 'I was tested, he tested me, I was Papa's favourite!'

She began to pace the confined space of the trailer, her hands clenching and unclenching. First Kellerman, now Luis, both wanting to take from her everything she had fought to get. She wouldn't let them, either of them. As she showered and changed, she talked down the blinding fury which boiled up inside her, forcing herself to think what she had to do.

Ruda did a last check of the cats, staying a moment longer with Mamon than the others. He was restless, as if he felt her own unease, and pressed close to the bars, then lay down totally submissive; she reached through to touch him, let his rough tongue lick her hand. She whispered to him. 'You know, you know, I won't be kicked, I won't take it, nobody kicks me, yes? *Yes?*' She loved this creature more than any other living being. It was Mamon, her angel, who had drawn from Ruda a love she had believed herself incapable of feeling.

She clung on to his bars. 'I'm ready for him, I can deal with him, I am strong, I am strong.' The bars felt cold to her brow, she pressed closer, closer. The voice whispered to her, soft, persuasive: 'You can do it, fight through the pain with your mind . . . that's my little girl, that's Papa's girl, you can do it, pain is sweet, pain is beautiful, come on, Ruda, give your papa what he wants. You love me, prove it!'

She was ready, ready to face out Kellerman, ready to go into East Berlin. She pushed herself away from Mamon. 'I'll be back.'

Ruda passed by her trailer and, through the lit window, saw Luis unwrapping a fresh bottle of brandy. She walked on, caught the bus into the city centre, went first to the taxi rank, and then changed her mind. She waited for another bus, to take her into East Berlin.

It was a strange experience crossing through the shabby Kreuzberg district. In the old days it hugged the Wall, but now it was home to most of the Turkish population. From the window of the bus she was shocked to see racist slogans daubed on the walls of the rundown houses. '*Ausländer* – foreigners – *raus* . . . get out!' Bricks were thrown at the bus as it passed through the district. The passengers were mostly women and children, and they cowered back in their seats. Anti-Semitic slogans were smeared on the sites of former synagogues and Jewish schools. Ruda began to sweat as a group of young skinheads spat as the bus passed, their hands lifted, their voices screaming, '*Sieg Heil!*' Their yells made Ruda bow her head. She hissed under her breath, 'Bastards . . . bastards!' but kept her head lowered.

A woman seated in front of Ruda began shouting and shaking her fist at the skinheads. She turned to her companion, and they began talking to the rest of the occupants of the bus. 'If your skin is the wrong colour, if it isn't pale enough, if your hair is too dark, too curly, these pigs will attack. Something must be done! Why has this hatred been allowed to continue and fester? Turn the machine guns on them, the fascist pigs!'

By the time Ruda got off the bus she was engulfed in a strange fear. Not two yards from the bus stop, she faced a massive poster of herself. The incongruity made her gasp . . . but the poster calmed her, comforted her.

She took out her street map, looking for the right direction to Kellerman's hotel. She hesitated, checked his scrawled note and passed on, heading down a dimly lit street to a small bed and breakfast establishment that could not be described as a hotel. It was almost ten when she entered the dingy reception area. There was no one around, and Ruda turned the guest register, or what was deemed a guest register but was scrawled across with memos and messages, to read it. 'T. Kellerman' was listed, occupying room 40. She waited another moment before she headed to the elevator, and pressed for the fourth floor. She stood outside room 40 listening to the sound of a television set, the volume turned up loud. She tapped and waited, tapped louder and the door inched open.

'They should have called from reception,' he said petulantly, but he swung the door open wider. He was in his shirt, the tie loosened, and he had on wide, cut-down red braces. Ruda closed the door, and looked around the small single room, dominated by the television set.

'Jesus, Tommy, what made you choose this dump?'

'It's cheap, nobody asks questions, and nobody's likely to come looking for me – that answer enough?'

'Yeah, I suppose so, but I'm surprised you've not had a brick through your window, or a turd in your bed.'

'Got scared, did you?'

Ruda shrugged, then, after a moment, 'Sickened, more like.' She placed her large leather bag on the edge of the bed. As she turned, Kellerman suddenly clasped her tightly round the thighs, his head buried in her crotch. She didn't resist. 'Still working the same foreplay game, are we?' she asked sarcastically.

He chuckled, and stepped back. 'Lemme tell you, that's turned on more women than I can count, they love it, hot breath steaming through their panties. Just a taste of what is to come, because when I ease the skirt down, really get stuck in, no woman can resist me, not when I've got my tongue working overtime.'

Ruda laughed and unbuttoned her coat, tossing it over her bag. 'You disgusting little parasite, I'd have thought at your age you'd have grown up, but then I suppose it's tough – not ever growing, I mean.'

Kellerman hitched up his trousers and crossed to the courtesy fridge. 'Want a miniature drinkie? From your own miniature lover?' He peered at the rows of bottles in the fridge and chose a vodka for himself.

'I won't have anything.'

'Suit yourself,' Kellerman said as he opened a tonic, and fetched a glass. His squat hands could reach only half-way round the tumbler.

Ruda sat on the bed watching him as he fixed his drink, dragged a chair from the small writing desk by the fridge, moved it closer to the bed, then waddled back to collect his glass, handing it to her as he gripped the chair by the arms to haul himself into it. Sitting, his feet hung just over the edge of the chair, child's feet encased in red socks to match his braces, his scuffed shoes on the floor.

'Cheers!' Kellerman took the glass, drank almost half

its contents, burped and wrinkled his nose. 'So! You came. I was half expecting you not to turn up.'

Ruda opened her handbag and took out her cigarettes. Kellerman delved into his pockets to bring out a Zippo lighter. 'Did you go to the cashier?' he asked, pointedly looking at the large leather bag.

'Yes.'

He flashed a cheeky grin. 'Good. I'm glad we understand each other. The licence, all our papers, are in that drawer over there. They still look good . . . guy was an artist!' He eased himself off the chair. 'You may not believe this, but I don't like asking for the money.'

Ruda laughed. 'Asking? Blackmailing is the word I would use.'

'You have to do what you have to do. I'm flat broke, and in debt to two guys in the US. It's been tough for me ever since you left.'

Ruda smiled. 'It was tough before I left. I'm surprised they employed you in Paris. Those folks worked hard for their dough. Way I heard it you were blacklisted – you'd steal from a kid's piggy bank. You've never given a shit for anyone but yourself. How long did you get?'

Kellerman shrugged. 'Five years. It was OK, I survived, the cons treated me OK. The screws were the worst, bastards every one of them, called me Monkey or Chimpy.'

'You must be used to nicknames by now.'

'Yeah, haw haw, sticks and stones may break my bones but—'

He leaned forward, a frown on his face. 'I'm shrinking, Ruda, did you notice? Prison doc said it was something to do with the curvature of my spine. I said to him, Jesus

Christ, Doc, I can't get any smaller can I? I said to him, if this goes on I'll be the incredible shrinking man, and he said—' Kellerman shook his head as he chortled with laughter. 'He said, that was done with mirrors! They built giant chairs and tables, then . . . fuck it! How could he know, eh? How could he know?'

Kellerman was referring to his obsession, a fun-fair mirror he used to haul everywhere he went. The mirror distorted a normal human being, but it made Kellerman look tall and slender, normal. In a fit of rage one night he had smashed it to pieces, and wept like a child at his broken dream image. He turned now to peer at himself in the dressing-table mirror, his head just reaching the top of the table. The effect was comical, even funny, but Kellerman was not a clown. He was a man filled with self-hatred, and obsessed with the idea that if he had grown, he would have been as handsome as a movie star, a Robert Redford, a Clint Eastwood.

He cocked his head, grinning. 'You know they got drugs now to stop dwarfism? They detect it early enough, pump you full of steroids, and you grow. Ain't that something?'

Kellerman loathed his deformity; when drunk he was always ready to attack anyone he caught staring at him. The circus had been virtually his only employment, his short body rushing around the ring, being chased and thrown around, drenched in water. He opened another miniature and drank the vodka neat from the small bottle.

'Did you work with the Frazer brothers in Paris?' Ruda asked the question without really wanting a reply; her heart was hammering inside her chest. She had to get him into a good mood – she didn't have the money.

Kellerman nodded. 'Yeah, the Frazers bought my

78

electric car just before I was sent down. So when I turned up and told them I just needed a few dollars they put me in the act. I timed it right, though. You know little Frankie Godfrey? He joined the Frazers about four years ago. Well he's been really sick, water on the brain maybe, I dunno. Some crazy woman, a few years back, got up from her seat and attacked him, just hurtled into the ring and began knocking him around. The audience thought it was all part of the act, but she was a fruit and nut case. Ever since the poor sod's had these blinding headaches. Still, it paved the way for me to earn a few bucks. Then the management found out about me, gave me my cards, or told the Frazers to get shot of me – cunts all of them.'

'Serves you right. If you steal from the only people who employ you, and virtually kill a cashier to get it, what else do you expect? I did that show – Monte Carlo, wasn't it?'

'I borrowed the dough, I was gonna pay it back. Yeah, Monte fuckin' Carlo, I only went there to date Princess Stephanie! Haw haw!'

Ruda laughed. 'Oh, yeah, where were you gonna find two hundred thousand dollars? From Prince Rainier?'

Kellerman chortled, and pointed to her handbag. 'I'm looking right at half that amount now. You know something? We made a good team, we could do it again. I'm good with animals.'

'Fuck off. You hate anything with four legs.'

He shrugged. 'No, I'm serious. You hear what that high-wire act got paid for a stint in Vegas? I mean, that's where the real dough is – cabaret. And there's a double act with big cats, you know, mix it with magic – they make their panthers disappear. I dunno how the fuck he does it, but it's got to be a con. You ever thought of trying the Vegas circuit? I got contacts there. I mean, maybe me in the act might not be a good thing but I could manage you. Grimaldi's washed up, or filled up with booze, so I hear, and you were shit hot with that magic stuff.'

'The day I need you to manage me, Tommy, *I'll* be washed up.'

Kellerman continued talking about acts he had managed, and she let him talk, only half listening. A long time ago now, Ruda had felt deeply sorry for him, because she had been in the same dark place. In retrospect she had made herself believe that their past experience was the reason she had married him – it united them. He was the only connection – now he was the reminder.

When they had first met, Kellerman was not as grotesque as he was now. He had seemed very boyish, innocent, his full-lipped mouth always ready to break into a wide smile, revealing white even teeth. But as he aged, the anguish inside him, his self-loathing, not only seemed to have deformed his body, but was etched on his face.

She was so engrossed in her own thoughts that Kellerman startled her when he suddenly hopped on to the bed beside her. 'You aren't listening to me!'

'I'm sorry, I was miles away.'

Kellerman rested his head against the pillows, his feet in their red socks pushed at her back, irritating her, so she got up and sat in the chair he had vacated. She was tense, her hands clenched, but the small voice in her head kept on telling her to be patient, be nice to him, she mustn't antagonize him.

'Strange coming back after all these years, isn't it?'

She made no reply. He tucked his short arms behind his head, and closed his eyes. 'You think it's all stored away, all hidden and then – back it comes. I've had a long time to think about the past, in prison, but being here, I dunno, it makes me uneasy, it's like a hidden drawer keeps inching open.'

Ruda began to assess how she should go about telling him there was no money, even trying to contemplate some kind of deal she could offer him. She was surprised by the softness, the sadness in his voice; he spoke so quietly she had to lean forwards to catch what he was saying.

'When my mama handed me over, there were these two women, skeleton women, I can remember them, their faces, almost as clearly as my mama. Maybe even clearer. One woman was wearing a strange green satin top, and a torn brown cloth skirt . . . filthy, she was filthy dirty, her head shaved, her face like a skull. She clawed at Mama, she hissed at her through toothless gums. "Tell them he's twelve years old, tell the guards he's twelve." My mama held on to me, almost hauling me off my feet, she was so confused. She said, "He's fourteen, he's fourteen but he's small, he's just small." The woman didn't hear because one of the guards hit her, and I saw her sprawled on to the station line, and I could see her shoes, she had one broken red high-heeled shoe, and a wooden clog on her other foot.'

'I've heard all this before! Come on, why don't we go some place for a meal?' She had to get him out, stop him drinking, talk to him, reason with him.

Kellerman continued, ignoring her. 'The next moment Mama and me were pushed and shoved into a long line . . . Eva was crying, terrified, and then the second woman passed us. The second woman whispered to Mama, she said "Twins . . . say your children are twins."'

81

Ruda arched her back. 'Shut up!' She gripped her arms tightly around herself. Her heart began to beat rapidly, as if she was being dragged under water. Her nostrils flared, she felt the damp darkness, the stench and she clenched her teeth, not wanting to remember. 'Don't, Tommy. Stop. I don't want to hear!' But she could hear the voice: 'Twins . . . twins . . . *twins*,' and she got to her feet still hugging herself. She moved as far away from the bed as possible, to stand by the window. She could feel the hair on the nape of her neck stand up, her mouth was dry, and the terror came back . . . The rats scurrying across her, the ice-cold water. In the gloom, the white faces of the frightened, the gaunt faces of the starving and the stinking sewer water which rose up, inch by inch, until they held her up by her coat collar. A blue woollen coat with a dark blue velvet collar: hers had been blue, her sister's had been red. 'Don't, Tommy, please don't . . .'

But he wasn't hearing her, he was too wrapped up in his own memories. He gave a soft, heartbreaking laugh. Eva, his little sister, was almost as tall as he, with the same curly black hair: she was only ten years old. Eva had always been so protective of him, so caring, how he had adored her. Ruda moved closer to the bed again determined to calm him, but it was as if he was unaware that she was in the room. He stared at the ceiling and began to cry.

'"My son is fourteen," Mama shouted, and all around us was mayhem, but all I did, all I could do, was keep staring at that second woman who had approached us. She had a pink see-through blouse, it was too small, the buttons didn't do up, you could see her breasts, her ribs, she was covered in sores, and she had a blue skirt . . . it had sequins on it, some of the sequins were hanging off by their threads, and the skirt must have been part of a ballgown, because it had a weird train. It was caught up and tied in a knot, a big knot between her legs. Like the other skinny woman, she had one high sling-backed gold evening shoe and what looked like a man's boot. I was so fascinated by these two skeleton women that I didn't really understand what was going on. But the next moment, this guard dragged Eva away, he kicked Mama, he kicked so hard she screamed in agony. She was screaming, her voice was screeching, like a bird. "He's fourteen, but he's a dwarf, he's a dwarf, please don't hurt him, he's strong, he can work, but don't hurt him, don't kick him in his back, please . . ."'

He sobbed. 'She said it, my mama said it, for the first time I heard her say what I was . . .'

Ruda sat on the bed, she reached out to touch Kellerman's foot, to stop him talking, but he withdrew his leg, curling up like a child. His voice was no longer a whimper, but deeply angry. 'He took me then, pointed with his white glove, first to me, and then to a line-up of children on the far side of the station yard. That was the first time I saw him, that was the first time. I've never told you that, have I?'

Ruda's nails dug into her arms. She was pushing shut her own memories with every inch of willpower she possessed. She forced herself to move closer to him. 'Stop it, Tommy, I won't hear. I won't listen to you.'

'Yes, you will,' he snapped. 'You will listen, because I want you to know, you more than anyone else. I want you to know.'

She wanted to slap him, but she kept tight hold of her mounting, blinding anger. 'I know, you've told me all this before, and we made a promise—'

He was like a child, his red-socked feet kicking at the bedspread. 'Well, fuck you! Won't keep the promise – I want you to know!' He clenched his hands, punching the bed. 'I was dragged away from Mama, and still she screamed, first for Eva and then for me, but no one took any notice, everyone was crying and shouting, but I heard Mama, I heard her clearly call out to me, "Wait for me at the station, I'll be at the station."'

Ruda snatched one of the pillows and held it over his face. 'Stop it! I know this, I don't want to hear any more!' She pressed the pillow down hard on his face, and he made no attempt to fend her off or push the pillow aside. After a moment she withdrew it and looked down into his face. His beautiful, haunted, pain-racked eyes looked up to her.

'No more, Tommy. Please.'

He nodded, and turned away, his cheek still red from the pressure of the pillow. 'Oh, Ruda, she never said which station. She never said which station.'

Ruda lay beside him, not touching, simply at his side. He was calmer now, and she heard him sigh, once, twice.

'You know, Ruda, no matter how many years pass, how long ago it was, I still hear her calling me. Every station, in every town I have ever been to, there is a moment – it comes and goes so fast – but no matter where I am, here or in America, in Europe, whatever station, I say to myself: "Which station, Mama, where did you wait for me? Did Eva find you? Why didn't you tell me which station?" It's strange, I know they're dead, long, long ago, but there is this hope that some day, some time I'll reach a station and my mama will be there, with Eva, walking the streets, and every corner I think maybe,

84

just maybe I'll see Eva. I never give up hope – I *never* give up.'

Ruda whispered she was sorry, and he turned to face her. 'Is it the same for you?'

He searched her eyes, wanting and needing confirmation that he was not alone in his pitiful hope. The amber light in her eyes startled him – cruel eyes. With a bitter, half-smile she said, 'It is not the same for me. It never was.' With some satisfaction she felt the chains, the locks tighten on her secrets.

Kellerman leaned up on his elbow, touching her cheek with his index finger. 'I'll tell you something else my mama said. She said never tell a secret to anyone, a secret is a secret, and if you tell it, it is no longer a secret. You are the only person I have ever told what they made me do, and whatever I have done since – I mean, I admit I have stolen, I am a thief, I know I did wrong. I stole from the circus, from my people, but they are not me, they don't know who I am.'

Ruda sat up, took a sneaking glance at his small alarm clock. It was almost ten-thirty. She knew she had to discuss the money he wanted, and that she didn't have it.

'I'm not blackmailing you, Ruda. All I want is my fair share.'

It was as if he had read her mind. He rubbed the small of her back. 'You don't hate me, do you? You know I've no one else but you.'

His touch made her cringe inside. He rested his hands on her shoulders and stood up behind her, planting a wet kiss on the nape of her neck.

'If you do that again, I'll throw you off the bed.' She pushed him away. 'Get off me!'

Kellerman began to jump up and down as if the bed was a trampoline. 'Oh, you liked it once. You couldn't get enough of me once!'

The next moment he slipped his arms around her neck; she could feel his erect penis pressing into the small of her back. 'Let me have you one last time, please, Ruda, the way you liked it, let me do it.'

Ruda didn't even push him away this time. There was no anger in her voice, just revulsion. 'I never liked it. I loathed it to such an extent I used to be physically sick. Now, take your hands off me or I'll elbow you in the balls – they are about the only normal-sized thing about you, as I recall – and I will make your voice even higher.'

He released his hold, but remained standing behind her. 'Did you mean that? Did you mean what you just said?'

She sighed, angry with herself. She had to be nice, she had to be calm. 'Oh, come on, Tommy, we both know why I married you so why pretend otherwise? Sit down and have another drink.'

'Physically sick? I made you vomit?'

She couldn't stop herself as she snapped back, 'Yes, as in puke.' Again, she could have slapped herself. Never mind him, why was she getting into this? She could so easily have laughed it off, teased him into a good mood, but it was as if she was caught on a roller-coaster, and out it came, her face twisted in a vicious grimace. 'Sick, you made me sick! Have you any idea what it felt like? To have you clasped at my back, shoving your dick up my arse? It was like I had some animal clinging to me. All I did was grit my teeth and pray for you to get it over with. I hated it, hated every second you touched me with those squat square hands, pawing me like a dog, rough hands, hideous rough hands like dogs' paws.'

Kellerman was stricken, backing from her on the bed, treading the mattress as if on water. Ruda glared. Her eyes frightened him because he almost knew what she was going to say next. 'But then you, Tommy, you must really know what it felt like, what it really felt like . . . because you know, don't you, Tommy?'

His small hands clenched into fists. 'You fucking bitch, whatever I have done, you, for you to throw that in my face—'

'I warned you to shut up, but no – you kept on and on. I warned you.'

Kellerman slithered off the bed, and punched Ruda hard in the groin, then he reached for her bag, shouting at her. 'Give me my money, and get out, I never want to see you again, you whore, you two-faced bitch!'

Ruda snatched back her bag, hugging it tightly to her chest. He made a grab for the handle, and again she stepped back but he had it gripped in his hand and he tugged. Kellerman was very strong and they struggled between them. Suddenly he released his hold and Ruda fell backwards. 'You haven't got it, have you? You lied, you haven't got my money.'

Ruda was shaking, she fumbled with the bag, lying. 'Yes, I have, but I want our marriage licence before you get it.'

Kellerman crossed to the wardrobe and opened a drawer, his back to Ruda. He delved around, and then threw the envelope at her.

'Take it – and you owe me more than one hundred thousand. I saved your skin, I gave you a life, you bitch.

If it wasn't for me you'd still be on the streets, you'd still be a whore, a cheap disease-riddled whore – taking it up the arse like a dog.'

She spat at him, and he spat back then kicked out at her again. 'Whore!'

She swung the bag and hit him in the face. He dived away from her and picked up the chair. 'Come on, lion tamer, try me, try and tame me, *come on*.' Kellerman pushed at her with the chair, she thrust it away, and he crashed it against her thigh. She stumbled against a coffee table, tripped and fell backwards. He came at her, the chair above his head. 'You can't fight me, Ruda, I'll fucking beat the living daylights out of you!'

She rolled to one side as the chair crashed down on to the table. The heavy green ashtray slid to the ground. Ruda grabbed it, and as Kellerman came forward to hit her again, she held one chair leg with her left hand, and with her right hit him with the ashtray.

Kellerman seemed stunned for a moment. He touched his temple, saw the blood on his hand. 'You asked for it now!' He started to shriek, jumping up and down like a chimpanzee, then threw the chair aside and grabbed the bright red candlewick bedspread from the bed, holding it up and out in front of him like a matador. 'Come on, come on, Ruda. Try – try to hit me!'

Ruda lunged at him, and he dodged aside, laughing, tossing the bedspread this way and that. The red blurred, like a red-hot fire in her brain. 'Stop it, Tommy, just stop it!'

'Oh, you never used to say that to me, you used to say, "More, more, I love it." That's what you used to say. You loved it from the dog in heat! Come on, bitch!'

The swirling bedspread swished this way and that, and

the next minute she was on top of him, throwing it over his head, and the heavy ashtray came down, again and again. The bedspread swamped him, he struggled frantically. She heard him laughing, shrieking that she had missed him and it drove her into a frenzy. Ruda thudded her hand down, over and over again. She could feel his head, at one point held it firmly in her left hand, pressing it down as she hit him. She could feel the blows finding his face, over and over again.

She didn't know how many times she had struck him, but at last he was still and she sat back on her heels.

'Tommy? Tommy? Get up!'

He lay still, and she pulled at the coverlet, drew it away from his head. His face was a mass of blood, bloody bubbles frothed at his mouth and nose. She pushed herself away from him. 'Oh, God. Tommy, get up! *Get up!*'

He was motionless, his body swathed in the coverlet. She felt for his pulse, could find no heartbeat. She backed away, terrified, and leaned against the wall. She could feel every muscle tensing, then giving way as she slithered down the wall to sit like a rag doll, her legs stretched out in front of her.

'Oh, God, now what do I do? Tell me what to do.'

The television screen flickered, and she crawled over and turned up the volume, afraid someone would hear. Slowly, as the sound of the television cut through her senses, she began to think logically, talking herself calm. 'Get out fast, save yourself, Ruda. Get out, be careful, no one must know you came here. You never came here.'

She picked up the envelope and checked that the marriage licence was there. She took all his papers and stuffed them into her bag – his passport, diary, address book. She dragged him by his feet to the side of the bed then attempted to lift him, and it was then that the terrible realization dawned. Cradled in her arms was the only link with her past. Only Kellerman knew, he was the only person she had ever told, and now she had killed him. She sobbed because she remembered what it had meant to be able to tell someone . . . someone who had been in the darkness. She hugged him tightly, hard, dry, tearless sobs shaking her body as she recalled how, shortly after they had arrived in the United States, Tommy had tried to purge the past which clung unspoken to each of them. In their small trailer he had banged down two tumblers and opened a bottle of bourbon, hitching himself up on to a chair opposite Ruda. He had poured almost to the rim before he pushed the glass towards her. 'Right. You and me are gonna get loaded, and we're gonna let the ghosts free, because I think we'll both go crazy if we don't. We got a new life. Now we open and close the old. So, cheers!'

It had been a long, memorable night as they tried to empty the terrors that haunted them both. The more they drank, the more fragmented horrors were whispered. They had cried, they had comforted, and they had promised to keep each other's terrible secrets.

Now Ruda rocked him gently back and forth. She had broken the pact, she had hurt him more than any living soul could have done. His anguished shame when he had told her what he had been forced to do she had thrown back in his face. She had done that to him. 'I'm sorry, Tommy, forgive me . . .' His blood stained her face, clung to her hair, but she held him close in a last embrace and eventually her gentle rocking stopped, because nobody knew now. Only Tommy had known that she had killed before; no one must know she had killed again.

She began to gasp with panic, unable to get her breath. She felt dizzy and had to fill the glass he had used at the sink. She gulped the water, her hands shaking uncontrollably. She saw her own reflection in the mirror, the bloodstains, her frightened eyes staring back at herself. 'It was always different for me, Tommy. For you, every station, every corner. For me, every mirror.' She put her hands over her ears as if to block out that voice, 'Twins . . . Twins . . . Twins.' Ruda shouted, 'I know she is alive. *I know, I know!*'

The fury seared up within her, the fury of betrayal which had kept her alive in the early years, a fury which now gave her an inner strength to survive. With a forced calmness, she began to clear all traces of her presence from the room.

Ruda packed all Kellerman's belongings in his own case, emptied every drawer, checked the bathroom and collected his shaving equipment. They would find out who he was soon enough, but they could also find out something else: Ruda held Kellerman's toilet bag in her hand and rifled through it, opened the razor, and looked back to his still figure. She hurried to his side, rolled up his left shirt-sleeve until she found what she was looking for.

The razor slit deep into his arm. She cut a square, and began to slice deep, cutting away the tattoo, but then fell back. As she sliced the artery his blood spurted over her face, her chest. Kellerman was not dead. Her rage went out of control.

She wanted to be sick, could feel the bile rising from her stomach. She picked up the ashtray and hit him again, and again, her teeth gritted as she used all her force. Then she waited, knew this time he had to be dead, and carried the heavy marble ashtray into the bathroom, washed it, dried it, left it wrapped in the stained bloody towel, sure it was clean of prints. Then she washed around the sink, the taps. Suddenly she caught sight of her reflection again. Her eyes were crazy, her face white, the blood splashes now running like tears over her face. She backed out of the bathroom, rubbing frantically at her skin.

She had to face Kellerman again. The force of the last blow had made his head jerk sideways: his teeth had fallen out, his top set of dentures. As she tried to drag and push his body under the bed, the heel of her boot ground the dentures into the carpet. Her breath came in short, sharp pants, but she kept on working. She cleaned the room, the door handles, anything she may have touched. Then she found Kellerman's hat, was about to tuck it into his case but changed her mind. She turned over the blood-soaked rug on which he had been lying and tucked the stained area beneath the bed. She then fetched the 'Do Not Disturb' notice, hung it on the door and, carrying Kellerman's belongings in his own case, wearing his hat, she slipped down the stairs, afraid to use the lift in case she was seen. There was still no one in reception; she grabbed the guest register, and tore out the page with Kellerman's name.

Ruda was back at her trailer by midnight but she could hear Luis snoring loudly, his door ajar. She slipped out as silently as she had crept in and went over to the freezer trailer. Knowing she couldn't sleep, Ruda needed to keep herself occupied and she began to prepare the morning's feed for the cats. She was so intent on her work that she didn't hear the door open. When Luis spoke she sprang back in shocked surprise.

'Jesus Christ, what are you doing? Do you know what time it is?'

Ruda returned to cutting the meat. 'I couldn't sleep.'

'I've only just woken up. I saw the lights on, I thought someone was breaking in. What are you doing? It's after midnight.'

Ruda continued cutting the meat. 'I couldn't sleep because your snoring drove me to distraction. You left your door open – I've told you to keep it shut.'

Luis grinned sheepishly, and offered to give her a hand. She refused, and he came to her side. 'I'm sorry, I know what I did this afternoon was unforgivable.' He backed away from her, her blouse was covered in bloodstains. 'Why haven't you got one of the rubber aprons on? Have you seen your shirt?'

Ruda looked at her hands, covered in blood from the meat, but her shirt was covered in Kellerman's blood. 'It doesn't matter, it was falling apart. I'll chuck it out in the morning. You go back to bed, I'll be a while yet.'

Again Luis offered to help her, but she ignored him, and after a moment he left. Ruda washed and scrubbed down the tables, scrubbed and cleaned the knives, hammer and hatchets before she washed her own arms, scrubbed them with a wooden scrubbing brush, paying particular attention to her nails. She stared at her own left wrist, and one more time the full impact of what she had done that night dawned on her, but she would not give in to it. She compressed it down further and further inside her, closing it tightly, locking it out of sight in her mind.

She took off her blouse, and stuffed it into Kellerman's

case. She saw that the inside of her raincoat was stained and knew she would have to destroy it, along with all his belongings.

Ruda returned to her trailer, grabbed an old sweater, took off her stained trousers and pulled on an old pair of Luis's. She then carried Kellerman's suitcase, her raincoat, shirt and trousers to the big garbage barrels. She tossed his case into the huge bins waiting for the morning collection, dug deep into the filthy garbage and covered up the case. She then carried Kellerman's papers, and her marriage licence, to the main incinerators and eased back the burning hot lid. She stuffed the papers inside, one by one, making sure each caught fire. She watched the flames slowly lick and eat his treasured green passport, watched the black letters disintegrate. The flames, the heat, the charred black smoke, the smell made her so desperate to replace the lid that she didn't use the holder, but picked it up, red-hot, in her bare hand. Her skin hissed, but she didn't even feel the pain.

There was a low rumble of thunder and the rain became heavier. The ground was still muddy underfoot, and she slithered over the gangplanks in her haste to get inside. In the vast animals' arena, all were sleeping, stored undercover for the night. The heaters were on full blast, and three night-lights made a warm, soft pink light. Ruda headed towards her cages as there was a second rumble. The animals loathed thunder, and lightning made it even worse. She paused, head tilted to one side, but the storm was still too distant for any concern.

Ruda passed the tigers, huddled together; a few raised their heads in recognition of her smell, then returned to sleeping. Only Mamon was awake, his amber eyes bright. Ruda pressed close to the cage and called to him; he crawled on his belly closer to the bars. She pressed herself against his bars as he rubbed at them with his head. She stayed with Mamon for a while, comforted by him, soothed by him.

By the time she got into her bed she was exhausted. She drew her clean sheet closer to her naked body, tired but relieved it was over. Kellerman's passport, their marriage licence, the hotel guest register, all his papers were charred to a cinder, gone . . . all gone. It was over at last, and there was no witness, no one to threaten her newfound fame and security.

Ruda concentrated hard, just as she had as a child, waited until she felt the weight ease over her body, covering her like a gentle drowning, creeping upward from her toes, to her knees, to her heart, to her arms. She breathed deeply, making her mind lose consciousness. Gradually she allowed the weight to cover and spread, from her lungs, to her mouth. She slept in a deep, dreamless whiteness, protected, peaceful; no one could break through.

CHAPTER 4

T HE NIGHT that Tommy Kellerman died was the night Baroness Maréchal experienced the horror of a living death, the terrible white weight she was powerless to control or stop. The attack had left her so exhausted she remained sedated for the next day. She had no memory of the visit by Dr Franks, or of how many people monitored her slow recovery to consciousness. She had no knowledge of the murder that had taken place, but felt a drugged relief. The violent rage that had gripped and twisted inside her was quietened.

Dr Franks had asked that Anne Maria be allowed time off to visit him at his office. He wanted, as well, another interview with the Baron and Helen Masters, to find clues to what lay behind Vebekka's mental disorder. It was finally agreed that Hylda be brought in to sit with the Baroness until Anne Maria returned.

Ruda Grimaldi felt refreshed, as if her deep dreamless state had revitalized and calmed her. She went over to the canteen and ordered a full breakfast. Hungry, she waited impatiently for the food. She sipped her hot chocolate smiling to herself; her hands were steady, not so much as a tremor. She felt rested, she felt in total control.

When Hylda reached the hotel suite, the Baroness was in a deep sleep. She sat down in a comfortable chair by the bed, and all that could be heard in the vast silent bedroom was the click-click of her knitting needles.

Vebekka slept peacefully, motionless, her hands folded on the starched white linen sheet. She was wearing a white frilly negligée, which did not disguise the sharp bones of her neck and shoulders, the thinness of her arms. Her face was drawn, deep dark circles beneath her closed eyes. The lines around her mouth, her eyes, gave a skeletal look to her face. Saline and glucose drips were still attached to her hands; the tubes and needles had left dark black bruises and a bandage was still wrapped around her left wrist. The room was filled with flowers and baskets of fruit, the air heavy with their perfume. Hylda would have liked to open the window, but it was a dark thundery day, with rain showers.

Half an hour after Hylda arrived, the Baroness stirred and turned her head to face the maid. 'Would you be so kind as to take the drips out of my hand? They hurt me.'

'I don't think I should do that, Baroness, and Anne Maria is not here, and the Baron and Miss Masters are also out.'

The Baroness sighed, as if in acceptance, and Hylda turned back to her knitting. In a second, her charge had pulled out the drip needles, ripped off the adhesive and tossed them aside. She smiled coyly at Hylda, drew her hands beneath the covers, and curled up on her side.

97

Hylda could do nothing but pick up the adhesive from the floor and hang up the drips, switching off the lock.

'Hylda, will you call room service? I want some vanilla ice cream, with chocolate sauce, nuts, and those chocolate Oliver biscuits, plain chocolate, white biscuits – if they haven't got chocolate Oliver, I'll have any plain chocolate biscuits, plain black chocolate.'

Hylda obliged, and in due course a trolley was sent up with an array of chocolate biscuits and ice creams. She helped the Baroness sit up, and watched in stunned amazement as she slowly began to eat, first a spoonful of ice cream, then a small bite of biscuit. Like a squirrel she nibbled and sucked at the spoon with such childish delight that Hylda felt even more motherly towards her; she tried to hint that perhaps eating so much sweet food was not good for her, but her pleas were ignored, and the entire tray of sweet food was, nibble by nibble, demolished.

The Baroness snuggled down, closer to Hylda, dark chocolate stains round her mouth, even some on her finger tips. The click-click of Hylda's knitting needles soothed her, and she slept again. When the roll of thunder came, she didn't seem to wake, but her hand slipped from the warmth of the covers to hold Hylda's, and the knitting was quietly put aside.

Anne Maria inched open the door, and crept into the room; she put her fingers to her lips, and looked at the dressing table. She began to take all the medicine and pills visible on it and then rifled the vanity cases. With her arms full, she came to Hylda's side, and whispered, 'The doctor said she is to have no more medication, no more sedation, unless from him.'

Anne Maria hurried from the room and returned with

a large packet, unwrapped it, and held it out to show Hylda. 'You know what this is?' Hylda shook her head, and put her fingers to her lips for Anne Maria to lower her voice. 'It's a straitjacket. I don't know about this great doctor – if you ask me he's yet another quack – so I got this just in case.' She put down the jacket and was about to leave when she saw that the drips were not attached. 'Who took those out?'

Hylda gripped the Baroness's hand and whispered, 'I did, they were causing her pain. Let her sleep, she's sleeping . . .'

Anne Maria pursed her lips. 'She needs glucose, she's got to keep up her strength, I'll have to re-do them.'

Hylda felt the Baroness's fingers grip her so tightly that it hurt. She was awake, listening, but Hylda didn't give her away.

'When she wakes, I'll call you, but she has just eaten, and I think it is better she sleeps.'

Anne Maria hesitated and then flounced to the door. 'But I have not seen them, and I will not take any responsibility.'

The grip relaxed, and Hylda gently patted the Baroness's hand. She straightened the bedcovers, leaning over, her face close to the Baroness's, and was touched when the sick woman slipped her arms around her neck and kissed her lips in gratitude.

'I have a terrible fear of needles – of things in my body – she knows, but she hates me. Thank you.'

Hylda smiled, returned to her chair. She picked up her knitting, and the Baroness laughed softly. 'Not knitting needles, though.'

*

Dr Franks tilted his chair, pulling at his hair. 'Your nurse, Anne Maria, says your wife has some kind of . . . not exactly an obsession, with boxes, vanity boxes. She always travels with three, sometimes four, yes?'

The Baron looked puzzled. 'Yes, they are part of her luggage, one is for her jewellery, one for make-up, one for medical and – I suppose it seems excessive, but not out of the ordinary. I can't understand why on earth the girl would even discuss my wife's travelling accessories with you.'

Franks leaned on his elbows. 'Because I asked. You and your wife travel extensively, yes? And these boxes always accompany her?'

'Yes, so do our cases and trunks. Perhaps you will find some ulterior motive in the fact I always have more—'

Franks interrupted. 'I am only interested in your wife at the moment, Baron. She always travels with an extensive wardrobe but rarely if ever wears three-quarters of the contents. According to Anne Maria, many items your wife insists on travelling with have *never* been worn, yes? What I am trying to determine is, does your wife appear, in your personal opinion, to have items of clothing in very different styles? Perhaps appear to you as different characters, or seem different to you at times?'

'That is the entire reason I am here. My wife has periods of sanity and insanity.'

Franks wandered around the room. 'Has anyone ever suggested to you that your wife may have a personality disorder? Could possibly be a multiple personality?'

The Baron shook his head and glared at Helen Masters.

Franks turned his attention to her. 'What do you think?'

'No, I don't think she is – or I didn't. But she

said something that'll interest you. I wrote it down, actually . . .'

Helen opened her bag and took out a small notebook. 'Quote, when I found her last night, she said, "We have done something terrible." Not I, but we.'

The telephone rang and Franks snatched it up, but spoke only for a second before he handed it to the Baron. 'It's for you, long distance. If you wish to be in private, I am sure Dr Masters and I can—'

The Baron gestured with his hand for them to stay as he listened to the caller. He then covered the mouthpiece. 'It's all right, it's Françoise, my secretary, from Paris.'

The doctor handed him a pen and notepad.

The call went on for some time, the Baron saying little but making notes. Helen whispered to Franks, 'She is very particular about her clothes, they are in many cases designed for her, but I have never noticed a marked difference in styles – say little girl to tart – I would simply say that the Baroness has a wardrobe any woman would be envious of. However, she does seem obsessive about the vanity cases.'

She was interrupted as the Baron dropped the phone back on the hook, and sighed. 'Gerard, my man in New York, has been having great difficulty tracing my wife's family. He started at her old model agency. They had no record of Vebekka ever having been signed with them. They then passed him on to someone who had run the agency before them. He said he had represented a girl called Rebecca Lynsey; he recalled she later changed her name to Vebekka, using just her Christian name for work. He had no records on hand but would see if he could trace his ex-wife who ran the business with him. But one thing he was sure about – or as sure as he could be . . .'

the Baron was very disturbed as he continued, 'He said that my wife's maiden name, Lynsey, was not her real name either, but one used for modelling. He could not recall ever having heard her real surname. Why would she have lied to me? I don't understand it.'

Franks rubbed his head. 'But when her father died, didn't you see a name, something to indicate that Lynsey wasn't her family name?'

The Baron shook his head. 'Gerard'll call again as soon as he has anything else. He's going to Philadelphia tonight. I don't understand, I mean Lynsey was the name on her passport, I'm sure of it. I've asked him to fax any new developments to the hotel.'

Franks raised an eyebrow at Helen. 'Well, this is getting very interesting. Vebekka is really Rebecca, and you have never heard her mention this, never seen it on any document? She has never referred to herself as Rebecca?'

The Baron shook his head. 'No, never. I have always known her as Vebekka Lynsey.'

Franks patted the Baron's shoulder. 'When she was in New York, did she meet anyone there, have friends there?'

'No, we have mutual friends, or family friends, but I have never seen anyone walk up to her and call her Rebecca, if that is what you mean. Also I have never seen her birth certificate, there never seemed to be a reason before now – that is, if there is a valid reason now.'

Franks's eyes turned flinty as he said, 'I am simply trying to find clues to your wife's mental problems, because I want to begin my treatment as soon as she is physically capable of walking into this place unaided.'

Franks sat on his desk, his heel tapping. The Baron's antagonism infuriated him, but he could not let his irritation show. Pleasantly, he asked, 'You recalled yesterday – Baron? Are you listening to me? – you recalled the first time you witnessed your wife's mental instability, yes?'

The Baron nodded. Franks asked if he could remember any other instances.

The Baron sighed, crossing his legs, staring at his highly polished shoe. 'I mentioned the circus. Er, to be quite honest there have been so many, over so many years and . . .'

He paused, and Franks knew something had come to him: he could see it, feel it in the way the Baron frowned then hesitated, as if recalling the moment and then dismissing it. Franks leaned forward. 'Yes? What is it?'

The Baron shrugged. 'It was in the late seventies, and this one had no connection to any of the children. We were in New York. We were at my apartment, we were both reading the *New York Times*. She was reading the real-estate section, I had the rest of it. She suddenly snatched the paper from my hands; it fell on to the table, the coffee pot tipped over me. I don't think she intended to spill the coffee, though at the time I believed she had done it for some perverse reason – perhaps because I wasn't paying her any attention, I don't know, sometimes she is exceptionally childish. Anyway, I suppose I behaved childishly too, because I insisted she give me the paper back. She refused, there was an argument, not a very pleasant one, and—'

The Baron shrugged his shoulders again, as if he suddenly felt the episode not worth continuing. Franks, however, leaned forwards: 'Go on . . . she took the rest of the paper, and then what?'

'Well, as I recall, I went into my bathroom, showered, and was dressing when the maid – no, it was my butler –

said there seemed to be a slight fracas in the foyer. The apartment was, still is, exceptionally well managed. The block has a foyer and a doorman. Directly next door to the building is a small news-stand. My wife, still in her dressing-gown, was, so I was told, in the foyer, her arms full of every conceivable newspaper, and when I went down I discovered her sitting on the floor ripping the newspapers apart, throwing pages aside. She was on her hands and knees, scouring each page, but to this day, I have no idea what for or why. All I know is that it was exceptionally embarrassing, and she took a great deal of cajoling and persuasion to return to the apartment.' Franks waited, expecting more, but the Baron clasped his hands together. 'That's it, really.'

'Did you ever ask her why she wanted the papers?'

'Of course.'

'Did she give you an explanation?'

'No, she didn't speak at all for over a week. She seemed elated, slightly hysterical, always smiling, but I couldn't get a word out of her as to why she was behaving in such a way, or what on earth had sparked the breakdown.'

'Breakdown?'

'Well, that is what the therapist called it, and Vebekka calmed down eventually, even seemed to forget the entire incident.'

'Did you ever check through the papers, find anything in them to give a reason for her behaviour?'

The Baron shook his head. 'I took it to be just another of her . . . problems.'

Franks remained silent for a moment before asking if the Baron could get his contact in the United States to check back to the exact date and obtain copies of the papers. The Baron looked to Helen Masters with an exasperated shrug of his immaculate shoulders, but agreed to try. Franks fell silent again, closing his eyes in concentration, and then asked, softly, whether when the Baron said his wife behaved childishly this meant her voice altered? That she sounded like a child?

'It was just a manner of speech, her act was childish. She didn't, as far as I can recall, speak in a childlike voice.'

Franks noted it again – the fleeting look of guilt or recall passing over the Baron's face. 'Yes? You've remembered something else?'

The Baron stared at the wall. 'She cried, in the night. I woke up, or was wakened by, her crying. I was confused because it sounded – dear God I've never thought of it before – but it was high-pitched, like a child. In fact, so much so, that for a moment, half asleep, I was confused and then I remembered the boys were in Paris.'

Franks said nothing, simply waited.

After a long pause the Baron continued. 'I went into her room and she was sitting up in bed. There was a shadow on the wall from the curtains, the lights from the streets. She was sobbing, pointing to the wall. She said, let me think, what was it now? . . . er . . . oh, yes, she said the curtains were a – no, they were a "Black Angel", then she said over and over, "It wasn't true! It wasn't true." I have no idea what she meant, but when I closed the curtains tightly and there was no more shadow she went back to sleep, but her voice . . .' The Baron looked this time to Helen, helpless. 'I would describe it now, it was . . . it was like a little girl's, the way she shook her shoulders, and . . . how would you say, that hiccup, you know, the way children do? It was as if she was a child having a nightmare.'

Franks clapped his hands. 'Now we are getting somewhere, and I think some tea would go down well. For you, Baron? And you, Helen?'

Before either had time to reply Franks had scuttled out, barking to some unseen assistant that he wanted tea. He returned to the room, and produced a child's picture-book; he held it like a piece of evidence, as if in a court of law. 'Your wife removed, stole, slipped into her handbag, a similar child's book when she was waiting in reception yesterday. Interesting?'

'When did she do that?' asked Helen Masters.

'When she was here, sitting with Maja. Maja saw her do it. Odd, don't you think? Especially as it's in German. Do you know if this book is also published in Paris, or the United States?'

The Baron was standing with his back to the room, staring from the window, his hands deep in his trouser pockets. 'How would I know?'

'Has your wife stolen or ever been involved in shoplifting?'

The Baron snapped, 'No, never, my wife is not a thief!'

Helen accepted the tea-tray from Maja at the door and carried it to the desk. Franks joked that kleptomania was about the only thing not diagnosed in the Baroness. His humour did not strike the right chord, and Helen quickly passed round the teacups, then sat on a hard-backed chair.

Franks seemed unaware of the atmosphere in the small room. He munched one biscuit after another in rapid succession until the plate was cleared. 'Would you say your wife suffered from agoraphobia?'

The Baron replied curtly that his wife was neither agoraphobic nor claustrophobic, turning to Helen as if for confirmation. She wouldn't meet his eyes.

Franks brushed the biscuit crumbs from his cardigan. 'But she is obsessive. Tell me more about her obsessions.'

'What woman isn't!' the Baron retorted, and then he apologized. 'I'm sorry – that was a stupid reply, considering the situation. Forgive me, but I find this – this constant barrage of questions disturbing, perhaps because . . . because I am searching for the correct answers and I am afraid that everything I say, when placed under the microscope, so to speak, makes me appear as if I have not been caring enough, when, I assure you, nothing could be further from the truth.'

The room was silent. The Baron had cupped his chin in his hands, his elbows resting on his knees. Helen Masters focused on a small brown flower-shaped stain on the wall directly in front of her. Franks looked from one to the other. 'Maybe we should take a break now.'

Helen picked up the files as Franks gave her a tiny wink. She went ahead to the waiting car and was about to step inside when the Baron announced that he had to return to the doctor's reception. 'I won't be a moment, wait for me here.'

Dr Franks looked up in surprise as the Baron tapped on his open door and entered, but did not ask if the Baron had forgotten something. He knew intuitively that the Baron wished to speak to him alone. Dr Franks cleared his throat. 'You know, if you would prefer to have these sessions with me alone, Helen is a very understanding woman, perhaps more than you realize. She is, after all, a very good doctor herself.'

'Yes, I know, of course I know, I have tremendous respect for her. I wanted to talk to you privately though.' The Baron could not meet Franks's eyes and turned his face away from him. 'I'd like to tell you something. It concerns my wife – obviously, I suppose.' He smiled, and Franks was struck anew by the man's perfect features, his strong aquiline nose, and deep dark blue eyes.

The Baron moved to the office window and stood with his back to the room. 'I have had many women, known many, I suppose you might call me a promiscuous man, but . . . I did love my wife. I say did, because over the years her behaviour, her illness, has gradually made me hate her. I have, may God forgive me, wished her dead more often than I care to admit, and yet, when she attempts to kill herself . . . my remorse, my dread of her dying and leaving me, is very genuine, and my relief when she recovers, very real.' He rested his head against the glass. 'She was, doctor, the most beautiful creature. I wanted to possess her the moment I laid eyes on her. She simply took my breath away. She was sweetness itself, she was naïve, she was nervous, like an exquisite exotic bird, and her fragility made me almost afraid of her, as though if I held her too tightly, kissed her too deeply, she would be crushed. The more I got to know her, the more delightful she became, but in those days my fear of—' He hesitated as if searching for the right word, then turned to face Franks. 'I had a fear of breaking her, that I could break her, hurt her. She soon assured me I could not, and during our courtship she became more vibrant, even more outgoing. She was very amusing with a wicked sense of humour, a great tease. She was, doctor, everything I had ever dreamed. I married her against tremendous opposition from my family, especially my mother. Perhaps Mama had some insight into Vebekka, but I would hear none of it. I refused to listen. The first few months of marriage, I don't think I have ever known such happiness,

108

such total commitment. I had never loved like that, or felt so loved, or been so satisfied.'

The Baron moved from the window, one, two paces, then turned back. His voice was hardly audible. 'I had my first sexual encounter when I was fourteen. I had countless women, from society to brothel. I was a normal and healthy man, I was obviously eligible, and known to be wealthy. I had very rarely, if ever, had to court a woman. Perhaps that was why I wanted Vebekka so much, because she was, to begin with, unobtainable and completely uninterested in me. We did not sleep together until after we were married. I know it may sound laughable but I presumed she was a virgin.'

Franks leaned back in his chair, waiting, but eventually he had to ask as the Baron seemed wrapped in his own thoughts. 'Was she? A virgin?'

The Baron drew out a chair and sat down. 'No . . . no, she was not, she was very experienced. I was a little – no, more than a little – I was shocked. My bride was sexually aggressive, demanding, explicit, and insatiable, a state that I quickly rose to and, as I have said, the first few months with her – I have never known anything so totally consuming, I never experienced such peaks of emotion, such sexual gratification, and then . . . then she became pregnant.'

Franks threaded his hands together, making a cat's cradle with his fingers, waiting.

After a moment the Baron continued, but was obviously very uncomfortable, running his index finger around the collar of his shirt, as if it constricted him in some way. 'A few months after she fell pregnant, she changed. She would not allow me to touch her, allow me anywhere near her, she was terrified of losing the baby by having sex. And then this illness, whatever name we want to call it, began. I was broken, she broke my heart, doctor. It was as if I had never known her, she behaved as if she hated me, and even when I was told that it was because she was ill, all I felt was rejection. My wife had rejected me.'

Franks stared at the church tower he had made with his fingers, then split his hands apart and placed them flat on the desk. 'But after the birth, she was herself again? Yes? Did you have your old sexual relationship again?'

'No, she continued to reject me as a husband for a long time, at least eight months. Then all of a sudden it was as if it had never happened. I returned home one evening and she was my Vebekka again. But I could not be turned on and off like a tap.'

'So you rejected her?'

The Baron laughed, it was a gentle, self-mocking laugh. 'My wife was a very persuasive woman. For two months it was like a second honeymoon, and then as quickly as it had begun, it was over – she was pregnant again.' The Baron explained that after his second son was born he had attempted to persuade his wife to use birth control, but she had adamantly refused. So the pattern had repeated itself yet again, but after that third time, when she had been ill for six months, he had no desire to be reunited, no desires left.

'So you stopped loving her, after your third child?'

'I realized she was sick, knew by then that she did not really know what she was doing during these periods. So I simply arranged my life around her.' His face flushed with guilt. He had not been at home as often as he should

110

have been, he blamed himself. There was nothing of great importance in anything the Baron was discussing, but Franks waited patiently.

And then the guilty expression in the Baron's eyes was replaced by an icy coldness. When he spoke, his voice grew quieter, almost vicious. 'I knew my wife had taken to leaving the house late in the evening. She never took the car, always hired a taxi, and on many occasions did not return home until the following morning. I began to have her followed, for her own good, you understand?'

'Were you considering a divorce?'

The Baron dismissed the question with a shake of his head. He spoke quickly, not disguising his disgust. 'She was picking up men, truck drivers, cab drivers, wandering around the red-light districts. As soon as I discovered this, I faced her with it, and she denied she had ever left the house, but she continued her midnight crawls. Even when I was threatened with blackmail, she denied she was – virtually soliciting.'

'You mean, she was paying for sex?'

'Occasionally, or she was paid. It was a terrible time, and I was at my wits' end. I have never considered divorce. She is my wife and the mother of my children. We are a Catholic family. It was out of the question.'

'Was? Have you changed your mind?'

The Baron picked up his coat, gave a distant smile. 'Just a slip of the tongue.' His arrogance returned, he was remote, icy cold. 'If you can do nothing, then I am – and I assure you I have never considered this before – but I am prepared to have my wife certified.'

The control slipped again. The Baron leaned over the

111

desk. 'I don't understand myself, you see, I just don't understand, after everything I have been through! I don't understand.'

Franks slowly stubbed out his cigar. 'Understand what exactly?'

'That I can . . . last night, I felt attracted to my wife. I did not believe myself capable of wanting her again. I must not allow her to manipulate me. I am tired, worn out by her. You are my last chance, perhaps hers. I ask you not just to help my wife, but me – help me!'

Franks nodded, it was time for dinner, his stomach rumbled. He hoped the Baron would leave.

At that moment, Maja tapped on the door and popped her head in. 'I'm sorry to interrupt, but Dr Masters said to tell you the car's still waiting, but not to worry, she has taken a taxi back to the hotel.'

Franks gave Maja a pleading look.

'And you have another appointment in half an hour, doctor!' Maja closed the door.

Franks rose to his feet, and the Baron was already by the door, his hand on the handle. 'Thank you for your time, I appreciate it.'

Franks clasped the Baron's hand in a firm handshake. 'I thank you for your honesty, and let us hope we will gain some results.'

At last Franks was alone and he slumped into his chair, buzzing the intercom for Maja. She appeared almost immediately, and smiled. 'My, that was a long return visit! I hope it was beneficial.'

Franks laughed, and rubbed his belly. 'I need food. I am starving to death!'

Maja brought in a tray of sandwiches and coffee, plus the paper which Franks hadn't yet had time to read. He settled back, making himself comfortable, his eyes roaming over the headlines, and then he flipped the paper open to the second page, glancing over the ads for the forthcoming circus, paying no attention to the short news bulletins. One five-line article stated that the *Polizei* had discovered a body in a small East Berlin hotel the previous day.

CHAPTER 5

THE CHAMBERMAID had not changed the bed linen of room 40, because the 'Do Not Disturb' card was hanging from the door. It was not until later in the afternoon when she was vacuuming the corridor that she tapped on the closed door, waited for a reply and, receiving none, entered using her master set of keys. The curtains were drawn, the television set turned on. The room was neat, except for the unmade bed, its coverlet bunched on the floor under the bed.

The maid fetched clean towels, sheets and pillowcases, and went back into the room. She tossed the clean linen down on the chair and drew back the curtains. She went into the bathroom, collected the dirty towels and dropped them on to the floor. Two were bloodstained and she picked them up between finger and thumb distastefully. She then replaced the towels with fresh ones, and was washing down the sink and bath when a friend popped her head round the door to ask if she was nearly through for the day as it was after three.

Both women were due off at two-thirty and both had other jobs to do in the early evening. Together they began to clean the room, and one pulled the sheets back. 'It's not been slept in. Christ! It's freezing in here, they must have turned off the central heating, some people are weird.'

Both women bent down to the rolled bedcover and tugged it from beneath the bed. They felt it catch on one of the wire mattress springs, and pulled together. And screamed, virtually in unison.

Tommy Kellerman's body rolled free of the bedcover, the section covering his head dried hard with black blood.

Screaming at the tops of their voices the women ran down the corridor towards the elevators. Someone carrying a loaded tea-tray of dirty crockery was about to step out of the lift when they appeared, arms waving and shouting garbled half-screams as they pointed frantically to the room. The laden man hurried to the room and was in no more than a few seconds, when he came out, his face drained as he stuttered, 'Dear God, it's a child – somebody's killed a child in there!'

By the time the *Polizei* arrived, the corridor was filled with gawping spectators, guests and the two chambermaids. The manager of the hotel was trying to keep some semblance of order, shouting for people to stand back, but he was very unsteady on his feet, having been dragged out of his quarters. The tails of his collarless shirt hung out over his hurriedly drawn-on trousers.

Polizei Oberrat Torsen Heinz pushed his way through the throng, holding up his badge. Three uniformed officers followed behind him, shoving people away. Torsen Heinz was the first to arrive at the open bedroom door. He asked if the doctor or forensic teams had been there. He could see the tiny body, the small foot in the red sock, and his stomach turned over. He did not attempt to remove the congealed mess beneath the bedcover, and trod gingerly and carefully around the body.

The manager hung at the doorway, peering into the room, demanding to know who had torn pages out of the registration book.

The doctor arrived and took only a second to certify the body as deceased, which was all he was required to do, but until he had verified the obvious work could not commence. The pathologist came in, followed by two technicians from the forensic department. They began yelling for everyone to clear out of the room.

Oberrat Heinz checked the room quietly, using a pencil to open a couple of drawers. The doctor looked over to him as he departed. 'It's not a kid, it's a dwarf or a midget and he's taken one hell of a beating, but that's rather stating the obvious. G'night.'

The pathologist carefully slipped plastic bags round the tiny red socks; he applied a bag to Kellerman's right arm and hand, and then reached for his left. He stood up rubbing his knee and, looking down, realized he was kneeling on a set of broken dentures. He beckoned Heinz. 'I'm sorry, I think I may have broken them. My mistake, but someone should have checked this area.'

Heinz stared at the broken teeth, and then stepped out of the way as the pathologist continued his work, about to wrap Kellerman's left arm in a protective plastic bag. 'Jesus, look at this, it's been hacked, a big chunk of skin removed, just above the wrist!'

Heinz sent one of the uniformed officers out to check for any rubbish that might have been removed. The pathologist finished wrapping the tiny body, and then his

116

team slipped a plastic sheet beside Kellerman, rolled him on top of it, tied all four ends and lifted the body up.

'He booked in early yesterday,' Torsen Heinz said to no one in particular. He tugged at his blond hair, watched as two men dusted door handles and mirror, then made his way down to the so-called reception area. The manager, now wearing a jacket, insisted he had been on duty and had seen no one who was not an official guest. Heinz listened, knowing that local tarts used the place for their clients, but said nothing, simply asked to see the guest register. The manager shoved it towards him, pointing with a stubby, dirty fingernail to the torn pages. He scratched his greasy head, tried to recall the dead man's name, but the name escaped him.

'What about his passport, did you see his passport, retain it?'

The manager was sweating. 'I saw it – checked it, I know the rules. He had luggage, a sort of greenish carryall, did you find it?'

'But you don't recall his name?'

'No, he just signed, and I gave him the key, told him what floor. I was on the phone when he checked in.'

'What nationality?'

'American – Kellerman!' The manager beamed. 'I remember, it was Kellerman.'

No one Heinz questioned had seen anyone entering the room and he and his sergeant took off for the mortuary to see what they could learn there. It had closed for the night.

Heinz returned early the following morning. Tommy Kellerman's naked body was even more tragic in death than in life, his squat hands spread out palm upwards, his

117

legs spread-eagled, his pride exposed, a wicked freak of nature to give this small, stunted body a penis any man would be proud to display: it was virtually down to the kneecaps on his twisted legs.

The bedcover had to be inched and cut away from his head as the blood had clotted like glue. There was hardly a feature left intact: nose broken, cheek, jaw and forehead completely concave; blood clotted in his eyes, his nose, his ears and his gaping mouth; the bottom row of false teeth had cut into his upper lip, giving him the look of a Neanderthal man, a chimp – even more so as his thick curly hair was spiky with his own blood.

The pathologist ascertained that Kellerman had died near to midnight the night before he was found and had eaten some four hours before he was hammered to death. He spent considerable time over the open wound on Kellerman's left forearm: he could tell it had been made while Kellerman was alive, and that the skin cut away was probably a tattoo, judging by the faint edge of blue left along one skin edge. The pathologist added that whoever killed Kellerman must have been covered in blood, as the main artery had been cut on the tattoo wrist.

Kellerman's clothes were spread out on the lab tables; again they gave a tragic impression of the wearer as they were so small, so childlike. In his underpants semen stains mingled with the final evacuation of his bowels: it was ascertained that he had ejaculated shortly before he was killed.

His pockets were empty, apart from a rubber band and a Zippo lighter. His clothes were tagged and listed, his body washed and tagged, placed in a child's mortuary bag, laid on a drawer and pushed into the freezer.

Torsen Heinz hung around for a while, then returned to the hotel to question the hall porter.

The toothless decrepit man could recall no one entering the hotel while he was working, or at least no one who warranted any special attention. He did recall seeing a big man, wearing a black hat, outside the hotel – in fact, the man could possibly have just left the main entrance, he couldn't be sure, he had simply passed him on the street as he emptied the rubbish. He could not describe him in any detail, just that he was tall, wearing a black hat, and it was around eleven or perhaps a bit later.

Torsen Heinz returned to his office and sat at his large wooden desk. The station was in a baroque-style building in the Potsdam district of East Berlin, and for equipment there were half a dozen old typewriters and an obsolete telephone system incapable of connecting with West Berlin. The principal piece of modern technology was a microwave oven, installed two months before to heat up the officers' lunches. Torsen and his men had been unable to keep up with the sharp increase in criminal activity since the fall of the socialist regime. Previously East Berlin's criminal behaviour had been hushed up by the Stasi secret police or played down by the state-controlled media. Now, Polizei Oberrat Heinz and forty-odd uniformed officers had to learn as fast as possible to make their own decisions.

Sitting with his microwave-heated breakfast sausages Torsen felt swamped. None of the officers he had assigned to the Kellerman case had made any report because they had clocked out promptly at six o'clock. No matter how much Torsen argued that they were no longer working from nine to six but if necessary round the clock, they were too used to the old regime to change their working habits. There was not one man on duty yet, and it was half past eight. Torsen had already been working for several hours.

Alone, he sifted through the statements and facts he had so far gathered about the dwarf. He surmized that Kellerman was possibly an American citizen as, according to the hotel manager, he spoke with an American accent. Without a passport or any documents to substantiate this, he decided he should first contact the US Embassy to see if they had any record of his arrival in Berlin. The next call would be to the main circus which was being heralded as the biggest event of the season. He tried to contact the embassy, but the telephone switchboard was still closed down, waiting for the telephonist to arrive. He finished his breakfast, carefully folded his cloth napkin and put it back in his briefcase, washed his hands at the cracked sink and returned to his desk. There was a photograph of his father on the wall behind the desk, wearing the same uniform as Torsen's. Gunter Heinz's picture was brown with age. Torsen gave the photograph a brief nod and determined that until it was absolutely necessary he would not go cap in hand to the West Berlin police; they had already been forced to assist him on a number of cases, and he had taken a lot of ridicule from his West Berlin 'colleagues' with their high-tech computers and fax machines. He wondered how well they would cope without so much as one single telephone connected after 6 p.m. or before 9 a.m.

He turned in his chair and looked at the memos taped to the wall beneath his papa's frowning face. 'Accept no coincidence – only facts.' He had stuck the typed scrap of paper up after he had been made chief inspector at exactly the same age his father had been promoted; his father's memo had been written when Torsen had first made the decision to follow his father into the *Polizei*.

Gunter Heinz was now residing in a home for the elderly, suffering from senility, for most of the time happily unaware of his surroundings – or for that matter who he was – but occasionally having strange flashes of recall, as if the clouds lifted, and in these moments Torsen was able to converse with him, even play chess. Torsen had arranged with the nurses that whenever his father was lucid, they call him. The last time he had hurried to visit, however, the old man had glared at him and asked who the hell he was. Torsen had replaced his chessboard in his case.

The nurse had apologized, whispering that she was sorry to have called him, but earlier in the day his father had asked to speak with his son on an important matter. Torsen had understood and was grateful for her kindness in contacting him. During Torsen's conversation with the nurse, his father was ripping small pieces of paper tissue from a box, carefully licking each tiny scrap, sticking it on his nose and blowing it off like a snowflake. A sad spectacle, but one that would have been laughable if it had not been his own father.

The desk phone pinged, signalling that the switchboard was now in operation. Torsen rang the US Embassy. They had no record of an American citizen named Kellerman in residence in East Berlin, but suggested that the border patrols be contacted, since if the deceased came across from Western Europe by train or even by bus then his particulars might have been recorded. The flow of refugees arriving in Germany was causing mayhem, and there was an attempt to record everyone travelling in by car or train. It was also possible that Kellerman had used the main airport and travelled to the East section; the airport authorities should also be approached.

Torsen sent two uniformed officers to try to discover Kellerman's origins and then set off with Sergeant Volker Rieckert for his first destination, the circus.

The patrol car got bogged down in the mud, but the attendant would not let them drive any closer to the private trailers and the performers' car park. Inspector Torsen displayed his ID, but it had no effect; the rain-coated attendant simply pointed to a railing, also bogged down in the mud.

Torsen and his sergeant sloshed across the space that would eventually be used by the customers, but which now resembled a bomb-site; deep holes and cinders made the long walk to the trailer sections and big tents a hazard. Their trousers were soaked at the bottom, their hair plastered to their heads, as they made their way towards the cashier's trailer.

The girl had dyed bright red hair, with a pink comb stuck in the top that matched her lipstick. She looked at his ID and blew a large pink bubblegum bubble, then pointed towards the manager's building. Torsen swore under his breath as he felt the mud squelch into his hand-knitted woollen socks.

The circus's administrator welcomed the men into his office. It was in a small building at the side of a massive tent, and the office itself was small and overheated. It was filled with neat filing cabinets, and the walls were covered in large circus posters. Romy Kelm, the administrator, a balding bespectacled man, introduced himself formally and ordered tea to be brought.

122

The two officers were settled on folding chairs, and Mr Kelm seated himself behind his pristine desk. He was quickly able to provide Torsen with a Christian name: the dead man could very well be Tommy Kellerman. Kelm hastened to add that Kellerman was not employed by the circus, but had been more than twenty years ago. He knew also that Kellerman had been in gaol in the United States, was prone to fighting and drunken brawls, and had stolen from his own people. He had absconded with a company's wages eight years previously when attached to the Kings Circus, a smaller touring company. The circus telegraph system of internal newspapers had given details of his theft and subsequent prison sentence. Kelm inferred that a number of people still resented Kellerman, to many of whom he owed money.

Torsen was given a detailed list of all the performers gathering for the opening night who may have known Kellerman or worked with him. Kelm told him that the dead man's ex-wife, Ruda Kellerman, was a star performer and was, in fact, still using the name Kellerman, although she had remarried long ago.

Torsen's head was reeling; it could take him a few weeks, even months, to accumulate all the data he was being handed. His sergeant was dumbstruck as he scrawled names and contact numbers endlessly on his pad. They spent more than two hours in the little office, and the small room became so hot that both police officers could feel their socks and shoes drying out, stiffening along with the bottoms of their trousers.

Finally, Torsen was assisted into his raincoat and handed a neat layout of the trailers, so that it would be easy for the two officers to get their bearings, and the dapper Mr Kelm reiterated his eagerness to help. The circus did not want any adverse publicity, their biggest show of the season was to open in a few days' time, their acts had come from all over the world, the opening night was to be a major occasion. Kelm was anxious to know whether anyone from his company was involved in the Kellerman incident and, if so, he wanted it dealt with as quietly and as quickly as possible. He was virtually saying to Torsen that if it was one of ours, get him, take him and get it over with. He kept gesturing to the posters as if to confirm what he was saying: 'Circus people often get a lot of ordinary folk against them, as if they are tinkers or gyppos. We are all good God-fearing people, who work hard for a living. Many of our people are world-famous and we are proud to present to a united Germany what we hope will be the finest display ever seen in this country. We have extended the main arena, and built a second and third ring . . .' As he ushered the policemen into the corridor, he said he felt sure no one in the present company was involved with Kellerman, that he was a man who had been virtually ostracized, a man who had turned against his people, who was unemployable . . . blacklisted.

Torsen suggested gently, without malice, that Kellerman's reputation surely meant that if many people detested him enough, perhaps one could have wanted to kill him. He received no reply, just a cold stare from the washed-out eyes behind the rimless glasses, but Kelm managed a tight smile, saying quietly he hoped Torsen was incorrect, and again offering any assistance necessary, saying that he was always available.

Torsen eased open the main exit door, and looked out at the downpour. He swore, then hunched up his shoulders and stepped out. His sergeant followed, tucking his thick notepad into his pocket, along with the free posters and cards that had been pressed into his hands by Kelm for his children – if they wanted to see the show, all they had to do was contact him and he would arrange tickets.

The inspector sloshed ahead and Rieckert quickened his pace, hunching his shoulders in his navy raincoat. 'Las Vegas, you see that poster on the high wire act! How much do you think a set-up like this costs?' He received no answer as he caught up with Torsen. 'That Kelm was pretty helpful, wasn't he?'

'Yeah he was, wasn't he? It's called get off our backs, schmuck! We've got our work cut out for us. You want to split up or shall we start it together?'

A string of horses draped in protective blankets was led past them on a single rein by a sour-faced boy. Rieckert stared with open curiosity, and then looked at four equally sour-faced men wearing dark blue overalls. They carried pitchforks, and one promptly cleared away some horse dung as the others hurried on towards the practice arena. Rieckert's jaw dropped again as coming up behind him were five massive elephants. He shouted to ask Torsen if he had seen them. Torsen looked at him – it was hard to miss five fully grown elephants.

The two men plodded on through the mud, heading towards the main trailer park. Torsen had decided he would interview the ex-Mrs Kellerman first. By the time he discovered they had been reading the trailer route upside down, he was sodden again and his hair was dripping. After asking a number of scurrying figures with umbrellas and waterproof capes, they arrived at the Grimaldi trailer. Torsen dragged his suede shoes across the grids outside and tapped on the door of the glistening trailer. Behind him Rieckert looked at it with admiration, wondering how much it was worth. The door opened, and Torsen looked up, still on the lower step.

'My name is Detective Chief Inspector Torsen Heinz, and this is Detective Sergeant Rieckert. Would it be possible for us to come in?'

Grimaldi stared, Torsen hesitated, asked politely if Grimaldi spoke German, and received a curt nod of confirmation.

'We would like to speak to a . . . your wife. She was Mrs Kellerman, yes?'

Grimaldi nodded, and then stepped aside. Torsen moved up the steps to enter. The officers were instructed to take off their shoes, and there was considerable fumbling around at the door, as Rieckert couldn't undo his soaking laces. The two men's coats were hung on a hook at the back of the front door while both pairs of shoes were propped up outside, promptly filling with rainwater.

Grimaldi gestured for the men to follow him and, now abreast of him, Torsen realized they were of similar height, six feet, but that Grimaldi was a big, raw-boned man, with very broad shoulders, whereas Torsen was bordering on skinny.

Grimaldi sat on a thickly cushioned bench seat, and offered coffee, but both men declined, sitting side by side on the opposite padded bench seat, grateful for the cushion after the hard-backed chairs in the administration office.

'Ruda's feeding the cats, should be back shortly.'

Rieckert took covert looks around the spacious room, greatly impressed, while Torsen stared at the posters and photographs, then gave a charming smile of recognition. 'I saw you – saw you performing, do you call it? Many years ago. I was just a kid, but I have never forgotten it, you were fabulous.'

Grimaldi's dark eyes were suspicious, brooding; he hardly acknowledged the compliment, but flicked a look in the direction of the posters. He pointed to the one of Ruda, and then looked back. 'This is Ruda, you see, Ruda Kellerman. She still uses his name. What's that little piece of shit done now?'

Torsen straightened his back. 'He's been murdered, sir, we are both from the East Berlin *Polizei*. He was murdered in East Berlin some time the night before last.'

Grimaldi smiled, showing big even teeth, a little yellowish, wolfish, then he laughed out loud and slapped his cord trousers with his huge hand. 'Well, you'll have a lot of contenders. He was a detestable creature, real vermin, somebody should have smothered him years ago. What was he doing in East Berlin?'

'We don't know, sir, and as yet we have had no formal identification of the body, but we are led to believe it was Tommy Kellerman. Would you mind me asking where you were last night? I mean, the night before last.'

Grimaldi banged his chest. 'Me?'

Torsen nodded. 'We will have to ask everyone at the circus if they saw him. Did you, by any chance?'

'Me?'

Rieckert's jaw dropped slightly, he had never come across anyone as large as Grimaldi. The man appeared to be built like an ox, his hands twice the size of any normal man's.

Grimaldi leaned back and then looked at Torsen Heinz. 'You serious? Night before last? Oh, yes. I was here, all night, ask my wife – she couldn't sleep because of my snoring. As to Kellerman, lemme think, I've not seen the creep for maybe five . . . no, more, I thought he was in gaol, last saw him – must be eight to ten years ago.'

'You have recently been in Paris? Was he working with you then?'

Torsen fumbled with his notes, giving Rieckert a cue to take out his notebook also. But it was in his raincoat pocket, so he excused himself and had a tough time retrieving it from the pocket – the pages tore slightly, damp from the rain. When he returned, he had to step over Grimaldi's outstretched legs.

Grimaldi was shrugging his massive shoulders. 'No one would employ him, he stole an entire week's wages, from . . . can't remember, but no circus would touch him. Besides, he was in gaol! I think he got extra time for beating up some inmate, that's what I heard.'

The door opened, and Ruda walked in. She leaned against the door frame, looking first to Grimaldi, and then to the two men.

'Kellerman's been murdered,' said Grimaldi.

Ruda eased off her boots. 'What do we do, throw a party?'

Grimaldi grinned, and introduced Torsen Heinz and Rieckert. Ruda walked further into the room and shook the officers' hands as they both stood up to greet her. Ruda's hand felt like a man's to Torsen, rough, calloused. She was almost as tall as he was but, judging by the handshake, a hell of a lot stronger. They made quite a pair, Mr and Mrs Grimaldi.

'Is this true?' she asked.

Torsen nodded. He had never seen such a total lack of

emotion. Kellerman had, after all, once been this woman's husband.

'Would you mind if I asked you some questions, Mrs Kell – er – Grimaldi?'

Ruda placed her boots by the door. 'Ask what you need to know. Is there coffee on, Luis?'

Grimaldi eased himself out of his seat, went into the kitchen and poured his wife coffee, again asking if either of the men would care for some. They both replied that they would, and he banged around getting the mugs and sugar together.

Ruda sat on the seat vacated by her husband, now rubbing her hair with a towel. Torsen rested his elbows on his knees. 'When did you last see him?'

She closed her eyes and leaned back. 'That's a tough one. Let me think . . . Luis? When did he come to the winter quarters? Was it six, eight years ago? I can't think.'

Grimaldi set down the mugs of thick black coffee; he didn't offer any milk, but a large glass bowl of brown sugar. As the two policemen spooned in their sugar, Ruda and Grimaldi had a short conversation about one of the cats. Ruda was worried that she was off her food: if it continued she'd change her feed, maybe put her back on the meat instead of the meal. They seemed totally unconcerned about Kellerman.

'Do you have a photograph?'

Ruda looked at Torsen and raised her eyebrow. 'Of the cats?'

'No, of Kellerman.'

'You must be joking. Do you think I would want a reminder that I was ever in any way connected to that piece of shit? No, I do not have a photograph.'

Torsen sipped his coffee. It was odd that neither had asked how Kellerman had died. They continued to be totally disinterested, and Ruda, when asked where she had been at the time of the murder, lit a cigarette and rubbed her nose. 'The night before last, shit, I dunno. Last night I was here working the act until after twelve.'

'No, the night before.'

Ruda thought for a moment then frowned. 'Guess I was here, worked the routines, then had supper over at the canteen, then came to bed. What time did I come in, Luis?'

Grimaldi took a picture of himself from the wall. He handed it to Torsen. 'That was the last time I played Berlin. You said you saw my act, more than fifteen years ago—'

Ruda interrupted. 'It would be more than fifteen, lemme see.'

She looked over the wall of photographs, and Torsen put his mug down. They were both discussing the exact time they were last in Berlin. Ruda suddenly turned to face him. 'You're sure it is Tommy Kellerman? I think he's still in prison.'

Torsen stood up and straightened his sodden trousers, the crease no longer in existence. 'We would be sure if you would be so helpful as to identify him. We have no one formally to identify him, so we ask your co-operation.'

Ruda hesitated. 'Don't they have fingerprints for that kind of thing? Contact the prison. I don't want to see him, dead or alive. Get someone else, there's many around the camp that knew him.'

'But you were his wife . . .'

Ruda stared hard at Torsen. 'Yes, I was his wife, but I'm not now, and I haven't been for a very long time.'

'For me to cable America and wait for prints could take a considerable time.' He did not add that it could take months as he had no fax machine, nor for that matter any facilities to send cables or check which prison. Gaining permission from Interpol to assist him could entail more paperwork, more time.

'If there's no one else . . .' Ruda said, obviously not liking the situation.

'Thank you. Thank you for your time, I may have to question you again. Oh yes, one more thing, the tattoo. Kellerman had a tattoo on his left arm. Could you tell me what it was like?'

Grimaldi laughed. 'Probably gave the size of his prick, he was so proud of it. Don't look at me, I never let the creep within two feet of me. Ask her, she was – as you so rightly say – married to him.'

Ruda looked at the thick carpet, her stockinged feet digging into the pile. 'A tattoo? He might have had it done in prison, he didn't have one when I knew him.'

Torsen shook their hands, and again felt how strong her grip was. 'Maybe he was looking for work. Ask at the main administration office,' Ruda suggested.

Torsen smiled his thanks, and just as he opened the door, Grimaldi asked how Kellerman had been murdered. Torsen dragged on his raincoat. 'Some kind of hammer, multiple blows to his head.'

Grimaldi wiped his mouth with the back of his hand. 'Ah well! Poor little sod had it coming to him.'

Torsen said tersely that no one had to be subjected to such a horrifying death. He then smiled coldly at Ruda, and asked if she would accompany them when he had finished taking statements from the rest of the people he needed to speak to. Ruda was tight-lipped, asking how long it would take – with the show due to open shortly she had very little time.

Torsen said he would be through as fast as he could, perhaps in two hours, if it was convenient. He did not wait for a reply, but left the trailer. The men's shoes were filled with rainwater, and they sat on the mud-caked steps to replace them.

From the trailer window, Ruda watched them hurry through the lanes between the trailers, pause to examine their map, and then head for the Giorgios' trailer. 'They've gone to the Giorgios'!'

Grimaldi chuckled. 'They'll last ten minutes. What do you make of it?'

Ruda sighed, making no reply, so he repeated the question. 'Maybe it isn't him!' she snapped.

'Well, you'll know soon enough, he'll not get anyone else to ID the body.' Grimaldi leaned back, then lifted his feet up to rest on the bench seat. 'You married him! Maybe he left some dough to you in his will.'

'Yeah. The only thing he's left is a nasty smell and a string of debts. He can get someone else to ID him, I'm not going.'

'But you were his wife.'

She swiped at him with the towel. 'You knew him, you identify him, it'll give you something to do.'

'Ah, but I didn't know him as well as you, sweetheart. You can't get out of that.'

Ruda sat down, pushing his feet aside. 'I can't do it, Luis. Don't make me, don't let them make me see him.'

Grimaldi cocked his head to one side. 'Why not? He's

dead. You telling me it's affecting you? I thought you detested his guts.'

'I do, I did, but I don't want to see him.'

Grimaldi pinched her cheek. 'You use his name, sweetheart . . . Serves you right.'

Ruda swung out at him, this time with the flat of her hand. She caught his face hard, and he gripped her wrist, shoving her roughly aside.

'Give me one good reason why I should do anything for you!'

'Fuck you!'

Ruda punched him, and Grimaldi swung off the bench, landing a hard, open-handed slap to her face. She kicked him, he slapped her again, and this time she didn't fight back. Her face twisted like a child's, and he drew her to him. 'OK, OK. I'll take you, I'll go with you!'

He began to smooth her hair from her face, massage the throbbing scars at her temples. Her body felt strong in his arms, strong as a man's, and for her to be vulnerable like this was rare. He held her closer. 'Ruda, Ruda . . . why do we torment each other the way we do?'

She whispered like a child, 'Just be with me, Luis, just stay with me, I don't want to go by myself.'

'Stay with you, huh? Until the next time you want something?' He couldn't help himself – as soon as he said it he wished he hadn't. She backed away from him, her hands in fists, and he threw up his hands in a gesture of impotence. 'We have to get divorced, Ruda, you know it. I can't live like this any more, we're at each other's throats.'

'I don't want to talk about that, not now.'

'Because of that shit Kellerman? Jesus Christ, Ruda, who gives a fuck if he's alive or dead? What concerns me is us, we have to settle the future, settle it, sit down and work out what part of the act you want. I'm through, Ruda, through standing around waiting, at your beck and call.'

'You can't have the act!' She glared at him.

Grimaldi clenched his hands. Like two fighters, they faced each other. 'Fine, you want it, then we arrange a financial settlement. Simple as that, Ruda.'

He saw the way her face changed, the way her dark eyes stared at him, and through him. Her voice was as dark as her eyes. 'Every penny I have earned has been put back into the act. You want out then you go, take your tart, your stupid little bitch, your whore . . . take her and *fuck off.*'

Grimaldi smirked. 'Takes one to know one.'

She went for him like a man, punching at him, kicking, and then she grabbed his hair. He tried to resist, but he couldn't; in the end they were slugging at each other. Crockery smashed, pictures crashed off the walls, and in the confined space they fought until they both lay sprawled, panting, on the floor. She still punched him, hard blows that hurt like hell. 'Take your clothes, take your belongings and get out! Without me you'd have nothing! Without me you'd be a drunken bum!'

She spat at him, and he staggered to his feet, began to open the overhead lockers, throwing not his things, but her belongings at her, around her. 'You take *yours*, you take *your* belongings and get out, go sleep with the animals, sleep with your precious angel! Sleep with any twisted, fucked-up thing that'll keep you!'

Ruda kicked him so hard in the back of his legs that he slumped forwards, hit his head on the side of the cupboard and fell backwards. He lay half across the bunk, half on the floor and she was on top of him, spread-eagled across his body. For one second he thought she was going to bite him: her jaw opened and shut, she was snarling like a wild cat, and then he rolled her – her head cracked back on the floor – and heaved his body on top of her. He bent his head closer, about to scream at her to stop. He felt her body grow limp beneath him, and her arms wound round his neck as she drew him closer. They looked into each other's faces, and there was a soft low moan, in unison, chest to chest, breath to breath, both their hearts thudding with the exertion. The kiss was gentle, his lips softly brushing hers, and then she buried her head in his neck.

They lay together on the floor of the wrecked trailer, their clothes and crockery around them, like lovers having found themselves after a long separation. They lay together with broken glass and shattered pictures of the Great Grimaldi and the fearless Ruda Kellerman.

When he spoke, his voice was filled with pain. 'Let me go, Ruda, because this is where it always ends. I want you now, you can feel I want you, but it always has to end.'

Her voice was muffled, a low half-plea, begging him to take her, to have her. She eased her hands down his body, began to unhook his belt.

He leaned up, gently turning her face, forcing her to look at him. 'Do you want me? Or is this – Ruda, look at me. *Look at me!*' His big hand cupped her chin, forced her to face him. Her eyes were expressionless, glinting hard eyes, dangerous eyes. She couldn't fake it, she had never been able to, she couldn't even do it now when she needed him. Slowly she let her hands drop to her sides. She made as if to turn over, for him to ease down her trousers, since she could not take him naturally, normally.

Small slivers of glass cut into her cheeks, the pain excited her, but she felt no juices, nothing to prepare her body for sex, for his hard erection. She gritted her teeth, waiting.

Grimaldi eased himself up, carefully avoiding the glass, stepping over her, tightening his belt as his erection pressed against his pants; the hardness left him by the time he walked into his own room and quietly closed the door.

Ruda lay in the debris. It had always been this way, they had always fought each other, that part had always excited her, but she had never felt any sexual desire beyond the fight; sex pained and hurt her too much, hurt her insides like sharpened razors. She felt a tiny drop of blood roll down her cheek and she licked it, tasted the salt, the blood, as if the drop of blood replaced a salted tear. She never cried, hadn't for a long time, too long even to remember.

She got up and went into her own room, closing the door as quietly as Grimaldi had shut his. She showered, feeling the hot needles pummel her, then gently began to soap herself. Her fingers massaged her shoulders, her arms, her heavy breasts, and then she began to soap her belly, her strong hands feeling each crude, jagged scar. She massaged and eased the foam down, until she soaped between her legs; the ridges of the scars, hideous thick whitened skin, hard rough skin, skin always a dark plum red, like a birthmark. She rinsed the soap away with cold water, reached for the bath towel, her hair dripping. She hadn't heard him come in, but he was there, holding out the big white bath towel. Gently he wrapped her, as if she were a baby, trapping her arms in the big white softness. He held her close. Her eyes were frightened, childlike, as if the animal in her had gone into hiding; there was no longer any ferocity, no anger. He guided her towards the bed and sat her down. She sat with her head bowed, her hair dripping, covering her face. Luis reached for a small hand-towel and began to dry her hair.

'I'll go to the mortuary, no need for you to do it, I'll go if they need someone.'

She nodded.

'Ruda, look at me. I need someone. I'm not talking about getting my rocks off, I'm talking about . . . needing – I need, you know? As it is now, I feel like half a man, and watching out for you every show isn't enough. It can't go on, this is my last chance. I'm old, maybe Tina can give me a few more good years, give me back my balls. I don't want to fight with you any more, I can't fight you any more. I will need to be able to keep Tina and the baby when it comes, so we have to work out an agreement, one we can both accept. I know how much money you've put in, I know how you've kept us going. I know, Ruda, but I can't go on like this.'

He rubbed her head gently, knowing the burn scars at her temples should not be irritated by the towel. He was so careful, showing more tenderness than he had in years.

There was a tap on the trailer door. It was the inspector asking if Mrs Kellerman could accompany him now to the mortuary. Ruda could hear Grimaldi asking if he could go instead, and she heard the inspector saying that Mrs Kellerman would be preferable. Grimaldi's voice grew a little louder as he said he also knew Kellerman. Then there were whispers, and the trailer door shut.

Grimaldi called out that she had better get dressed, they needed her, but he would accompany her. She began to dress very carefully, choosing a dress, high-heeled shoes

137

and, for the first time in many years, she applied make-up other than her stage make-up. She took her time, a soft voice inside her telling her to stay calm, take things one at a time, she would deal with Luis when the time was right, this was not the right time.

Grimaldi had a quick shave and stared at his reflection, uneasy with the interaction between himself and his wife. He had felt such compassion for her, it confused him, she confused him, but then she always had. He rinsed his face and sat for a moment, remembering ... remembering Florida, how many years ago he couldn't recall, but shortly after they were married. Ruda had wanted a child so badly, he knew how she must feel now with the Tina situation. He understood, but what could he do? It was not his fault.

Luis had held her when she told him, wrapped her in his arms when she came out of the doctor's waiting room, but she had pushed him away. Then, he had so much love for her that he hadn't been angry, just saddened that she pushed him from her. He knew she was fighting to keep control of herself in that way she had – her head up, her jaw out. She didn't cry, he had rarely ever seen her crying; somehow it had been more touching, her desperation to speak matter-of-factly, as if she was not affected.

'I can't have a child, artificially or any other way, so that is that.'

She had put on her coat and walked out of the doctor's waiting room, and he had waited a moment to accept the news for himself, then followed her to the car. They had driven back to their winter quarters, Ruda staring ahead, giving him directions as she always did – Luis was never good at routes and their quarters were far out of the main city. But he would never forget that journey, the Florida heat, the quiet calm voice, flatly telling him to go right, then left . . .

Ruda had become deeply depressed: nothing he said or attempted to do seemed to interest her. It was then that he had suggested she play a bigger part in the act; up until that point she had simply helped his boys muck out the cages. He had never contemplated her working in the ring with him, only suggested it to give her something else to think about. He had begun to train her, and to his relief her depression lifted, the dark sadness dispersed, but since then their personal relationship had deteriorated. Ever since the visit to the specialist she shrank away from him whenever he touched her. He let it go, hoping that in time she would come back to his bed.

The animals, his cats, had brought out a side in her that at first impressed him: she worked tirelessly, showed no fear, no regard for her own life. No matter how he reprimanded and warned her she continued to take foolish risks. She almost dared the cats to attack her, dared them to maul her. Luis was a good trainer, and a well-respected performer, a man brought up around animals. It was he who persuaded her that she must love the cats, nurture them; she would gain no results from threats or impatience. Everything took time but, above all, it was the caring, the loving which would pay off. At first, she had refused to listen to him, and the fights had begun then, the violent arguments, but he kept on warning her that unless she listened, showed him respect as well as the cats, she would never learn. Constantly he told her she was not to tame the animals, but to train them: there was a vast difference.

He gave her so much of his time, so much patience . . . and when she gained results, she began to smile again, and he heard her wonderful, bellowing laugh return. But she did not come back to his bed. When he took a mistress, one of the stable girls at the winter quarters, she had said nothing, and so the pattern had begun then, all those years ago.

And then Ruda bought Mamon, and their relationship took a terrible turn. They had been looking at cats to buy for the act, and they had seen a number, turned down many. Luis was intuitive when buying cats for his act: he had been taught by his father to be very choosy, often declining ten or twelve before he found an animal he felt would work well. One look and he could tell the young lion was trouble: Mamon had been in too many homes, too many circuses, moved too many times. His history would give any trainer a clue to his temperament, but Ruda had not listened – even when Luis had refused to pay for him – and argued to such an extent that he had driven off and left her.

A week later Luis had gone to inspect four Bengal tigers being sold by a trainer he knew well. These were four cats he was quick to buy because he trusted the owner and liked the act into which they had already been worked. He had bought them on a handshake, though his money was running short. Then he had returned to discuss the purchase with Ruda.

Ruda had taken the opportunity of his absence to go back to buy Mamon. Luis had been furious, but she had shouted that Mamon was not his but hers, and she would train him – with or without Luis's help – it had been her money, not his. Mamon was hers. The argument had grown into a fist-fight, and in the end he had given way. When she had said Mamon was her baby, he had walked away, walked into the arms of . . . he couldn't even remember the girl's name now. He sat trying to recall it, and suddenly realized Ruda was calling him. She then banged on his door, shouting that she was ready, the *Polizei* were waiting. He fetched a clean shirt and began to dress.

Luis had never told Ruda that he had returned to the gynaecologist. He wanted to know for himself what Ruda's diagnosis had been, as she had refused to discuss it. He wanted to know if they should try for a second opinion. He had cared that much. At first the doctor had refused to discuss his patient with Grimaldi, even though he was her husband. He said that Ruda had asked him not to, and simply stated that there was no hope of his wife being able to conceive, and no amount of second opinions or other specialists could help.

Luis had accepted the gynaecologist's word, but at the same time, from his manner, he knew the man was not telling him the entire truth. When he tried to push for further details, the doctor, without meeting Grimaldi's eyes, said quietly, 'Your wife is unable to have normal sexual intercourse, and even if insemination took place, there is no possibility of her carrying a child. I am sorry.' Though he would not discuss Ruda's condition with Luis, he showed her X-rays and tests to two colleagues. He gave them no name, nothing to identify the woman, just the appalling X-rays and photographs of her genital area. All her organs had been removed, as if her womb had been torn from her belly. The internal scar tissue was even worse than her external body scars. Nothing could be done to eliminate them. The entire genital area had been burnt by what the surgeon felt was possibly an early form of chemotherapy.

The colleagues listened in silence – appalled silence.

The clitoris had been severed, the vagina covered in scar tissue, the crudeness of the stitches and the scar tissue formation had left no opening. The only form of sexual intercourse the woman could have was anal; her urinary tract had been operated on to enable her to pass liquid, and a plastic tube inserted when the infected tract had festered. The anal area was large, denoting that sexual practice had obviously occurred on a regular basis over a period of years, stretching the colon.

The three men discussed the X-rays. What they had on their screens was a shell of a woman. She had been stripped of her female organs, and what made all of this even more horrible was that the butchery had been performed when the woman was a small child. They talked about the resilience of the human body to have withstood so much, but did not deal with the patient's present state of mind. They couldn't. Ruda Grimaldi had refused to discuss what had led to her condition, and she never returned to the gynaecologist.

Grimaldi knew something of Ruda's past, but she would never tell him all of it. Only Kellerman had known more, but Ruda had told Grimaldi the first night he had met her that she wouldn't have straight sex. She had told him in that stubborn way she had, head up, jaw stuck out. Grimaldi combed his hair. It was strange to think of it all now. At that time he hadn't cared, he had no thought of marrying her then. That had come many years later. He slipped his jacket on, brushing the shoulders with his hands. He had married her – not out of pity, Ruda hated pity. Grimaldi had married her because by the time she had come back into his life, he had been in desperate need of someone. He was slipping down the slopes, drinking too much, and his act was falling apart.

He sighed, knowing he was lying to himself. For a reason he couldn't understand, he had married her because he had loved her. He had believed she loved him, and it was many years before he realized Ruda loved no one, not even herself. No, that was wrong: she loved her angel, she loved Mamon.

By the time he was dressed and ready to leave the trailer, Grimaldi had talked himself into a corner. He had to leave Ruda, but fighting her and making ridiculous demands wouldn't work; he had to make it a fair split. He determined that after the Kellerman business was sorted out, he would discuss it calmly and realistically, and this time he would not back down.

'Luis, come on, what are you doing? You've been ages, that inspector is waiting.' Ruda banged on his door again. 'What are you doing in there?'

Grimaldi came out of his bedroom. He gave her a smile, made her turn around, admiring her, flattering her; he had not seen her so well dressed for years. He had also not had a drink for more than twenty-four hours. He felt good, and he teased Ruda as he admired her dress. 'How come you dress up for a corpse?'

Ruda wrinkled her nose, and hooked her arm in his. 'Maybe I need to give myself some confidence. I'm scared.'

Grimaldi laughed, and assisted her down the steps. Then, because of the mud, he held out his arms and carried her to the waiting patrol car.

By the time Inspector Heinz and his sergeant had returned to their bogged-down patrol car, they were both reeling from the statements given by all the people who had known Kellerman. Not one had a nice word for him, all seemed rather satisfied he was dead, none had been helpful, none had seen Kellerman on the day or night of his death, and everyone had a strong alibi. Torsen was grateful that the ex-Mrs Kellerman had agreed to identify the dead man.

He held open the back door, and Grimaldi assisted his wife inside. She looked very different from the woman Torsen had visited in their trailer. She was also in a good mood, laughing with her husband – a strange reaction, considering she was being taken to a mortuary to identify her ex-husband's corpse.

Ruda had been determined to make sure she could not be recognized in case someone had seen her enter Tommy Kellerman's hotel. She had dressed carefully in a flowered dress and a pale grey coat. She had left her hair loose, hiding her face, and with her high heels she seemed exceptionally tall. Torsen looked at her through the car mirror. It was hard to tell her exact age, but he thought she had to be close to forty, if not more. It was her manner, the direct unnerving stare of dark, strange amber-coloured eyes: he felt as if they were boring into the back of his head as he tried to back out of the mud-bound parking area.

Ruda wasn't looking at the inspector, but past him, about fifty yards in front. Mike, one of their boys, was hurrying towards the canteen section, a rain cape over his shoulders, but what freaked Ruda was that he was wearing Tommy Kellerman's black leather trilby. She remembered she had left it in the meat trailer when she had returned – left it and forgotten about it. The car suddenly jerked backward free of the mud, turned and headed out of the car park. Ruda didn't turn back, she couldn't: her heart was pounding, her face had drained of colour. Grimaldi gripped her hand and squeezed it. He murmured it was

144

all right, that he was there, and there was no need for her to be afraid.

The rain continued to pour throughout their entire journey to East Berlin. The patrol car's windscreen wipers made nerve-racking screeches as they worked. Grimaldi and his wife talked quietly to each other, as if they were being chauffeured. Torsen began to listen to their conversation. They spoke in English and he could only make out the odd sentence, wondering idly what the word 'plinth' meant. His sergeant sat beside him in the front seat, thumbing through his notebook in a bored manner, then he muttered, patting his pockets, that he had lost his pencil. Torsen continued to listen to Ruda, passing Rieckert his own pencil.

In an attempt to calm her nerves, Ruda was talking about the new plinths for the act, having tried them out that morning. She was telling Luis she had had a lot of trouble, particularly with Mamon: he seemed loath to go near them, had played up badly. Grimaldi said the return of the old plinths was out of the question, they couldn't get them returned in time for the act. They would tone the colours down. Ruda snapped at him, telling him the smell of the fresh paint would be just as disturbing, and to pull out the main part of the act would be insanity. They discussed asking for more rehearsal time before the show, and then both fell silent.

Torsen surmized that plinths and pedestals were the large seats the animals sat on and climbed up and down during the act. They drove on in silence for a while, through Kreuzberg, passing refurbished jazz cellars, Turkish shops, bedraggled boutiques and small art galleries.

It was the same town Ruda had passed through on the bus the night she had murdered Kellerman. A heavy foreboding in her mind reflected the greyness of the town.

Torsen looked back at them through his mirror. 'It was perhaps naïve of us to expect the new freedom would unleash some exciting new era overnight. People who have lived in cages get used to it and people in the East feel afraid – this new financial insecurity spreads a panic. The people here have been denied creative and critical expression for so long, they suffer from a deep inferiority complex. In the old regime many cultural institutions were built up, very well funded – we have good opera houses, two in fact, but now the West holds our purse strings and a number of our theatres have been closed for lack of funds.'

They continued to drive on in silence. The inspector felt obliged to talk, as if giving a guided tour. 'In the old days we had no unemployment – of course, there was much overstaffing, but that was the GDR's way of disguising unemployment. Everything has doubled in price since the Deutschmark took over but I believe we are on the threshold of a new beginning.'

Ruda sat tight-lipped, staring from the window, wishing the stupid man would shut up. They crossed into East Berlin. Ruda turned to her husband as her fear, mingled with the thought of having to see Kellerman, made her angry. She had to unleash it, she was going crazy. They passed a building with JUDA scrawled over its walls, and it was the perfect excuse. She suddenly snapped, her voice vicious, 'Some new beginning, look what they daub on their walls. He should stop the car and grab those kids by the scruff of their necks, better still take a machine gun and wipe them out! *Fuck you, bastards!*'

Inspector and sergeant exchanged hooded looks; the

146

screech of the windscreen wiper was giving Torsen a headache, and the rain wouldn't let up.

Grimaldi stared at the anti-Jewish slogans, and touched Torsen's shoulder. 'How come this kind of thing is allowed?'

Torsen replied that no sooner did they wash down the walls than the kids returned. His sergeant turned. His pale blue eyes and blond crew-cut made him at first appear youthful, but there was a chilling arrogance about him. He spoke with obvious distaste, his pale eyes narrowed. 'The city is swamped with immigrants, the Rumanian gypsies have flooded in, women and children sitting on every street corner, begging. The Poles are not wanted either. They fight like animals in the shops, they park their tatterdemalion cars any old how, they steal, they urinate in the entrances of apartments – this new Germany is in chaos. Eastern Europe is poverty-stricken, and they come in droves. We have more illegal immigrants than we know what to do with. We have no time to wash down walls.'

They drove on, past peeling buildings, collapsing sewer systems, electricity cables hanging from broken cages on street corners. The patrol car passed vast acreages of grimy nineteenth-century tenements that had withstood the bombing, their occupants staring now from filthy windows in their grey shabbiness. Ruda was tense, shifting her weight, one buttock to the next, crossing and uncrossing her legs. She took out her cigarettes and lit up, her hand shaking. She opened the window. She didn't care if she got soaked . . . just to be able to breathe. She tossed the cigarette out, breathing in through her nose, exhaling, trying to stay calm.

Torsen noted her discomfort and began pointing out

sights, a few new art galleries. The atmosphere in the car was tense and he was trying to lighten it but now he had a gale blowing down the back of his neck. No doubt, to add to his headache he'd have a crick in his neck the following morning.

They went past a greystone hospital building, and around a drive to a low cement building, with empty parking places freshly painted in white, but there was no other vehicle to be seen. The inspector pulled on the handbrake, and turned to his passengers. 'We are here, this is the city mortuary.'

Ruda and Grimaldi were led to a small empty waiting room – green plastic seats and a low table with torn newspapers – and were asked to wait. Sergeant Rieckert remained with them, his eyes flicking over Grimaldi's jacket, his shoes, his Russian-styled shirt with its high collar, mentally sizing up how he would look in the same apparel.

Inspector Torsen Heinz walked down a long, dismal corridor into the main refrigerated room. 'Can you get Kellerman ready for viewing?' He shut the door again, returned to the waiting room and beckoned Ruda to follow him down the corridor. Grimaldi asked if he should accompany them, and Torsen said it was entirely up to him. The three walked up the long corridor, their feet echoing on the tiled floor. They reached a door at the very end, which was opened by a man wearing a green overall. He stood to one side, removing his rubber gloves. They entered the cold room. Three bodies were lying on tables, covered in sheeting, and Grimaldi tightened his grip on Ruda's elbow. Her heart was pounding, but she gave no other indication of what she was feeling. Grimaldi looked from one shrouded body to the other, then to the

148

bank of freezers, with their old-fashioned heavy bolted drawers. He wondered how many bodies they kept on ice.

The inspector stood by a fourth table: the small figure, shrouded like the others, seemed tiny in comparison. In a hushed voice he addressed Ruda. 'Be prepared, the dead man had extensive wounds to his face and head . . .'

Grimaldi moved closer to Ruda and asked if she was all right. She withdrew her arm, nodding. Slowly the inspector lifted the sheet from the naked body, revealing just the head. Grimaldi stepped back aghast, but Ruda moved a fraction closer. She stared down at Kellerman's distorted face, or what was left of it.

'Is this Kellerman?'

Ruda felt icy cold, but she continued to stare.

The inspector lifted the sheet from the left arm. 'The tattoo was on his left wrist. As you can see, the skin was cut away. It would have been quite large.'

Ruda stared at the small hand, the open cleaned wound, but said nothing. Torsen waited, watching her reaction, saw her turn slowly to Grimaldi.

'Is this Kellerman, Mrs Grimaldi?' he asked again.

Ruda gave a hardly detectable shrug of her shoulders. She showed no emotion whatsoever. It was difficult for the inspector to know what she was thinking or feeling. She seemed not to be repelled by the corpse, or disturbed by the grotesque injuries to the dead man's face.

Grimaldi stepped closer, peered down. He cocked his head to the right, and then left. 'Well, I think it's him.'

He returned to Ruda, leaned close and whispered something, and she moved away from him, nearer to the dead man. She looked at Torsen. 'I can't be sure, I'm sorry . . . it has been so long since I saw him.'

'It's him, Ruda, I'm sure even if you're not.' Grimaldi seemed impatient. Turning to the three shrouded bodies he asked if they, too, had been murdered. He received no reply. Torsen lowered the sheet further to unveil Kellerman's chest.

Again Grimaldi whispered to Ruda, and this time he smiled. The inspector couldn't believe it – the man was making some kind of joke.

Grimaldi caught the look of disapproval on Torsen's face and gave a sheepish smile. 'The little fella was very well endowed, I suggested my wife perhaps could remember . . .' He shut up, realizing the joke was unsuitable and tasteless.

Ruda touched Kellerman's hair, a light pat with just her fingers to the thick curly grey-black hair. She spoke very softly, hardly audible. 'He had a mole, on the left shoulder, shaped like a . . .'

The inspector pulled the sheet down, exposing the left shoulder to reveal a dark brown mole. Ruda nodded. She whispered that the dead man was Kellerman, then she turned and strode out of the room – had to get out because she could hear Tommy's voice, hear him telling her not to switch out the light. He hated the dark, was always afraid of the dark and of confined spaces. She had teased him, calling him a baby, but she had always left the lights on. He didn't need them now.

Back in the waiting room Inspector Torsen thanked Ruda for her identification. He opened his notebook and sat on the edge of the hard bench; he searched his pockets and looked to his sergeant. 'Have you got my pencil?' He snatched it from Rieckert and looked at Ruda. 'We have been unable as yet to trace any documents on the deceased, how he entered Germany, and if

150

there are relatives we should contact. Was he an American citizen?'

Ruda nodded, told the inspector that Kellerman gained his American citizenship in the early sixties, that he had no relatives and there was no one to be contacted.

'Where did he come from originally, Mrs Grimaldi?'

Ruda hesitated, touched the scar at her temple with her forefinger. 'Poland I think, I can't recall . . .'

Grimaldi frowned, almost waiting for her to tell the inspector that she had met Kellerman in Berlin, but then she surprised him: she suddenly asked about Kellerman's burial, suggesting he be buried locally as there were no relatives to claim the body. She also said that she would cover any necessary costs, and asked for a rabbi to be called. Although, Ruda said, Kellerman had not been a practising Jew, she felt that he would have wanted a rabbi present.

The inspector wrote down her instructions carefully, but looked up quickly when she said in a low sarcastic voice, 'I presume there is a rabbi in this vicinity. Or one left in Germany who could perform the funeral rites. He must be buried before sunset.'

Torsen said he would arrange it. Then he asked if Kellerman was the deceased's real name. Ruda looked puzzled, said of course it was. He saw at last she seemed disturbed. She lit a cigarette, inhaled deeply before she replied again to his question, apologizing for her rudeness. As far as she knew it was his name, that was the name she had always known him under and the name she had taken when she married him. Torsen snapped his notebook closed officiously, and offered to have the couple returned to West Berlin. They refused the offer of a patrol car and asked instead for a taxi.

Grimaldi suddenly asked if they had a suspect, and Torsen shook his head. 'We have no one as yet. We have also not discovered his suitcase, the hotel room was stripped.'

'But didn't anyone see who killed him? That was some beating the little guy took, I mean someone must have hated his guts, and surely someone must have seen or heard something?'

The inspector shrugged. They had nothing, possibly a number of motives. Kellerman was not a well-liked man.

'Well liked is one thing, but you don't beat a man's head in because you don't like him. It must be something else.'

Torsen nodded, said quietly that until he continued the investigation, there was no further information he could give. He excused himself and left his sergeant to arrange their transport.

The sergeant, irritated at having to walk back to the station, called two taxi companies but no cars were available. He suggested that they could get one from the Grand Hotel: it was not too far, if they wished he could walk with them.

Ruda refused his offer to accompany them, and turned back to stare out of the grimy window. Grimaldi came to her side, whispered to her that she should have kept her mouth shut – now she would have to fork out for the little bastard even in death. She glared at him in disgust and, keeping her voice as low as his, she murmured that what he was really pissed off about was her asking for a rabbi. She turned back to the window. 'That little blond-haired Nazi prick will probably send us in the wrong direction anyway, now he knows I'm Jewish!'

Grimaldi gripped her elbow so tightly it hurt. 'Shut

up, just keep it shut! And since when have you been a fuckin' Jew!'

Ruda smirked at him and shook her head. 'Scared they may daub us on the way back to the trailer?'

Grimaldi glared back at her, he would never understand her. She was no more Jewish than he was, certainly not a practising one. She had no religion, and he was a Catholic – not that he'd said a Hail Mary for more than twenty years.

The sergeant handed directions to Grimaldi and, with a curt nod of his head, left them. He'd heard what she had called him and he smarted with impotent fury: foreigners, they were all alike, and Detective Chief Inspector Heinz bowed and scraped like a wimp to that Jewish bitch! What kind of pervert was she to have been married to that animal on the mortuary slab? She repelled him.

Luis and Ruda walked together, arm in arm; it took a lot longer than the sergeant had suggested – over an hour to arrive at the newly refurbished Grand Hotel. It was such a sight that they decided – or Grimaldi did – that they should order a taxi and have a Martini while they waited. At first Ruda resisted, but then, being told there would be no taxi available for another hour, she relented.

They walked into the foyer and headed for the comfortable lounge. They made a striking couple. Grimaldi began to enjoy himself. Guiding Ruda by the elbow, he inclined his head. 'Now, this is my style, and I think, since we're here, we might as well order a late lunch. The restaurant looks good, what do you say?'

Ruda looked at her wristwatch. She had to get back to rehearse and feed the cats, but they had to wait for the taxi so she suggested they just have a drink and a sandwich.

Grimaldi decided this was as good a time as any to have a talk, out of the trailer, away from the circus. In the luxurious surroundings they might have a civilized conversation. They sat in a small booth, with red plush velvet seats and a marble-topped table. Ferns hid them from the rest of the hotel residents, mostly American as far as Grimaldi could tell.

They sipped their Martinis in silence, and Ruda ate the entire bowl of peanuts, one at a time, popping them into her mouth. Grimaldi took an envelope from his pocket and opened it. 'I have been working out our financial situation, how much the act costs, living expenses, and what we will both need to live on. Maybe we should sell the trailer and buy a smaller one each.'

She turned on him. 'Your priority is to get back the old plinths! I can't work with the new ones.'

'We've already discussed that, for Chrissakes. Just go through this with me, we have to sort it out some time.'

Ruda snatched the sheet of paper, and looked over his haphazard scrawl. It was quite a shock to her that even after their closeness, he was still intent on leaving her.

'She's pregnant, Ruda. I want to get a divorce and marry her.'

Ruda tore the paper into scraps. 'I'll think about it.'

Grimaldi signalled for the waiter to take another order. Ruda's foot was tapping against the side of the table leg. 'I don't want to have an argument here, Ruda. OK?'

She stared at him, her mind ticking over, telling herself to keep calm. She had to deal with things one at a time. She had dealt with Kellerman, next would be Grimaldi himself, but her main priority now was to get the act ready for opening night. One thing at a time, this show was the biggest she had done, and if she performed well she knew that with the television live coverage there would be no more second-circuit dates: she would be an international star. She wanted above all to get to the US again and win a contract at the mammoth New York circus, Barnum and Bailey's big top, one of the finest in the world.

'Ruda, we have to discuss this . . . Ruda!'

'I'll think about it. We'll work out something.'

As the waiter arrived at their table, passing directly behind him was a very handsome man accompanied by an attractive blonde woman. They were both deep in conversation, not giving Grimaldi or Ruda a glance. They seated themselves in the next booth, and the waiter, after taking Grimaldi's order, moved quickly to the elegant couple's booth.

'Good afternoon, Baron.'

Helen Masters asked for a gin and tonic, and the Baron a Scotch on the rocks. He spoke German, then turned back to continue his conversation with Helen in French. They paid no attention to the big broad-shouldered man seated in the next booth. They could not see Ruda.

Grimaldi had ordered two more Martinis. Ruda had said she didn't want another but he had ignored her. He looked around the lounge, then noticed she was playing with the bread. It always used to infuriate him, the way she would pick at it, roll it into tiny little balls, twitch it and pummel it with her fingers . . .

'Stop that, you know it gets on my nerves. We'll sort out the plinths when we get back. Now, can we just relax, Ruda?'

She nodded, but her hands beneath the table began to roll a small piece of bread tighter and tighter, until it became a dense hard ball, because she kept on seeing the

155

boy, Mike, wearing Kellerman's hideous leather trilby. Mike, Grimaldi and his bloody divorce ... It was all coming down on her like a dark blanket, and suddenly she felt as if her mind would explode. Her fingers pressed and rolled the tiny ball of bread as if out of her control. She swallowed, her mouth had dried, her lips felt stiff, her tongue held the roof of her mouth. It was seeping upward from her toes ... she fought against it, refusing to allow it to dominate her – not here, not in public. 'No ... no!'

Grimaldi looked at her, not sure what she had said. He leaned closer. 'Ruda? You OK?'

She repeated the word, 'No!' like a low growl. He could see her body was rigid, and yet the table shook slightly as her fingers pressed and rolled the tiny ball of bread.

'Ruda! *Ruda!*'

She turned her head very slowly; her eyes seemed unfocused, staring through him. He slipped his hand beneath the table. 'What's the matter with you? Are you sick?' He held her hand, crunched in a hard knot. She recoiled physically from him, pressing her back against the velvet seat.

'I have to go to the toilet.' Suddenly she rose to her feet. 'I'll meet you outside, I need some fresh air.'

Grimaldi made to stand, but she pushed past him and he slumped back down in the seat, watching as she walked stiffly towards the foyer, hands in tight fists at her side. She brushed past an elaborate display of ferns and then quickened her pace, almost running to the cloakrooms. There was only one other occupant, a tourist applying lipstick, examining her reflection in the mirror. Ruda knocked against her, but made no apology, hurrying into the vacant lavatory. She had no time to shut the door, but fell to her knees, clinging to the wooden toilet seat as she began to vomit. She felt an instant release, and sat back on her heels panting; again she felt the rush of bile, and leaned over the basin, the stench, the white bowl – she pushed away until she was hunched against the partition.

'Are you all right? Do you need me to call someone?' The tourist stood well back, but very concerned.

Ruda heaved again and forced herself once more to be sick into the lavatory bowl.

'Should I call a doctor?'

Ruda wiped her mouth with the back of her hand, and without even looking at the woman, snapped, 'Get out, just get out and leave me alone!'

Ruda slowly rose to stand, pressing herself against the partition, then crossed unsteadily to the wash basin. She ran cold water and splashed it over her face, then patted herself dry with the soft hand-towels provided. She opened her handbag and fumbled for her powder compact. Her whole body tingled, the hair on the back of her hands was raised, the same strange, almost animal warning at the nape of her neck. Was it this hotel? Something in this hotel . . . ? The white tiled walls, the white marble floor – had she been here before?

She seemed to step outside herself, look at herself. What was wrong? And then, just as she had always done, she began to work the calm, talking softly, whispering that it was just the whiteness, it was the white tiles, it was seeing Tommy, it was nothing more. It was a natural reaction, it was just shock, delayed shock at seeing him, seeing Tommy.

*

157

Ruda passed through the large foyer, her composure regained. She paused, wary, as if listening for something, to something, but then she shrugged her shoulders and headed towards the main revolving doors. She made no attempt to return to Grimaldi, just walked out, had to get out of the building.

As Ruda stepped outside, Hylda was scurrying towards the staff entrance, a small hidden door at the side of the large hotel. She stopped in her tracks, seeing the tall woman standing on the steps. For a moment she thought she was seeing the Baroness, but then she shook her head at her stupidity; this woman was much bigger, her dark hair long. Still, as she continued through the staff entrance, she wondered where she had seen the woman before. She unpacked her working shoes and slipped them on, carefully placing her other shoes in her locker. As she closed the door and crossed to the mirror to run a comb through her hair, she remembered. The circus poster. It was the woman from the circus poster, she was sure of it and rather pleased with her recall. She wondered if she was staying at the hotel; perhaps, if she was, Hylda could ask for her autograph.

A chambermaid coming off duty called out to Hylda, and scurried over to her. She asked furtively if it was true that the Baroness was insane; rumours were rife and she was eager to gossip. Hylda refused to be drawn into a conversation, and the young girl pulled a face and changed the subject, moving on to further news. Yesterday a dwarf had been found murdered in the red-light district just behind the hotel, his body beaten. They had first thought it was a child, his body was so small; she knew about it because her boyfriend worked with the *Polizei*. She came close to Hylda and hissed: 'He was a Jew!'

158

CHAPTER 6

GRIMALDI LEFT the Grand Hotel, unable to find Ruda. He walked a while, then caught a bus back to the circus.

Baron Maréchal and Helen remained in the hotel bar. The Baron knew he had been rude to leave Helen waiting so long, and attempted to explain his reasons. She said no explanation was necessary, that if he needed to speak with Dr Franks alone, that was his business. He kissed her hand, saying that her understanding never ceased to amaze him.

The Baron sipped his drink, placing it carefully on the paper napkin. 'Franks knows that the present situation cannot continue.'

The manager approached their table, and excused his intrusion. For a moment the Baron half rose from his seat, his face drained of colour. 'Is it my wife?'

The manager handed the Baron a folded envelope containing faxes that had been sent that morning. Helen saw the relief pass over Louis's face, and he tipped the manager lavishly before he opened the envelope. He read through the five fax sheets, handing each one to Helen as he did so.

There was no record of a Vebekka Lynsey in Philadelphia,

159

and the woman who had once run the model agency that first employed Vebekka confirmed that her real Christian name was Rebecca. Still, checks on Rebecca Lynsey in Philadelphia produced no results. Two girls who had once been employed by the same agency had been tracked down. They remembered Rebecca, and one thought her real surname was Goldberg, but could not be absolutely sure. She had shared a room with Rebecca, and remembered her receiving letters in that name.

A Mr and Mrs Ulrich Goldberg had subsequently been traced to an address in Philadelphia, and though they had no direct connection to the Baroness, they were able to give further details. Ulrich Goldberg's cousin, Dieter, or David, Goldberg, had run a successful furrier business until 1967. He and his wife Rosa had arrived in Philadelphia from Canada in the fifties. They had one daughter, Rebecca Goldberg. Was Rebecca Goldberg Vebekka Lynsey? Ulrich Goldberg, when shown recent photographs of Vebekka, was unable to state that they were definitely of her, but admitted there was a great similarity.

According to Ulrich, Rebecca was last seen at her father's funeral in January 1972. She had been distant and evasive, speaking briefly to only a handful of mourners, and had soon departed. No one had seen or heard from her since. A number of photographs were being forwarded by express mail, taken when she was about ten or twelve years old.

Mr and Mrs Ulrich Goldberg had arrived in the United States in the late 1930s from Germany. They knew that David Goldberg's wife was or had been a doctor, born in Berlin, but the time when she had married and emigrated to Canada was something of a mystery. Although the two

Goldberg families were related, Ulrich openly admitted that he and his wife had not been on close terms with David Goldberg – and found his wife a very cold, distant woman.

The Baron finished reading the last page and handed it to Helen. She read it in silence, then folded the fax sheets and replaced them in their envelope. The Baron lit a cigar, and turned to Helen. 'This could all be some kind of confusion. These are not from a detective, he's my chauffeur!'

Helen nodded, and then chose her words carefully. 'The date of the funeral, is that when Vebekka left Paris?'

The Baron frowned, picked up the envelope, and after a moment nodded.

Helen spoke quietly. 'First you have to deal with the lies Vebekka has told, or the cover-up. Perhaps she simply didn't want you to know anything about her family, for whatever reason, but if she really is Rebecca Goldberg, and her mother was born in Berlin, we can do some detective work of our own. Maybe there are relatives still living here, maybe someone who knew them. We could try to trace them.'

The Baron pinched the brow of his nose; everything was too much for him to take in.

Helen twisted the stem of her glass. 'Perhaps the reason, or a possible reason, was that your family were against your marrying Vebekka.' She hesitated. Would Vebekka's being Jewish have been one of the reasons why the Baron's family disapproved of the marriage? She decided not to broach the subject; after all, she was sure Vebekka was Catholic. She sipped her drink and put down the glass. Perhaps, as Louis himself had said, this was all a misunderstanding. But if Louis was hesitant to check out this Goldberg connection, there was no reason why she shouldn't.

Hylda had almost finished a sleeve and was beginning to check the measurements on her knitting when Vebekka stirred, and opened her eyes. Slowly she turned to face Hylda and smiled. 'Have I been sleeping long?'

Hylda nodded, said it was after two, but that she needed all the sleep she could get. She helped the Baroness out of the bed, and wrapped a dressing-gown around her thin shoulders. She assisted her into the bathroom, where big towels were warming on the rail. She had to help her into the bath, but Vebekka slid into the soap- and perfume-filled water with a sigh of pleasure.

Hylda had gently towelled Vebekka dry, feeling protective and motherly as the thin frame rested against her, and Vebekka seemed loath to let her go, clinging to her as they returned to the bedroom. Then the Baroness sat in front of her mirror and opened one of her precious vanity cases. 'I need my hair done, Hylda.'

Hylda said that she would try, but she had never done this blowing and combing and was not sure how to go about it. Vebekka had giggled and begun taking out small pots and brushes. 'No, no – my roots! I need my roots done. See, the grey hair is showing through.'

Hylda watched as Vebekka mixed her tint, stirring it into a plastic container. 'It's called Raven. It looks sort of purple, but it comes out black, see. Mix the two, now stir them together.'

With Vebekka parting her hair and clipping sections, Hylda began to brush the thick purplish liquid into the hair line. Then Hylda sat and waited, timing to the last second: the tint had to be left on for twenty minutes. Meanwhile, Vebekka manicured her hands, creamed her elbows and neck, then her legs, and her arms. Together they returned to the bathroom and Hylda shampooed and washed out the tint. Her hands were covered with the dye, but she soaped and rinsed and conditioned, under Vebekka's instructions. Then she wrapped a towel around the clean, tinted head and they returned to the bedroom. Next Vebekka directed Hylda to hold the dryer while she used the brush. 'I'm young again, Hylda, see? You were very good. Now I want to look beautiful, a little make-up, rouge . . .'

Hylda was fascinated at the transformation, even more so when she helped the Baroness into a flowing silk and lace garment, so delicate it floated when Vebekka moved, the lace on the sleeves trailing like a medieval costume.

Hylda ordered a light luncheon of boiled fish, some milk and vegetables, and she was pleased to see that Vebekka ate every morsel. Just as she was ringing for room service to take the trolley away, the Baron entered to find his wife sitting like a princess at the window. His face broke into a smile of delight. 'You look wonderful! And you have eaten? Good, good . . . do you feel better?' Hylda made herself scarce, entering the main bedroom to tidy the room and remake the bed.

The Baron bent to kiss his wife's cheek, she smelt sweet and fresh, her hair gleamed like silk. She smiled, and looked up into his concerned face. 'Did you come in to see me earlier?'

'No, I had a cocktail with Helen. If you need her she is in her room.'

She cocked her head to one side. 'Well, don't you two get too familiar!'

He turned away, irritated.

'I was just teasing you, Louis, it was just – well, strange. I was sure someone came in . . . maybe I was dreaming.'

With her husband's assistance she stood up, clinging to his hand. 'I think I will rest for a while now. You don't have to stay, I have Hylda. Maybe Helen would like to go sightseeing? She must be very bored.'

They walked slowly to the bedroom, and suddenly she leaned against him. 'Remember in that old movie with Merle Oberon, when she said, "Take me . . . take me to the window, I want to see the moors one last time!"' Vebekka did such a good impersonation of the dying heroine from *Wuthering Heights* that she made Louis laugh; he swept her in his arms and gently carried her to the bed.

He stood by watching as Hylda fluffed up her pillows, remained watching as Hylda gently drew the sheet around her and then closed the curtains, leaving the room in semi-darkness. Then she asked if she might take a break for an hour as she had not had her own lunch. He nodded, dismissing her with an inclination of his head, and sat in the chair she had vacated.

Vebekka lay with her eyes closed, as if unaware he was there. She could have been laid out at a funeral home she was so still, the perfect make-up, the long dark lashes, her hair outlining her face, framing its beauty. The Baron took out his gold cigarette case, opening it silently, patted his pockets for his lighter, and kept his eyes on her as he clicked it open. Still she didn't stir. He inhaled deeply and let the smoke drift from his mouth to form a perfect circle above his head. Had she woven all these lies about herself? Why? He couldn't think of a reason for not telling him – unless she was ashamed, but ashamed of what? The more he stared at the still figure, the more unanswered questions crossed his mind. Was it his fault? He could hear her, as if she was saying it to him now: 'My father's dead. I have to go to America to see to the funeral.'

She had said it so matter-of-factly, as if suggesting she fly to New York for a dress fitting. He had asked if she wished him to accompany her and she had smiled, shaking her head, reminding him that he was flying to Brazil for a polo game. All he could remember was his relief at not having to alter his plans. He had not been in Paris when she returned, so the funeral was not discussed. She had bought so many gifts for the children and for him, and had laughed at her extravagance, saying she was surprised at how much her father had left. Louis knew it was a considerable amount, because his own lawyers had telephoned to discuss the matter, but she had been uninterested in the money, as he was. She had been happy, she had been well – above all, happy.

These infrequent episodes always remained vivid to him, because when Vebekka was happy the entire family's spirits lifted. She was so energized, arranging secret outings and surprise parties, like a child. Her good spirits extended beyond the family circle: she arranged dinner parties, dressed up for masked balls. As a hostess she was a constant delight, charming and making everyone feel immediately at ease.

He leaned forward, noting in the semi-darkness the contours of her face. The way her long exquisite fingers rested like an angel's, one hand on top of the other – the perfect nails, her tiny wrists. It was hard to believe that those long tapering delicate hands could become like vicious claws.

The Baron pondered on his conversations with Dr Franks. Was he in some way to blame? Was it his fault? In the quietness of the room he could honestly ask himself if he was guilty and why the glimpses of sun in her life were so shortlived now, so rare, and why, when she changed, there was such anguish.

He got up to stub out his cigarette. From the dressing table he looked at the still sleeping woman; she had not moved. He had to think not just of himself, but of Sasha, the boys; they too had suffered, they had been forced to care for their mama, watch out for the signs. His eldest daughter had retreated into a social life that left little or no time to spend at home. The boys had drawn very close to each other. The real damage had been done to his younger daughter, so much younger than the others that she had seen fewer good periods.

Louis would perhaps never know what damage had been done to his sons and daughters. He sighed. It would be easy to slip the pillow from the side of the bed, press it to her face, and it would be over. No one could say he had not been driven to it, that she did not deserve it.

She stirred, her hands fluttered, lifted a moment, and then rested again. She turned her head towards Louis, slowly opened her eyes. He wondered if she knew he was there, wondered if anyone could understand what it was like to turn to someone you loved, and then face a stranger, and worse – be afraid. That awful moment of awareness when he knew it was happening. When the face he loved became distorted, the mouth he kissed pulled back like an animal, the voice he loved, snarled – and the gentle arms lashed out like steel traps.

He pressed his back against the dressing table, watching. Was he about to see the transformation now? The slender arms stretched and she moaned softly, then smiled with such sweetness. 'I thought you were going out? How long have you been here?'

'Not long,' he lied, and sat on the edge of the bed.

'Where's Hylda?'

'She's having something to eat.'

'She's so sweet.'

'How do you feel?'

'Good . . . refreshed. Have I eaten? Where's Helen?'

'I don't know, she may have gone shopping, I don't know.'

Vebekka sat up and shook her head. 'We did my hair, Hylda and I. What time is it?' She looked at her bedside clock, and then threw back the sheet. 'We can call Sasha and the boys.'

He watched her slip her feet into satin slippers, and then yawn, lifting her arms above her head. 'I feel hungry, I am ravenous! Hot chocolate, I need something sweet, we call room service? Where is Hylda? Oh, you said . . . and Helen? Oh, shopping, my mind's fuzzy.'

Louis hesitated, then told himself not to draw back now, to go through with it. 'I'm glad you feel better, and hungry. Dr Franks will be pleased too.' He saw the cat-like reaction, her eyes narrowed. He continued, 'Franks is waiting for me to call him. He said for me to contact him as soon as you recovered.'

'Really?' she said flatly, and turned away.

'Yes, really. So, my dear, shall I call him?'

She pursed her lips. 'Oh, I can't see him yet. I'm still too weak. Can you get Hylda for me?'

Louis opened the curtains, warned himself not to

back off, not this time. 'Shall I tell Dr Franks maybe tomorrow?'

'Oh, I don't know. Is Anne Maria in?'

Louis crossed and took her hand, drew her to him. 'Come and sit down. I'll get Hylda and Anne Maria, but first we need to talk.'

She sat on the dressing-table stool, looking up at him.

'I'm going to call Dr Franks, right now. What shall I tell him?'

She hunched her shoulders. 'I can't see him for a while.'

He sighed and stuffed his hands into his pockets. 'What does that mean? A day? Two days? A week? How long do you expect us all to wait around here? This is the entire reason—'

She retorted angrily, interrupting him, 'I know why we came, and I have agreed to see him, but not just yet!'

When the Baron suggested they ask Franks to come and see her later in the afternoon, she pursed her lips. 'I have to rest.'

He walked to the door, saying he would call him anyway.

'I *don't want* to see him, I've changed my mind. Besides I feel as if I am getting stronger. Without all those pills that wretched woman makes me take, my system is getting cleansed – I am detoxifying, it's always a slow process, I am bound to have some withdrawal symptoms and—'

'That's right, keep on with the excuses, but this time I am not taking no for an answer. If you want to stay here a month I'll arrange it, but you are going to Dr Franks.'

'Don't be so nasty to me. Why are you being so nasty?'

'For God's sake, I am not being nasty, you are being childish. I'll call him now.'

'No.'

He looked at her, opening the door.

'I *said no*.'

He slammed the door shut – hard. '*You* have no say in the matter, do you understand?'

'I won't see him.'

The Baron crossed the room and gripped her arm. 'You will see him, do you hear me, you will see him, we agreed, *you* agreed and you cannot change your mind now.'

'Why not? It's my mind.'

He released her arm. 'Right, *now* it is! But for how long? I've told you, this is the last time, it's your last chance.'

'Don't you mean yours?'

He had to control his temper. 'We have nothing left, Bekka, you and I both know it. I am doing this for you – not for me, for you.'

'Liar. You want me certified and dumped.'

'I don't want to fight with you, Bekka, I want to help you. Can't you understand it? That is all I have ever wanted to do – help you.'

She stared at him, pouting childishly. He kept his voice low, trying to be controlled. 'You need help, you know it. If not for me . . .'

'Oh, shut up! I've heard that one too many times.' She mimicked him, '"If not for me, do it for yourself."' She turned on him. 'This is for you, Louis, I am here in this bloody awful country for *you*. *You* want to get rid of me, don't you think I know it? Well, one, I will not give you a divorce, two, I will go to see Dr Franks when I feel up to going to see him, in my own time when I feel fit and well enough, and I will not be pressured by you, or by that whore Helen. I will not be forced into seeing this crank because *you* want to get rid of me and run off with that tart.'

'Tart? You mean Helen? For God's sake, she is your friend, your doctor – and, Bekka, I am not running anywhere, I never have before, and I don't intend to now.'

'But you are leaving me? Aren't you? You've decided, haven't you?' She plucked a tissue from its container, and wiped her face, slowly removing her make-up. She had only done her hair and made herself look pretty for him. She murmured under her breath about Helen again.

'Helen has nothing to do with any decision I make.'

She smiled. 'Ah, you're making a decision all by yourself, are you? Well, that does make a change.'

He refused to be drawn into an argument, and their eyes met in the mirror. 'No, Bekka, you make the decision this time, it's up to you. If you refuse to see Dr Franks, then . . .'

She held his gaze with a defiant stare. 'Then what?'

'You cannot return to the children.'

'They are old enough to make their own decisions.' She said it with a pout, but he could see her eyes were beginning to flick, blinking rapidly.

'Sasha is not.'

Her hands trembled and she began to twist the tissue, but still she didn't look away from him. 'You can't do that to me! I love Sasha, she needs me.'

'You give me no alternative. I've told you, this is your last chance.'

He walked out. Even after he had closed the door, he felt as if her eyes were on him. He poured a brandy, his hands shaking as he lifted the glass, his body tense, waiting. Would she begin throwing things, screaming, was she going to come hurtling out of the bedroom? The brandy hit the back of his throat, warming him. He poured another measure, and then froze. The telephone extension rang once, he knew she was making a call, and he hurled the glass down, breaking the stem. Was she calling Sasha? He hurried to the bedroom, about to fling open the door. He could hear her talking; he pressed his head to the door to listen.

Vebekka's palm was sweating, small beads of perspiration glistened on her brow. She could feel a trickle of sweat slip from her armpit, but she waited, licking her lips, her mouth as dry as her body was dripping. She gripped the telephone tighter, afraid she would unconsciously replace it.

'Dr Franks? This is Baroness Maréchal, I—' She could hear him breathing, then asking how she was. She had to swallow once, twice before she could reply. 'I am very much better.'

'Good, I am glad to hear it.'

The sweating made her feel weak, her whole body trembled. Her hair was wringing wet – she could see the clear drops, became mesmerized by them.

'Hello? Baroness? Hello?' Dr Franks could hardly hear her, but he knew she was still on the line. 'Are you experiencing any adverse effects? Any withdrawal symptoms? Baroness?'

'Sweating, I am sweating—'

She gasped and had to reach for the dressing-table top to steady herself; she felt as if she was going to faint.

'That is only to be expected. You must drink, can you hear me? You must drink as much water as possible, spring water, keep drinking. Would you like me to come and see you?'

'No!'

Franks couldn't hear her. He asked again, 'I can be with you in half an hour. Would you like me to come to see you?'

There was a long pause. He could not tell if she was still on the line or not.

She whispered, 'I would like to come to see you.'

'Pardon? I can't hear you.'

'I want you to help me, I want to come to you.'

Franks punched the air. 'That is good, I can arrange for you to have the entire morning. Shall we say nine in the morning? Baroness?'

'Thank you.' Carefully she replaced the phone, it felt heavy. Her hands clasped tightly together. Vebekka felt nothing but fear, she had hardly been able to finish the call.

The Baron was elated that she had called Franks herself. He had not expected her to have the strength. He called down to the desk to ask for Hylda to come to their suite immediately. He then called Anne Maria to check on his wife. He was banking on Dr Franks, as if on a miracle cure; it was naïve of him, and he knew it. But even if Franks could not help Vebekka, at least the Baron could honestly tell himself that they had tried. And then he could, without guilt, have her placed in an institution. Facing the prospect no longer gave him any regrets, it was the only choice he had. From the open door to her bedroom, he watched for a brief moment as Anne Maria attended to Vebekka. He could see that her nightgown was sodden, her face dripping with sweat and she was mumbling incoherently. The Baron saw Anne Maria check his wife's pulse, then take her temperature. He continued to watch as Vebekka struggled a moment, her arms thrashing at her sides, and then she grew listless, still sweating profusely. He turned away as Anne Maria began to remove his wife's delicate nightgown. Vebekka seemed unaware of the nurse, and when Anne Maria realized the Baron was watching she hesitated, the gown half removed.

He bowed his head. 'I'll be in the foyer if you need me.'

He didn't go to the foyer but to the small bar at the rear of reception. There was no mistress for him to run to; instead, he sat hunched in the corner of the bar with a cognac.

Vebekka seemed grateful when Hylda bustled in and quickly began to help Anne Maria change the bed linen. They changed her nightdress, and continued to place cold compresses on her head. Bottles and bottles of mineral water were brought up. Hylda helped her to hold the glass, encouraged her to drink as much as possible. Vebekka began to shiver, and more blankets were piled on top of the quilt.

Hylda was sitting close to the bed, wringing out the cold compress – Vebekka had gone from shivering with cold to sweating with fever. At least she was sleeping deeply now, but Hylda grew more and more concerned. She gestured for Anne Maria to move closer to the bed and watched as she took Vebekka's pulse. It was rapid, but nothing to be too concerned about. She felt the skin on the underside of Vebekka's wrist. There was a shiny area of skin, whiter than the rest. Anne Maria pointed it out to Hylda.

'What is that mark on her wrist from?'

Anne Maria whispered, 'She told me it was a burn, it looks more like a skin graft.' She continued whispering as she pointed out that it was the same wrist Vebekka had cut the night they had arrived. She smirked, suggesting that perhaps Vebekka had attempted it before. Hylda said nothing, she could see the fresh wound already healing, but the white, neat scar tissue was higher up, about four inches from the base of the Baroness's palm.

Ruda shouted out orders to Vernon and Mike, and they rushed to finish attaching the locks to the arena cages. She attempted to work on the new plinths for an entire hour but could not concentrate, could not give the rehearsal her full attention. She had a headache: the harder she worked the worse it became, and the cats picked up on her tension. Mike had not seen Ruda so obviously tense in the ring or take so many risks as she put the cats through their paces. She snatched a towel left stuck between the bars and wiped the sweat from her face and neck.

'And again, Mike. Let's go from the top again! *Vernon*, get Mamon's cage in position, *now* . . . move it the pair of you!'

It was just after four when Vebekka woke, and she reached out for Hylda's hand, struggled to sit up, drank thirstily from a glass Hylda held, then rested back on the pillows.

She looked to the window, asked for it to be opened as she wanted some fresh air. Hylda obliged. 'Is this too much?'

'No, it feels good. Has it stopped raining?'

'Yes, just. But there are dark clouds, I think there could be a storm.'

Suddenly Vebekka's body went rigid and blinding colours flashed across her brain. Hylda rushed back to her side. 'What is it? What is it?'

The thin hands clutched the sheets, her body seemed in spasm, and Hylda ran out to call for Anne Maria.

The colours screamed in her head, red . . . blood red . . . green . . . they were coming fast, flashes of brilliant reds, greens and blues. When Hylda returned, Vebekka was struggling to get on to her feet, she kept repeating, '*Up . . . up!*'

Neither woman could restrain her; she struggled to get to her feet, her hands pushing them away. Then, as quickly as the spasm had occurred, it stopped. She flopped back on to the pillows, clutching her head as if in agony. Hylda tried to put an ice-cold cloth on her brow but Vebekka swiped at her, screamed for her to get away, to stay away from her.

Hylda stepped back, frightened by the force of that skinny arm. Shocked, she looked to Anne Maria, but she was well back, not attempting to go anywhere near the thrashing figure.

'Should we call someone?' Hylda asked.

Anne Maria walked out of the room, warning over her shoulder for Hylda to stay away from the bed. Vebekka was rubbing at her hair, banging her head with her fists. 'Stop it! Stop it! Make it stop, please God, make it stop!' The colours hammered, flashed, and she couldn't get her breath. Panting and gasping, she reached out to Hylda, trying to get hold of her. Anne Maria came back with the straitjacket, unwrapping it from its plastic case. 'I told them she could have one of her turns. That doctor should be here now, never mind her husband!'

Hylda stood guard by the bed, her arms open wide, protecting Vebekka. '*No*, no! Don't put that on her, I won't let you!'

Anne Maria looked at the bed, and tossed the jacket aside. 'They shouldn't have taken her off the sedatives. This has happened before. Well, I am not taking any responsibility, she'll attack you . . .'

She stormed out, and Hylda kept hold of Vebekka, calming her, stroking her hair, saying over and over that she was there, she wasn't going to leave her. The thin arms relaxed and Vebekka rested her head against Hylda's shoulder. 'Oh, God, help me, what is it? What happens to me, Hylda?'

Hylda coaxed her to lie back on the pillows, and Vebekka didn't struggle – she was too exhausted. She whispered, like a frightened child, 'It is closer. It is so close, I can't make it go away . . .'

Hylda made soft shushing sounds, as if to a little girl. 'What is it? What are you frightened of? Is it something in the room?'

'I don't know. It takes me over, controls me, and I can't fight it any more, I'm so tired . . . so tired.'

Hylda continued stroking Vebekka's hair. 'What do you think it is? If you tell me, then maybe it won't be so frightening.'

Vebekka turned away, curling her knees up, her arms wrapped around herself. How could she answer when she didn't know? All she knew was that it was closer than it had ever been before.

Hylda closed the window, drew the curtains, and in the semi-darkness returned to the bedside, bending down to try to see Vebekka's face. She talked softly all the time, saying she was there, nothing could come into the room, nothing in the room could frighten her. She stood by the bed, waiting, but Vebekka didn't move. Gradually, she crept out, closing the door silently behind her.

Hylda stood in the empty suite lounge, not knowing what she should do – stay or try to find the Baron or Helen Masters. She looked at her watch, it was almost five, glanced at Anne Maria's closed door and back to the bedroom. The suite was silent, she could hear the clock ticking on the marble mantelpiece, but outside the taxis tooted, the noise of traffic drawing up outside the hotel was intrusive and she was afraid it would wake Vebekka.

Hylda crossed to draw the wooden shutters closed. They were heavy and she moved from one window to the next before she lifted the fine white curtains to look into the street below. Hylda's hand was on the shutter when she saw the solitary figure. She could not see whether it was a man or woman, because a car drew up and obscured her view. The driver appeared to say something to the dark figure, who bent down then straightened up, gesturing for the car to drive on. Hylda could tell now that it was a woman, but her hair was drawn back tightly from her face. The collar of her thick overcoat was turned up. But what caught Hylda's attention was the way the figure seemed to be staring towards the hotel, her head moving very slightly from side to side, as if looking from window to window, floor to floor. At any moment now she would face Hylda, and Hylda could catch a better view of her – but just then the doors to the suite were thrown open.

Helen Masters strode in and asked brusquely if the Baron was with his wife. As Hylda turned back to close the shutters, the woman on the pavement below had vanished. 'No, Dr Masters, he is not.'

At that precise moment the Baron walked in. Helen smiled a greeting. He seemed a little unsteady. 'Helen, I called your room, have you been shopping?'

'No, Louis, you must come with me. I've traced a woman, a relative of David Goldberg's wife, Vebekka's mother. She said she would see us.'

'Excuse me, Baron . . .'

They both turned to Hylda, as if only then realizing she was in the room. When she nervously repeated what had occurred, the Baron slumped into a chair, then turned to Helen. 'She called Franks herself, earlier this afternoon, said she would see him tomorrow. And now this!' He opened the bedroom door and went into the darkened room.

Helen asked if Anne Maria was with Vebekka, but Hylda shook her head. She was twisting her hands nervously, and Helen went to her side. 'Are you all right, did she frighten you?'

Hylda whispered to Helen that she would like to speak with her, that she did not mean to say more than she should, but felt Helen should know what Anne Maria's intentions had been.

Helen moved her further away from the bedroom, patting Hylda's shoulder. 'It's all right, you can tell me. I want to know what happened. It's very important.' Briefly, and in a hushed voice, Hylda related to her the story of the straitjacket.

Louis bent down to try to see Vebekka's face. She appeared to be sleeping. He gave a feather-like touch to her head and then joined Helen. 'She's sleeping.'

Helen gestured for him to come close and repeated everything Hylda had told her. The Baron strode to Anne Maria's room, knocked and without waiting for an answer entered and closed the door behind him. Anne Maria looked up from her book, flustered, trying to straighten her blouse.

'I would like you to leave, you can arrange a flight at the reception desk.'

He opened his wallet, and before Anne Maria had time to reply, he left a thick wad of folded banknotes on her bed. She snapped her book closed, wanting obviously to discuss the matter, but he walked out. She stared at the money, her lips pursed. Then she counted it, looked at the closed door and swore under her breath.

The Baron and Helen Masters were sitting in the lounge when Anne Maria came out of her room, with case packed and coat over her arm. Her face was tight with anger. 'Thank you for your generosity, Baron. Perhaps when you return to Paris, you would be kind enough to give me a letter of recommendation.'

The Baron threw the straitjacket at her feet. 'There will be no letter of recommendation.'

Anne Maria stepped over the straitjacket, and crossed to the suite's double doors. She opened the right-hand side, about to walk out without a word, but then she turned back. 'I would be most grateful for a letter. I will require one for future employment.' Helen put out her hand to restrain the Baron. Anne Maria looked at them both with disdain. 'I will be only too pleased to give *you* a letter of recommendation – to enable you to have the

Baroness certified. She should have been, years ago! Dr Franks is just another quack, another fool who'll take your money like all the rest of them. There will be no cure, it is a fantasy. Your wife, Baron, is insane. She has been since I have been in your employment. Next she will kill someone – and that will be entirely your fault.'

Helen's hand was thrown from the Baron's arm as he leapt up and strode across the room. 'You had better leave before I throw you out. *Get out!*'

'As you wish, Baron. I will collect my personal belongings from the villa.'

He pushed her out and slammed the door shut. 'I should have done that months ago.' At his feet was the straitjacket. He picked it up and stared at it. He seemed totally defeated.

'Don't give up, Louis, it isn't true. I believe in Franks.'

He sighed, laying the jacket on a chair. He kept his back to Helen. 'Maybe she is right, maybe this is all a waste of time. I am so tired of it all, Helen.' His whole body tensed. 'I wish to God she was dead!'

'That's not true.'

He turned to face her. 'Isn't it? I was sitting by her bedside, earlier today, thinking if I had the guts I would put a pillow over her face and end it, for her, for me, then—'

'Then?'

He sighed, slumping into a chair. 'She was lucid, understood that I cannot allow her to be with Sasha, and she did it. It was her decision to call Franks.'

Helen crossed to her handbag and took out her notebook. 'I am sure he will help her, but I think we should at least talk to this woman. The more we know of

180

Vebekka's background the better. Franks will need as much information as possible. Louis?'

He cocked his head to one side and gave a rueful smile. 'Fine, whatever you say.'

Helen picked up her coat, heading for her own suite. 'I'll have a bath and change. We can leave when Hylda returns. Perhaps I'll order some coffee to be sent up.'

The Baron nodded, and then gave a delightfully boyish smile. 'Yes, I think some coffee would be an excellent idea.'

The coffee arrived moments later, and the Baron downed two cups before he felt at all revived. He checked the time, first on his wristwatch and then the clock on the mantelpiece. It was five-thirty. He put in a call to his sons, and spoke to Sasha for a while. He said they missed her, and that he would tell her mama that she was being a good girl. The high-pitched voice hesitated before asking if her mama was being a good girl. He told her that everything was fine, and her mama would talk to her very soon. He managed to keep his voice calm and relaxed, but he was crying.

'Will she be coming home better, Papa?'

Louis pinched his nose between thumb and forefinger. 'I hope so, but she hasn't been very well for a day or so, which means we may be here longer than we anticipated.'

Sasha sighed with disappointment, but then changed the subject, talking about school and her new pony and that she was practising dressage and entering a gymkhana – she was sure she would win a rosette this time. Angel – her pony – was living up to his name. 'Papa, we jumped a two-foot fence. He's wonderful!'

Louis congratulated his daughter, and then said he had

to go, there was another call on the line. Sasha made kissing sounds, and he waited for her to replace the receiver before he put his down. He heard the click, then another click. He frowned, replaced the receiver and walked into Vebekka's bedroom. She was propped up on her pillows, very pale, deep circles beneath her eyes.

'I will go to see the doctor tomorrow, Louis, even if you have to carry me there.' She sipped a glass of water, then replaced the glass on her bedside table. It took all her willpower to be calm, she needed something to help her, something to make her sleep, but she asked for nothing. She wasn't going to drug herself, not this time; she was determined she would see it through.

'I've dismissed Anne Maria. Hylda will be here shortly.'

She leaned back, closing her eyes. 'I never liked Anne Maria, she was so ugly. Will you hold my hand?'

He sat on the edge of the bed, lifted her hand to his lips and kissed her fingers; they were so thin, so weak.

'Will you promise me something, Louis?'

'Depends on what it is.'

She didn't open her eyes. 'I understand what trouble I cause, and I know I am always asking you to forgive me, but I always mean it, I always need your forgiveness. But if – if this doctor – if he thinks I will get worse, that these good moments will get fewer, and . . . you are right, that I shouldn't be with Sasha, I understand that, but you must understand, I never . . . I never intend to hurt anyone. I don't know what takes me over, but it unleashes such terrible—'

'I know . . . I know, but you must rest now, regain your strength.'

She withdrew her hand, turning away from him. 'Louis, if nothing can be done, you know, if after the hypnosis you find out things, I want no lies, no cover-ups, no new tests, because I don't think I can stand it any more. I'm getting worse, I know that, hours go by and I don't know what I have done, who I've hurt, so promise me.'

He knew what she was going to ask of him and he leaned over the bed to kiss her cheek. 'Sleep now . . .'

She opened her eyes: they pleaded, they begged him. 'Don't put me away, Louis, help me to end it – promise me?'

He kissed her again, tilted her chin in his hands, looked deep into her eyes. He didn't answer, and her eyelids drooped as she fell asleep, her chin still cupped in his hands.

They were still together like a loving couple when Hylda slipped quietly into the bedroom. Gently the Baron drew the covers to Vebekka's chin, and Hylda saw the way he brushed her cheek with the edge of his index finger.

'She was so frightened, sir, of the dark. Frightened someone was out there.'

The Baron patted Hylda's shoulder. 'Hylda, my poor darling is frightened of her own shadow. Thank you for your care and attention, good evening.'

Hylda whispered, 'Good evening,' as he quietly closed the door. She began to knit, then looked to the closed shutter and remembered the woman, the one she had seen outside earlier; she had been like a shadow, waiting, watching . . . The click-click of her knitting needles soothed and calmed Hylda.

Vebekka did not seem to be awake, but her hand moved closer to Hylda, and she said very softly: 'Ma . . . angel.'

183

Helen was still getting ready, so the Baron lit a cigarette, pacing the sitting room, tormented by his wife's request. He picked up the paper that Helen had left in the room, and a front-page article caught his attention. 'Murdered Man Identified.' He started to read the column. The man was called Tommy Kellerman, a dwarf, a circus performer, who had recently arrived in East Berlin from Paris. The *Polizei* requested anyone seeing Kellerman on or during the night of his murder to come forward.

Helen walked in, refreshed and changed. The Baron lowered the paper and smiled. 'You look lovely.' He was about to toss the paper aside when he passed it to Helen. 'Did you read this? A circus performer was murdered.'

Helen took the paper and glanced at the article. 'Yes, I was talking to one of the doormen. The hotel is only a few streets away from here, in the red-light district. Apparently they have no clues as to who did it – it happened late the same night we arrived. He was horribly beaten, the doorman was very keen to pass on all the gory details.'

The Baron drew on his fur-collared coat, and said he would call down for a taxi. Helen went to the window, drew open the shutter to look at the weather, then had a moment of *déjà vu* so strong that she had to step back from the window. Vebekka had been curled by the window, her nightgown covered in blood. Helen recalled the exact words she had said – 'We have done something terrible tonight' – and remembered thinking she was referring to Louis. But now something else came back to her: she had seen a man, a tall man, passing in the street below. She was sure of it.

'Good heavens, Louis, is there a description of the man

they are looking for?' She picked up the newspaper again, rereading the article, then something else jarred her memory, the word Paris leaped out from the paper, and she turned to Louis. 'When we were at Dr Franks's you said you remembered an incident with Vebekka and the children . . . something about a circus.'

But Louis did not hear her, he was on the telephone. 'There's a taxi waiting for us. I need to tell Hylda we are leaving.'

Hylda was given instructions that, should Vebekka awake, need anything, she should call Dr Franks. The Baron thanked her profusely for being such a caring companion and slipped some folded banknotes into her hand. She blushed and replied that she was happy to look after the Baroness. She added hesitantly, 'I hope she will be assisted by this Dr Franks, that whatever demons torture and frighten her will be driven away.'

The same taxi that the Baron and Helen used had just returned from the circus, having driven Ruda Grimaldi back to her trailer. The driver kept up a steady flow of conversation about the price of the circus tickets, and that there were already lines of people waiting for them. He was about to launch into telling them that the previous occupant of his taxi was one of the star performers, but Helen and the Baron began to speak to each other in French, ignoring him, and, as he couldn't understand a word they said, he concentrated on driving to the address in Charlottenburg. It was a long drive and he hoped the rain would keep off as they were about to get into the rush-hour traffic. The Grimaldi woman had been strange, said hardly a word, and she hadn't gone into the hotel but stood outside on the pavement, waiting, watching, looking up at the window, the collar of her big overcoat pulled up as if hiding her face. Then, after a while, she had asked him to return her to the circus. He thought it odd, because he had seen her leaving earlier in the afternoon – perhaps she had caught a bus then, been incognito, the famous often acted up – but stranger still, was the fixed expression on her face. Standing, so still, almost as if listening for someone to call out to her. Ruda Grimaldi had ordered him to pick her up the following day. He wondered if he could ask her for a couple of complimentary seats.

CHAPTER 7

AFTER RUDA GRIMALDI had identified her ex-husband at the mortuary, Inspector Torsen returned to his rundown station in the slum area of East Berlin. He and Rieckert proceeded laboriously to type out all the information about the people they had interviewed.

Kellerman's immigration papers had not been found at Customs. All Torsen knew to date was that he had arrived from Paris, booked into the hotel, eaten a hamburger and been murdered. Nobody seemed to have seen him or noticed anyone else either enter his room or leave it. Everyone who had known him from the circus felt his death was deserved. His ex-wife had not seen him since he had been in prison and was unable to describe the tattoo sliced from his left arm.

Rieckert put his typed report on Torsen's desk and since it was almost one-thirty went to collect his raincoat.

Torsen watched him. 'You know, for a few nights we may have to work overtime on this.'

'I have a date tonight. You coming out for a sandwich?'

'No, but you can have a toasted cheese and tomato sent over, just one round, rye bread, tell her I'll pay tomorrow.'

Rieckert shrugged and walked out. Torsen completed his own reports, adding that the hall porter from Kellerman's hotel should be questioned again. His stomach rumbled – he'd eaten nothing since breakfast and he hoped Rieckert wouldn't forget his sandwich. He put the kettle on to make himself an instant coffee and, waiting for the water to boil, he turned in his reports to the empty *Polizei Direktor*'s office, and filed a second copy for the *Leitender Polizei Direktor*, who was away on holiday.

The coffee jar was virtually empty and, someone having previously used a wet spoon, he had to chip away at the hardened coffee powder. He then fetched his own sugar supply, but could find no milk. He sighed, even thought about joining Rieckert, when his cheese on rye was delivered, wrapped in a rather grubby paper napkin but at least it was what he had ordered. He kept an eye on the delivery boy who hovered by the missing persons photographs, and not until he had left did Torsen return to his desk.

The bread was stale, he noticed as he chewed thoughtfully, reading the autopsy report. The heaviness of the blows indicated they were more than likely inflicted by a man – to have crushed Kellerman's skull must have taken considerable force. Whoever had killed him also ground his false teeth into the carpet. A heel imprint, retained in the pile of the carpet, was still being tested at the lab. The print was of a steel-capped boot heel, again probably a man's because of the size. Samples of mud and sawdust found at the scene of the crime were also still being tested.

Torsen made a few notes:

(a) Where did Kellerman go for his hamburger?
(b) How many dwarfs were attached to the circus?

(c) Were any dwarfs missing from Schmidt's circus? (Just in case they had lied about him not being employed there.)

(d) Sawdust – was it from the circus?

(e) Get the ex-Mrs Kellerman to give a written positive ID for burial to take place (Rabbi).

(f) Why was Tommy Kellerman in East Berlin?

Torsen wondered why she still used Kellerman's name and not Grimaldi's. Then he remembered something that had been nagging at the back of his brain. He scrambled for his notepad and scrawled a memo to himself. 'Check unsolved dossier – the magician.'

When Torsen's father had been detective inspector at the same station as his son, they had often discussed unsolved cases together. It had begun as a sort of test between the old policeman and his eager son, but the two men had eventually grown to enjoy discussing what they thought had happened, and why the case remained unsolved. One case they had nicknamed 'The Magician', because the murdered man had been an old cabaret performer. He too had been found brutally beaten and stabbed. The magician – he could not even recall the man's real name – had been discovered in the Kreuzberg sector; he had been dead for many months, his decomposed body buried under the floorboards . . . and his left arm had been mutilated. It was suspected that the mutilation had taken place because the discovery of a tattoo would have assisted police enquiries, may even have helped them identify him. They would have required a lot more assistance if his body had not been wrapped in a wizard's cloak. They had been able to identify him, but his killer had never been found.

It was, Torsen surmized, just a coincidence . . . but he could hear his father's voice, see that forefinger wagging in the air. 'Never believe in a coincidence when you are investigating a murder, there are no coincidences.'

Torsen picked up his notepad again.

(1) Discover any persons residing in East Berlin or in the vicinity of the dead man's hotel recently arrived from Paris.
(2) Call the Hospice Centre.
(3) Magician.

Torsen checked his watch, then demolished the rest of his lunch, carefully wiping the crumbs from his desk with the napkin. He sipped his coffee, draining the cup and then, unlike anyone else at the station, returned it to the kitchen, rinsed it out and left it on the draining board. He had a quick wash and brush up in the cloakroom before going back to his office, where he sifted through the work requiring immediate attention. Then he checked his watch again: he had taken exactly one hour, no more no less.

Rieckert was late back, by a good fifteen minutes. Torsen could hear him laughing in the corridor and snatched open the door. 'You're supposed to take one hour!' Rieckert held aloft a new jar of coffee as an excuse, asking if Torsen would like a cup. 'No thank you, now get in here on the double!'

Torsen left his door open and began to gather up all his half-completed vehicle-theft reports, at the same time shouting again for Rieckert to join him.

He was looking very authoritative when at last he

strolled in. 'I was just going to get some milk. We haven't got any.'

'These are more important – get them sorted. I want the lot filed and checked.'

'But I'm off at five-thirty!'

'You can leave when these are completed and not before. I have to go out later myself so the faster we get through them the—'

'Where are you going?' Rieckert interrupted sullenly.

'The Grand Hotel. I am, in case you are unaware of the fact, heading a murder investigation. I have to have further discussions with the manager and list all guests and, if the hall porter saw someone leaving the hotel around the time of the murder, perhaps I should have a look at the alleyway – the distance the porter would have been from him, if that is permissible with you!' To bring home his point Torsen began furiously jotting down further ideas in his thick notebook.

(a) How did the killer get to the hotel?

(b) Question taxi drivers.

(c) Question bus drivers.

(d) Question doormen at the Grand: very well lit-up reception area outside, within spitting distance of Kellerman's hotel.

(e) Discuss guests with hotel manager.

Ruda had been soaked to the skin standing outside the Grand Hotel yet she still went to see Mamon before she changed. As she turned to head towards her trailer, she saw Mike – and froze. He was still wearing Tommy

Kellerman's black leather trilby. She swore at herself again, at her stupidity for not remembering to burn it along with the rest of Kellerman's belongings. She watched Mike heading towards the meat trailer, but she couldn't do anything about him. She had to change and get ready to rehearse the act, already behind schedule. When she reached the trailer Grimaldi was already there, with an open bottle of brandy.

'Why don't you stay sober, at least until I've worked the act?'

'I just need something to warm me up, all right? I'm freezing. I looked all over the place for you. Why didn't you wait for me at the hotel? You just upped and walked out. Where the hell have you been?'

Ruda pulled on her old boots, ignoring his question, and suggested nastily that all he had to do was try to retrieve the old plinths, then slammed out of the trailer. Grimaldi cursed at her as she passed the window. Ruda didn't even turn her head, but gave him a V-sign. So much for thanking him for going with her to the mortuary. He didn't know where the hell he was with her. 'And you never have, you old goat,' he muttered to himself.

He really had not intended getting loaded, but he had just one more, then another, and then Tina tapped on the trailer door. She wore a raincoat over tights and a glittering bodysuit, and carried a feathered headdress. 'I hear you and the bitch went to see Kellerman this afternoon.'

Grimaldi nodded, offered her a drink which she refused. She surveyed the broken crockery, the smashed pictures, and half smiled when she said, 'Did you talk to her about us, then?'

'Yes, and it's settled . . . well, up to a point.'

'What's that supposed to mean?'

'We discussed it. She's not going to be easy.'

'But you knew that. Did you show her what we worked out?'

'I reworked bits of it. I can't just give her an ultimatum. She's worked her butt off for the act. It'll take a while to sort out.'

'Take a while! *Take a while!* You've been fobbing me off with that line for weeks. I'm pregnant, Luis, how long do you think I can get myself bounced around in my condition? You promised – promised you'd talk to her about it, about us.'

He drained the glass. 'And I just told you we talked about it. She's got a lot on her mind.'

'And I haven't? *I am pregnant!*'

He sighed, opening his arms, but she wouldn't come near him.

'I want you to get it written down, on paper, I want her out of this trailer, I'm not rooming with the girls any longer.'

He hung his head, his big hands clasped together. 'As soon as the opening's over, you and I can sort out the living accommodation.'

'There's nothing to sort out – we agreed. You give her half, that's fair – it's your act, half those animals are yours, this is your trailer. Just see how far she can go without you and your name.'

'She doesn't use my name. Now shut up.'

Tina hit the wall with the flat of her hand. 'She just uses you, and I can't bear to see it, everyone laughing at you behind your back – and what are you drinking for? What are you getting pissed for at this hour?'

She was giving him a thudding headache. 'I am not

193

getting pissed, I am just having a drop to warm me up – I've been standing around a freezing mortuary for half the fucking day. I've been wanderin' around lookin' for her, gettin' soaked to the bloody skin. She's been actin' like a bear with a sore arse. I dunno. Everybody is naggin' me, drivin' me nuts. So don't you start, just shut up! I dunno where she goes half the time, I dunno what she's doing.'

Tina sat down and began to pluck at the feathered headdress.

'Was it him, then?'

Grimaldi nodded. 'Yeah, it was him.'

'She must be sick in the head. How could she have married that grotesque, malformed creature?'

'Because he had a big dick.'

Grimaldi grinned, and she flung her headdress at him, but she smiled. 'So have you . . .' She went to him then, and sat on his knee. 'I want us to be married, and with me behind you, you could take over the act.'

He smiled ruefully. 'You think so?'

'I know so. You were the best, everyone tells me. They all say at your peak you were the best in the world.'

'Ah, yes, at my peak . . . that was quite a while ago, sweetheart. I've peaked and come up for air a few times, and I've plummeted. Maybe I'm too old.'

Her heavy breasts were pushed up by her costume and he bent forward to kiss them. She was so young, too young ever to have seen him perform. He had been at his peak before she was even born.

'I want to have the baby, and then you can begin to train me, teach me what to do. I want to be in the ring, I want my face in the centre of that poster.'

He laughed, a low rumble. 'I bet you do . . . but it takes a long time.'

'I'm young, I have time to learn.'

He eased her off his knee and filled a glass. 'She learned so fast, Tina. I've never seen anyone adapt to working with cats like Ruda.'

Tina pouted. 'Well, that was because she had the best to teach her – that's why I want you.'

He smiled. Sometimes she was so blatantly obvious it touched him. He leaned his back against one wall staring at the posters. 'See that one from Monte Carlo? That was her first solo performance. Then there's Italy, and France . . .'

Tina put her hands over her ears. 'I don't want to hear about her, all I want to know is if you are ditching her, getting a divorce.'

'Ditching her?'

'Well, separating, whatever you want to call it.'

The trailer door banged and Mike, wearing Kellerman's hat, popped his head round the door. 'We're almost set up, sir, if you want to come over, we're ready to go in about fifteen minutes.'

'Thanks, Mike. I'll be there.'

Mike gave Tina a good once-over, and she glared at him as he closed the door. Grimaldi was checking some of the broken pictures. One was of Ruda with Mamon, she was sitting astride him as if he was a pony – she was laughing. 'You know, she hardly ever laughed when we first met, was always so serious.'

Tina swung one foot up and down. 'Oh, please, no past glories. I get bored with all your past glories. All I am concerned with is the present, and the promises you make and don't keep.'

Grimaldi replaced the broken frame, hung the picture up without the glass. 'I'll talk to her some more after rehearsal.'

Tina clasped him in a hug from behind. 'Will we keep him?' She pointed to a picture of Mamon.

Grimaldi shook his head. 'No, she'll never part with him.'

She clung tighter. 'I'm sorry, I forgot, I'm sorry.'

He wanted to shrug her away, wanted her out of his way, but he stood there, her soft body curled around him, her pink young lips kissing his back, rubbing her nose across his jacket. 'You'd better go, I've got to get ready. We're trying out some new plinths, the cats could get tetchy.'

She picked up her headdress, and slung her coat round her shoulders. 'OK, I'll be by later. Can we have dinner?'

'Sure.'

She stared at his back, waiting for him to turn, but he didn't. She sighed, opening the trailer door. 'Be about nine, Luis?'

'Yes, nine's fine. See you then.'

'I'll talk to her with you, if you like.'

'No . . . no, that won't be necessary. I'll work it out.'

He sighed with relief when the door closed, and then bowed his head. 'You stupid bastard, what the hell are you getting into?' he asked himself.

Another glass and the bottle was half empty. Still he stared at the wall of photographs. Tina was such a child – he was old enough to be her father, he laughed to himself, her grandfather even. He lit a cigar knowing he should be going across to the arena, but he couldn't move. The more he drank the more each photograph recorded his past. He took sly glances at Ruda riding Mamon, as if he was drawn back to that single memory more than the others. He leaned over and unhooked it, ran his fingers across her face, and then smashed the frame against the side of the table, smashed it until the photograph itself was destroyed. 'I've got to get to the arena,' he kept telling himself – but he couldn't move. It was as if the brandy was opening up the scar down his body, opening it stitch by stitch until he felt as if he was on fire.

It had been late afternoon, winter quarters in Florida. He had watched her working the act, saw she was making extraordinary strides, knew he should have been in the ring with her. He saw her lifting the hoop, training Mamon to leap through it; the fire was lit on top, and Mamon jumped like the angel she called him. Next, he watched her edging the padding for the flames further and further around the hoop, each time Mamon leapt through. Now the entire hoop was alight. Mamon hesitated, and then he jumped straight through it. She hugged Mamon as if he were a puppy! And the hands standing around watching applauded and cheered. Mamon began a slow lope around the arena, and then on a command he moved closer and closer.

Luis had watched, genuine interest mingled with envy, as she held on to the massive creature's mane of thick black fur, and then sat astride him. One of the boys had taken the photograph, not Luis, but it was as clear a picture in his mind as it was in the frame. The way she had tossed back her head and laughed that deep, wonderful full-bellied laugh; he had never been able to make her laugh like that, had never witnessed her so free, so exhilarated, and he was consumed with jealousy.

Mamon was Ruda's baby, Ruda's aggressive, terrifying love. She worshipped him, and Luis knew she was too close to him, that no trainer should get so involved with one of the cats. The danger was that the animal could become too possessive of her, that when she was working with the others and fondled one, or gave it a treat, Mamon might become jealous and in his jealous rage he would attack.

Ruda and Grimaldi had argued about her training of Mamon. He had insisted she must refrain from treating him as if he was a pet. 'He is a killer, a perfect killing machine, if you forget what he is, then you place yourself in danger.' She had smirked at him, insinuated that he was jealous because he was too afraid even to get into the ring with Mamon – he was jealous of the way she was handling him. He had turned to her angrily. 'Wrong, Ruda. What I'm trying to do is to make you see. You treat Mamon differently. All the other cats, you're working as I taught you, but with that bastard you constantly give in to him. What you refuse to see is that he is dominating you and, lemme tell you, the first, the very first moment he sees he has you, he will attack. You must not treat Mamon differently, because he will automatically think he is stronger than you.'

Ruda had stood in sullen silence before she had answered. 'Mamon is different, I understand him, and he understands me.'

Luis had shaken his head in disbelief. 'You are being naïve, childish and foolish. He is not human, he is an animal.'

She had walked out, giving him one of her snarls, twisting her face. 'Maybe I'm one, too . . .'

But Ruda knew Luis was right, and she attempted not to be so familiar, to spend less time with Mamon. Still, he was the one she could train faster than the others.

They had introduced two more lionesses, and allowed Mamon to mate with both of them. Ruda watching him released into the compound, his powerful body loping round the two lionesses as he courted and showed himself off. The three disappeared into the huts, and she had sat outside all night, waiting. Luis had told her she should stay away from him the following morning, he would be all male, all animal – wild.

Mamon had walked out as the sun rose, his head low, his massive paws carefully crossing his pathway in a perfect, steady rhythm. His eyes caught the sun like amber lamps and Ruda stood up, her hands tight on the netting. Mamon rose up on his hind legs and roared, and she could feel his hot breath on her face. 'You perform well, my love? You screw the arses off them, did you? Who's a beautiful boy?'

He had banged his body sideways on to the meshing, and then loped off to drink at the trough, turning with water dripping from his mouth to see if she was still watching.

Both lionesses were pregnant, and Ruda watched over them until the birth. Two female Bengals were pregnant and a Siberian; Ruda had her time cut out watching over the cubs, and began to see less and less of Mamon. He became distant, defiant, more and more uncontrollable. Luis blamed Ruda, but she refused any assistance. Working in the ring with sixteen tigers, two lionesses and two lions, she was still confident that she could control her Angel.

Luis had been right behind her the first time she had taken over the main part of the act. Twice he broke up squabbles between two Bengals, but Ruda seemed to have the act under good control, until Sasha misjudged a leap and fell. She reared up as Jonah, a massive Bengal, tried to attack her, and Sasha fought back and somehow caught her right paw in the top of the meshing. Her claw held firm, and she hung, paws off the ground – open and vulnerable – as the tigers, only too ready for a scrap, moved in for a hoped-for kill. Luis shouted for pliers to be brought – and fast – and helped Ruda force the rest of the cats back into their positions on the plinths.

The lions remained seated, with Mamon at the top of the pyramid, seeming to survey the situation. Luis kept up his commands as Ruda obeyed him. The clippers were brought and with Ruda moving in front of Luis to cover for him, he unclipped the wire caught in Sasha's claw. She was away fast, unharmed, lashing out a warning to the others not to come near her.

'Keep them in position, Ruda . . . hold the positions, Ruda!'

She faced the cats, sweating, her whole body on fire with adrenaline. Sasha shook her head, became very vocal but moved back into position. The danger was over and Luis, at Ruda's side, put his arm around her. He was smiling. 'OK. You did OK!'

That was the moment Mamon chose to make his attack. He sprang down from the twenty-foot-high plinth, his body seeming hardly to touch the ground as he sprang again. Both front paws caught Luis in the chest, throwing him back against the railings, but he was back on his feet again fast. Mamon's right front paw ripped through Luis's shirt, cut open his chest and dragged him forwards. His face was close to the massive jaws, and Ruda was on Mamon's back, clinging to his mane, screaming her commands. Off his back again she lashed out with the whip, and Mamon turned his attention to her, stalked her, but she kept up the command for him to move off. Turning on her heels to keep the rest of the cats in her sight, she screamed out, '*Red* Mamon . . . *Red!*'

Luis's hands clutched the open wound of his chest as he backed towards the trap gate. He managed to stay on his feet, still ordering Ruda to get the cats in line ready to be herded out, before he collapsed half in and half out of the trap gate. Mamon went for him again, Luis's blood dripping down his jaws as, snarling, Mamon shook him like a rag doll, his teeth cutting through Luis's leather belt, ripping open his belly, trying to drag him like a piece of meat further into the arena. The boys got him out just in time.

When Ruda got the cats back down the traps to their cages, Luis was already aboard the ambulance and on his way to the emergency ward. She arrived at the hospital shortly after he was brought out of the operating room. His wound had taken one hundred and eighty-four stitches: he had been ripped from his throat to his groin. He remained in intensive care for eight days, as the wound festered and he suffered blood poisoning.

Ruda was at his bedside when he regained consciousness. His voice was barely audible as he told her to shoot Mamon, that he had warned her the cat would do something like this. She had wept, promised she would get rid of him, had even lied to him at other visiting times, saying that Mamon was gone, that the most important thing was for Luis to get well.

Grimaldi had recovered slowly, very slowly; the wound constantly reopened and he suffered from persistent infections, caused by rancid meat caught between Mamon's claws. His weight plummeted, he caught hepatitis, and then pneumonia put him back on the critical list. The hospital bills took every penny he had. Ruda worked at making as much as she could, but nothing covered the costs of the feeding and winter quarters. She began to sell off the cubs – and anything else she could lay her hands on. Some of the cats were the prize part of Grimaldi's act, but she had no choice. The bills kept on coming in, even though many of Grimaldi's friends rallied round and helped.

Grimaldi's main man went to visit him in hospital, and announced that he was quitting. It was a severe blow, they had been together for thirty years. It was not that his wages had not been paid – that he could understand. What he could not deal with – and refused even to clean out his cage – was Mamon. Ruda, he told Luis, had never made any attempt to get rid of him: when any buyers came, he was towed to the back of the quarters.

As sick as he was, Luis had ranted and raged at her. Why had she lied to him? Lost him a man he had worked with for all those years? Ruda had listened with eyes lowered so that he couldn't see her expression and then had said it was not Mamon's fault; he had been vicious because he had an abscess on his tooth, and since it had been removed he was as gentle as a lamb.

Grimaldi languished in the hospital as the bills mounted. Ruda came less often, claiming she was too busy trying to keep a roof over their heads. She succeeded in retaining nine of the cats – and Mamon, of course.

On his release from hospital, she had driven Grimaldi back to the quarters. He was determined to see the cats, and with the aid of a cane he had walked from cage to cage. 'Where is he? *Where is he?*'

She had stepped back, warning him, 'Don't you touch him. I mean it, Luis, don't touch him.'

He had pushed her aside, determined to find him, and she had stood guard over the cage, arms outstretched. 'Please don't, Luis, please. I have never asked you for anything in my life, but don't touch him.'

Mamon was lying like a king, yawning, as Luis stared at him. Grimaldi had turned away and limped to their trailer. Ruda called out that she would show him just what a sweetheart Mamon was, he must watch from the trailer window. Luis got the shotgun, would have shot him then, but instead he had watched her, been afraid for her, loved her, and watched . . . until the fear crept up along the jagged scar, a fear that had crippled him. He had never been in the ring since, and Mamon had proved him wrong. He had never mauled or attacked Ruda, but she had never forgotten Luis's words. She used everything he had ever taught her, and went beyond it, working out her own methods and her own commands. Even if Luis could make it back into the ring now, she would have to teach him a new act, the complete new set of commands she now used.

As for Mamon, he was both an obsession and a constant test of Ruda's capabilities. The controller and the controlled. Theirs was a strange battle of wills that thrilled her beyond anything she could have imagined. Mamon was the lover she could never take, and they had reached the perfect union, one of total respect. But she knew if she broke their bond, weakened, if she gave him an opening, he would attack her. She liked that.

Luis stared at his bloodshot eyes, began to clean his teeth, angry at himself for drinking so much. He heard the trailer door bang and he sighed, hoping it wasn't Tina again.

'Yeah! What is it?'

Mike's voice called out and intuitively Grimaldi knew something was wrong. He ran out of the small bathroom. The boy was panting, waving his hat around. 'You'd better come over to the arena, she's having a really rough time. It's those new plinths.'

Grimaldi ran with Mike across to the big tent, Mike gasping that it couldn't have come at a worse time: the big boss was in, up in the gallery looking over the rehearsals.

Hans Schmidt, wearing a fur-lined camel coat, sat back in his seat, his pudgy hands resting on a silver-topped cane. Below him, way below, he could see the main ring, the cages erected and the caged tunnel. The spotlights were on, and Ruda's figure seemed tiny as she turned, calling out to the cats.

Mr Kelm eased into the vacant seat next to Hans Schmidt. 'You wanted to see me, sir?'

'This Kellerman business, has it been cleared up?'

'I don't know, sir, the *Polizei* were here, I told you. I gave them every assistance possible, but I heard they asked Mrs Grimaldi to identify him this afternoon.'

Schmidt nodded his jowled head, his eyes focused on the ring. 'Very disturbing, bad publicity. Very bad!'

'Yes, I know, but I'm sure it'll all be cleared up.'

'It better be. This is the costliest show to date. What do you think of the Kellerman woman?'

'She's stunning. I've seen parts of her act in Italy and Austria, she is very special.'

'Doesn't look so hot now . . .'

Kelm peered down, and then told Schmidt about the

new plinths, that the animals were playing up, they always did with new props. Schmidt stood up. 'Jesus God, is that part of the act?'

Kelm looked down to see the cats milling around Ruda, he nodded his head and then waited as she did the jump, spinning on the tigers' backs. Schmidt applauded. 'I have never seen anything like it . . . she must be insane!'

Kelm nodded again, his glasses glinting in the darkness. 'She takes great risks.'

Ruda felt her muscles straining as she lifted one plinth on top of the other; the sweat was streaming off her, her hands in their leather gloves were clammy. She backed the tigers up . . . gave the command for them to keep on the move, and then tried for the third time to get them seated in the simple pyramid. They went up to the plinths, hesitated and turned away.

'Goddamn you . . . *up red edededddd! Roja!*' She knew if Roja obeyed her the rest would follow, but he was playing up badly. She was exhausted. Grimaldi moved slowly to the rails, asked if she was OK, and she backed towards him.

'The owners are up in the main viewing box, it's been mayhem. But I think I'm winning. Can you give me the long whip?'

Luis passed it through the bars. She took it from him without looking and began again, her voice ringing round the arena. '*Red–red–blue Sasha blooooooooot* . . . good girl, good girl, *Roja up* . . . *yup yup* . . . Red! thatta good boy . . . good boy . . .' Luis kept watch as at last she got them on to the plinths, leaving one vacant ladder to the top.

Ruda gave the signal and the tigers remained on their

plinths as she gave a mock bow, looked to the right, to the left. The gates opened. In came one male lion and, a beat after, she heard the click again and knew the second one was hurtling down the tunnel. The two lions came to her, one to her right side, one to her left, and she herded and cajoled them on to the lower seats. They were unsure, backed off . . . but they were not as uneasy as the tigers.

She gave the signal, and Mamon, spotlighted in the long tunnel, came out at a lope. Ruda pretended she did not know he was there. Mamon was trained to come up behind her, to nudge her with his nose, and then in mock surprise she would jump, on to his back. She had a semi-circle to go before she gave him the second section command. The act centred on Mamon's refusing to do as he was told; it was always fun, the audience roaring their approval as Mamon played around.

Mamon refused, once, twice . . . Ruda called out to him but he swung his head low. Again she gave him the command: '*Up* . . . Ma'angel up Mamon . . .'

Mamon refused the jump. He began to prowl around the back of the tigers. They got edgy, started hissing, and then two of them began to fight. Ruda called out, '*Down*,' herding out all the cats, leaving Mamon to her right. They behaved well, moving back down the tunnel, but Mamon refused to leave.

Luis waited, watching, swearing to himself about the plinths, but it was too late now. Ruda gave the signal for Mike to get the cats herded back into their cages. She was going to have to work Mamon with the new plinths, cajoling and talking to him, all the while trying to get him on the lower plinth. He refused, sniffing, unsure, smelling, circling, giving a low-bellied growl.

'Come on, baby . . . up up . . . *yup red red red red!*'

Mamon lay down, ignoring her, staring at her. She stood with her hands on her hips. They eyed each other, and Ruda waited.

High up at the back of the main circle seats Tina sat eating a bag of crisps, watching as Ruda sat on one of the plinths, patting it with her hand, softly encouraging Mamon to come to her. He refused. Ruda checked the time, knew she was overrunning, and suddenly stood up. 'Angel . . . *Angel up*, come on – *up*!'

Mamon slowly got to his feet, walked very, very slowly to the new plinth, sniffed it, walked around it, and just as slowly eased himself up and sat. Ruda looked at him. 'You bastard, now stop playing around – *uyup blooooo*.' He shook his head, and then just as slowly mounted the blue plinth. He sat. Ruda encouraged him, flattered and cajoled him until he had sat on each plinth and sniffed it – twice he pissed over them. He was in no hurry, his whole motion was slow, leisurely, constantly looking to Ruda as if to say, 'I'll do it. But in my time.'

Ruda gave him the command for his huge jump down; he hesitated and then reared up and sprang forward, heading straight for Ruda. Tina dropped her bag of crisps as she stood up, terrified.

Ruda shouted at Mamon, pointing the whip. 'Get back . . . back!'

Mamon paid no attention. Ruda spoke sharply to him – and suddenly he turned. Grimaldi gasped as the massive animal churned up the dust. Now he was not playing, now he was the star attraction. In wonderfully co-ordinated jumps he sprang from plinth to plinth, showing off, until he reached the highest point. Then he lifted up his front paws and struck out at the air.

By the time Mamon was moving back down the

tunnel, Ruda had unhooked the latch to let herself out of the arena. She slumped into a seat, taking the proffered handkerchief from her husband to wipe her face. He sat next to her and she could smell the brandy.

'That was tough going!'

'You said it, Luis. I'm going to need double rehearsal time before we open, you could see. They're all over the place. They hate those bloody plinths. I hate them!'

'It was your idea to get new ones, I warned you but you wouldn't listen.'

'I said get them the same *fucking colours. These are too bright!*'

They argued and Tina looked on. Her vision of herself taking over the act had paled considerably. She watched as Grimaldi and the boys began to dismantle the arena cages, then she went over to the horses and got ready for their practice. Grimaldi hadn't even looked in her direction.

Ruda was still in a foul mood, and exhausted, when she walked into the freezer trailer. She began chopping up the meat for the cats' feed. By the time Mike appeared, still wearing the hat, she had all the meat ready.

'The arena cages are stacked, we got two extra hours tomorrow.'

'That's marvellous, this'll be a nightmare. You saw them, they were all playing up.'

Mike shrugged, giving a funny cockeyed smile. 'But you handled them. Word is that Schmidt was impressed! You want me to take the feed through?'

Ruda shook her head. 'No, I'll do it, just double-check that their straw is clean, their cages ready.'

'OK. Will you need me later tonight? I reckon if I get

their night feed set out me and a few of the lads will go round to the clubs.'

'I hope not in that hat. Where did you get it?'

'Oh, I found it, it was in here.'

Ruda smiled. 'Well, just leave it, will you? It's one of Luis's I kept here so he wouldn't wear it, it's disgusting.'

Mike tossed Kellerman's hat aside. 'Sorry, it was just that it was pissing down earlier ... Oh, about this guy Kellerman.'

Ruda froze, staring at the blood-red meat.

'Somebody said he was a dwarf, used to work the circus, is that right?'

Ruda nodded.

Mike flushed slightly. 'He was found in East Berlin. One of the lads told me he had been murdered.'

Ruda lifted the trays. 'Yes, he was, we had to go and identify him today. You ever meet him?'

Mike shrugged, shaking his head. 'Nope. I don't know anything about him, just that someone said he used to be your husband.'

'Yes he was, a long time ago.'

Mike watched her carry the trays down between the trailers, stacking them on to a trolley. She returned for the next batch and said sharply, 'You going to stand watching me work or are you going to earn your pay?'

'Oh, sorry.'

Mike began to put more feed trays out, and Ruda worked alongside him, until suddenly she banged down an empty tray. 'Mike, if you've got something to say, why don't you come out with it?' He flushed pink, unable to tell her what was bothering him. He was sure he had seen Kellerman the day he died, but he said nothing. She continued heaving out the hunks of meat. 'Maybe you can feed Sasha and the two buggers with her.'

'OK,' he said, already carrying out the second batch of feed. Ruda picked up Kellerman's hat and put it into her bag, then continued heaping the meat into the trays. Mike was still watching her and she stopped abruptly.

'OK, I married Tommy Kellerman. I needed a marriage certificate for a visa for the United States. Tommy offered it, I accepted, I went to the United States. End of marriage – or is that fertile imagination of yours working overtime?'

He laughed, and then paused at the open door. 'More kids arriving for the tour of the cages. Look at the little gawking creeps.'

Ruda walked with Mike to the loaded trolley. Stacking the last of the big trays, she chatted nonchalantly. 'There was one of those kids hanging around the cages the other afternoon, did you see me talking to him? Only came up to my waist, trying to put his hand into Mamon's cage. I had to give him a ticking off.'

Mike grinned. 'I remember, yeah. It was a kid then, was it? I wondered, you know . . .' He went on with his business and called to her that he would return as soon as he parked the trays. Ruda returned to the freezer. That was Mike sorted out, he hadn't known it was Kellerman with her, and now that she had the little bastard's hat, she was safe. Ruda stared at her hands, her red-stained fingers, the blood trickling down almost to her elbow. She was thinking of Tommy, seeing his crushed, distorted face on the mortuary table, and she whispered: 'I'm sorry I broke our pact, Tommy, but you just wouldn't stop.'

It was as if he was calling out to her from the cold marble slab, calling to her, the way he used to when she teased him, but hearing his voice in her mind, hearing it now, made her feel a terrible guilt.

'Don't turn the light out, Ruda, please leave the light on!'

CHAPTER 8

THE RAIN had started again, the traffic jams had built up and the journey to Charlottenburg became a long and tedious drive. The Baron looked from his rain-splattered window and checked his watch. It was after six. Helen spoke to their driver in German. 'I have never seen so many dogs!'

Their cab driver looked into his mirror. 'We Berliners love animals, bordering on the pathological. There are more dogs in Spree than anywhere else in Germany – they say there's about five dogs to every hundred inhabitants.'

The Baron sighed, resting his head against the upholstered seat. Helen stared from her window. 'Why is that? I mean, why do you think there are so many?'

The driver launched into his theory, welcoming the diversion from the inch-by-inch crawl his car was forced to make. 'Many people living in the anonymous council flats, many widows, a dog is their only companion. A psychologist described the Berliners' love of animals, dogs in particular, as a high social functional factor.'

Louis grimaced, taking Helen's hand, and spoke in French. 'Don't encourage him! Please ... the man is a compulsive theorist!' Helen laughed.

They passed by the Viktoria-Luise-Platz, heralding

the West Berlin Zoo, and their driver now became animated.

'The zoo, you must visit our famous zoo. In 1943 the work of a hundred years was destroyed in just fifteen minutes, during the battle for Berlin. When the bombing was over, only ninety-one animals survived, but we have rebuilt almost all of it. Now we have maybe eleven or twelve thousand species – the most found in any zoo in the world!'

At last, they were near the centre of Charlottenburg itself. 'Bundesverwaltungsgericht,' the driver said with a flourish, and then he smiled in the mirror. 'The Federal Court of Appeal in Public Lawsuits.'

Helen passed over the slip of paper with the address of Rosa Muller Goldberg's sister, a Mrs Lena Klapps. The driver nodded, turned off the Berliner Strasse, passing small cafés and alehouses, and rows and rows of sterile apartment blocks, their shabby façades dominating the rundown street, before he drew up outside a building. He pointed, and turned to lean on the back of his seat. 'You will require for me to take you back, yes?'

The Baron opened his door, saying in French to Helen, 'Only if he promises to keep his mouth shut!'

Helen instructed the driver to wait, and joined the Baron on the pavement. They looked at the apartment numbers painted above a cracked wide door leading to an open courtyard. Their driver rolled down his window, pointing. 'You want sixty-five. Go to the right . . . to the right.'

The lift was broken, and they walked up four flights of stone steps. Dogs brushed past them, going down, and one bedraggled little crossbreed scuttled ahead, turned and yapped before he disappeared from sight. There were

213

pools of urine at each corner, and they had to step over dog faeces. Helen muttered that perhaps the residents were all widows. 'Dogs are . . . what did he say? . . . a social function? More like a health hazard.'

There was a long stone balcony corridor, the apartments numbered on peeling painted doors . . . sixty-two, sixty-three was boarded up, and then they rang the bell of apartment sixty-five.

An elderly man inched open the door; he was wearing carpet slippers, a collarless shirt and dark blue braces holding up his baggy trousers. Helen smiled warmly. 'We are looking for Lena Klapps, née Muller? I am Helen Masters.'

The old man nodded, opened the door wider and gestured for them to follow him. They were shown into a room containing antique furniture mixed with a strange assortment of cheap modern chairs, and a Formica-topped table. The room was dominated by an antique carved bookshelf, covering two walls, its shelves stacked with paperbacks and old leather-bound books.

The old man introduced himself as Gunter Klapps, Lena's husband, and gestured for them to be seated. He stood at the door with his hands stuffed into his pockets. 'She is late. The rain – there will be traffic jams. But she should be here shortly, excuse me.'

He closed the door behind him, and Helen unbuttoned her coat. The Baron stared around the room, looked at the threadbare carpet, then to the plastic-covered chairs. Helen placed her handbag on the table. 'Not exactly welcoming, was he?'

The Baron flicked a look at his watch. 'Maybe we should call the hotel?'

Helen nodded, and crossed to the door. She stood in

the hallway, calling out for Mr Klapps. The kitchen door was pulled open, and he glared.

'Telephone – do you have a telephone I could use?'

'No, we have no telephone.'

He continued to stare, so Helen returned to the room. The Baron was still standing, his face set in anger. 'I hope this is not a wasted journey. I am worried about Vebekka, leaving her alone.'

'They have no telephone. Shall I go out, make a call?'

He snapped, 'No,' and then sat in one of the ugly chairs. Helen took off her coat, placing it over a typist's chair tucked into the table. She looked over the bookcase; some of the leather-bound volumes were by classical authors, but many of the books were medical journals. She was just about to mention this to Louis, when they heard the front door open.

Lena Klapps walked in. She was much younger than her husband, but wore her hair in a severe bun at the nape of her neck. The grey hair accentuated her pale skin and pale washed-out blue eyes. 'Excuse me, I won't be a moment, my bus was held up in the rush-hour traffic. May I offer you tea?'

The Baron proffered his hand. 'Nothing, thank you. I am Baron Louis Maréchal.'

Lena retreated quickly, saying she would just remove her coat and boots.

She returned a few moments later. She wore a white high-necked blouse, a grey cardigan and grey pleated skirt. Her only jewellery was her wedding ring. 'I must apologize for my husband, he has been very ill.' She shook Helen's hand, and nodded formally to the Baron, gesturing for him to remain seated. She then withdrew the typist's swivel chair, lifting Helen's coat and placing it

215

across the table. She seemed to perch rather than sit, her knees pressed together, hands clasped in front of her.

Helen looked to the Baron, but he gave a small lift of his eyebrows as an indication she should open the conversation. She coughed, and chose her words carefully. 'May I call you Lena?'

Lena nodded, looking directly at Helen. Her pale eyes were cold, ungiving, as unwelcoming as her husband's.

'The Baron's wife, Vebekka Maréchal – we are trying to trace her relatives, and as I said to you in my telephone call, we think she may have been your sister's daughter. Your sister was Rosa Muller?'

'Yes, that is correct.'

Helen continued. 'She married a David Goldberg? And they lived in Canada and then Philadelphia, yes?'

'Yes, that is correct.'

The Baron cleared his throat. 'Do you have a photograph of their daughter, of Rebecca Goldberg?'

'No, I lost contact with my sister before she left for Canada. I know they emigrated to Philadelphia, but we did not keep in touch. Her husband's cousin, a man named Ulrich Goldberg, wrote to me that she had passed away.'

Helen bit her lip. 'We need as much information as you can give us about Rebecca and your sister.'

Lena swivelled slightly in her seat. Her toes touched the ground, the folds of her pleated skirt falling to either side of her closed knees. 'I know nothing of . . . Rebecca, you say? I cannot help you.'

'But Rosa was your sister?'

'Yes, Rosa was my sister.'

Lena suddenly turned to the bookshelf, reached over and took down a thick photograph album. She began to search through the pages of photographs. She spoke in English, heavily accented, as if she was proving some kind of point. 'I find it somewhat strange that after forty years I am asked about Rosa. You say it is in reference to your wife, Baron? Is that correct?'

Helen went to stand by Lena. 'The Baroness is very ill, and we have come to see a specialist in East Berlin who may be able to help her. It is his suggestion that we should try to discover as much about her past as possible.'

Lena nodded. 'And this is Rebecca? Correct? But there must be some confusion. She could not be my sister's child.' She paused, turned back two pages, and then showed Helen the photograph. 'This was Rosa when she was seventeen, 1934 . . .'

Helen stared at the picture of a pretty blonde-haired teenager, with white ribbons in her hair, white ankle socks and a school uniform. Next to her stood Lena, taller, fatter, and not nearly as pretty. She had been as stern-faced a teenager as she was now in middle age. Helen passed over the photograph album to the Baron. Lena hesitated, her hand out, obviously not wanting the Baron to take possession of the album. 'That is the only photograph, there is no point in looking at any others.'

'Lena, is there some way we could contact any of David Goldberg's friends or family? Do you know if any of his relatives are still living in Berlin?' Helen asked.

'No. I did not know Rosa's husband, they met at university. As I said, I have not spoken to my sister for more than forty years.'

The Baron turned over a few pages, and Lena got up and retrieved her book. She stared at the neatly laid-out photographs, some brown with age. 'Berlin has seen many changes since these were taken. My family home,' she pointed to an elegant four-storey house, 'it was bombed, all our possessions, we lost everything but a few pieces. The other photographs are just my family, my mementoes – nothing to do with Rosa.' She held on to the book, touched it lovingly before she replaced it on the shelf, and then hesitated. 'I agreed to see you, because I know Rosa was well off . . . as you can see, money is short. I thought perhaps she had made provision for me. Obviously I was wrong.' She stared from Helen to the Baron and then, tight-lipped, remained standing. 'I am sorry, but it seems very obvious that I cannot help you.'

Helen reached for her coat, making as if to prepare to leave. 'Rosa was a doctor? Is that correct?'

'She was a medical student. She did not qualify here, she continued her studies in Canada, after the war.' Lena folded her arms.

'Was her husband a doctor?'

Lena shook her head. 'No. My father, my grandfather were also doctors.'

'But Rosa and David met at university?'

'Yes, but he was studying languages, I believe. When they went to Canada, I heard he began to trade as a furrier.'

Helen looked at Louis, wishing he would say something, ask something; but he sat on the edge of his seat, obviously wanting to leave.

'Er . . . you said earlier that Rebecca could not have been Rosa's daughter. Was she perhaps David Goldberg's daughter?'

'I don't know.'

'But why are you so sure she could not have been Rosa's child?'

218

Lena pursed her lips. Then she carefully pushed her chair under the table. 'Rosa could not have children.'

Helen persisted. 'Could you give me the reason?'

Lena faced her. 'Because she had an abortion when she was seventeen years old, a backstreet abortion, paid for by that creature she ran off with and married. She nearly died, and she broke my father's heart. When he discovered her relationship, he would have nothing to do with her. He begged her to give David up, but she refused. He tried everything, he even kept her under lock and key to stop her from seeing him. She was obsessed by David and so she ran away, and my father never spoke to her again.'

'This was when?'

Lena rubbed her head. 'She ran off on the second of June. It was 1934 they ran away together. We discovered they had married.'

'They went to Canada?'

'Yes. His family were wealthy, they must have had contacts there to help him set up in business. They always help each other.'

Helen began to put on her coat. 'Did they ever come back?'

Lena nodded. 'I believe so, but not for a long time, not until just after the war. The Goldbergs had property here.'

'So they came back to Berlin?'

'Yes, yes, I believe so.'

'And you didn't see him or speak to him?'

'No.'

'Did you see Rosa when she came back?'

'No.'

'And you cannot give us any clue to relatives?'

Lena stared hard at Helen, her eyes expressionless. 'He had no one left but his cousin, Ulrich Goldberg, who was already residing in the United States. Rosa never contacted her mother, never visited her father's or her brother's graves. As far as I am concerned, my sister died a long time ago, the day she ran away. Now I should be grateful if you would leave.'

The Baron gripped Helen's elbow, wanting to get out, but she stood firmly. 'Do you think your sister could have adopted Rebecca when she returned to Berlin? Could she have adopted a child then, knowing she could not have children of her own?'

Lena pushed past Helen and opened the door. 'I have told you all I know, please leave now.'

Helen snatched up her handbag and walked out, as the Baron folded some money and handed it to Lena. 'Thank you for your time, I appreciate it.'

He followed Helen to the front door. Lena watched them, her hand gripping the thick wad of folded notes.

'She worked in a hospital for three months. I don't know where, I have told you all I know.'

The stale smell of cabbage filled the hallway, as they hurried along the stone corridor. The Baron guided Helen down the stairs, holding her elbow lightly in the crook of his hand. 'The family album was interesting. Did you get a chance to see any of the other photographs? The father was like an SS officer, the brothers were all in uniform too.' He shook his head. 'Can you believe it? She wouldn't see her sister for forty-odd years, and then thinks she may have left her something.'

Helen stopped and turned to him. 'We can get Franks to check hospitals, and we can contact someone from the

Canadian Embassy to see if they can trace a birth certificate – but you know something, I don't think they'll find one. I think they adopted a child here. God knows, there must have been thousands of children needing help.'

The Baron snapped, angrily, 'We don't know if this Rosa was Vebekka's mother, adopted or otherwise. We're just clutching at straws.'

They came out from the apartment building, and their driver tooted his car horn, having parked across the street. Louis slapped his forehead. 'Dear God, I'd forgotten him! I don't think I can stand his guided tours all the way back.'

Helen found it a little strange. Louis seemed more relaxed, even good humoured, now they had left the apartment. They got into the car and he asked the driver to stop at the nearest telephone kiosk. They drove only half a mile before he went to call the hotel to check on Vebekka. Helen watched him from the window, and then leaned back closing her eyes. She was sure the jigsaw was piecing together: the Mullers had turned their back on Rosa not because she was pregnant, but because the father of her child was a Jew.

Louis returned and signalled for the driver to move on. 'She has eaten, she is resting, and Hylda says she is calm, sleeping most of the time.'

As they crossed into East Berlin, their driver became even more animated. 'You know the Communist regime may have tried to squash artistic freedom but, like the West, we always had circuses – you like the circus? At one time it was all provided for, classical music, opera, everything funded by the state. Now we need many millions of marks to sustain it and all our artists, our best talent and producers run to the West. A leading ballerina from the

East Berlin Ballet is having to find work as a stripper to cover her rent – it's true!'

Helen leaned forwards, trying to stop the constant flow of dialogue, and asked if he had heard about the murder, the dwarf found in the hotel not far from the Grand.

The driver nodded his head vigorously. 'Yes, yes I heard, the crime wave is unstoppable here, we don't have enough *Polizei*. Maybe he was working at the Artisten-schule, you know, teaching circus acts. We have many famous circus performers from Berlin – you know there is a magnificent circus about to begin a new season? If you want, I can get you tickets, I have contacts.'

The car drew up outside the hotel, and still the driver talked. 'I have many contacts for nightclubs, for shows. If you want something risqué – you know what I mean – this I can arrange . . .'

He had exhausted them both. Helen rang for the lift while the Baron enquired at the desk for any letters or calls. He was handed a package, a special delivery, just arrived.

Standing next to the Baron was Inspector Torsen Heinz, also waiting at the reception, but he gave him no more than a cursory glance, more interested in the contents of the parcel. Torsen was mentally counting up the cost of the small salad he had eaten in the hotel bar: he'd never have another, not that it hadn't been fresh and well served but it had cost more than five times his cheese on rye at lunch.

Torsen had been waiting patiently for more than half an hour for the manager to give him a list of residents who had arrived at the Grand Hotel from Paris on or near the night of Kellerman's murder. The Baron and Helen stepped into the lift as the manager bustled across the foyer gesturing for the inspector to follow him.

He ushered Torsen into his private office, then closed the door. 'I have had to speak to the director of the hotel over this matter. I am afraid you place us in a very difficult situation. We do have guests, and they are from Paris, but whether or not I can ask . . .'

Torsen opened his notebook officiously. 'I have been able to gain a positive identification of the murdered man, sir, and I will require from you the date these guests arrived. Does it coincide with the dates I gave to you?'

'Yes, yes, but these guests are Baron Maréchal, his wife, a nurse and I think his wife's physician, a Dr Helen Masters.'

Torsen closed his book. 'Could I speak with the Baron?'

'I'm afraid that won't be possible. His wife has not been well and she is resting in their suite. I really don't like to disturb them. Perhaps if you return in the morning, I will speak to the Baron. He is not available now.'

'He just came in.'

'Pardon?'

'I said the Baron just arrived at the reception desk. I saw him.'

The manager pursed his lips, referred again to the conversation he had just had with the director, and suggested Torsen returned in the morning. In the meantime he would speak to the Baron.

Torsen was shown out into the elegant foyer, and checked the time by the array of clocks behind the reception desk. He wondered if he could squeeze in a quick visit to his father before interviewing the hall porter at Kellerman's hotel. It had started to rain again, and the inspector decided he would treat himself to a taxi. He asked the doorman to call him one, but he pointed at the waiting rank.

The Baron's and Helen's driver was snoozing, his cap drawn over his eyes, but he jumped to attention when Torsen tapped on his window. Torsen got into the passenger seat next to him, gave the address of his father's home, and was treated to a detailed blow-by-blow account of the rise in price of hospital beds and facilities for the elderly. 'This city will be in deep trouble – you know why?'

Torsen made no reply, knowing it would make no difference.

'The avalanche of poverty-stricken immigrants is heading this way. Our young have all flown to the West. I was telling the Baron, he was in my cab today, I was telling him about the circus, the Artistenschule, once the most famous in the world for training circus performers. It'll close, mark my words, it'll close . . .'

Torsen frowned. 'Did the Baron ask about the circus?'

The driver nodded. 'We were discussing the murder, the dwarf. He was asking about the murder.'

Torsen listened, interested now, and instructed the driver to change direction. He wanted to go to the Artistenschule.

The driver did a manic U-turn in the centre of the road. 'OK, you're the boss. I said to the Baron, I said, they'll never find the killer.'

'Why is that?' asked Torsen.

'Because we've got a load of amateurs running our *Polizei*, they never made any decisions before, they were *told* who to arrest and who not to, you can't change that overnight. This is it, the main door is just at the top of those steps.'

Torsen fished in his pockets for loose change, then asked for a receipt. The driver drew out a grubby square notepad, no taxi number or official receipt. 'How much do you want me to put on this? Travelling salesman, are you?'

Torsen opened his raincoat to reveal his uniform. 'No. I just need to give it to my *Leitender Polizei Direktor*.'

The driver said nothing, scribbled on his notepad, and shook Torsen's hand – too hard, too sincerely. For a brief moment Torsen saw fear pass over his face, and then it was gone. So was the Mercedes in a cloud of black exhaust fumes. In the old days he could have been arrested for slandering the state.

Torsen tapped on the small door marked 'Office Private' underlined twice. He waited, tapped again, and eventually heard shuffling sounds. Then a rasping voice bellowed to some animal to get out of the way. The door opened, and Torsen was confronted by a massive man wearing a vest and tracksuit bottoms. Clasping his hand was a chimpanzee. They rather resembled each other, the vest hardly hiding the man's astonishing growth of body hair.

Fredrick Lazars beckoned Torsen to follow him, saying he was just eating his dinner. Torsen was seated on a rickety chair, covered in dog hairs, as Lazars sat the chimp in his baby's high chair and fetched a big tin bowl and large spoon. He tipped what looked like porridge into the bowl, and then took out of an oven a plate piled with sausages, onions and mashed potatoes. He offered to share his dinner with Torsen. As the dinner looked started, the sausages half-eaten, Torsen refused politely, adding that he had just dined, 'At the Grand Hotel!' He made no mention that it had been just a side salad and, as Lazars didn't seem impressed that he had eaten there, dropped the subject. Lazars opened two bottles of beer and handed one to Torsen, just as the chimp swung his spoon, flicking Torsen's uniform with porridge. Only two years old, the chimp was called Boris, but was really a female – all this was divulged in a bellow from a food-filled mouth.

'Did Tommy Kellerman come to see you?'

The big hands broke up large chunks of bread, dipping them into the fried onions. 'He did ... the night he died.'

Torsen took out his notebook, asked for a pencil, and Lazars bellowed at Boris who climbed down and pottered to an untidy desk where he threw papers around. 'Pencil ... *pencil, Boris*!' Torsen was half out of his seat, ready to assist Boris, when a pencil was shoved at him, but Boris wouldn't let go of the pencil, so a tug of war ensued before Lazars whacked Boris over the head and told her to finish her dinner. Boris proceeded to spoon in large mouthfuls of the porridge substance, dribbling it over the table, herself and the floor.

'Kellerman came to see me about six, maybe nearer seven.'

'Why have you not come forward with this evidence?'

'He came, he ate half my dinner and departed. What's there to tell in that?'

Torsen scribbled in his book. 'So what time did he leave?'

Lazars sniffed and gulped at his beer. 'He stayed about

226

three-quarters of an hour, said he had some business he was taking care of, important business.'

'What did you do after he left? Or did you accompany him?'

'No, he left on his own, I stayed here.'

'Do you have any witnesses to substantiate that?'

'Yep, about two hundred. We were giving a display, just a few kids trying out, but I started at eight-thirty, maybe finished around ten or later, then we had an open discussion, finished after twelve. We went on to O'Bar, about six of us, then we stayed there.'

Torsen held up his hand. 'No, no more . . . if you could just give me some names of people who can verify all this.'

Lazars reeled off the names as Boris banged her plate splashing Torsen with more of her food. She started screeching for more, and received it, giving Lazars a big kiss as a thank-you.

'I love this little fella . . . mother died about a year ago – you know we had to close part of the animal sector? Well, she's moved in with me until I find someone to buy her.'

Torsen asked Lazars what he knew of Kellerman's background, and the massive man screwed up his face, his resemblance to Boris even more staggering. 'He was an unpleasant little bastard, nobody had a good word to say about him, always borrowing, you know the kind, he'd touch a blind beggar for money, but, well he'd had a tough life . . . you forgive a lot.'

'Did he ever work here?'

'Yeah, long time ago – I mean, a really long time ago, early fifties, I think. He turned up one day, sort of learnt a few tricks, just tumbling and knockabout stuff, but he never had the heart. Got to have a warm heart to be a clown, you know? Kellerman, he was different, he was never . . . I dunno, why speak ill of the dead, huh?'

'It may help me find his killer. Somebody hated him enough to give him a terrible beating.'

Lazars lifted Boris down and carried her to the dish-piled sink. He took a cloth, ran it under the water, rinsed it and wiped the chimpanzee's face.

'Look, Kellerman was a bit crazy, you know? Mixed up. He hated his body, his life, his very existence. Kellerman was somebody that should have been suffo-cated when he was born. He couldn't pass a mirror without hating himself. And when he was younger, it was tragic – he looked like a cherub. Like a kid . . . See, when he first came here he must have still been in his twenties.'

Torsen nodded, finishing the dregs of his beer. Boris, her face cleaned, now wanted her hands washed. 'I'm trying to train her to do the washing up!' roared Lazars, laughing at his own joke. 'But she's too lazy! Like me!'

Lazars sat Boris down, and cut a hunk of cheese for himself. 'The women went for him, always had straight women – you know, normal size.'

Torsen hesitated. 'I met his ex-wife.'

Lazars cocked his head to one side. 'She's a big star now, doesn't mix with any of us, but then who's to blame her? She's been worldwide with the Grimaldi act. He's a nice enough bloke, part Russian, part Italian – hell of a temper, nice man, but I'm not sure about Ruda. But then who's sure about anybody?'

Torsen flicked through his notebook. 'Did you know them when they were married?'

'No, not really. I don't, to tell you the truth, even know where she came from. I think she used to work the clubs, but don't quote me. Kellerman just used to turn up, we never knew how he did it. I think he was into some racket with forged documents, he seemed to be able to cross back and forth with no problems. We had a bit of a falling out about it. You know, he'd come over here, check over the acts – next minute they'd upped and left. I think he made his money that way, you know – paid for fixing documents and passports. He always had money, not rich, but never short of cash either in those early days, so I just put two and two together. He had a place over in the Kreuzberg district, so he must have had contacts. Not circus people, he was only ever attached to circuses because of his deformity – when he couldn't make cash on rackets, he joined up with a circus.'

Torsen rubbed his head. 'Did he have money when you last saw him?'

Lazars shook his head. 'No, he was broke, told me he had been in gaol but I knew that anyway. All he said was he had some business deal going down. Maybe he'd got in with the bad guys again, who knows? I do know he let a lot of people down.'

'How do you mean?'

'Promises, you know, he'd get them over the border, get them work. They'd pay up front, end up over there, and no Kellerman – he'd pissed off. Any place he turned up you could guarantee there would be someone waiting to give him a hiding.'

'Or kill him?'

Lazars had Boris on his knee; the chimp was sucking at her thumb like a tiny baby, her round eyes drooping with tiredness. Torsen reached for his raincoat; it was covered with animal hairs. 'There is just one more thing, then I'll get out of your way.'

Lazars stood up, resting Boris, fast asleep, on his hip.

Torsen almost whispered, afraid to wake Boris. 'Do you recall a tattoo on his left arm?'

Lazars nodded, and the bellowing voice was a low rumble. 'I remember it, they're the ones you never forget.'

Torsen waited, and Lazars sighed. 'Maybe that was why we all put up with his shit. Tommy Kellerman was in Auschwitz – the tattoo was his number.'

Torsen bowed his head, answered softly, 'I see. Thank you for your co-operation.'

For once the rain had ceased, and Torsen took a bus back to Kellerman's hotel. He sat hunched in his seat, making notes in his book. He put a memo for Rieckert and himself to visit Ruda Kellerman and question her again: it was important, he underlined it twice. She had lied about Kellerman's tattoo, she must have known what it was. He closed his eyes, picturing Ruda Kellerman as she touched the dead man's hair at the mortuary that afternoon. She had lied.

He spent the rest of the journey mulling over why she would have lied, but came to no conclusion. He stared from the grimy window of the bus at a group of punks kicking empty beer cans along the street. They had flamboyantly blue and red hair; they wore torn black leather jackets, and black boots that clanked and banged the cans along the street. He felt old, tired out, bogged down, trying to find the killer of a man nobody seemed to care about. Was it all a pointless waste of time? The men at the station had implied that it was; nobody would give any overtime to assist him.

He interrupted himself, swearing. He should have asked Lazars if the dinner he had shared with Kellerman was hamburger and chips. He'd have to call in the morning, and again he swore – he couldn't call him before nine because of the switchboard. He also wanted a telephone.

Torsen began another of his lists. He was going to start throwing his weight around; he wanted a patrol car for his personal use, plus fuel allowance, and, as from tomorrow, he was going to work out a rota – none of this nine to five from now on. They would work as they did in the West, day and night duty officers, round the clock. The bus rumbled on. Torsen sniffed his hands – they smelt of Boris, he smelt of Boris, and the remains of the chimp's food had hardened into flecks all over his jacket. The bus shuddered to a halt and Torsen stepped down, checking the time, sure the porter must have started work by now. He felt even more worn-out as he headed for Kellerman's hotel, passing the ornate and well-lit Grand Hotel's entrance, hurrying down the back streets tallying up how many girls he saw lurking in the dark dingy doorways, even wondering if one of them had seen the killer. But he didn't approach the girls because he was alone and didn't want his intentions to be misconstrued. He made a mental note to add to his lists: check out the call-girls. No doubt Rieckert would jump at the chance.

The Baron had ordered dinner to be served in his suite, and the manager himself had overseen the menu. He bowed and scraped at the lavish tip, the Baron thanking him for his discretion; he understood the *Polizei* would have to take statements. He shut the door, sighing, and turned to Helen. 'This place is unbelievable. They want me to meet with someone from the police here because we arrived from Paris on the same night that circus dwarf was murdered!'

Helen frowned, but said nothing. She was sifting through the package of letters and photographs that had just been delivered. She held up a small blurred snapshot. 'I am sure this is Rosa Muller, she's even got the same pigtails, and you can see where it's been cut in two, so maybe we were right after all . . . Louis?'

He sat beside her. 'Yes, yes . . . I hear you.'

Helen pointed out the cut edge of the photograph, sent by the Baron's chauffeur from the US. 'I am sure Lena was on this photograph. It's very similar to the one she showed us, and just look at the other snapshot, Louis. I'm sure it's Vebekka.'

Louis looked again at the snapshot of a girl in school uniform who was glaring at the camera. She had two thick plaits, her arms rigid at her sides. And she was very plump: her face, even her legs seemed rounded. 'I just don't know.'

Helen took the photograph. 'We could always ask her, show it to her?'

Louis snapped, 'No, I don't want her upset, I don't want anything to upset her, she's calm, she's sleeping, she's eating, she's going to see Franks tomorrow. You talk to him about it, see what he says. I just don't want these games we're playing to upset—'

'Games? Louis, we're not playing games, for God's sake.'

He shoved the papers aside. 'I used the wrong word then, but we have come here to have Vebekka see Franks, she's agreed, now all this detective work . . .'

Helen pushed back her chair. 'This detective work was, if you recall, specifically requested by Franks himself. I don't understand your attitude. You have no knowledge of her past, and you have said it is your main priority to find out whether there is any history of mental instability in Vebekka's family. But, Louis, unless we try to trace her goddamned family, how do you expect to find out?'

Louis rubbed his brow, his mouth a tight, hard line. 'Perhaps some things are best not uncovered.'

'Like what?'

He stared at the ceiling. 'I don't know . . . but all these photographs, this woman this afternoon, what have we gained? We still know nothing of Vebekka's family. Her mother, or adopted mother, is dead, her father, or adopted father, is dead. How can they tell us what, as you said, is my priority? And it is not just *my* priority, but my sons', my daughters'.' He sighed. 'Look, maybe I'm just tired, it's been a long day.'

Helen carefully gathered the photographs together, the letters from Ulrich Goldberg, the lists of Goldbergs she had contacted to trace Lena, and stuffed them into the large brown envelope. 'Perhaps you're right. I think I'm tired too, maybe I'll make it an early night.'

The Baron poured himself a brandy. 'Do you want one?'

'No, thank you. I'll look in on Vebekka if you like.'

'No, that's all right. Hylda's staying overnight, she's using Anne Maria's old room.'

'What time are the police coming?'

'First thing tomorrow morning.'

'I'd like to sit in on the meeting, if I may, just out of interest. What time will Rebecca be going to Dr Franks?'

'Vebekka!'

'What? Oh, I'm sorry, what time is her appointment with Franks?'

Louis shrugged as he lit a cigar and began puffing it alight. 'I doubt if it will be before ten – he has set aside the entire morning.'

'Goodnight then.'

He stared at her, then inclined his head. 'Goodnight.' Louis noticed she took the envelope with her; it irritated him slightly, but he dismissed it. He turned the television set on, standing in front of it a moment, switching from channel to channel.

Hylda came out of Vebekka's bedroom. 'She is sleeping.'

He smiled warmly. 'Good, you are very good for her, and I am grateful for your assistance, also for agreeing to stay. Thank you.'

Hylda crossed the room, head bowed, and slipped into Anne Maria's room. As she went into the small adjoining bathroom, she could hear a bath being run from Helen Masters's suite.

Helen wrapped the thick hotel towelling robe around herself, and then sat at the writing desk, taking the photographs out, studying them and staring at the wall. She picked up the photograph of the plump schoolgirl, turning it over. On the back was written in childish scrawl, 'Rebecca'. She stared at the photograph angrily, and then let it drop on to the desk. Why was she so angry? Why?

She looked again at the photograph, and this time she took a sheet of paper and held it across the bottom part of the child's face, hiding the nose and mouth. They were Vebekka's eyes, she knew it!

Inspector Torsen had to wait at Kellerman's hotel until after eleven o'clock before the porter came on duty. He stood waiting impatiently as the scruffy man rummaged through the rubbish bins in the alleyway. Eventually, and very disgruntled at his work being interrupted, he led Torsen to where he recalled seeing the tall, well-built man. He pointed from the alley towards the street – not, as Torsen had thought, the other way round.

'But it's well-lit, you must have got a good look.'

'I wasn't paying too much attention, I'd just started work. I clear the rubbish bins at a number of hotels around this area. I don't start workin' until after ten, but I remember seein' him, and he was walking fast, carrying this big bag – a sort of carryall.'

This was something new. The porter was able, after some deliberation, to describe a dark hat, like a trilby, worn by the man. 'It was shiny, sort of caught the light, yes, it was black and shiny.'

'Did you see his face?' Torsen asked.

The porter shook his head, asked if he could continue his work and Torsen nodded, standing a moment longer as the man turned on a hose and began to wash down the alley.

It was almost twelve, but Ruda worked on. She swilled around the sides of the sink, then rinsed out the cloths, filled a bucket of water, and carried it to the chopping table. She scrubbed the surface, shaking the brush, dipping it into the boiling water. Her mind raced, had she covered any possible tracks, any possible connection to the murder? As hard as she tried to concentrate she knew, could feel, something else was happening. It had begun in the hotel, when she was sick in the toilets. Why did she feel the compulsion to return to that hotel? She hurled the brush into the bucket, yanked the bucket up, slopping water over the floor and herself as she tipped it down the drain . . . white tiles, splashes of the red, bloody water . . . white tiles. The same tingling started. Her hands, the nape of her neck, the dryness in her mouth. She rubbed her hands dry on the rough towel, then, as she threw it into the skip used for the laundry, she saw the bloody towels and cloths and caught her breath. It wasn't Tommy, it wasn't the murder, it was something else.

She swore, muttering louder, she must not allow this to happen. She had controlled it for her whole life, she would not allow it to break into her mind, not now, and she punched out at the walls, punched with all her strength, right fist, left fist. But nothing would make the memory subside, return it to the secure, locked box imagined in her mind. Her fists slammed against the wall and she turned her fury to Kellerman: it was his fault, all his fault. Why did he have to come back? Why now? But Ruda knew it was not Kellerman who was back. It was the past.

Louis was sitting in a comfortable chair, a magazine held in his hands. He was wearing half-moon glasses, but he had been unable to concentrate. The glasses took Helen by surprise, she had never seen him wearing them. It was a moment before he realized she was in the room. 'Can't you sleep?' he asked softly.

Helen glanced at the clock on the mantelpiece. It was after twelve, she hadn't thought it was so late. 'No, no, I can't. I'm sorry, it's late but . . .'

He put his fingers to his lips, then indicated Vebekka's room. He gave no indication of his own surprise at Helen's intrusion, but he was none the less taken aback: she was wearing only a rather flimsy nightgown, her robe undone, and her feet bare.

'She's sleeping, she looks very well.'

'Good, I'm glad.'

Helen sat on the edge of the sofa. 'Louis, I need to ask you something, I am just not sure how to phrase it . . .'

'Do you want a brandy?'

'No, nothing, thank you . . .' She stared at his slippered feet, suddenly aware that in her haste she had not put on her own. 'Vebekka has said repeatedly that she is afraid of hospitals, nurses and doctors in white coats, yes?'

He nodded, pouring a glass for her even though she'd said no. He went over to the sofa and held it out. 'Here, it'll help you sleep.'

Helen took the glass, cupping it in her hands. 'So even though she was afraid of needles, of doctors, she had plastic surgery to her nose, her face. I read it in Dr Franks's reports.'

He frowned. 'Yes, it was not extensive, and I suppose when she had it done she was well. I never thought of it. It was done in a private clinic in Switzerland the first time, and then, I think, in New York.'

'Were you with her on these occasions?'

He touched his brow, coughed lightly. 'The first time,

but not the second. She had no adverse effects – quite the contrary, she was very pleased with the results. She's always been very conscious of her looks.'

Helen sipped the brandy. 'The photograph is of Vebekka, Louis. The girl is plump, fat even, but her eyes – I recognize her eyes. She could never change her eyes.'

He slowly stubbed out his cigar, his back to her. Helen took another sip of the brandy, she licked her lips. 'But that is not what I wanted to ask you.'

As he turned to face her, he removed his glasses, carefully placing them in a case.

Standing up, she put down her glass. 'I think you were, to begin with, prepared to try to discover everything about her background until . . .'

He moved closer. 'Until what?'

She looked at him, met his dark blue eyes. 'Until you heard the name Goldberg.'

'What's that supposed to mean?'

Helen backed further away from him. 'I know how important your family is, your family heritage. I know you have put up with your wife's illness because they would not approve of a divorce.'

'They?' He said it quietly, but with such sarcasm. 'My dear Helen, I am the family, I am the head of the family, and I can't for the life of me think what you are trying to say.'

'I think you can, Louis.'

He shook his head in disbelief, and then walked to the windows, drawing the curtains to one side. 'You really think I would care?'

Helen cleared her throat. 'I think the old Baroness would have, perhaps your father. It was common knowledge that he allowed the Gestapo to take over your villas.'

He drew the curtains, patting them into place. 'I think, Helen, you should try and get some sleep, before you say or insinuate anything else.'

'You have not answered me.'

He was at her side, gripping her arm so tightly it hurt. 'You know nothing, nothing, and your insinuation insults me, insults my family.'

She dragged her arm free. 'It's always your precious family. I think you, Louis, hate the thought of your precious family being Jewish as much as you hate the thought of producing more insanity.'

His slap sent her staggering backwards, she cried out more with shock than pain. He rushed to her, touched her reddened cheek. 'Oh, my God, I'm sorry . . . but you don't understand.'

Helen put her hand up to indicate for him not to come close, and he flushed, gestured another apology with his hands. 'I am so sorry.'

She watched as he took out his handkerchief, touched his lips, the brow of his head, and then crossed to the window and unhooked the shutter. He remained with his back to her as he reached through the half-open shutter to the window. 'I don't care if Vebekka is Jewish. How could I? She's the mother of my children, I only care about their future.' He opened the window, breathed the cold night air, but still seemed loath to turn and face her.

Helen twisted her ring around her finger. 'Then surely you can understand my confusion. Why don't you want to try to find out as much as possible, Louis? Please, look at the photograph. Look at it.'

He walked briskly to the table and snatched up the photograph from where Helen had left it. He turned it over, then let it drop back on to the polished wood surface. He saw the childish looped writing, the name 'Rebecca'.

'Helen, if she is this little girl, if she is in some way connected to that dreadful woman this evening, to these people in Philadelphia, then we must do whatever you think is right. But please don't ask me to show enthusiasm. Show this to my wife, if you wish, or preferably ask Franks to, because if she looks at it and admits it is her, then she has lied to me, to everyone. Let Franks do it, but don't ask me to.'

'Don't you see, Louis? It is the reason *why* she has lied that may be important – it has to be, and when we discover why, maybe—'

He snapped then, his face taut with controlled anger. 'Maybe what? Everything will fall into place? Have you any idea, any knowledge of how often I have hoped for that? Let Dr Franks handle this photograph and any further developments.'

'As you wish.'

As Helen crossed to the door, he said her name very quietly, making her turn. 'I obviously appreciate all you are doing for my wife, and any financial costs to yourself will be met. I had no conception of how – well, how much we would be seeing of each other, or how much my own personal life would be placed under scrutiny. I ask you, please, to realize at all times that you are privy to very personal emotions, traumas – whichever terminology you wish to label them with. But please do remember that you are my guest, and that you are here because my wife asked you to accompany us. You are therefore free to leave at any time you wish to do so.'

Helen felt as if he had slapped her face for a second

time; his cold aloofness made her feel deeply embarrassed. 'I arranged my vacation to enable me to spend time here.'

'How very kind. But I will, as I said, make sure you incur no extra costs. Now, if you don't mind my asking, in future, if you wish to join me in my suite, you will be good enough to dress accordingly. Hotels are notoriously scandalous places. My wife has already managed exceptionally well in making a spectacle of herself since we arrived.'

Helen gave a brief smile of apology. 'Anything we have discussed is, and will remain, completely confidential. Goodnight, Baron.'

He saw the glint in her eyes, and flushed, moving back to the shutters once more. He switched off the lights, leaving the shutters ajar, the street lamps outside giving the only light in the spacious drawing room. Helen would never know what a raw nerve she had touched, he assured himself. His mama had accused him of marrying not only a fortune hunter, but a Jewish bitch with no breeding, no education, just a pretty face. She had ranted at him, shouting that men in his position took women like Vebekka as a mistress, never as a wife, and the reason the bitch had never let him make love to her was because that was all she had to hold him, sex . . .

Louis could see his perfectly coiffured mama turning to point with her cane at the paintings, the tapestries. 'Your papa would turn in his grave. She is a tramp! And you cannot see it. What kind of name is Vebekka? Eh? Tell me that? I tell you, she is trouble. Marry your own kind, Louis, marry a woman who can run this estate, bring money to this estate. Marry a woman who will make a wife.'

Louis had ignored his mother, had married Vebekka and when he had confronted her, knowing it was too late for her to do anything about it, she had opened her Louis the Fourteenth writing desk, and tossed a thick manila envelope at his feet. His face drained of colour as he read the contents and his mother glared at him contemptuously. 'You should have learned this before you acted so rashly. Now it's too late. Now you have made your bed and you must lie on it. I hope for your sake it works, because there can never be a divorce. I don't want the family name dragged through the courts, the press outside the château. I don't want to know about your private life, that is your business. But if you want your inheritance, you will, in future, do as I ask.'

So Louis had learned that Vebekka had lied, had known all those years that she was really Rebecca Goldberg, but he had chosen never to find out the truth or face her with it. He had burnt the contents of the private investigator's notes, and then left for a trip abroad.

Now the ghosts were catching up with him, as his eldest son, wanting to marry, waited to hear if his mother was clinically insane, waited for the Old Baroness's inheritance to be released, waited to see if he was socially acceptable to marry one of the richest heiresses in France. Waiting – the entire family, most of all her son, had waited for the Old Baroness to die and she had never released his fortune.

Louis laughed softly: his whole life had been spent waiting. His mama had tied up the bulk fortune in trust funds for his children, leaving Louis an allowance for life. His second son, Jason, was courting the daughter of a rich German industrialist, his eldest daughter engaged to a Brazilian multi-millionaire. He laughed again, a soft humourless laugh, all waiting, the massive wealth their cross in life.

Dear Helen, how very little she knew. Louis had been able to continue his luxurious lifestyle, to create one of the finest polo stables in the world, only because of David and Rosa Goldberg's inheritance. It wasn't his money that he squandered so lavishly, but Vebekka's.

He yawned and rubbed his hands. He felt chilled – the window was still open. As he reached to close the shutters he saw a figure standing near the brick wall opposite the Grand Hotel. He could not see if it was male or female, just the dark outline leaning against the wall, waiting. He paid no further attention, thinking it was probably a prostitute from the red-light district.

Ruda stared at the window, saw the light extinguished. Her eyes flicked to the next window. It was still dark. What had compelled her to return to the hotel in the middle of the night? What was here? She felt cold as she walked slowly to the cab rank and stepped inside a waiting taxi, giving one last look to the dark window, the window with the shutters firmly closed.

Her driver was a small, withered-looking man, who seemed delighted to have a fare at that hour. 'Do you know what night it is tonight?'

Ruda lit a cigarette and made no reply.

'Tonight is November the tenth. In 1938 the Nazi mobs destroyed Jewish property and murdered and abducted twenty thousand Jews. They paved the way for the Holocaust – the Night of the Shattering Glass, the Kristallnacht. And tonight, you know what is happening in Leipzig? Fighting! Hundreds arrested, the outbreak of violence is a nightmare. Some of my friends they've gone there for business, but me? Nobody will shatter the windows of my cab.'

Ruda closed her eyes. She spoke not one word, remaining motionless in the centre of the back seat, aware of his dark eyes peering at her in his mirror – suspicious, darting black eyes.

When finally they arrived back at the circus, she paid him, leaning into his cab as he carefully counted out the change. Suddenly she touched his cheek. 'Keep it. If they break your windscreen, you get a new one.'

CHAPTER 9

GRIMALDI HAD been drinking steadily all evening. He and Tina had been out for dinner, and now they went around the nightclubs. He had demanded that the taxi stop when he recognized a street, and then excitedly leaned against the driver to direct him to where there was loud music and crowds of kids thronging around a doorway. He couldn't believe the club would still be in existence. He had paid off the taxi before he realized he was wrong, that it was not the same club he remembered.

Tina moved down the murky stone corridor lit by a naked light bulb. She shrieked above screaming music that it was a terrible place. A young punk passed them, laughed at Tina and then shouted to his friends. 'What did he say?' shrieked Tina.

Grimaldi put a protective arm around her. 'He said, welcome to the Slaughterhouse!'

The club was throbbing with life where once it had been filled with the screams of slaughtered animals. Tina squealed happily and pushed and shoved her way to the bar. The music was so loud it was impossible to hear. Grimaldi felt his age among all these kids, dancing and drinking, smoking pot and openly passing drugs. He suggested they drink up and leave.

Tina pouted. 'Don't be so *boring*! This is the only opportunity I'll have. When the show starts, I won't be able to get out.'

Grimaldi shrugged and made his way to a small alcove where a couple of crude benches were stacked against the wall. Tina sat on his knee as he squashed himself on to the edge of a bench. She tipped back her bottle of beer, her feet tapping to the music. All around them young men and women prowled in black clothes, dark faces, white make-up. They screamed and they danced and Grimaldi leaned back on the old white tiles, giving a dig to the girl behind him as she fumbled with her boyfriend's trousers.

A boy asked Tina to dance, and she kissed Grimaldi, passed him her handbag and her half-empty bottle of beer, and dived on to the dance floor.

He sat waiting, getting hotter and hotter. He finished Tina's beer, and began to look around the crowd of thrashing kids to see if he could see her. He got up, looked over the heads of the dancers and saw her flinging her body around, dancing with her eyes shut, loving every minute of it.

Grimaldi made his way up the crowded staircase, and then he pushed and shoved like the rest. He heaved for breath on the pavement, and looked right and left. He was trying to get his bearings, sure that the old club he remembered had to be near. He grabbed hold of the beefy doorman and, shouting to make himself heard, tried to describe Tina if she came out looking for him, and said that he had her handbag. He said that he was looking for a club called Knaast, which used to be in the same area. The doorman pointed down the street, and Grimaldi thanked him and walked off, still carrying Tina's bag. He walked for about ten minutes, stopped, turned this way and that, had decided to give up and return to the Slaughterhouse when he saw the club door. He grinned, and crossed the road.

The venue was the same, but the clientele had changed a lot. It was now a well-known leather bar; he had never in his life seen so many chains and leather jackets crammed into such a small space. Beefy barmen, with T-shirts and muscles, wearing spikes and God knows what attached to their chests and throats, and chained to bars, served customers. Some men were chained to each other, yet carrying on animated conversations as if their chains were part of the décor.

Grimaldi pushed his way to the bar, asked for a beer, and turned to face the main club floor. Only then did he realize the occupants were all male. He was asked to dance by an ageing homosexual in a strange leather helmet, jock strap and white tights. He downed his beer fast, and tried to edge his way towards the exit but it took a great deal of pushing. Inadvertently he shoved a large, muscular man wearing an SS hat, who turned and gripped Grimaldi by the testicles. 'Don't push me!'

Grimaldi grimaced and the man's grip tightened. 'I just want to leave, I don't want any arguments.'

'You don't, cocksucker?'

Grimaldi was eye to eye with the SS officer's handlebar moustache. 'I don't, but you will get a lot of trouble if you don't get your fucking hands off me!'

'Make me ...' lisped the pursed lips through the handlebar moustache. Grimaldi back-handed the SS queen, then gave him an elbow in his throat. He could still feel his testicles burning, as the man went sprawling.

Suddenly a blond-haired boy tried to swipe Grimaldi

with his whip. Grimaldi snatched the whip and began to crack it, his actions creating a mixture of hysteria and applause. A bottle of champagne was waved at him from behind the bar, the chained barman screaming it was on the house, and Grimaldi suddenly broke up laughing. It was so crass, so hideous he had to laugh, and everyone joined in. He kept on saying he had only fallen into the place by mistake, he was straight. 'Just get me out of here, somebody get me out!'

Suddenly he could hear his name being shouted, bellowed: '*Luis . . . Luis . . . Luis!*'

Grimaldi shook his head. His name was being yelled by a bloody chimp!

Fredrick Lazars had Boris up on his shoulders, the little animal's arms and legs virtually covering his face, and she was pursing her lips. She looked as if she was the one calling Luis, not Lazars. Grimaldi broke up, roaring with laughter, and the two men clasped each other in a bear-hug as Boris whooped and screeched with excitement. Lazars introduced Grimaldi to a few of his friends, and ordered drinks, dragging Grimaldi to a brick alcove.

An hour later, Tina stood waiting outside the Slaughterhouse Club in tears. She spoke no German, and was still with her young dancing partner, who was trying to persuade her to come back into the club. She pushed him away and shouted she was looking for someone, but he couldn't understand and began to pull at her arm.

'I'm looking for somebody . . . *Leave me alone!*'

'I help you . . . I find for you, OK?'

Tina was so relieved he spoke English, she hugged

him, and kept tight hold of his hand as he talked to the doorman, who pointed down the street.

'Your friend, ze big man, go there – you come? I show you, come with me, yes?'

Tina teetered after her young friend, looking back doubtfully to the doorman, who then nodded, gestured back to the street with his hand. 'Zat way . . . he go zat way.'

As Tina disappeared down the dimly lit alleyway, Grimaldi was staggering out of a taxi with Lazars. Boris was riding on Lazars's shoulders; the two men stumbled around the pavement, Lazars trying to get his wallet out of Boris's hand while Grimaldi took out a thick wad of notes and paid off the taxi. Tina's handbag was still hooked over his arm, but he seemed unaware of it. He was very drunk, lurching against the side of the taxi; Lazars bellowed for him to follow as he entered his apartment.

Lazars passed Boris over to Grimaldi and opened two bottles of beer. He drew up two chairs and then, weaving slightly, opened both his arms, beaming. 'She's a good girl, you won't regret this, and I'm giving you a good price!'

'I don't want a fuckin' chimp!'

'But you know somebody who would want her! You got more contacts than me, somebody'd want her. She's two years old, lot of years in her, she's intelligent, sharp, an' I've got all her papers, her certificates, her inoculations, it's a hell of a deal, I can't keep her here, shake on it! Look at her. You don't have a heart for human beings and a heart for animals. A single sense of compassion . . . I love her, my friend, but I am willing to let you have her.'

Grimaldi shook his head. 'I can't . . .'

'Put her in the act.'

Grimaldi drank the beer, banged the bottle on to the table. 'Just leave it, I don't want a goddamned chimp!'

Standing Boris on the table top, and pulling a worn old cardigan over her head, Lazars showed the little chimp as much affection as if she was a child. 'She's toilet-trained, she could live in your trailer, heard it's like a palace.'

'You been up to the grounds?'

'No, Tommy Kellerman told me. You know he's dead?'

Grimaldi yawned, scratching his head. 'Ruda had to identify him.'

Lazars tucked Boris up in the old horsehair sofa, gave her a teddy bear to cuddle, patted her head, and waited for the animal's eyes to close before he opened two more beers. 'You know my attitudes have changed, I never thought they would, but . . . eh, you remember the mad Russian, Ivan the Crazy Horse?'

Grimaldi nodded. 'He's a tough one to forget, you been over there? I hear he's still with the Moscow Circus.'

'Yeah, he's still with them, earning peanuts and working in that jungle of concrete and glass. He's got eighteen tigers, ten lions and two panthers. Act's good, he's good – one of the best – but . . .' Lazars drank thirstily, and then stared at the bottle in his massive gnarled hands. 'Not the way it used to be. Ivan took me round his cages, steel cages on wheels, hardly enough room for the poor creatures to turn round in. You know, I dreamed of working with big animals all my life. I never had the money or the breaks, and then – just like that!' Lazars slapped the table with the flat of his hand. 'I changed my mind . . . my whole outlook changed. I didn't want it any more. I talked to the Soviet Union's society for the protection of animals, SSPA, I said there should be more control. You know they lost three, *three* giraffes a few years back. They transported them around in railway carriages. They couldn't stand upright, hadda travel with their necks bent, crouched on their knees, for five days. But they said to me that against the power of the Soyuzgostsirk – I mean, they run most of the circuses in Russia – they could do nothing. It sickened me! For the first time I began to think we should look again, try again to find the heart of the circus.'

Lazars opened more beer, and gulped half a bottle down before he continued. 'Then, my friend, my eyes were opened. You ever seen France's Circus Archaos? You seen it?'

Grimaldi shrugged. 'Yeah, but it's not everyone's taste.'

'They got chainsaws, punks, Mad Max and *fire*! Rock music – it's new, it's exciting!'

'*Bullshit*. What kids wanna see clowns in dirty mackintoshes and rubber boots, *bullshit*!'

Lazars banged the table. 'No, you are wrong, my friend. They have got some of the finest performers because the heart of their circus is still juggling, the trapeze, tumblers – but it's all updated. It caters to the new audience, the kids, the teenagers that don't want to see fucking bears pedal bikes, chimps like Boris forced to become entertainers. They've seen through it, they know it's a fucking lie. You train a dog to sit and you've got to use force. Animals are no longer wanted.'

'*Bullshit again!* Don't give me this arty-farty crap about the French. They tried an animal-free circus in England and it flopped belly upwards. Nobody came ...

251

you stand by a box office and you hear every other caller, they all ask the same thing. What animals? *They come for the animals!*'

'No, not any more. They see, Luis, they see with their own eyes, they see man trying to prove he is top dog. They see man only wanting to dominate other species, they see the tragic animals hemmed into their cages, *they see . . .*'

'I should get back.' Grimaldi tried to stand up, and slumped back into his chair again.

Lazars took no notice, passing over a bottle. 'So, how is Ruda? She's come a long way – she's queen now, huh?'

Grimaldi nodded, and Lazars began to reminisce about the old days, referring back to the time when Grimaldi himself was a star attraction. They swapped stories, recalling past glories, the two massive men seated either side of the small table in the filthy cluttered kitchen. They laughed, they slapped each other's shoulders, and ploughed their way through the crate of beer. They fell silent, suddenly caught up in their own private memories.

The first time Grimaldi had seen Ruda was with Lazars: Grimaldi was with a group of performers having a night out. He had been drunk that night, had been drinking for the best part of the evening when they all stumbled down to the basement club. The bombed-out, crater-filled city – the abject poverty was everywhere, the only escape was in drinking and attempting to keep the show on the road. The people were dazed, hungry, and the aftermath of the terrible war hung like a sickening cloud. Memories of pre-war times, of affluence, of dreams were pushed roughly aside; living and being alive was all that mattered, making a living the only priority.

Grimaldi had money then, one of the few who had.

He had been just a young boy of fifteen when the war started, had travelled with his father to the United States. His father had died, and it was in America that Luis learned his two brothers had been killed on the Russian front. He built up the act, and was one of the first performers to return after the war. It was the mid-fifties, and already word had spread among the circus scouts that young Luis Grimaldi was someone to watch. Those he was out with that night had all seen his act, and everyone was slapping him on the back, toasting him. Then Ruda and the Old Magician had appeared on the basement cabaret stage in a pitiful puff of green smoke. This had caused general catcalls and yells, a bottle was hurled at the old man, but he attempted to continue his act.

The audience paid little or no attention to the act until there was a taped drumroll, and the old man with the ragged satin cloak asked for their participation. This was greeted with whistles and lewd remarks. Ruda had been dressed in a cheap black bra and panties, with laddered black tights and high-heeled shoes. She seemed disinterested in the entire performance, passing the tubes and hoops with a half-hearted smile on her face. The magician had drawn from various pockets small silk handkerchiefs, red, blue, green. With great showmanship he had thrown them into the air and called to the audience to hide the silks. Grimaldi's friends had taken a bunch of the silk squares, blown their noses on them, tossed them aside, and Grimaldi had tucked one down his right boot.

Ruda had stood impassive, her head half turned from the blinding spotlights. The silk squares hidden, the magician slipped a thick black blindfold around her eyes. He began to thread his way through the audience, as Ruda in a low monotone began to name the colours as

253

each was retrieved. 'Red, blue, red, red, red, blue, green, red, blue, green . . .' She seemed at one point to be ahead of the magician as the coloured squares were caught and held aloft. She turned her head slightly as if listening, and yet kept on intoning the colours. The audience had grown quiet, caught up in the scene as the old man pushed his way through the club, gathering the squares fast; at times he had his back to her, it was impossible for her to cheat.

He stepped in front of Grimaldi. 'Red . . .' Grimaldi shrugged his shoulders, smiling, gestured with his hands as if he did not have a silk square. 'Red . . .' They had all cheered as he suddenly retrieved a red silk square from his boot.

Grimaldi and his friends had continued to another club until almost dawn, and then Grimaldi had hailed a taxi. As he waited he saw her, standing on a street corner; she still wore her costume, only now she had an old brown thin coat around her shoulders. He saw her stop two men, and then shrug as they passed on.

The taxi pulled up and Grimaldi got inside, then the cab did a U-turn coming alongside Ruda. She stared dull-eyed at it, and then stepped forward. Grimaldi wound down his window, about to say he had seen her act, when she stuck her head in the window and asked, 'Do you want oral sex?' He shook his head, reached for the handle to wind up the window. She hung on. 'Come on, you can name your price!'

Grimaldi had told the driver to move on, but she still clung on to the window. 'You were the guy, it was in your fucking boot, you like to make people look like shit? *Fuck you!*'

Grimaldi shouted for the driver to stop. He got out

and she backed away from him, afraid. But he smiled and complimented her. 'You know, that was quite good, you should get rid of that old man, work up a real act, you're good! I know it has to be some kind of trick, but it works.'

She hung back, pressing herself against the wall until he returned to the taxi and drove off. But the following morning she was there, hanging around his trailer. 'I'm looking for work.'

Grimaldi had virtually brushed her aside, but nothing deterred her. Every day she came by, and he used to give her a little money, more to get rid of her than anything else, but she still turned up. He would find her sitting on his trailer steps, no matter what the weather, waiting, asking for a job, or if he wanted oral sex, masturbation. He had told one of the stewards to keep her out, but she still came back. If she wasn't hanging round his trailer, she was waiting by the cages. She seemed always to be available, always in the worn brown coat, and always hungry. Grimaldi had been having a relationship with an attractive trapeze artist, a cute little girl from Italy, who began to scream at him to get rid of the whore. He had got nasty with Ruda, physically shoving her away; but still she came back.

There were only a few more days left on his contract before he travelled on, and so he had given in, become more pleasant to her, tried to find out where she came from, if she had a home. She just used to shrug her shoulders. Then he had done a foolish thing. Seeing her huddled outside his trailer in pouring rain, he had asked her inside.

Once inside she seemed genuinely interested in his

255

photographs and his reviews. He offered to take her sodden coat, but she refused, sitting in it, smoking, her wet hair hanging.

'Can you take me with you when you go?'

He had laughed, saying it was impossible, he was going to Austria, then on to Switzerland, crossing back to Italy and then, he hoped, America.

She had offered to be a groom, sweep up, do anything if he could get her a job, and he had told her she would have to get permission from the circus bosses. But he had allowed her to follow him into the tent to watch the show.

She turned up the next day – he found her sitting in his trailer. He chucked her out, but after the show she was back. He was exasperated by her persistence, and then said that if she had the right papers, passport and exit visas, he would see what he could do, maybe ask the circus boss if he could get her a job. She had stood with her hands dug deep into the pockets of her coat, then had upped and left. But later that night she came back, tapping on his window to let her in. He shouted for her to get the hell away, but she kept on tapping and in the end he had dragged open the trailer door. 'Look, I said I don't want you around. If you got the papers, leave them, I'll see what I can do, now go. I'm taking a shower – go – just go!'

She had brazenly walked past him into the small bedroom, taking off her filthy coat. Beneath it she still wore the black brassière, black panties with a suspender belt . . . and the stockings were even more laddered.

'I've got someone with me, OK? So whatever you have to say, make it quick.'

'I've got no papers, I need you to help me. I need money.'

She stared at him defiantly, and he almost laughed at her audacity.

'My husband won't let me have any money.'

'Your husband?'

'Yeah, the old man. I work for him, it's his act – you know, the magic man?'

Grimaldi hitched up the small towel around his waist. 'Well, like I said, part of the act – the part with the coloured silk squares – you should work it up. I mean, I don't know what the signals are, but it's good.'

'Signals? What do you mean?'

'Well, how you do it, how you get all the colours in the right order, and so fast.'

'Oh . . . that's no trick, that's just something I can do. I can do that easy, ever since I was a kid.' She was looking around, peering into his bedroom.

'Well, it's good. The old boy's not so good though. You should get a new partner.'

The next moment she was in his arms, coiling around him. She pinched his cheek in her finger and thumb. 'You lied. There's no bleedin' woman here. You lied. Who's a bad boy, then?'

He didn't want to kiss her, touch her even, but he stood there, he let her go down on him, let her take him there in the middle of his trailer.

After it was done, she wiped her mouth with the back of her hand. 'That was for free! I'm going now.'

He had felt guilty, thrust money into her pocket. She seemed surprised, taking out the folded notes and counting them, and then she had looked up and smiled. He had never seen her smile before. 'Maybe next time I come I'll have a visa, you can take me with you then. Oh, my name is Ruda ... R U D A, you won't forget that, will you? Thanks for the money.'

He travelled on the next day, but he didn't forget her – he was able to recognize her immediately five years later when she turned up again. This time it was in Florida and she was accompanied by her husband: Tommy Kellerman.

Grimaldi woke up. For a second he had no idea where he was, his head throbbed so hard he couldn't lift it. He felt something warm and hairy curled by his side, lifted a stinking blanket and peered into Boris's face. 'Whoop ... Whoop.' Grimaldi let the blanket fall back over the chimp. A loud snoring was coming from across the room. In the darkness he could just make out the sleeping Lazars, his legs propped up on the table, his head on his chest, still sitting in the upright chair.

Grimaldi swore ... how in God's name had he got here? ... he couldn't remember. He sighed, and the strong hairy arm patted his chest gently. He inched up the blanket again, and the round bright button eyes blinked ... 'What time is it, eh?' Boris sucked in her gums, and Grimaldi tried to sit up – he slumped back again, better to sleep it off. He doubted if he could stand up anyway.

Ruda was wakened by the trailer door being banged and tossed her sheets aside. She lifted the blinds and saw a bedraggled Tina waiting outside. 'What do you want?'

Tina peered through the window. 'Is he here? I can't pay the taxi. He took my handbag. Will you let me in?'

Ruda pulled on an old wrap, stuffed her feet into worn slippers. She fetched her wallet, and opened the trailer door. 'You know what time it is? How much do you need?'

Tina was red-eyed from crying. 'He just left me, he took my bag.'

Ruda laughed. 'That's my husband. Here, take this.'

'Is he back? Did he come back?'

Ruda shook her head, about to close the door, her hand on her hip.

'I can't get into my trailer, the girls lock the door.'

'What do you expect me to do?'

'Can I come back, after I've paid him?'

Ruda shrugged and left the door ajar, returned to the bedroom and closed the door. She heard Tina return, then heard the clink of cutlery. She stormed out. 'Eh! What do you think you're doing?'

'I was making a cup of tea?'

'Oh, were you? Don't you think it would have been polite to ask? You wake me up, get money out of me and now start banging around in my kitchen. You've got a nerve, a lot of nerve.'

'I'm sorry, do you want one?'

Ruda hesitated. 'Yeah, white, one sugar.'

She got back into her bed and turned on the bedside light. It was after four; she leaned back, hearing the girl banging around searching for the tea, then she heard the rattle of teacups and her door inched open. Tina had a tray with the two cups, a pot of tea, sugar and biscuits. She poured Ruda's cup, spooned in the sugar, then stirred it carefully.

Ruda took the cup, watching Tina pour her own, then she laughed softly. 'Well, isn't this cosy? You fancy keeping the baby in my room, do you? Little pink elephants on the curtains, frilly crib, white baby wardrobes?'

Tina edged to sit on a small stool in front of Ruda's dressing table. 'I got really frightened, he was with me one minute and the next he just disappeared, and he's got my handbag, all my money, my cards, chequebook – everything. I'm worried about him, do you think he'll be all right?'

Ruda opened her bedside drawer, took out a bar of chocolate and broke it into pieces. She sucked at a large piece, not offering any to Tina. Tina took a biscuit and nibbled it. 'I mean, he had been drinking.'

Ruda said nothing, kept on staring at Tina.

'Actually, I wanted to talk to you, Ruda. Is it all right if I call you Ruda?'

Ruda took another bite of chocolate, sipped her tea, felt the thick black slab melting slowly in her mouth. She found it amusing to watch the stupid little bitch squirming. She said nothing.

'I know he's talked to you about the baby, and we've never really spoken. He said you'd agreed to a divorce.'

Ruda licked around her mouth, leaving a dark brown chocolate stain.

'I know how much the act means to you, Ruda. I was watching you in rehearsal. I mean, I was really impressed. I don't know all that much about training, but—'

'Impressed! Well, I *am* flattered—' Ruda held out her cup for more tea, and Tina scuttled to the tray and poured, spooned in more sugar and then started for the door.

'I don't want any milk, never have milk in the second cup, thank you.'

Ruda smiled, and Tina sat on the edge of the bed. 'I love him . . .'

'You love him. How old are you?'

'Age doesn't matter.'

'Doesn't it?'

'No, and I think I can make him happy. He's really excited about the baby.'

'Is it his?'

Tina flushed, and her petal mouth pursed. 'That's a terrible thing to say. Of course it's his.'

Ruda slowly put her cup down and leaned forwards. Tina backed slightly, and then allowed Ruda to take her hand. 'What tiny little hands you've got. Let me see your palm. Oh yes, really interesting! My, my! What a lifeline.'

Tina moved closer, allowing Ruda to press and feel her open palm. 'Do you believe in that stuff? I think it's all mumbo-jumbo.'

Ruda suddenly gripped Tina's hand so hard it hurt, but she still smiled, as if she was joking. 'And I think everything you say is a load of crap – you little prick-teaser. You don't love Luis. You don't love that big bloated old man, that drunken has-been, you want . . .'

Tina tried to draw her hand away, but Ruda held her in a vice-like grip, pulling her closer and closer . . . and then, there was no smile. Her face twisted with anger, and with her free hand she punched Tina's belly, pummelled it as if it was a lump of dough. Tina twisted and tried to drag herself free. She started screaming – terrified, trying to protect her belly.

Ruda hauled Tina almost on top of herself. Tina kicked out with her legs, but Ruda dragged her closer and covered her mouth. Tina could feel Ruda's body beneath her, and she twisted again, tried to turn.

'Don't struggle or I'll break your neck.'

Tina began to cry, her body went limp. She knew she couldn't fight, Ruda was too strong.

'Promise not to cry out? Promise me? *Promise!*'

Ruda jerked Tina so hard she gasped. 'I promise . . . I promise . . . just don't hurt me, don't hurt my baby, please . . .'

'If you scream or cry out, then I will hurt you, maybe even kill you.' Slowly Ruda released her grip, easing Tina from her, and then rolled away, leaned up on one elbow. She smiled down into the frightened girl's face. Tina was like a rabbit caught in the poacher's beam of light. Her eyes were wide, startled and terrified. She was transfixed, unable to move, too scared to cry out. Now, Ruda's strong hands stroked and caressed, with knowing assurance, gently easing down Tina's skirt to feel between her legs, her voice soft and persuasive, a half-whispered monotone, hardly audible.

'The nights when they had their entertainments, when they had their drinks, their music, we knew we were safe for one or two hours. We'd hear the laughter, we'd hear the singing, the applause, the shouting . . .'

Ruda unbuttoned Tina's blouse, cupping the heavy breasts in their white lace brassière. Her skin felt soft, so soft, and Ruda had an overwhelming desire to hold her, as if she was some long-forgotten lover she wanted to protect. She no longer frightened her, she knew that, and she cradled Tina in her arms, drawing her closer, her lips close to Tina's face. She gave gentle, almost sweet kisses to her neck, to her ears. Tina felt the sadness sweep over her like a wave, a terrible sadness. She could not stop herself giving a return, child-like kiss to Ruda's neck.

'Where were you?' Tina asked hesitantly, unsure what was happening, why it was happening.

Then Ruda rested her head against Tina's breast, and Tina continued softly to stroke the back of Ruda's head, as if to encourage her to continue. 'Where were you?' Tina repeated.

'Oh, I was some place, some place a long time ago. The older ones discovered there was a flap beneath the main hut, that we could wriggle beneath, hide under the trestle benches, hide and wait to see the show . . .'

Ruda moved to rest her head on the pillows. Tina could easily have got up then, but she didn't move. The big strong woman's sadness had mesmerized her.

'What was the show? Was it your first circus?'

Ruda sighed. 'Yes, it was a sort of circus. They had animals, they had dancers, and they had hunchbacks and giants. They had every imaginable human deformity, but they had chosen only the prettiest girls. They were thirteen, maybe a little older, but each one had their head shaved, their body hair shaved, and they were given coronets of paper flowers . . . red flowers, like bright red poppies . . .' Ruda's eyes stared to the ceiling, her face expressionless.

'They made the dwarfs fuck the giants, they made the hunchbacks fuck the pretty sweet virgins, they forced the dwarfs to ride the dogs' backs with their dicks up their arses . . . and they clapped and applauded, laughed and shouted for more. Then they began to beat the pretty, weeping girls and they kept on beating them until their white bodies were red with their own blood, as red as the paper flowers on their scraped and scratched bald scalps . . . One of the trestles moved, cut into my leg. The

263

others escaped, they crawled back under the feet of the bastards, inching their way out. But I couldn't. I was trapped, I had to keep on watching. When I shut my eyes, it made it worse because I could hear them, hear the cries, hear the dogs . . .'

Ruda seemed unaware Tina was there, and Tina inched away, slid from the bed until she knelt on the floor trying to retrieve her clothes. Ruda made a strange guttural sound, half sob, half cry, and she covered her face with her hands. 'Oh, God, my poor Tommy, poor Tommy!'

Tina slipped her blouse round her shoulders. Ruda remained on the bed, not attempting to stop her leaving. She wiped her cheek with the back of her big raw hand. 'Not until the show was over, not until they were too drunk to stand, too drunk to care, could I crawl back. Next morning, I saw what they'd done to the older ones. They were on the cart, the skin of their little bald heads burst open, clouds of flies stuck to their blood, purple-black-rimmed eyes. I only wanted to see the show, to see what made everyone laugh.'

Tina crawled towards her skirt. Suddenly Ruda rose from the bed, her hand outstretched. 'Don't go. Please stay with me, just for a little while.' She reached over and placed her hand on the unborn, the rounded belly of the young girl. 'I will see you have money to travel, but you are leaving.'

Tina backed away from Ruda: the expression in the woman's eyes made her afraid again. 'You will be leaving, Tina, but without my husband.'

Tina blurted out a pitiful, 'No. No!' She would never forget the look on Ruda Grimaldi's face, the strange hissing sound before she spat out the words: 'He is *mine*!'

The slap sent Tina reeling against the wall. At the same

time Grimaldi eased open the trailer door, silently, so as not to wake Ruda. He heard the cry, turned towards Ruda's bedroom, inched along the narrow tiny corridor, opened the door, and for a moment was unable to comprehend what he was seeing.

He slammed the door, slammed out of the trailer and, still drunk, began to vomit. He turned as Tina ran out hysterically, half undressed, sobbing. She gasped, 'My handbag. I want my handbag.' She snatched it from him, and ran. She stumbled once, flaying the air with her hand, and then ran out of sight.

Ruda was at the trailer door, looking at him shaking, his vomit trickling down the trailer. 'You better get some coffee down you. Come on, I'll get Mike to clear up in the morning.'

Grimaldi, dazed, allowed himself to be helped back up the steps, stood as she took his jacket and peeled off his shirt.

'Christ, you stink. What the hell have you been doing?'

'I met Fredrick Lazars, we got drunk . . .'

'Sit down and let me take your trousers off, you stink like a dog.'

Grimaldi sat as she heaved off his boots and unbuttoned his trousers.

'I slept with Boris, a baby chimp.'

He curled up on the cushions. She fetched a blanket, dropped it around him, placed a bottle of Scotch ready for him to drink when he came round – she knew he would be unable to face the day without one. When she was sure he was asleep, Ruda returned to her own room and slumped on to her crumpled bed, confused by the evening's events. What had she just done?

She rubbed her arms with revulsion, growing more

angry with herself. She had told Tina, stupid little Tina, about a part of her life that she had never told anyone before. Why? She bit her knuckles. Tina had made her feel something, the girl's soft body in her arms had reminded her of a warmth, a loving, she had forgotten. But it wasn't the same, it was stupid even to think of it now, she had to get her mind straightened out, had to think straight. She had even offered to pay Tina to leave. Why? 'What do you want, Ruda?' she asked herself. Whatever Grimaldi had become, even if she didn't want him, was the real truth that she didn't want anyone else to have him either? That surprised her.

'What do you want?' Ruda said it aloud as she started her pacing walk, up and down the small trailer bedroom. Her pace quickened, and she paused twice looking up to the cupboard. She could feel it drawing her, but every time she got to it she turned and walked back across the room. She paused by her own picture, her poster. She pressed her hand against her face, and then she couldn't stop herself. She stepped up on the small stool by her make-up mirror, and opened the small cupboard above. She had to balance on tiptoe to reach it. Her hands pushed boxes and hats aside until she felt the cold sides of the black tin box. She hugged it to her chest, secretive, child-like, and then got to her hands and knees, lifting the carpet until she found her hidden key. She always felt a strange sensation on opening the box: pain pierced her insides. The odd assortment of treasures, her secrets that meant so much to her, were of no value to anyone else. She spent a long time fingering, touching her things, unaware of the low humming sound she made, her body rocking backwards and forwards. 'Mine, mine . . . mine . . .' She licked the small oval grey pebble-like object, then replaced it, and looked to the poster of herself. 'Mine, mine, mine.' Her own face in the centre of the brightly coloured poster became a distorted skeleton head. She could see the loaded truck, weighted down, being dragged through the muddy yard, teetering dangerously to one side. Beneath a hastily thrown tarpaulin, she glimpsed the stacked, bloated bodies, and from the crushed bellies of the corpses came the hideous hissing sound of escaping gas. As the truck tilted a body slid from beneath the tarpaulin, and fell to the ground, rolling to one side. The guards shouted to the orderlies to get the corpse back on the truck, but then in the darkness something glittered on the fat bloated hand, with fat purple fingers. The guard tried to wrench the thick gold wedding ring free, but try as he would he could not release it. He picked up a spade and, holding it above his head, brought it down blade first across the dead woman's hand. The fingers jumped, as if they had a life of their own, and they rolled in the mud. The guard dug this way and that, swearing and shouting but unable to find the ring. He gave up and screamed for the truck to move on. An orderly unhooked his coat belt, made a loop and flicked it over the dead woman. He dragged her by her neck back on to the truck, and then tightened the tarpaulin down. The guards and the Kapos began to push and shove the truck forwards through the freezing muddy ground.

As it disappeared, the ragged men, hidden like nightmare shadows, appeared like a pack of dogs, scrabbling in the mud until one man, on his hands and knees, found the ring. 'Das gehört mir!' 'Mine!' But the others tore at him, beat him, he screamed and kept on screaming: 'Das ist der *meine, meine, meine!*' The pitiful man clung to his

267

treasure, fought like a demon, then desperate to save himself he threw the ring and it shot through the air, sinking in a puddle not two feet away from a tiny little girl, a little girl crying with the pain in her leg, terrified by what she had just witnessed . . . a frightened Ruda, crawling between the alleyways of huts, safe from the shadow men, on the other side of the barbed-wire fence. The man clung to the meshing with his skinny hands, his mouth black, gaping and toothless, like a starving jackal he screeched, 'Das ist der meine, das gehört mir, das ist der meine!'

Ruda had crept back to her hut, silently lifting the worn blanket, slipping to lie beside her sister, needing her comfort, needing to feel the warmth of the tiny plump body and, in her sleep, Rebecca turned to cuddle Ruda, to kiss her with sweet adoring childish kisses. Ruda felt safe and warm, and they had a prize worth a fortune. A golden ring. The music, the red paper flowers, the screams and the anguished faces merged and distorted as Ruda, not old enough to comprehend the misery, felt only the burning pain in her leg, and she repeated over and over in her mind: 'Das ist der meine, das ist der meine . . . meine, meine . . .'

Ruda carefully relocked her treasure box, hid the key and returned the black tin box to its hiding place. She knew she could not sleep, and as it was after five decided she would shower and get ready for the first feed of the day. As she soaped her body, turning round slowly in the small shower cabinet, she felt the tension in her body begin to ease. But she could not rid herself of the deep anger which lingered inside her. She carefully wrapped herself in a clean soft towel, patting herself dry, then pointed her left foot like a dancer. The small scar where the trestle bench had cut into her leg was still there. She poured some body lotion into her cupped hand and massaged her leg with long, soothing strokes. The wound had festered. She had been so frightened of telling anyone and eventually she had been taken to the hospital bay. They had put a paper dressing on it. Days, perhaps weeks later the pain had become so bad that she had been carried back to the hospital by an orderly. Lice had eaten into her leg beneath the pus-soaked bandage and she had been forced into the delousing bath, screaming and crying out in pain. It was as a result of the festering wound that she came to the attention of Papa. She had been taken to see him that afternoon, washed, her hair combed, wearing clean clothes, her wound well bandaged with a proper dressing. That was the first time she had been alone with him, the first time he had asked her if she wanted to play a game, a very special game. He had sat her on his knee, given her a sweet and jiggled his knee so she bounced up and down. But she didn't unwrap the sweet, and he had asked why not. He had smiled, asking, didn't she want the sweet? He even playfully tried to take it away from her.

'Das ist der meine!' The little girl's fist clamped over the sweet and she glared into his handsome face, her determined expression delighting him, and he smiled, showing perfect white teeth.

Ruda tossed the towel aside. She continued to cover her body with the moisturising lotion, then she dressed. The anger had gone now. Thinking of Papa always made the anger subside. It was replaced, as it had always been, with a chilling, studied calmness. Ruda braided her hair, gave a cursory look at her reflection. She passed the poster of herself and, in passing, lightly touched it with her hand. That poster represented everything she had fought so hard to attain, and nothing would take it from her. She didn't even look at it as she passed, but she whispered quietly to herself, making a soft hissing sound: 'Das ist der meine!'

Luis was still deeply asleep where she had left him. She drew the blinds, pulled the blanket further round his shoulders, and left him. Outside she picked up the hose and washed down the trailer herself, then began to whistle, stuffing her hands into her pockets as she strolled over to the cages. She looked skywards, shading her eyes. It still looked pretty overcast.

Ruda passed between the trailers, calling out a brisk good morning to the early risers. There was movement now, trainers, performers, some heading to the canteen for breakfast, some, like Ruda, getting ready to prepare their animals' feed. She made her routine morning check, passing from cage to cage, calling every cat by name, and then she stopped by Mamon's cage. He was lazily stretching, easing his massive body away; he threw back his head and yawned. 'You're mine, my love.' She leaned against the rails, and he swung his head low, stared at her and then threw his black mane back with a roar that never ceased to delight her. He seemed to roar her inner rage. 'Everything's all right now, ma'angel!'

CHAPTER 10

TORSEN WOKE refreshed and prepared to put everything he had listed into order. The moment he got into his office, he pasted up his memos, his suggested rota for the men. It was still only seven-thirty, but he had brought in fresh rolls and was brewing coffee. He typed furiously the past evening's reports and distributed them around the station.

At eight forty-five when the men began to trickle into the locker rooms, they saw a large memo requesting all station personnel to be in the main incident room for a briefing.

Torsen was placing his notebook and newly sharpened pencils on the incident room's bare table when he overheard Rieckert laughing as he entered. 'No, I said, it's not just a dwarf but a Jewish dwarf and . . .'

He beckoned to Rieckert to join him. He kept his voice low, his back to the main room. 'If I hear you make one more anti-Semitic remark – in the station, in the car, at any time you are wearing your uniform – you will be out, understand?'

Rieckert smiled, said that he was just passing on a joke.

'I don't care, I don't want to hear, now sit down.'

Torsen gave out the day's schedule, and suggested that

they should all review the new rota of times for on and off duty periods, and anyone with any formal and reasonable complaint should leave a memo on his desk. He then discussed in detail his findings to date regarding the murder of Tommy Kellerman.

The meeting was interrupted by the switchboard operator, who slipped a note to Torsen. It was an urgent request to call his father's rest home. Torsen placed the call, and the nurse informed him that his father was exceptionally lucid, and had requested to see him.

Torsen returned to the incident room. 'I will not, as listed, be on the first assignment. Rieckert and Clauss take that, and I will join you at the Grand Hotel. Please remain there until I arrive.'

Torsen had made clear that they must all remain in contact with each other throughout the day so that they could confer and discuss their findings. He declined, however, to tell them where he was going, feeling that after his pep talk a visit to his ailing father should not, perhaps, take precedence over the murder enquiry. But everyone found out anyway – the switchboard operator told them. She was very miffed at being told to come into work an hour earlier than usual: she had children to get off to school, a husband to feed, it was all very well for Inspector Torsen to throw his weight about since he wasn't married.

Nurse Freda was a pleasant dark-haired girl in her late twenties; she was waiting for Torsen at the main reception. 'He seemed very eager to speak to you.'

'I appreciate your call, but I cannot stay long. I am involved in a very difficult case.'

He followed her plump rear end along a corridor, and into his father's ward. Nurse Freda turned, smiling. 'He's been put by the windows today. It's more private, you can draw the curtain if you wish.'

The old man was looking very sprightly, hair slicked back, checked dressing-gown and clean pyjamas. He had a warm rug over his frail knees, and his usually sunken jaw was less so today because they had put his teeth in.

'Took your time, took your time, Torsen . . . I don't know, only son and he never comes to see his poor old father.'

Torsen pulled the curtain and drew up a chair to sit next to his father.

The old man crooked his finger for his son to come closer. 'This is important, woke up thinking about it and I've been worried stiff . . . can't sleep for worrying. Then I had a word with Freda, my nurse's name's Freda, and it clicked, just clicked.'

'What did, Father?'

'You need a wife, you've got to settle down and have a couple of kids. You've got a good job, good pay and a nice apartment. Now Freda, she's not married, she's clever, make you a good wife, she's got good, child-bearing hips.'

Torsen flushed, afraid they would be overheard. 'Father, right now I don't have a telephone.'

'Why haven't you got a telephone? Did they take it out?'

Torsen sighed – he had had this conversation before. 'No. Remember, when you moved here, I was delegated a smaller apartment. The telephone remained in the old apartment – I was not allowed to take it when I moved.'

'How can you work without a telephone?'

'With great difficulty, Father. I put in for one months ago, and today I left a memo to the *Direktor*. In fact today I instigated many changes, some I am quite proud of . . .'

The old man stared out of the window, plucked at his rug a moment, then turned frowning. 'No telephone? Tut tut.'

Torsen checked his watch, then touched his father's hand. 'I am in the middle of an investigation, I have to leave.'

The old man sucked in his breath and turned round, staring at the ward, leaning forwards to enable himself to see the row of beds. Then he sat back. 'Dying is a long time in coming, eh? There are many here, waiting, and afraid.'

Torsen held the frail hand. 'Don't talk this way, I don't want to go away worrying about you.'

'Oh, I'm not afraid, there are no ghosts to haunt me, but the dying here is hard for some. They have secrets, the past is their present, and they remember . . . You understand what I am saying? When you pass by their beds look at their faces, you'll see. You can hide memories surrounded by the living, but not in here. Still, soon there will be none left and then Germany can be free.'

Torsen wondered what his father would think if he saw the packs of skinheads screaming out their Nazi slogans. 'I hope you're right.'

The old man withdrew his hand sharply. 'Of course I am. We have been culturally and politically emasculated by Hitler, devastated by the Allies and isolated by the Soviets for more than half a century. Now it is our second chance, the city will be restored as the capital of reunified Germany. We are perfectly placed, Torsen, to become the West's link with the developing economies of the democratic East. You must marry, produce children, be prepared for the future . . .' The old man's face glowed, his hands clasped tightly.

'Father, I have to leave. I will come again this evening.'

'What are you working on?'

Torsen told him briefly about the murder of Kellerman, and the old man listened intently, nodding his head, muttering, 'Interesting, yes, yes . . .'

Torsen leaned close. 'In fact, I was going to ask you about something, remember the way we used to discuss unsolved crimes, Father?'

The old man nodded, rubbing his gums as if his teeth hurt.

'There was an old case, way back, maybe early sixties, late fifties, we nicknamed it the Wizard case . . . do you remember? The body was found midway between your jurisdiction and I think Dieter's. There may be no connection, it was—'

'How is Dieter?'

'He's dead, Father, ten years ago.'

The old man frowned, Dieter was his brother-in-law, and for a moment he was swamped with confusion; was his wife, Dieter's sister, dead too?

'Father, can you remember the name of the victim in the Wizard case?'

'Dieter is dead? Are you sure?'

Torsen looked into the confused face and gently patted his hand. 'I'll come and see you later.' He drew back the curtains and waved to Nurse Freda to indicate he was leaving. His father began singing softly to himself.

Torsen proceeded to walk down the aisle between the beds. He paused, watching Freda finish tending a patient, then waited until she joined him. 'I wondered if perhaps, one evening, we ... if you are not on duty, and would like to join me, could go to a movie ...'

Freda smiled sweetly. 'Your father has been playing Cupid?'

Torsen flushed and fiddled with his tie. She laughed a delightful warm giggle and then asked him to wait one moment. She disappeared behind a screen with a bedpan.

Torsen stared at a skeleton-thin patient, plucking frantically at his blanket, his toothless jaw twitching uncontrollably, eyes wide and staring as if at some unseen horror.

Torsen turned and hurried out, unable to look at the dying relic of humanity, too agitated to wait and arrange a date with Freda.

Rieckert was waiting in the hotel foyer. Torsen hurried to his side, apologized for his lateness and then crossed to the reception desk to ask if they could go to the Baron's suite.

The Baron himself opened the doors to the suite, and pointedly looked at his wristwatch. Torsen apologized profusely as they entered the large drawing room. Rieckert gaped, staring at the chandelier, the marble fireplace – the room was larger than his entire apartment.

The Baron had laid out his wife's and his own passport and visa on the central table; he then introduced them to Helen Masters who proffered her own documents. Torsen leafed through each one, and asked if they were enjoying their stay. The Baron murmured that he was, and sat watching Torsen from a deep wing armchair.

Torsen noted that their papers were in order. Then, standing, he opened his own notebook. 'Would you mind if I asked you just a few questions?'

The Baron shrugged but looked at the clock on the mantelpiece. Helen Masters interrupted to say they were late for an appointment. Torsen smiled and said it would take only a few moments. He looked to the Baron and asked whether the Baroness was feeling better.

'She is. Will you need to speak with her?'

Torsen coughed, feeling very uneasy, and drew up a chair to sit at the central table. 'If it is not too much trouble. But if it is not convenient for her I can return at a later date.'

The Baron strode towards the bedroom, tapped and waited. Hylda came to the door. 'Is the Baroness dressed?'

Hylda murmured she would only be one moment, and the door was closed.

Torsen directed his first question to Helen Masters. 'You arrived by car on the evening in question, that is correct?'

'No, I think we came just before lunch.'

The Baron sighed. 'We ate in the hotel restaurant, then returned to the suite. Then we left at about three o'clock to visit Dr Albert Franks's clinic. We remained with Dr Franks, and then returned to the suite. We dined here, and remained in the hotel all evening.'

Helen nodded as if to confirm part of the Baron's statement. Torsen looked to her, and she hesitated a moment before saying, 'I remained with Dr Franks and had dinner with him, but I returned here at about ten-thirty, maybe a little later.'

Torsen asked if on her return she had seen anyone in the street outside.

Helen laughed softly. 'Well, yes, of course, I saw a number of people – the doorman, the taxi drivers and . . .' She looked to the Baron. 'Your chauffeur, we have forgotten about him. He returned to Paris and then flew to New York, but he would have left before early evening.'

'On your return to the hotel did you see a very tall man, about six foot, wearing a dark raincoat, and a shiny, perhaps leather, trilby hat?' Helen shook her head. Torsen looked up from his notes. 'Did you see anyone fitting that description at or near the hotel entrance on the night in question?'

'No, I did not.'

'Did you see anyone fitting that description in the lobby of the hotel?'

Helen gave Louis a hooded smile. 'No, I am sorry. Is this man suspected of the murder?'

Torsen continued writing. 'I wish to talk to this man about a possible connection to the murder.'

Helen moved closer. 'Do you have any clues to his identity?'

Torsen folded his notebook. 'No, we do not. I think that is all I need to ask.'

'What time was the murder?' Helen asked.

'Close to eleven or eleven-thirty. We know he was carrying a large bag and that his clothes, if he was involved in the murder, would have been heavily bloodstained.'

Helen asked how the victim was killed, listening intently as Torsen described the severity of the beating. She asked if the victim was with the circus, and Torsen gave a small tight smile, wondering why she was so interested, but at the same time answering that the victim was not, as far as he had been able to ascertain, an employee of any circus.

The bedroom doors opened, and Torsen rose to his

feet as the Baroness, assisted by Hylda, walked into the room. The Baron sprang to his feet, crossing to his wife, arms outstretched. 'Sit down, come and sit down. The car is ordered.'

Vebekka wore a pale fawn cashmere shawl fringed with sable, a fawn wool skirt, a heavy cream silk blouse and a large brooch at her neck entwined with gold and diamonds. She also wore her large dark glasses. Her face was beautifully made-up, her lips touched with a pale gloss sheen. She held out her hand to Torsen.

'I am sorry to inconvenience you, Baroness. I am Detective Chief Inspector Torsen Heinz, and this is Sergeant Rieckert.'

The Baroness's hand felt so frail he did no more than touch her fingers. She smiled at Rieckert. Hylda helped her to sit and brought her a glass of water. Torsen noticed how thin she was, how her body seemed to tremble, her hands shaking visibly as she sipped the water. He found it disturbing not to be able to see her eyes.

'I need simply to verify your husband's account of the day you arrived in Berlin.'

She sipped, paused, sipped again and Hylda took the glass.

'What day?'

The Baron coughed, drawing attention to himself. 'The day we arrived from Paris, darling.'

She nodded and then looked at Torsen. 'What did you ask me?'

'If you could just tell me what you did, during the afternoon and the evening.'

She was hardly audible, speaking in a monotone, as she recalled arriving, taking lunch, and then going to see a doctor. She reached for the water again and this time Hylda held the glass as she sipped. 'We dined in the suite, and then I had to rest, I was very tired after the journey.'

Torsen placed his notebook in his pocket, gave a small nod to Rieckert as an indication they were leaving.

'Why are you here? Has something happened? Is something wrong?' She half rose, looking at the Baron. 'Is it Sasha?'

The Baron hurried to her side. 'No, no, nothing wrong, just something happened close to the hotel the night we arrived, and the *Polizei* have to question everyone who booked into the hotel from Paris.'

Torsen noticed that he spoke to her as if she was a child, leaning over towards her, touching her shoulder as if shielding her from harm. 'There was a murder, everyone in the hotel is being questioned.'

'Is this true?' the Baroness asked, and looked in concern at her husband. 'But why? Why have we to be questioned? I don't understand, did I do something wrong?'

The Baron patted his wife's hand, gently telling her they were asking all the guests in the hotel the same questions.

'You didn't happen to see anyone, perhaps looking out of the window down to the street, at about eleven o'clock – a tall man wearing a shiny hat, carrying a holdall?'

The Baroness seemed unable to comprehend what he was talking about. She stared at her husband. 'I didn't do anything, did I? I was in the suite, I never left the suite.'

Torsen shook Helen's hand and thanked her. He gave a small bow to the Baron. His sergeant was already holding open the door. As they waited for the elevator, Rieckert whispered to Torsen, 'She's a sicko. That doctor,

Albert Franks, he's a famous shrink. Deals with crazies, hypnotizes them, that's what they must be here for, she's a sicko . . .'

As Rieckert went to collect their patrol car, Torsen waited on the whitewashed steps. He saw the line of taxis waiting for hire and recognized the driver from the previous night. He crossed over to his Mercedes. The driver jumped out, started to open the rear door.

'No, no, I just wanted to ask you to spread the word around for me – ask if anyone saw a tall man, wearing a shiny trilby hat, dark raincoat, boots, carrying a bag on the night the dwarf was murdered, it was—'

The driver stopped him with an outstretched hand. 'I know the night, we've all been talking about it, but I never saw anyone fitting that description, sir.'

Torsen persisted. 'You ever pick up Ruda Kellerman? The lion tamer? Her husband is Luis Grimaldi.'

The driver nodded his head vigorously. 'Yeah, picked her up from this hotel yesterday, took her back to the West, to the circus.'

Rieckert drew up in the patrol car giving an unnecessary blast of the horn. They drove off as the driver went from cab to cab asking if any of them had seen or given a ride to a huge man in a big trilby, with high boots – the killer! As he conferred with each driver his description grew . . . scarred face, huge hands and covered in blood. One cab driver recalled driving Ruda Kellerman from the hotel, and then remembered it was after the murder, so he didn't mention it, or that he had seen her standing on the opposite side of the road, looking up at the hotel windows. He didn't think it was of any importance.

*

Ruda was feeling a lot happier. The act had run smoothly, the animals getting more used to the new plinths. She saw to the feeds, checked that the cages were clean and the straw changed, and then, still in her working clothes, went to Tina's trailer. She rapped on the door, and waited.

A big blonde woman with gapped teeth inched open the trailer door.

'Can I see Tina?'

'She doesn't want to see anyone, she's been very sick.'

Ruda stuffed her hands into her pockets. 'Tell her it's me, will you.'

After a moment the girl returned, said Tina's room was at the end of the trailer and she had half an hour before practice. The girl stepped down and walked off. Ruda went inside.

The trailer was small and cramped, costumes and underwear littering the small dining area. Ruda stepped over the discarded clothes and pushed open the bedroom door. Tina was huddled in a bunk bed, her face puffy from crying, and she wore a flowered cotton nightdress.

Ruda hitched up her trousers. 'You seen him?'

'No . . . I can't face him. What did he say?'

Ruda shrugged. 'Nothing much. Actually, he sort of suggested I come and check on you. If you want I can fix you something to eat.'

'I'm not hungry, oh, God!' She buried her head in her hands and sobbed. 'It must have looked disgusting. I mean, I dunno why I let you.'

Ruda began to tap the toe of her boot with her stick. 'Look, I didn't come here to talk about last night. I just want to tell you something. He will never leave me, Tina, and I will never divorce him. He's old, sweetheart, he's an old man, he's washed up, and without me he's fucked.'

Tina stood up. 'I don't want to hear any more. Just get out, leave me alone.'

Ruda leaned forwards and pressed Tina's belly. 'How far gone are you?'

Tina backed away, her hands moving protectively over her abdomen. 'Three and a half months.'

'You're lucky . . . they don't like terminating after four months.'

Tina gasped. 'What did you say?'

Ruda smirked. 'You heard me, now stop playing games and listen.'

'I don't want to listen to you – you are evil, you are sick. Get out – *get out!*'

Ruda cocked her head to one side and kicked the bedroom door closed. 'I am here to help you, you stupid little bitch. I can help you, I can give you names, good people you can trust, they'll take care of it for you.'

'I want my baby! I want my baby.'

Ruda shrugged her shoulders. 'OK, that's up to you . . . but I am going to make you an offer. Now, listen to me. I am going to give you fifteen thousand dollars – dollars, Tina! You can leave Berlin, go back to wherever you came from, you can have the baby, abort it – whatever you want. But—'

'I don't want your money.'

Ruda dug into her pockets. 'It's the best offer you'll have, sweetheart – fifteen thousand dollars, in cash, but the deal is, you leave before twelve. If you hang around, the money goes down every hour, so . . . you got until twelve o'clock noon, Tina. Think about it. I'll be in our trailer. OK?' She half opened the bedroom door, then hesitated, swinging it backwards and forwards slightly. 'You know, I'm doing you a big favour. I was married to an old man once, as old as Luis ... decrepit, senile, pawing at me. You turn the offer down, Tina, and I guarantee your life will be a misery. He's a failure, he's washed up, and you wouldn't last a season with any act he tried to get together. He's scared, Tina, he'll never go into the ring again. Everything he's promised, all the lies, are just an old man's dreams.'

Tina sat hugging her knees, rocking backwards and forwards. Big tears trickled down her cheeks. She cringed as Ruda stepped towards her, looked up, almost expecting to be slapped. Instead, Ruda gently brushed the girl's wet cheeks with her thumb. 'Take a good look round this hovel. Now, imagine a cradle, a little baby bawling and clutching at you, needing you, and your body feels bloated, your face all blotchy. You want to bring it up in this? Get rid of it, walk away. It won't even hurt.'

Tina turned her face away. 'I want my baby.'

Ruda swallowed. Tina surprised her. 'Then go home, Tina. Take the fifteen thousand dollars and get out.' Ruda was almost out of the door.

'Make it twenty.' Tina tried hard to meet Ruda's eyes, but they frightened her. She bowed her head, but quickly looked up again when she heard the big deep laugh.

'You're gonna be OK, sweetheart. An' you know somethin' – I like you. It's a deal.'

Ruda whistled as she threaded her way between the trailers. When she reached her own, she eased off her big boots, stacking them outside. She looked skywards, the rainclouds were lifting. She let herself in silently and eased open drawers as she collected the money, counting it. She slipped it into an envelope. She heard Luis stirring.

'Hi, how you feeling?'

He needed a shave, his eyes were red-rimmed. She gave a quick look at the bottle – it was a quarter full – and crossed to him, pulling up the blanket. 'Sleep it off, then I'll fix you something to eat, eh? Rehearsal went well, they're calming down, getting used to the plinths. You were right, you said they'd work out OK.'

'That's good . . .' he mumbled. 'Do you want a chimp? Lazars's got a chimp.'

She cocked her head to one side, handed him the bottle. 'Here, is this what you want?'

He moaned, said he didn't want a drink, but he took the bottle, drank. Some of it trickled out of his mouth. She walked out and left him, turned on the shower for herself and began to undress.

The bottle fell from his hand, he stared at the ceiling, one arm across his face. In his drink-befuddled mind, he kept on seeing the fear on Tina's face, her wretched submissiveness, but worse – he couldn't forget the way Ruda had looked at him, because Ruda had looked at him the same way, the exact same way, when she had ridden on Mamon's back, daring him, mocking him. He lowered his arm, tried to sit up, but the room began to spin, he couldn't get to his feet, couldn't stand. He sank back, then reached for the bottle. He held it by the neck, unable to focus. '*Rudaaa! Ruda!*'

Ruda came in and held the bottle out for him. He eased himself up, and stared at her. 'Thank you.'

She was soaping herself when she heard the light tap on the door. She smiled and peeped round the shower curtain. It was almost twelve. She wrapped herself in a towel, was about to call out, when she heard the main trailer door opening.

Tina walked in. It was dark, the blinds drawn. She stood in the doorway, unable to adjust to the darkness.

'Want a drink?' He was stretched out on the bench seat, his fly undone, his shirt hanging out. Tina edged further into the room as he held out the bottle. 'Have a drink?'

Tina took a step back, whispered his name and then, in a half sob, repeated it. She had somehow not expected him to be there.

'Chimp . . . got a two-year-old chimp, called Boris . . . *oi Boris*!' He laughed, and continued to drink, he didn't even know she was in the room.

She jumped when she felt a light touch on her shoulder, and Ruda drew her close. 'Look at him, take a good look, Tina.'

Tina squeezed past Ruda into the tiny corridor by the front door. 'I did love him. I did.'

Ruda pressed the envelope into her hand. 'I know . . . I know you did but, you know as well as I do, it would never have worked out.'

Tina fingered the thick envelope. 'Because you would never have given us a chance. I'll take your money, Ruda, not for me but for my baby – Luis's baby.' The young girl's eyes stared up at Ruda. This time she didn't look away. 'We agreed twenty, don't make me have to count it. You said twenty.'

Ruda smiled, touched Tina's cheek with her hand. 'Don't push your luck, little girl. I have done only what I had to. It's called survival. You got off lightly. Now get out of my sight before I kick you out.'

Tina let herself out. Ruda shut the door fast, even faster than she had intended, because right outside the trailer she could see the wretched little inspector. She swore under her breath. Why had she been so foolish? She should have just smiled at him. It was getting rid of Tina that had made her react suspiciously. She took a deep breath and waited. Was he coming to see her?

Torsen and his sergeant were looking at the large pair of boots outside the Grimaldi trailer. They had steel tips. Torsen gave Rieckert a few instructions, had to repeat them as Rieckert was so interested in the pretty girl who had just left the trailer, then tapped on the trailer door.

Ruda inched open the door and smiled.

Torsen gave her a small bow. 'Mrs Grimaldi, could I please speak to you for one moment? Oh! Are those your husband's boots outside?'

Ruda hesitated, and then drew her gown tighter around herself. 'Yes, why, do you want to borrow them?'

'No, no. May I come in?'

'I'm afraid he cannot see you right now, he's indisposed.'

Torsen cocked his head to one side. 'It is you I wished to speak to, Mrs Grimaldi.'

Ruda shrugged her shoulders and stepped back from the doorway. She gestured to her husband, still sprawled out, and then suggested they go into her bedroom. She tossed the duvet over the unmade bed. 'What is it this time?'

Torsen remained in the doorway. 'It is with reference to your husband.'

'He won't be able to talk sensibly for hours, maybe days. He's drunk.'

'No, it is about Mr Kellerman. You see, when I

287

questioned you, both here and at the city mortuary, I asked about the dead man's left wrist. You said you had no knowledge of a tattoo, and you repeated that at the mortuary. I have subsequently discovered that the dead man was a survivor of Auschwitz, and the tattoo was his camp identification number. So you must have known what the tattoo was when I asked you. Now I ask you, why? Why did you lie to me, Mrs Grimaldi?'

Ruda sat for a moment, her head bowed, and then slowly she began to roll up her left sleeve, carefully folding back the satin, inch by inch, until her arm was naked. She looked at Torsen. 'Is this a good enough reason for not talking about it?'

She turned over her wrist, her palm upwards, displaying a jagged row of dark blue numbers: 124666. Her voice was very low, husky. 'When they reached 200000 they began again – did you know that? They were confident that by that time there would be no confusion, no two inmates carrying the same number. You know why? Because they would already be dead.'

Torsen swallowed, shocked by the confrontation. He had never met a holocaust survivor face to face. He had to cough to enable himself to speak. 'I am so sorry . . .'

She stared at him, carefully refolding the sleeve down to cover the tattoo. Her eyes bored into his face. In great embarrassment he stuttered that she must have been very young, so very young. 'I was three years old, Inspector. Is there anything else you want to know?'

Torsen shook his head, mumbled his thanks and apologies, and said he would let himself out. He hurried to the patrol car, where Rieckert grinned at him. 'I did it, took a shoe box, one of the performers gave it to me. I filled it with mud, then pressed the boot down hard.

We've got two good clear prints. I took the right and the left because I wasn't sure which heel we got the original print from.'

Torsen started the engine. 'Left, it was the left heel, and they're Grimaldi's boots.'

The car splashed through the mud and potholes and on to the freeway. Rieckert opened his notebook. 'I got samples of sawdust from the cages, from all over the place, got it all in plastic bags as you told me. So, what did she say? Why did she lie?'

Torsen stared ahead, continued to drive. After a moment, he said, 'She had a reason for not wanting to remember. One I accepted.'

Ruda carried her boots to the main incinerator, the one used for the massive amount of rubbish left after a show – old ice-cream cartons and leaflets, chocolate boxes. She checked the grid: the fire was low, it wouldn't be built up until after the show opened, but she tossed the boots inside the oven and waited by the open door to see them catch. They took a long time – the leather was tough, hard to ignite. Gradually they began to smoulder, to give off a heavy odour. She slammed the oven closed.

So many years she had controlled the images, fought them, but the smells . . . they were the worst, they could sneak up on you unexpectedly, and they were stronger because they were unexpected, more difficult to repress. The pictures they conjured up were more powerful, more horrific . . .

Ruda walked blindly through the lanes of trailers, her hands in fists, taking short sharp breaths to keep herself from falling into the darkness. She made her way to the cages as if by instinct, until she was at Mamon's cage. He sprang to his feet, swinging his head from side to side, and she clung to the bars, gripping them so tightly that her knuckles turned white. 'Ma'angel, ma'angel!'

Mamon's tongue licked at her through the bars, rough, hard. She closed her eyes, comforted by his growled affection, a low heavy-bellied growl, and she answered him, releasing a part howl, part scream of release, as the pictures faded.

Vebekka had been calm all the way to the doctor's, seated between Helen and Louis, holding their hands. She clung to Louis as they went into the reception, where Maja greeted Vebekka warmly. Dr Franks, wearing a green cardigan and an old pair of grey flannel trousers, sauntered in, kissed Vebekka, and said he felt they should talk in his private lounge area. She allowed herself to be led along a corridor into the comfortable room. Vebekka was relieved: there were no white coats or nurses.

'Sit where you will, my dear, and Helen, Baron, if you wish to stay with us, by all means do. We are only going to have a friendly discussion.'

Helen touched Louis's arm; she knew Dr Franks wanted them to sit in the adjoining room and watch through the glass. Vebekka seemed a little afraid when they left, but then sat in a comfortable easy chair.

'And how are you?' Franks asked softly.

'A little better, still weak, and thirsty. I keep on drinking as you told me to.'

'Good, good.' He drew up a chair, not too close, but within touching distance, and then fetched a stool, winking at Vebekka. 'Make myself nice and comfortable. Now, let's get you some nice iced water, do you want a cigarette?'

Vebekka began to relax. He would not offer her a cigarette if he was going to hypnotize her, would he? She opened her case and he clicked open his lighter. She bent her head, inhaled the smoke, at the same time easing her body back. Franks settled himself in his chair, and propped up his feet.

'Tell me,' he said quietly, 'if you were to describe, with only one word, how you feel mostly – like happy, moody, sad – what word would it be?'

She let the smoke drift from her mouth, and then cocked her head to one side. 'One word? Mmmm – that is very difficult.'

The room fell silent, Franks sitting with his arms folded over his chest, Vebekka cupping her chin in her hands.

She flicked the ash from her cigarette. 'One word?' she asked again and he nodded. She continued to smoke for a while, obviously thinking, then she sipped the iced water and replaced the glass.

'Can you think of a word, Vebekka?' He looked at her directly, and she turned her face away from him, sighed.

'Longing.'

He savoured the word, repeated it, and then smiled. 'That is very interesting, nobody has ever said that to me before . . . longing.'

'I long for . . . always I feel I am longing for . . .'

His voice was soft and persuasive. 'What, Vebekka, what are you always longing for?'

'I don't know.'

The clock was ticking, ticking. She could hear a soft voice telling her not to be afraid, she had nothing to fear, and that perhaps she would like to lie down, rest for a while. She wasn't sure if she got up, or if she floated, but she was glad to lie down, it was so comfortable . . .

Helen and the Baron watched intently, saw Vebekka smiling, smoking, and then saw Franks help her lie down on the couch. He took a soft blanket and gently covered her up. Her eyes were open, wide open.

Franks now flicked on the microphone connecting the two rooms, and looked to the two-way mirror. He said, very softly, 'She is under. I am going to begin now.'

CHAPTER 11

D R FRANKS began by asking Vebekka simple
questions, what she liked to eat, what her
favourite drink was, and she answered coherently and directly. Then he reached for his notes, made
reference to doctors she had visited and asked for her
reactions to the tests. Again she answered directly, referring to the last medical diagnosis with sarcasm. Franks
asked what she understood to be meant by panic attacks,
did she feel she suffered from some form of panic? No
answer, so he asked if she often felt afraid.

'Yes, I am afraid.'

'Do you know what you are afraid of?'

'No . . .'

'How does the fear begin?'

'As if someone I am frightened of has entered the
room.'

Franks pursed his lips. He did not want to push
Vebekka too far on their first session so he changed the
subject, directing his questions away from her fear. He
asked how she liked to travel, what cases and clothes she
liked to take with her, and he was given a long list of
favourite items from her wardrobe: shoes, wraps, furs.
She continued for ten minutes, and he saw that she

was relaxed again, her hands resting on the top of the blanket.

The Baron looked at Helen, raised his eyebrows and sighed. He could see no point in the session whatsoever. Helen whispered, 'Wait . . . just wait.'

'Now tell me about your cases, your trunks, Vebekka.'

She described her various handmade leather cases, how she liked to pack everything with tissue paper. Franks asked her about her small boxes, her many vanity cases, and without any sign of undue stress, she listed her jewellery, her make-up, the photographs of her children and her medicine.

'Do you feel these cases, or boxes, have any other meaning, that you separate everything you own into compartments?' He received no reply. He asked, 'Do you have similar boxes inside you? For example, shall we say the make-up box is your head. Do you think that way at all?'

She hesitated, and then smiled. 'Yes, yes I do.'

'Can you explain this to me?'

'I have many compartments inside me.'

'Do they all have keys?'

'Oh, yes!' She seemed pleased.

'Will you unlock them for me? Tell me what is inside each layer? Can you do that?'

She sighed and moved to a more comfortable position. 'Well, there's the first compartment, that contains my special make-up, make-up I use only on rare occasions.'

'Tell me about the second.'

'My children, their letters, their photographs, things I treasure. I have Sasha's first baby tooth and I have . . .'

'Tell me about the third box . . . what's in there?'

'My jewellery, all the pieces I am most fond of, the

most precious pieces. There is an emerald and diamond clip and a bluebird made of sapphires and—'

'Go to the next box . . . open the next box.'

'Medicine, sleeping tablets and my pills . . . I have them all listed.'

'You make a lot of lists?'

'Yes, yes, lots of lists.'

'Go to the next. Open the next box.'

Vebekka began to become a little agitated, her hand clutched at the blanket.

'Go to the next box.'

'No.'

'Why not?'

'Because it's private.'

'Please, open it. Or does it frighten you to open it?'

'No, it's . . . just personal, that's all.'

Franks waited, she was breathing very deeply. 'Open it, Vebekka, and tell me what is inside.'

'Rebecca.'

Franks looked to the two-way mirror, and then turned to Vebekka. 'Rebecca?' he asked softly.

'*Yesss*, she's in there.'

'Do you have any more boxes?'

Vebekka was more agitated now, chewing her lips.

'Go to the next box, Vebekka, tell me about the next box.'

'No . . . it is not a box.'

'What is it?'

'Locked, it is locked, I can't open it.'

'Try. Why don't you describe it to me?'

'It's hard, black, it's chained, I don't have the key.'

She began to twist, her hands clutched tightly together. 'Rebecca won't open it.'

Franks talked to her softly, saying he was there to help her and whatever was in the box he would deal with – all she had to do was open it.

'*It's not a box.*'

'Whatever is there, we'll leave it for a while. No need to get upset, if you don't want to open it then we won't. But tell me about Rebecca, who is Rebecca?'

Her breath hissed, she seemed exasperated. 'She guards it, she protects it, so nobody can open it, nobody must know.'

'Know what?' Franks could feel her strength of mind, it astonished him. She was fighting his control. She began breathing rapidly, her eyelids fluttering, she was trying to surface, trying to come out of the hypnosis. Franks changed the subject. 'Vebekka, tell me about Sasha.'

Vebekka relaxed and began to tell Franks about her daughter, that she was riding, and had a pony. She described Sasha's bedroom and her clothes, giving Franks a clear picture of the little girl.

'Tell me about Sasha's toys. Her dolls.'

Vebekka described the different dolls, where they had been bought. How many were for birthdays, for Christmas.

'Why did you destroy Sasha's dolls, Vebekka?'

'I did not.'

'I think you did. You took all Sasha's dolls, you took their pretty frocks off and you stacked them up like a funeral pyre, didn't you? You set light to them, you burned them—'

'*No, she did that!*'

'Who? Who burnt the dolls, Vebekka?'

She tugged at the blanket, her body twisted. 'Rebecca . . .'

'Who is Rebecca?'

Vebekka vomited, her whole body heaved and she leaned over the couch. Franks fetched a bowl and a towel. He pressed for assistance and Maja entered. She went quickly to Vebekka as Franks put down the bowl.

'I am so sorry . . .' Vebekka turned to face him, their eyes met for a moment, and then she looked away.

Franks checked her pulse, frowning, and helped her to lie back on the cushions. He drew his chair up. She smiled and whispered again she was so sorry, then she closed her eyes. Franks touched Maja's shoulder and whispered for her to clean up the room. He slipped out.

He joined the Baron and Helen Masters. 'Firstly, I have to tell you I have never known this before, she is able to move into the waking cycle by herself. She forced her vomit attack, her will is quite extraordinarily strong. I had quite a hard time taking her under – usually it's a matter of seconds but she took a considerable time, did you notice, Helen?'

Helen looked at the Baron, and then asked if she could speak to him alone. Franks seemed slightly taken aback, and then said by all means, he would wait in the corridor. Helen turned to the Baron and said quietly that considering what Vebekka had already said during the session she felt they should now pass on the information to Franks regarding the discovery of the photograph.

She went to Franks, who was talking quietly to Maja. She told him about the photograph, passed him the black-and-white snapshot. He studied it, turned it over to read the inscription 'Rebecca', then asked if Vebekka was aware of the discovery. Helen was sure that she was not. The Baron came out into the corridor. Franks looked at him. 'I must ask if you are sure your wife has had no hypnotherapy treatment before.'

'None that I know of.'

'I ask because I feel that she is very aware, and I did not take her too deeply. But now, now I would like to try.'

The Baron gave a shrug of his shoulders. 'You are the doctor, I will go along with whatever you suggest.'

Franks returned to Vebekka. Helen and the Baron took their seats again in the viewing room. She whispered, 'He was trying to find out if she could be a multi-personality . . . the boxes, taking her through the different internal protective layers.'

He sat tight-lipped, irritated when Helen added softly, 'I was right, Vebekka is Rebecca!'

Vebekka sipped the iced water, resting back on the cushions, and Franks checked her pulse again. She was very hot, and he removed the blanket. Returning to his seat he paused a moment before he began to hypnotize her again.

'Longing, repeat the word to me, Vebekka.'

She did, but it was hardly audible, and she did not resist him.

'So you feel a longing . . . yes? Listen to me, Vebekka. Just listen to my voice, don't fight my voice, just listen . . . you feel very relaxed, you feel calm and relaxed, you know no harm will come to you, and the feeling of longing . . . longing . . .'

She was under again. This time her eyes were closed, and she breathed very deeply, as if sleeping. Franks waited a few moments before he asked if he could speak to Rebecca. Would Vebekka allow him to speak to her?

She sighed. 'You don't understand.' She sounded irritated, as if he had asked her something stupid.

'Then help me, let me talk to Rebecca.'

'I am Rebecca,' she snapped.

'I'm sorry, you were right, I didn't understand.'

'Oh, that's all right, you wouldn't like her anyway. She's not very nice, she has very bad moods, very dark moods and a very bad temper. She is ugly and fat, always eating, always wanting sweet things – not nice, Rebecca is not nice.'

'But you said you are Rebecca?'

Again there was the irritable sigh, as if his incomprehension of what she was telling him annoyed her. Her voice became angry. 'I *was* Rebecca, but I didn't like her. Don't you understand? I am Vebekka, I am not Rebecca any more.'

'I see. So which of you would you say was the stronger? Rebecca or Vebekka?'

She hesitated, then gave a strange sly smile. 'Rebecca was, but not any more.'

Vebekka went on in a low unemotional voice, describing how she had made the decision to shut away Rebecca because she did not like her. She left home, left her parents and went to live in New York. Nobody knew Rebecca there, so it was very easy; she created a new person, someone she liked. She lost weight, became slim and joined a model agency as Vebekka.

'How did Rebecca feel about this?'

'Oh, she couldn't do anything about it. I locked her up, you see, I shut her away.'

Franks began to try to pinpoint dates and times, discovering that the change of name or personality change occurred when Vebekka was seventeen. Then, because she had changed, she did not want any connection with her old self, and as she became successful in her career as a model she started to travel on modelling assignments, eventually securing work in Paris.

'When did Rebecca start to come back?'

Vebekka turned on the sofa, wriggled her body, her face puckered in a frown. 'She started to get out, you see, she wouldn't stay locked up.'

'I understand that, but when did you find she was very difficult to control?'

She held her hands protectively over her stomach. 'My baby . . . she said there wasn't enough room inside me, not enough room for the two of us, she kept on trying to get out, but I fought her, she said terrible things, terrible things about the baby, she said it would be deformed, it would be deformed . . .'

Franks spent over an hour with her, and then decided he needed a break. He did not wake her because he wanted her to rest as much as possible. He replaced the blanket and tucked it around her, checked her pulse, and told her she would sleep for a while.

Helen poured a black coffee for the doctor. He sipped it, sighing with pleasure, and then slowly replaced the cup. 'Let me explain something to you, Baron. What you have heard may seem extraordinary to you, that your wife created another being, but it is a very common thing. Every person, at some time or another, has his or her mind split into two factions. The easiest way to understand it is to think back to a moment of fear – for example a near miss in a car accident if you have ever had one – a voice will begin talking you down, talking your fear down, telling you

300

it's all over, everything is fine, that it was a narrow miss etc. etc. Your wife created Vebekka because Rebecca was as she described, moody, bad-tempered, fat. She was, in other words, someone she did not like, did not want to be associated with. As yet we do not know the reasons for Rebecca's moods, or why she needed to become a split personality. All we do know is that for Vebekka to be able to exist, to live normally, she had to lock Rebecca away. There will be a reason, one that will come out, but it will take time. I will begin taking her back to her childhood, perhaps something occurred with her parents that instigated this dual personality.'

The Baron drained his cup and replaced it on the tray. 'You mean she was mistreated?'

'Quite possibly. Often the safety barrier created is due to sexual abuse. We shall find it out – but as you can see it is slow, a gradual stage by stage process to ascertain the truth.'

Helen was excited. 'If Rebecca began to resurface when she was pregnant, it ties in with what Louis has discussed, that her breakdowns began when she was three to four months pregnant.'

Franks nodded. 'We shall see.'

Helen looked at the Baron, then told Franks about the meeting with Vebekka's mother's sister, and that she was sure Vebekka was adopted.

Franks said, 'You know you must keep me informed, I have asked you to report back any information you gain, as everything could be of value. Have you received the newspapers, the ones I asked for?'

'Not yet,' said the Baron.

'Please try to contact whoever you have working for you in New York to send you copies. I would now like to be left alone for a while. If you would care to take some lunch and return, you may go straight into the viewing room.'

Franks walked out, and went first to sit with his sons, who worked with him and were recording and filming the session. They discussed what they had seen and heard to date, then Franks went to lie down in his office. But he did not sleep, just allowed the interaction between himself and Vebekka to replay slowly in his mind. He was sure he would discover severe child abuse, sure that it would have taken place over a period of years. What amazed him was that none of the many therapists and doctors who had already seen Vebekka had been able to uncover such a simple, basic and very common trauma. He hoped there were more layers to be uncovered, something deeper, because in truth he was somewhat disappointed.

Vebekka slept deeply, totally relaxed. Maja checked her pulse, and drew the blanket closer around the still figure. She emptied the ashtrays from the viewing room, and then went to have a quick lunch herself, peeking into Franks's office to tell him she was leaving. He was fast asleep on his own couch.

Grimaldi slept like a dead man. Ruda had opened the trailer windows, thrown out the empty bottles, and he had not stirred. She prepared to get ready for the afternoon's rehearsal. That evening would be the big dress rehearsal for the opening of the show, full costumes, lights and ringmaster. And she still needed as much time as possible to get the cats working with the new plinths. She hung up her costume, got the ironing board out ready to press the jacket. She opened the blinds and looked skywards. The sun was still trying to break through, but more rainclouds had gathered. She crossed her fingers, hoping that the storm which had been forecast would not happen, and then she left to feed the cats.

Grimaldi heard the door close, as if from some great distance away. He slowly opened his eyes, and moaned as the light blinded him. He lifted his head and fell back with a louder moan. His body ached, his head throbbed, if he shut his mouth his teeth came together like hammer blows. He let his jaw hang loose; his tongue dry and rough. One hand gripped the edge of the bunk seat and slowly, inch by inch, he drew himself into a sitting position. The room spun round and round, and his heart pounded in his chest. He needed another drink. He looked around bleary-eyed, but could not see a bottle within reach.

He got to his knees, moaning all the while, and then pushed himself upright. He fumbled in a cupboard for a bottle, knocking over glasses, sauces, tins of food. He began to retch uncontrollably and staggered into the shower. Turning on the cold water he slumped again on to his knees and let the icy water drench him, the sharp jets bouncing on to his tongue.

Grimaldi peeled off his soaking shirt and trousers. His head was so bad that tiny white sparks were shooting, dancing around his eyes. He moaned and swore but eased his pants off and propped himself up under the shower, turning on the hot water. He began to feel the life coming back into his limbs, his chest, but the headache was as if unseen hands were pressing his ears together. He could not remember how he had got into such a state and did not begin to piece it together until he sat hunched up in a towel sheet with a mug of black coffee and began to recall the previous night. He hung his head and half sobbed, but the action made his head scream, so he gulped more coffee, and more coffee and a handful of aspirin. The pills stuck in his gut and he burped loudly. Weaving unsteadily to the washbasin, he looked at himself. His eyes were bloodshot, his face unshaven with a yellowish pallor. 'Dear God, why do I do this to myself? Why?'

He began to shave. Jagged memories of the past evening made him feel disgusted ... poor little Tina, he had to see her, had to talk to her ... and then he saw Ruda's face smiling at him, he saw little Tina huddled half naked against the wall, and he bowed his head with shame. He remembered now he had left her in that club, the Slaughterhouse; no club could have been better named, he had led her like a lamb to the slaughter. He finished shaving and got himself dressed. The effort exhausted him. He sat morosely, trying to find the strength to get himself out of the trailer and across to Tina's. He put on a pair of dark glasses and, still unsteady, crossed the trailer park, knocked on Tina's door and waited. He knocked again, and a voice inside yelled for whoever it was to wait. Tina's girlfriend opened up, she was wearing jodhpurs and pulling on a sweater over a rather grubby bra. She looked at Grimaldi and tugged her sweater down.

'What do you want?'

'Tina in?'

'You must be joking.'

'Where is she?'

The girl went back into the trailer and came out

again carrying a rain cape. She slung it around her shoulders, and he stood there like a dumb animal. The girl looked at him with disgust. 'She's gone, packed her bags and gone, you bastard!'

He tried to reach out for her arm, to stop her moving off. 'I don't understand, what do you mean she's gone?'

'Ask your wife, shit-head, ask your bloody wife!'

'Gone where?'

'Home. She's gone back to the States.'

'Did she leave a letter?'

'What you want? A forwarding address? Dickhead! She's gone – left, understand? You'll never see her again.'

His mind reeled, and he leaned against the side of the old trailer. The girl sauntered off, calling out to two lads leading a couple of horses through to the ring.

Grimaldi walked a few paces and then stopped, turned back to the trailer, sure for a moment the girl was lying.

'Tina? *Tina!*'

He kicked at the set of steps in a fury. He felt impotent, angry, unable to believe she would walk away, leave him without a word. He turned towards the big tent and began to weave his way towards it, swearing loudly, striking out at the sides of trailers as he passed.

Mike ran into the meat truck, shouted for Ruda, and was told she was feeding, was in the cages. Mike took off, calling out for Ruda, dodging this way and that past the animals as they were led into the ring.

She came out of Sasha's cage, locked and bolted the

door, and wheeled the feed trolley on to the next cage. Mike was shouting for her and she turned to look in his direction. She entered the next cage and put down the food, talking softly to the tigers as they came towards her. She rubbed their heads, tossing chunks of meat to them. Mike continued to call, and she let herself out and bolted the cage again, wheeling the trolley to the next cage. 'I'm here, Mike.'

He ran towards her, his face flushed. 'It's the guv'nor, he's screaming and yelling over at the main ring, you'd better get him out. The big boss is walking around, and there's a party of schoolkids just arrived.'

Ruda muttered to herself, 'I have to finish the feed.'

'He looks kind of crazy, Ruda, breaking up chairs, no one can get near him.'

Ruda picked up Mamon's big bowl and unbolted his cage. She stepped inside. 'Be right with you ... Ma'angel ... come on, dinner time, come on, baby.'

Mike leaned against the bars. 'He's thrown a punch at Willy Noakes, kicked a hole in his trailer.'

Ruda's attention wavered from Mamon to Mike, and the big cat snarled, swiping a paw at her, as if demanding her entire attention. 'Get back ... *no* ... don't you dare! Here – eat.' She tossed another hunk of meat. Mamon caught it in his jaw and lowered his head to rip it apart.

'*Rudaaa* ... *Ruda!*' Grimaldi bellowed for her and Mike turned, startled. He was heading towards them, carrying a pitchfork, dragging it along the cage bars. '*Ruda!*'

Ruda moved further into the cage, still facing Mamon, but tossing out more meat. She rested her back on the bars, turning to her right. She could see Grimaldi staggering along with the huge pitchfork. 'Mike, get him away from the cages!'

Mike, terrified of the big man, stuttered out to him to keep back.

'You want to make me?' Grimaldi shoved the boy aside, and came to Mamon's cage. 'She's gone, she's left me, she's gone!'

Ruda threw another chunk of meat, but Mamon lowered on to his haunches, no longer interested in eating. He began a low rumbling growl; Ruda was trapped in the small cage, the exit door behind Mamon. 'Good boy, back . . . back off . . . *get back*!'

Grimaldi banged the bar with the pitchfork. 'What did you do to her, *you bitch! What have you done?*'

Mamon was up at the bars, snarling, trying to slice through with his paws, snarling and snapping at Grimaldi. Ruda dodged around him and out of the trapdoor. She slapped it shut, bolted it and ran to the front of the cage. 'Get away from the cages – *get away from the cages!*'

Grimaldi turned all his pent-up anger on the big lion snarling and snapping at him. He pushed the pitchfork through the bars and caught Mamon on the rump: the cat went crazy, lunging and screaming with rage at the bars.

Ruda tussled with her husband, trying to get the pitchfork out of his hands. They fought like two men, the big fork between them, pushing and shoving each other. 'Let it go – *Luis, let it go!*'

'She's gone, she's left me, you did it! You did this to me!'

Ruda brought her knee up, slammed it into his groin. He gasped with pain, let go his hold on the fork and doubled up in agony. She dragged the fork clear and then turned it, the sharp iron prongs at Grimaldi's chest. 'Get back – *get out of here!*'

He tried to grab hold of one of the sharpened prongs, gripping it with his bare hand, and Ruda yanked it free – the prong sliced into his palm. He stumbled back, blood streaming from his cut hand.

Ruda tossed the fork to Mike and pushed Grimaldi with her hands. 'Get out – go on, go back to the trailer – *back, get back.*'

He stared at her, but took two steps back. 'I'm not one of your lions, one of your cats. *You pushed too far this time, you pushed too far!*' Grimaldi turned on his heels and stumbled away.

Ruda turned on Mike. 'What the fuck you gaping at? Get that fork back to the truck and bring the feed trays – go on!'

Not until she had fed every cat personally did she take off to her trailer, but half-way there she was stopped by the administrator. Mr Kelm asked that she come over to the offices immediately. The chairman wished to speak to her. Ruda followed, the sweat still dripping off her.

The big man was standing, his coat draped over his shoulders, his silver-topped cane propped against a large oval table. Ruda walked in and he snatched the cane. Brought it down with a crash on the highly polished table.

'*We pride ourselves – understand me, Mrs Grimaldi – we pride ourselves* . . . that everyone working here is the best, the best in the world! We have millions riding on this show, millions in advertising – we have school parties coming through, I want every child to go home and say they want to come to the show, that's parents, sisters, brothers. And today those schoolchildren witnessed a brawl – *a brawl*! involving one of my top acts. Now, if you and your husband have domestic problems, sort them out in private – *not* in a disgusting public display. You may be a top act, Mrs Grimaldi, but I will not have the name of my company – this circus – damaged, even if it means ending your and your husband's contract. Do I make myself clear?'

Ruda nodded, furious at being spoken to like a child. She turned as if to leave.

'Every act is replaceable, Mrs Grimaldi – remember that!'

She faced him. 'Not every act. You show me one cat trainer, one act on a par with mine—'

'Yours?'

'Yes, mine. My husband no longer works in the ring.'

'I see. If your husband has a problem – get rid of it! Do I make myself clear?'

She nodded, and stood glaring at him. He dismissed her with a wave of his hand. She turned and walked out, carefully closing the door behind her.

Schmidt turned to Kelm. 'That woman is trouble – any further problems and they both leave. We can hire the lion act from Moscow Circus. Just keep your eyes on the pair of them and feed it back to me!'

Ruda tore back to the trailer in a rage, only to find Grimaldi, his hand wrapped in a towel, clumsily loading one of his rifles. As soon as she saw what he was doing, she slammed the door shut and locked it. 'Put that away, Luis, put it away!'

He turned, sneering, cocked the gun and released the safety catch. He then pressed the barrel to his neck. 'I was going to shoot that beast, that crazy fucking animal. Then I decided I should kill you. Now I think I'll blow my own head off, because that's what you want, isn't it? *Isn't it?*'

She sat on the bunk, forcing herself to remain calm. 'If that's what you think, then do it – go on, shoot.'

He wavered, but did not remove the gun.

'Why do you think I want you dead?' she snapped.

'Give me one good reason you don't.'

She shrugged. 'That might be tough, but if pressed I'd have to admit that maybe I need you.'

He lowered the gun. 'You haven't needed me for ten years.'

She watched the gun lower with relief – she couldn't take a scene, not after that lecture. 'I don't need you for the act, that's true . . . but maybe I need you.'

He slumped down, the gun loose in his hand. 'Bullshit, you don't need anyone, you never have – unless you want something, *then* you pretend to need.'

Ruda stared at him. 'Why don't you give me that gun and stop playing around? Come on, give it to me.'

He cocked his head to one side, asked why she had done it.

'Why did I do what?'

'Make Tina run away.'

She laughed, shaking her head. 'I made her? *I* made her? You don't think maybe you had something to do with it?'

'I loved her, I loved her . . .'

'You left her without money, without anything. Left her in the middle of the shittiest place in Berlin, and now you tell me *you loved her?* The only thing you love is booze. She came here crying her heart out and all I did was comfort her.'

'Comfort? *You filthy whore!*' He lurched to his feet and came closer. 'I saw you together – *I saw what you were doing to my little girl.*'

'She wasn't your little girl, and don't think for two seconds that baby was yours – she told me it wasn't. She came here asking for money, threatened to tell that fat slob Schmidt about you, about you screwing all the young kids, and you know what he just told me? He told me that if you play around with any more of the teenagers then you and I will be out, contract or no contract.'

'I don't believe you.'

'Ask him, go and ask him. Kelm was there, he heard, I just got a lecture from the fat-assed bastard. Tina was a little tramp. I am telling you the truth, the baby was not yours – she admitted it to me.'

Grimaldi leaned back, closing his eyes. 'I don't believe it.'

Ruda moved quickly, grabbed the gun from him, and put the safety catch on. He made no effort to stop her. He held his face in his hands, saying over and over that she was lying to him. Then he looked up. 'I could have had a life with her, I could have started again.'

'Doing what? Changing someone else's brat's nappies?'

'I could have been happy with her.'

Ruda sighed. 'And what was going to keep you? You know I would never have parted with the act. I tell you something, you would have had to shoot me to get them, it was just a fantasy on your part.'

He got up and poured a glass of water for himself. 'I talked to Lazars, spent hours talking to him. We argued and yelled a lot, but he's changed, too, he's changed.'

'I don't follow. Can I have a drink?'

He handed her a glass of water, and then stared at the posters. 'I tell you, the circus, as we know it, it won't last, it can't last. You remember the Russian, Ivan? Spent fifteen years of his life training his tigers, been in the circus business since he was six years old, but he couldn't afford to keep them in the out-of-season periods. He shot the poor bastards, shot all twenty-four of them so nobody else could have them ... said they were no use to anyone and he wouldn't let a zoo have them, didn't think it was fair ... he told Lazars he shot them because he loved them. Now what crazy mind is that?'

Suddenly he laughed his old rumble laugh, leaning back, his eyes closed. 'Maybe I should have shot myself – can't be put out to grass, can't get any other work.'

Ruda's heart was hammering. She had never heard him talk this way, ever. She sat next to him, close to him. 'Don't ... don't talk like this.'

'It's the truth, maybe I've known it for a while now. I see them cramped in their cages. I keep on telling myself that it was different when I was working the rings, that it was better, but I know it wasn't, if anything it was worse. You, we, are living on borrowed time, because it will come, one day soon, when all wild animals will be barred from being used as cheap entertainment.'

'No, no, I don't believe it. I love them, I care for them, I love every single one of them.'

Grimaldi cocked his head to one side, gave a slow sad

smile. 'No, you don't. You love the feel of dominance, you like the danger, the adrenaline, but you don't love them.'

'I do, you know I do.'

'Caged, locked up twenty-four hours a day, you call that love?'

He stretched out his long legs, resting his elbows behind his head. 'You know this little Boris, the little chimp Lazars had? Well, he got it from a troupe of Italians, spent his savings on her. Boris was too young to work in the ring, she was being trained, and Lazars sat in on one of the training sessions, kept on watching the Italian rubbing the chimp's head . . . he thought it was with affection. But the little fella got very upset. After the rehearsal Lazars checked her over. Boris's head was scratched, it was bleeding – this so-called trainer, his little finger, he'd got the nail sharpened to a point, like a fucking razor – he wasn't patting his animals and encouraging them out of kindness, he was sticking his nail into their heads . . .'

Ruda stared at the toes of her boots. 'Lazars was always a second stringer, a soft touch, you shouldn't listen to his bullshit.'

'I haven't before. I just think what he's saying may be true, that acts like ours have a short time to go.'

Ruda sprang to her feet. 'I won't listen to any more . . . I've got to go and get ready to rehearse.'

'Yeah, make them jump through hoops of fire – great, they love it. Get their manes singed, they fucking love it . . .'

Ruda paused at the door. 'Will you give me a hand in the ring? They're still nervous about the plinths.'

He looked up at her. 'You don't need me, Ruda.'

'What are you going to do?'

He turned away, unable to face her. There was such a helplessness in the big man, it touched her, unexpectedly. She hesitated, then went and slipped her arms around him. 'You're hung over, go and lie down. I'll come back later and cook up a big dinner, yes? Luis?'

He patted her head. 'Worried I'll run off, go after Tina?' She wriggled away from him, but he pulled her close. 'You are, aren't you? Is it me you want?'

She tried to get away from him, but he wouldn't let her go. 'Is it me?'

She eased away from him, her face flushed red. 'I guess I'd miss you, I've got used to you being around.'

He watched her reach for the door, unlock it. He gave a hopeless smile, he knew she didn't really want him – she just didn't want anyone else to have him. The door closed behind her and he sat down, once again staring at the posters and photographs over the wall.

The forensic laboratory had made a plaster cast of the mud and heel print taken from the Grimaldi boots. They were good impressions, very clear, but the print off the carpet was not. Even so, they were reasonably sure the heel print had been made by the same boot. Torsen asked whether it could be used as a piece of evidence, would it stand up in court? He was told not: the print taken from the victim's hotel room had only a section of the heel.

'But you think it was from the same boot?'

'Yes, I do, but that is just my personal opinion.'

Torsen sighed. It had been a long, fruitless day of waiting for results. The second disappointing non-evidence was that the sawdust taken from the victim's hotel room matched with fifteen samples taken from the circus, all from different cages. The sawdust was also discovered to be similar to samples brought in from the Berlin Zoo. The main sawdust factories had sent supplies to both the zoo and the circus.

Torsen's next enquiry was at the bus station. The night-duty staff had still to be questioned regarding bus passengers the night Kellerman was killed. The three conductors could remember no man fitting the inspector's description; two could recall no passengers alighting from a bus on the night in question at or near the Grand Hotel; the third conductor could only recall a female passenger who had picked up the bus from the depot and alighted at the stop close to the Grand Hotel; but he could recall little about her except long hair, dark. He remembered that it had been a particularly unpleasant journey, mostly filled with Polish women and children who had been greatly disturbed by a group of young punks hurling bricks at the bus, shouting Nazi slogans. The conductor spent considerable time berating the *Polizei*, saying they should give the buses, their drivers and passengers better security.

Torsen returned to the station, heated up a bowl of soup in the microwave and ran down his lists on the Kellerman investigation. He had a motive – the man was disliked by everyone he seemed to have been in contact with, possibly owed money to whoever killed him. But from there on it went downhill; not one person had seen a man fitting the description of the possible killer.

Torsen sipped his soup . . . it was blindingly hot and he burned his lip. He almost knocked it over when his desk phone jangled. It was the nurse, Freda, she was coming off duty at five and wondered if she could see him, or if he could come to the hospital. His father had written a note which he had made Freda promise to deliver. Torsen suspected it his father's ploy to get him to Freda. He stuttered that he would try to pass by the hospital, asked again about his father's health and Freda laughed, said he was making snowflakes again. He did not find it amusing – the vision of his father plucking the bits of tissue, licking them, sticking them on the end of his nose and blowing them off again. He spoke rather curtly, repeated that he would call by when he had an opportunity, but that he was very busy investigating a murder.

'I know, the note has something to do with it. Would you like me to read it to you? It would save you a journey.'

Torsen fumbled for his notebook.

'Are you ready? Shall I read it?' Freda asked.

'Yes, yes, please go ahead.'

Freda coughed, and then said: '"One" – it's very scrawled – "no coincidence". Would that mean anything to you?'

Torsen muttered that it did, and asked her to continue.

'"Two" – and this is very hard to decipher, it looks like "magic man", or "magician" – does that make sense?'

'Yes, yes, it does. Please continue.'

'It's a name, I think . . . Dieter? Yes?'

'Yes, yes, that was my uncle, is that all?'

Freda said she was trying to puzzle out the next few words. 'Ah, I think it says, "Rudi" . . . "R – U – D – I". Yes, it's Rudi and then there's a J. I think the name is Polish, Jeczawitz. Yes, I am sure it's Rudi Jeczawitz. Would you like me to spell it for you?'

Torsen jotted down the name, thanked Freda, and

apologized if he had sounded brusque. She laughed and said no matter. She replaced the phone before he plucked up courage to ask to see her. He let the receiver fall back slowly. He swivelled around in his desk chair to look at the photograph of his father, murmured 'Thank you!' and finished his soup. He had to think carefully how to set about tracking down the old records of Jeczawitz. He would have to go cap in hand to the West Berlin *Polizei* with a story to cover his enquiry.

Torsen and Rieckert crossed the old border and passed through Kreuzberg, drew up outside a new building housing a section of the West Berlin *Polizei*. The building was a hive of activity, the reception area alone busier than the entire station the pair had just left. They were directed towards the records bureau through a long corridor. Outside was a counter at which a stern-faced woman heard Torsen's request for the record of a Rudi Jeczawitz, checked over his identification and handed him a formal records request sheet to fill in.

Torsen hesitated, as if uncertain whether it was necessary. 'The man is deceased, perhaps twenty to twenty-five years ago.'

He was told he must fill in the form, so he pored over the list of questions and alongside the request for case details he wrote 'last will and testament of relative query'.

They did not have to wait long as the station was fully computerized and the grey-haired, dog-faced woman soon returned with three sheets of paper clipped together. They had to sign the release request to say they had received the documents and Torsen asked if they wanted them returned.

'They are just copies, computer printouts. You can keep them.'

They hurried back to their patrol car, Torsen skimming the pages as they walked. He got in, and continued to read. He then sat bolt upright, turning back one page, returning to the next.

Rieckert waited patiently, having no idea why they had come to the station in the first place. 'Where next?'

Torsen lowered the paper. 'Better head back to the station. I have to speak to the *Leitender Direktor*.'

'He's still on holiday.'

'I have to speak to him. Just drive.'

Rieckert drove to their station, flicking looks at Torsen who read, lowered the pages and muttered to himself. His cheeks had two bright pink spots. The car had hardly drawn to a halt before he was out and running up the steps.

The records gave details of the dead man. The corpse had been found in a derelict building used by vagrants for many years and considered 'unsafe'. His body had been squashed inside a small kitchen cabinet, not, as Torsen had thought, under floorboards. The body, because of the freezing temperatures, had barely decomposed – yet Torsen was sure his father had described the body to him as exceptionally badly decomposed. It was almost intact, apart from deep lacerations to the left wrist and forearm. The victim was naked, apart from the cloak he was wrapped in. The skin had been hacked off with a crude knife with a serrated edge, but no weapon had been found. They had been unable to identify the body for a considerable time until a newspaper article requesting information on the deceased gave a clear description of the strange cloak wrapped around him. A club owner had come forward, identified the dead man as 75-year-old Rudi Jeczawitz, a one-time magician who had performed in his clubs. The man was an alcoholic, known to deal in forged documents. He had also been a procurer of very young girls, and shortly after the war had run a string of prostitutes. His drinking had made him fall on hard times, and at the end he had been working for little more than free drinks, using his wife as part of the act. His wife, a known prostitute, had disappeared; she had not been seen after the murder. It was supposed that she, too, may possibly have been murdered. No one was ever charged with the murder of Rudi Jeczawitz, his case remained on file. A few further details were listed: informants had said that he had been held in the death camp at Birkenau. He had survived the camp by entertaining the camp guards with his magic act.

Torsen felt his heart hammering inside his chest as he kept staring at the name, reading and rereading the name of Jeczawitz's wife: Ruda. Coincidence number one. Coincidence number two: Rudi, like Tommy Kellerman, had been involved with forged documents. And then there was a third coincidence: all three were survivors of concentration camps. He paused, the fourth coincidence: both men had been tattooed, and both had had their tattoo slashed from their arm.

Torsen scribbled down a list. He had to find out if they were legally married, find out the maiden name of Ruda Jeczawitz, see if there was still anyone alive who knew the old magician and could describe him. But most important was that he had to find out whether Ruda Kellerman was in fact the woman involved with Jeczawitz ... Torsen was sweating, his lists growing longer. Next he scribbled 'boots'; he had supposed the boots had belonged to a man because of their size, had even asked Mrs Grimaldi if they were her husband's boots. But what if they were her boots? Torsen let out a small whoop. He thumbed through his book, until he found the page he had written that morning. A conductor was sure no male passenger had alighted from his bus the night of Kellerman's murder, only a woman, described as . . . he stared at his scrawl, for a moment unable to read it, then snapped the book closed. He knew he would have to go back: all he had written was female, dark-haired. He grabbed his coat, shouted for Rieckert, his voice echoing in the empty building.

He stormed through the vacated offices and then banged into the switchboard operator's small booth. 'Where in God's name is everybody?'

She looked up at him in astonishment. 'Tea break! They have gone across to the café for their tea break. It is four o'clock, sir.'

CHAPTER 12

'I AM GOING to take you back now, Vebekka. You can see a calendar, the years in red print, we go back, '91, '90 . . . can you see the red date, Vebekka?'

'Yes, I can see it.'

'Go back, '89, ten years before, go through the dates . . . what year do you have on the calendar?'

Vebekka sighed. '1979 . . . it is 1979.'

Franks looked towards the two-way mirror, and then turned back to Vebekka.

The Baron tapped Helen's hand. 'That was the year of the newspapers . . .'

Franks continued. 'Go to the morning in New York when you were reading the newspaper, sitting having breakfast with your husband. Can you remember that morning?'

She sighed, gave a low moan, and then nodded. 'I am reading the real estate pages . . . Louis is reading the main section. I talk to him, but he pays no attention. I tell him . . . an apartment is for sale, but he doesn't listen to me.'

'Go on.'

She sighed and her brow furrowed as if she was trying to recall something.

'Go on, Vebekka, you see something in the paper?'

She breathed in quickly, gasping. 'Yes ... yes ... Angel, *Angel, Angel.*'

She twisted and turned, shaking. 'They have found him.'

'Who, Vebekka? Whom have they found?'

She ran her hands through her hair. 'It's in the paper, it's in the papers, I have to find all the papers, I have to know if it's true. Angel, the Dark Angel of Death will find me, he put the message in the paper to find me.'

'It's all right ... it's all right, no need to be alarmed. Who is the angel? Is it the angel who makes you so frightened?'

She thrashed the sofa with her hands, fists banging at the upholstery. 'They will know what I have done. *He knows what I have done! ... Oh! God help me!'*

Franks lifted his voice, and told her to go to the next morning, to tell him what happened the next morning. She calmed, said that the next day she remained very quiet, said nothing to anyone about what she had seen. But she had a nightmare, she had thought the Angel had come into her bedroom and was going to make her tell, but it was just a shadow, it was just the curtains, he wasn't there.

Franks scribbled in his notebook that they must trace the newspaper. He was sure he was dealing with a woman traumatized by an event in her childhood, but when he began to discuss her childhood she became very calm again, seemed relieved. And when he asked if she was Vebekka or Rebecca she giggled, told him not to be stupid, she was Rebecca.

She began to talk quite freely to Franks as Rebecca. She described her home in Philadelphia, discussed her parents. She said they were kind but never very affectionate. She said that they were very close to each other, that she had often felt like an intruder.

'Did this upset you?'

'Not really, they always gave me what I asked for, they just seemed more interested in each other. My mother was often unhappy, she used to say she missed her home, her family, but they would never speak to her, they sent back all her letters unopened. She was often crying, and often ill – she used to get bronchial troubles, that was why they moved from Canada, it was very cold, and Mama was always ill.'

Franks asked if she loved her parents. She hesitated, and then shrugged with her hands. 'They loved each other, and they fed and clothed me.'

'So you never felt a great affection for them?'

'No . . . just that they kept me safe, they watched out for me, no one could hurt me while I was with them, they told me that.'

'Who wanted to hurt you?'

She wafted her hand. 'I don't know.'

Franks asked her to recall her first memory of her mother.

She pursed her lips and said, 'She gave me a blue dress, with a white pinafore and a teddy bear.'

'How old were you then?'

She seemed to be trying to remember her age, but in the end she shrugged her shoulders and said she was not sure. He asked if she was afraid of her parents, and she said very promptly that she was not. 'They were afraid of me! Always afraid, afraid . . .'

'Had they reason to be afraid of you?'

'Yes, I was very naughty, had terrible tantrums.'

'What did they do when you had these tantrums?'

'Oh, Mama would talk to me, get me to lie down, talk to me, you know, so I would calm down.'

'Did they try to stop you leaving home?'

She laughed. 'Oh, no, they were pleased, I think they were pleased, when I left.'

'Did you miss them when you left home?'

'Yes . . . yes, sometimes, but Mama helped me often, told me how to handle Rebecca.'

'What did she tell you to do?'

'Oh, put her in a cupboard, throw away the key, forget her.'

'So it was not your idea to change your name?'

'Yes, it was, it was all my idea. I never told Mama what I had done, and I never told Papa. I just did what Mama said, put her away.'

'Is the other box inside you?'

She started to twist her hands, plucking at the blanket. 'Yes, yes, that is always there.'

'Did your mama put somebody in the box?'

'*It's not a box!*'

Franks was growing tired; he rubbed his head, checked his watch. 'What is it, then?'

She remained silent, her face taut as she refused to answer.

'Why don't you want to tell me about it?'

She seemed to be in terrible pain, her face distorted. She opened her mouth as if to scream, but no sound came out.

Franks stood close by the couch. 'It's all right, ssh, don't get upset, I won't ask you about it any more. It's all over . . . unless you want to tell me. Do you want to tell me?'

She cried, her mouth wide open like a child's, her face twisted, and the blanket was wrung into a coil between her hands. He waited, and in the viewing room the Baron rose to his feet. He hated the way his wife seemed to be in such pain; he pressed his hands to the glass. 'Stop him, tell him to stop this!'

She was clawing at her arms, trying to get up; Franks gently held on to her shoulders. The scream made him step back; it was a scream rising in such pitch, a terrible howling, her body shook in spasms. Franks asked over and over again what was happening to her, but the torture continued, her body thrashed around, she was out of control.

'Vebekka, listen to me, the longing time, come back into the longing . . . can you hear me? Longing . . . come on, come on, awake, everything is all right, you've just been sleeping, you'll wake up refreshed, relaxed.' But her body was stiff, he was not able to wake her. He began again to give her the key word between them, but whatever it was held her, and she was fighting it, fighting to get it out of her.

The Baron turned helplessly to Helen. 'It's as if she were possessed. Can't he stop it? Tell him to stop!'

Vebekka gasped, panting, that she was coming up the stairs, rounding the spiral staircase, but she could not find the door . . . Franks picked up fast, said the door was in front of her, she could open it. She began to relax, her breathing quieted down, and she sighed. He moved back as she sighed again and her eyelids fluttered.

Awake, she stretched her arms above her head and yawned, like a cat. She stretched her whole body, and then curled up. 'I am so thirsty . . .'

Franks rang for Maja and poured her a glass of water.

325

She drank thirstily and held out the glass for more. He refilled it and she drained it again. Maja came in, smiled at Vebekka and asked how she was feeling. Vebekka laughed. 'Good, I feel very relaxed and refreshed.'

Franks was exhausted, Helen and the Baron drained. They left Maja with Vebekka while they conferred in the small office.

'She has been through deep hypnosis before – when, I don't know, but she knows how to hypnotize herself, bring herself through the waking cycles. I had no control over her for some considerable time. I have never witnessed anything like it, it is quite extraordinary. But we must try to ascertain when this occurred because it can be very dangerous. You saw for yourself her own internal trouble. Whatever she has locked away inside she refuses to unleash. God only knows what she was involved in, or subjected to – the key to her lies in that box, chest, the thing that is so hidden inside her, with chains, locks, God knows what else . . . but it is inside her. It is imperative that we find out what hypnosis she has been subjected to on previous occasions. Somebody at some time treated her, made her lock away horrors, and what you have witnessed, Baron, what we have both seen here today, is the danger of enforcing this. Vebekka, Rebecca, has pressed down a trauma inside her, hidden it deep inside her mind, and it rears up. When this occurs, it sends her to the edge of a breakdown. If we find out what it is, your wife may, with time and medical attention, be able to face and deal with the trauma. But also we must face the fact that we are dealing with the unknown. Others may argue that she has only survived by locking this trauma away. It will have to be your decision whether we continue or not.

I would only add that I sincerely hope you will agree to continuing the sessions.'

The Baron stared, nonplussed. He could not tell whether Franks believed he could help his wife, or whether he was saying that to continue would cause irrevocable mental damage. He turned helplessly to Helen, who looked away.

'It must be your decision.'

'But what about Vebekka, doesn't she have a say in this matter?'

Franks stared at his shoes, his hands stuffed in his pockets. 'Your wife will have no memory of what occurred in that room, none whatsoever. As her husband, it must be your decision.'

'But what happens if she goes crazy? As you said, if you open up this trauma, and she cannot face it, then what?'

Franks still refused to look up. 'Then she will continue as she has done, sane periods, insane periods, spasmodic logic, violent moods. Who knows how this can continue? All we know is that she has, in your own words, grown steadily worse over the years, has attacked your daughter, you, your sons.'

The Baron pinched his nose, looked again at Helen, wanting, needing confirmation – anything to assist his decision, but she turned away.

'What time would you like to see her tomorrow?'

Franks shook his hand. 'Good, you have made the right decision. Let's say nine, to have an early start.'

Vebekka felt better than she had for a long time, even though she had taken no drugs for two, almost three

327

days. She wanted to dine out, go to some of the clubs, and Louis conceded. But first they should return to their hotel in case there were any messages. Perhaps she should call Sasha. Then, when they had dined, they could decide what they wanted to do. He was exhausted, had no desire to go clubbing. Nor had Helen, but she giggled. Their patient was filled with energy, having slept most of the day. She suggested to Vebekka that maybe she should rest, take care of herself, and she got a pinched cheek. 'Don't be such a fuddy-duddy, Helen. If my darling husband is too tired, then you and I will go on a trip. Some of the clubs here are the most famous in the world.'

There were letters and two packages for the Baron at the hotel desk. Helen went up in the lift with Vebekka, but returned to her own suite for a shower. Louis read through the further details pertaining to his wife's background: names of school friends who could be contacted, school teachers.

He tapped on the door of Helen's suite and entered with the parcels. She read over the letters and then asked if the newspapers had arrived. The Baron nodded, they would have to check through them. Helen had already decided that she would see what she could find out about Rosa Goldberg, née Muller. He asked if they should dine in the suite or in the restaurant, and Helen said she would prefer the restaurant. He booked a table for eight-thirty and returned to his own room to shower and change. He heard Vebekka on the telephone in her suite talking to Sasha, and called out to send his love, said they would be dining at eight-thirty.

Shortly before eight Louis went to see if Vebekka was ready to dine, but she was not in her room. She had changed clothes; those she had been wearing were left on the bed. He called down to reception to see if she had gone ahead of them into the restaurant, but she was not there. Helen came in and they searched the suite, and spoke to Hylda, who said she had dressed the Baroness and presumed she had gone down to the restaurant.

The manager signalled to the Baron as soon as he saw them walk out of the lift. He gestured to the main foyer. 'The Baroness has just left. I am so sorry if I misled you, but I did not know she had ordered a car.'

The Baron went pale. 'Did she say where she was going?'

'No, Baron, I think she took a taxi from the rank outside. Would you like me to enquire?'

The Baron shook his head, gripped Helen by the elbow and guided her through the circular door. He was furious, swearing under his breath. As they stepped on to the red carpet, he spoke curtly to the doorman and was told that the Baroness had just taken a taxi.

'To where? Do you know where?'

The doorman looked perplexed and hurried to the rank, signalled for the Baron to join him by a waiting taxi. The driver popped his head out. 'She asked to be driven round the clubs, I heard her asking. We can catch them, no problem.'

The Baron turned back to the hotel, and Helen hurried after him. 'Louis, what are you doing? Don't you want to go after her?'

'I have been going after her all my life. She can do what she wants. I am hungry, I want to eat.'

Helen hesitated; she could tell that despite his attempt to appear unconcerned, Louis was very distressed. He made a half-hearted approach to the dining room before he stopped. 'Perhaps I should wait in the suite, have something sent up. I'll wait half an hour and if she has not returned I'll contact the *Polizei*.'

They turned back to the reception, the Baron reaching out to call the lift, then his hand moved back to his forehead. 'Why? Dear God, why does she do this? I don't understand . . . I had hope, I hoped . . .'

Vebekka sat in the back of the taxi feeling like a naughty schoolgirl who had escaped from her teachers. She wore her dark glasses, her sable cape and a pale green cashmere top with matching trousers. She had also taken great care in applying her make-up: thick eyeshadow, a dark, obvious foundation, her lips outlined in a bright, unflattering crimson. Make-up from her special box, make-up she only used on special occasions. She lit a cigarette and as she dropped the lighter back into her bag, realized she had no money. She tapped the glass. 'I have no money. Can you give me some?'

He stopped the car, turned back to her. 'You want to go to the hotel? Yes? Get money? Yes?'

She shook her head. 'No, you pay for me, OK? I am borrowing from you.'

The driver turned and hit the wheel with his hand. 'You must have cash? *Cash only, understand?*'

Vebekka opened her bag, took out her solid gold lighter. 'Take this, gold . . . good gold.'

The driver looked at the lighter, back to Vebekka, then put the car in gear with a beaming smile. 'OK . . . where you want go?'

Vebekka looked from the window. 'Clubs, take me to clubs.'

CHAPTER 13

TORSEN'S EYES were becoming bloodshot reading the screens; he had been at the bureau for hours and still had not traced the marriage certificate of Jeczawitz. Many of the files were incomplete, and the further back he went, the worse they became. Listed time and time against names was 'no document available to establish birth certificate granted'.

Torsen looked up as the woman in charge of the records bureau gestured to her watch. She wished to leave. 'The building is empty, Inspector, and the watchman wishes to lock up the main gates before nine.'

He began to collect his belongings. She came to stand by his side. 'You still have four more files on the Js. Will you return tomorrow?' When Torsen said he would, she promised to have the files set out for him. 'Without knowing the year this man was married it is very difficult, especially in the fifties – so many refugees, so many homeless.'

They walked to the door, and she sighed as she turned off the overhead lights. 'Four million inhabitants, more, and you know how many were left after the war? Just two million, this city was devastated, everywhere corpses, burnt-out tanks. You are too young to remember, but the survivors were mostly children, old men and old women, making homes in streets buried by rubble, in the cellars, in the old bunkers.'

They walked to the main building exit doors. She went to a small closet and opened the door. 'There was something so frightening about the terrible emptiness in the city – even the survivors crept about, no one believed it was over, and behind the half-alive were vast cities of dead . . . I lost my father, my brothers, my family home – all my possessions . . .'

Torsen waited while she collected her coat and hat and rang through to the watchman to lock up. He took her arm, and they walked slowly across the courtyard.

'I began working here just after the war and I have worked here nearly all my life, recording the marriages, the births, and trying to trace the dead. I think that was the worst, trying to get the papers organized. You see, the building caught fire, there was nothing left. In those days the main priority was to find food, everything was so scarce, and without documents people could get no food coupons. So the black market trade flourished, forged documents, so much confusion. And still it continues, but now we have people arriving from all over the world trying to trace their relatives, coming back year after year to learn about a son, a daughter. It is impossible, but we do what we can.'

Torsen paused and took out his notebook. 'May I ask you a great favour? If you could, when you have a spare moment, see if there is anything recorded for Rudi Jeczawitz's wife? All I have is a Christian name, Ruda, I don't know her age.'

They walked on, she seemed glad of his company. 'Ruda? Is that Polish? Maybe Russian? We had many,

many refugees, they poured in daily, they were starved . . . many so young, and all they had was their body. Now we have them again, refugees from the borders – they come every day, no papers, no money. It is getting bad, begging on the street, gypsies – Romanian, Czech, Polish. Dear God, it seems it will never end!'

Torsen nodded. 'I have been told she was a prostitute. Perhaps they did not marry legally, I don't know . . .'

'Many did marry for papers. If they had none they would marry for a name, for an identity. You know, many children roaming the streets in those days knew only their Christian name, nothing more – and some only a number. It was a terrible sight to see these young children every-where, their shaved heads, their skeleton bodies, and now when I see these punks . . . this new fashion it stuns me, they do not remember. Maybe, maybe it is best they don't, because it haunts the living, I know that.'

Torsen continued walking. 'My father said that to me, he's in a clinic. He said there were many there finding dying hard, that they had memories, they clung to life afraid to die.'

She turned to him, a tight smile on her face. Her blue eyes searched his for a moment, and then she pointed to a bus stop. 'I leave you here, my friend, and I will do what I can, but no promises. I have enjoyed speaking with you.' They shook hands, and Torsen was apologetic, he did not know her name. 'Lena. Lena Klapps.'

Torsen waved to her as she stepped on to her bus, and then got on at his own bus stop, in the opposite direction. He felt worn out, and wondered if he had been wasting his time; the days were passing and he had made no arrest. He was behind in his daily *Polizei* work – all the paper-work he knew must be piled up in his trays. He closed his eyes. 'There is no coincidence in a murder enquiry.' And then, by an extraordinary coincidence, he looked out of the bus to see Ruda Kellerman stepping from a taxi. He craned his neck to see more clearly, sure it was her, but he could not see her face as she wore dark glasses, a fur draped around her shoulders. She was standing outside Mama Magda's – a notorious nightclub, a hang-out for gay, lesbian and mixed couples. He moved to the back of the bus to see more clearly, and watched her entering the dark paint-peeling doorway. He wondered what she was doing in such a place, then returned to his seat, his mind churning over the day's events, asking himself if there was some connection between Ruda Kellerman and the two murders? Suddenly he realized he was almost at his stop and rushed from his seat calling out to the conductor as he rang the bell. Hurrying along the aisle he came face to face with the night conductor he wished to question again. As he paid his fare, he asked if they could halt the bus for just a few moments.

For privacy they conferred on the pavement. Torsen asked for a better description of the woman who got off his bus near the Grand Hotel the night of Kellerman's murder. The conductor removed his cap, rubbed his head and tried to remember what he had first told the inspector while the disgruntled passengers glared from within the bus.

'She was foreign, dark-haired, definitely dark-haired . . . and wearing a dark coat – no, a mackintosh. It was raining, and she was tall, yes, tall . . . taller than me, say about five foot eight, maybe a fraction more.'

Torsen moved in close. 'That is very tall, are you sure she was that tall?'

The conductor backed off and sized up Torsen, asking

him how tall he was, and they then stood shoulder to shoulder, until the man was satisfied he had been correct . . .

Torsen let himself into his apartment, put on his electric fire. He checked his empty fridge and swore, slamming the door shut. He brewed a pot of tea, sat at his kitchen table, and began his laborious notes again. He had a suspect, one he underlined three times. Ruda Kellerman-Grimaldi – but where were the reasons?

(1) Motive: None.
(2) Gain: None.
(3) Alibi: Good.
(4) Did she have help?
(5) Could she have inflicted the hammer blows?

Torsen rubbed out number five, then wrote it down again. He just remembered her handshake, she was very strong, she was also very tall. Could she have been mistaken for a man leaving Kellerman's hotel?

(6) Check if Ruda Kellerman has a trilby.
(7) Check if Kellerman had a trilby.
(8) Stock up fridge – coffee and milk.

The more he thought of food the hungrier he felt, so in the end he took himself off to buy some rolls from the all-night delicatessen. He ate standing at the window at a small bar provided by the shop for their customers.

When he returned to his apartment it was after ten, and a note was pinned to his door. Freda, the nurse, had popped by to deliver the note from his father in case he needed it. She had also left her home phone number and address, and a neat list of duty times, days on/days off, evenings on/evenings off. He liked that, liked that she was methodical, made lists like himself. He decided he would call her in the morning and ask for a date.

That same evening, Ruda was ironing her jacket lapels, the iron hissing over the wet cloth. Luis woke up and sniffed. He loved the smell of freshly ironed clothes: they reminded him of his mother. He wrapped his dressing-gown around himself and wandered into the lounge. 'How did rehearsal go?' he asked.

'I thought Mamon was adjusting, but he still hates the new plinths. He's been playing up again, I really have to push him.'

Grimaldi looked into a large frying pan left on the stove. There was bacon, sausages and onion rings, all of it now cold in its grease. She turned off the iron. 'I did call you, but decided not to wake you. There's a baked potato in the oven. Do you want a beer?'

He forked out the food on to a plate and refused the beer, said he'd stick to water – for that night. He carried his plate to the table and sat down. She called out that he would have time to shower and change, the dress rehearsal was not until nine as some of the acts didn't have their time during the afternoon. She came in zipping up her tight white trousers. 'We're the last act before the inter-mission, and we open the second act. It's a good spot – well, the one before the intermission is. I'd like to close the show, but he won't let me have the time to reassemble the cages.'

She put on her jacket, checked it in the mirror, and then arranged her hair in a tight braid down the back. She oiled it away from her face, so it looked sleek, almost Spanish. She leaned against him as she put her boots on, stamping her feet into them. He looked sidelong at her, and gave her bottom a pat.

'Don't!' she snapped. 'Your fingers are all greasy.'

'You look good,' he said with his mouth full, and she did a small pirouette, then gathered up the short whip, her stick and, with a final glance at her reflection, went to the trailer door.

'Get dressed, Luis, I want you on display, sober and looking good. Everyone heard about that scene, so let's put up a good front. It's almost seven-thirty.'

He laughed. 'This crowd thrives on what the Grimaldis did, what they said, who hit who – tell them to go fuck themselves.'

She picked up her hat, twisted it, and placed it on her head. 'Over and out, big man! See you in the ring.'

Grimaldi shaved and dressed, and stood in exactly the same position she had, to give himself the once-over. He looked beat, even after a shave and a long sleep: his eyes bloodshot, his skin puffy. He checked the regrowth in his hairline. He needed a tint, the grey was showing through.

He tightened his big thick belt, aware that his belly hung over the top, and hitched the shirt up so it almost disguised the extra pounds. And as he stared at himself in the long mirror, he asked himself where it had all gone wrong. He couldn't blame it all on the mauling: it was falling apart – he was falling apart – a long time before that. Out of habit he looked at the wall of photographs, saw his papa, his brothers, remembered holding tightly to his dying father's hand. 'You keep it going, you marry, you have sons, don't let the Grimaldi name die. Have many sons! For your brothers, Luis, God rest their souls.'

He thought about little Tina. It had been a foolish dream, and yet he had been thrilled to think at last he would have a son, an heir. He had even wondered what it would feel like to hold his son. He never considered it could be a girl, it was a son he had always wanted. Yet he had married Ruda . . .

Luis opened a drawer and took out an old folder, small snapshots. He sifted through them, not even sure what he was searching for – memories maybe?

He inched open Ruda's wardrobe door and looked inside, wondering where she had stashed all his albums. He looked up: there was a row of cupboards on top of the wardrobe. He was tall enough to reach up and open one. It contained her show hats; he flipped open the second, it had an old winter coat, a plastic rain cape. He slapped the doors shut and tried the next. It was stuck firm, so he stepped up on the stool and pulled hard. He almost lost his balance as the albums tumbled out, paper clippings spilled everywhere, loose photographs. He swore as he bent to retrieve them.

He sat on her bed and began to flip through the books, chuckled and smiled as the memories flooded back. His had been such good times, he had had a wonderful childhood. She never talked of her past; she had said without any emotion that some things are best left buried. She would talk about her life with Kellerman, even the old magician up to a point, but then she would change the subject, as if her life before that was not worth mentioning, or, as he guessed, too painful to mention, because, if he pressed, she would roll up her cuff, thrust the scar in his face. 'I have this to remind me. I am reminded every time I stand naked, every time my head aches, that is enough. Why talk about it, why open up memories I have fought to forget?'

When she had been in one of her moods, when she had thrown one of her rages because money was short or his drinking out of hand, she would turn on him with a fury, screaming that whatever pain he was in, she had known worse. She would thrust her tattoo under his nose, use it like a weapon. 'This is my proof, what is yours, Luis? What right have you got to complain about anything?'

She had taken over. He slowly turned the pages, asking himself how he had allowed it to happen. The first time he had met her, he was a star act, he had money – he had success.

He lay back on her hard pillow, closed his eyes, seeing the old winter quarters he had booked in Florida, remembering how he had stood in front of the cages as the vet went from one animal to the next. He had been working in England, just before all the quarantine laws came into effect, and his act had gone down well. He had travelled to Manchester, to Brighton, and then to Wembley for the big Chipperfield contract. He was at his peak in the early sixties – what a time that had been – and then he had returned to America, on the invitation of Barnum and Bailey's scout. With the winter season coming on he had arrived in Venice, Florida, confident that he was a star: the great Luis Grimaldi was an international act.

Knowing the contract was forthcoming, he continued to spend freely, and even bought two more tigers. Then the bombshell: first to go down was his lead cat, a massive Siberian tiger trained by his father. The big animal began sweating, his eyes running, and his coat quickly began to look dull. The vets diagnosed a virulent, dangerous flu – perhaps one of the animals in England had been contagious.

The cat flu spread like a forest fire, they went down one by one; the act was disappearing before his eyes. He worked every hour God gave him, but no matter what care and attention he gave to his beloved animals, they were dying. No injections saved them, his only hope was to segregate the animals fast. Then he had a second nightmare, the surviving animals had been placed in spare cages with hay from a farm barn where they had used poison to exterminate rats and mice. The fittest of his cats now became dangerously ill, and Luis worked himself into a state of exhaustion, remaining in the contaminated areas all day. He watched his beasts sweating, coughing, their breathing rasping as they choked and grew listless, eyes and noses running, paws sweating, refusing their food. They died in his arms. A funeral pyre was built, and he stood by watching as the prize and the pride of his life burned in front of him. He felt as if it was his own life blazing.

Out of eighteen tigers only four were left, with one fully grown male lion and a small sickly panther. The cost of replacing the animals was astronomical and no insurance covered the epidemic.

Then, when he believed nothing else could go wrong, a hurricane swept through the state. His trailer and two more cats perished. He lost his home, his cages were wrecked, his props and plinths crushed.

Luis Grimaldi could not sign the contract, his most coveted prize; he had not the finance to buy new cats. He was finished. He moved into a run-down trailer donated by the circus folk residing at the winter quarters. His drinking began then, and for weeks his old retainers fed and cleaned the few remaining animals, without wages, understanding. Eventually they had to seek work elsewhere – they had wives and kids to support – and the only one left was Johnny Two Seats, so nicknamed because of his wide, fat ass. He cared for Grimaldi as best he could, saw that at least he ate the odd meal or two.

Winter came and went, the circus performers moved on, and Grimaldi stayed. He had nowhere else to go and, out of pity, the owners and managers let him stay on. Ruda Kellerman had appeared, in a rusty old jeep, with her obnoxious husband. They were travelling on to Chicago: Kellerman had a contract to join a troupe of acrobats. She wasn't skinny or half-starved any more, but well filled out – twice the size of her diminutive husband. Kellerman was only there a few hours before he got into a brawl and was asked to leave. He yelled that he hadn't wanted to come to the rundown shithole, he'd only come because his wife wanted to see Grimaldi.

Ruda appeared at Grimaldi's trailer – or shack, as it didn't have any wheels. She banged on the window and, hung over, unshaven and stinking to high heaven, he flung open the door, shouting for whoever it was to leave him alone. She was shocked to see him in such a state, this man who had been her fantasy figure for years.

She brought him food, brewed some coffee, told him how she made pin money doing astrological charts, reading palms. She had laughed at how easy it was to make money. Grimaldi wasn't listening, he sat in a stupor, drinking the thick black sweet coffee. She dug deep into her old trouser pockets, took out a wad of dollars and stuffed them into his hand. 'Here, you were kind to me once. I've never forgotten that.'

Kellerman had banged on the door and yelled they were on their way. She had shouted back for him to wait in the truck, and stood staring at Grimaldi, her face concerned. 'I got to go, you take care now, maybe see you around some place.' She had offered her hand to shake, like a man, and he had turned away, embarrassed at taking her money, but unable to give it back.

For the next four months Ruda and Kellerman had travelled around, stopping off at small-time circuses, never for long. Kellerman held on to his dream of working in one of the main venues in Vegas, but when they eventually arrived there they were so broke that he had to sell all his so-called props. He had no act to offer, at least, not one that would earn them any cash, and none of the high-class acts would consider his type of performance. Ruda had to work as a waitress, at a roadside truckers' stop, doing twelve-hour shifts to earn enough for them to live on.

The gambling bug took hold of Tommy: slot machines attracted him like a drug, and he began to borrow more and more money. Then he made the mistake of getting in with loan sharks. He owed thousands, and gambled in a feverish panic to try to cover his losses. Three weeks after their arrival in Vegas, Ruda returned home, worn out after a late-night shift, to discover Kellerman had sold their mobile home at the trailer park – sold it, when they didn't even own it. But he had at least left word where he had bolted to and she tracked him down to a small, seedy rooming house. The only possessions he had been unable to sell were a few of her clothes. Ruda had told Grimaldi, albeit a long time after, how she had opened her cheap trunk, rummaged through her things, and then slammed down the lid. She told him how angry she had been, demanding to know what Kellerman had done with her albums and notebooks. Kellerman, so Ruda had said, didn't seem to care, he had simply got out as fast as he could.

Grimaldi remembered asking Ruda if that was why she had left Kellerman, why she had eventually come back to Grimaldi, and she had told him . . . He frowned, trying to recall exactly what reason she had given, then suddenly it came to him, he remembered exactly what Ruda had said: 'I was pissed off so many times with Kellerman, and the thought that he had left my boxes, the ones with all my letters, my contact numbers, my box numbers for when I wrote out my customers' charts – that really got me mad.'

She had grown silent, and Grimaldi had asked about the boxes. Had Ruda got them back? She had shrugged, tried to sound dismissive. 'Yeah, the little shit had that much decency – *he*'d got my boxes. Oh, Luis, I was so angry, I beat the hell out of him and I really went crazy when I found out he'd searched through them. He knew I didn't have any money, but what got me so mad was that he couldn't even leave my boxes alone. I guess it was that that finally made me leave him – that he didn't give me any respect. You see, they're mine. They're all I got.'

Grimaldi could have no knowledge of the importance of the boxes to Ruda. He could not know that Kellerman had watched her checking each item: the little pebble, a piece of string, a heavy gold wedding ring and all the tiny folded squares of newspaper, some of them brown with age, their edges tattered from being opened and refolded so many times. Ruda had never told her husband of the fight that had followed.

Ruda was always placing adverts in newspapers. In every city, every town, she would always place the same one, just two lines: 'Red, Blue, Green, Ruda, Arbeit Macht Frei' and then the box number where she could be contacted. Kellerman had given up trying to persuade her it was a waste of time. Finally he had been so angry he had torn up the neatly cut square of newspaper, ripped it into shreds and screamed: 'She will never contact you. She is dead, *dead*, *dead*!'

Ruda had looked at him, then calmly opened the kitchen drawer and taken out a carving knife. She seemed to fly at him from across the room, and he had only saved himself by crawling beneath a table. She kicked at him, began to stab the knife into the wooden tabletop; her frenzied attack continued until she had slumped exhausted on to the floor beside him. She had allowed him to take the knife from her hands and, like two children hiding, they huddled together under the table.

Kellerman never brought up the subject again, or admitted how much it hurt him to see those words: 'Arbeit Macht Frei'. They had been the words printed above each hut in the concentration camp. He knew, therefore, more than anyone else, the importance of the black box, but he had not realized it meant more to her than he did.

The morning after the fight, Ruda had given Tommy some money from her previous evening's tips. He had promised he would not gamble, he would look for a job. But he hadn't even attempted to find one, he had already

344

planned what he was going to do. He used Ruda's money to buy a gun.

Kellerman and two men he had befriended planned the robbery together. They would travel to a circus where he had once been employed. Kellerman knew when and where the takings were counted. The robbery, seemingly so simple on paper, got out of hand and the cashier, a man who had himself lent money to Kellerman at one stage, was shot and died on his way to hospital. Kellerman had planned to move on fast with Ruda, but he had barely arrived back at the rooming house with the takings when the police came for him. Ruda had been arrested along with Kellerman and held in gaol on suspicion of being his accomplice.

Perhaps one of the few decent things Kellerman had ever done in his grubby, miserable life was adamantly to deny that Ruda had played any part in the robbery. She was released. She saw him only once, and had listened as he begged her to find a good lawyer. Then she had looked at him and asked how she was to pay for a lawyer. He had pleaded with her: 'You got to help me, Ruda, please. Help me get out of this! I got a contact, guy runs a decent whorehouse, please . . . Turn a few tricks – help me.'

She hadn't even waited for the visiting time to be over, instead she had said, with a half-smile: 'No, Tommy. I'm finished helping you. You see, Tommy, you should never have opened my box. It's mine.'

Ruda never tried to contact Kellerman. She read in the newspapers he had been sentenced to eight years in gaol. By this time she was already heading back to Florida, having used his contact to make some quick bucks. It had been easier whoring than in the old days, and, as

Kellerman had said, it was a decent brothel. Ruda had almost enjoyed the whips and domination scenes she had created for the fetish clients. They were always easier to take care of and they paid better than the straight ones. Ruda could have stayed on but she had no intention of returning to whoring full time. She had made up her mind to return to Florida, to Grimaldi.

She arrived at Grimaldi's winter quarters on the same day he had been asked to leave. Grimaldi was as broke as Kellerman: the people who had befriended him could extend their charity no longer.

Ruda acted as if he was expecting her, putting down her suitcase at the side of the table, picking up his notice to leave, and walking over to the manager's office. She paid over two thousand dollars in cash and asked if she could use Grimaldi's shack as a contact base for her fortune-telling business. They all knew about Kellerman, about the robbery and his arrest – he had stolen from his own people – but Ruda stood her ground, saying although she was his wife she had walked out and filed for divorce as soon as she knew what he had done.

Grimaldi had run up huge debts, and just to have some rent paid off made Ruda's appearance in some way acceptable. She promised that, from that moment on, she would take care of Grimaldi. As if she had substituted one loser for another. Now, Luis asked himself, why? Why had she come back to him?

Ruda had returned to the rundown trailer and ordered Luis out while she began to clean the place up with buckets of water and disinfectants, washing and scrubbing as he sat on the steps drinking beer. She borrowed a van and carried the filthy sheets and laundry to a launderette in town; she ironed and tidied, brought in groceries and

346

cans of paint. She was up at the crack of dawn, painting the outside of the old trailer, forcing old Two Seats to lend a hand. Grimaldi never lifted a finger.

Ruda slept on the old bunk bed in the main living area of the trailer; Grimaldi had the so-called bedroom. She was never still, stacking bottles and garbage into big rubbish bags, carrying them to the bins. One morning, Grimaldi leaned against the open door, watching her working and sweating with the effort. It was a blistering hot day and he had caught her arm as she was about to push past him.

'Where's Kellerman now?'

'Still in gaol. We're finished. He's history.' She released her arm and went inside. It was dark, flies everywhere. She poured water from a bucket into the sink – they didn't have running water. 'We got a quickie divorce, only cost a few dollars. If I'd known how cheap it was to get rid of him, I'd have done it years ago.'

Grimaldi slumped into a chair. 'So you married him?'

She turned, hands on hips. 'Yeah, I married him. I had no way of getting out of Berlin – he was my way. That answer your question?'

He looked up at her helplessly. 'I don't know what you want from me. Why are you doing all this?'

'You got somebody else?'

He laughed. 'Does it look like it? I'm just trying to get a handle on what you want.'

Her eyes were a strange colour – amber – they reminded him of his cats, and even in his drink-addled mind he felt she was dangerous. She had moved close to him: it was not sexual, it was a strange closeness. She put out her hand and covered his heart. 'Marry me.'

He had started to laugh, but her hand clutched his

chest. 'I'm serious, marry me. I'll get you back on your feet, I'll get you started again. All you need is money, I can make money, I can get enough so you can start again, but I want some kind of deal, and if I am your wife, that's a good enough contract.'

'My wife?'

She returned to the sink, began scrubbing. 'Think about it. I don't want sex, sex doesn't mean anything to me. It'll just be a partnership.'

Grimaldi grinned, not believing what he was hearing. 'You any idea how much cats cost? Feed? Transportation? Then there's the training – it'll take months to get an act, any kind of a decent act, together.'

Ruda scrubbed a pan with a wire brush. 'Yeah, I'm sure it's a lot, but we can do it gradually, and I am willing to learn. I can muck out, do anything you tell me to do. I've been around circuses now for long enough, I know the ropes, and I know it's hard work, but I can do it.'

He sighed, shaking his head. 'No way, I couldn't do it . . . I'm finished.'

She threw the pan across the room. 'You were the best, *the best*, and you can be again. I'm giving you a chance.'

He grabbed her hand, dragged her out of the trailer and crossed to the back of the sheds, to the pitiful remains of his once fine act. He shoved her against the bars. 'Look at these animals. They're as fucked and as finished as I am. You don't know what you're talking about, you have no conception of what an act the likes of mine took – *years. My father, his father before him* . . . and that's what I'm left with.'

She back-handed him one hell of a punch. 'They'd turn in their graves if they heard you. Go on, get another bottle, go on, get drunk . . . you weak bum!'

He stormed off in a rage, wanting to hit out at her, but wanting even more to hit himself. Left alone, she had stared at the bedraggled unkempt cats, their cages filthy, their ribs showing through their matted coats. She grabbed a bucket of water, and headed back to the trailer.

The water hit him in the face, then the bucket. 'You bastard. You can get yourself as drunk as you want, you can let yourself go, but what you've done out there is a crime – they're starving to death.'

'*I have no money to feed them. I got no money, and nobody wants to buy them!*'

She rolled up her sleeve, shoved her tattooed arm under his nose. 'See this? I've been caged, I've been starved, I've been beaten, I've been to hell and back and I am still here. I am still fighting, and I have enough for the two of us. You've got ten minutes before I take a gun and shoot what's left of those poor creatures, and then I'll leave a bullet for you. You don't let them suffer another hour, you hear me? *You hear me?*'

She had slammed out of the trailer, banging the door so hard it came off its hinges. She went around to the cages. Having never been inside a cat's cage in her life, she unbolted the door, stepped in, and took out the empty meat trays. She then rebolted the door and went back to the trailer. He was sitting, head bowed, hands held loosely in front of him.

'What do they eat?'

'Meat, horsemeat. Maybe I should put myself in there, let them have a go at me.'

Ruda stormed out and went into town. She came back an hour later, carrying a stack of wooden boxes. She found him mucking out the cages, Two Seats using a hose to wash them down. She cleaned out the bowls, and carried the fresh meat to the cages. Two Seats gave a toothless smile to Ruda, and he touched her hand with his gnarled, crusted fingers. 'I don't know what you said, but I thank God for you, young woman.'

They mucked out and cleaned, fed the cats and went back into town for fresh bales of hay and sawdust. Neither of them brought up the question of marriage. Luis began to exercise the cats. Two Seats collected the old plinths from the storage huts and dusted and washed them down. The heat was oppressive and the small trailer airless; they continued to sleep separately.

Four months after Ruda had arrived, Grimaldi disappeared into town. Old Two Seats sat on the steps glumly muttering that he doubted if the guv'nor would come back that night, he'd be getting plastered at the local whorehouse.

Ruda went and sat down on her bunk, flopping back. 'Shit! *Shit!*' She had traded one bum in for another. She wondered if she had made the wrong decision in coming to Florida, but then she heard Grimaldi calling out for her. Luis had returned, stone cold sober, and he placed on the kitchen table an envelope and a small red box. It was a marriage licence and a wedding ring. He said nothing, just pointed to the table.

He hovered outside the trailer watching her from the window as she opened first the envelope. He saw her smile – she who so rarely smiled – and then slowly she opened the ring box. She snapped it shut, was about to walk out to him when she heard Grimaldi ask the old man if he had a suit.

'A suit! You must be jokin', it's at the pawnbroker's.'

'Well, get it out, and by Wednesday, 'cos you're gonna need it.'

'What fer?'

'Wedding, you old bugger.'

'What?'

'We need a witness. Me and Ruda are getting married, next Wednesday.'

There was a loud guffaw, and then a lot of back-slapping. She came to the door, and Grimaldi held out his big hand. She took it, gripped it tightly as the old man wrinkled his nose and then threw his hat up in the air with a yell.

'By Christ – that's the best news I've heard in years!'

The wedding had been a quiet affair with just a few people from the winter quarters. They had lunch at a local restaurant, and then returned to feed the cats. Ruda had been very quiet; she had smiled for a photograph, but as the day drew to a close she continued to make excuses, anything to keep busy, delaying the marital consumma-tion, even unsure if that was what he wanted. She had arranged a platonic partnership with Kellerman, but after six months in the States he had demanded sex with her. Kellerman revolted her, the thought of his touching her made her shiver with revulsion, but nevertheless the marriage had been consummated, in so far as it ever could be, but then Kellerman liked kinky sex. Her physical problems had never bothered him: he liked to have her give him a blow job, liked her on her knees in front of him.

Luis had brought flowers and champagne, and she noticed her bed linen had been removed from the couch she had always slept on. He was in high spirits, partly as the aftermath of the wedding party, and although he wasn't drunk, he was obviously merry. Also, having made the decision to marry Ruda, he was now more than willing to take her into his bed. He opened the champagne, and then produced a box, presenting it to her with a flourish. She opened the gift, and the delicate nightdress, its lace and frills carefully snuggled in white tissue paper, made her bite her lips – she didn't want even to take it out of the box.

'Don't you like it? It's silk, the lace is from France, is it the right size? Take it out, go on take it out . . .'

Slowly she had held the delicate nightgown against herself.

'You like it?'

She whispered that it was beautiful, and he asked her to put it on. She hesitated, and seemed so distressed he wanted to put his arms around her, but she stepped away from him. 'Nobody ever gave me anything . . .'

'So let me see you in it,' he said gently.

'You want this to be a proper marriage?'

Luis was a trifle confused; he said that he thought that was what she wanted, and she had turned away from him, hunching up her shoulders.

'I guess that is what I want, Ruda, I mean . . . maybe I've not been the best person to have around, not said the right things, but you wanted to marry me, didn't you?'

She nodded, but remained turned away from him, and when he tried once again to hold her she fended him off. 'I want to tell you something, I sort of thought you knew . . . but I guess you don't.'

Again he tried to make her turn to him, look at him, but she hunched further away. 'Don't, please don't touch me.'

She held the soft silk to her face, almost caressing the gown, and then she sighed. 'Luis, I *can't* have normal sex. Something was done to me when I was a child. I can give you . . . make it all right for you, but that is all.'

Luis had visions of her having had a sex change, that she was a man. He couldn't hide his revulsion, his confusion. 'Jesus Christ, what a fucking time to tell me. Are you kidding me?'

She turned to him, unbuttoning her shirt, her face rigid. 'You don't think this is something to kid about, do you?' She began to undress in front of him, and he now backed away from her. She undid her blouse, took off her bra, and then began to unzip her trousers. 'Look, don't, Ruda, don't do this to me, I can't deal with it, please, Ruda!'

She continued to undress, easing her trousers down, and then kicking off her shoes. She had a pair of thick cotton pants on, and he really believed she was going to show him a penis. Instead, she drew down the pants and showed him the terrible scars on her belly. He stared in disbelief, deeply shocked but not repelled.

Ruda then held up her wrist, showing him the tattoo. He looked from the row of numbers to her belly; he couldn't look into her eyes.

'I'm surprised you've never seen it before, the tattoo.'

He swallowed, and gave a half-smile, but his hands were shaking. 'I guess I'm just not very observant.'

She stood before him with such helplessness, such shame, her head bowed. He picked up the gown, and slipped it over her head. Then he stepped back. 'Now you look like a bride.' The small space between them was like a chasm; he did not know how to cross to her. Seeing her standing there in the white floating gown made him want to weep, but she shed no tears.

Her voice was husky, her head still bowed. 'I'll make up a bed for myself on the sofa. You don't have to be with me. I understand, I can understand.'

He gathered her in his arms and held her tightly. His voice was thick with emotion. 'What kind of a man do you think I am? We said to each other for better or worse, didn't we? Well, I don't think you got such a great bargain, so maybe you're a bit damaged too, that's OK, we'll make out.'

Ruda had clung to him, her whole body shaking, and when he cupped her face in his big hands, two tears rolled down her cheeks. He told her then that he loved her. Maybe it was those two tears – he had never seen her cry before – and he had carried her into the small bedroom and gently laid her down. He undressed as she watched, and then he got in beside her, and he reached out and cradled her in his arms.

'Don't ask me about it, Luis, don't ever want to know what was done to me, because it might open up a darkness inside me that I could not control. It happened, and now it's over.'

He had never felt so protective to any living soul. He kissed her head as she rested against his chest. 'I will always take care of you, Ruda, nobody will ever hurt you again. You are my wife, this will be our secret, no one will ever know.'

He made her feel secure, a strange new emotion. She felt warmed by this big soft man, and gently she stroked his chest, and then rolled over to lie on top of him. She smiled down into his face, and then whispered to him, that she could make him happy, there were ways, she would teach him how to make love to her, he would like it, he would be satisfied.

The old hand and the few workers left at the winter quarters gave knowing winks and nudges as a very happy Grimaldi greeted them the morning after the wedding. He was a man who appeared infatuated with his new marital status. Maybe it was indeed love.

The big album dropped to the floor, and Grimaldi woke with a start. For a moment he was disorientated, couldn't even remember coming into Ruda's bedroom. 'You're gettin' old, you soft bugger, noddin' off . . .' He yawned and leaned back. He could smell Ruda on her pillow. He nuzzled it and then slipped his arm round it sighing. 'Oh, Ruda, where did I go wrong, huh?' He knew she would play hell with him if she found him in her room, but he chuckled and eased himself into a more comfortable position. His last thought before he fell into a deep sleep was of Ruda, his wife. 'What a bloody wife.'

Ruda had intended to apply for a divorce as soon as she had the opportunity. That she had married Grimaldi bigamously never concerned her. With Kellerman in prison, he would not find out; by the time he was out she would have secured a divorce. She wished she had done it in Vegas, as she had told Grimaldi she had, but then she had been in such a hurry to leave that divorce had been the last thing on her mind.

Grimaldi began to earn money by training other acts, travelling around the United States. He returned with gifts, and cash to begin buying new cats for his own show.

Ruda worked at the winter quarters, learning how to groom and feed the animals, and they thrived under her care and attention. She and Luis began to breed the tigers and their first summer together as man and wife saw four new cubs born. Ruda was a doting surrogate mother, bottle-feeding two lion cubs, and was heartbroken when Grimaldi sold them. He said they needed the sale because it would help build up their savings, but he also demonstrated his knowledge of the cats – the cubs were not a good colour. He taught Ruda how to detect the best of the litters, how to test their strength, their health always the main priority, and she was a willing pupil. She worked tirelessly, nothing was too much trouble. Everyone said that Grimaldi had found the perfect wife and that Ruda was getting him back on his feet.

Ruda continued with her star-gazing sideline. The letters arrived every week and she would spend hours every evening typing replies, giving predictions. She typed very slowly with two fingers, her face puckered with concentration. She had a dictionary beside her, always thumbing its well-worn pages. Grimaldi used to tease her, and at times was stunned when she asked him to spell the simplest of words. He believed at first it was because she was German and typing in English, but then watching her studied concentration, he understood she was almost illiterate. She had caught him watching her and given him a V-sign. 'I never went to school, dickhead, so no jokes!'

He leaned on her chair, and began to read a letter. She tried to cover it with her hand, and he snatched it out of the roller. '"Dear Worried From Nebraska", my God, what in God's name is somebody writing to you from Nebraska for?'

Ruda had tried to grab the letter back, but he held it away from her. 'I've done her charts, now give it back.'

Grimaldi dangled the letter jokingly. 'Her charts? What in Christ's name do you know about all this junk?'

He continued to read on, and roared with laughter as he read Ruda's predictions. She folded her arms. 'You laugh, but they pay ten bucks a letter, and they pay for the cats' feed. You got any better ideas how to make dough that fast?'

Grimaldi slapped the paper down, and rubbed her head. 'Keep working, keep working!'

She carefully rolled the paper back into the typewriter and he was about to walk out when he paused at the doorway. 'You never did tell me how you did that scarf trick, you know, with that old magician.'

She began typing again, and without looking at him said that it wasn't a trick. He told her to pull the other leg, but she turned to face him. 'That wasn't a trick, I'm telepathic.'

'Oh, yeah? Prove it!'

Ruda shrugged and said she couldn't be bothered, but he had hovered around, teasing, asking her to prove it. She sighed, pushed the typewriter away. She had picked up a stack of envelopes, containing all the letters she had received that week. She handed them to him, first flicking through the stack like a pack of cards. She then turned her back and told him to flick each envelope up and she would tell him what colour the stamps were. She repeated, in rapid succession: red, blue, red, red, green, blue, red, red, red, red ... then swivelled round in her chair and cocked her head to one side.

'You already knew! You cheated!'

She held out her hand and shrugged. 'Yeah . . . now can I get on with my work?'

'Don't let me hold you up, carry on.' But he remained leaning at the doorway watching her, until she looked up at him and pulled a funny face.

'Is it just the colours, then? I mean, can you do anything else?'

She laughed. 'If I was to say yes, what are you gonna do? Set up a booth and make me wear a turban? Just get out, go on, don't you have anything to do?'

Grimaldi laughed. As he stepped down he called out, 'I'll get myself a cloak like that old boy you worked with. Old Two Seats can bend over and give us a good fart, I'll set light to it!'

She could hear him laughing as he passed by the window, and then he stuck his head against the glass. 'I tell you today how much I love you, gel. Eh? Cross my palm with silver . . . and I'll tell you how much!'

She stuck up her finger, shouted for him to 'Sit on it!', and he gave his marvellous, deep-bellied laugh, as at last he went about his business.

Ruda began her laborious typing once more but, after a moment, she sat back and slid out from beneath the typewriter a slip of paper. It was another advertisement, another place: Florida. She stared at the two lines, remembering how Tommy Kellerman had told her she was crazy. Slowly she crumpled the paper, then straightened out the creases, kept on reading and rereading the two lines, 'Red, blue, green, Ruda . . .' and the message Tommy had hated so much.

Ruda crossed to her dressing table, opened a drawer, eased her hand to the back and drew out the small black tin box now fitted with a new lock. She fetched the key, hidden behind a book in the bookcase and unlocked her treasure box. She looked at the stack of small, folded slips of newspaper clippings. The date of the last one, Vegas, was the longest time between all the many cuttings, perhaps because, for the first time she could remember, she felt a sense of security.

She locked away her treasures again, carefully hiding the tiny key, and returned to her typewriter. She sat staring at the white sheet of paper in the roller and lifted her hands, about to begin work, but she couldn't concentrate. She went into the bedroom, slipping the bolt across as she passed the trailer door, and drew the curtains so the small room was in semi-darkness. She sat in front of the dressing-table mirror, a three-sided, free-standing mirror that she slowly drew towards herself, closer and closer until she could see her breath form tiny circles on the glass. By turning her head a fraction she could see her left profile, turning the opposite side, see her right, and then she stared directly ahead. She breathed deeply through her nose, mouth shut, and kept on breathing until she felt the strange, dizzy sensation sweep over her. Her shoulders lifted as her breathing deepened . . . first came the red, as if a beam of a red light focused on her face. She breathed deeper, concentrated harder, until the red merged into a deep green, then a blue. The colours, dense now, began flashing and repeating: red, blue, red, red, green . . . They never merged, each was a clear block of single colour. Her body began to shake, her hands gripped tightly the edge of the dressing table. The bottles of cologne shook, the entire dressing table began to sway, and she held on tightly, held on for as long as she could, before she regulated her breathing again, bringing herself slowly out of the trance.

Her body felt limp, exhausted, but she remained sitting, then tilted her face forward to kiss the cold glass, kiss her own lips. Slowly she sat back, and traced with her fingers the faint impression of her lips lingering on the mirror.

She had received nothing back, and she was consumed by an overpowering feeling of longing; the desire to feel warm lips return her kiss was like a pain inside her, a pain that, like her scars, would never heal. She could never give up, never, because on three occasions she was sure she had felt a contact.

She lay down on the bed, closed her eyes, needing to be enveloped by sleep. But now a low, nagging pain at the base of her spine made her feel uncomfortable. She turned on her side, but the pain grew worse, began to feel like a dragging sensation, as if something was being drawn out of her belly. Ruda panted, became frightened as she sweated, the pain intensifying. She gripped her stomach – it felt swollen and she began to rub her hands over her belly. As quickly as the pain had begun, it subsided. Ruda lay back. Then the pain began once more. She called out for Grimaldi, her body twisting in agony, the rush of pain centred in her belly and as she tried to sit up, she screamed with all the power in her lungs.

Grimaldi was in the barn, using a pitchfork to heave up the bales of hay. He paused, listened, and looked towards the barn doors. 'Did you hear that? Eh, you toothless old bastard, was that one of the cats?'

Two Seats shrugged and carried on working. Grimaldi stood for a moment, listening intently. Hearing nothing more he resumed his work, but after a moment he tossed down his pitchfork and walked back to the trailer. He peered in through the window, saw the typewriter, then crossed to the door, dragging his feet on the grid to wipe off the mud. He was just about to enter when he heard the bolt on the door drawn back. 'Ruda? You OK? Ruda?'

She opened the door, her face pale, shiny with sweat.

'What you lock the door for?'

Ruda gave a weak smile. 'I just didn't feel too good. I think it must be something I ate. I've been sick.'

'You running a temperature?' He reached out to touch her face and she stepped back.

'No, I'm fine now, you get on with your work. I'll lie down for a while. Go on.'

'I'll check on the cats, I swear I heard screaming. Did you hear anything?'

'Get back to work, you lazy old so and so. I'll bring over some food. It was just something I ate, now off . . . go on!'

He smiled, walking back to the barn, calling her a slave-driver. He didn't notice that she hung on to the door for support, so weak she could hardly stand.

As soon as Grimaldi was out of sight, Ruda inched herself back to the table and slumped into the chair by her typewriter. She had felt this same pain before, although she couldn't remember the exact date, but the pain had been the same, the terrible dragging sensation. She tried to type, forcing herself not to think about what had just occurred, because it frightened her. She was terrified of doctors, especially hospital doctors in their white coats – they made her shake with terror.

She felt her energy returning and just as she had pushed the pain from her, she forced herself to continue working, listing what the week's itinerary would be, what work she had lined up for Grimaldi. Almost immediately she felt better. She never did make an appointment to see a doctor, but a few months later she went to see a specialist, not at her own instigation, but her husband's.

With Ruda pushing him, Grimaldi continued taking on more training work. As the money came in, they began to buy more and more animals. At weekends he would begin training them, and she sat and watched his every move. Gradually she began to work alone when he was away, putting everything she had seen him do into practice.

They bought a new trailer and a truck, and then one night he sat her down. 'I know your injuries, the scars, but I was wondering, with you being here, and me away working until we have enough finances, whether maybe this would be a good time . . .'

'For what?' she had asked, dragging out the typewriter.

'Maybe we should see a specialist. They have all kinds of newfangled equipment now, and maybe we should go see someone about having a baby.'

She continued fetching papers, stacking them neatly at the typewriter, carrying her boxes of mail to the table. Over the past few months her little sideline had grown into quite a lucrative business. Having a semi-permanent address helped, and she worked each evening after the animals were settled. Grimaldi sometimes sat and watched her – he never read any of the letters, he was never that interested. Tonight, though, he wasn't prepared to sit. He didn't want her working, he felt this was too important.

'Ruda, listen to me. Maybe, just maybe, you can have this done medically, you know, artificial insemination. We could at least try.'

'I have enough work cut out for me, without bringing a kid up.'

'I want a son, Ruda. I mean, we're breaking our backs to get an act back together, so why not? We'd have a hell of a boy, Ruda. Don't you want even to give it a try?'

She rolled a sheet of paper into the typewriter, and started to type. He came and stood behind her, massaging her shoulders. He felt her shoulders shaking. She tried to type, and then folded her hands in her lap.

'If it hurts you, then we walk away. I don't want anything to hurt you, but we should just go and see somebody.'

He kissed the top of her head and left her. Slowly she began to type. 'Baby-baby-baby-baby . . . MY BABY. MY BABY. MY SON.'

She stared at the word until it blurred. She touched the paper, the word 'baby'. Nothing had prepared her for this, for Luis wanting a child, her child. She whispered, 'My child, he would be mine. My baby.' It had never occurred to her that perhaps there was a way. The more she thought about it, the more excited she became. Would it be possible? Dare she think it could be?

She ran out of the trailer, shouted to old Two Seats asking if he'd seen Grimaldi, and he pointed to the barn. She ran, calling for him, and hurtled into the barn. He was using a pitchfork, heaving the bales of hay. She dived at him, throwing him back on to the bales.

'Luis, Luis, I want a baby! *I want a baby. I want I want I want!*'

They had kissed, and held each other tightly. She was excited, almost feverishly so, asking him to fix an appointment. She would do anything necessary, and then she had leaned up on her elbows, looking down into his delighted face. 'You love me, don't you? You really love me!'

Luis knew what it meant to her the day she learned she

could not conceive. She had not spoken a word since they returned from the clinic, and he was incapable of comforting her, needing comfort himself. Even when he tried to reach out to her in bed she had turned her back on him. 'Don't touch me, please leave me alone.'

He was almost grateful that he had to leave for a two-week stint in Chicago.

After he left she didn't want to get up, didn't even open the blinds, and remained in the darkened trailer. She remembered little Eva then, a girl she had hardly known, but a girl much older than herself. Eva had been in the camp too, had survived like Ruda, but when Ruda had been taken to the mental institution after the liberation, when the doctors at the hospital no longer knew what to do with her but certify her as mentally deranged, she hadn't known Eva was still alive – not until she caught sight of her in the mental ward. Eva had a beard, like a man. The teenage girl who had always had stories and jokes to tell the little ones now sat on a stool with her head bowed and her face covered in hair. Her eyes stared to some distant place.

Like Ruda, Eva had not spoken since she had been found, but Eva was docile while Ruda showed violent signs that she was greatly disturbed. They had to sedate her. Ruda found it impossible to speak, impossible to believe it was over; every night she had waited for the men in white coats to take her back to the hospital ward in the old camp. She had forced herself to remain awake. The screams and weeping from the inmates didn't frighten her – she was used to screams. What she was terrified of was being taken back – back to the camp. A key turning in a door sent bolts of terror shuddering through her body, and she could not speak her fear, could not cry tears. If they tried to comfort her, she was sure it was a ruse; if they spoke kindly to her, they had another motive. She spat out the pills they gave her, refused the food. Suspicious of everything, everyone, from the moment she had arrived in the institution, her paranoia manifested itself when she saw Eva. Poor little Eva Kellerman. At least Ruda had spared Tommy that, she had never told him, but it was because of Eva she had run. Eva had put an end to her own misery: she had torn a strip of cloth from her hospital gown and hanged herself in the showers. Ruda had discovered her pitiful body and knew then for sure that it was not over. She had run, had to escape some way, because any day, any hour, it could be her turn and she would become an animal, become like Eva, whose only freedom had been death.

In the end, Ruda made herself think that her inability to conceive was for the best. Maybe she could only produce a monster, an Eva. She would not think of a baby, her baby, any more, she would forget. As it was, the entire episode had dragged her back again to the darkness of her childhood; she was angry again, she was fighting again, determined that nothing would ever drag her back, it was to be forgotten.

Ruda had no real idea of how long she had been unreachable, how many times Luis had attempted to embrace her, show his love and concern. She wasn't aware he had slept on the couch, tried to tempt her to eat, or that she had kicked the tray from his hands. She was oblivious that when Luis had tried to tell her that he had to leave for a few weeks she had told him to fuck off, go wherever he liked, she didn't care . . .

Grimaldi had discussed her behaviour with old Two Seats, who suggested that all Ruda needed was time, she was just hurting, and this hitting out at Luis was her way of dealing with it. 'She's just like one of 'em cats, Luis. They get injured, and by Christ you'll know it, they'll go fer you! She's just hurtin'.'

Luis punched the old man's shoulder, said perhaps he was right. He never mentioned his own hurt, how much he had wanted a son . . . and he had left. He hadn't said goodbye because he hadn't wanted to disturb her. Ruda had been sitting on the bunk bed, with the old tin box.

Luis sighed, his face still pressed into Ruda's pillow. He rolled over, awake now, and sighed again. 'I wanted a boy, a son, so bad, Ruda, but, most important, I wanted him to be ours.' He sat up and ran his hands through his thick hair; it stuck up on end. He got off the bed and straightened the cover. The photo album had fallen open at an old picture of himself with his father. He picked it up, touching the picture lightly with his finger. 'Ah, well. Maybe the circus days are numbered, and, maybe I'd get a kid who wouldn't want to go into the ring. It happens . . .' Luis stepped up on the stool, talking away to himself. 'The Karengo brothers got a kid who's studying law! Mine'd probably end up in gaol some place . . . who knows? Can't all be warriors, eh, Dad?' About to shut the cupboard door, he saw the box, the old square black tin box at the back. He stretched and reached out, drew it close, and then stepped down with it. He tried to open it – it was locked. He went into the kitchen and took a knife, but when he tried to prise the box open, he buckled the lid. He swore as he wrenched and pulled, but it wouldn't open.

The trailer door banged. Luis turned guiltily: he was behaving just like Kellerman – had he reached this point with Ruda, too?

Mike called out that they were due on in ten minutes. 'Ruda said to get over to the ring, the big boss is in the viewing room, and he's got a scout from Ringling Brothers' Circus with him. We're all set to go.'

Luis shouted he would be right there, and quickly hid the box under his own mattress. Mike was waiting at the door, and raised his eyebrow to Grimaldi; he admired the old man's resilience, there he was all done up like a Christmas dinner, and not long before he had been well plastered.

'Your hand OK?' Mike asked, as they walked towards the big tent. Grimaldi gave a big rumbling laugh and hooked a huge arm round Mike's slim shoulder. 'Son, I've been slashed by a lot more dangerous species than a pitchfork!'

Mike laughed, then lifted the tent flap. 'She's all steamed up as usual, pacing out there like a panther. Mamon's playing up, I hope to God he'll play ball tonight. It's those plinths, he hates them. Did I tell you the Ringling scout is in?'

Grimaldi nodded his head. 'Yeah, you told me, son. You know once I had a contract with them, some years back, but they offered me a . . .'

Mike had gone, and he was alone, talking to himself. He stood in the semi-darkness amid the empty rows and rows of seats. A juggling act was moving through its paces in the ring, the coloured costumes spangled, catching the spotlights. He looked to the lighted viewing box; he could see Schmidt conferring with a man sitting next to him, gesturing down to the ring. Then Grimaldi saw a third man, seated just behind Schmidt. He shaded his eyes to get a better view. It was Walter Zapashny, rated as probably one of the finest animal trainers in the world.

Grimaldi wondered why he was up there; it made him feel uneasy.

Grimaldi inched down the aisle between the empty seats; he saw one of the hands standing by to erect the cages around the ring. He moved quietly to his side. 'Have you seen who's in the viewing tower?'

The man nodded, he whispered that everyone knew, it was the big Ringling scout. The word was out that the great Gunther Gebel Williams was about to retire. It meant that the most lucrative circus job, a possible ten-year contract with the powerful Ringling Brothers of New York was coming up for grabs. Williams had been top of the bill as one of the greatest showmen for almost twenty years.

Grimaldi nodded, his heart pounding in his chest. What he had dreamed of all his adult life, that coveted position for himself, could now be Ruda's. He felt a rush of pride. 'Tell Ruda I'm here, tell her to make this the best show she has ever given. Hurry!'

CHAPTER 14

As RUDA KELLERMAN prepared to begin her act, Vebekka Maréchal sat at the cramped dingy bar, its red light giving everyone an eerie pinkness. It was still only nine, and the club was almost empty; three girls wearing mini-skirts and tight lace tops chattered quietly at the end of the plush plastic-covered bar. Vebekka had gone from club to club until she found Mama's. A doorman came out of the men's toilet, looked at the elegant woman sitting alone, gave her a good once-over; he was sure she was after young blood – male or female. He sniffed, she'd get it – if she had enough Deutschmarks. He passed through the arch, its green and red beaded curtain held back by a ribbon, went up the flight of stairs leading to the main club entrance, then flattened himself against the wall as Mama began her heavy descent. He saw the swollen ankles first, the fat rolling over her gold sandals, as the tiny feet moved down one step at a time.

Mama Magda Braun's massive frame squashed against her doorman, but she didn't even acknowledge him. She was talking loudly to a small queer who had followed her down, clutching her poodle. 'I am sick to death of those ugly bastards, I don't wanna see those bitches stealing my girls' jobs. The smell of them! Emptying the store shelves, bringing crime and bad taste, I hate them! Everything used to be a good tight scene. Now, Jesus Christ what a mess!'

His high-pitched lisping voice squeaked out from behind her bulk. 'Now, Magda, the shops are doing a roaring trade, you know it, I know it . . .' He was referring to Magda's sex and porn shops in East Berlin. She was making money hand over fist, but hated it when the girls from the East tried to come to her clubs in the West. Magda was the biggest single porn-shop owner in the West. Now with the Wall down, she had been one of the first to see the potential money-making machine; the sex-starved Easties, as she called them, needed an injection from the Westies, and she was giving them what they wanted in the form of shops – but they didn't have to come swarming over into her clubs. Magda Braun owned four nightclubs: she was a multi-millionairess.

Magda's peroxide curls turned bright pink in the light, her diamonds glittered, as did the large beaded necklace dangling over her massive bosom. But she gave a bad-tempered glance around the half-empty club. It was early, she told herself, but she hated it when it was empty. This was her main club, the one in which she had her small cramped office. Eric, her diminutive husband, called out to the girls, waved to a few couples and continued to follow Magda, to a door marked private. The effort of walking across the small dance floor had exhausted what little breath was able to squeeze through her nicotine-polluted lungs. Her chest heaved, and she gave a phlegmy cough. She could still be heard coughing as the door closed behind her.

Magda checked the takings on the computer, a cigarette in her crimson-painted lips. Years of smoke had created a yellow tinge on one side of her jowled face. 'Our take is down again this week. You think those bitches are at it again? I tell you, Eric, you have to watch them like a hawk. Give me a barman any day, trust a man better than those tarts.'

Eric was peering through a small spyhole. 'You seen the class act at the bar?'

Magda paid no attention, continued tapping out the accounts. The boys handling the girls over in the East were short-changing her, she knew it. They'd have to have a short sharp lesson.

'I'm gonna check on the class, be back in a minute.'

Magda picked up a pencil and dialled, hooking the phone under her chin. 'It's Magda, can you get over here, bring a couple of the boys, and the handy ones, yeah? . . . Yeah, he'll do. No, . . . give me another.' She listened and agreed to three of the names supplied by the caller, then replaced the phone, sighing. They never learn their lesson, they should know you don't get to be near eighty, and as rich as she was, without learning every trick in the trade.

Eric scuttled back, gesturing for Magda to come to the spyhole. 'She's asked for water, just sits there, she may be a fruit. You want to take a look? She's wearing good jewellery – that's sable on the edge of her wrap, Magda.'

'I don't give a fuck about her, if she's paying, then what's the problem?'

'That's it, she's been there over half an hour, said she's not got any money she just wants to sit. She didn't pay any entrance money, doorman wasn't on duty . . . Magda!'

Magda shoved him aside, peered through and kept on looking, her heaving breath seeming to stop suddenly.

She straightened up. 'I just seen a ghost. Fuck me!' She laughed, and thudded down into a wide cushioned seat. 'Eric, bring me a bottle of champagne, good stuff, and ask the lady to come in.'

'You know her?'

Magda nodded, 'I know her, she may look like class now but, honey, believe you me that was one hell of a tart. You know something, Eric? They always come back . . . some day, one day, they come back, maybe to see where they came from, or how far they've left us behind . . . but they always come back to Mama. Get her in. This one I've been waiting for, so long now I can hardly remember.'

Eric crossed to Vebekka, asked if she would join Madame Magda for a drink. He pointed back to the office, the door left ajar. Vebekka hesitated and looked towards Magda, who was smiling, beckoning her to come, but Vebekka shook her head. 'Thank you, no. I don't speak German.'

Eric asked if she was English. She told him she was French, and he attempted to repeat his invitation in French.

'*Ruda!* Come in here, Ruda!'

Vebekka felt strange, a little faint, as the fat woman kept calling to her, waving her over. She slid from the stool. 'Excuse me, I must go.'

Eric ordered champagne, took Vebekka's elbow. 'Please, you come.'

'No, thank you, no . . .'

'*Ruda! Ruda!*'

Eric insisted, holding her arm firmly, as one of the girls carried a tray with a bottle of champagne and two glasses across to the office. Vebekka was ushered into the small room and the big woman held open her arms. 'Come here. Come and give me a kiss!'

Vebekka stepped back, repelled by the grotesque woman. Eric pushed her further into the room, the waitress squeezed out, and Magda wafted her hand at Eric. 'You, too, get out.'

Disappointed, Eric walked out, pouting. He crossed to the bar and ordered a Martini. The club began filling up, and he perched himself on the stool vacated by Vebekka. He noticed she had left her handbag on the bar.

Magda poured the champagne. Vebekka remained standing. Magda handed her a drink, but she shook her head. 'No, I don't.'

Magda smiled and set the glass down, lit another cigarette from a stub, offering the case to Vebekka. She took one, and Magda flicked a Zippo lighter across the desk. 'You look very good, I didn't recognize you at first.'

Vebekka remained standing. 'I am so sorry, I don't understand, I don't speak German.'

Magda smiled again, shrugged her plump shoulders. 'What then?'

Vebekka spoke in French, introducing herself as Baroness Vebekka Maréchal, asking if they had met before. Magda kept her eyes on Vebekka, heavily made-up eyes, the mascara so thick her lashes were spiked. 'You want to speak in French, Italian, Spanish that's OK by me. You been away so long, huh? That long?'

'I don't understand, I am so sorry, but I think there is some confusion, I don't think we have ever met.'

Magda leaned her fat elbows on the desk. 'OK, I'll play, have a drink, sit down.'

Vebekka eased herself on to the proffered chair; she felt very uneasy, but she sipped the champagne. Magda

373

suddenly reached out and took Vebekka's left wrist, turned it over. Vebekka tried to withdraw her hand, but the old woman, for all her heavy breathing, was as strong as an ox. Her long nails scratching at Vebekka's wrist, she turned her palm upwards, and traced the fine skin graft with the tip of her nail. She let go, and smiled.

'Why did you do that?' Vebekka rubbed her wrist.

'So I know I am sure. Drink, drink – it's good, the best money can buy,' Magda answered in French.

Vebekka sipped the champagne, the old woman looking at her, scrutinizing her. Magda tapped her own nose, and then pointed to Vebekka's face, said that the work was good, she looked good, looked young. She asked where she was staying, why she was in Berlin, and Vebekka said she was with her husband.

'And you couldn't resist it? Had to come back and see Magda? And now you're a what? A Baroness? Well, well – face changed, name changed, what did you call yourself? Vebekka? What kind of name is that?'

Vebekka smiled, a sweet coy smile, and sipped more champagne. Magda picked up her vodka, drank thirstily, and shook the glass. 'I still take it neat, with ice, but now I own a warehouse full! Times change, huh? Times change, Ruda, little Ruda. Just look at you, and married to a baron! Does he know you're here?'

Vebekka began to feel uneasy, a little frightened. Why did the woman keep on calling her Ruda? But all she said was that her husband did not know.

'I bet he doesn't. So you got to America? I heard you had, and then what? You met a prince and a baron – all the same thing. Is he rich?'

Vebekka drained her glass. Magda poured more and

asked again if her husband was rich. Vebekka shrugged. 'I suppose so, I don't know, I never think about money.'

Magda laughed, her body shook and she had a coughing fit that seemed to be calmed by a drag on her cigarette. 'You don't think of money. I do, every second of every day, I count it every night on this little baby computer – cuts a lot of time, and accountants' fees.'

The two women drank in silence. The sounds of a Madonna record could be heard from the club, the low murmur of voices and shrill laughter. Magda's eyes watered. 'You know, it hurt, Ruda, it hurt when you ran off – I never thought you would steal from me, not after all I did for you. I never thought you would do that to Mama, maybe that's why I have never forgotten you. You forget lovers, forget husbands, forget children even, but when someone hits your pocket, you don't forget. I never forgot you, Ruda, and maybe I just guessed one day you would come back.'

Vebekka listened, her head cocked to one side. Sometimes she understood what she was saying, but Magda's French kept slipping back into German. 'I don't understand what you are saying, but I know I have never met you before. I am not this – Ruda? You are mistaken . . .'

Yet Vebekka felt a strange sensation when she said the name Ruda, it seemed to ring through her brain like a tiny ominous bell. Magda heaved herself to her feet and looked at Vebekka with distaste. 'Don't play games with me, I am a master player, sweetface. You don't speak German? We've never met? Who the fuck do you think you are kidding, eh? Because you got a few fancy clothes on, call yourself a Baroness?'

'I don't understand.'

Magda was losing patience. She slapped the desk with her fat hand. 'Don't make me angry, it's been a lot of years, a lot of changes, Ruda. I run this city, hear me? You stop this act right now – *I have had enough!*'

Vebekka gulped at the champagne. The woman frightened her. 'I have never met you before! Please, there is some misunderstanding, perhaps I should leave.' She started to stand but Magda was up beside her, pushing her into the seat, leering over her.

'You want something to refresh your memory? Huh? I didn't want to do this, I was prepared to be hospitable, maybe forget, but me? Never, I forget nothing, no one. You owe me a lot, Ruda, you owe me!'

Magda waddled to a large built-in cupboard, heaving for breath as she opened up the double door. The cupboard was stacked with boxes and files, she stared up and down, up and down, reached out for one box, and then withdrew her hand. Suddenly she yelled at the top of her voice. 'Eric. *Eric!*'

The club was in full swing now, Madonna still blared out from the speakers.

'Just sit, sweetface, I'm gonna jog that memory of yours.'

Eric tapped and entered, looked to Magda, to Vebekka, then asked if everything was all right.

'There was a box, old cardboard box from the Kinkerlitzchen, taped up, big brown cardboard box.'

'What about it?'

'I want it. Where is it? It used to be stashed in there, in that cupboard. Where is it now?'

Eric hovered at the open cupboard doors. 'I haven't moved anything for years from here, everything you wanted brought over should still be here, unless when they computerized the club somebody threw it out. What do you want?'

'*I never gave permission for one thing to be chucked out!*'

Magda was heaving for breath, and Eric got down on his hands and knees. 'Shit, this place is filthy. It's dusty in here.'

Magda stood behind him. 'Just find the fucking thing.'

Vebekka looked on, not understanding what they were saying, looking from one to the other. Eric suddenly heaved at a box beneath a stack of files. 'Is this it?'

Magda peered over his shoulder and told him to put it on the desk. Eric dumped the dirty dusty box on the table and then restacked files as Magda tore it open. She rooted around, hurling things to the floor, and then took out an old torn thick envelope. 'Put it all back and get out!'

'Shit, Magda, I'll have to take all the files and restack them again, it won't fit now.'

Magda screeched at him to leave – she would sort it out later. Eric tripped over the dog, which yelped and scuttled under the desk, then slammed out of the office, very peeved.

Magda filled Vebekka's glass again, then settled herself back on her cushions, lighting another of her cigarettes. 'You don't remember Mama, huh? You don't remember what I did for you, what Mama did to help Ruda? Well, tell me, you remember this, sweetface?' Magda tore at the envelope and pulled out a parcel wrapped in old newspapers.

Again Vebekka felt the name pass across her mind . . . Ruda? She suddenly turned to stare behind her, she had the sensation that someone else was in the room . . . close to her; but there was no one. Ruda, she repeated to herself, not even listening to Magda. Then she sipped the champagne; it was chilled, icy cold, it tasted good. She had not been allowed to drink for years. She turned again, sure someone was near to her, but as she turned she saw Magda watching her, and she gave a nervous laugh. 'I have not been allowed to drink. I had forgotten how lovely it tastes. Are you all right?'

Magda was coughing, ripping open the newspapers. She withdrew an old wooden-handled carving knife, a knife with serrated edges, and snarled, 'You forgotten this?'

Vebekka looked at the knife, puzzled. 'I don't understand.'

'You don't understand, and you are not Ruda? And you didn't come bleating to Mama? Didn't come begging me to help you clean up? Help you to strip him, help you hide him? You couldn't even lift him, you had to come running to Mama, stuffing him into the kitchen cupboard? That perverted piece of shit still moaning and begging us to save him, begging you, begging me, but you couldn't do it, you were fucked up, so you started begging Mama – *you remember Magda now, tart?*'

Magda staggered slightly, heaving for breath again. Vebekka began to shake, both hands clasping her champagne glass. She could hear Louis shouting at her, he was dragging her to their car, she was trying to button her blouse, pulling at his hand. Where was it? Was it here? She couldn't remember. All she could hear was his voice as he pushed her roughly into the car. 'You tart! *You cheap tart!*' He had driven off so fast, the car tyres screaming, his face white with pent-up anger, shouting how he had been searching for her, and then he had pulled over and punched the steering wheel with his hands. 'Why, why do you do this?'

'You remember, tart? *Answer me!*'

Vebekka's head began to throb. She gulped the champagne. 'Did my husband tell you?' she asked Magda. She felt hot, the cramped office was stifling and she began to sweat. 'Water, could I have a glass of water?'

Magda leaned back in her chair, clinking the ice cubes in her tall glass of neat vodka. 'What you had done to your face? You done something to your face . . . you had a nose job? That's what's different, you had some work, sweetface?'

Vebekka touched her face. 'Yes, yes . . . I had, er, surgery.'

Magda chuckled patting her own fat jowled cheeks. 'I knew it, I knew it, I can always tell . . . Ruda.'

'Please, I need a glass of water!'

Magda reached over to the champagne bottle and banged it down in front of Vebekka. 'You want a drink? You need a drink?' Her fat face twisted, and she leaned forwards and threw the contents of her glass into Vebekka's face. The vodka burned her eyes, and she knocked over her chair as she sprang to her feet, her hands covering her face.

Magda dragged herself up. 'Get the hell out, and think about this!' Magda waved the carving knife in front of her. 'Think about this, Ruda, then come back and see me, you owe me, maybe now's the time to pay me off. *Out – get out!*'

Vebekka stumbled to the door, fumbled, trying to open it. Magda pressed the button at the side of her desk. The door buzzed open, and Vebekka ran out, as Magda

379

picked up the phone and screamed for Eric to come in to her.

Magda's face was sweating, her eye make-up running. She didn't even give Eric time to shut the door, but snapped at him to follow the tart, find out where she was staying and report back. 'I want to know everything about that one, you understand me? Go on, get out!'

Eric straightened his hand-printed silk tie, smoothed his hair with his hands and made his way quickly to the club exit, not even acknowledging the calls from customers he knew. He thudded up the stairs, looked for the doorman and saw him examining two young kids' driving licences. 'You see a woman come out, dark-haired woman, few seconds ago?'

The doorman nodded, jerked his thumb along the street, and Eric took off, swearing loudly that he should have got his overcoat. It started to rain, coming down in a deluge; the doorman swore and huddled in the doorway.

Magda opened the small soft leather clutch bag. It contained only a gold and diamond embossed compact, a matching lipstick and a gold cigarette case. There was no wallet, no credit cards, nothing. She felt the lining, sniffed it; there was a faint smell of expensive perfume. 'You sure it was hers?'

The barmaid who'd brought the bag in nodded, said the woman had left it on the bar in front of her when she came into the office. 'OK, you can go.'

The girl departed as Magda took a magnifying glass from a drawer and examined the compact. She squinted, then lifted her eyebrows; it was gold, so the diamonds must be real. She checked the cigarette case; it too was eighteen carat. Maybe the bitch wasn't lying, maybe she was a baroness. Magda laughed, lit another mentholated cigarette, then turned the cigarette case over in her hand. She'd hang on to it and the compact; they would cover what the little bitch had stolen all those years ago. Hell, she sniffed, nowadays the leather bag would cost two hundred dollars. She opened a drawer and placed the bag inside, slamming it shut. It was funny, but she wouldn't have turned nasty, wouldn't even have wanted her debt repaid, so much water had passed under the bridge since then.

Magda sucked at her cigarette, the room stinking of smoke. It was the way the bitch refused to admit who she was that really pissed Magda off. Who did she think she was kidding? All the handouts she'd given, all the helping hands to the young slags; they always turned round and slapped you in the face. She thought about the girls and the pimps she had set up, buying their trailers out of her own pocket, all they had to do was stand outside them, pick up their customers. She paid off the police, she, Big Mama, covered everything, even the bitches' clothes – and they still robbed her when they could.

Magda picked up the carving knife. The blade was eight inches long, the handle carved but worn; Ruda probably stole even that, or found it in one of the bombed-out houses in the rubble of the old cellar she had lived in. In those days it was surprising what you could find, picking around in the rubble. Magda ran her fingers along the serrated edge; it was brown with rust. She had always given a hand, helped the kids get started, and somehow had always survived, even the total wipe-out of the city.

It was after the war that she had come into her own. She gulped her vodka, slowly feeling herself calm down as she remembered the good times. The Americans, the English . . . those soldier boys wanted women, young, fat, thin, they wanted them, and Magda supplied their needs, every sexual need she could fill from under-age kids, boys and girls. The children were roaming the streets, hundreds of them, hungry and homeless; they'd turn a trick for a meal, for a crust. That's how she got her nickname 'Mama', even that bitch Ruda had called her Mama.

Magda squeezed her eyes closed, could see Ruda as clear as yesterday. Ruda, no more than eight or ten years old, crawling with lice, dressed in rags, her skinny legs covered in open sores. She had been like a stray dog. No matter how often Magda and her boys sent her packing, she returned, hand out, begging. Magda had taken pity on her, let her scrub out the cellars she had started to convert into makeshift brothels. She clothed her, fed her, and the child never said a word. They never even knew her name for weeks – or was it months? She couldn't remember how long it was before the girl had started talking, and when she did she had an odd gruff voice, used a strange mixture of languages, Polish, German, Yiddish. They never even knew her real nationality; all they knew was that she had survived one of the death camps, because of the tattoo. Which camp they never discovered.

They nicknamed her Cinders, after Cinderella, and they wondered if she was deaf as she spoke so infrequently. Then one day she hit one of the young lads who was messing around with her, hit him with the broom, knocked him unconscious and Mama Magda had been called in to attend to him. Ruda had huddled in the corner, clutching the broom, and then in her odd gravelly voice said that her name was Ruda. Magda had clipped her hard, told her she had to behave herself if she wanted to be fed.

'My name is Ruda.'

Magda asked if Ruda had another name; she always worried about the police checking up on her kids, rounding them up. At every bomb-blasted corner there were long notices of missing children, and Magda always kept an eye on these lists just in case one of the missing children was working for her; if any were she got rid of them fast, even dragged them to the depots. If the children had families searching, they could cause a lot of aggravation; soldiers, convoys of doctors and nurses from all the orphanages being set up tried to get the kids off the streets. It was a difficult operation; they were no sooner picked up and housed than more took their place, the pitiful, bedraggled aftermath of war, diseased and sickly. Some kids simply died on the streets. The ones who knew their way around landed with Mama Magda.

Magda often asked Ruda if she had another name, but the child acted dumb. Then once she had lifted her wrist, as if the number was her surname. Maybe that was what had touched Magda, that the kid didn't even know her own name. Maybe that was what made her take such an interest in the skinny wretch. Magda began to let her work in her own apartment, washing and cleaning. She was all fingers and thumbs, but the good thing about her was she still didn't talk, just got on with her work. She put weight on, her hair was cleaned of the lice and her sores healed. She was never a pretty girl, but there was something about her, and Magda's men friends soon started to take an interest in her.

She would probably have kept Ruda on as a maid, but

she had one of the usual visits from the health inspectors, checking on missing kids. They had a long list with them of kids who had absconded from the orphanages. Magda listened to the names, shook her head. 'I check the lists, I make sure none of them are around here. I find one, you know me, I drag them to the depot. I'm known there.'

Then they asked if she'd come across a girl called Ruda, they had no surname and they were still trying to trace any living relative. She had been held in a mental institution for four years directly after the war. She was a survivor of Birkenau, would be recognized by her tattoo; they described her as possibly eight to twelve years of age. They had a place for her in an orphanage but she had run away. Magda said she had no girl of that age working for her; she was sorry she couldn't help but would keep her eyes peeled. For a moment she was scared they were going to start searching her squalid apartment, but they folded their papers.

'I hope, Magda, you haven't got any under-age girls working for you, because if so, we'll keep on coming, and we'll bring the *Polizei* with us.'

Magda had passed over a black-market bottle of Scotch, laughing and joking, telling them she drew the line at kids. 'You think I'd use kids? What kind of a woman you think I am?'

They had no illusions about her, but what could they do? They had no search warrants, no time to look properly, there were too many . . . Even the threat of the *Polizei* was empty, but they had to make a show, at least try to salvage some of the young children roaming the streets. They took their Scotch and left.

Afterwards, Magda had to search for Ruda, guessed she was hiding somewhere. She went into her bedroom and opened the wardrobe. Ruda was scrunched up inside. 'Don't send me back there, Mama, please. Please don't.'

'I can't keep you here, sweetface, they'll close me down. I don't want trouble. I said I didn't know you – they find out I lied and I get aggravation.' Ruda had clung to her, sobbing. It was the first time Magda had seen her shed a tear. 'I can't keep you here, but I'll see what I can do.'

Even though she now knew just how young Ruda was, she got one of the older girls to start taking her around the brothels, got her to break Ruda in. But then, after a few weeks, Magda was told that there was something wrong with the girl's vagina. She couldn't have straight sex. Magda had shrugged; she was still a kid, maybe too tight. She suggested they teach her a few other tricks, to get her working. 'Just don't bring her back, I don't want her here. If she can't earn her keep, kick her out.'

Ruda was taught about oral sex. She was grateful it didn't hurt her insides. She would do anything to prevent being sent back to the mental institution. She learned fast, and was given a small percentage of the money she earned. She ate well, and started living with a few of Magda's whores in a rundown house. The customers often asked for her, since she was exceptionally young. But she was forever stealing from them; no matter how often she was beaten she still stole wallets and food coupons. Magda put her on the streets, to see if that would teach her a lesson – out on the bomb-sites, giving head wherever there was a dark corner, a derelict truck or car. It was a step down from Magda's filthy cellars, at least they had mattresses there, but being on the streets Magda never knew just how much she earned, even though she sent her heavy thugs around to collect. Ruda could always lie, hide a percentage of her takings, even put up her price.

Ruda worked the streets for almost three years, scrimping and saving her money, never buying the black-market clothes the other girls coveted; she couldn't care less. She wore the same old brown coat Magda had given her and her underwear, opening her coat as a come-on to the soldiers. The few items of clothes she bought from secondhand dealers were neatly folded and pressed in a battered case she salvaged from a tip. She found a derelict house occupied by a few tarts, girls so low down they didn't even have a Magda to look out for them. These girls would fight and claw at each other to safeguard their lamp-post, doorway, wrecked car. The house had no electricity or running water and no roof, but Ruda's room was dry, and she slept on a burnt mattress she had also retrieved from a tip. She began to bring back clients to the room, but then one night a US Marine had wanted more than oral sex. When she had said she couldn't have straight sex, he had tried to rape her. Unsuccessful, he had buggered her. It had hurt her, made her bite the edge of the mattress to stop herself from screaming out loud, but after it was done, he gave her a handful of dollars, tossed them on to her naked body. The pain went, as she sat counting her money, realizing that she could ask more, she could do more.

Ruda used to pay for a bath a week at the local bathhouse. She always paid more for a private, number one bath – this meant she was the first to use the water. The bath was her only luxury; she saved, hoarded her earnings, dreaming of one day going to the United States. She plied any American soldier she met with questions about America. She was naïve enough to believe that when she had enough money saved she could just buy a ticket and leave. When she discovered that without documents, visas and a passport she could never go anywhere, she stayed in her hovel for two days, then went to talk to Magda.

'You want papers? Visas? You any idea how much that kind of thing costs, sweetface? There's lines, hundreds, thousands lining up waiting . . . go find somebody with papers, marry them – that's the fastest way you can get a legitimate passport. You'll have to wait in line, but you'll get one eventually.'

Ruda begged Magda to help her. Where was she going to find anyone who would marry her? Magda asked how much she had saved. Ruda halved it fast, knowing she would be suspicious. Even so, Magda asked if Ruda had been holding out on her, it was a lot of money. Ruda had opened her coat. 'I got no clothes but these, I don't cheat you, not any more. I don't smoke, I don't drink, Jesus Christ, Magda, I hardly fucking eat, I save every cent, I wanna go to America.'

'What's so special about America?'

Ruda buttoned her coat. 'I need some surgery, I can't pee straight, I get pains every time I piss. I'm not going to any hospital here, they'd drag me off to some mental hospital, but they can fix me up in America.'

Magda arranged for Ruda to meet with Rudi Jeczawitz, a cabaret artist, who knew certain people dealing in forged papers. Jeczawitz had been in Auschwitz and maybe he'd be prepared to help Ruda.

Magda made a deal with him; he needed a girl to help him in his act. Magda made a deal with Ruda. She wanted half Ruda's savings for setting it up, so Ruda was pleased she had not told Magda the exact amount she had saved. In some ways Magda was relieved she had got rid of her

– she had a girl working Ruda's pitch within the hour. She knew Jeczawitz had contacts, but as to whether or not he could get Ruda to her beloved America was neither here nor there. Magda pocketed the money, she did nothing for anyone for free.

Jeczawitz was not actually involved with forged papers. He worked the clubs, and anyone needing forged papers passed their requests to him. Then he forwarded the requests to a man named Kellerman, a dwarf.

Jeczawitz took Ruda into his act and for the rest of her savings agreed to marry her. That way she would have a marriage licence and a surname. Ruda paid, believing that it would only be a matter of time before her husband gained the visas and documents for her to leave for New York. Rudi Jeczawitz was in his late sixties, and crippled with arthritis. He had lost his wife and children at Auschwitz. He made no sexual approach to Ruda; it was a marriage of convenience. She cooked for him, washed his tattered belongings, and he moved into her derelict room. He had nowhere to go; he had been sleeping rough for years. He had a battered cardboard suitcase filled with his hoops and magic tricks – he had been allowed to keep them when he was in the camp. The officers had even found him a cloak to wear, and a wizard's hat. The case represented everything to him and he guarded it obsessively. He always wore his cloak, the hat was kept in the case.

It was Ruda's job to hand him the hoops, the hats, the silk scarves he dragged from his sleeves, night after night. The clubs were seedy, rundown, most of them only employing him because of his contact with Kellerman. If they were caught passing on illegal papers they could be closed down, but by using Jeczawitz as the go-between they could always plead innocent, and he would take the blame. After every show there would be some desperate figure waiting to speak to him.

One night, just before a show, he had been arguing with Ruda about preparing his handkerchiefs when she had grabbed them, called out the colours, and stacked them in a heap. He began to notice how quickly she could get them into order; he tried it out a few times, holding them up to her, then behind his back – she was able to tell him the order of colours. If he spread them on to a table, she needed look only once and then she could tell him each colour in rapid succession. He asked how she was doing it, and she had shrugged, told him they used to play games in the camp, it was a test they did.

He stared at her. 'You played games? My babies died, my wife died, thousands died – and you played games?'

That was the first time he beat her, took a stick to her and kept on hitting her. She took his beating, she was used to them, she just shut her mind off. No incoming pain signals registered on her brain. She just waited for him to exhaust himself. Bruised, she had gone on stage, hating him, but held him to his promise of getting her papers.

Jeczawitz beat Ruda regularly, and then he would weep inconsolably for hours, calling out names. Jeczawitz was as pain-racked as his wife, bleeding internally, his mental wounds never healing. He had no peace, but he lived somehow, day to day, dragging his old suitcase to the clubs and brothels. At night he passed on the pitiful messages, the folded money, the names. Some nights he was so drunk she had to help him to their room.

One night he was too drunk to make it to the club. Kellerman arrived at their hovel in his flashy clothes, and Rudi offered him Ruda for a night.

'I don't want your whore, hear me? I want names, money that's been paid to you.'

Ruda had followed Kellerman out on to the waste-ground outside their house, offered herself. He turned and spat at her; he never paid for women, he didn't want a whore.

'I want papers,' Ruda said. 'Can you get them for me? My husband said you could, I have money.'

He had stuck his thumbs into his braces. 'I can get anybody anything they can pay for. You got the money – I'll get you the visas, passport, anything you want.'

'I've got my marriage licence, I've got proof of who I am.'

He had laughed in her face, told her he needed nothing but money. He would supply a name, get tickets for anywhere in the world she wanted to go – all she had to have was money.

When she learned how much, her heart sank, but she tried to earn as much as she could. But then Jeczawitz's drinking got out of hand, they lost two spots, and she got him sober enough to do the third. Their audience that night was a rowdy bunch, all shouting and yelling. She was told they were performers from the big circus. Ruda discovered who the big man was, she even tried to pick him up after the show, but he had virtually knocked her off her feet before his taxi drove off. She had found his trailer, learned by now he was important. She was certain he could get her out of Berlin. She had pushed her way into his trailer and he had given her money, told her he was leaving, that he couldn't get her a job.

When she got back to her room she found Rudi huddled on the bed. 'Kellerman's been here. He's not coming back, they kicked me out of the club, Ruda.' He opened his arms up to her, wanting comfort, and she slapped his face.

'He was my only hope. You've ruined everything. Where is he? Tell me where I can find him!'

Rudi lay down, said there was no way Kellerman would do business with her, he hated whores.

She went to her hiding place, tore at the ground with her hands. Her tin box had gone. All the money she'd saved had gone. 'Oh, no, please – please tell me you didn't take my money, please tell me you didn't.'

He hung his head, shamefaced. 'I owed Kellerman, I had to give him money, it had been paid to me. I'm sorry, I'm so sorry—'

She punched him, and he fended her off. He screamed out that Kellerman had a place in the Kreuzberg district, that was all he knew. He never went to his place, Kellerman always contacted him. He began to cry, covering his face with his hands, blubbering his children's names.

'Shut up. I don't want to hear about your fucking children, your wife, your mother – you survived. *You're alive!*'

He sat up. 'No. I am dead, I wish to God I was dead, like my babies, my wife – oh, God, help me, why did they have to die?'

Ruda smirked at him. 'You made them all laugh, didn't you, playing out your stupid tricks, Mr Wizard? What else did you do, huh? With your act you had to do something else at the camps. You think I don't know? *You named names . . . you gave those bastards names. You killed your own babies, you bastard!*'

'So help me God I did not!'

Ruda danced around him. 'Liar, why would they let an old man live?'

He reached for his stick, but she snatched it from him, started thrashing him, and he fought back, kicking out at her. He raged at her, screaming, 'You played games, you were his children, in your pretty frocks. I saw you all, I saw you all fat and well fed. My babies died, but you—'

Her rage went out of control. How could he know what they had done to her, what they had forced her to do? She kept on hitting him with the stick, over and over. She hit his head, his weak bent body. She was panting, heaving for breath, but at last he was silent, and she began to panic. She felt for his pulse – and then ran out.

Magda could hardly understand what she was saying, begging her on her knees to help, asking what she should do – somebody had to help her. 'Mama, please, he lied to me, he took all my money, and he never got me papers – all my money – please, please help me. He said he would go to the *Polizei*, tell them about you, tell them about the forged papers, he's really sick.'

Magda sighed, threw on her coat, said she would look at the old bastard, get a doctor if he needed one. 'This is the last time, Ruda. You don't come to me for anything ever again, understand?'

Magda looked over the old man. He was alive, just, but she doubted that he would last long. She told Ruda to strip him and stuff his clothes into his case. Ruda did as she was told. Magda began to collect all the pitiful possessions from around the room, scooping everything into an old sack. She then opened a cupboard. Jeczawitz moaned, his eyes opened, and he begged Magda to help him. She gestured for Ruda to grab his legs, and they heaved him into the cupboard, drawing his legs up, pushing and shoving him into the tiny space.

'He's alive, Magda, he's still alive, what if he gets out?' Magda snatched a piece of rag, stuffed it into his mouth. 'Hold his nose – *hold his nose so he can't breathe, you stupid bitch!*'

Ruda pinched his nose as he twisted, made weak attempts to push her away, and then his chest heaved, once, twice . . . still Ruda held his nose, then he gurgled. There was no more movement. He was dead. Magda looked around the room, saw the old knife, picked it up. 'Use this, cut it out.'

Ruda was panic-stricken, not understanding.

'The tattoo, his number, they can trace who he is. Cut it off his arm, and hurry up. I'll take his case, dump it, just clean everything out, cover him up, shut the door.'

Ruda averted her face as she sliced into his frail arm, hacking at the skin. The knife was serrated, it seemed to take a long and terrible time. Magda shouted for Ruda to hurry. 'Gimme the knife, come on, hurry!' She tied a knot in the top of the sack.

Magda left Ruda, telling her to make sure to leave nothing that could be traced back to her. Ruda cleared everything up, and pushed the cupboard door shut, pressing her body against it. His hand was caught between the doors, and she had to open them again. Then she saw his old cloak and threw it over his head, slamming the doors shut. She got a block of wood and dragged it against the cupboard, then bricks, anything she could lay her hands on. She scrabbled in the filth and dirt. Ripping up newspapers, she lit the fire, stacking wood on top of the papers. She heaved the heavy broken door to the room closed, and prayed the fire would ignite.

The fire smouldered, and it was the smoke that eventually drew the attention of a passerby. The fire was extinguished, having only partly gutted the room. Anything of value left intact was swiftly taken, and a new occupant was ready to take over the squalid blackened room, but then it was boarded up, as unsafe. The dead man would remain undiscovered for weeks.

Magda seemed almost surprised when Ruda showed up; she poured her a vodka, neat. Ruda was still shaking, thanking Magda, grovelling to her, saying she would do anything – she would work for free if that was what she wanted. Magda laughed, told her she just wanted her gone, that she should clear out fast.

'I've no money, I've nothing.'

'That's how you came, sweetface, so that's how you leave. I reckon I've done more for you than for anyone else in my life, why I dunno, but I'm a Gemini. What star are you?'

'I dunno, I don't know when I was born, we were in hiding when they took us, my sister—'

Magda cocked her head to one side. 'You got a sister, sweetface?'

Ruda felt icy cold, as if her body was slowly freezing over. She couldn't speak, the room began to spin. 'Sister? Sister?'

When she woke up Magda was sitting next to her and she was lying on her red satin bedcover. 'Jesus Christ, sweetface, where in God's name have you been? You went out like a light. I've had smelling salts under your nose, even lit a feather . . . you gave me a fright. I thought you were dead!'

Ruda smiled weakly and reached for Magda's hand. Magda held the dirty skinny hand in hers. 'You got to go, Ruda. I can't let you stay here, I want no more troubles than I got. You can have a bath, get some food from the kitchen, but then you are out.'

'Don't throw me out, Mama, please, please, I need you.'

Ruda had reached up, held the big fat woman, smelt her heavy perfume. She wanted to lie in this woman's arms, wanted her to comfort her, and Magda rocked her gently. 'I can't let you, it's too much of a risk, just get yourself cleaned up, like a nice good Mama's girl.'

Magda had cupped Ruda's face, and then kissed her lips. Her tongue thrust into Ruda's mouth, she was smothering her, pulling Ruda's hand beneath her skirts, between her big fat thighs. 'Oh, yes . . . yes, press your fingers inside me, Ruda, yes . . . yes!'

Ruda let the woman paw her body, rip off her cheap dirty clothes, lick at her, and when Magda began to peel off her own tent dress, when she saw the mounds of flesh, the mountainous breasts released from their brassière, she closed her eyes. She felt nothing but revulsion, but Magda kept on talking, kept on telling what she wanted her to do, her breasts flattened against Ruda's face, as she demanded she be sucked. She wanted her nipples sucked like a man's cock, she knew how good Ruda was, all the men said she was the best.

Magda sweated and moaned, and Ruda pressed and could feel the wetness dripping from Magda, seeping down her thick thighs. She began to moan and groan as she climaxed, and then she sighed, her body shuddered. Ruda prayed it was over, she could hardly breathe.

Ruda had to wait for Magda to bathe before she was

allowed to wash. Magda tossed a few clothes from a trunk, told Ruda she could have them. They were good clothes, hardly worn, and Ruda clutched them tightly. Magda was dressed in one of her tents, slipping on gold bangles, and redoing her make-up. 'Go on, sweetface, get yourself all cleaned up and out of here. When you're through, come into the office. I'll give you some money, don't expect a lot, I need every cent I earn, but I'll see you have enough to get to another big city, maybe give you a few contacts.'

Ruda slipped into Magda's water in the bath, it was still quite warm, and she soaped her body, leaned back. She dreamed of the lion tamer, dreamed of Luis Grimaldi. She had to get to America, she had to find Kellerman, she had to find Luis Grimaldi wherever he was.

She buttoned up the dress: it was too short and the neckline gaped on her thin shoulders. She had on a pair of silk camiknickers, the crotch hung low and they were many sizes too large, but they were silk. She pulled on the nice checked coat with padded shoulders, then crossed to the dressing table to brush her hair and see if she could find a safety-pin to fix the neckline of her dress. She looked over the powder-strewn dressing table, with pots of cream and make-up jars littered everywhere. There was a large box of coloured beaded necklaces and cheap bangles, but no safety-pin.

Ruda inched open the small drawer beneath the mirror; a leather jewel-box was open. She stared at the rows of rings, picked one up and squinted at the shaft. It was gold. She looked at the rings again. They were Magda's famous diamonds, the rings she wore on every finger.

Ruda took a handful, then started for the door. She went back and took a necklace, stuffing it into her pocket.

Her heart was pounding. She eased open the door and crept down the stairs, past the kitchens, past the lavatories. She saw no one, but as she reached the entrance to the club she heard voices. Magda was giving the barman hell about not watering the drinks enough.

She was out and down the street, running in a panic, not sure which way to go, or where. She kept putting her hands into her coat pocket, making sure the rings were there.

She returned to a club where she had worked with Rudi and spoke to the manager who gave her the once-over. She was looking very classy – he fingered her coat. 'Found yourself a rich American, have you?'

Ruda smiled. 'No, something better. I got people, a family with money, and they want a contact for passports.'

The manager shrugged and said he couldn't help her; he knew of no one dealing in any foreign documents or currency.

'Kellerman. I want to talk to Kellerman. I know you know him and I know he's somewhere in the Kreuzberg district. Now you tell me, or I tip off the authorities. I know this club is a contact drop . . .'

Ruda found Kellerman sitting in a bar playing poker. It had been a long walk, four hours. She didn't have money for a taxi, even for a bus. He didn't recognize her, and she didn't remind him of where they had last met. He took her into a back room and eyed her, leaning against the wall, like he was some American movie star – all three feet of him.

'So what do you want?'

'Visa, passport, ticket to America.'

He laughed out loud. 'Oh, yeah, what makes you think I can get them?'

Ruda sat down and swung her leg. Her legs were good and she inched up her skirt. 'Friend told me. I got something to trade.'

Kellerman touched her knee. 'Baby, if it's your cunt, forget it. What you want costs a lot more than a fuck.'

'Maybe I've got a lot more . . .'

Kellerman shoved his hands into his tiny pockets. 'Let's see what you got.'

Ruda was no fool, she had already stashed the bulk of the stones under a broken-down truck outside the bar. She brought out a couple of rings and held them in the palm of her hand. Kellerman picked one up, examined it, then prodded her palm with his short squat finger. 'Good stones . . . but this isn't enough.'

'I have more, a lot more, and I've got a marriage licence.'

'You'll need a birth certificate, inoculation, visa, passport, then a ticket.'

Ruda deflated. How much was this going to cost? She held out her hand again. 'I've got more, a necklace, diamonds. How much do I need?'

Kellerman touched her palm again, and then drew up the sleeve of her coat. He saw the tattoo. She tried to withdraw her wrist, but he held on to her. ''S OK, I won't hurt you. Where were you?'

Ruda bowed her head. 'Does it matter?'

'I guess not, all that matters is you survived, eh, I'm not prying, see, I got one too.' He pulled up his shirt-sleeve. Then he flushed and pulled his cuff down. 'I don't show it to anybody. I was at Birkenau.'

'So was I . . .' She virtually whispered it.

He looked up into her face, reaching to touch her cheek with his short stubby hand. He had no need to say a word, there was mutual understanding in their eyes. It was not compassionate, or loving, it was a contact. Ruda bent down, to kneel, and he cradled her in his arms. Still they did not speak, and it was Kellerman who broke the embrace. Stepping back he said, softly, 'You never get down on your knees to anyone. Look at me, show me a fist, show me some fire in those eyes. I'll get us out of this shit. Get up, up on your feet, girl.' He began to pace up and down, strange blunt, short steps. 'We got to find a buyer first, sell the stones, turn them into cash, then we can do the deal. If you got more like the ones you showed me, we can get enough.'

'We? I don't understand, what's with this we?'

He gave her a cheeky wide smile. He had perfect white teeth, his face was cherubic under the thick black curly hair. 'Yeah, that's the deal – Ruda, you said your name was?'

'Yes, Ruda—' She could not mention the last name.

'The deal is, Ruda, I get the documents, make all the arrangements, but I want to come with you. We both go to America, and I'll get us a licence. We get married, you go as Ruda Kellerman, it'll make it a lot easier. I already got my papers, I just never had enough dough to get out of this shit-hole.'

She hesitated, and then smiled. He looked up at her. 'You know, when you smile it changes your whole face.'

'Same could be said of you.'

He chuckled. 'I guess maybe we've neither had too much to smile about, but have we got a deal?'

She nodded, but then held up her hand. 'But it's just a marriage of convenience, right? And where the stones go, I go? Agreed?'

He laughed and then, reaching up, swung the door

open wide with a flourish. 'Let's go, partner, and America here we come!'

It had taken two months, a nerve-racking time. Ruda and Kellerman stayed together in his small rented room. He never made any advances towards her; instead they played cards together, and he started to teach her how to read and write. They felt safe with each other, they liked each other. He found out about the magician, and said she would come to no harm, he would take care of her. And he did. He pocketed a lot of the money for himself, but he kept his promise. He got them to America.

Magda had sent all her boys searching for Ruda, sure she would turn up on some street corner some place, some day. The days turned into weeks, months, and Magda had to admit she was wasting her time and money searching for the little bitch thief. But she never forgot Ruda: every time she slipped a ring on to her finger she remembered the little bitch thief. She had never told anybody of her part in the murder, but she had kept the knife – as a memento, a warning never to turn soft on any of her tarts, on anybody else for that matter. The knife had travelled from apartment to apartment, club to club, until she had stowed it away. She somehow knew that one day Ruda would come back, one day she would see her again . . . and when she did, she would think about cutting her throat open.

Magda ran her nail along the serrated edge. She had been right, she had come back. But when she had seen her . . . it was strange, she hadn't hated her, had really wanted to talk to her. She had been ready to forgive but Ruda had played a stupid game, pretending she couldn't understand German, that she didn't know Magda. Well, the Baroness, or whoever Ruda pretended she was, would be sorry. This time she wouldn't be able to hide away, there would be no place in Berlin she could hide. Remembering made her head throb and she searched for her tablets.

Eric slammed back into the office. He was soaked, his hair dripping wet. 'I lost her, she was going from club to club, she was very drunk. Then I went in one door, and she must have walked out another. She disappeared.'

Magda hurled papers from her desk. 'You fucking little queen, all you had to do was follow the bitch!' Her face was puce with rage.

'I followed her, I've been up and down the fucking streets. I'm soaked – it's comin' down in torrents out there!'

'Get out of my sight, you useless piece of shit!'

Eric leaned on her desk. 'I'm all you've got – you big fat cow. You haven't got a friend in the world, Magda. I am the only person who can put up with you.'

'There's the door, Eric, and that thing attached is the handle. Turn it and walk. Go on, I don't need you, I don't need anybody – I never have. I have never depended on anyone or anything but *me*! Because that's all I've ever had, *me. I made me and my money is mine!*'

Eric hesitated, and she laughed, her heavy phlegmy laugh. How many years had he put up with that hulk? But he had no other place to go, she kept him, and he had an easy life. Besides, she couldn't last many more years. She was eighty, maybe even more. So he laughed, and she held open her arms, her mammoth body shaking.

'Come on, make up, come and give me a hug.'

He let her embrace him, her beads clanking against his head. He could hear the rattle of her chest, her heavy hideous breathing that he had lain next to for fifteen years. She settled back on the cushions, and said she'd start calling the clubs, she'd soon trace her.

'Who is she? I mean, what's so important about her?'

Magda dialled, and waited. 'She stole from me, Eric. I was like a mother to that girl, and she pretended she didn't know me. Well, she's going to know who I am.'

Eric eased off his tie, removed his Gucci loafers with their little tassels. They were stained round the edges. Magda made call after call, club after club, getting more angry, breathier, lighting a cigarette, puffing and panting, describing Vebekka, even the clothes she had worn, down to the cape with the sable trim. She kept on saying it was urgent, she had to find her.

Eric pulled off his socks; his feet felt cold. He was so intent on inspecting his feet he didn't even hear anything strange; he only looked up because the room was so quiet. She sat well back in her chair, her head lolled on her bosom, a cigarette still burning in her fat hand.

'Magda? Magda?'

Eric inched around the desk, peering at her. The poodle suddenly started clawing at her leg, wanting attention. Eric took the cigarette from her fingers, stubbed it out. He called her name again, then felt for the pulse at her neck. He withdrew his hand and gave her body a little push. She slowly sagged to one side, and her arm slid from the desk and hung limply over her chair.

He gave a brief, dry laugh like a hiccup, and quickly covered his mouth. He shooed the dog away and it scuttled beneath the desk. He was about to rush out of the office when he remembered he was barefoot. As he slipped his feet into his loafers, he had another good look at Magda and giggled. It was his club, all his now, and he wanted to hug himself.

The phone rang. He hesitated, deciding whether or not to answer, and in the end he snatched it up. It was the barman at the Vagabond Club returning Magda's call. The woman she wanted to know about had just walked in. 'It doesn't matter, Magda's dead,' said Eric. He heard the shocked voice asking how and when, and he beamed, but kept his voice to a hushed whisper. 'I have to go, I have to get the *Polizei*.'

'Jesus Christ, what happened?'

'Heart attack, I think.'

'My God, when?'

'Oh, about five minutes ago.'

'Oh, shit, will you be closing the club?'

'No . . . no, I don't think so, she wouldn't have wanted that. Nothin'll change, just that I'll be running the show from now on. So, if you'll excuse me . . .' Eric carefully replaced the receiver, looked at the peroxided head of his wife. He couldn't see her face – he was glad about that. He whistled to the dog, and grabbed it by the scruff of its neck. 'Your life, sweetface, hangs on a thread. You had better be very, very nice to me.' Eric didn't even notice the carving knife on Magda's desk as he walked out of the office.

CHAPTER 15

VEBEKKA EASED her way to the bar. This was the third she had come to. The champagne had dulled her senses, she was confused and disorientated but she wanted something, anything, to wake her. The rain had begun again, a downpour. Her hair was wet, her cape soaked, but she pushed her way through the customers, calling to the barman.

She felt a man brush against her. He smiled apologetically and then signalled to the barman, clicking his fingers impatiently. His heavy gold bracelet and thick ring gleamed, his cheap suit and white polyester shirt were picked out in the fluorescent light.

'It's raining again?'

He said it pleasantly and smiled, his teeth as white as his shirt. She could see speckles of dandruff on his shoulders, and she giggled. 'I don't speak German, I'm American – or French.'

He spoke in pidgin English, leaning his elbow casually on the bar facing her. He asked Vebekka if she would like to drink with him. She nodded, asking for champagne. He hesitated, and moved closer.

'It's very expensive here.'

She looked at him with a half-smile, and asked for a

cigarette. He patted his pockets in search of his packet but she leaned against him, slipped her hand into his trouser pocket, withdrew the cigarettes and giggled. Confident, he slipped his arm around her shoulders and then, as the barman came over, asked for champagne.

She drank the entire glass in one gulp and banged it on to the bar.

'Let's sit down.'

She shrugged and wandered off. Taking her hand, he guided her to a booth and she tossed her cape on to the seat.

'What's your name?'

'Vebekka.'

She drank another glass, again gulping it down as if it were water. He moved alongside her; his hand began to feel along her thigh. She suddenly felt sick, and she pushed his hand away, mumbling that she needed to go to the bathroom. He eased her past himself, feeling her thighs and backside. She stumbled, and he caught hold of her. 'Maybe you need some help . . .'

They headed towards the door marked 'Toilets', and by this time he had one arm around her, the other feeling under her cashmere sweater. The door led into a small corridor, ladies' and men's toilets to either side.

Vebekka staggered into the ladies'. She vomited into the toilet, the room began to spin, her legs went from beneath her. She swore, pushing herself up against the wall. She began to pant, trying not to be sick again. The cubicle door opened – she hadn't bothered to lock it.

'You OK?'

'I have to go. Can you call me a taxi?'

He closed the door behind him and locked it. 'Sure . . . in a few minutes.'

She didn't even attempt to stop him pulling down her panties, heaving up her sweater, she just leaned against him. He undid his flies and pulled her hands to hold his penis. Her head lolled against him, and he rammed her against the wall. She half laughed: it was as if she was on a train, her back thudding against the wall. She kept on half laughing, as he forced himself inside her. It was over, and she laughed louder. He buttoned up his trousers, listened in case anyone had come in, and then unlocked the door.

'You call that a fuck? When's the next train through here?' She laughed loudly, and then slowly slid down the wall, her underwear round her ankles. The tiles felt nice and cool; she lay down and rested her cheek on the nice cold tiles.

She was hauled to her feet. The man literally dragged her out – she was only semi-conscious. He dumped her in the corridor and went back into the club. He crossed to the bar, told the barman there was a drunken woman lying outside the toilets, went back to the booth, snatched his champagne bottle and made his way out.

The barman crooked his finger to the bouncer hovering at the main club entrance.

Vebekka was thrown out of the club, fell into the gutter, staggered up and stumbled away. She managed to pull her pants up, but she had lost her cape and her sweater was still half off. She kept on walking in the pouring rain. She stopped and looked upwards, holding her mouth open to catch the water: she felt almost happy.

Three skinheads passed and, seeing she was drunk, began messing around with her, pushing and shoving her until she fell against a wall. She put up her hands in a pitiful attempt to save herself, but one of them kicked, kept on kicking her, called her a filthy tart, and they walked on.

Vebekka sat hunched for a while, and then helped herself up by the wall; she began to be violently sick again.

The Baron slammed the taxi door. Helen didn't ask if he had found Vebekka, but instructed the driver to go to the next club he knew of: so far they had been to four, each one more tawdry than the last. They sat in silence, the Baron clenching and unclenching his hands as Helen stared from the window, glancing this way and that in the hope of seeing Vebekka. Then she leaned forwards and asked the driver to stop. Turning to look out of the back window, she could see the reeling figure stumbling along. Helen shouted, 'We've found her!' She was the first out, catching Vebekka in her arms as she fell again.

The Baron took off his coat and wrapped it around his wife. 'Put her in the back.'

Vebekka rested her head against Helen's shoulder.

'Dear God, look at her face. Have you got a hankie, Louis? She's bleeding.'

He snatched his handkerchief from his pocket. 'Aren't we all? Here.'

Helen gently dabbed the cut on Vebekka's forehead. 'She's been drinking.'

'I would say that is obvious.'

They arrived back at the Grand Hotel, Louis and Helen holding Vebekka between them; they almost had to carry her in. The manager rushed forwards, his face concerned, and the Baron brushed him aside. 'My wife fell, but she is all right. Just call the lift please.'

407

The lift operator stared hard: the woman was so drunk she virtually fell to her knees. He eased open the lift gate and stepped back. The Baron scooped up Vebekka in his arms and Helen hurriedly opened the doors to their suite. She followed Louis to the bedroom, and he called out for Hylda, dumping Vebekka on the bed. She moaned, and turned her face into the pillow.

Helen tapped on Hylda's door, and she whispered she would only be a moment, she had changed for bed.

'It doesn't matter, Hylda, just put on a dressing-gown. It's the Baroness. She . . . she's had a little accident, she fell.'

Helen rejoined the Baron, who stood staring down at his wife. 'Look at her, take a good look, Helen. So much for your damned doctor.'

He had such fury building inside him that he had to walk out – he couldn't speak to Hylda. He didn't even want to face Helen, but she followed him out, closing the door behind her. 'Hylda's bathing her, she's bruised all over her stomach, as if she's been kicked. Louis? Did you hear what I said?'

He stood with his back to her, his hands in fists at his sides. 'She stinks like a whore.'

Helen poured a drink, asked if he wanted one, but he shook his head. She sighed. 'I blame myself, the moment we knew she had left the hotel we should have gone out and searched. We wasted time.'

He whipped round. 'Have you any idea how many times, how many nights I've had to go looking for her? Searching every seedy rundown club, every red-light district? She's been found in alleys, in back rooms, she's been fucked for the price of a drink, and tonight was probably no different. You smelt her, she smelt of sex and booze – vomit. She sickens me, disgusts me, she's been picking up men—'

'You don't know that!'

He looked at Helen as if she were an idiot. 'I don't? She has played these games for years – *for years!*'

'I don't think she knows what she's doing. Are you asking me to believe she *likes* what she has been doing? Likes to be beaten up, kicked . . . She looks as if she's been kicked.'

He snapped, 'That's what she goes out for, Helen, she wants to be beaten, she *wants to be treated like a whore, she likes it – she is a whore!*'

Helen faced him, becoming really angry. 'Don't shout at me, Louis. I'm right here, OK? No woman likes to be treated like a whore – that is a male chauvinistic, ridiculous statement! Women who work the streets don't necessarily like what they are doing.'

'Oh, please, Helen, don't. Don't give me your psycho-analytical theories, I don't want them tonight, I don't want them period.'

'It is not a theory, it's a fact. No woman likes to be beaten, but if you beat her long enough, you will—'

He gripped her tightly. 'I have never beaten, struck or hurt her, I have had reason to, God knows, I have had reason, you don't understand . . .'

'I am trying to.'

The scream made them both freeze. Helen ran to the bedroom, as Hylda ran out. Her face was stricken. 'It is happening again! Please—'

Vebekka was rigid, her hands clenched, her teeth clamped together. The colours were cutting across her mind, terrible bright flashing colours, reds, greens . . . and she felt each flash. They kept on coming, blinding, as if her brain was going to explode . . .

Helen tried to talk to her, but the pain was so intense Vebekka didn't know who was there. All she wanted was the pain in her head to stop. Louis went to the other side of the bed, leaned over his wife, and she rose up. The scream was low, as if trapped inside her, her hands were like claws as she hit out, attacked the pain, clawed at the pain. Louis backed away, his hand to his cheek. She had scratched his face, drawn blood. Helen ran to the door, shouting that she would call Dr Franks. Vebekka was thrashing at the bed, her body rigid.

Hylda was terrified, she hung back at the door, shaking, holding one hand in the other. Helen called Franks, who said he would be there within half an hour, then slipped her arm around Hylda, whispering that she could go back to her room. Hylda clutched her hand. 'She bit me, she bit my hand!'

Helen forced Hylda to show her hand, and was shocked – the toothmarks were clear, the blood forming in deep red bruises. 'Dear God! Run cold water over it, Hylda, and I'll get you a bandage.'

Louis stood at a distance from the bed, searching his pockets for his handkerchief, then remembered he had given it to Vebekka in the taxi. He drew out a tissue from a box on the dressing table and dabbed his face. He stared at Helen in the mirror.

'Franks will have to take her into his clinic. I'm finished, Helen, this is it.'

Helen nodded. 'Yes, yes, I think so too. I'll pack her things, maybe if I call him back now I can catch him before he leaves. Perhaps he will be able to make arrangements tonight.'

The first spot had made even Schmidt stand and applaud. Ruda was on form – she was brilliant. She had been flushed with excitement as Grimaldi had helped her change. 'Ringling's scout's in, did you know, Luis?'

He told her he did. 'You got them to their feet. It was the cartwheel – you should have seen Zapashny's face, he was open-mouthed. I could feel his envy!'

She began to redo her make-up. 'Zapashny? What's he doing here?'

Luis laughed. 'Getting jealous! I've heard Gunther Gebel is retiring. They must be looking for someone to replace him at Ringling.'

She turned in a panic. 'Oh, God, he's not here to replace me, is he?'

'Don't be stupid, you'll see them coming here in droves to get to Ringling's man – get him to see their acts, bribe him, you know the scene.'

Ruda brushed her hair, her hands shaking. Luis held out her black shirt, but she pushed it away, drawing on her tight black jodhpurs. She stamped into the gleaming, polished boots, then held out her arms as he eased the shirt over her head, careful not to disturb her hair. She buttoned the collar. 'God, I'm so nervous. This is supposed to be a dress rehearsal!'

'Everyone else will be nervous, too, you can bet on it. You look wonderful! Now – make them get on their feet for the next spot. You pull it off and we'll be in New York, guarantee it!'

411

Ruda checked her appearance and tightened the wide black leather belt. She breathed in deeply, forcing herself to relax. All in black, her hair drawn away from her face, her eyes thick with black eyeliner, she looked like a cat herself – her strong lithe body was taut with nerves.

'OK, I'm ready. How long have I got?'

Luis checked his watch, told her she had plenty of time. All the acts were running over time, everyone playing to the visitors, pulling out the stops. She pulled down her shirt, seemed to give herself a small nod of approval. 'OK, I'm ready.'

Luis stood back and gave her a smile. 'Good luck! I'll be right by the ringside. You'll need an umbrella, it's pouring.'

Ruda carried a large black umbrella and carefully side-stepped the puddles as she hurried to the tents. Luis ran from the trailer and entered the big tent via the audience flaps. He made his way down to the ringside and sat waiting. The clowns were throwing their foam-filled buckets, chasing and tumbling, skidding on the plastic protective floor covering, an electric car bursting into smoke and flames as they reached their finale. The lights dimmed . . . It was strange to end in silence; usually the sound of thunderous applause accompanied the clowns, along with the high-pitched shriek of children's laughter.

Luis looked up to the viewing box, could see the Ringling Brothers' scout standing with his back to the ring, talking animatedly, drinking champagne.

The crew moved like lightning, clearing the props, buckets and ladders, rolling the floor covering, raking up the sawdust. As the ringmaster announced the Polish group of bareback riders, they virtually stampeded into the ring, twelve of them, wearing brilliantly coloured

412

American Indian headdresses, whooping and screaming, covering the last inches of clearance of the ring. Then the lights beamed on the riders, picking them out as they formed a fast-moving semicircle. Luis moved into position, saw their boys carrying in the cages, getting ready to erect the safety cage around the ring.

Dr Franks waited impatiently by the lift at the Grand Hotel, carrying a small medical bag. He barely gave the operator time to open the gates before he snapped out that he wanted Baron Maréchal's suite. As the lift moved up, he checked his watch, hoping the ambulance would arrive quickly.

Helen let him in, and they hurried to Vebekka's bedside. 'She's been quieter for about fifteen minutes.' Franks nodded, and Helen closed the bedroom doors. 'She left the hotel, she's been drinking.'

Franks held Vebekka's wrist and took her pulse, his face set in concentration. 'How did you let that happen?'

Helen blushed. 'She seemed so well, we were going to dine in the restaurant, and she was dressing. Next moment she had gone.'

Franks withdrew the bedclothes. 'Have you given her something? Anything to sedate her?'

'No, nothing, she was behaving as if she was having some kind of epileptic fit and then she calmed.'

Franks took out his stethoscope, examined her chest. 'How did she get these bruises?'

'We don't know. We were out looking for her and found her in the street.'

Vebekka moaned softly. Franks sat by her. 'Are you awake? It's Albert, Dr Franks.'

She opened her eyes and whispered softly that she knew who he was. He explained that he just wanted to examine her bruises, to make sure there was no internal damage. He rolled up her nightdress, saw the dark bruises on her belly, and gently pressed her body. 'Well, what have you been up to, huh?'

He eased her nightdress down, and drew the covers over her. She smiled sweetly. 'I went out. I had too much to drink.'

She looked past Franks to Helen, and turned away. 'Do you want to leave us alone, Helen, do you mind?'

Franks waited until Helen had left the room, and then he leaned close. 'What were you up to?'

The Baron sat impatiently in a chair, his foot tapping, waiting, waiting for Franks to come out of the bedroom. 'What in God's name is he doing in there?'

Helen looked towards the bedroom. 'They're talking.' The telephone rang and she answered it. The ambulance was downstairs, she told them to wait.

Franks came out of the bedroom, closing the door quietly.

'The ambulance is downstairs.'

He nodded, placing his bag down. 'I don't like to disturb her, she's sleeping now, she didn't need anything, she's exhausted.'

The Baron kept his voice low, afraid to wake her. 'I want her out of here, tonight.'

Franks sat on the edge of the sofa. 'She remembers everything she did, where she went, even the name of the clubs – Mama Magda's! Notorious old woman. She remembers, Baron . . .'

The Baron pointed to his cheek. 'She knows she did this?'

Franks shook his head. 'No, she remembers up to the point she was brought into the hotel. Would you like me to look at the—'

The Baron interrupted, 'It's just a scratch, but Hylda – she bit her hand! Don't you think you should call whoever is necessary and take my wife away?'

'I am not sure—'

'I am, doctor. I want her out of the hotel – tonight.'

Franks looked at Helen and asked what she felt. She hesitated. 'If I hadn't seen with my own eyes, seen how violent she was, how incredibly strong – neither of us could hold her down.'

'I see,' he said, not waiting for Helen to finish. He pursed his lips. 'You know I am loath to lose her to a hospital, be it mental or otherwise. I really think we had some interesting things come out of the session today, and I would very much like to continue.'

The Baron stood up and straightened his jacket. 'I refuse to take any further responsibility for my wife. If you wish her to be taken to your clinic, that is up to you. I want her out of the hotel.'

'Out of your life, Baron?'

'Yes. *Yes!*'

Franks nodded and looked at his watch. 'Very well, I will take her. She can stay at my clinic.' He opened his bag, and sifted through it, taking out papers. 'I will need you to look these over and sign them, releasing Vebekka into my charge. This will mean it will be my decision to certify her if, and only if, I feel there is nothing more I can do. If this is the outcome, you will have to cover all financial costs for her to be sent to—'

'Doctor, just give me the papers.' The Baron took them to the writing desk and searched for his pen. Franks looked at Helen, raised his eyebrow slightly and then went into the bedroom.

Vebekka was lying with her hands resting on the cover. She turned to him and smiled. 'I'm hungry.'

Franks took her hand. 'Vebekka, I am going to take you with me to my clinic. There is no need to be afraid, but I think it would be for the best.'

She closed her eyes. 'Oh, God, what did I do?'

Franks kept hold of her hand. 'Nothing too bad, but you need to be cared for, need to—' Her hand began to grip his tighter, tighter, he was astonished at the strength.

'It's coming back—'

Franks could not release his hand. Her body twisted, he tried to stand but she was so strong that she pulled him down beside her. She was panting and her body began to go into spasm. The pain in her head – it was coming again, the bright lights, the colours. Franks wrenched his hand free and ran to the door. He shouted to get the ambulance attendants up immediately, then he returned to the bed. She gave him such a helpless look, opening and shutting her mouth, unable to tell him what was hurting so much. Her hands were shaking as she touched her temples. On and on went the piercing flashes of colour.

Franks leaned over her. 'Tell me. Tell me. What is it?'

Her mouth opened wide, but she was becoming rigid. The terror on her face became a frozen mask, the cement was creeping upwards, reaching her knees, her belly, pressing down on her chest. Any moment it would reach her neck, and though she could hear Dr Franks, could see him, she could not communicate, could not tell him that the oozing thick whiteness was inching up into her throat, suffocating her. Franks saw her eyes glaze over but remain open, her hands become rigid. He turned with relief as the attendants carried in a stretcher.

Standing by the open doors was the Baron. He watched as they wrapped blankets around his wife, eased her stiffened hands to her side and then strapped two thick leather belts around the stretcher.

Luis moved closer to the caged arena. A massive single spotlight picked out Ruda. The tigers moved in a circle around her in the darkness. Twice she gave the command for the circle to break, for the tigers to begin forming the pyramid on the stacked plinths, still in the darkness. Their faces entered and disappeared from the carefully orchestrated spot, its light spreading inch by inch as the electrician saw the cats obey the command.

Ruda was sweating. She gave the command to Roja again and he kept on running, picking up speed. '*Roja, upppp uppp . . . blue . . . blue . . .*' Roja suddenly sprang back, and Ruda kept up the commands as, one by one, the tigers moved to their plinths. Blue, red, green . . . the spotlight spread and they were all in position. Ruda gave the command for 'Up!' and they sat back on their haunches, their front paws swiping at the air. She gave the command 'Down!' and they perched. With her left hand she gave Mike the signal to release the lionesses. They came down the tunnel within seconds, and she had to give her commands over and over again as they refused the plinths.

Luis could feel the sweat trickling down his back; he gripped the steel bars, swearing at himself. It was his fault, she had been right, the new plinths were putting them all off their stride. Luis looked up to the viewing room. Zapashny was deep in conversation with the Ringling Brothers scout, pointing to Ruda in the ring, back at himself. He would know she was in trouble, and Luis guessed he was taking pleasure in giving his professional opinion to the scout, eager to tell him how much better his own act was.

The lionesses had reached their plinths. Ruda gave them the command to rest their front paws on the pyramid above them. Once, twice, they refused, snarling and growling; the tigers began to spit, but they held their positions, and Mike got the signal for the two massive male lions to enter the tunnel.

Three positions on the top part of the plinth were still vacant. The two lions ran to either side of Ruda, as rehearsed and, as rehearsed, she looked to the tunnel, bent down to one lion as if asking him a question, back to the plinths: three places, only two lions. She walked to the tunnel, followed by one lion, turned back to admonish him – all rehearsed. As she looked down the tunnel, she got a push from the lion – rehearsed. She turned and wagged her finger.

The children would be screaming by now, hysterical with unabashed delight at the big lions teasing her. Ruda had her hands on her hips in mock temper; she gave the two lions strolling around their command to get up on the plinths, calling out down the tunnel.

It happened again. Both lions refused their jump, once . . . twice. Grimaldi wanted to scream out, but Ruda was holding her own, keeping calm. Again she gave the command; now they obeyed and Grimaldi sighed with relief. He looked up to the viewing tower, the Russian was staring into the ring; he had to know what exceptional training it took to retain the pyramid of sixteen tigers, four lionesses, two lions, all seated.

Ruda gave the signal for Mamon to be released. He came down the tunnel at full run and galloped in. As soon as he entered the ring he came to Ruda as if he were late, and lay down in front of her – again perfectly rehearsed. He rolled over, legs in the air. Ruda stamped her foot, pointed to the plinth, and Mamon rolled and rolled.

Unrehearsed, two tigers started to swipe at each other. She crossed over and shouted, and they turned on her. Again she yelled at them and they calmed down. Now she began the carefully practised act with Mamon, pointing to the top twenty-foot-high plinth. He looked up and shook his huge head, she wagged her finger at him. He turned round and made as if to run back down the tunnel. Ruda grabbed his tail, began to pull him back – all rehearsed.

Mamon and Ruda had a tug of war; all the while she was feeding the commands to the cats still waiting on the plinths. Mamon appeared to be on form, he didn't hesitate over a single command, he was on time, in position, even when she rode his back. To the onlooker, he was performing faultlessly, but Ruda could detect he was impatient, as if pacing himself; like any star, he seemed to be withholding an energy. She kept an eye on him, but he continued working well, right up until the final command for him to jump to the highest point of the pyramid. All the cats were seated, all under control, waiting. Ruda gave the command, then a second time. '*Red – yup* ... *Ma'angel, up, up!*' Mamon tossed his head.

Luis knew Ruda could not hold the pyramid formation

much longer: they were starting to pick up on Mamon's unrest. Suddenly Mamon backed away, prowled around the back of the plinths. He stared at Ruda from beneath the pyramid, and then went low, crouching on his haunches.

Up in the viewing tower, all three men were standing, looking down into the ring. Ruda stared angrily at Mamon, *'Red, red, red . . . Ma'angel!'*

He suddenly leaped forwards, as if he were going to spring at her, then he veered off, and like lightning he sprang from one step to another, up and up, until he was on the top plinth, up on his haunches. At a command they all rose up, some placing their paws on the plinth next to them. They looked like a mountain of brilliant colours. On command they moved again, jumping down in perfect order, and Roja led them out and back down the tunnel.

As rehearsed, Mamon held his position at the top. Ruda stood by the plinths, slapping the bottom one with her hand for Mamon to come down. He shook his head, refused to move – rehearsed. Ruda sat down giving a shrug of her shoulders to the audience as, behind her, Mamon moved down plinth by plinth. Ruda was giving him commands: *'Red – green – blue'*, but pretending she did not know he was directly behind her, within a foot of her. The children would always scream out, at this point, aided by the ringmaster, *'He's behind you!'*

Mamon eased his body back, balancing himself, and then gently placed his front paws on her shoulders. Ruda feigned surprise, turned virtually in his forelegs. Mamon was dependent on his own balance – in no way would Ruda be able to take his weight – it appeared as if he was resting against her. Slowly she slipped her arms around him in an embrace. The spotlight shrank down, down, until the two were framed like lovers, the huge lion's body swamping Ruda's. She gave the command for him to know she was stepping away, and then he came off the plinth. As she took her bow, she held her left hand out, towards Mamon's mouth. This was very dangerous, more dangerous than putting her head into his mouth – then the trainer would place a hand over the animal's nose, who wouldn't shut his mouth if he couldn't breathe! Mamon held her hand gently in his mouth, as she continued her bows. Finally, she pretended he was dragging her to the tunnel.

Blackout, the lights went, and the hands ran to dismantle the arena. The lights came on, Ruda took her bow, and then left the arena. Grimaldi looked up to the viewing tower, the scout from Ringling Brothers was applauding, even though they couldn't hear him as the box was soundproofed. Grimaldi punched the air with his fist.

Ruda made sure the animals were back in their cages, fed and settled down for the night before she made her way back to the trailer. Luis had helped take down the cages, stack and prop them up ready for the show the following night. He returned to the trailer with a bottle of champagne. Ruda came in, her shirt soaked in sweat, and he swept her up into his arms. 'They were applauding, they were cheering you!'

She smiled and slumped on to the benches. 'They asked to see me, want to see me right away but get me the bandages and the disinfectant, quick!'

Luis looked puzzled.

'Do as I say, they want me over there in a minute.'

Ruda unbuttoned her shirt cuff, removed the protective

wad beneath her sleeve. There were deep indentations of toothmarks, the dark bruises forming fast. 'Jesus Christ! Did he break the skin?'

Luis carried over the first-aid box and knelt down beside her.

'No, no, it's just bruised. It was really tough out there, they were all playing up.'

Luis looked up at her, and carefully pushed her sleeve up her arm. 'You mean your fucking angel was, you'll have to cut that part of the act. Jesus God – he could have taken your arm off.'

'But he didn't. Just put some antiseptic over it, then get me a clean shirt.' She wrapped a bandage around her arm, and got into a clean shirt, an identical black one. The old one was torn, Mamon's teeth had sliced the silk. She flung a coat around her shoulders; he went to get his, to accompany her, but she patted his cheek. 'They just want to talk to me, Luis, you wait here. I won't be long.'

He stepped back and flushed, saying he understood. He'd wait, maybe cook dinner. She smiled, said that she was hungry and then left him. He watched her holding the coat above her head against the steady rain.

Luis knew her arm must hurt like hell. She never ceased to amaze him, all the cuts and knocks she'd taken during training and never complained about. He stacked the first-aid equipment away, and then remembered the black tin box he had taken from her wardrobe. He had better replace it before she discovered it was missing. She'd know he had tried to open it: he had damaged the lid – maybe he could fix it.

Luis was about to press back the damaged lid without opening it, but then his curiosity overcame him. He took a screwdriver and began to loosen the tiny screws at the back. He inched the lid open. There was her wedding ring, still in its box: she had only worn it for a year, then said she had to take it off because she used the stick and whip and the ring cut into her finger. There was another wedding ring, maybe the one Kellerman had given to her; he had never seen it before. There was their marriage licence from Florida, still in the envelope, and then beneath that, tied up in a pale blue ribbon, were newspaper clippings, brown with age, neatly folded, as if treasured. Luis thought at first they would be reviews from one of her shows. He untied the ribbon; the cuttings smelled musty, the creases almost splitting the paper in two. He carefully unfolded the first, and stared at the headline: 'MENGELE STILL ALIVE IN BRAZIL'. He checked each tiny scrap of paper; every one of them referred to Joseph Mengele, the Angel of Death. He read snatches of the articles, one describing how Mengele had made sure the chimneys of Birkenau always blazed, heated by thirty fires. The ovens had large openings, one hundred and twenty openings, and each one could take three corpses at a time; they could dispose of three hundred and sixty corpses every half-hour – all the time it took to reduce human flesh to ashes. Seven hundred and twenty people per hour, 17,280 in twenty-four hours. Dr Joseph Mengele made sure the ovens were filled to capacity; he and he alone had the power to choose who lived and who died, to direct the terrified masses to the ovens with his murderous efficiency.

Luis felt his blood grow cold, as he read the dates and figures. May 1944, 360,000; June 1944, 512,000; July 1944, 442,000.

Ruda had written over some articles, in her childish scrawl: 'Joseph Mengele, Papa'.

Grimaldi refolded one scrap after another. Some were articles cut from journals, describing the diabolical experiments the Angel of Death had performed on tiny children, with or without anaesthetic, depending on his mood or the availability of medication. Article after article described Mengele's passion for furthering the Aryan race, this fanatical killer of babies, of women, of men – all defenceless, desperate human beings. He had embraced cruelty beyond a sane person's credibility, had been a madman let loose. One newspaper piece was around a small pebble, or stone, he couldn't tell; as he opened it, the cracks made the paper split in two, as if this particular piece had been read and folded, opened and folded. The article described the reported death of Dr Joseph Mengele, his body found on a beach in Brazil; the paper was dated 1976. The article discussed the possibility that it was not the real Joseph Mengele; forensic scientists had left for Brazil to begin tests.

Luis began to restack the clippings, wrapping them in the same way as he had found them, tying them with the worn ribbon. She had kept them as a woman would keep love letters, as if they were treasures. He carefully replaced each item in the tin box, rescrewed the back, and returned the box to her wardrobe. As he stepped down from the stool in front of her dressing table, he remembered some of the things she had said to him, often in rage: how he would never know what pain she had suffered, that the worst scars were those inside. He bowed his head and sighed, he had never even attempted to understand. But, he told himself, Ruda had never wanted to discuss the past.

He looked around the kitchen, opening cupboards to see what he could cook, wanting to do something special for her. He decided he would go out and buy some groceries from one of the all-night shops, maybe get some champagne. He felt a need to start afresh, wanted a second chance and, if she got the Ringling contract, they could have a new life. He wouldn't fight her any more, he would fight alongside her, for her.

He passed the meat trailer. The lights were on, and he went inside.

'Mike? I'm going out for some groceries, taking the jeep. If you see Ruda, tell her I won't be long.'

Mike grinned, said the word was already going round, the Ringling Brothers scout was having talks with Ruda. Grimaldi winked, said not to count their eggs before they hatched. He looked out, the rain was still pouring down. 'You got a spare umbrella, Mike?'

'No, guv'nor, I dunno where they all disappear to, but I got a rain cape you can borrow.'

Grimaldi shook his head, drawing his collar up. Mike continued chopping up the meat, saying that his hat was around somewhere – in fact, he had borrowed it. Grimaldi held his hand out. 'OK, I'll pinch your hat, give it back later.'

Mike shook his head. 'No, I said I used yours, that old black leather trilby. Ruda said she hated you in it, so she stashed it in here someplace. Caught me wearing it!' He looked at the row of rubber aprons on the hooks and searched under the table. 'I dunno where it is now. I tell you what, wrap one of the rubber aprons round your head.'

Grimaldi laughed, hunching his shoulders. 'I'll wrap it around yours, son. Never mind, I'll make a dash for it.'

Grimaldi ran to the jeep and started to drive out. He passed the lighted administration offices and slowed down to look over at the window. He could see Ruda with the boss, the Ringling scout ... they were drinking champagne, talking, and the Russian was with them. He stared for a while, he couldn't help feeling hurt, even rejected, but then he punched the wheel. 'Go get dinner, go and cook for your woman. Come on, get your fat ass into gear!' He had started the engine and was about to drive off when Ruda shouted out to him. He turned, she was running from the administration office, leaping over the puddles like a young girl. She yanked open the passenger door. The rain still poured down, but she wasn't even wearing a coat.

'I did it, Luis! *I did it! They want me to go to New York straight after this contract ends!*' She spun round, hands up, face tilted to the rain. '*I did it!* ... I did it!'

'And if you stay out there any longer you're gonna catch pneumonia. Come on – get in the jeep!'

She dived inside and slammed the door, flung her arms around him. 'Luis, I did it! He loved the act, he thought it was great!'

Luis said he would drop her off at the trailer, and go on in to pick up groceries, maybe some champagne.

'I've had champagne. Just take me to the cages!'

'But you're soaked.'

'I don't care, I want to see my baby. I want to tell him!'

Grimaldi drove to the animal tent, and she was out running to the entrance. 'Get me chocolate, *black chocolate*!' She turned back, as he started to roll up the window, and she cupped his face in her hands. 'I told you Mamon was a good guy, didn't I? Was I right?'

He had thought she was going to kiss him, for a second he'd hoped she would, but then she was off running full

426

pelt to the cages. Mamon leered at her from the back of his cage, bared his teeth, and she pressed close to the bars. 'Angel, ma'angel – what's the matter, huh?'

His eyes glittered, and then he went back to ripping his meat apart, his whiskers and his jaws bloody. She rubbed her arm, as if only now conscious of it. He had held too tightly; tomorrow she would have to rehearse him, rework him, make him know she was stronger than he was. She remembered always Luis's instructions: never let them know how strong they are, never let them know their own power, never give them the opportunity to know. Ruda stared hard at Mamon. 'Until tomorrow, my angel.'

CHAPTER 16

VEBEKKA'S ATTACK was unlike any other Dr Franks had ever witnessed. He was convinced it was not an epileptic fit, but he looked through her files to make certain. He was sure he recalled a reference to a test for epilepsy. He found the date. In 1979, the doctor had written: 'Nervous system characterized by periods of loss of consciousness, with serious convulsions. Epilepsy brain scan negative.' Franks rechecked: the date of the attack coincided with the newspaper incident, and he called the hotel.

Helen Masters answered the phone; the newspapers were in the package that had just arrived, but they had not as yet checked through them. Franks requested she do so and call him first thing in the morning. Helen replaced the phone, feeling inadequate: seeing Vebekka taken away looking so defenceless had upset her more than she liked to admit. Yet she couldn't talk to Louis – he had asked her to leave him alone. Helen knew that the package containing the newspapers was in Louis's room; she would leave it there until morning.

She sat for a while thinking about the meeting with Lena Klapps, then frowned and went to her desk. She had Ulrich Goldberg's phone number in Philadelphia. She placed a long-distance call to him. She told him that she was sure the Baroness was Rebecca, his cousin's daughter, that she was very ill, and they needed to know as much about her background as possible in an attempt to help her recover. The line went silent. Then after a moment Ulrich said that he did not understand what assistance he could give. 'My cousin and I were not on very friendly terms, it is a personal matter and one I decline to speak of to a total stranger.'

'Rebecca is very ill, Mr Goldberg.'

There was a pause, but then he told her that the rift had been to do with the fact that his family were Orthodox Jews. His cousin's wife Rosa had never converted, and they had not made any attempts to bring up Rebecca as a Jew. It became a matter of bitter contention between the cousins, who had once worked together but split up. David Goldberg moved on to more successful ventures whereas Ulrich failed, and when he asked his cousin for help, it was offered only on the understanding that they invite his wife to their house, that they accept Rosa.

'You perhaps cannot understand what this would have meant to me, to my wife and my sons to have to accept Rosa. My wife was the daughter of a rabbi, one of my sons was to be ordained. My brother left me with no option but to ostracize him. It was a sad day.'

'Can you tell me what Rosa was like?'

Ulrich hesitated, and then said sharply, 'She was a very cold, aloof woman. Exceptionally intelligent, but deeply disturbed. She felt we were persecuting her husband when nothing could have been further from the truth. She was exceptionally cruel to both myself and my wife about some small debt. She was bedridden for the last fifteen years of her life. She was not a happy woman – in fact, Rosa was a deeply unhappy woman.'

When Helen asked again about Rebecca, there was the hesitancy. 'I was told they had a great deal of trouble with her in Canada. She seemed to settle down when they came to the United States, but I saw her very rarely, maybe three or four times.'

'They adopted her?'

Ulrich Goldberg coughed, asked her to repeat the question.

'Rosa Goldberg could not have children, did you know that?'

'I believe so.'

'Then you *knew* they had adopted Rebecca?'

'I was never told that was the case.'

'Was it, perhaps, because she may have been adopted illegally?'

'I was not privy to my cousin's affairs. We lived here, we did not see my brother and his wife until they arrived in Philadelphia.'

'Mr Goldberg, I am very grateful to you for talking to me. If you think of anything which may help my patient, would you contact me? Can I give you my hotel number?'

Helen passed on the hotel and suite extension, and then almost as an afterthought asked how well he knew Lena Klapps. She was surprised when he answered that he had never met her – had traced her via Rosa Muller's address book. The only telephone number they had for Lena Klapps was at her workplace, the Bureau of Records. After the death of his cousin he wished to contact anyone who might know who was his cousin's heir. As he had not heard anything of Rebecca, he did not even know if she was still alive. 'As it turned out, my cousin left everything to Rebecca, and it was at his funeral that I last saw her. She refused to allow me to enter the house. At the funeral she spoke to no one, and when we went to hear the reading of David's will, she left almost immediately after she was told she was the only beneficiary. We were obviously disappointed, had a perhaps misguided belief that David would forget our past differences ... but he left everything to her. We knew he was wealthy, but the fortune was far and above anything I had ever contemplated. I believe her husband's lawyers settled the sale of the house and business.'

After Helen hung up, she began to pace the room. Louis had remarked on a number of occasions that his wife had inherited her father's estate. What he had never disclosed was the vast amount of wealth. Helen knew he had lied about not knowing Vebekka was really Rebecca. If his lawyers settled her father's estate, it was obvious that he had to know. She found herself wondering if Louis intended to divorce Vebekka, or simply have her placed in an institution so he would gain total access to her money – or had he access to it already? Did he control her fortune?

Helen's mind reeled, so many unanswered questions, and such unpleasant ones. She knew she had to speak to Lena Klapps knowing she had no home telephone number. She decided the best thing to do was get a taxi first thing in the morning before breakfast, before Lena went to work.

Helen jumped as Louis tapped on her door. He seemed almost embarrassed, and excused his interruption by saying he had seen her light was on and knew she was still up. He was very hesitant. 'I wondered if you'd like a drink – I feel in need of some company.'

Helen smiled, said he was not interrupting her, in fact she was glad that he had appeared as she wanted to read through the newspapers. Louis looked puzzled for a moment, and then remembered the package. 'Oh, yes, of course.'

'I promised Dr Franks I would check them through before tomorrow, he wants to know the dates. We can do it together.'

Helen followed Louis into his suite. He asked if she was hungry, and she realized that she was. 'Yes, maybe a sandwich.'

Louis picked up the phone and asked room service to send up some coffee and some chicken sandwiches, then went to get the newspapers.

They sat at the large oval table. Louis opened the package and took out five newspapers, chose the *New York Times*. 'OK, I was reading the front few pages, and Vebekka was reading the real-estate section. Helen? Helen, did you hear me?'

Helen stared at him, folding her arms. 'Why did you lie? You've known all along she was Rebecca Goldberg. I just don't understand why you have lied to me.'

Louis searched in his pockets for his glasses. Finding them, he slipped them out of their leather case. 'Haven't we been through this?'

She leaned towards him slightly. 'No. Why did you never tell me Vebekka was an heiress?'

His eyes flashed angrily over the half glasses, but he spoke with calm detachment. 'Perhaps, my dear, I did not think it was any of your business.'

Helen was stunned. 'Not my business? I see. Why am I here, Louis?'

He opened the paper. 'Because, at your suggestion, we brought Vebekka to Dr Franks.'

'And you didn't think it was *important* that I know who she really is? Louis, Ulrich Goldberg told me about the money, he said your lawyers settled the estate.'

'They probably did, and very well. They have cared for my finances since I was a child.'

The room service arrived and the coffee and sandwiches were placed on the table, but Louis continued to look through the paper, not acknowledging the steward or Helen as she poured his coffee and placed it by his elbow. She sat opposite him, and reached for the paper.

'If Vebekka is certified insane, institutionalized, will you gain access to her personal fortune?'

Louis still did not lift his head from the paper. 'It will be immaterial, there is not very much left, I have not given it much thought either way, and I would presume the costs of keeping her in a home, any kind of nursing establishment, would eat into what little money remains.'

He continued turning the pages of the paper, muttering that he could see nothing of any importance, or possible significance. His refusal to look at her or speak to her directly infuriated Helen. She suddenly reached over and snatched the paper. The Baron's right hand tried to retrieve it but knocked over his coffee, which spilt on him. He sprang to his feet swearing. 'That was a bloody stupid childish thing to do!'

Helen hit him with the newspaper. 'Was it? *Was it?*'

He stared at her coldly. 'Yes, it was.' He removed his glasses, placing them on the table, picked up a napkin and began to wipe the coffee from his dressing gown.

Helen patted the table dry with her napkin. 'I keep

trying to understand you, Louis. You knew all along Vebekka was David and Rosa Goldberg's child, but you never admitted it to me. You let me continue making enquiries, like an idiot, a total waste of my time. Now I find out your wife inherited millions – another small fact you deliberately did not tell me.'

Louis swiped the air with his hand and snapped in fury, 'Leave me alone, just leave me alone!'

Helen watched in exasperation as he slammed into his bedroom. She reached down to try to salvage the papers. The front page of the *Times* had fallen beneath the table. She was not really concentrating, but telling herself she should pack her belongings and leave. She could explain to Dr Franks.

Helen folded the page. It was stained with coffee and she dabbed at it with her napkin. It was a small article at the bottom right-hand corner: 'ANGEL OF DEATH FOUND'. Helen glanced over the single paragraph, which stated that Joseph Mengele, the most wanted Nazi war criminal, had been found dead on a beach in Brazil . . .

Helen began frantically to open the other papers, searching each page, tossing them aside, as Louis returned, shamefaced.

'Helen, I'm sorry. You are right, perhaps we should talk.'

She turned to him. 'Louis, I think I've found it. Remember you told Franks how terrified she was about a dark angel? You heard her sobbing that night, just after the newspaper incident. Look at the bottom of the front page.'

Louis looked at the stained paper, picked it up. 'What am I looking for?'

Helen leaned over his shoulder and pointed. 'Angel of Death, Joseph Mengele, it's mentioned in two papers, just small paragraphs, but it's all that links with her screaming, with her nightmare of the Dark Angel!' He scrutinized the articles as Helen paced up and down. 'If she was adopted from Berlin, maybe that is the connection, and I am sure she was adopted, Louis.'

He held out his hand to her. 'I did not know she was adopted, I *didn't* know . . . and I don't understand where all this is leading to, but if you think there is a connection, then tell me what to do.'

'Be honest with me. And trust me, you must trust me, because if you don't then there is no point in my being here.'

He kissed her hand, gave a small bow. 'I apologize, and believe me, I am truly grateful for your presence. I don't really know how I would have coped without you.'

He gave her one of his boyish smiles, and his hesitancy was touching, he seemed so vulnerable. 'I know how her wealth must appear to you, Helen. But my mother left me a small allowance – everything is tied up in trust funds for my children. When the money came, it was a relief, it meant I could care for Vebekka, continue to live as I always had, but my decision to have her taken away is in no way connected to her fortune – it's gone. In fact, I will be dependent on my sons for the upkeep of the château, the apartments. They in turn will need the added finances of their brides.'

'And your life, Louis? What about your life?'

He drained his coffee, returning the cup to saucer thoughtfully. 'I still have my allowance, I can sell the polo stable. It will break my heart, but if it comes to that, then

435

so be it. Now I think it is time I went to bed, if you will excuse me.' He slipped his arm around her shoulder. 'Goodnight, Helen.' He kissed her cheek lightly.

She walked towards her own bedroom, not even turning back as she said, 'Goodnight, Louis.'

Helen knew how easy it must be to be drawn into a life of luxury, the Rolls-Royces, the fabulous restaurants, the flowers and expensive gifts. Louis was a very handsome man, his light, almost careless kiss to her cheek made her realize that he excited and attracted her, too, and it would not be hard to take their relationship a step further. She knew he had mistresses, but she knew, too, that such a life could not satisfy her. What she had to face was her own loneliness: before she had been only half aware of it, always able to justify being alone because she determined it was her choice; she even made the excuse of being a very private person. 'You are so private, Helen, that no one even knows you exist!' She said the words out loud, to herself, to her own reflection in the bathroom mirror. She cleaned her teeth, washed her face, and returned to her bedroom – everything neat and tidy, the bed cover turned down in expectancy. She lay for a long while staring up at the ceiling. It was time she returned to Paris. This was her vacation, she had given enough of her time – and with very little thanks. But then, guiltily, she thought of Vebekka. It had been at Helen's instigation that Vebekka had come to Berlin; she was too deeply involved to extricate herself. But from now on she would distance herself from Louis.

Helen left the hotel very early the next morning. She did not wake Louis, but left a note saying she would meet him at Dr Franks's clinic and to be sure he took the newspapers with him.

She looked along the taxi rank, and found the over-talkative driver who had taken them to Charlottenburg. He was dozing in his Mercedes. She tapped the window, and got in beside him.

'Same address as before?'

'Yes, the same address. Lena Klapps. I want to get there before she leaves for work.'

'We'll do it easy, no traffic at this hour, we'll miss all the rush.'

Inspector Torsen was at his desk by seven-thirty. He began to plough through the vast amount of paperwork; there were more reports of cars stolen in the West and brought to the East than they could handle. He worked on until eight-thirty, then opened the morning paper. There was a large article on the front page with a picture. 'MAMA MAGDA DIES'. He read the article, turned to the next page, and then flicked back. Now there was a coincidence: he had seen Ruda Kellerman the same night Mama Magda had died – entering Mama's club. He scribbled a note on his ever-ready pad, and continued to read, checking on the time as he wanted to be at the records bureau when they opened at nine.

Rieckert appeared, with a black eye and plaster on his cheek. Torsen looked at him, asked if he had been in trouble. Rieckert slumped into a seat. 'Acting on your orders, sir! We tried to clear up some of the hookers working from the trailers, we warned them to clear off, get their trailers out, and the next minute four big bastards jumped on us – the girls' pimps – and they had iron bars . . . bloody beat up Kruger, he's in hospital.'

'Did you make any arrests?'

Rieckert swore. 'You must be joking – we only just made it into that station courtyard. We radioed for them to have the gates open. They chased us, were on our tail for miles, their car was a hell of a lot faster than ours, it was a big four-door Mercedes! We only just made it back in time, and they banged and hammered on the gates. Have you seen the damage they did?'

Torsen rubbed his nose. 'This is madness, are you telling me the pimps *chased* . . . *chased* the patrol car?'

'Yeah! Overtook us twice, it was a near thing, one got me through the window – I had to have a stitch, cut my head open!'

'Would you recognize them again?'

Rieckert sat bolt upright. 'I'm not going back there, they'd bloody kill me, they're huge blokes, musclemen!'

Torsen returned to his desk. He flipped open the paper. 'There will be war out there soon. Mama Magda's dead, last night, and most of those trailers are hers, so God knows what's going to happen now.'

Rieckert glanced over the paper. 'She must have been worth millions. I'm surprised nobody bumped her off before.'

'It was a heart attack, she was over eighty and the size of an elephant.'

'They open tonight, will you be using your ticket?'

'Pardon?'

Rieckert tossed the paper on to Torsen's desk. 'The circus, they gave us free tickets, you going? They open the big show tonight.'

Torsen had forgotten about the free seats, and he chewed his lip, opened a drawer and took the tickets out. 'I'd forgotten . . . Yes, yes, I think I will use my two.'

Rieckert left for the kitchen and Torsen called the

nursing home and asked to speak to Nurse Freda. 'I have two tickets for the circus . . . tonight, I'm sorry it's short notice, but I was wondering . . . if you aren't on duty, if you would care to . . .'

Freda shrieked that she would love it, and generated such excitement that Torsen went pink with embarrassment. They arranged to meet at seven.

He gave out his orders for the day, and said if he was required for anything urgent he would be at the records bureau. He left, taking one of the few patrol cars in good condition – to the aggravation of the *Polizei* instructed to check over the prostitutes.

Tommy Kellerman had been buried by a rabbi from the Oranienburger Tor area. His body was taken to the rundown quarter inhabited by the Eastern Jewish community. No one attended his burial. The plain black coffin was carried from the city mortuary before sundown, as Ruda Kellerman had requested. The costs for the burial were delivered to the station, and Torsen forwarded the receipt to Ruda Kellerman, care of the circus.

Vebekka had slept soundly and had eaten a little breakfast. She was in a small room, white-walled, with an old iron bedframe painted white. There was a white chest of drawers, but a bowl of fresh flowers gave colour to the room. The door had a peephole, and no inside handle. A white-tiled bathroom cubicle, with bath and toilet, led off the room, without a door. The room was devoid of mirrors, of any adornment. There was no telephone.

Dr Franks drew up the only chair in the room. 'How are you?'

'I'm fine, do I have to stay in this room?'

'Only for a little while, then we'll go into my lounge. You remember you were there yesterday?'

She nodded, it seemed years ago. Franks told her that her husband had called and he would be in soon after he had breakfasted. If she felt like it she could have a bath and get dressed.

He asked if she needed anyone to help her, and she shook her head. He said all she had to do was ring the bell by her bedside, and Maja would be with her in moments.

She rested her head back and sighed. 'They should never have brought me here. It's very close here, I feel it . . .'

Franks cocked his head to one side, and held her hand. 'Feel what?'

'I don't know, a presence. I've felt it before, but not this close.'

Franks threaded his fingers through her long perfect slim hands, soft, beautiful skin, perfect nails. 'Maybe we will find out what this presence is, send it away from you . . .'

She gave him a sweet sad smile. 'They've sent me away this time, haven't they? Ah, well . . . I suppose it had to come.'

'You are not away anywhere, Vebekka, you are here, in my clinic, until we sort things out. You do want me to help you, don't you?'

Tears welled in her eyes, and she turned away. 'I don't think anyone can help, I hoped . . .'

He stood up and leaned across her. 'I want more than hope, my dear. I want everything you want, want you to get well, want you to help yourself, help me to help you. OK?'

440

He returned to his office and picked up his notes, carefully transcribed for him by his son. Two passages he had underlined:

(1) Get me to lie down and talk to me, so I would be calm.
(2) Put her in a cupboard and throw away the key.

Vebekka's own words, describing what her mother had done and had told her to do. Franks was sure that the key Vebekka's mother had said to throw away was at the root of her problems. He was so engrossed in thinking through his approach for the day's session that it was a moment before he realized his phone was blinking. Baron Maréchal had arrived, bringing with him the copies of the newspapers Franks had requested. He told his receptionist to show the Baron in, a little irritated that he was so early.

Lena Klapps opened the front door while eating a slice of toast. Seeing Helen, she was about to slam the door shut in her face, but Helen put her foot across the threshold. 'I know this is an intrusion, but I had to speak to you. Please, I won't take more than a few moments.'

Lena turned and walked into the hall, pushing open the door. 'I have to leave in fifteen minutes. I have to get my bus.'

'I understand, but I can give you a lift to the records bureau in my taxi.'

Lena hesitated and walked out, calling to her husband to finish his breakfast. She returned carrying a cup of coffee, but did not offer Helen one. She stood with her

441

back to the large bookshelf. 'I told you everything I know. I do not see how I can assist you any further.'

'You have worked at the records bureau for many years? Is that correct?'

Lena nodded; she picked at a food stain on her skirt with her fingernail, the same grey pleated skirt she had worn on Helen's last visit.

'I have checked the hospitals for any possible record of your sister. You said she worked at one of the main hospitals just after the war, after she returned to Berlin. Everyone I spoke to referred me to the main records bureau. You head the department, don't you?'

Lena nodded, and continued to sip her coffee. When Helen asked how long she had worked there, she swivelled slightly in the seat. 'You have no right to pry into my personal affairs, Miss Whatever-your-name-is. I have told you all I know. Now, please, I would like you to leave.'

'If you refuse to help me then you leave me and Baron Maréchal no alternative but to make enquiries as high up as we need to go. I want to find out if your sister Rosa Muller adopted a child, I want to know the background of this child – I do not care, Lena, if the adoption was legal or illegal, all I am interested in is trying to help a woman who lives in a nightmare.'

Lena stared into her empty coffee cup. Two pink dots appeared in her cheeks, a small muscle twitched at the side of her mouth. 'We all have our nightmares.'

'No, no, we don't. But are you really telling me that a sister, a sister you grew up with, didn't make any contact with you when she returned to Berlin, didn't try to see you?'

Lena looked up, her eyes filled with hatred – whether

for Helen or her sister, Helen couldn't tell. She banged the cup down on the table.

Helen was losing patience; she didn't mean her voice to rise but she couldn't help herself. 'All I want is to know more of Rebecca's background, I am not interested in yours.'

Lena whipped round. 'Please keep your voice down, I don't want my husband to hear you.'

She clasped her hands together. 'No one has ever been interested in me. When I was a child it was always Rosa this, Rosa that – she was always the beautiful one, always the clever one. She had everything, looks, brains . . . She had everything, and you know something else? She was always happy, always smiling, like she had some secret, something filling up her life. My father doted on her, he worshipped her. She broke his heart.' Lena pursed her lips. Helen said nothing. 'She refused to listen to him. He begged and pleaded with her to break off her relationship with David Goldberg. It was very embarrassing for him, for all of us. My father was a very well-respected scientist, with many connections, my brothers—' She wafted her hand, as if unable to continue, turned her back, facing the bookshelves. 'I cooked and cleaned and waited hand and foot on him when Mama died . . . but he wanted Rosa, always wanted Rosa. She made a fool of him, a fool of all of us, but she refused to listen . . . and then . . . then she became pregnant.'

Lena remained with her back to Helen, her arms wrapped around herself. Helen had to know more. 'You told me Rosa had an abortion, but I need to—'

'It was not an abortion.'

Helen half rose to her feet: Rebecca was their daughter after all?

'My father and my brothers locked her in the house, and my father . . . he performed the operation himself, he sterilized her.'

Helen sat back, shocked.

Lena's hand shook as she patted the coiled bun at the nape of her neck, but she looked defiantly at Helen. 'This Rebecca is not my sister's child.'

Helen showed not a flicker of what she felt, pressed her hands flat against her thighs.

Lena moved closer, until she stood in front of Helen. 'I did lie to you, I did see my sister again. She was working at the main refugee hospital with some of the children picked up from the streets, picked up from the camps, from everywhere. It was my job to try to keep a record of how many, if they knew their names. My father was dead, my brothers dead. I lived in the cellar, in the rubble of our old home, for years . . . and I hoped . . . hoped she would one day come back. I saw her, and she was smiling, she was still beautiful, still happy, she was playing with a group of Jewish children.' Lena repeated the same wave of her hand, a dismissive wave as if she was shooing away a fly. 'She smiled at me, and then . . . then she drew this child forwards, she said, "This is my daughter, Lena, this is Rebecca."'

Helen stood up. 'You have a record? The child's family name? The adoption papers?'

'There were no papers, no documents. The child couldn't even talk. She was from Birkenau.'

Helen closed her eyes, pressed her fingers to her eye sockets. Suddenly she heard a loud banging, and her eyes flew open. Lena was hurling books from the bookcase.

'She left me, she left her family, she left me, and all I

444

have are these – these, and a broken-down man! Rosa was happy, she was always happy!'

Helen reached for her purse, picked up her coat. Lena began to weep uncontrollably. 'Why – why did you come here? Go away, leave me alone . . .'

Helen asked if she could take Lena to work, but she shook her head, wiping her face with her hands. 'No, just go away.'

One of the large medical books had fallen in front of the door. It was an old medical journal, and it was open to a picture of a man's head, his brain, with diagrams pointing to the front lobe. 'The World of Hypnosis'.

Helen picked up the book. 'Hypnosis? Lena, do you know if Rosa ever—' The book was snatched out of her hand before she could say another word. Lena held the book close to her chest, hugging it tightly. 'This was my father's – this was my father's book, go away . . . *go away*!'

Helen left, the door slamming shut behind her. She ran down the steps to the waiting taxi, eager to pass on her findings to Dr Franks.

Ruda was in high spirits, singing in the shower. She washed her hair and tied a big towel around it. She called out to Luis that she would only be a moment longer. He shouted back that coffee was on the table, he was going over to check the meat delivery truck, it had just arrived.

Ruda whistled as she sat down to breakfast – fresh rolls and black coffee; the newspaper lay folded on the table with a large bunch of flowers. Luis had made a card with 'Congratulations!' scrawled across it. She smiled and poured herself coffee. She bit into the roll, opened the paper – then slammed it on to the table. 'MAMA MAGDA DEAD'.

She read the article and leaned on her elbows, staring at the fat woman's face. Then she laughed, it was very fortuitous. With Kellerman dead, it was as though fate had suddenly started to turn good for her. She had the promise of a contract with Ringling Brothers, the show opened that night, she was feeling good and even Luis had remained sober, had seemed as pleased for her success as she was.

Ruda finished her breakfast, then took a pair of scissors and cut out the article. Folding it neatly, she got up and went into her bedroom. She pulled the stool up, and stood on it to find her black box, felt around the cupboard and withdrew it, putting it down on her dressing table. She reached down to fold back the carpet and get the tiny key, then straightened up, staring at the old tin box. She turned it round, saw the scratches on the hinges, the indentation where Grimaldi had tried to force it open. She had fitted a new lock after Tommy Kellerman had broken it open, now Luis had done the same. She knew it could be no one else. Luis.

She unlocked the box, knew by looking that the contents had been taken out. Her heart hammered inside her chest, she held up the small ribboned package of clippings. She slipped the new cutting about Magda under the ribbon, then relocked the box. She felt as if the contents were burning into her hand ... the memories began, like scars opening, bleeding ...

Inspector Torsen checked his watch, it was after nine.

He asked the receptionist again if he could be allowed

446

into the record room, and she apologized. Mrs Klapps had never been late since she had worked there, and she was sure she would have called in if she was not coming. She suggested Torsen have a cup of coffee somewhere. Torsen scribbled a note asking for both records to be ready for him, together with any record of a marriage licence between T. Kellerman and a woman of the same name, Ruda.

Torsen, having use of the patrol car, headed for Mama Magda's club; he wished to know who was taking over and if they could discuss the matter of the influx of prostitutes.

He pushed through the beaded curtain, getting one section caught in his lapel. Eric was checking over orders for flowers, and at the same time looking at coloured swatches of material for redecorating the club. Eric looked up fleetingly, then returned to his colour charts.

'I am Chief Inspector Torsen Heinz from the East Berlin sector.'

Eric turned and sighed. 'Not another one. The *Polizei* have been in and out of here all morning already, last night there were more *Polizei* than customers. What do you want?'

Torsen asked if they could talk in privacy. Eric led him into Magda's office. It smelled of stale tobacco, as did the entire club. He perched himself on Magda's cushions and Torsen sat on the chair opposite the untidy desk.

'I would like to talk to you, since you are taking over the clubs, and we have to try to stop the prostitution getting out of hand. I believe Magda controls the—'

'Did. I am her main beneficiary, Inspector, I was her husband, so let's get down to basics. How much do you want?'

447

Torsen frowned. 'I am giving you a warning, I am not here for money, bribes are against the law. You were not attempting to . . .'

Eric screwed up his face, trying to recollect if he had seen this one with his hand out. He sat back and listened as Torsen said that four of his officers had been attacked and chased. Eric interrupted him. 'I'm sorry, I don't follow, you say your men were chased?'

Torsen elaborated. His men had been chased by four men in a high-powered Mercedes, the number plate was being checked. He was there simply to warn the new establishment that he would not allow such things to continue.

Eric pretended great concern, agreed that he would personally look into what girls and their pimps were working over in the West.

Torsen was about to leave when he remembered to offer his condolences. Eric murmured his thanks with downcast eyes, and then regaled Torsen with the details – how he had just been sitting exactly where the inspector was when she just keeled over . . . 'It was a strange night, there was this woman Magda insisted she knew and the woman insisted she didn't know her. I think it was this woman's fault she had a heart attack. Magda really got agitated about her, screaming and carrying on, as only she could do.'

Torsen rose to his feet, hand outstretched. Eric jumped up.

'Ruda, that was her name, shot out of here, and Magda hit the roof, wanted her boys to get her, you know the way Magda was, but I'd never seen her before.'

Torsen hesitated. 'Ruda Kellerman?'

Eric shrugged. 'Don't ask me, but she put Magda in

448

one hell of a mood. Eh, I should grumble, she's dead, and I don't mind telling you, telling anybody, I've waited a long time for that to happen.' Eric continued talking as he led Torsen out of the club. Torsen headed up the stairs and back to his patrol car.

Eric waited until he saw the inspector's shoes disappear up the staircase, and then returned to the bar, clicking his fingers at the barmaid. 'Can you get Klaus in? I need to know who we've got working over in the Eastern sector, how many girls, etc. Do you think this plum would look good on the wall?' He held it up. Not waiting for a reply, he returned to the office to order the fabric. It was a coincidence that Torsen had been sitting not two feet away from the carving knife which had sliced through Jeczawitz's arm . . .

Torsen waited as Lena put down the file discs for the rest of the Js. She then handed him two more files on males listed with the name Kellerman.

'Thank you, this is very kind of you.'

She nodded, but walked out without saying a word. Torsen looked after her, and then turned his attention to the files. Perhaps she had had a bad morning.

Two hours later, his back aching from straining forwards to see the screen, Torsen found what he was looking for. He found the registration of the marriage licence between Rudi Jeczawitz and a Ruda Braun. Stamped across Ruda's name was 'No documentation available'. She had signed her name with a strange childish scrawl.

He was even luckier with Thomas Kellerman and his wife, also Ruda Braun. He took copies of both licences and matched the handwriting. Ruda Braun's signature was identical to Ruda Jeczawitz's. His heart was thudding in his chest as he looked from one document to the other. He gathered up his papers to put them into his briefcase. As he did so, he realized his newspaper was tucked inside; he was about to throw it away, when he looked again at the 'MAMA MAGDA DEAD'. The first line of the article leapt out at him. 'Last night one of the most well-known women of West Berlin's red-light district, the infamous Magda Braun, known as Mama Magda . . .'

Torsen's head was spinning with coincidences as he made his way back to the station. He was sure he had enough evidence to interrupt his *Direktor*'s holiday, and ask for permission to arrange a warrant for the arrest of Ruda Kellerman.

As usual, the station was virtually empty, the main bulk of officers having taken off for their lunch. He had to wait five minutes before they opened the yard gates to let him drive in. Once in his office he began to lay out in front of him all the evidence he had accumulated. He had to make sure he made no mistakes. Ruda Kellerman was now an American citizen – and a famous performer. This would be his first murder arrest, he could not afford to be wrong. He ran his fingers through his hair, flicked through his notes, and then tapped with his pencil. He should have commandeered the boots. He still didn't know if they were Grimaldi's or Ruda's, or if they were in it together. He swore, checked his watch; it was almost one o'clock. He needed a search warrant – had to get a search warrant.

His desk phone jangled and he snatched it up. It was the manager of the Grand Hotel who wanted to discuss with someone the nightly invasion of prostitutes hanging around outside the hotel entrance; they were even walking audaciously into the foyer of the hotel itself. Torsen said he would send someone over straight away. He was then caught up in calls: there were more burglaries from tourists' cars than they could deal with, and the rabbi rang, asking when he would be paid for Kellerman's funeral. Torsen diverted the calls, then dialled the receptionist. 'I have to go to the circus.'

'Yes, I heard you and Rieckert have free tickets.'

'I'm going on business, I'll be using the same patrol car, contact me if I'm needed. And have you got another girl to take over from you?'

'We've got three applicants, but this is a very old board, you have to have experience with this one.'

'I want someone on that switchboard day and night, is that understood?'

The receiver was slammed down and Torsen stared at his phone; he hadn't had any lunch and it was already two o'clock. He picked up the rabbi's bill for Kellerman's funeral; he would use it as an excuse to talk to Ruda, and then ask if he could take the boots. If he waited around for a search warrant to be issued, it could take hours.

Grimaldi was looking for Ruda: he'd not seen her since breakfast. She was late for feeding time and, as she always fed the cats herself, he was worried that something had happened to her. When he saw the inspector easing his way round the puddles, he hurried towards him. 'Is something wrong?'

'No, no, I was just coming to see you, or your wife. I have the receipt for Kellerman's funeral costs. You recall she said she would pay for the funeral?'

Grimaldi shrugged. 'I don't know where she is, but come on inside.'

Torsen stepped into the plush trailer, wiping his feet on the grid and noticing that there were no boots. He sat on the cushioned bench turning his cap round and round, as Grimaldi opened the envelope from the rabbi. He looked up after reading, and delved into his pockets. 'I'll pay you now, cash – that all right?'

Torsen nodded. Grimaldi counted out the notes, folded them and handed them over. 'Not much for a life, huh?'

Torsen opened his top pocket, asked if Grimaldi required a receipt. He shook his head, and then crossed to the window lifting up the blind. 'This isn't like her, she's never late for feeding, I wonder where the hell she has got to?'

Torsen tried to say it nonchalantly, but he flushed. 'Perhaps she has gone to Mama Magda's funeral?'

Grimaldi started. 'Who the fuck is she?'

Torsen explained, growing more embarrassed at his attempt to be a sly investigator. 'She was a famous West Berlin madame; she died last night at her club, Mama's. I believe your wife was there last night.'

'What are you talking about?'

'She was at the club, Mama Magda's, last night. I was told about nine, nine-thirty . . .'

'Bullshit! She was in the ring, we had a dress rehearsal last night, you got the wrong girl!'

Torsen pointed to the newspaper on the table. 'It was in the papers this morning, Mama Magda . . . photograph.'

Grimaldi snatched the paper and opened it. 'I've never heard of her, and why do you think Ruda was there?' He looked at the paper, could see where the article had been, but it had been cut out. He said nothing, tossed the paper back on to the table.

Torsen felt exceptionally nervous: the big man still scared the life out of him. 'Do you mind if I ask you a few questions? I'm sorry to inconvenience you.'

Grimaldi sniffed and rubbed his nose. 'She's never late.'

'Do you have a leather trilby, or a similar hat – a shiny black hat?'

Grimaldi turned. 'Do I have a what?'

Torsen stuttered slightly as he repeated his question. Grimaldi shook his head. 'No, I never wear a hat.'

'Does your wife?'

'What? Wear a hat? No, no.'

Torsen explained the reason why he had asked, that their suspect in the Kellerman murder investigation wore a black shiny hat, but it was possibly Kellerman's own hat, worn as a disguise.

Grimaldi sat on the opposite bunk, his legs so long they almost touched Torsen's feet. 'So you think I had something to do with Kellerman's death? Is that why you're here?'

Torsen swallowed, wishing he'd brought someone with him. 'I am just following a line of enquiry and elimination. An unidentified man was seen leaving Kellerman's hotel.'

Grimaldi nodded, his dark eyes boring into Torsen. 'So why do you want to know if Ruda's got a trilby?'

Torsen tugged at his tie. 'Perhaps our witness was mistaken, perhaps the person leaving, er, the man with the hat, was in fact a woman.'

Grimaldi leaned forward and reached out to hold Torsen's knee. His huge hand covered it, and he gripped tightly. 'You suspect Ruda? I told you, she was here with me all night, I told you that, and I don't like your insinuations.'

Torsen waited until Grimaldi released his kneecap. 'We also have a good impression of a boot, or the heel of a boot. Would it be possible for me to . . . to check the – if I could look at your boots, and your wife's boots . . . ?'

Grimaldi stood up, towering above Torsen. 'The only boot you will see is mine – as it kicks your ass out of my trailer, understand? Get out! *Out! Fuck off out of here!*'

Torsen stood up, folded his notebook and stuffed it into his pocket. 'I just need to check your boots for elimination purposes. If I am required to return with a warrant, then I shall do so.'

Grimaldi loomed closer, his voice quiet. 'Get out. Come back with your warrant and you'll fucking eat it – get out.'

Torsen slipped down the steps as the door slammed shut so fast behind him it pushed him forwards. He returned to his patrol car, his legs like jelly. Next time he would get a warrant, but he'd send Rieckert in for the boots.

Grimaldi went over to the meat trailer. All the trays were ready, Mike and the other young hands finishing preparing the meat. Grimaldi leaned against the chopping board. 'She still not shown up?'

Mike said nobody had seen her, but the cats were getting hungry. Grimaldi checked the time, said to leave it another half-hour. Then he looked at Mike. 'Eh, where did you say you put my hat?'

Mike chopped away, not even looking up. 'Mrs Grimaldi took it from me, I dunno where it is.'

Grimaldi stood at the open door, cracked his knuckles. 'You ever meet that little dwarf, the one that got murdered?'

Mike flushed slightly, because he knew that Mrs Grimaldi had been married to that dwarf. He covered his embarrassment by carrying the trays out to the waiting trolley. 'No, I never saw him.'

'I think *I* did.'

Mike jumped down, not hearing the other young hand who was running water into buckets. Grimaldi turned, easing the door half closed. 'What did you say?'

The boy turned off the taps. 'Day we arrived, I think it was him, I dunno, but he came in here, well, came to the steps, asked for Ruda, she was out by the cages.'

Grimaldi nodded. 'You told anyone this?'

The boy started to fill another bucket. 'Nope. Nobody's asked me.' He turned back to Grimaldi. 'I saw him later talking to Ruda so I presumed she must have said he was hanging around here. Have they caught the bloke that did it, then?'

Grimaldi rubbed the lad's shoulder with his hand. 'Yeah, they got the bloke, so don't open your mouth, we don't want those fuckers nosing around here any more than they need to. OK?'

The boy nodded, and Grimaldi strolled out. 'I'll just see if I can find that bloody woman.'

Grimaldi walked through the alley between the cages, and then stopped. She had lied, Kellerman had not only been to the circus, but he had talked to her! He shrugged it off. Maybe she just didn't want anyone to know she had been married to him. He walked on, worrying about the hat, and then his heart thudded. He remembered seeing her in the meat trailer, the night of Kellerman's murder. She had been covered in blood, it was over her shirt, her trousers. Shit! He remembered asking why she wasn't wearing one of the rubber aprons. He stopped again. Dear God, he had been so drunk that night he wouldn't have known if she was in the trailer or not.

Grimaldi ran back, slammed the door behind him, and went into Ruda's bedroom. He opened the wardrobe, searching for the shirt, trying to remember what clothes she had worn that night, but gave up, he couldn't remember. He rubbed his head. What did that little prick want to check their boots for?

The sound was half moan, half sob, but low, quiet, it unnerved him. He looked around, heard it again. He inched open the small shower door. She was naked, curled up in the corner of the shower, her arms covering her head, as if she was hiding or burying herself.

'Oh, sweetheart . . . baby . . .'

He had to prise her arms away from her head, her face was stricken, terrified. She whispered, 'No, please . . . no more, please no more . . . red, blue, red, red, red . . . blue, green . . .'

Grimaldi was unsure what to do, she didn't seem to know him, see him, her body curled up so tightly. Her voice was like a child's. He couldn't understand what she was saying. Some sort of list of colours – the plinths? It didn't make sense. Then he heard distinctly: 'My sister, I want my sister, my sister, please . . . no more . . .'

He took a big bath towel, gently wrapped it around her, talked quietly, softly, but she refused to move. He tucked the towel around her and eased the door shut. The cats had to be fed if there was to be a show that night, they had to have their routine.

He went back to the meat trailer, and then, for the first time in years, fed the cats. They were very suspicious, snarling and swiping at him, but they were hungry and the food became their priority . . . except for Mamon. If Grimaldi even went near the bars, Mamon went crazy; he couldn't get within an arm's length of the cage to throw

456

in the meat. Grimaldi swore and cursed him, then got a pitchfork and shoved the meat through the bars. Mamon clawed at the fork, his jaws opened in a rage of growls and he lashed out with his paws. He didn't want the meat, he never even went near it, but prowled up and down, up and down, until Grimaldi gave up trying and returned to the trailer.

She was in exactly the same position, curled up, hiding now beneath the bath towel. He knelt down, talked to her, keeping his voice low, encouraging her to come out. He was talking to her as if she was one of his cats. 'Come on out, that's a good girl, good girl, give me your hand . . . I'm not going to hurt you, that's a good girl.'

Slowly inch by inch she moved towards him, crawling, retracting, and he kept on talking, until she allowed him to put his arms around her. Then he carried her like a baby to the bed, held her in his arms and began to rock her gently backwards and forwards. 'It's all right, I'm here . . . everything's all right, I'm here.' He wanted to weep, he had never seen her like this.

'Sister, I want my sister . . .'

She felt heavy in his arms as he continued to rock her, and then he eased the towel from her face; she was sleeping. He was afraid to put her down in case he woke her; he held her as he would the child he had always wanted, sat with her in his arms, and said it over and over. 'I love you, I love you, love you . . .'

Then he saw the box on her dressing table, saw beneath the old ribbon the newspaper clipping, 'Angel of Death' and he whispered, 'Dear God, what did they do to you? What did they do to you, my baby?'

CHAPTER 17

HELEN ARRIVED at Dr Franks's apartment just as he was leaving. He was on his way out to see a patient. Helen asked if he could direct her to his library. He gave her a quizzical look when she told him what books she wished to read. 'My house-keeper will make you comfortable, bring you some coffee.'

Helen was shown into Franks's drawing room. The comfortably furnished room was dominated by book-shelves on every wall. Helen began to look over the books, moving slowly along the ranks of books carefully listed in alphabetical order until she had a stack to take to the table.

She turned the pages slowly, very slowly, sickened by what she was reading. She didn't want to, but she had to go on reading about the experimentation carried out under the auspices of Joseph Mengele at Birkenau concentration camp. He had used shortwave rays, administered by placing the plate on his female victims' abdomens and backs, in determining the rapidity of cancer production cells. The electricity was directed towards their ovaries, the X-rays given in such huge doses that victims were seriously burned. Cancer invariably followed, and then the gas chamber. The women suffered unspeakable agony as the waves penetrated the lower abdomen. Women's and children's bellies were cut open, the uterus and ovaries removed to observe the lesions, and the victims left, with no medication or pain relief, to determine how long they could stay alive.

Mengele paid particular attention to women and young girls, his experiments purporting to discover the fastest means of mass-sterilization and, incongruously, to study fertility. Mengele attempted to produce an impressive report to send back to Berlin, his 'Special Mission' to reproduce a genetic master race, using his pitiful patients as guinea pigs. His experiments had no apparent order, no rules. So-called gynaecologists used an electrical apparatus to inject a thick whitish liquid into the genital organs, causing terrible burning sensations. This injection was repeated every four weeks, and was followed each time by a radioscopy.

Sometimes selected women and small female children were injected with 5cc of a serum in the chest – no one has since discovered what the serum contained – at the rate of two to nine injections per session. These produced large swellings, the size of a fully grown man's fist. Certain Birkenau inmates received hundreds of these 'inoculations'. The children were often injected in their gums because Mengele wanted to speed up the reaction. Depending on his mood, he would change from one experiment to another, no one ever knowing what new, diabolical test he would demand that his nurses and physicians carry out next.

The Germans were experimenting with sterilization in many other camps; it was a sickening race between madmen who believed they would win the war, and, once victorious, ensure they would never be threatened by a new generation of an inferior race.

Mengele raged when he discovered typhoid epidemics spreading through Birkenau. He ordered vast amounts of serum, directed the medical orderlies to begin vaccination, then demanded they vaccinate outside the hospital, not to bring the creatures inside for fear of contamination. He would scream abuse at his 'helpers', insinuating they were sabotaging his programmes. One day he would reproach the orderlies for not seeing enough patients, the next day he would be in a violent rage about their wasting time and precious medicines on the sick.

Typhoid was followed by malaria. Mengele decided that it was the Greeks and Italians who had been the carriers, and, on the pretext of curbing the disease, sent thousands to the gas chambers. Whatever concept lay behind Mengele's work in the camp, his experiments lacked any scientific value, all his actions full of contradictions. He would take every precaution during a childbirth, noting and observing that all aseptic principles were rigorously observed and that the umbilical cord was cut with care. Half an hour later mother and new-born infant would be sent to the gas chambers. He carried out serious health treatments on internees, whom he then immediately dispatched to the gas chambers. He would order phenol injections at random, to curb the fevers, and then, when supplies ran out, substituted petrol. To his actions there was a zealot's energy not for life, but for wretched, agonizing death.

Helen had to stop reading, she simply could not take in any more. She checked her watch, it was almost ten, and she began to collect the books she had removed from the shelves. One book she had not had time to read was a small slim volume, written by an Auschwitz survivor; it chronicled specifically the work and brutality of Joseph Mengele, and Helen was about to replace it when she saw the words 'Angel of Death'. The nickname had, she read, been given to Mengele because he was always charming, always smiled as he sent thousands to their deaths. Mengele wore white gloves, his uniform was specially designed by his own tailors. He was a high-stepping peacock of a man, handsome, dark-eyed, high-cheekboned. The description surprised Helen – she had assumed the man would be as physically repellent as his crimes.

She stared at his photograph. It was unnerving: there was a similarity to Louis, the same haughty stare. But Mengele was a monster, a terrifying killing machine, a nightmare man with no morals, no feelings; he sent babies to their deaths as easily as he sent old men, young men, women, even pregnant women. No one escaped him . . . except twins – identical twins.

Helen looked at her watch again, knew she should leave, but now she could not stop reading. Mengele had one passion, the author wrote, one specific experiment that he first pursued in the privacy of his deathly hospital. Telepathy. He was determined to discover the powers of human telepathy, and he centred his experimentation on identical twins. Male and female twins were separated from their families, placed in a well-run camp hut, well fed and, according to the author, treated kindly. That word made Helen gasp: this monster sent thousands to their deaths, yet could still be described as 'kindly'. The author contended that many desperate mothers pretended that they had twins, lied that sisters and brothers were twins in a misguided attempt to 'save' them, unaware of the sickening experiments that were being prepared for those selected. Mengele became very particular, personally inspecting the children, rewarding a guard if he had 'salvaged' twins from the gas chamber. Soon, all the guards awaiting new arrivals would scream at the tragic passengers asking if there were any twins . . .

Mengele, it seems, became frantic if a twin died during his experiments; he would send the other to the gas chamber, but only after he dissected and matched the internal organs of the dead with the living twin. He operated on these children, sometimes without anaesthetic, on their eyes, their ears; he switched their organs, he starved one and overfed the other to watch their reactions. He personally tortured and mutilated these children in the name of science. Eight thousand identical twins passed through the camp. Only seven hundred children survived.

Helen walked to the clinic, needing to breathe fresh air. But when she sat down with Franks in his office, she was close to tears. He listened, his hands forming a church tower, staring at the index fingers, until Helen calmed down.

'I'm sorry, perhaps everything I have told you, you know already. It's just – to see it written down in black and white, to read it, to know it happened, to read him described as "kindly" – it is beyond my conception of a human being. I'm sorry.'

Franks gave Helen a steady stare and, in a soft quiet voice, his eyes fixed to a point on the wall ahead, he said, 'People in the camps lived from day to day, their only concern to stay alive until the next day. But, Helen, in order to live through each day one needed such courage, such toughness and, perhaps most of all, luck. Anyone who collapsed physically would die quickly, or be finished off by the Kapos, block seniors and the SS men – all of them experts in brutality, it was their trade. The ones who stayed alive were, as a rule, young. Some of the older men grew used to camp conditions, managed as best they could. It was always worst for the new arrivals, they had no idea what a concentration camp meant. It was, Helen, a completely alien atmosphere. The key was to discover the art of staying alive, and it was an art, Helen, unless you were exceptionally lucky. The survivors were often men with no scruples – those men advanced rapidly inside the camp. They came to power, could not afford to be squeamish about the means they chose, the human suffering, even the loss of human life. The most important thing was to make sure of your position. You filled your stomach with stolen rations, you were forced to become criminally minded to survive. You had to become cruel and ruthless – if not, the hopelessness of your position gave you only one alternative, to run at the electrified barbed wire fences.

'I often thank God, Helen, that I was one of those whom fate spared. But it was many, many years before I came to terms with what I had been forced to become, simply to survive, many years before I was able to hold my head up high . . . many years.'

He sat back in his seat, his eyes met Helen's, a strange direct stare, before he looked away, clasping the wooden carved arms of the old desk chair. 'I think the worst thing is that we forget – Germany, every German, should carry the cross of what was done. But memories fade, scars heal, and now we have adolescents not even born when this took place. This city, this country is a monument to a savagery that still makes one weep with shame. But life goes on ...' He hesitated a moment, as if about to continue, then decided against it, not wanting to discuss his own past any further. He motioned to the newspapers on his desk.

Franks told Helen that the Baron had brought them, spent time with Vebekka, and then gone for a bite to eat. He gave a half-smile, and a shrug of his solid shoulders. 'He is very confused, guilty, I think, and perhaps frightened. Perhaps you would like to see her before we start, it'll give me a few moments to get myself something to eat. Are you hungry?'

She shook her head and picked up her handbag. 'I'll see her, I'd like to.' She then reached over and touched his hand. Franks smiled.

'We all have our secrets, Helen, but, thankfully for me, they are no longer a nightmare, but a reality. Whatever is in Vebekka's past, must also become her own reality.'

It was a few moments after Helen had left the room before Dr Franks looked at the old framed photograph of his parents and grandparents, his brothers and sisters. He was fourteen years old, it was his parents' wedding anniversary. There he was, leaning against his mother's chair, smiling to the camera and wearing plus-fours, a hand-knitted sweater and socks. He could even remember their colour, a mixture of brown and green wool, and his shoes, highly polished dark brown lace-ups. It was the only photograph that existed, just as he was the only member of the entire family who had survived the holocaust.

*

Vebekka was dressed, sitting on the edge of her bed staring out of the window. She didn't turn when Helen entered, but seemed to know it was her. 'I'm glad you came. Come and sit beside me.'

She seemed very calm, very rational. 'I asked Louis, I said to him, if things don't go well for me, I asked if he'd make sure I had some sleeping tablets. Of course he won't, he may think about it, but in the end he won't be able to help me, so, I'm asking you.'

'Please don't, because you know I couldn't do that.'

'I couldn't bear to be locked up in a little room like this for the rest of my life ... and I know that is a possibility. I know, Helen.' She got up from the bed and walked around the small white-walled room. 'You know what is so awful? I never know – never know when it will take me over, and now I can't stand it any longer, to see the fear in that sweet-faced Hylda, the same fear in my children's eyes. I can't tell you what that does to me, to know I've hurt them, but not to know what I have done.'

Helen twisted her ring round her fingers. 'Do you know what you did last night?'

Vebekka giggled. 'Yes, I got very drunk, and I think I got screwed in a toilet, but that often happens to sane people – they get drunk and screw, don't they?'

Helen laughed softly. 'Yes, I suppose they do.'

Vebekka was working her way gradually round the walls towards the door, to be directly behind Helen, and Helen suddenly felt wary. She turned quickly. Vebekka was leaning against the wall, her eyes on the ceiling.

'I met this big fat woman, and she kept on calling me by somebody else's name ... It was strange, frightening, because I knew I didn't know her, and yet I was sure I had been there before. Do you ever feel that way?'

'You mean *déjà vu*?'

'Yes, yes, that you are in a place that you have been to before, do you feel that way?'

Helen nodded, said she did sometimes, and Vebekka did a delighted quick twirl, like a dancer, ending up flopping on to the bed. 'I feel it all the time, all the time!'

She rolled on to her back, her arms spread out wide. 'You know, Louis loves me, he told me so, he's such a child, like a schoolboy. I think he's – he's afraid, Helen.'

She sat up and wrapped Helen in her arms. 'Take care of him, please, and Sasha, look after my baby for me.'

Helen hugged her tightly. 'Now, don't! You talk as if you were going away, but you're not.'

Vebekka rested her head on Helen's shoulder. 'I feel as if I am, Helen, I am so frightened. Please don't let him open the trunk, please tell him not to do that.'

Before Helen could answer, Dr Franks walked in. He made a mock bow and gave Vebekka his arm.

Torsen waited for the *Direktor* to come to the phone. He cleared his throat in preparation for his speech, but the rasping voice snapped out what the hell did Torsen want? This was his holiday, the first he had taken in Switzerland since he had been married. Whatever it was had better warrant the interruption of his lunch. Torsen flicked a look at his watch, it was after three. Why on earth was he still eating lunch?

'Well, what do you want?'

Torsen began his laboured explanation of the investigation into the murder of Tommy Kellerman, his evidence and suspicions, constantly asking if the *Direktor* was still on the line, as he remained silent. At last he finished, turning to the last page of his copious notebook.

'And that's it? What's your most concrete piece of evidence? Sounds as if it's all supposition to me. The woman has an alibi, she has no motive, she's an American citizen. You need more, you need an eyewitness – the one you've got says he saw a man not a woman, you're going on a fucking imprint of a boot! That's your main evidence, isn't it? Have you got the boots? Do you know if they're hers?'

Torsen stuttered out that he required a search warrant to get the boots.

'So you haven't got the boots? As far as I can tell you've got fuck all – and you've seen too many American movies.'

Torsen asked his *Direktor* what he felt the next move should be. He was instructed brusquely to wait, told that the woman was not going anywhere, she was performing at the circus, so, until he had more concrete evidence, he should wait. The telephone was slammed down, and Torsen was about to replace his receiver when he heard the click from the switchboard and knew the operator had been listening. It infuriated him.

He tore out of his office and stormed into her booth. 'You were listening to a private call! Don't ever do that!'

She made a great show of removing the wires and plugs. 'I have a call for you, I was simply trying to put it through. This exchange is antiquated, sir, and we need an extension buzzer. Would you like me to place the call through to you now, sir? It's the manager of the Grand Hotel.'

Torsen snapped at her to tell the man he was busy, and

to call back. He burst into his office, kicked the door shut and swiped at his desk. His accumulated lists scattered, his notebook fell into the wastepaper basket, and his report sheets, neatly typed up for the *Direktor* to inspect on his return, received the dregs of his morning coffee. 'Shit! *Shit!*'

He sat in his chair, refusing to clean up the mess he had just created. He knew Ruda Kellerman was guilty of murder, knew it, and he should have taken the bloody boots. He dragged open his desk drawer, fished around for the envelope he had been given by the circus administrator containing his free tickets. At least he had got something out of all the hours he had put in. Attached to the tickets was an advertising leaflet, a coloured picture of Ruda Kellerman's face with the cats grouped behind her.

Torsen stared hard at her face, and then grabbed his coat. It was a chance, a long one, but if he could break Ruda Kellerman's alibi for the night of the murder, he knew he had enough to charge her, with or without the *Direktor*'s approval. His one hope was the bus conductor who had described the woman passenger the night Kellerman died; he might recognize her from the leaflet.

The Baron slipped into the viewing room, Helen turned and smiled, patting the seat next to her. They could see Vebekka lying on the sofa in the lounge area, eyes closed, a blanket covering her body.

'Rebecca, I want you to tell me about your mother, the way she used to say lie down, lie down and talk to me, so you would be calm, do you remember that?'

Franks waited, it had taken much longer this time to put her under, but she was now deeply hypnotized. He waited, leaned forwards a fraction. 'Tell me about your mother, Rebecca, how she used to encourage you to—'

She interrupted him, lifting her hand lightly and then resting it on the blanket. Her voice sounded strangely tired, as if Rebecca the woman was formulating pictures, seeing herself as a child. 'Yes, it was in the study, in Papa's study, the big couch, he used to sleep on it, when he was working late.'

Franks waited again, then gently coaxed her to continue. 'What did she used to say to you?'

'Close your eyes, listen to my voice . . .'

'Do you know why she asked you to lie down?'

'Yes, because of my nightmares.'

'Did she take you from your bed to talk to you?'

'No, it was our name, we called them my nightmares, but I was not asleep, they happened in the day.'

'Can you tell me about one, about what happened?'

'Oh, Papa was playing his records, and . . . it started, I was very naughty, I broke Mama's china, all her precious china, every single piece. It was the music.'

'Why did you break your mama's china because of some music?'

'I remembered it.'

'What music was it? Do you know the name?'

'Wagner . . . he never played it again.'

'Why do you think Wagner upset you so much?'

She whispered, still speaking as the adult Rebecca, her voice conspiratorial. 'Uncle played it all the time, all the time.'

Franks frowned, looked to the glass and shrugged his shoulders, and then remembered. 'Your uncle Ulrich?'

'No, no. Uncle, uncle!' She plucked at the blanket, very distressed. Franks waited, and then softly told her to listen to her mama's voice, to stay calm, to be calm, and she sighed deeply.

Franks leaned forwards and checked her pulse. He frowned. 'Can you hear me, Rebecca?'

'Yes . . .' She sounded very distant, very quiet.

'What did your mama mean when she said put her in the cupboard and throw away the key?'

'Me.'

Franks asked if Rebecca was in the cupboard. She plucked at the blanket, seemed to be growing disturbed again. 'No, it was my other me.'

'You mean the one who broke your mama's china?'

'Yes, put her in the cupboard, lock away the key, forget her, forget the bad Rebecca, she was a naughty girl, she did bad things.'

'Is it Rebecca locked up? Is it Rebecca in the trunk with chains on?'

She started to struggle, very agitated. Again he told her to listen to her mama's voice, to stay calm. Again she calmed, and he checked her pulse, she was going deeper and deeper, breathing through her nose, making a pursed lip as she released the air.

'What is it in the trunk that frightens you so much?'

Her face pulled down like a child's as she started to cry; he let her cry for a while and asked again. She tossed and turned, and he repeated the question. She mumbled something and he didn't catch what she had said, he asked again, and this time the pitch of her voice was higher. 'My sister's in there.'

'Why is that so bad?'

'Because I ate her.'

'You hate your sister?'

'*No, no, I ate her.*' She twisted her body, squirming,

her face distorted, and then she began to sob, and her words tumbled out. She had eaten her sister, they told her she had eaten her, that was why she was fat, she had eaten her alive.

Franks had to tell her to calm again, to listen to the calming voice of her mama, and slowly she rested again, her head bending forwards.

'But you know that is impossible, people don't eat each other, so maybe that isn't true.'

Her voice was strong, it took him by surprise. '*Hah!* You don't know, you don't know ... They stack the babies up, big pile of babies, and they put them in the ovens to eat them. *Hah!* See, you don't know!'

'Did you see that, Rebecca?'

'Yes.'

'And this person, this person inside you, did she see that?'

'Yes, we see it, we see it.'

Franks looked to the two-way mirror, gave a small shake of his head. 'Does this person—'

'Sister, she is my sister.'

'Ah, I see, your sister.'

'*Yes! Yes!*'

'And she is inside you because you think you have eaten her?'

'*Yes. Yes.*'

'Does she have a name?'

'*Yes. Yes!*'

'Will you tell me her name?'

Vebekka's face pulled down in a clown-like show of heartbreak. 'Ruda.'

Franks looked at the mirror. Both Helen and the Baron stared back at him. Then Helen jumped up and left the room. She called for Maja, asking her to pass a message to Franks. Maja asked her to write it down, and then she put her fingers to her lips, and entered the lounge area.

Helen returned to the viewing room and stared at the glass. Maja held up the note, he looked towards Helen and smiled. Maja crept out, closing the door behind her soundlessly.

'Is Ruda your twin?'

'*Yes! Yes, Ruda and me, me and Ruda!*'

'I see. I understand now, and Ruda is inside you?'

'*Yes! Yes!*' She pulled at the blanket, her brow furrowed. She twisted again, began the wringing motion.

'What are you doing? Rebecca? Can you hear my voice? Tell me if you can hear my voice. Rebecca?'

She was in the dark airless room. It was so cold outside but in this room it was always hot.

'Hot, I'm hot . . .'

'Where – can you tell me where you are?'

The reply was fast, as if an order had been given to her. The child's voice remained: 'Hospital, C 33 wing, hospital hut 42.'

Franks removed the blanket. She seemed not to notice.

She was seeing him, remembering him, watching the white gloves lay out the cards, one by one, she could hear that persuasive voice, she could smell him, he was telling her to concentrate on the cards, to look at the cards. 'Remember the cards, Rebecca, keep on looking at the cards, remember the cards . . .'

Franks asked Rebecca to listen only to his voice, whatever else she was seeing, but she sat up, bolt upright, and her head began to swivel, right left, right left. Franks asked what she was doing. She didn't answer. He told her to hear her mother's voice, to stay calm. She kept on flicking her head from side to side, a set expression on her face. She saw the white gloves move to the curtain, she wasn't ready, she wasn't ready, but the curtain began to move slowly, and then she saw Ruda, poor Ruda. She was held up by the woman; seeing Rebecca she gave a tiny wave of her hand, but she was too weak to stand up, she was so thin, her body was covered with sores, and Rebecca had to remember.

Franks became concerned: Vebekka was dragging at her clothes, still sitting upright, dragging and pulling at her clothes. 'Rebecca, listen to me, can you hear me?'

Again she made no answer, she had to get the colours right, she had to get the colours right, she had to get the colours. The same soft persuasive voice was talking to her again. 'Feed your sister the colours, feed them to her, make her call out the colours and she will have sweeties, she will have toys . . . Come along, my pretty one, the curtain will be closing, I am closing the curtain.'

Vebekka was rigid. Franks checked her pulse, it was very fast, she was not responding to him, seemed not to hear him. 'Rebecca, listen to me, start to come through the years now, listen to my voice.'

She began to speak in German for the first time, still paying no attention to Franks, her words like small rapid bullets: 'RED, RED, BLUE, RED, GREEN, BLUE, RED, BLUE, RED, RED, RED, RED, RED, BLUE, GREEN . . .'

Franks pressed his emergency button for Maja to enter. Vebekka continued to call out the colours, as Maja moved to his side. She carried an electrode box.

The Baron looked to Helen. 'Dear God, what is happening in there?'

Helen, unsure herself, tried to calm him. 'It's all right, he knows what he is doing.'

'Red, blue, green, red, red, red, green, blue, red, green . . .' She suddenly grew quiet, her voice trailing away, her head slumped on to her chest.

'Rebecca, *Rebecca*, can you hear me?'

She murmured, and he signalled to Maja that he didn't need the electrode box. He moved close to the bed, held Vebekka's hand, and spoke softly to her, bringing her through the cycles. She seemed drugged, her voice slurred. 'Yes, I can hear you . . .'

Franks asked where she was. She made no answer, and he asked again, telling her to listen to his voice, her mama's voice was gone, just to hear his, he wanted her to remember what she had been telling him, it was important she remember . . . They watched her as she came closer and closer to the surface, and then he held her hand. 'Sleep for a little while now, sleep and when you wake you will feel well, you will feel able to discuss everything we have talked about, do you hear me?'

'Yes, I can hear you.'

'Who am I?'

'Dr Franks.'

'Who are you?'

'My real name is Rebecca, but I call myself Vebekka.'

Franks relaxed; he dabbed his head with his handkerchief. He ordered Maja to sit close to the bed, then he walked out.

Helen and the Baron joined Franks in his office where he was sipping a glass of water. 'Well, now we know. Your wife, Baron Maréchal, had been hypnotized by her mother to forget, possibly in an attempt to help her. But the outcome, as you know more than anyone else, has been catastrophic. She is deeply traumatized by her childhood. I will need many sessions, we have only just begun.'

Helen could not sit down and paced up and down. 'As you know, Mengele experimented with tiny children, in particular identical twins, more with the females than the males – he discovered females were more telepathic, but first he had to decipher which twin was the more adept at receiving.'

Franks took a number of books from his shelves. 'We will need to examine every possible record of Mengele's tests. I think Rebecca was repeating some kind of code – the colours were spoken not in French or English, but German. Yet she has always maintained she did not speak German, did not understand it.'

The Baron stepped between them. 'I don't think you have any idea what you are doing. I saw her in there – how can you allow this to continue, don't you think she has been used enough – experimented on as a child? Now as an adult you want to take it another step. I refuse to allow this, I refuse!'

Franks sat heavily in his chair. 'You cannot do this – you cannot leave her in limbo because that is where she will be. We have opened up the horrors inside her and she will need extensive therapy to be able to control them and come to terms with—'

'*No*, I refuse, I refuse!'

Franks looked at Helen. 'You had better discuss this in private.' He walked out, furious. The man was a fool – they had made incredible progress and he was sure, with therapy, Rebecca could come to terms with her past, face it head on.

He walked down the corridor, as Maja came out of the lounge area. 'Is she still sleeping?'

She nodded, and looked past him to his office. 'Trouble?'

475

He sighed, and gave an exasperated gesture. 'Isn't there always? He wants us to stop.'

'But you can't – doesn't he realize what you accomplished today?'

Franks smiled ruefully. 'I think Vebekka's mother accomplished a great deal today, tomorrow I will begin work, I hope. Go talk to him, persuade him for me.'

Franks let himself into the lounge area. Vebekka was already sitting up, her feet on the ground, but she looked tousled, her hair standing up on end, as if she had been deeply asleep.

'How is my sleeping beauty?' he asked gently.

'A bit bruised, shaky, but she's still here.'

She looked up to him and he opened his arms, she went to him and held him tightly. Her voice was muffled. 'I want my sister, I want my sister.'

He stroked her hair. 'I know, I know, and you've hidden her away for all these years, haven't you? But you know now you didn't hurt her, it wasn't you, Vebekka. It was not you.'

She gave a wobbly smile, and asked for a drink. He went to a side table, and poured some iced water. 'Your husband is very afraid, for you. He wants to end the sessions.'

She took a cigarette from a box provided and he lit it for her; she inhaled deeply, and then picked up the glass of water. 'Do you think this longing I have felt always . . . is it for Ruda?'

He nodded his head. 'Of course – she was part of you, she was your twin.'

She nodded as if trying to assimilate the fact, and then sat down on the sofa. 'I feel a terrible sense of loss.'

'That is only natural, you have lost your safety barrier, your trunk, the one with all the chains, the one you were so afraid to open, you've lost that.'

She stubbed out the cigarette. 'What did they do to me?'

He crouched down in front of her. 'We'll find out, we'll find it all out, my pretty one, and gradually you will understand. But it will be hard going, we have a long way to go.'

She nodded again. 'I don't remember ... I don't remember.'

He touched her head, moving a strand of hair away from her brow – she felt hot. He stood up. 'Drink up, drink the water.'

'I'm tired.'

'Then sleep, you can sleep in here, no need to go back to your room, rest here.' Franks settled her down, tucked the blanket around her and waited as she lay with her eyes open. 'Don't try to remember, just rest. We will take it stage by stage, year by year until all the pieces are back in place. You have a lot to catch up on, your mama—'

'She wasn't my real mama, I know that.'

He smiled down at her. 'I think you will know everything, I sincerely believe it, and there will be no more rages, no more violence, it was, if you like, poor Ruda – you locked her away, but she wouldn't lie quiet. Now you will be able to give her peace.'

She frowned. 'Peace,' she repeated. Her eyes closed, and she seemed to have fallen asleep. Franks quietly let himself out and signalled to Maja to be close by. He felt tired himself.

Maja went to her office, the desk exactly opposite the

lounge, giving her clear access to the door. She was just about to sit down when Helen called out to her. 'Do you have some aspirin? Baron Maréchal is feeling ill.'

Maja went into the medicine cabinet, took out a bottle of aspirins and fetched a glass of water. The Baron was very pale, and thanked her profusely, saying he had a bad headache. She smiled understandingly, and said it must have been a difficult afternoon for him. She had been gone from her desk no more than five or ten minutes at most. She returned to her desk, and looked around for her handbag. It had gone. She returned to the office, then looked into reception. She was sure she had left her handbag by her desk, but went and checked in the viewing room to make sure. She did not see her handbag, but that became of secondary importance because when she looked into the lounge area, Vebekka had gone.

Maja ran back to the office. She called for Helen, the panic rising. 'Is she with you?'

Helen joined her in the corridor. 'She's not in the lounge, I'll try Dr Franks's son's room.'

Helen walked into reception. 'Has the Baroness been through here?'

The young nurse looked up and smiled at Helen. 'Yes, about five minutes ago.'

'Did she leave the building?'

'Yes, yes, she said her taxi was waiting. Is something wrong?'

Dr Franks came into reception. 'I don't believe this. Helen has just told me – is it true? – Vebekka has gone, just walked out and nobody stopped her.'

Helen said that she could not get far. She had no handbag, no money on her, but Maja said she was wrong – her own handbag was gone.

478

Louis looked up, his head thudding, as Helen walked in. She held the door. 'We have to go, quickly. Vebekka just walked out, nobody knows where she has gone, she's taken Maja's handbag. We'll get a taxi and start searching the streets, Dr Franks will remain here. We have to find her.'

Vebekka sat in the back of the taxi, opened Maja's handbag, removed some money, and got out of the cab at the Grand Hotel. She handed Maja's handbag back to the driver. 'Would you return with this to the clinic – but in about an hour? They'll pay the fare for the delivery. Thank you.'

Vebekka strolled through reception, asked for the key to their suite, and then rang for the lift. She hurried to their suite, locked the door behind her, ran into the bedroom and began to pick out a few garments. She fetched a purse and rifled through Louis's bedside table to find some cash. She froze as there was a light tap on the main door to the suite. She crept towards it and the light knock was repeated.

'Who is it?' Vebekka whispered.

'Hylda, it's just Hylda, Baroness. I saw you down in reception and . . .'

Hylda stepped back as the door inched open. 'Hylda, I am afraid I can't see you. Wait, please, wait one moment.'

The door closed and was relocked. Hylda looked around. Had the Baron returned, too? She had not seen him. She tapped the door again. 'Are you all right? Baroness?'

The door was unlocked and Vebekka opened it, only a

fraction. 'This is for you. I have no money. Please, please take this.'

The leather box was thrust into Hylda's hands, but she was not interested in the contents, more concerned for the Baroness. 'Where is your husband? And Dr Masters? Baroness?'

'They are due any moment. I must go. God bless you, dear Hylda, take care, goodbye.'

The door was shut and locked once again. Hylda hesitated, only now opening the gift. She gasped. The beautiful bluebird brooch nestled in the velvet-lined box. She snapped it shut. She would return later, give it back, if not to the Baroness then to her husband. Hylda went slowly towards the staff staircase, opened the box again. It was, she knew, one of the Baroness's favourite pieces. So like her, the bird, as if in flight, so fragile, and she knew she would have to return it. What she did not know, could not have known, was that she would never see the Baroness again.

Vebekka slipped out of the suite fifteen minutes later. She was looking refreshed and elegant.

She went downstairs and asked the doorman to call her a taxi. One drew up at the red carpet within moments.

'The club, Magda's, Mama Magda's, quickly, please. I am in a great hurry.'

She sat well back in the seat and took out her dark glasses, afraid she would be seen. She knew they would be looking for her but she had to know why the big fat woman had called her Ruda. She knew now that Ruda was free – she had released her – and she felt a strange sensation inside her. The feeling of loss was disappearing because, she was sure, Ruda was alive.

CHAPTER 18

Luis had let Ruda sleep, was sitting as if on guard in the trailer. He was very concerned, and kept an eye on the clock; she had already missed any chance of a pre-show rehearsal. He had explained her absence by saying she had a migraine. Would she be capable of doing the main show that evening? Her first spot was at eight forty-five, and he knew that if she was no better, he would have to withdraw the act.

'Luis? What time is it?' She stood in the doorway, her face very pale, and she was shaking badly.

He rushed to her and helped her sit down. 'You've missed the rehearsal, sweetheart, but don't worry.'

'Oh, God!'

She hung her head, and he slipped an arm around her shoulders. 'They've all been fed, and after last night they won't need a run this afternoon. You just rest, I've got you a hot chocolate.'

She closed her eyes, leaning on the bench cushions. He held out the mug of hot chocolate, a thick skin on top. She smiled, and pushed it aside with her finger. 'You always burn the milk.'

He crouched down in front of her. 'What happened?'

She sipped the chocolate, her hands cupped round the mug, and gave a wan smile. 'Ghosts . . .'

'You want to talk about it?'

She shook her head. He went and sat opposite her. 'Will you be fit enough for the show tonight?'

'Try and stop me!'

He chuckled, but he was very concerned; she seemed to have no energy, her body was listless, her eyes heavy as if weighed down.

'Is it about the box? The tin box? I wasn't prying, I was looking for my old albums, you know me, always looking to the past. I found it, I know maybe I shouldn't have opened it, but to be honest I didn't think you'd find out.'

'No, you shouldn't have opened it, but you did, so that's that.' She put the mug down. 'I'd better check on the cats.'

'No, I've done it, and the boys are there. You just rest, you'll need all your strength for the show.'

She nodded, and again he was deeply concerned; it was unlike her to agree to anything he suggested. He snatched a look at his watch: there was time. She stared through him, beyond him, her eyes vacant.

'Do you want me to tell you what you said?'

'What?' She seemed miles away.

'I found you all curled up in the shower, carried you in my arms like a baby – bet you haven't let anybody do that for a long time, huh?' He was trying to make light of it, attempting to draw her back.

'Nobody ever held me when I was a baby, Luis, nobody, only . . . only my . . .'

He waited but she bowed her head. 'Sister?' he interjected. 'You said you wanted your sister, I've never even heard you talk about a sister before, I mean, were you dreaming? You were freaked out!'

Her whole body shuddered and she clasped her arms around herself, staring at the floor, her voice so soft he had to strain to hear her. 'You know when we went to the Grand Hotel? After we'd been to the mortuary, something sort of happened inside me. I had a feeling . . . so many years, Luis, I've tried, tried to find her, but – she was called Rebecca, and I was called Ruda. We were taken in a train, hours and hours on a big dark train. Rebecca slept, but I kept guard over her, I watched out for her, she . . . she didn't talk too good, I used to talk for Rebecca.'

She leaned back with her eyes closed, remembering the noise of the iron wheels on the rails. She could remember someone, someone crying all the time, the rat-tat-tat of the wheels and the weeping, but everyone was crying, howling, screaming, rat-tat-tat . . . hand in hand they were crushed and pushed and trodden on as the big doors were inched back. Had it been days or hours? She lost count, but at last the rat-tat-tat had stopped. Rebecca was crying because she had messed her panties, done it in her panties, she cried for Mama, but they had no mama, she was gone, and then the voices, screaming, screaming voices.

'Women to the left, men to the right, women and children to the left, men to the right.' So tiny, so young they didn't know right from left.

'Any twins? Twins over here, twins here, dwarfs, giants . . . twins . . .'

Ruda was picked up and thrown to a group of screaming women. Rebecca fought and shouted to her sister, and the guard had picked Ruda up by her hair and tossed her across to another group. The screaming went on and on, and, pushed and kicked, they were herded towards a long, long path, at the end of which were gates, big high gates. Fences, with barbed wire as high as the sky, surrounded hundreds and hundreds of huts.

Ruda dodged between legs, squeezed under the marching, bedraggled, weeping women and screeching children. At the gates she caught up with Rebecca, holding a strange woman's hand, and the guard started shouting orders. Ruda tugged at his sleeve. 'My sister, my sister!'

The guard had looked into their identical faces, grabbed them and hauled them into the back of a truck, just inside the perimeter of the gates. '*Twins! Twins!*'

The truck rumbled and swayed over potholes and ditches, a truck filled with children, clinging in pairs, identical faces clung in terror to each other – boys, girls, all shapes and sizes, but with one thing in common: they were twins.

Luis sat next to her; he wanted to hold her, comfort her, but she remained leaning back with her eyes closed. He heard only part of what she was saying; she lapsed into silences, and then odd words came out, disjointed words, some in Polish, Russian, Czech and German, but she remained motionless. Seeing with her adult's eyes what she had seen as a two-year-old – the carts of dead skeletons, the strange eerie women with their shaven skull-like heads . . . the screaming women giving birth on a stone slab, and the babies taken, still with the afterbirth covering their tiny bodies, and thrown on to a seething mass of babies, dying, taking their first breath with their last, and the weeping and wailing never stopped, and the cold icy wind never stopped, the snow and ice freezing, freezing the memories like crystals.

They clung together, slept together, and played together. No mother, no father, no brothers, no religion, no surname, all they knew was that they were sisters, Ruda and Rebecca, and, protected by being a pair, they fought when needed as one.

The normal ration for all prisoners was a bowl of soup, and anything could be found in this watery filthy liquid, tufts of hair, buttons, rags – even mice. The soup was their nourishment for the day. The evening meal was black bread, a ration of six and one half ounces, with more sawdust than dough. Hunger-ravaged faces, clawing hands begging, pleading for food.

In comparison with the other inmates, the twins were fed well. They were given not only clean clothes but toys, and their childish laughter tore into the tortured minds of the rest of the inmates, made them weep and scream for their lost babies. Men and women clung to the wire meshing that segregated these special children, clung and screamed abuse at them, hating them because they were playing. Some mothers clung on in desperation to see the faces of their children, and some crept out in the freezing night and twisted their rags to hang themselves.

But the twins who were old enough to understand knew it would be only a short time before the innocent laughter stopped. They knew what was to come, they had seen the twins carried back to their bunks in the dead of night from the hospital. Tiny, broken bodies lifted from the trolleys, minus limbs, blinded, bruised and disorien-tated by drugs and chemicals pumped into young veins . . . and those that knew wept in silence, because they knew that one day it would be their turn.

Gradually even the tiny ones, the new inmates, the fresh twins, the ones as young as Ruda and Rebecca, began to understand. When the nurse called out the numbers to go to the experiment wing, they trembled in fear . . . The fear made the children grow old fast – only the fit survived, only the strong survived the mutilations, the drugs. Hundreds came and went, but those who survived grew an inner strength, learning to interchange with each other to save the agony. They switched places, they stole to feed each other; they each became a single unit.

Papa Mengele had a particular liking for the two tiny girls; he had them called out regularly. To the jealousy of the other children they had sweets, and a very special treat – they had chocolate. Ruda and Rebecca began to trust the man who said they could call him 'Papa' or 'Uncle'. They liked him, and went to the experimental wing hand in hand.

Mengele was fascinated by the way they interacted. Rebecca, slow to talk, began a sentence and Ruda completed it. They were so close, they often spoke in unison, moved in unison. Their closeness absorbed him, and for many weeks he simply examined them, monitored them together.

Ruda reached out and held Luis's hand, she clenched it tightly now, as words and sentences seemed to be dragged painfully from her memory. At times her voice was so soft he had to bend close to her to hear. 'She was always smiling. He even let her play with his precious white gloves; she would sit on his knee and hug and kiss him, and he teased her, said she could call him "Papa", and she would put her arms around his neck and kiss him

. . . But his eyes, Luis, his eyes were like the Devil's, and he would stare at me. I was afraid of him, I tried to warn her, he knew I didn't trust him, he knew it. I couldn't go near him, I was always afraid of him, but Rebecca had no fear, and then, one day, he said he was going to show her something pretty. I tried to stop her, and she slapped me, said to leave her alone, she was going with her papa to see something nice, and she held his hand, and she left me . . .'

Ruda got up, she went to the window and stared out, her hands hanging limply at her sides. 'She didn't come back for three days. For three days my body burned, my head ached, I screamed with the pain, cried out for them to stop. I knew . . . I felt every single injection, I knew they were hurting her. Then they brought her back, the nurse carried her in, pushed her on to the bunk bed. Her eyes were glazed, she was burning hot, and she just lay there. I didn't know what they had done to her – her face was bloated, her belly distended, her cheeks flushed bright rosy red. They didn't call us for a long time. I stole what food I could, slept with her in my arms, warmed her with my body . . . and just as she was better, able to get up, they came back for her. When they called her number, I took her place.

'But they knew who I was, and I was punished for trying to fool them.' She covered her face with her hands. She couldn't tell him what they had done that had hurt . . . but what had been worse was not being with Rebecca, and each day they promised she would see her soon. They gave her no food, nothing, and every day came the interminable agonizing X-rays, the electrodes to her head, the drugs. They burnt her insides, kept on asking her questions she didn't understand, asking the same question over and over, 'Tell us what your sister is doing, tell us. If you tell us you will be given sweeties.'

Ruda sobbed, wringing her hands. 'I didn't know what they wanted, I didn't understand. I hurt so much, I was in such terrible, terrible pain, all I did was cry. Luis, they hurt me so much, and then . . . then they took me to this little room, locked me inside, all alone, all by myself, nobody came to see me, nobody gave me any food. And then the new pains began, my head, my arms, my knees were on fire. I screamed, louder and louder, begging them to stop, to stop hurting her.'

Luis leaned closer. 'I don't understand.'

She almost screamed it, her face puce with rage: 'I felt what they were doing to her, I felt every pain. I knew what they were doing to her, because I felt it.' She gave a sobbing laugh, stood up to pace around the trailer. 'Papa was very pleased with me. They came to me then, and I was carried into another room. They gave me hot milk and cookies, kept on telling me what a good girl I was.'

Ruda stared from the trailer window, then pressed her head against the cold windowpane. 'They took care of me, bandaged my knees, put ointment on my legs and stomach, dressed me in clean clothes. Then they took me into his office, made me sit in front of him. He had . . . a – ' she turned back to Luis, 'telephone, and he was smiling at me. They were playing music on a gramophone, he spoke to someone, told them to begin. Oh, Luis, I screamed out – my head, I said they were hurting my head, then my stomach. The more I cried out in agony, the more agitated he became, shouting into the phone, again . . . again, until I fell to the floor. Then he replaced the phone, picked me up and sat me on his knee, told me what a good girl I was. Then she came in.'

'Your sister?' asked Luis.

'No. Papa's assistant. She came in, and he said to her: "This is the strong one. Say hello, Ruda, say hello to—"'

She couldn't continue, slumped on to the bench. Luis reached out and drew her into his arms. 'Did you ever see her again?'

She whispered: 'Through the glass window . . . they used to show me her through the glass window. Her face was like a stranger's, she was fatter, more bloated, but she still tried to smile at me. Then they would draw the curtain, and she was gone. The nurses would tell me that if I was a good girl, if I could tell them what Rebecca was thinking, they wouldn't hurt her any more.'

He held her close, his cheek resting against hers. She kept on staring ahead, whispering, 'You remember the silk scarves? The old magician? That's where I learned it, Luis. They said they wouldn't hurt her if I could tell them the colours, and I used to try so hard, try to tell them what they wanted to know, but they still would never let me see her, touch her.'

'But why, what did any of it prove?'

'They wanted me to read her mind, they showed her all these colour charts, cards, and . . . and I failed, I couldn't get it right, so many, they wanted so many. I tried, I used to try very hard. When I failed they would burn me, make me try again, and I did, because then they didn't hurt her. If they had done, I would have known, but she wouldn't concentrate. I'd always been able to think for her, talk for her, but she . . . didn't concentrate hard enough. And then one day they came to me, clearly, one colour after another. Papa applauded and shouted, and they let me see her. They told me I was a good girl, that I had saved my sister and if I continued to be a good girl she would not be hurt.'

'Did they continue to torture you?'

She nodded. 'Not so much – but they would not let me hold her. I was kept all by myself, but you know, I knew she was being taken care of, so it was all right. But then, I got so tired I couldn't, I couldn't do it. They took her away, it was my fault.' Her voice was hardly audible, as she whispered, 'They hurt her . . . but all I could feel was her terror.'

Luis felt so inadequate. He held Ruda tightly. 'You listen to me. From now on, when something hurts you, when you remember, you tell me. Because no ghost is going to touch you, blame you. I love you, Ruda, do you hear me? You have done no wrong, you have done nothing wrong, you can't blame yourself, you were just a baby.'

She broke from him, and gave him a strange look. He could feel her mistrust.

'It's true, Ruda, you have done nothing wrong! You have to believe that!'

She reached the door leading to the small hallway. 'I had better rest before tonight.'

'You sure you will be all right to do the show?'

She nodded. 'I do care for you, Luis, you know that. I think I always have. Maybe, in my own way, I—' She couldn't say the word.

'Ruda, maybe it's taken me a long time to realize just how much I need you, that I'm nothing without you . . . but I understand that you need me, you need me, Ruda, and it makes me feel good.'

'Don't tell anyone what I have told you.'

'As if I would . . . but, remember, you have nothing to be ashamed of.'

She gave him that look, her eyes slightly downcast. 'I didn't tell you all of it, some things you can never tell anybody, you know why? Because nobody could really believe it ever happened.'

'Can I ask you something?'

She looked at him impatiently.

'Did you know Kellerman at the camp? Was he at the same place?'

'Yes, Kellerman was at Birkenau with us. I didn't know him there . . . He had it bad, they made him fuck dogs for their entertainment – and you thought it was funny to make jokes about the size of his dick, didn't you? See, look at you, you don't really believe it, do you? Kellerman the clown, *haw haw*! They degraded him, defiled him, and treated him like an animal, *haw haw*. Kellerman was not a clown, not in his heart.'

'You did see him, here in Berlin. You saw him, didn't you?'

She stared at him directly, not a flicker of an indication she was lying. 'No. I suppose he came to try to squeeze money out of me, but I didn't see him. Look, I'd better go and rest, then I'll check on the animals.'

She closed the door of her bedroom. Grimaldi cleared away her half-finished mug of hot chocolate. He ran the water into the sink and turned off the taps, then strode across the trailer, rapped on her door. She pulled it open. 'What?'

'The *Polizei*, that little prick of an inspector was here. He wanted to know about the night Kellerman died, something about a pair of boots, the ones he'd seen outside.'

She shrugged, gestured to her closet. 'He can take whichever ones he likes. Is that all you wanted to say to me? I got a lot to do.'

He looked at her and started to walk out. 'I'll go and check over the props – and, Ruda, if you still have Kellerman's hat, get rid of it, they asked about that, a leather trilby. Mike borrowed it, he said that you had said it was mine. Get rid of it, Ruda.' Grimaldi slammed out of the trailer.

Ruda kicked her door shut. 'Shit! Shit!'

She paced up and down. She had got rid of everything, she was safe, they couldn't connect her to Kellerman's murder. Then she realized that maybe the *Polizei* had not made any connection, but Grimaldi had. She stood, hands clenched at her sides. 'Shit!' She talked herself through, making herself calm. Well, she could handle him . . .

Torsen hovered around the bus station, checking his watch. He had been there over an hour and he was getting edgy. He had to get back to his apartment, bath, change and collect Freda; he wouldn't make it if the bus didn't come soon. There was a loud bang as a car backfired, and Torsen looked out. His man had arrived in a cloud of exhaust fumes. Torsen hurried towards the conductor as he slammed the door shut. 'Eh, you'd better be careful, slam it too hard and the engine'll fall out.'

Torsen smiled. 'Could I have just a word?'

The conductor nodded, said he would have to make it quick as he was due out of the depot ten minutes ago. Torsen produced the leaflet showing Ruda Kellerman's face, having carefully cut around the circus name and cut out the lion's head. 'Can you look at this? It's not a proper photograph, but it's a very good likeness of someone we think may have been the passenger on your bus the night the dwarf was murdered. You remember we spoke about it?'

The conductor nodded again, clocking in with his card, and collecting his money bag from the office. Torsen trailed after him, back to the waiting bus. 'Would you have a look, please?'

'You know, it's a while back now, I dunno if I can remember her, let me see . . .' He squinted at the picture of Ruda, tipped his hat up. He held it this way and that. 'I'm sure I've seen this before . . .'

'But is it the woman on your bus that night?'

'I have definitely seen this woman's face before, but whether it was her or not, I couldn't honestly say. I just took her fare, I didn't even have a conversation with her . . . It could be, but I wouldn't say it was.'

Torsen slipped the picture back into his wallet. 'Thanks for your time. Have a good night!'

Torsen returned to his car and was unlocking it as the bus rumbled past. Displayed on the side of the bus not seen by Torsen was a large poster – of Ruda Kellerman's face about a *foot high*. Torsen threw up his hands. So much for a valued eyewitness. He drove back to his apartment. On the way he radioed in to see if there were any messages, and said he would be requiring the patrol car for some work that evening. Everybody in the station knew he was going to the circus and using the patrol car in off-duty periods was against the regulations. Rieckert called back to Torsen asking if he could pick him up. There was just his girlfriend and himself. Torsen snapped that he thought he was giving the tickets to his wife and kids. Rieckert laughed. 'Nah, they hate the circus. See you about seven, over and out!'

Mama Magda's was empty when Vebekka pushed open the door. She called out and, receiving no reply, crept down the dark unlit staircase to the basement club. She passed through the arch with the beaded curtains and called out again. The office – the room where she had sat with Magda – had a light on. Eric opened the door.

'Could I see Magda, the woman who owns this club?'

Eric squinted in the darkness, unable to see her face clearly.

'I just want to talk to her.'

'That would be very difficult. Who are you?'

Vebekka said who she was, and Eric opened the door wider. 'Please, it is very important I speak to her.'

Eric gestured for her to come into the office. She stood in the doorway. 'You're twenty-four hours too late, she died last night.'

Vebekka sighed and leaned on the door frame. 'Oh, no, no, please, no!'

Eric offered her a chair, but she refused. 'Can I help in any way? I've taken over the club. Sit, please sit.'

'She called me Ruda . . .'

Eric remarked that Magda called a lot of people names, and then he saw how distressed Vebekka was. 'Look, I'm sorry, I can't help you.'

Vebekka walked out, Eric watched her leave, then remembered the handbag he still had. If she was who she said she was maybe she could cause trouble. He opened the drawer, picked up the bag and scuttled after her. He could see her up ahead of him on the pavement and he called out. She stopped and turned back. 'You left this last night, your handbag. No money, there was no money in it, OK?'

She stared at the bag, uninterested. Eric thrust it towards her. 'It's yours. Eh, are you OK?'

She took it and tucked it under her arm. She seemed close to tears. 'It was perhaps just a coincidence, you see ... Ruda – Ruda was my sister. The big woman called me Ruda, kept on calling me Ruda.'

'I can ask around for you. What's her surname?'

'I don't know.'

Eric backed away. She was a fruitcake. 'Well, I can't help you then, goodbye. Any time you're passing, drop in.'

He made his way back, and heard a screech of tyres. She had walked out into the street and a car had narrowly missed her, but she kept on walking, not even turning to the shocked driver.

Helen hurried to the Baron; she was out of breath, having run from the hotel forecourt and back to reception. 'She came to the hotel, she went up to the suite, and then took a taxi. The manager spoke to her, the driver has just got back. He said Vebekka went to a club, "Mama Magda's", he's waiting to take us there now.'

When they reached Magda's club, Eric explained that the Baroness had been there, but swore he had returned her handbag left from the previous evening.

'We are not interested in that, we simply want to know where she went. Do you know?'

Eric explained she was looking for her sister, someone

called Ruda, and the next minute she almost got herself killed, walking across the central road, straight into the traffic. He followed them out to the pavement, and watched them virtually get knocked over as well as they ran across the road, car horns tooting at them. He shook his head. Crazy foreigners, all of them crazy.

Vebekka walked on, bumped into passersby, kept on walking, walking ... she turned into a churchyard, unaware of where she was, where she was going. Pictures kept cutting across her mind, fragments, disjointed memories. She walked into the church and sat in a pew at the back. Rosa used to take her to church on Sundays; her adopted father never accompanied them. Vebekka closed her eyes, bowing her head. She used to call Rosa 'the woman', she had not known who she was, but the woman worked at the hospital where they had taken her after the camp was liberated, when she had been very ill.

The woman had been so kind, the way she had explained she was just examining her, trying to see if she needed any medication. She was so kind, gently touching her arms, asking what her name was, asking if she remembered her name, but Rebecca was too terrified to talk. Any moment she expected the needle, any moment they were going to stick needles into her arms. When the needles didn't come, she was in terror they would bring the electric pads, and she hid beneath the sheets, but after a few weeks, maybe even months – she knew only night and day, not weeks or months, she lived only for each day – eventually, she had begun to believe she was safe; then they had taken her to an X-ray department, and she had screamed and screamed.

The woman used to come every day with little presents, and Rebecca would refuse to take them: she knew it was a trick. She had been in the hospital for six months before she was transferred to an orphanage; she had still not spoken, and she had begun to get used to the nice woman's visits. She had explained to Rebecca that she was in Berlin with her husband, that she was not a qualified doctor, just helping in any way she could. She had held the frightened girl's hand, saying she just wanted to help her, she must not be afraid, and she would keep on coming to see her, if Rebecca wished. She had asked Rebecca if that was what she wanted and Rebecca had slowly nodded . . .

The older children used to tell terrible stories, steal her things, pinch her; she was so fat – they called her a pig, she was a fat pig. They were too young, too bruised themselves to know she had been injected and tortured, they had all suffered, but for Rebecca – who looked fit and healthy – the teasing and jokes ostracized her. She rarely spoke, she mourned her sister, cried for her every night. Then the nice lady arrived with her husband. She asked if Rebecca would like to come away with them, if she would like to live with them.

Rosa and David Goldberg had many children to choose from, but Rebecca had touched Rosa deeply; she was also the most outwardly healthy of the children, and Rosa was sure that, in time, she would overcome her terror, and they knew she was not dumb.

They had attempted to trace Rebecca's family but to no avail; she could not remember her surname, they only knew her first name because one of the children told them. Rebecca left with the Goldbergs a year and a half after her release from Birkenau, but it was months before she began to believe they were not going to hurt her.

Rosa made the decision never to speak of Birkenau. What she had so far learned of it was too much for her to accept and she felt it was better for Rebecca to forget, never to speak of the past. They had a plastic surgeon remove her tattoo, and although the operation had distressed her, the doctors and nurses terrifying her, she recovered remarkably quickly.

Nevertheless, three years after the adoption, Rosa was beginning to despair. Rebecca still hid food, urinated on the floor, wet her bed every night. She remained suspicious and uncommunicative, retreating into sulking silences for so long that Rosa began to think she would never settle down. And she had nightmares: virtually every night she woke screaming hysterically and would let no one near her. At school she disrupted the class. She had no friends, she fought and spat and kicked at other children. She stole the children's toys and their luncheon boxes.

Her eating habits varied from refusing food for days on end to eating binges; Rosa would find her sitting on the floor by the fridge eating everything she could find – mustard and jam, raw eggs, anything her hands could reach for, she would stuff into her mouth.

Rebecca was sly, she lied, she would fly into terrifying, uncontrollable rages, and she wore Rosa Goldberg down. No care, no love seemed to break through her resistance. She was as cruel and vicious to pets as to the smaller children at the school. The Goldbergs began to feel they had adopted a monster.

Therapy sessions followed, and in some way helped; through the therapy her adoptive parents discovered she had a twin sister. Rosa had tried to trace Ruda in a desperate bid to help Rebecca, but it was a long, fruitless search, financially exhausting as well. Ruda, it was presumed, had died in the camp. There was no record of her leaving Birkenau, no record in any orphanage; she had, like thousands of others, disappeared; no grave, no name, no number was ever traced.

David Goldberg was at his wits' end; under the strain of caring for Rebecca his wife was becoming a nervous wreck, obsessed with helping the child. As a last resort, when they arrived in Philadelphia Rosa arranged a session with a hypnotherapist. For the first time Rebecca calmed, and then Rosa read every book she could find on the subject. She trained at a local clinic until she could give Rebecca sessions at home, and gradually she began to blank out from the child's mind the memory of her past.

Rebecca did not transform overnight. There were setbacks when Ruda was remembered. So Rosa found the solution. She talked Rebecca into locking her sister away, so she would not come out, would not make her do bad things. She would lock her away and lose the key. It was, in some ways, justified, because from then on Rebecca was able to study at school and she caught up well . . .

Vebekka sat back, staring at the altar. She understood now why she had been so afraid for her babies, afraid they would be born with two heads, born twisted, with ropes. She had been too young to understand what an umbilical cord was. She had seen the skeleton-headed women cut at the twisting baby rope with a rusty knife; she had seen and looked with the curious fascination of a young child at all the babies she'd seen the skeleton women deliver, and at the rows of deformed, tragic foetuses held in the hundreds of jars in the hospital.

In the silence of the church Rebecca let the past play out its grotesque dance, the darkness passing into the lightness of her moments of happiness – the relief and joy she had felt holding her newborn, touching their fresh perfect bodies. She whispered, her voice echoed softly round the dark empty church, 'I'm so sorry . . .' She had never meant to hurt them, it was beyond her control. She thought of Sasha, and for a moment felt panic-stricken: sweet innocent Sasha. She had wanted Sasha to see the burning babies in the hidden secret compartments she had stored in her mind. She had wanted Sasha to understand. Rebecca moaned, remembering how she had frightened her daughter, frightened Louis, poor dear Louis. He was such an innocent. How could a man with such a pampered, charmed existence be expected to understand? He had only wanted her to love him, but Ruda demanded her love, ached inside her. The powerful longing to be reunited had dominated everything in her life, but it had been locked away, Rosa had locked Ruda away.

She sat back, feeling the hard bench of the church pew against her. The colours of the stained-glass window drew her attention, the red, green, blue glass sparkled in front of her. She laid her hands flat against the prayer shelf and kept on staring at the colours. She heard his voice, that soft persuasive voice, she heard the music . . . He played the same Wagnerian recording over and over, he even whistled it as he walked through the camp, he used to hum it to her when he laid out the cards . . .

'Clear your mind of everything, look at the cards, red,

green . . . look at the cards, there's a good girl, now more cards . . .'

The white gloves snapped down the coloured cards. At first she had liked the game – it was fun, and Papa Mengele had kissed and cuddled her when she remembered each one, and when she could pass the exact colours to Ruda he rewarded her with chocolate, breaking off pieces, popping them into her mouth.

Then the games had become frightening. She was forced to pass more and more colours. It had begun with just three cards, then next day it had been six. She found it hard to concentrate, she was hungry. Once she had complained, said she couldn't remember them because she was hungry, and she had been force-fed until she was bloated. Now, he had told her, you are full. Now show me how clever you are. This time there were twenty cards; she had concentrated as hard as possible. The card sessions went on every day and gradually Rebecca was able to pass telepathically up to twenty-five colours, in correct order, primal red, blue and green, to her sister.

If Ruda made a mistake, if Ruda could not repeat the exact order of the colours, she would be punished. They told Rebecca that was her fault, she was hurting her sister. Papa displayed fifty cards, and Rebecca started to cry. That day Papa had withdrawn the curtain and made her see what she had done to Ruda.

Ruda sat on a high chair with things clipped to her head. They could see each other, but they couldn't touch, they couldn't hear. Poor, sick Ruda held up by nurses. When the curtain was drawn again, she concentrated even harder and was duly rewarded, told that as she had been such a good girl, Ruda would also be rewarded.

Rebecca rubbed her temples, staring at the coloured

glass. It began to blur, her head throbbed. She was trying to reach Ruda, just as she had as a child. Rebecca began to weep. She could not hope to reach out to her, it was too late. She held her hands to her face, could not help but feel embittered by her mama's foolishness. If only Rosa had understood, had not been afraid, if only she had allowed Rebecca to open up her past, then she might have been able to find Ruda. Instead, Rosa had buried Ruda alive inside Rebecca's mind.

Ruda looked over the props, even though Grimaldi had done so already. Next she went to the meat trailer, asked if all the cats had eaten. She was on her way to Mamon's cage, when she remembered the time, and checked her watch. The crowds would soon be starting to line up. She was heading back to the trailer when, suddenly, her head felt as if it was bursting open. She gasped with the pain and leaned against the side of a trailer. A young girl jumped down, asked if she was all right. Ruda nodded, and pushed herself to carry on, telling herself it was because of all those old memories of her past. She was tired, she had to lie down again, rest again, she hadn't eaten – that's what it was, she had to have something to eat.

Torsen arrived at Freda's apartment building and, giving a quick brush of his hair with his fingers, rang the bell. She opened the door before he had time to take his finger off the buzzer. She had her coat over her arm, and her handbag in her hand. Freda remarked on the patrol car. She asked if it meant he was on duty, and he shook his head. They drove off as he explained they were to pick up his sergeant and then his girlfriend.

The two couples talked animatedly, looking forward to the show. Rieckert kept taking out his free tickets, showing the price, and replacing them in his wallet. Torsen kept giving Freda small sidelong glances. 'How was my father today?'

'Well, he was fine at breakfast, but then it was snowflake time again.'

Rieckert asked what she meant, and Freda explained, pulling a little bit of tissue from her purse, licking it and sticking it on the end of her nose, then blowing it off. 'He does it for hours until the bedcover and the floor look like there's been a snowstorm.'

Rieckert laughed and nudged Torsen, said he would keep his eye on him, it could be hereditary. Torsen seethed. He would have to speak to Freda about this snowflake business, it wasn't funny. As Rieckert started to do it in the back seat, making his girlfriend shriek with laughter, Torsen got more and more uptight. 'If it was your father, you wouldn't think it was funny! It is *not* funny!'

Rieckert blew a fragment of tissue off his nose. 'I agree! But it's one hell of a hobby!'

As the Baron and Helen continued walking, they passed one of the circus advertisements. Helen stopped, looked at the face surrounded by lions. She hesitated . . . Louis turned back to her and she pointed to Ruda Kellerman's name. 'Ruda,' she repeated, and then stepped out to hail a passing taxi.

Louis joined her. 'Why a taxi? He said she was walking.'

Helen bent down to the driver. 'The circus, please take us to the circus!'

The circus car park was filling up, crowds began walking from the train stations, the coaches deposited parties near the fenced perimeter. The main ticket office was crowded with lines of people waiting to buy their tickets. Children waited impatiently to have their photograph taken on top of the elephant's back. Clowns passed leaflets, sold balloons, the speakers roared music, and two drum majorettes paraded up and down banging their drums, their red costumes covered in sequins.

Ruda sat in the bedroom of her trailer. She wore her boots and white trousers; she did not have her jacket on, there was plenty of time for that and she didn't want to crease it. She was shaking, her body wouldn't stop trembling. She pressed her hands together, they were wet with sweat, she had never felt this way before. She didn't know what the matter was, she was beginning to get frightened. Luis hurtled into the trailer.

'Standing room only, they're going to have to turn away hundreds, it's pandemonium out there. Have you taken a look? Come on, come and see the crowds, they're going to let go with the laser beams, it's one hell of a sight! Come and see!'

'Luis, something's wrong with me, look, I'm shaking, I don't know what's the matter with me!'

He caught her in his arms. 'It's just nerves, because they are coming to see you, Ruda. Look – see, it's your face on every poster, your face, your act . . .'

Ruda heard the roar of the crowds as Luis opened the trailer door.

'*Jesus Christ* . . . Ruda! Look at the laser beams. My God, I've never seen a show like this, that old bastard knows how to draw the crowds!'

High in the sky, in brilliant colours, the lasers wrote:

RUDA KELLERMAN, THE MOST FAMOUS FEMALE WILD
ANIMAL TRAINER IN THE WORLD . . . RUDA
KELLERMAN, RUDA KELLERMAN, RUDA KELLERMAN!

Rebecca quickened her pace; she seemed buffeted along by the crowds heading towards the massive circus. She could feel the urgency of the crowd following behind her, see more people way ahead. Even if she wanted to turn back she would find it difficult, but she was not attempting to turn away, she was frantically pushing her way forwards, as if someone was calling out to her, someone was telling her to hurry. She had an overpowering urge to run, to push with all her strength. Suddenly the stream of people ahead stopped, they began pointing upwards to the laser beams in the sky. They gasped and called out, still surging forwards, but now with faces tilted skywards, but all Rebecca saw, all her mind focused on, was the name 'Ruda'. She could hear a child's voice calling out, screaming, 'I'm here, I'm here . . . I'm over here.' Lost in the milling people a little girl screamed for her mama, but to Rebecca it was a sign, a signal, and she had to get to the front of the crowd. 'Let me through, please, please let me pass!'

Ruda stood in the open door of her trailer, staring at the sky. Slowly she looked back to the crowds. Thousands of people were milling around, eating candyfloss, carrying balloons, surging toward the massive triple-ringed tent . . .

But there was someone else, she could feel it with every nerve in her body.

Rebecca stood with her face tilted to the sky, her head spinning at the blazing name. 'RUDA KELLERMAN!' She began desperately heading towards the trailer park. A steward at the gate was about to stop her, then waved her through with an apology – he thought she was Ruda Grimaldi.

Luis was like a kid, clapping and shouting. He turned to Ruda. She stood motionless in the open doorway.

'Are you OK, honey? Ruda?'

She stared ahead. He asked again if she was all right, but she didn't answer, she couldn't. She didn't even hear him, she didn't hear the crowds, the band, anything, because standing within yards of her was Rebecca.

Rebecca could not move, she could hear nothing, no sound, no voices. All she could do was look at Ruda, framed in the doorway, standing as motionless as she was. The sisters had not seen each other since before the liberation of the camp, and yet they knew without question, without hesitation, that they were confronting each other, were within yards of each other, both hearing in their frozen minds the other's childish voice, screaming as, hand in hand, they entered the nightmare of Birkenau.

'She is *my sister. She is my sister.*'

Luis was not sure what was happening. He saw the tall elegant woman, but so far away he couldn't see her features clearly. 'Who is it?' he asked, but Ruda stepped down from the trailer. He watched as she moved, step by step, closer and closer. She moved into the lights from the trailer windows, and still he did not connect, but she continued to move, step by step, closer and closer. 'Oh, Mother of God!'

Shadows played across her face, but he saw her eyes. They were Ruda's eyes, and he knew then . . . but he was immobilized, unable to move. All he could do was stand and look on . . . look as Ruda and the woman came steadily closer, oblivious to everything that surrounded them.

There was one pace, one step between them. They stood, the exact same height, but Ruda was more powerful, her body blocked Rebecca entirely from Luis. It was as if he saw only Ruda, as if the other woman did not exist. He moved sideways, trying to see, but he could only see Ruda's back shielding, hiding, as if protecting her other self.

They did not speak as their hands moved in unison to touch each other's face. But they spoke each other's name in their minds, in unison, as they melted into each other's arms, every touch like a mirror image.

Way past their heads, past the car park, out in the road leading to a circus entrance, Luis saw the ominous blue flashing light of a patrol car. 'Please, dear God, no. Please don't let them have come for Ruda, not now, not tonight.'

CHAPTER 19

ThEY LAY together like long-lost lovers, devouring with their identical eyes the physical changes in their faces.

They felt the rapid beating of their hearts. They had so much to impart to each other, to ask of each other and yet they could not break from the embrace. It had to be broken, and by Ruda. Inch by inch she released her hold, then rolled over to lie on her back. She felt Rebecca shudder.

'No, don't . . . don't cry, please don't.'

It took all Ruda's willpower to move away from the bed. She reached for one of the posters pinned to the wall, and turned back to Rebecca, holding the poster up for her to see. 'I am Ruda Kellerman.'

'I am . . .' Rebecca's lips trembled, she couldn't say her name.

Ruda held out her hand. 'Come. Come with me!'

Hand in hand, side by side, they looked at the photographs framed on the walls. Ruda pointed, speaking softly, odd descriptive sentences, and then their mind communication began.

'Chicago, London, Florida . . .'

Rebecca made soft, hardly audible 'Mmm' sounds,

nodding her head, and their interchanges became repetitive. Ruda would begin a sentence, and Rebecca would finish it.

'This was taken in . . .'

'Summer, taken in . . .'

'Yes, Mexico, this was the old . . .'

'Trailer. Who is . . . ?'

'That's Luis, he is . . .'

'Your husband, yes . . .'

'Yes, husband, you . . .'

'Yes, I married too . . .'

'Your husband?'

They both spoke at the same time, as they repeated their husbands' names – different spellings but the same sound. Then they giggled, at exactly the same time. As if they were regressing to their only memories of each other, their voices took on a childish intonation, and their words were no longer spoken in English but in disjointed mixtures of made-up languages; sometimes a word in German, or Polish, even Czech, their own language began to emerge. Every move was mirrored by the other. When Rebecca put her hand to her cheek, Ruda automatically touched hers. They were held in a world of their own.

But the outside world was closing in. The entire showground was a heaving mass of bodies. The car park was jammed to bursting point. Lines of people were waiting to buy ice creams and circus memorabilia; more lines formed by the ladies' and men's toilets, and the mass of ticket holders surging towards the big tent entrance was four to five abreast.

In all the mayhem some children were lost, a few screaming for their parents. Meanwhile the announcements

509

continued, describing the biggest circus acts ever to come to Berlin, while lasers lit up the sky.

Luis was pushing and shoving his way towards the stream of waiting cars. He could still see, about half a mile ahead, the *Polizei* car with its blue light flashing. He had made up his mind what he had to do and say. He began to run as best he could towards Inspector Torsen's patrol car.

Torsen was red-faced. Twice he had turned off the flashing light, but Rieckert had shouted that unless they used it, they would not make it in time for the opening parade. Rieckert was as excited as a child, urging Torsen on, digging him in the shoulderblade. 'Go on, put the siren on, make them pull over for you.'

Torsen banged the steering wheel. 'Look, there's hundreds ahead of us. They won't start the show, it's not due to begin for another three-quarters of an hour. We just have to wait like everyone else!'

Freda turned angrily to the back seat. 'He's right – we'll get there. They won't start the show before everyone's seated. Look up ahead, you think they won't let everyone inside first? Just sit back and enjoy the fireworks!'

Their car inched forwards, now minus the flashing light. It was frustrating to see passersby hurrying past on foot. Then the line came to a complete standstill. A car up ahead had overheated, and there were roars of laughter and calls of abuse as four young boys tried to push it over to one side.

Far back in the long line of cars was a taxi. Louis and Helen began to think they should turn back; after all, it seemed so far-fetched. Yet Vebekka was looking for a sister named Ruda, and one Ruda Kellerman was starring in the circus. There was, at least, a chance . . .

Helen suggested they get out and walk, they would certainly move a lot faster. Louis agreed, but the driver argued, as he could not turn back. Louis paid him more than the fare would have come to, and the well-dressed couple began to hurry alongside the cars.

The rain started, lightly at first, but after a while it began to come down steadily, so now there were umbrellas adding to the crush. Torsen could see Luis Grimaldi coming towards him, and he lowered his window. Luis was soaked, his hair wringing wet, and he was out of breath as he called out, 'Inspector . . . Inspector . . .'

Torsen smiled, and turned to Freda. 'This is my friend, Freda, I think you know Sergeant Rieckert . . .'

Rieckert leaned forward to shake Grimaldi's hand. 'I keep telling him to put his siren on, just to get us through the crowds. Will they start on time?'

Grimaldi looked puzzled, but then Torsen waved his tickets. 'We have complimentary seats, Mr Grimaldi, front row. Will everyone get in, do you think?'

Grimaldi walked alongside the car. 'Yes, yes. There are always enough seats or, if not, there's standing room. The show can be held maybe ten, fifteen minutes – but it's not usual. So, you are just here for the show?'

Torsen nodded, slamming his foot on the brake as they almost ran into the back of the vehicle in front. 'I am greatly looking forward to seeing your wife's act.'

Grimaldi walked away, relieved, but turned back again as Torsen called to him through the window. 'Mr Grimaldi . . . *Grimaldi*! You are welcome to ride with us. I don't suppose I could have a word on our behalf? It looks as if the car park's full,' Torsen said.

Grimaldi hesitated, then suggested that when they got to the barrier they ask to use the staff parking area. He would talk to the gatekeeper.

'Satisfied now?' Torsen said rather smugly to Rieckert.

The Baron and Helen held up their collars as they pressed on, surrounded by cars and people, many in such good spirits that they shared raincoats and umbrellas.

Grimaldi did not speak to the gatekeeper, but hurried back to his trailer. He passed Mike and two of the boys and asked why they were not in the animal tent.

'We've got to pull the barriers back to make more room for the crowds.'

Grimaldi nodded, and kept going. His mind churned over how narrowly he had come to making what could have been a disastrous mistake: the inspector wasn't coming for Ruda, just for the show. He gave a mirthless laugh, told himself he was a foolish old bastard. As he scraped the mud from his boots, he remembered again the query regarding Ruda's old boots. He sighed. Best just to ignore it, he told himself, forget it.

Luis banged on the door and let himself in.

The women turned towards him in unison. Ruda smiled. 'This is my . . .'

'Sister,' said Rebecca.

Ruda's cheeks were flushed, her eyes brilliant. Her mouth was tremulous, quivering; torn between smiling and crying.

They spoke as one: 'We are sisters – sisters . . . She is my sister, sister!'

Luis found it unnerving, the way they moved together, spoke in the same high-pitched singsong voice.

'We are twins.'

'Twins,' repeated Rebecca. They both lifted their right

hand, touched their right cheek, and laughed. They laughed as one, and it was exactly the same pitch.

Luis looked from one to the other. 'But – you're not identical.'

They sat down at the same time. Crossed their left legs over the right. Ruda leaned forwards, Rebecca leaned forwards. 'We were, we were, we were, but Rebecca . . .'

'I had my nose altered.'

'Plastic . . .'

'Surgery.'

'Yes.'

'Yes.'

Luis poured himself a brandy. When he offered them a drink, they both shook their heads and said, 'No,' at the same time. For a moment he wondered if they were playing some kind of game with him.

'Just remember, Ruda, you've got a show to do!'

They talked together, heads very close. They made soft shushing sounds and there were jumbled words. Then they both looked towards him.

'Rebecca want to see . . .'

'Show, yes.'

'Yes!' They said, in unison.

Their eyes were identical in colour. So were their lips, their cheeks.

Luis felt uneasy. 'I see it now . . . the likeness. I see it.'

They nodded, smiling as if very pleased that he could see they were twins.

Luis looked at Rebecca. 'How did you find Ruda?'

Ruda answered, 'She went to the church in the city.'

'The lights . . .'

'Yes.'

There followed a conversation that Luis could not

make head nor tail of. He just heard the name Magda repeated, then watched as they both put their hands over their faces and laughed.

Luis leaned forward. 'Ruda, keep an eye on the time.' She ignored him. He got up and looked out of the window. 'The lines are thinning out.'

Their eyes seemed to follow him around the trailer. He sat down again, then half rose. 'Do you want to be alone? Left together?'

He saw the way they pressed closer, and he sighed, looking at Rebecca.

'She must start to get ready. Do you understand?'

They stared back, with their identical wide eyes. He sipped his brandy. 'Where are you from? I mean, do you live in Berlin?'

Ruda answered saying that Rebecca was staying in a hotel. 'Her husband is called . . .'

They both said, 'Louis!' and then giggled, bending their heads.

Their interaction began to irritate Luis. He drained his glass, putting it down. 'I'll go and check on the boys.'

As he opened the door, he asked, almost as an afterthought, 'Do you work in a circus, Rebecca?'

'No,' said Ruda. They both said the one word, 'Mother.'

'I'm sorry?' Luis didn't understand.

Ruda said her sister was a mother. Rebecca nodded, and shrugged her shoulders. Ruda gave the same shrug, but Rebecca answered. 'I am just a mother.'

'Mother,' said Ruda.

Luis had his hand on the door handle. He wanted to leave them, and yet there were so many questions he wanted to ask. 'Does she know where your parents are? I mean, if they're alive?'

They both looked at him, turned to each other, then back to him.

'For God's sake, stop this! You're acting crazy, Ruda. I mean, can't she speak for herself?'

'Yes,' they both said, and Luis yanked open the door.

Then Ruda answered solo. 'She was adopted.'

'Adopted, yes,' chimed in Rebecca.

'After the war,' said Ruda, firmly.

'After the . . .' Rebecca's voice trailed off.

Luis sighed, it was too much for him to handle. 'Well, I'm glad – glad you've found each other.' He didn't mean it to sound so hollow, so lacking in warmth, as if they had been apart for only a few hours, days, weeks – not a lifetime. He felt guilty, forced a smile. 'You two have a lot to catch up on, but don't delay too long, Ruda.'

They stood up, hands still held tightly. 'Nothing will ever separate us again.' They spoke as one, turned and held each other, lifting their arms, so synchronized it was like a slow dance.

Luis closed the trailer door behind him, rested his back against it, not sure what he should do. A feeling of dread swamped him and his hands were shaking. Seeing the sisters together upset him. In some ways he was angry with himself, knew he should have stayed to make sure Ruda got herself ready.

The rain was bucketing down and Luis had no coat. He muttered to himself. It was stupid, all he had to do was turn around, walk inside the trailer to fetch one. But he didn't want to see them again, not just at this moment. He looked at his watch and knew Ruda should be getting ready. Then he looked over towards the main tent. Just a few stragglers stood at the box office now, and the last cars to be parked were being directed towards the car park, the gatekeeper in his bright yellow cape making authoritative, sweeping gestures.

Luis passed by the lighted window of his trailer. He peered into it, but the blinds were down, he could see nothing. The laser beams continued to spell out the acts, and he looked up, waiting for Ruda's name. Suddenly the sky blazed with the looped, magical writing: RUDA KELL-ERMAN. He said a silent prayer that being united with her sister would not distract Ruda. He, more than anyone else, knew just how important it was for Ruda to have all her wits about her. He plodded heavy-footed through the sodden ground and made up his mind that, just in case, he would be more diligent outside the performance ring tonight, would carry a loaded rifle. He stopped, unconcerned that he was getting soaked to the skin.

'I love her.' He said it out loud, helplessly, to no one. The dawning of how little he really knew about Ruda and her past shamed him. 'I love her.' Of course he did. Hadn't he been prepared to tell that strait-laced inspector that he had killed Kellerman himself? He, Luis, could have been in handcuffs by now. It was just sad that after all the years they had been together, it was only now that he realized just how much he loved Ruda. He shook his head, smiling to himself, and then chuckled.

They would be on the move soon, out of the country. She would be safe, he had time to make up for the bad years. Luis hesitated again, wondering if Rebecca would be coming with them . . .

'I love my wife . . .' he said again, out loud. Anyone who had witnessed his slow stop-start progress from the

516

trailer would have concluded he was drunk, talking away to himself in the pouring rain, without a coat on.

Helen and the Baron reached the barrier and asked the way to the administration offices, sure they would be able to gain their information there. The ground was slippery; Louis held Helen's elbow tightly to ensure she did not fall. They stepped on to duckboards leading to the offices.

Their arrival was not welcome. At first the secretary believed the Baron was simply trying to get tickets in the main guest arena, to be invited to the small champagne party the owners had organized. She politely asked if they would wait while she tried to reach one of the administrators, inferring that it was an inopportune moment for anyone to request a private meeting.

The Baron, charming as always, gave a winning smile and said that rather than wishing to interrupt anyone, and far from wanting tickets to see the show, he simply wished to speak to Ruda Kellerman.

The girl beckoned the Baron over to a layout map of the trailer park. 'Ruda Kellerman is Luis Grimaldi's wife, but whether or not she will agree to see you, sir, I can't say. She will be getting ready for the show.'

The Baron smiled gratefully, and ushered Helen out, back down the slippery boards. They stood trying to remember which direction they should take. 'Perhaps, Helen, this was not such a good idea.'

Helen tucked her arm in his and said that as they had come this far they might as well try to speak to Ruda Kellerman.

*

Mike showed off the meat trailer, the freezers and the massive carcasses to Torsen and his party. He had been the one Torsen had approached to enquire whether Grimaldi had mentioned they could park in the artists' private parking area. Mike had signalled them through. 'I work for the Grimaldis,' he had told Torsen, and had been flattered at their interest. As they began to head towards the main entrance, Mike had offered to show them a short-cut. He had led them behind the trailers, pointing out the ones owned by the big acts, and then offered to show them the meat trailer. Until the show started he had nothing else to do.

Torsen checked his watch, worried he would miss the opening parade, but Mike had assured him there was plenty of time. He told them that the 'Big Boss' would make sure every single ticket was sold, every seat taken, before the parade began. 'You think they'll never get everyone seated in time, but they always do. Maybe five, ten minutes late – never more. Besides, I'll show you the artists' entrance – if your tickets are for the front row, it'll be much easier.'

As they peered into the freezers and looked over the cleavers and hammers, Vernon came in, already in costume. Mike made the introductions, and was about to suggest they follow him to the big top when Torsen asked nonchalantly if Mike had ever met Tommy Kellerman. Mike said he had seen him the day he was murdered – briefly, up by the lions' cages. Torsen turned to Vernon and repeated his question. Vernon flushed, shrugged his shoulders, muttered he was not too sure whether he had seen him or not.

'You know he was brutally murdered?' said Torsen.

Freda looked at Torsen, and he could see that she was impressed. He decided to elaborate. 'Yes, Kellerman was brutally murdered. So if you saw him, anything you can tell me could be of great importance. I am heading the homicide investigation.'

Mike gave Vernon a warning glance, then checked his watch. 'Look, I'd better go and change!'

Vernon suggested that, since he was already dressed, he could show Torsen to the big tent, and Mike, after another warning look at him, skipped off. As they hurried across the muddy ground towards the big tent, Torsen asked again about Kellerman. Vernon said nothing, holding open the tent flap and instructing them to turn right through the main arena entrance. 'I hope you enjoy the show.'

Torsen smiled and was about to step inside, when the boy called out to him. He turned. The boy held the umbrella down, the rain glanced off the black-soaked canvas. 'I did see Kellerman, sir, but only for a brief moment. He was standing talking to Mrs Grimaldi, up by Mamon's cage. It was early afternoon the day I think he was killed.'

Torsen stepped closer. 'Were they having a friendly chat?' He felt water trickle down his neck, and inched beneath the umbrella.

'I don't know, I couldn't hear, sir. In fact I thought, at first, that he was one of the kids, you know, from the school parties. They take them around the cages. She looked as if she was telling him off. She had been in one of her moods – Grimaldi had been hitting the bottle a bit, on one of his binges, so he was pretty useless and she'd had to do everything ... and the plinths, the new

519

pedestals were wrong. She's got a right temper, has Mrs Grimaldi, and she's always telling the kids off for getting too near the cages, but then – I noticed his hat.'

Torsen stepped further under the umbrella. 'His hat?'

'Yes, sir, it was a trilby, black leather trilby.'

'How did you know it was leather?'

'Oh, well, I saw it again, in the meat trailer. Well, I think it was his hat – Mike was wearing it.'

'Mike?'

'Yes, sir, the other helper, sir. He was wearing it. He said he'd found it in the trailer, but Mrs Grimaldi took it off him, she said it was her husband's, but it looked like the same hat I saw Kellerman wearing. Dunno why I remembered it, but then everyone around here's been talking about the murder, so it sort of stuck in my mind, you know, wondering if it was him I had seen.'

'But you said you did see him?'

'Well, I don't know for sure if it was Kellerman, sir. Just, well, he wasn't with this circus – I know that. He wasn't with any of the acts, or I would have recognized him.'

They heard a loud fanfare, and Torsen looked at the big tent.

'That's the parade starting, sir, you'd best hurry or they won't let you get to your seat this way.'

Grimaldi had seen them all leaving the meat trailer, had followed Vernon and Torsen towards the big tent, had watched them huddled beneath the umbrella together. As Vernon hurried away, he stepped out and caught the boy by his coat.

'I want to know what he asked you. What did he want sniffing round the freezer truck like a stray dog?'

Vernon backed off, terrified of Grimaldi. 'He said

you'd told him he could park in the artists' car park, then he asked about the cats. Mike brought him in, he offered to show him the trailer. That was all, sir.'

Grimaldi patted Vernon's shoulder. 'I'm sorry, son, just that I'm a bit on edge tonight, it's a big occasion. Have you seen Ruda?'

Vernon said that he had not, and was relieved when Grimaldi started to walk away.

'Oh, Vernon, tell Mike I'll be watching the cages tonight.'

'Yes, sir.'

Grimaldi looked back, his eyes narrowed. 'You sure that prick wasn't asking questions about Tommy Kellerman?'

'Yes, sir.'

'Cats all lined up ready, are they?'

'Yes, sir, I'll double check them before we go in.'

Grimaldi nodded and waved his big hand to indicate that Vernon could carry on with his business. In truth, he was not sure what he should do himself. He looked at his watch; there was still a good three-quarters of an hour before Ruda went on with the act, but she had to be dressed ready for the parade. He didn't want to go back to the trailer, not yet, so he meandered around, making his way towards the line-up of cages. He heard his name called, turned and saw Mike waving to him.

'Boss, there's a bloke and a blonde woman. They've been asking the way to your trailer. They went towards it about two minutes ago.'

Grimaldi hurried to Mike. 'They say who they were?'

'Yeah, I think the guy was a baron, maybe one of the celebrity guests. There's a bit of a bash in the main conference room over in the administration block.'

521

Grimaldi pulled a face. There were always the stars, the rent-a-celebrity, at these big opening shows. He ran his hands through his soaking hair. 'Sod 'em. Oh! Mike, in future you want to show any bloody people around the freezer and meat trailers, you get permission, OK, son?'

'Yes, sir.'

They walked on to the covered tent attached to the big tent housing the animals.

'What did he want to go in there for, anyway?'

Mike was uneasy, he knew he should have got permission, so he lied. 'Oh, he asked us a few questions, you know, if we'd seen Kellerman, Mrs Grimaldi's ex—'

'I know who he was!' snapped Grimaldi.

'As it was raining, we took cover in the trailer.'

'What did you tell him?'

Mike wiped his face. 'Nothing, sir. I'd better check the props.' He tried to move away, but Grimaldi held onto his arm.

'The cats all settled and in order?' Grimaldi asked.

'Yes, sir, everything's in order.'

Grimaldi walked from one cage to the next. As always, the cats touched him with wonder; their wild beauty, their menace, affected him deeply. The big cats had been part of his entire life, he truly loved them. He checked each cage, and then he heard the low heavy growl, like a dull rumble.

Grimaldi stood about two feet away from Mamon. Even waiting for the act, he was solo. Grimaldi paused.

Mamon's eyes glinted, his head hung low, feet splayed out, sensing the man's fear, enjoying the domination.

*

Their voices spoke together. 'Sasha! Sophia! Jason, Luis . . .' Four of Ruda's cats had the names of Rebecca's children. They hugged and laughed at the coincidences. Grimaldi hid behind Mamon's cage, watching them. They walked in step. But from a distance, Grimaldi could detect that Rebecca was just a fraction behind Ruda, as if the movement was not instinctive, but copied. She was like Ruda's shadow, and because she was so slender – willowy almost – the shadow effect, in the low lights of the animal arena, made them appear even more like one being.

They had not caught up the lost separation years, they could not in so short a time. Only disjointed sections of each other's lives had been snatched and clutched at. Ruda knew Rebecca was married with four children, Rebecca knew Ruda was married and trained big cats. The scars held firm, but a thin layer had already slipped from them both . . . There were many layers to uncover, many questions to ask, but all they wanted now was this closeness. They constantly studied each other, touched each other, to make sure they really were reunited.

Rebecca showed no fear of the cats, only an extraordinary excitement. She wanted to touch them, put her hands through the bars, and Ruda had to hold her back, whispering that it was too soon.

'Too soon, yes, yes, too soon . . .' repeated Rebecca.

Ruda's physical strength made Rebecca weak with adoration, to feel the powerful body, the rough hands, made her want to be constantly wrapped in Ruda's arms. Ruda felt the dependency of her sister, it awoke in her a gentleness, a protectiveness that made her body tingle. She showed off her life with pride, wanting Rebecca more than anyone else to see her loved ones, to see her perform.

'This is everything I dreamed . . .'

'Yes, you dreamed this, and I want . . .'

'You to see me, with my children.'

'Yes, they are my children,' Ruda paused, realization dawning, and gave a strange half laugh. 'Sasha, your last daughter, she is twelve, yes?'

Rebecca nodded. Ruda recalled the pains she had felt at the time of each birth, each child. Sasha's birth pains she remembered most clearly, they coincided with the time she had been told she could never carry a child herself. As if she knew this, Rebecca clasped her sister's hand in comfort. In some ways it was as if they had never been apart. Rebecca accepted Ruda without question. She had reverted, unknowingly, in that one hour to the way the relationship had always been. Ruda was dominant, Rebecca passive. Ruda had been born first, by two minutes.

The fanfares grew louder, and Grimaldi watched Ruda lead Rebecca towards the artists' entrance. By now he was soaked, and knowing the trailer would be empty he made his way back to change for the show.

The fanfare was deafening. Torsen couldn't see Freda or Rieckert and his girlfriend anywhere. Apologetically, he edged his way through a group of jugglers waiting to enter. The waiting performers stared suspiciously at him, and he mumbled his reason for being there. A painted clown gestured to him to go through the entrance flap quickly. 'You shouldn't be here, hurry.'

Torsen moved cautiously along the sides of the tiers of seats. He stood at the edge of the ring and looked around the audience. He could see walls of lights, tiers and tiers, thousands of seats. He didn't have his seat number – all he knew was that they had front-row seats – and he squinted through the semi-darkness, searching the sea of faces. Beyond the small ring was the vast central main ring, beyond that the third ring. Dear God, he thought, I'll never find them. Suddenly the huge big top was in complete darkness. The crowd murmured, sensing the show was about to begin. The fanfares blared, once, twice: 'LADIES AND GENTLEMEN, SCHMIDT'S WORLD FAMOUS CIRCUS WELCOMES YOU! THREE RINGS, HUNDREDS OF ARTISTS. WE WELCOME YOU TO A NIGHT OF UNPARALLELED EXTRAVAGANZA! FROM ARGENTINA, THE WORLD FAMOUS BAREBACK RIDERS – THE COMANCHEROS . . .'

Torsen, his eyes at last accustomed to the darkness, made out his companions' faces. They were seated at the side of the main ring's entrance. He bent low and scurried along the narrow alley between the front-row seats and the ring itself; he tripped and stumbled so he stepped on to the rim of the ring and ran the last few yards, to fall into his vacant seat just as the horses thundered into the ring.

Freda clasped his arm. 'Isn't this exciting? You know, I have never been to a circus before!'

Torsen inched off his wet coat, and wriggled it down beneath his seat. Freda moved away to give him room and then as he sat up, rested close to him, slipping her hand through the crook of his arm. Torsen touched her fingers. 'I am glad I asked you to come with me, Freda.'

She looked in awe at the massive ring as the Argentinian riders screamed and called out at the top of their voices. Twenty-five horses, groomed and gleaming, galloped around carrying a sparkling banner. The bareback girls whooped and yelled as they bounced and bobbed, leaping in one fluid move to stand upright on the horses' backs with nothing more than a glittering red ribbon for a rein. The smell of the horses, the sawdust, the resin added to the excitement.

Torsen felt happy. His father had been right: Freda was lovely.

Grimaldi had pulled on his clean shirt, was buttoning the high collar, listening to the fanfares. He knew exactly how many there would be before the parade ended, and he quickly tucked his shirt into his trousers. Then he opened the bunk seat, and looked over the rifles, searched around for ammunition . . .

The Baron and Helen approached one of the car-park stewards, and the Baron asked which was the Grimaldi trailer. He was taken aback when the man turned on them. 'Where's your pass?'

'I don't have one, I am Baron—'

'You don't have a pass, then please leave the artists' section.'

'No, I wish to speak with Mr Grimaldi – his wife Ruda Kellerman. It's very important.'

'No way. See the big tent – they'll be in there. I'm sorry, please leave. I can't let you wander around here. Go on, through the barrier.'

The Baron was about to argue some more when Helen suggested that perhaps they should wait; it was obvious they would not be able to speak to either Grimaldi or Ruda Kellerman now.

'Sir! Mr Grimaldi!'

Luis turned, quickly hiding the rifle beneath his rain cape.

The steward ran to Grimaldi. They conferred, then the steward pointed back to the Baron and Helen. 'I told them to wait, sir. They got no pass, but they said it was important.'

Grimaldi walked up to the Baron. 'What do you want?'

The Baron asked if they could talk somewhere in private, but Grimaldi shook his head. 'Not before the show. What do you want?'

'It is very important. I need to speak to you about my wife.'

'Your wife?' Grimaldi held his hand up to enable him to see better as the rain lashed at his face.

'Yes. This is Dr Helen Masters. My wife is her patient. Have you met Baroness Vebekka Maréchal? We think there may be some connection between her and Ruda Kellerman.'

Grimaldi hesitated.

Helen moved closer. 'Please help us, she is very sick. We think she may have tried to see Ruda Kellerman.'

'Is the woman called Rebecca?'

'*Yes!* Yes.' The Baron stepped closer, but Grimaldi moved back sharply. 'Is she here? Have you seen her?'

Grimaldi had to shout above the noise of the circus orchestra, the rain. 'She came here. She was with Ruda, but I don't know where she is now. Come to the trailer after the show.'

'Did you speak to her?' asked Helen.

'Yes, yes, I did. She's sick, you say?'

The Baron gripped his hands tightly. 'This is very important. Please, we must talk to her.'

527

Grimaldi looked back to the tent. 'I can't talk to you now, the show's starting. Your wife, she says she is Ruda's sister; they were together earlier, they said they're twins.'

Helen grabbed hold of Grimaldi's rain cape. 'Is Ruda Kellerman here?'

'She is about to go into the ring. Look, I don't know what you can do now. I'll try to find her, tell her you're here. Wait at the trailer, the big silver one over there – but after the show. I have to go!'

'Please, please, wait – your wife, Ruda—'

Grimaldi backed away, pointed again to his trailer. 'Meet me here, after the show.'

The Baron and Helen watched him hurry away, then stop and turn back. He shouted for them to mention his name at the box office, to go into the big tent.

Helen and the Baron crossed towards the box office. All the tickets were sold, but there was still standing room left. The Baron was soaked, his shoes muddy, and he was about to insist they return to the Grimaldi trailer, but Helen ignored and opened her handbag. 'Louis, we'll do as he said, just wait until the end of the show. We'll take two standing-room tickets, please.'

'You will have a very good view, it'll be worth it,' said the cashier, and pointed towards the tent. 'I'd hurry, the parade's already started.'

The artists were lined up, waiting at the edge of the entrance to the rings, watching for their lights: red for stand by, green for go. The music blared from massive speakers as the live orchestra, its conductor in a tuxedo, gave each act in the parade its set piece of music as the ringmaster introduced it, his red frock coat, his black silk top hat and whip caught in the spotlight.

528

'FROM RUSSIA – THE GREATEST HIGH-WIRE ACT IN THE WORLD . . . THE STRAVINSKY FAMILY!'

Ten men and four women in crimson robes ran into the ring, bodies fit and muscular. They paraded with a marvellous arrogance, strutting and twirling their cloaks, eyes flashing.

Ruda Kellerman never did the parade with her cats, but she walked it. Now she waited her turn to enter. The hectic swirling events buffeted and frightened Rebecca, but also exhilarated her, made her whole body tremble. Ruda kept tight hold of her twin's hand, describing some of the acts. Anyone close was proudly introduced. 'This is my sister!'

Ruda had dressed for the parade in a tailored black evening suit, a white silk shirt with heavy ruffles at her neck, and a flowing black cloak with white satin lining. The trousers were skin tight, and she wore black polished high Russian riding boots. She held a pair of white gloves and a top hat, and smiled broadly, joking with friends as they passed her to enter the ring. Her red warning light flicked. The Tannoy warned: 'Stand by, Ruda Kellerman.'

She whispered to Rebecca that any moment it would be her cue. But when she released her hand, Rebecca clung to her. Ruda cupped Rebecca's face in her strong hands. 'Just for a moment. Watch me!'

'LADIES AND GENTLEMEN, THE MOST DARING, THE MOST FAMOUS, THE MOST AUDACIOUS, FEARLESS, FEMALE, WILD ANIMAL TRAINER IN THE WORLD . . . PLEASE WELCOME TO BERLIN THE STAR OF OUR SHOW. WELCOME TO BERLIN, RUDA KELLERMAN! RUDA KELLER-MAN, LADIES AND GENTLEMEN!'

The spotlight hit Ruda who stood with arms raised

above her head, the cloak swirling around her. She stood motionless, held in the brilliant beam of light, then strode to the centre of the ring. She turned to the right, to the left, bowing low, taking her applause. She continued across the ring. The cheers and applause had never felt so sweet.

Torsen stared at the confident figure, leaning forwards slightly. Having met Ruda, to see her now was fascinating. Rieckert turned to Torsen. 'Eh, she's something else isn't she? I can't wait to see her with the big cats.'

Helen and the Baron were five rows behind, in the standing-room section. Helen could not even see the ring. Louis looked at her.

'I told you. This is a waste of time, we can't see.'

Helen beckoned to Louis to follow, as she pushed and shoved her way through the section. 'Look, Louis, there's four seats vacant in the second row. Why don't we just take a seat? If the ticket holders arrive, then we'll move. Come on.'

'FROM FLORIDA, AMERICA'S ARABIAN NIGHTS – THE FINEST ARAB HORSES IN THE WORLD . . . THE FINEST HORSEMEN . . . THE FRANKLYNN BROTHERS!'

No one stopped them. Louis and Helen now had a perfect view of the centre ring. They took their seats as Ruda Kellerman left the ring. Helen leaned across to the couple sitting next to them and asked if she could borrow their programme. Louis was astonished at her audacity. Helen looked down at it and passed it to Louis.

'Ruda Kellerman is on last, just before the intermission.'

Louis looked over the programme, holding it at a slight angle to enable him to read in the semi-darkness.

His handsome face was caught in the half light, his high cheekbones accentuated. He leaned across Helen to thank the owner of the programme. Helen saw his charming smile, saw the woman blush as she said, 'Any time!'

'THE BELLINIS! PLEASE WELCOME – FROM ITALY – WELCOME DIDI AND BARBARA BELLINI . . . AND THEIR TEAM OF DOGS!'

Ruda was hurrying round the back of the tent when she saw Luis. She called out to him, with a broad smile, 'What a house, can you hear them?'

He nodded. As they drew close, he could see her eyes were shining. 'I can't wait . . . *I can't wait, Luis! Tonight, I will be the most magnificent, the best . . .*'

She was walking so fast he almost had to jog to keep by her side. She drew off her white gloves and flicked them at him. 'You know what it means for me to have her here? For her to see me? You know, Luis, we used to make up stories and always, always, Luis, I would say: I am the lion tamer!'

She hurried back to the artists' enclosure, talking nineteen to the dozen, unbuttoning her cuffs and the buttons on her shirt. Then she stopped and turned to him. 'You made my dreams come true, Luis. Did you know that?'

He had never seen her so happy, so relaxed. She seemed to dance, light quick steps as she hurried on, tossing the cloak to him. 'You made my dream come true. *I am here, Luis,* and . . . and my sister is here. My heart, Luis, my heart is breaking open!'

'I love you, Ruda.'

But she had moved on. With his arms full of the heavy cloak, her hat and gloves, he couldn't keep up with her.

He trailed behind like a lackey, tripping, stumbling and then he watched as Rebecca ran to Ruda. They embraced, Rebecca giving Ruda frantic childish kisses.

'Rebecca! Wait! Your husband was here looking for you with a woman, a doctor!'

Rebecca stared wide-eyed at Grimaldi. She seemed terrified, but Ruda, impatient to change for her act, drew Rebecca towards the exit.

'Did you hear what I said? I told them to meet us at the trailer. Ruda?'

They ignored Grimaldi and ran out, step for step. He saw Ruda stopped by the steward, saw him point at Rebecca, and Ruda fling a protective arm around her shoulders. No one was allowed guests at the back of the arena unless with a special pass. Ruda pushed the steward roughly out of her way, holding the flap open for Rebecca. 'She is not anybody, she is my sister!'

Torsen flicked through the programme and turned to Rieckert, pointing out when Ruda Kellerman was on. He then put his arm around Freda's shoulders. She was laughing at the clowns who rushed around with a bucket filled with soap suds. Torsen's initial genuine enjoyment suddenly palled. The small clown, with his short legs and funny bowler hat, was the same size as Kellerman. It could have been Kellerman – except he was dead and buried. Torsen watched the diminutive figure hurl himself around the ring. Everything he had been told began to niggle and eat away at his pleasure. Seeing Ruda in the black suit had not really meant anything, but now he felt sure it was she who had walked away from the murdered Kellerman's hotel, who had worn the dead man's hat to disguise herself. He knew she had lied to him, not once but many times. She was strong enough to have killed Kellerman, he knew that. The question was, how in God's name could he prove it?

Everything going on in the ring blurred as Torsen concentrated on piecing together what little evidence he had accumulated against Ruda Kellerman. All three rings were bursting with activity, chimpanzees, clowns, acrobats . . .

'THE WONDERS OF THE ANIMAL KINGDOM . . . RAHJI THE ELEPHANT MAN!'

Grimaldi had given her an alibi, but the young boy, Vernon, had said Grimaldi had been on one of his binges. What if he was drunk on the evening of the murder? Would he have known what time she came or went? Had Grimaldi lied? And where were the boots?

'It's the elephants next!' Rieckert shouted, his tie loose, his face flushed pink.

Torsen pursed his lips. They did not sleep in the same room. How could Grimaldi give his wife an alibi if he was drunk? Torsen remembered Ruda saying Grimaldi was snoring, that he had kept her awake. So obviously he had been sleeping. Could she – did she – leave the trailer, return . . . while Grimaldi slept through?

Freda clutched his arm as the elephants started to enter the ring. They came so close, they were within touching distance. Rieckert shouted excitedly to Torsen, 'I hope they don't let the lions this close, eh?'

An elephant's trunk swung dangerously close to Torsen, and he pressed back in his seat – much to the delight of Rieckert who shrieked with laughter. The giant animal gently placed his front feet on the ring rim: giant feet, carefully, delicately placed down, then the massive trunk swirled above their heads. They screeched and cowered as the elephant slowly turned back, and all eight elephants began to waltz.

Freda suddenly sighed.

'You OK? You weren't afraid, were you?' Torsen asked.

'It's sad in a way, isn't it? They are so wonderfully huge, and I don't like to see them looking foolish, dancing. It's not right.'

At that moment a baby elephant began to perform what could possibly have been termed a pirouette. The crowd roared its delight. But Freda obviously did not approve. Torsen began to like her more and more. He leaned in closer. 'If I get rid of Rieckert, would you have dinner with me? Tonight, after the show?'

She nodded her head, and his grip tightened. She rested her head on his shoulder and he wasn't thinking of Ruda any more.

Helen was laughing, amused by the antics of the baby elephant. Louis turned to watch her. She had such a lovely face, such neat features, she was a very attractive woman. It was as if he had never really noticed her before this evening. He reached over and held her hand. 'You know, I don't think I have ever really said how much I appreciate your kindness, your care of Vebekka. You must think me a very—'

Helen withdrew her hand. 'I think you have been under tremendous stress. I understand, and I hope—'

'I love her, Helen, I always have . . . I always will.'

'Yes, I know.' Helen knew no one could take Vebekka's place. He was a weak, delightful man. A charming man who had always found solace in women. Louis had

534

turned to other women to survive – that was all his infidelities were, substitutions. His weakness was his inability to face reality; instead of seriously trying to help Vebekka, he had others take that responsibility for him.

'THE FEARLESS, DARE-DEVIL DUPRÉS – FROM PARIS, FRANCE . . . NO SAFETY NET, LADIES AND GENTLEMEN! THE FLYING DUPRÉS DEFY DEATH!'

The main ring darkened as slim, white-clad figures climbed the ropes to the roof of the big tent. Louis looked up, watched the young beautiful boy expertly swing the trapeze backwards and forwards, his eyes on the catcher who dropped down, his arms free, his legs hooked over the bar of the swing. The swing picked up momentum, the boy continued to push out the free swing, and then sprang forwards, flying through the air. The swings passed each other, high above the audience's heads, and the crowds gasped, 'Ohhh!' and 'Ahhh!' as the young boy flew from his swing and performed a perfect triple somersault, the catcher reaching out with split-second timing to clasp his hands.

Louis looked at Helen. 'You know, that is how she makes me feel – like I am supposed to catch her. I almost touch her hands, almost get to hold her, save her, but she slips away, she falls. Helen?'

She patted his hand. 'We'll find her. You'll hold her, and maybe next time she won't fall, if she feels you are strong enough, but—'

'But?' he queried.

Helen smiled. 'But maybe we will need Dr Franks as a safety net.'

Louis nodded. 'Do you think this Ruda Kellerman really is her sister? It would be an extraordinary coincidence, wouldn't it? That she should be here in Berlin?

And my wife may be here somewhere in the circus with her?'

Helen edged closer, whispering, 'You know, Vebekka, I mean Rebecca, kept on saying, "It's close, it's very close." What if "it" meant her sister was close? I mean, if they were twins, then ... like it was some kind of telepathy between them. She knew her sister was close, but because of what had been done to her, she didn't, or couldn't remember she had a sister, or one that was alive.'

Louis gasped as, way above him, a trapeze artist slipped. The crowd gasped too. But it was a very carefully rehearsed mistake, one designed to make the audience afraid. The tent was silent as the artists prepared for a dangerous jump: springing from the swing on to a high wire in the darkness, not even seen by the audience. He seemed to fly downwards and then swung his body over and over the taut high wire, twelve feet below.

Helen stared high into the roof of the tent, trying to recall everything Rebecca had said. She felt her palms begin to sweat. She recalled the incident at the circus in Monaco. Rebecca had attempted to get into the ring. Could it have been instinctive, telepathic connection to her sister? Helen leaned against Louis. 'Louis, the time Rebecca attacked the circus clown. Do you know if Ruda Kellerman was also with the circus then? Louis?'

He did not hear the question. 'I wasn't there for her, Helen. I should have found out more about her past, cared more. Now I feel as if I have a second chance, and I intend to be there for her from now on. All I hope is that I am not too late.'

*

Rebecca helped Ruda into her costume, and then delight-
edly agreed to change into trousers and boots herself, and
wear one of the boys' red jackets.

'Good, it looks good. Now you don't have to stay by
the entrance, you can come right into the ring! Stand
outside the cages. Luis will look after you, won't you?'

Luis was not happy about it, said that Rebecca would
only get in the way and besides it was too dangerous, she
might distract Ruda or make her concentration waver.
Ruda dismissed his fears with a sweep of her hand.
'Rubbish. You take her in, she can stand by you and then
you take care of her, yes?'

Rebecca repeated, 'Yes?' and when he shrugged his
compliance, they both gave an identical gleeful giggle.

'But you must go now, Ruda. I'll bring Rebecca.
Please – you haven't been near the cages.'

Ruda nodded, then took Rebecca's hand. 'We're
ready!'

Grimaldi stood beside Rebecca as Ruda went over to
the boys. At last she seemed to be concentrating, checking
the props and cages as usual. Then she gave a signal for
the boys to start stacking the tunnel sections to the
entrance. Two more acts and they were on.

Ruda went from cage to cage. She had changed into
tight white trousers tucked into her black shiny boots,
and a white frilled Russian-styled shirt. The simplicity of
her costume made her appear smaller, slimmer, more
vulnerable. She carried only a short stick. Rebecca stepped
forward as if she wanted to follow Ruda, but Grimaldi
held her arm firmly. 'No, no, you must leave her alone
now. This is very important, she must pace herself now,
get herself ready.'

'Yes, yes, I understand. Get herself ready, she must be ready.'

Ruda was starting her pacing, up and down, up and down. Twice she stopped and looked over at Rebecca. She smiled, then returned to walking up and down, asking the boys if the fire hoop was set up, the pedestals stacked. Like her old self, she went over every detail. Grimaldi felt relieved as he saw the transformation, saw her twisting her head from side to side to relax her neck muscles, clenching and unclenching her hands over her stick. Then her pacing began in earnest, and as sharp as ever she pointed out to Vernon that one button was undone on his tunic.

Mike stood by the mass of stacked railings; four circus hands waited for the signal to move into the main ring. There would be two sets of clowns and jugglers covering the mounting of the cages in the central ring. The main ring would be in darkness as the safety barrier was erected; the boys waited for their standby light.

Red light on. Mike looked to Vernon. 'Stand by. OK, boys, stand by, we got the red light. Red light, Mr Grimaldi.'

'Two minutes for Kellerman's act. Stand by, you have red light . . . *go green, Miss Kellerman, please stand by.*'

Luis looked at Rebecca. She was shaking; he patted her shoulder. 'When the red light comes on over there, that is our cue to go into the ring. We go in first, then Ruda will get her own red and green light.'

In the darkened ring, the cages were brought into position, the tunnel erected. The first cage was positioned at the trapdoor of the tunnel.

Mike checked the trapdoor and used his walkie-talkie. 'Cages in position for tunnel over . . .'

'LADIES AND GENTLEMEN! SCHMIDT'S ARE PROUD TO

ANNOUNCE FOR YOUR ENTERTAINMENT TONIGHT, THE MOST FAMOUS, THE MOST DARING WILD ANIMAL ACT IN THE WORLD. PLEASE REMAIN IN YOUR SEATS. DO NOT ATTEMPT TO MOVE FROM THE RINGSIDE ANYWHERE NEAR THE BARRIERS. PLEASE DO NOT MOVE DOWN THE AISLES DURING THIS ACT. ANY ONE OF THESE WILD ANIMALS CAN KILL, PLEASE REMAIN SEATED . . . ANY MOVEMENT OUTSIDE THE BARRIERS CAN DISTRACT THE ANIMALS, CAN ENDANGER THEIR TRAINER.'

The crowds murmured, excitement increasing as the orchestra now began a slow drum beat.

Grimaldi got his green light to enter the ring. He picked up his rifle and beckoned for Rebecca to follow him. She kept close as he entered the darkened arena, making his way carefully to the far edge of the barrier to take up his watching position.

Vernon was already in his watcher's position opposite Grimaldi, and he lifted his radio. 'In position, Grimaldi on the far side with the woman. Eh! Looks like he's got a bloody rifle!'

Mike kept his eyes on Ruda as she paced up and down. He lifted the radio. 'He's just showing off, Vern. OK, we got the red! Stand by for green!'

Ruda pulled on her leather gloves. She seemed to make small jumps on the spot.

'LADIES AND GENTLEMEN . . . RUDA KELLERMAN!'

Green go! Green go!

Vernon heard the command and withdrew the bolts from the trapdoor leading from the tunnel into the ring. The entire ring was still in total darkness. Ruda entered from the side trapdoor, and made her way in the gloom towards the open trap from ring to tunnel. She backed into the tunnel ten paces, exactly ten paces.

'She's in position, over!'

Vernon heard Mike tell him the cats were released. *Bang!* Up came the central spotlight, pinpointing Ruda Kellerman running from the tunnel into the centre of the ring while close on her heels came Roja, her lead tiger. Packed behind him came fifteen more tigers. The crowd murmured. It looked, as it was supposed to, as if the tigers were chasing Ruda into the ring.

The act began. Rieckert gasped, 'Holy shit!'

Helen gripped hold of Louis's arm. 'My God, look at her, look at her face! Can you see, Louis?'

Louis half rose out of his seat. From where they were sitting, Ruda could have been Rebecca. Totally, utterly stunned, he couldn't get his breath. Helen pulled on his arm. 'I know, I know. I can see. My God, they're almost identical!'

Torsen released his arm from around Freda, and stared at the ring in astonishment, awe. There she was, surrounded by a mass of terrifying cats, running around her like sheep, their bodies so close they seemed to brush against her legs.

Ruda was in perfect control as she gave her commands. In perfect co-ordination they kept up the tight, circular move; tightening, faster and faster.

'Good, Roja . . . Roja, good . . . *Roja, break!*'

The massive tiger broke to his right. Now the sixteen tigers formed two circles as Ruda backed to the barrier and picked up the reinforced ladder. The spotlight spilled over to the barrier, picking out Grimaldi and Rebecca. It was only a split second, but it was enough for Helen to stand up. 'She's at the side of the ring, Louis. I saw her!'

Helen's jacket was pulled by the man behind her and she was sharply told to sit down. But Louis had seen too.

White-faced, he turned to Helen. 'I saw her, I saw Vebekka. She's with Grimaldi.'

Torsen was on the edge of his seat. He leaned across to Rieckert. 'Did you see her? The woman across the ring, on the opposite side?'

Freda turned to Torsen. 'What did you say?'

Torsen stared into the ring, and then gasped. 'My God! Look what she's doing!'

Ruda was backing up the ladder now. Roja turned inwards, the circle getting closer, tighter round the ladder. The ladder rocked dangerously – assisted by Ruda.

'Roja! Move move . . . *right* . . . *right! Sasha! Sasha, down!*'

This was the most dangerous part of the sequence. Ruda poised and ready to make her famous flying leap, the cats forming the tight group in front of her. Grimaldi moved closer to the bars, Rebecca pressed her face against them.

'Sasha, *down.*'

Grimaldi looked at Rebecca. She was repeating word for word: 'Sasha . . . Sasha . . . Sasha!'

Grimaldi looked back to the ring. Sasha was playing up. '*Down!* Sasha. Down, down!'

At exactly the same time Ruda gave the command to Sasha, Rebecca repeated it. Grimaldi grabbed her arm. 'Shut up! Shut up!' he hissed.

Rebecca turned to him, seemingly unaware of who he was.

'*Down! Down!*'

Grimaldi kept his grip, then sighed with relief. The sound was lost in the roar from the crowd as Ruda sprang forward and lay across the cats' backs. The cartwheel turn, then Ruda jumped back on to her feet. She gave the command to spread out. The applause was deafening. Now the cats were running like a wild pack. Ruda bowed, gave the animals the command for them to form the chorus dance line . . .

Sasha played up again. This time she refused to back up on to her hind legs, swiping at Ruda, snarling and growling. Then she started after the tiger next to her. They swiped and snarled at each other, and Ruda crossed over. '*Sasha, no* . . . up, up, *up!*'

Rebecca was shaking, repeating over and over, 'Sasha, Sasha . . .'

Vernon became very tense. The cats were refusing the commands repeatedly. Fights were breaking out, instigated by Sasha. Then Sophia, the big female at the end of the line, broke out of her place and joined in. Sweat streamed off Ruda's face.

Ruda pushed, Ruda cajoled, she shouted and ordered. At one point she cuffed Sasha's nose – hard. Sasha lashed out, but at last they were in line, behaving. They began to form the pyramid, then the roll-over, as Ruda moved one of the pedestals into the centre of the arena. It was a bright red pedestal, with a gold fringe. As rehearsed, Roja broke from the row and nudged Ruda from behind. She turned round to face him, shaking her finger, then returned to setting up the next pedestal.

Vernon kept his eyes glued to the waiting tigers. At a command, they all sat back on their haunches, paws waving in the air. Ruda looked as if she was gesturing to each to keep in the sit-up position, but she moved in and out of their territory, giving small hand signals for one or other to try to get off their pedestal. They swiped at the air with their paws, as if refusing. Ruda put her hands on hips in mock frustration.

Vernon got the radio message from Mike. 'Mamon's on his way down.'

With her back to the tunnel, still pretending to admonish the tigers, Ruda got a large bottle of milk and fed Roja, then looked back as if pleading for him to sit on the pedestal. The children in the audience shrieked with laughter, unaware just how dangerous it was not only to feed the big cat, but to take the bottle away.

A small spotlight spilled out to hit mid-centre of the tunnel. Now Mamon crept slowly down the tunnel, as if sneaking up behind Ruda. When she turned, she appeared not to see him, but actually gave Mamon the command to move behind her, while still pretending to encourage Roja to sit on the pedestal.

Roja refused. Ruda pretended to get angry. The children, as expected, began to shout, 'He's behind you!'

As trained, Mamon kept moving stealthily behind Ruda. Every time she turned she gave the command for a tiger to head back down the tunnel. Each time she turned back to her row of tigers, there was always one missing. Ruda made an elaborate show of counting tigers, looking puzzled, but she knew exactly where each cat was. Roja feigned an attack, Ruda sidestepped him, and the audience hushed as Roja made another run at her. This time she crouched down and he jumped over her head and ran into the tunnel. Ruda took out a bright red handkerchief and wiped her forehead. When she turned back, she stared in astonishment – all the pedestals were empty! All the tigers had gone down the tunnel!

Vernon whispered into his microphone. 'All clear . . . all clear. Bolt on, wait for Roja, over. OK, he's clear, he's out.'

The children screamed once more. 'He's behind you!'

Mamon roared. Their screams went silent. Ruda turned in mock fear to face the big lion. Vernon got the radio message. 'All back. Trapdoor down.'

Ruda was now left with Mamon, who was supposed to go and sit on the red pedestal all by himself, as if that had been his intention all the time, to clear away all the other cats and be the star.

Ruda gave Mamon his command, using the single word: 'Red!' and continued to play-act, bending to the empty tunnel, puzzled that the others had all disappeared.

Grimaldi tensed up, Vernon moved closer. Mamon was behind Ruda, but he was nowhere near where he should be, nowhere near the pedestal. His head hung low, he was moving stealthily forwards.

'Red . . . Ma' angel . . . Ma' angel . . . !'

Grimaldi heard Rebecca gasp. She broke free of him, clung to the bars. Her face was rigid. '*Red . . . red . . . red!*'

The sawdust churned up behind Mamon as he made a fast U-turn, and at a terrifying full gallop careered across the ring, flinging himself at the railings, at Rebecca. He seemed crazed, swiping at the bars . . . snarling, pushing forwards.

The audience went silent. Ruda moved to the centre of the ring. Only the ring was lit, not the barrier, so the audience could hardly see Grimaldi or Rebecca. But Rebecca fell back, terrified.

Ruda kept the pedestal between herself and Mamon. '*Yuppp Mamon . . . up up . . . red red . . . Ma' aangelll!*' He was too far across the ring to force back to the tunnel again. He began a crazed run around the barrier, teeth bared, his eyes crazy . . .

'Red, *good boy* . . . ma' angel . . . red!'

Rebecca was scratching at Grimaldi, saying over and over, 'Red, red, red . . .'

Vernon snapped an order for someone to get over to Grimaldi, get ready to let Ruda out of the trapdoor on that side. Mamon was going crazy.

Torsen bit his knuckles, his face white. 'It's out of control . . . look at it, it's going for her!'

Rieckert was pressed back in his seat. 'Bloody hell . . . she must be crazy! It's going to attack her—'

Mike sent one of the boys to stand by the trapdoor. Grimaldi signalled for him to get to his side. He pushed Rebecca forward. 'Take her out, just get her out of the way. I'll handle it, I'll see to the trapdoor.'

Rebecca called out to Ruda, but the orchestra was playing at full volume. Only the few rows close to Grimaldi could hear, could sense something was very wrong.

Rebecca was dragged out, her eyes turned back to the ring. Grimaldi cocked the rifle. There was a gasp from the rows and banks of seats close by. They could see him aiming it into the cage. The whispers spread, the fear was picked up around the vast tiers and tiers of seats.

Helen gripped the Baron's hand. 'Can you see him? He's got a rifle, but I can't see Rebecca. I think something is wrong. Do you think this could be part of the act?'

Mike listened as Vernon repeated into the radio that Mamon was going crazy, Ruda couldn't control him . . .

'He's acting up! No . . . no . . . hold the panic.'

They faced each other. Without Rebecca's presence Mamon seemed calmer. He still wavered, but Ruda moved in closer. She felt her whole body sweating, tingling, the adrenaline pumping through every vein. She faced him out, dared him. 'Come on . . . come on, ma' angel. Up red . . . red *up*! *Mamon*.'

She moved closer, closer. His massive jaws were open and drooling as he tossed his head from side to side. There was silence now. The orchestra had quietened, not because there was panic, but because towards the end of the act they played a soft, gentle piece of Wagner's *The Ring*, the moment when Siegfried discovers his beloved . . .

Ruda knelt on one knee and bowed her head. There was a gasp as Mamon sprang as if to attack her, but leaped over her head and landed perfectly on the pedestal. He eased his paws around to gain his balance, then sat, in a comfortable position, and slowly lifted his front paws up in the air. Ruda crossed to the pedestal and stood in front of him. Directly beneath him, she opened her arms to accept the applause, facing him.

'Mamon . . . good, good. Gently now, good boy.' Ruda turned, giving Mamon her back, and slowly he lowered his massive front paws to rest on her shoulders. The spotlight shrank . . . shrank until it shone on the great animal's head above Ruda's. Then she turned again to face him. The position was lethal, his paws on her shoulders. She could smell his breath, hear his heart pumping.

'Good boy . . . good, *kiss*!'

Ruda stepped quickly away. On command he was off the pedestal and running for the tunnel. She was left alone to bow, to take the thunderous applause. Many in the audience gave her a standing ovation.

'LADIES AND GENTLEMEN WE NOW HAVE AN INTERMISSION . . . BUT HURRY BACK TO SEE THE SECOND HALF OF THE FEARLESS, THE EXTRAORDINARILY DARING RUDA

KELLERMAN'S ACT. MEET WANTON, THE PANTHER. MEET MORE OF RUDA KELLERMAN'S AMAZING FAMILY OF WILD BEASTS.'

The lights came on as the ice-cream girls streamed down the aisles. Many of the audience remained in their seats dazed, unsure of what they had just seen, uncertain whether they had really been afraid or not.

Ruda was panting, patting her face dry with a towel as she ran across to her trailer to change in readiness for the second half of her act. Grimaldi was waiting. 'Don't take him into the second half, he's crazy. He refused time and time again.'

She turned on Grimaldi. 'I can control him, *I did*. Now back off from me, I know what I'm doing.'

Only then did she stop, look around. 'Where is she? *Luis, where is she?*'

Grimaldi snapped back that she was by the cages with Mike and Vernon. He continued to follow. 'She became as crazy as the bloody animals. Ruda – *Ruda, will you listen to me!*'

Ruda was splashing through the mud towards the trailer. 'I hear you, Luis. But please don't ask me to *listen to you!*' She exploded into fury. 'I saw the rifle, Luis! I don't want you in or near the ring for the second half, hear me? You are pitiful, *pitiful! So desperate to be part of the act you have to stand there like something out of a Wild West show!*'

She ran on. The sweat she had worked up in the ring now mingled with the cold rain, making her shiver. She entered the trailer leaving the door open for Luis. 'I'm cold. *I'm cold. Run the shower.*'

*

Rebecca was not with Mike, as Grimaldi had believed, but on her way back to the trailer. She was about to open the door when she heard Ruda's angry voice. She stood motionless as Grimaldi shouted, 'You don't give me orders like I was a dog!'

'Then what are you? What possessed you to stand like a prick with that bloody rifle?'

'Maybe, just maybe I was worried about you – you hadn't rehearsed, you were all uptight because of this Rebecca business.'

'She is my sister, *my sister, Luis*! You know what that means to me? Can you even contemplate what it means to have found her? She came to me, *she came to me, Luis*!'

Grimaldi sat heavily on the bunk bed, wiping his hair with the towel Ruda had tossed aside. She was pulling off her boots as she talked. Outside, Rebecca was frozen, unable to move from the trailer steps, huddled in Vernon's rain cape.

'Boots, help me with my boots.'

He held the toe and heel and jerked hard. 'She took a long time finding you. Why has she never appeared before?'

The boot came away in his hand and Ruda fell back. She pushed her other foot out to him, and he began to pull off the boot. 'She didn't know I was alive.'

'She tell you she looked for you?' he asked.

Ruda pushed against him. 'I looked for her, she looked for me. *Yes, yes, yes!* Oh, come on, pull, Luis, I've got to change.'

'There's something wrong with her, Ruda. I tried to tell you earlier. There was a man, said he was her husband, he was with a woman, a doctor. They said she was sick. I think they meant crazy sick, you know!' He pulled hard

548

at the boot-heel. The boot came away and Ruda fell backwards again.

'What did they tell you?'

'Nothing much. I just felt it from the way they were so desperate to find her. They knew about you, came looking for you. I said they'd best come to the trailer after the show.'

'Why did you do that?'

'What else was I supposed to say? I knew she'd been here – Christ! They wanted to try to find you there and then. If it wasn't for me they'd have been wandering around—'

'You should have just minded your own business.'

'You are my business.'

'Since when?'

Luis hesitated. 'Since . . . since you killed Kellerman.'

She stared at him and he sighed. 'I know, Ruda, so don't deny it. I know you killed him.'

Ruda unbuttoned her shirt. 'Ah, I see. You're going to blackmail me, is that it?' She pulled her sweat-soaked shirt off. 'Try it and I'll get your bloody rifle and I'll shoot your fucking head off . . .'

Luis grabbed hold of her. 'You know what I was prepared to do for you? That inspector – when I saw them arrive, you know what I wanted to do? Say it was me, say I killed Kellerman! I was going to do that for you, Ruda, because—'

Ruda let the shirt drop. 'Oh, God, what did you tell him, you fool?'

'I told him nothing. They were just coming to see the show, they had free tickets. I said nothing.'

She seemed almost amused. 'You were really going to do that for me?'

He pointed to the clock. 'You got ten minutes. I'll get the boys ready.'

She unzipped her pants slowly, never taking her eyes off his face. 'He took a long time to die. I never meant to kill him – but he threatened me and . . . there was this big ashtray, green, very heavy. I kept on hitting him and his teeth fell out. I remember seeing his teeth, on the carpet. It sort of made me real angry, funny. He was always so proud of his white teeth, but they were as false, as fake as he was.' She took a strange hard intake of breath, blinking rapidly. 'Oh, God, Luis. He took such a long time to die.'

Ruda drew down her trousers and kicked them off. The terrible jagged scars were heightened by the sweat and the tightness of her clothes. She looked up at him, held out her arms to him, and he hugged her tightly. 'Nobody will hurt you. I won't let them.'

She stroked his face. 'So if they come for me, you'll say you did it? You'd really do that for me?'

Luis kissed her forehead; the vicious burn scars at the side of her head were shiny red with perspiration. He touched them. 'Yes, yes, I'll say it was me. Nobody will ever hurt you again, I promise you.'

She cupped his face in her hands, and kissed his lips. Her eyes searched his face, her expression unfathomable, and he flushed like a boy, covering his embarrassment, his love. She traced his lips with her fingers. 'Be nice to her, Luis, she was always the weak one.'

'Yes, I can tell that.'

She gave a strange smile. 'Can you now? I have underestimated you.'

Luis tapped his wrist to indicate the time, started to

fetch her costume. He heard the shower being turned on, and eased off the plastic cover from the white jacket, glad to be needed.

Outside, Rebecca sat hunched on the steps. When she heard Ruda call out for her costume, she moved away, afraid to be seen. She lost her footing, falling in the thick mud. She crawled along then tried to stand, but she had slithered half beneath the trailer. The door opened. She could see the polished boots, hear Ruda telling Grimaldi to bring her to the ring.

'And, Luis, no gun! Promise me?'

As Ruda hurried away, Rebecca could see Grimaldi's feet. She crawled a few inches, called out after him. The mud oozed beneath her, she could smell it, smell the wet earth, and she was lost. The dank stinking tunnel, the stench of the sewers, the scurrying rats. Two tiny girls forced to stay silent. They clung to each other, could hear above them the heavy feet, the clank of the steel-edged boot-heels against the rim of the manhole cover. They were waist-deep in the filthy water. The water pulled at their coats and scarves. Rats swam around them. They heard the echoes of boots, screaming voices.

The darkness began to swallow her. Rebecca's heart beat rapidly as she tried to force the smells, the memories, away. She tried to concentrate on where she was, to get herself out from beneath the trailer, but the fragmented memories were stronger than the present.

Ruda snapped at Vernon that she could handle Mamon, all they had to do was their job, she would do hers. Vernon backed off and looked at Mike. They were radioed up to the main soundboard, ready to start the second half of the show. Ruda looked at Mike. 'Where is she?'

Mike was so concerned about Mamon that for a moment he looked blank.

'My sister. She was with you, wasn't she?'

Mike shook his head. 'She went back to the trailer.'

'Go and get someone to fetch her, she might have got lost. Tell her to stand by Grimaldi.'

Ruda was pacing up and down as the orchestra started the introduction to the second half. 'Mike! I don't want him with that bloody rifle. If he comes in with it, get it off him. Don't let him go in the ring with that god-damned thing.'

Mike nodded. He didn't even know where Grimaldi was, and he would not risk looking for him now. He signalled to one of the helpers to go and search for both Grimaldi and Rebecca.

Ruda edged closer to the entrance. She stamped her feet. She was wearing her second costume, a white jacket, black trousers and black boots, with black leather gloves. The white shoulders of the jacket were padded as she would be working with Wanton. He was very unpredictable and could give a nasty scratch. She was, in fact, always more worried about Wanton, though he was only a quarter of the weight of Mamon. Panthers were more difficult to train by far.

The release cages, used for the cats ready to enter the ring, were lined up. Three fully grown male lions paced up and down, as eager to get into the ring as Ruda. Behind the lions came the lionesses, behind them the tigers. The last two smaller cages held Wanton and Mamon.

'LADIES AND GENTLEMEN – PLEASE TAKE YOUR SEATS FOR THE SECOND PART OF THE SHOW. TAKE YOUR SEATS, PLEASE . . .'

Ruda peeked through the small aperture. The audience was still settling down, the orchestra ready to switch to her intro music. She turned to the standby board. The red and green lights were not on. She looked back to the ring, it was growing darker.

Ruda eased her head from side to side. Her neck was tensing badly. 'Come on, come on,' she murmured, her hands clenching and unclenching.

Mike received the radio control signal that Grimaldi was in position on the far side of the ring. Alone.

Vernon came to Ruda. He pressed his earpiece. 'Bit of a delay with a big party on the left bank of seats.'

Ruda clenched her hands. 'Shit! Any money it'll be the bastards that haven't paid to get in anyway.' She eased her weight from one foot to the next. She sighed impatiently, then gave a fleeting look around for Rebecca and asked again if Mike had located her. He smiled, gave the thumbs up. Ruda nodded. 'Make sure she's OK, will you?' Again he nodded, and Ruda breathed in deeply, exhaling on a low hiss. She looked again to the lights, then over to Vernon. He shrugged.

She closed her eyes trying to concentrate on the act, but she couldn't stop thinking of Rebecca. Her clothes . . . when she'd helped her change, she'd noticed they were of the finest quality, even her underwear. She had worn a big diamond ring! Ruda tapped her stick against her leg. Rebecca had four children, a rich husband. Her life must have been very different from her own. She wondered if Rebecca *had* tried to find her, tried as hard . . . Ruda opened her eyes, forcing herself to concentrate.

'Are the pedestals set up?' Ruda asked no one in particular, as if she were on automatic pilot. Vernon replied that they were. Ruda looked again to the lights. 'What the bloody hell's going on? Come on, light up! Red, come on red . . . green, red, green!'

Rebecca curled her body into a tight ball, hemmed in beneath the trailer. The colours came in rapid succession. She had to catch them, remember them. She had to remember each colour, she had to give them to Ruda. If she didn't give them to her sister, Ruda would be given no food, they would hurt her. She heard Papa's voice, saw the cards being laid out, red, green, blue . . .

The red light flickered. 'Stand by, Miss Kellerman.'

Ruda stood rigid. She didn't see the draped entrance to the main ring, but instead the dark green curtain. The hand that drew the curtain open was always clean, nails painted red; manicured oval nails, and the beautiful blonde hair swept in a perfect coil. Her face with the painted eyelids, cheeks rouged and powdered as if she were an actress. The dark red lips were often parted in a half-smile. Ruda could see him behind the glass, he used to stand just a fraction to the right of Red Lips, one of his gloved hands resting against the high dentist's chair. They made a handsome couple. His oiled, slicked-back, ebony black hair, his chiselled features and immaculate uniform. When he smiled his teeth were even, white. As white as Red Lips's large, square teeth.

Rebecca looked like a doll: frilly dress, white socks and little black patent shoes. Once, when the curtain was drawn back Ruda saw that she had been holding a doll, and she had held it up for Ruda to see. A doll with orange hair and a china face, pink-cheeked, pink-lipped, with delicate china hands. Ruda had pretended that when they drew the curtain back she was looking into a mirror, seeing herself. It had calmed her, made the pain go away.

He made the unwrapping of a toffee like a gift from God, holding each end of the wrapper delicately between finger and thumb, as if afraid to get so much as a trace of toffee on his white gloves. Ruda's mouth was always dry, rancid, tasting of metal. She longed for the sweet, watched the elaborate unwrapping of the treat with wide desperate eyes. When he smiled, when he touched Rebecca's chin to indicate she should open her mouth, when he looked through the glass to Ruda and smiled that smile as he popped the sweet into Rebecca's mouth, Ruda could taste the sweet, soft caramel. The green film over her tiny baby teeth became sweet and delicious.

Days, weeks later when Red Lips drew back the curtain, Ruda could see Rebecca changing. The frilly white dress was dirty. What were they doing to her that made her mouth gape open? She could see the tears, see her fighting and scratching and sobbing, but she couldn't hear because the curtain draped a soundproofed cage. She was desperate to get to her sister, desperate to know what frightened her so much, what terrible things they were doing to her. She, too, would scream and scream, but Rebecca couldn't hear. No one could hear on the other side of the curtain.

What Ruda could not have guessed was that Rebecca's hysterical outbursts, her screaming, were because they were showing her what they had done to Ruda.

Vernon shook Ruda's shoulder, once, twice. She turned, startled. 'My God! Hurry, you've had the green light twice! Are you OK?'

Ruda took a moment to get herself focused, then she nodded, licked her lips. They were repeating her intro music. She waited a beat, then walked into the ring. Cheers and loud applause greeted her entrance.

'LADIES AND GENTLEMEN – RUDA KELLERMAN!'

CHAPTER 20

REBECCA REMAINED hunched beneath the trailer. Her head started to throb and she whimpered, prayed for it not to happen, not here. Someone was squeezing her brain. Then through the throbbing pain she heard his voice. He was saying over and over that she had been a bad girl, she had not tried hard enough, now she would see what she had done. They tied her to the chair. She was rigid with terror, screaming for them not to draw back the curtain. But back it moved, slowly, inch by inch. And there was Ruda.

Ruda's body was covered in weeping sores. They had cut off her hair. Rebecca could see the sores on her scalp, the wires attached to her head. She could see Ruda through the glass panel, see them propping her up – she was too weak to walk, too weak to stand up.

The little girl, unable even to hold up her head, smiled through the glass. The effort of lifting her hand drained her, but she gave a tiny, pitiful wave as if to say, 'I am still here. I'm still here, Rebecca.'

The pain was excruciating. Rebecca sobbed, buried her face in the mud. All she could see was Ruda's tiny wretched face. Was this the memory she had blotted out of her mind? The more she held on to the picture of

Ruda, the more agitated she became, scratching the muddy ground with her fingers. She wanted the pain to stop, wanted the memories to stop – but they squeezed through, kept on coming. 'Please help me, somebody help me . . .'

But no one could hear, everyone was at the big top. She couldn't stop them coming, another memory squeezing out. Rebecca could see herself in the frilly white dress, feel her bladder empty, urine trickle down her legs. She was afraid they would open the curtain, afraid to see what she had done to Ruda, and she tried desperately to remember what Papa wanted. Her face pressed into the ground as she sobbed. What was it he wanted? What *was* it?

Red – red – green – blue, red – red . . . roses are red, violets are blue, pass the colours from me to you . . .

Sixteen tigers, three lions and the black panther. The massive ring seemed to seethe with cats. Twice Ruda attempted to give the command for Roja to move to the red pedestal. Instead she repeated four colours rapidly. It was as if her mind was locked. Command after command was confused and the cats started to veer away from the pedestals and meander around the ring.

Vernon moved close to the bars and whispered urgently into his microphone. 'Hold back Mamon. Is he in the tunnel yet? Shit! Don't open the trapdoor yet, keep him in the tunnel. Repeat. Don't release Mamon, don't let him through. Get Grimaldi.'

Mamon moved stealthily down the tunnel and reached the midway gate just as it clanged shut in his face. He backed, ran at it again, angrily this time. Vernon used one of the long sticks, prodding him backwards. Mamon growled and swiped at the stick, but they got him moving back down the tunnel to the safety of his cage.

Ruda remained motionless, the pain across her eyes blinded her. The massive spotlights began to haze and stream out brilliant colours. Her voice was hardly audible as she began to repeat in a monotone: 'Red red green blue red red green.'

The cats became seriously disorientated. Almost in slow motion the tigers, led by Roja, reverted in their confusion to the first part of the act, moving from the arena bars closer to Ruda, forming a circle around her motionless body. The audience was mesmerized, silent. No one knew anything was wrong. The orchestra played on; the conductor, who took his music changes with the act as it progressed, repeated the same music used for the pedestal pyramid. He turned, baton up, and seeing the cats forming a circle cut the music to a low drum beat . . .

Grimaldi opened the side trapdoor leading into the arena. He carried a long whip stick and the cats immediately turned their attention towards him.

'Roja, *up* . . . *red up* . . . *Sonia*, green, *Sophia*, blue . . . *up!*'

Ruda stared ahead, still mumbling colours as if unaware Grimaldi was in the arena. He came quietly, authoritatively to her side and took her left hand, smiling – but his eyes were focused on the cats.

'Jason . . . green. Good boy . . . *up, up!*'

The cats seemed relieved that order had returned. They began to return to the pyramid formation, Grimaldi all the while drawing Ruda gently back from the centre of the ring. He felt her hand tighten in his, but he kept his attention on the cats . . .

'You OK?'

Ruda gasped. She had completely blanked out and the realization of what was happening made her freak for a second. Then she was back in control. They worked together, like a team, and the audience applauded as the cats sat poised on their pedestals. Grimaldi slowly handed more and more of the commands back to Ruda, standing a few feet behind her just in case he was needed.

Wanton began to leap from one high pedestal to the next, and the audience cheered. Grimaldi saw Ruda turn towards the trapdoor, expecting Mamon.

From behind her he said softly, 'No Mamon, Ruda. Finish the act on Wanton.'

Ruda was startled, confused again. Then she looked to Luis and gave a brief nod. As Wanton made his final leap to the top rung, Vernon passed the hoop of fire between the bars. Ruda took the flame torch and showed the audience the massive hoop. The orchestra picked up again. Ruda fixed the hoop to its stand, then stood back as she touched the cloth to set it alight. The entire hoop blazed, spotlights pinpointed the cats who held their position, waiting for the commands. The trapdoor to the tunnel was slid back in readiness.

Back at the cages the helpers, under Mike's supervision, cajoled and pushed Mamon back into his small cage. They had to move fast, push the cage out of the way in readiness for the cats coming back down the tunnel from the ring. The men were sweating with the exertion. Mamon was frantic, lunging at the bars, trying to swipe through his cage.

'Don't even try to put him back in his main cage, let him calm down. Get him out of the way. Come on, move it!'

The tractor was hooked up to Mamon's lightweight cage and wheeled out of the clearing. In the ring, Roja led off from his pedestal. He jumped through the hoop and ran straight to the tunnel. One by one the cats followed, leaping through the flames as the lights flickered and spun, their massive bodies moving with grace and agility, herding back down the tunnel to their cages, on command and in perfect formation.

Last to leap came Wanton. From forty feet in the air the cat sprang and for a moment the spotlight caught him in midair. He sprang from the lowest pedestal and upwards through the hoop in one fluid move, his sleek black body bursting through the blazing hoop, as if leaping into darkness.

The ring went black, and came up with Wanton draped over Ruda's shoulders. He remained relaxed, resting across her, impervious to the wild cheers. Ruda slowly bent on one knee, dropped her head down and Wanton sprang off and returned down the tunnel.

Ruda took Grimaldi's hand and they bowed together. As she leaned forwards she felt the ground give way beneath her feet. Grimaldi swept her into his arms, and smiling, waving, he carried Ruda from the ring, acknowledging the rapturous applause.

The safety barriers were dismantled fast and as the helpers carried out the gates, they saw Ruda assisted to a chair by Grimaldi. Water was brought and she drank thirstily, resting against her husband. She covered her face with her hands. 'Oh, God. Oh, God . . .'

She rocked backwards and forwards on the chair. Grimaldi angrily waved away Vernon as he came near. 'No. Leave us alone. Leave us alone, she's OK.' He didn't want anyone to see her this way, he knew how gossip ran wild and he didn't want anyone saying Ruda Kellerman was sick. They had six more weeks, the chance of going back to the States. Grimaldi lifted Ruda to her feet. 'Right, we'll go and get changed for the final parade, OK, Ruda? All right, lads, everything's under control, no problems. All the cats back in their cages?'

The tractor was drawing all the cages into their covered tent to be put back into their regular heavier cages. Mamon growled and hissed, swiping and butting the bars. Grimaldi assisted Ruda from the arena, then gestured for Mike. 'Be careful with that bastard, he looks mean,' he whispered. 'Don't move him if you're worried, we'll deal with him when he's calmed down.'

Mike nodded, murmured that he'd get the feeds ready, then looked back as Mamon roared out his fury. Mamon's cage rocked dangerously as it disappeared. Grimaldi didn't have to repeat his order: no one would go near him.

The cold air made Ruda gasp. Grimaldi put a protective arm around her shoulders. She took in gulps of air, her chest heaving. 'You were right, Luis. I should have listened to you. Seeing Rebecca again my mind went, but I'll be OK . . . maybe need to lie down for a while. I'll be OK.'

As Grimaldi walked her to the trailer he stepped on Vernon's yellow rain cape, left by the side of the steps. He chucked it aside and helped Ruda in. She sat down on the bunk, her head between her knees. Grimaldi poured a brandy and held it out for her. Ruda took the glass, cupping it in both hands. 'You did OK out there, you old bastard.'

He grinned and fetched himself a drink. 'Well, you know me, always did like a challenge.' He caught his reflection in the mirror, gave a chuckle. 'I felt good. It was good. It's been too long. Maybe if we did the first half we could work something up together. But I won't work with Mamon, he's your baby. If you look at the show tonight, you don't need him. You know what, we could maybe try and get another panther. Wanton's a great crowd-puller, they loved him. Did you hear that applause?'

Ruda inched off her leather gloves. Grimaldi was staring at himself in the mirror. 'I'll start working out, get this fat off me.' Grimaldi slapped his belly.

Ruda sipped her brandy, turned her face away. 'Where's Rebecca?'

He sat opposite her, the way they used to in the old days, his long legs propped up beside her. She didn't even notice his muddy boots on the cushions.

'Vernon's taking care of her, you just relax now.' Grimaldi cocked his head to one side. 'So, you want to tell me what happened? I mean, you blanked out, Ruda. In the middle of a bloody big act! It made the old ticker jump.'

He smiled, but Ruda paid him no attention, rested back against the cushions. 'You sure she's with Vernon?'

'Yes, just relax. Eh! Did you see how fast I shot through that trapdoor? They were going into the first part of the act again, Ruda. Ruda?'

She frowned, turned her head as if listening. 'You sure she's with Vernon? I feel her. God, it's hot, I'm so hot.'

Rebecca felt so cold. Her head ached and she didn't know how long she had been there. Had she fainted? She sighed, this had happened before so many times – hours

563

blanked out, even days. She tried to clean her face, afraid if Ruda knew she was sick she wouldn't want her. She was about to crawl out from beneath the trailer when she heard Ruda's voice and the darker, heavier tones of Grimaldi. They were directly above her.

Ruda pushed open the trailer window. 'She has no memory of what happened. Strange, she remembers nothing. But she is to blame for what happened tonight, I know it.'

'Oh, come on. I don't think you realized the emotional impact it had on you to see her. I told you, I warned you.'

'You don't understand,' Ruda snapped.

'Well, why don't you help me understand, Ruda? I want to.'

She laughed. 'Oh, aren't you Mr Wonderful all of a sudden! You think I don't know why? Got your balls back tonight, did you? I may have fouled up, but you'll never replace me. It's my act, Luis, it's mine.'

'How the hell do you think you'd have got out of there tonight without me? Maybe I did get my balls back, but it's good I still had them! I admit I've been scared, Ruda, but tonight I faced it, didn't even think about it. The fear went, I had no fear, Ruda!'

'What the fuck do you want me to say? You did great, you did good. Now leave me alone. I need to think about something. Just leave me alone.'

'One of these days, Ruda, I might do just that.' He patted his pockets for a cigar. Finding one on the coffee table, he glanced around for some matches, and found some in the ashtray. He puffed the cigar alight, then turned back to her, prepared for a fight. He was surprised by the soft tone of her voice.

'I kept on seeing colours. I couldn't give the right commands – the pedestals, the colours of the pedestals.'

Luis looked at the burning tip of his cigar. He drew the ashtray closer and was about to interrupt when she continued. 'We were so young, they could only do the tests with colour cards . . .'

'You told me.'

'No, you don't understand. We could transmit coded colours – don't you realize how our minds are linked? That's what was wrong tonight. It was me, Rebecca—' She suddenly stood up. 'Oh, my God, where is she?'

'Look, just forget her for a second, OK? Sit down.' He poured another brandy, but Ruda was edgy, she knew Rebecca needed her – she could feel it.

Grimaldi handed her the brandy, stood over her. She stared into the glass. 'What was any of it for, Luis? We were just another one of his insane experiments. He tried with other twins, used to be able to discover which one could receive – it was always the stronger of the two, the weaker one was the transmitter.' She stared at the brandy, then passed him the glass. 'I don't want this. Here, you have it.' She breathed in heavily. There was a slight tremor to her entire body. She began to rub the scars at the side of her temples. 'The pain in my head. They clamped these wires to my head, they used to burn me, hurt my head. I didn't understand what they wanted. When I finally did, it was easy, I always knew what she was thinking. If she bruised a knee I felt it, could soothe her. I always knew, Luis, as if she was inside my head, you know?'

He said nothing, simply watched her.

'After – years after – I sometimes felt she was close. It was strange. You ever had the feeling? Like you know you are about to meet someone, see someone, and you do. Well, I would often have a strange feeling she was close by. It would just be a feeling, and I would concentrate on her, as I had at the camp, picture her face. But then the feeling would go away and we'd travel on ... But so many times I was sure I had her. I remember once in New York, I was so sure she was close, and then here – remember me saying I had this feeling? Well, she's staying at the Grand Hotel. So close ...' He saw her hand tighten into a fist. 'I knew, always knew she was alive.'

'Why did you never tell me about her? If you knew she was alive, we could have searched for her together, put ads in the papers, there's even organizations that—'

She interrupted him. 'I searched, I never gave up hope, that's why I started all my astrology letters, remember them? I was always thinking about her. You know, hoping maybe one letter would be from her. Everywhere I went I'd put ads in the papers, things that only she would understand, and I thought about her, concentrated on her.'

He sipped his brandy and waited, then encouraged her to continue. 'Go on, you concentrated on her and . . . ?'

'Oh, I would think about what she owed me, what I had done for her. Then I would become angry, so angry because I knew she had to feel me too, had to know I was alive, and I would curse her, hate her for not coming to me. I wanted her to come to me, I wanted to put my hands round her throat and squeeze her to death.'

'What?'

'She left me ... she left me, Luis, she left me.' Her voice was hardly audible. He poured himself another measure of brandy, uncertain if what he was hearing made any sense. Ruda was silent, staring from the window.

When she continued her voice was stronger, but her hands still clenched and unclenched. 'I kept her alive. But when the Russians liberated the camp, I saw her from the hospital window hand in hand with a soldier. She was able to walk. Then the soldier lifted her up on to his shoulders. I saw him give her chocolate. And she never turned back, never came back for me . . .'

She began to bite her fingernails. 'She never tried to find me, Luis, I could have forgiven everything, if she'd just tried to find me. With her rich husband, her children, she had money, she could have found me. I know that now.'

'It was a long time ago, she was just a child. Maybe you . . .'

'Maybe I nothing, Luis. Everything with you is always maybe this or maybe that. I know she knew what they were doing to me, she knew because she could *see*. They starved me and fed her like a pig. They put these things on my brain, and they gave her dolls. She knew what they were doing to me.'

He wanted to comfort her, to put his arm around her, but she shrugged him away.

'Ruda, what difference does it make now? She's here, you're reunited. Now you can make up for all the—'

She screamed at him, '*You don't understand!*'

Luis put his hands up. 'Jesus Christ – I am trying, Ruda! I wasn't there, Ruda. All I know is what I hear, what you tell me.'

Ruda kicked out at the table. 'Shut up! You don't know. You weren't there.'

'I know that, sweetheart, of course I don't know.'

'No, you don't know. How could you? Nobody can even imagine what happened there. The longing, Luis, I

567

longed for her so much, like a well inside me, that filled up and drowned me. I drowned with longing for her to come to me, to . . . make what had happened real.'

'Who told you? I can't follow what you're saying. Who are they?'

She sighed. 'The doctors, the nurses, the stupid fat-faced nurses in the asylum, they put me in with crazy people because there was nowhere else. Just forget, just forget. Take this, swallow this, this'll make you sleep. Nothing happened, it's all over. Forget? How could I forget when every white coat made me remember, every needle, every whispered voice terrified me.'

Her mouth was trembling. 'Forget? Tell me how? There were all these babies, newborn babies. But not one was alive, they were blue from the freezing cold. Some were bloody, some still had their cords dangling out of their bellies. Rebecca thought they were dolls. She asked if she could have one. But I knew, I knew they were dead babies. I knew, because from my window, where they kept me, I would see them being born, outside on the slabs in the snow. Don't touch them, Becca, they're not to play with. Don't touch them. But she had one, Luis, she had one in her arms.'

Her face twisted into a silent scream. She covered her mouth as if she couldn't stop opening the wounds which had been locked up inside for so many years. 'Every time I see a baby I remember. Papa told me it was all right, he used to stand with me and watch the babies coming. He was holding my hand, and I didn't think anything was wrong because he whistled. He whistled. He was always whistling.'

Luis felt sick. The image of the dead infants already

haunted him. Ruda's hands plucked at her jacket. 'He liked me to call him Papa.'

She tried to say the name of the man whose face was buried inside her mind, the man who had tortured and tormented her and instigated an anguish that was indescribable. Deep beneath her scarred body, beneath her entire adult existence lay a consuming, confused and heart-breaking guilt. Slowly it began to surface. She was the little girl sitting on his knee, hands clasped round the sweet he had given her. The little girl who said, 'It's mine!' He had kissed her cheek, pinched her chin, teased her. She could hear his voice.

'Open it, you can open it!'

'No.'

'Don't you want it?'

'My sister, want it for my sister.'

He had laughed, jumped his knee hard so that she fell to the floor. 'What is your sister's name, I forget?'

'Rebecca.'

'Ah, yes. Is she well?'

Ruda nodded, and he crouched low, resting on the heels of his polished boots. He traced her cheek with his white-gloved hand. 'Tell me, do you feel pain when your sister is hurt?'

'Yes.'

He seemed delighted. He brought out a box of sugared almonds with a pink ribbon, gave a small bow, clicking his heels. 'These are for you and your sister.'

She reached out, but he withdrew the box. 'I want a kiss.' She stood on tiptoes, slipped her arms around his neck and kissed first his right, then his left cheek. He smelt of limes. With the box of almonds tucked under one arm, her hand in his, they walked into the hospital wing.

'Bring her sister. I want her sister! These are going to be my special twins.'

Grimaldi had said nothing, simply sat watching her, her head bowed. She stared unseeing as the face of the monster emerged. The face of the man who had embraced the child with love, and yet committed heinous crimes against her tiny body. The being who had distorted and twisted her mind for some foolish experiment that meant nothing, benefited no one. Why had he never stood trial? Why had he never been punished? He had been free, the Dark Angel's wing had overshadowed her life. Alive, he had been living proof that no one cared, it had not happened. But it had. And the rage against him began to unleash.

Rebecca pressed her body against the side of the trailer. She could feel the rage rising inside her. For the first time she felt apart from it, as if watching it manifest itself. She could see her hands clenching and unclenching. When this had happened before, she had always lost control, had no memory of what occurred. But now she knew the rage was not hers, but Ruda's. Now their minds entwined, like an electric circuit fusing, ready to ignite . . .

Rebecca fought against its taking over, tried to reach for the trailer door, to call out that she was there, that she had not tried to find Ruda because she didn't know she existed, she had been forced to forget. Now the memories opened in a blinding, red-hot blaze.

*

Luis saw it happen and was helpless to stop it. He saw the rage explode from Ruda. Every muscle in her body tensed, the veins in her neck throbbed, her hands flayed the air, her mouth drew back in a terrible silent scream. But, above all, it was the madness in her eyes which made him freeze.

The rage she had held inside for so long, and the fury of her torment, made her blind to the fact it was Luis she attacked – she believed him to be the Papa, and she had to destroy him.

Mamon lay with his massive head resting on his paws. Mike, easing open the trapdoor, pushed the feed tray inside. Vernon was carrying bales of clean straw. He called across to Mike. 'Eh! I wouldn't try that, Mike. Leave it for Mrs Grimaldi. She's not in the arena, they'll be going into the parade any minute.'

Mike half turned, his hand still on the bolt of the trapdoor. At that moment Mamon lunged forwards, his whole weight hitting the side of the cage: the trapdoor flew open, knocking Mike off his feet, and Mamon was out.

Vernon dropped the bale of straw and threw himself out of the way, but Mamon wasn't interested in either of them; he was loping towards the open tent flap, churning up the sawdust. His roar of rage was terrifying in its volume and intensity.

'Oh, shit! Oh, my God! *Get the nets – fucking get the nets!*'

Word spread fast; within minutes the area was cordoned off and gatekeepers and parking attendants warned that no one was to be allowed beyond the barriers. The helpers ran towards the trailer park, their flashlights flickering as they questioned anyone who might have seen where Mamon had run.

As the panic spread the security men were alerted.

The grand parade was just drawing to a close, the audience cheering, flowers tumbling from the very top of the massive tents, balloons cascading down.

Thousands of chattering, laughing people streamed from the big tent exits. They gathered alongside coaches, or made their way on foot back down the road. Some ran to their parked cars. Children were carried in arms, overwhelmed by the excitement and now fast asleep, others ran whooping and screaming, carrying circus maps, toys and balloons.

The sky opened again with a heavy roll of thunder and more rain came lashing down.

Mike, in a state of nervous hysteria, made his way to the Grimaldi trailer. At the same time Torsen and his group headed back to their car, via the trailer park and inside the barriers.

Helen and the Baron were pushed and buffeted along by the crowd at the main circus entrance. They fought their way against the crowds to head for the trailer park barriers.

Inside his trailer Grimaldi tried desperately to control Ruda. She had overturned the table, ripped at the cushions. It was difficult to move out of her reach in the confined space. Twice he had caught her arms, but she had forced herself free. She scratched, kicked and tore at him. She herself heard nothing, the violent rage consuming her. She was biting, her jaws snapping like an animal's, her fury giving her an even more terrifying strength.

Grimaldi had hold of her by the hair. Ruda twisted,

punched her elbow into his stomach and, as he released his hold and buckled over, dragged his head up, forcing him back. Her hands gripped his throat.

Rebecca banged and pushed at the door, hit it with the flat of her hand and then ran to a window, screaming to be let in. Ruda turned to the window. For a moment she was frozen, then she picked up a chair and hurled it at Rebecca's face. It shattered the window. Grimaldi got to his feet, but Ruda was going for him again. And Rebecca now punched at the glass, trying to heave her body through it into the trailer. A jagged slice of glass cut into her cheek, blood mingling with the mud. It made her look as crazed as Ruda. Her hand flew up to her face.

Ruda backed away, held her hand to her cheek as if she had cut herself. Then she reached out and hauled Rebecca inside, crushing her in her arms, holding her so tightly Rebecca couldn't breathe. It was a killing embrace, a furious protection. They were locked into each other, totally one.

Grimaldi grabbed hold of Ruda from behind, wrenched her away, but Rebecca screamed, making no effort to fend for herself, to escape. She felt as if she was being plucked out of her own body.

Grimaldi slapped Ruda's face hard, jerking her head from side to side.

'*You're killing her! Ruda! Ruda!*'

She seemed to deflate. He gripped her face in his hands. 'Ruda, it's me, *it's me*!'

Running towards the trailer, Mike screamed out, '*Ruda! Ruda!*' He appeared at the shattered window. 'He's loose, Mamon's loose! Nobody can find him, we've got the nets standing by.'

Ruda's punch sent Grimaldi crashing into the wall, banging against Rebecca. They fell in a tangled heap as Ruda ran out.

Rebecca started to scream and he crouched down beside her. 'Listen to me, stay here. Do you understand? Don't leave the trailer, I'll get someone here to help you, but stay inside.'

'Ruda, I want Ruda. Ruda, *Ruda*!'

Grimaldi lifted her off her feet, sat her down. 'Just do as I say. Don't leave the trailer. We'll sort everything out.'

Rebecca was shaking with terror as he threw the bench cushions aside, searched for his gun. In her confusion she believed he was going to shoot Ruda. She lurched towards him, clinging to his arm. '*No!* Please – please don't hurt her!'

Grimaldi pushed her roughly away. 'The hurting's been done. Just stay inside, *stay inside*!'

'She needs me. I have to go to her.'

He turned on her in a fury, wanting to slap her face. '*You are too late. Stay in the goddamned trailer!*'

Grimaldi slammed the door shut and ran towards the torchlights and shouting voices. Every available man formed a human wall cutting off the trailer area from the crowds. A disembodied voice shouted that Mamon had been spotted. He was behind the animal tents. Hand in hand the men walked forward, step by step, alert and watchful, drawing the chain of arms tighter as the helpers with the big nets ran to the clearing by the tents.

Ruda was running ahead of Mike, repeating over and over, 'Don't hurt him. Don't let them hurt him.'

*

574

Helen and the Baron were confronted by two parking stewards. The men pulled a barrier across the opening. 'Stay outside the barrier. No one is allowed inside.'

The Baron demanded to be let through.

'I'm sorry. No one can come into this area until we have clearance. Please wait!'

Helen tried unsuccessfully to explain they were to meet Grimaldi at his trailer. She was brusquely informed that no one was allowed beyond the barrier. The Baron stepped back and took Helen's elbow, pulling her away.

'But this is ridiculous, Louis, we've been told we can meet him.'

'Look over there. Can you see?' Louis pointed to the lights. Helen looked across the barriers. She could see the human chain of men, some still in costume, linked hand in hand, moving closer and closer.

'What's going on?'

The lights of the disappearing cars, the noise of tooting horns, car doors slamming, people shouting, all added to the confusion. The Baron and Helen saw a group being ushered by two gatekeepers.

'It's the inspector, Louis. Maybe he can help us.'

They hurried to Torsen, but he was unable to help them, as he too had been asked to leave. They all stared across at the lights. Two men ran into view carrying a large net. They shouted to the gatekeeper. 'They got him cornered on the open ground over by the rubbish bins. We're getting the nets around the back, just in case!'

Torsen stepped forward. 'I am a police officer. What's happened?'

The gatekeeper waved his hand to indicate they should all stay behind the barriers. 'Everything's under control now, sir. Just keep moving, please leave this area.'

Torsen looked to Rieckert, then to the Baron. 'What do you think's wrong?'

Again the Baron approached the gatekeeper. 'My wife is with the Grimaldis. Has something happened?'

The irate man banged the top of the barrier. 'Please. Just stay out until I've got clearance. It'll soon be all over.'

'What will, for God's sake?' Louis was furious. He looked back to the lights, and caught sight of Rebecca. He shouted, called to her but she disappeared out of sight. 'That was my wife. Please, please let me through!'

'No, sir. I'm sorry, this is for your own safety.'

'WOULD ALL CUSTOMERS PLEASE LEAVE THE PREMISES AS QUICKLY AS POSSIBLE. NO ONE IS ALLOWED NEAR THE ARTISTS' TRAILER ENCLOSURE. FOR YOUR OWN SAFETY, PLEASE REMAIN OUTSIDE THE BARRIERS.'

The Baron and Helen waited impatiently. Torsen and his group began to make their way back to the patrol car. The loudspeakers repeated the warnings. The barrier was now heavily guarded. A group of boys in jeans and T-shirts soaked from the rain tried to climb over. The gatekeepers ran to throw them out. Over-excited and unaware of the dangers, the boys dodged the gatekeepers, as if it were all a game.

Helen and the Baron eased back the barrier and made a run for it, just as Torsen returned to assist the gatekeepers in ejecting the boys. They made their way towards where they had seen Rebecca. They could now see clearly the human chain edging closer. They went towards it.

Torsen and Rieckert found themselves in an ugly scuffle as the boys fought back. One boy threw a wild punch which caught Torsen on the nose and knocked him to the ground. He shot to his feet and gave the boy a good belting. 'I am a police officer. Now, do as you're told or I'll arrest you for disturbing the peace. Go on – out, get *out*!'

The boys trudged away. The gatekeeper thanked Torsen. 'There's a big cat loose, sir. That's what all the panic is about. Obviously I can't tell the kids, it'll cause mayhem, and then that kind will think themselves tough, try to get back in. But they've got it under control now. He's over on the open ground by the rubbish bins, that's what the nets were for.'

Torsen wiped his bloody nose. 'You sure they don't need a couple of extra hands?'

'Thank you, sir, but for your own safety just stay back there. It's all under control now. He's probably in the nets already!'

One of the clowns, his make-up still on, ran past shouting that they needed more men over on the far side. Torsen called Rieckert over. 'Come on, let's give them a hand.'

Rieckert and his girlfriend clung to the barrier. 'Maybe I should stay with the girls. No need for both of us to go!'

'Fine. You do that. Get them into the car. I'll see if I can help.'

He smiled at Freda. She told him to take care, and he kissed her. 'I will.'

Mamon had moved out in the open, then eased back, weaving in and out beneath the big trailers, his body low to the ground. They kept the burning torches stuck in the ground as the nets were set up. As long as they could see him, there was no panic. They preferred to wait until all the crowds had gone.

The human chain remained, the torches lighting the area reasonably well, and the nets began to be linked up, cornering Mamon.

Ruda pulled on a pair of heavy gloves and picked up a long pole, Mike following with a bucket of meat, as she pushed her way through. 'Thank you. Thank you everybody. But please stay back, please stay back! And keep quiet. Thank you.'

'He's under the big trailer with the red shutters, been there a good five minutes.' The trapeze artist was still in his tights and T-shirt. Ruda smiled her thanks and continued on. She entered the circle, two men breaking their hands apart, rejoining them as soon as she was through.

Ruda looked around at the strained, fearful faces. 'OK, everybody. I want to see if I can encourage him back out into the open. Those with the loose nets get in closer, but everybody stay back until I give the word. Please stay well back, he's probably panicky, but I can control him. Just stay back . . . and please keep silent.'

They did not need to be told twice: no one wanted to get in close. The boys began to bring out the barriers used in the act, to make an open-air caged arena. A tractor towed Mamon's main cage in close. When everything was quiet, Ruda moved further and further into the clearing.

The back wall of the tent cut off one route and now the barriers were cutting and hemming Mamon in on all sides. He eased between the trailer wheels, his fur flattened, his paws muddy. He squeezed out and darted under the second trailer, but the lights picked him out clearly, and the trailer was low. He struggled and began to swing his head, easing out backwards.

'Ruda, he's between the two trailers,' Mike called, then turned as Grimaldi moved behind him. Mike saw the gun, but said nothing, looking back at Ruda. 'They've got him trapped, sir. He's between the trailers on the far side.'

The cage was drawn closer, the trapdoor open. Mamon could see it directly ahead of him. He was fifty to sixty feet away from the clearing, standing in an alley and hemmed in by the trailers on either side. Behind him were the nets. The only clear route was ahead. He began a very slow walk, his front paws crossing over each other as he moved closer and closer to the arena. He paused, sniffing the air. He could smell Ruda.

'Good boy! Come on, come on, ma' angel . . . Good boy. Come to Mama, come on . . .'

Mamon was approaching her slowly, his eyes like glittering amber lights, his teeth gleaming. Panic made his chest heave, saliva dribbled from his open jaw. He was coming to her, she knew it and smiled encouragement. Ruda bent down slightly, whispered to him. He kept on coming, her voice quietening, soothing him. 'Come on, good boy. Come to Mama! He's coming, please keep silent. Don't unnerve him.'

Rebecca slipped under the linked arms of two men. They were confused for a brief moment, thinking she was Ruda. When they realized their mistake, it was too late to stop her – she was already hurrying between the trailers.

Rebecca saw the torches, saw the nets, but they meant nothing to her. She wanted to get to Ruda and she could see her, standing in the clearing.

Helen and Louis, now aware that the panic was

because of an escaped lion, stood outside the ring of men. They watched, unable to see Mamon, but they could feel the electrifying tension.

Torsen joined them. Helen pointed across the ground, told him they were still trying to get the lion back in his cage, but she hadn't seen him, just knew he was still loose. Louis tried to make out Rebecca in the flickering lights, but he couldn't see her, and looked back at Ruda. He was struck by the eerie likeness, her shadow streaming behind her, making her seem like a giant . . .

Mamon made his slow journey down the aisle between the trailers. Rebecca ran the last few yards between the trailers adjacent to Mamon and burst into the clearing.

'Ruda! *Ruda!*'

She was caught between Ruda and Mamon, unaware that the big cat was no more than twenty feet behind her. Mamon froze. Poised, head up, he sniffed the air, then swung his head low and growled, darting back fast. He ran crazily to the nets, turned again snarling with anger, wheeled around, ready to charge back into the clearing.

The men held the big nets in readiness: fifteen feet wide, six feet high, heavy poles linking the nets. If Mamon came close they could release the poles to drop the nets over his entire body . . . but he was wily, keeping his distance, moving further into the clearing. Now there was nothing – no men, no nets – between him and Rebecca. He snarled, lashed out with his paw.

Rebecca turned, saw Mamon, and looked back to Ruda in terror. Ruda's voice was soft, persuasive, cajoling and calm. 'Don't move. Stay perfectly still. Don't move, keep your hands at your side.'

She inched forward, moving a fraction to her right, keeping Mamon directly in her line of vision. Mamon tilted his head to the right, to the left. He stepped forwards, stopped. Crouched. He was ready to spring.

'Move to me, one step at a time . . .'

Grimaldi knew the cat was enraged enough to attack. He was sure of it and his face went rigid. He swore to himself at the stupid bitch, his heart thudding, but he knew that if he were to make a single move now it could be fatal for both women. So, like everyone else, he remained totally still, his hand gripping the rifle.

Rebecca took one step forward, her back still to Mamon. He was watching her. She moved forwards again, and he followed, still low on his haunches . . .

Grimaldi lifted the rifle, trying to release the safety catch silently, but the click made Mamon lift his head.

Ruda heard the slight noise, but did not take her eyes off Mamon. Her voice remained soft, calm.

'Don't touch me, just move very slowly behind me. You can do it, nobody will hurt you, Becca. Come on, I'm here. Ruda's here.'

Slowly Rebecca moved behind Ruda, becoming part of the giant shadow streaming behind her. 'Good, Becca, good. Now, when I step forward, you step back. But slowly, very slowly. Wait!'

Mamon hurtled from the aisle, his outline clear to everyone. He seemed to begin a lunge and then stop, his chest heaving as he glared around. The sisters remained together.

'Back! Mamon, back . . . *Ma' angellll!*'

The Baron tried to break through the human chain, but he was pushed back, forced to watch with everyone else the way Ruda slowly but surely moved closer to Mamon, placing herself in danger as, step for step, Rebecca eased away to safety.

Louis pushed forward and grabbed hold of Rebecca.

'Is she safe?' Ruda kept her voice calm, never taking her eyes off Mamon. 'Is she safe?' she repeated.

Grimaldi eased a step into the arena. 'I've got her, Ruda. Now back up to me, I'm about four feet behind you, just start backing towards me, sweetheart, I'm here . . . Ruda?'

Luis thought she was going to do as he asked. First Ruda slowly lifted her right arm, let the whip drop, but remained in the same position. She lifted her left arm, both arms open wide, and there was a moment of total silence. No one moved, no one spoke. Luis, expecting Ruda to go back, stepped a fraction to his right, aiming the rifle and it happened in a split second.

Afterwards, everybody had a different version. Ruda did not move back, she stepped forwards. Mamon and Ruda seemed to move in unison towards each other, but he reared up on to his hind legs, then sat back on his haunches. His front paws seemed to embrace Ruda. Perhaps he was simply obeying a command, a command he was used to being given in the ring . . . *kiss*, and Ruda was in exactly the same position that she took in the ring when Mamon laid his paws on her shoulders, but now she was facing him and he was not on his pedestal. His massive paws enveloped her head and shoulders in what appeared to be a terrifying embrace. Did she give him the command? Nobody heard it, but she did say something. They clearly heard her say, 'Ma'angel.' Then the shots rang out.

The first bullet hit him in his right shoulder. He keeled forwards, and she was wrapped in him, his black mane hiding her face. His jaws screamed open as the second

582

bullet hit him just above his right ear. The third bullet –
all three in rapid succession – entered his right side, just
below the elbow of his right paw. It struck his heart, but
he was already dead. The big animal crashed forward still
holding her, his weight crushing her, snapping her neck.
She made no sound, no cry.

Four men had to ease him away from her. Both her
hands held tightly to his fur, his blood covering her shirt.
At first they thought one of the bullets must have hit her.
Only when Grimaldi lifted her in his arms did they realize
her neck had been broken. The big man held his wife,
rocking her gently, sobbing. The men moved in closer, as
if protecting him, shielding him. They formed a circle
around him, and they bowed their heads.

Mamon's carcass was dragged away in the nets. In
death he seemed pitiful, all power gone. His limp body
was sodden from the rain, his claws and feet caked in
mud. The three bullet wounds were hidden beneath his
thick fur, but the dark blood matted his coat.

Helen and Louis Maréchal helped Rebecca to the first-
aid room. She said nothing, seemed dazed, robot-like. By
the time the doctor came to see her, she was in a complete
catatonic state. She did not understand where she was,
did not recognize Louis or Helen. When Dr Franks
arrived an hour later, they arranged for her to be taken to
his clinic.

Torsen sat in the patrol car, his face so pale it seemed
almost blue. 'She's dead. The lion attacked her, she's
dead . . .'

Rieckert swore. 'Shit! What a thing to miss. Wish I'd
been there.'

Torsen shook his head. 'No. No, I don't think so. It

was one of the saddest, most horrifying things I have ever seen. I don't think I can drive home. Will you drive us back?'

Rieckert drove and Torsen sat in the back seat, Freda holding his hand. She knew he was crying, but that made her feel even closer to him.

'She seemed to give herself to the animal. She had no fear, she seemed to embrace death. From where I was standing I could see her face . . . and she smiled, I am sure of it. She smiled, as if she knew she was going to die.'

Freda snuggled against his arm. 'I see it every day. I see those who are afraid to let go, and those who welcome the end. It's strange, when it's over for them all the pain in their faces is gone.'

He was quiet for a moment, rubbing his chin against her hair. 'I know she killed once, maybe twice. No one will ever know exactly what happened and I doubt if I would ever have been able to prove it.'

Luis Grimaldi, wearing a big overcoat, stood by the stonecutter, whose overalls were white with dust. Even his face was ingrained with a fine film. The man's large, gnarled hands held the sheet of paper, the wind tearing at it, and the rain that had not stopped for days made the ink drawing run.

'Can you do it?'

'Yes. It'll take a while, and I'll need a very large block. It will cost – black marble is the most expensive. I have to have it shipped in from Italy.'

'That's immaterial. I'll pay whatever it costs. I've

brought you photographs. If there's anything else you need, you know where to contact me.'

The stonecutter watched the big broad-shouldered man walk out of his yard. He carefully folded the damp sheet of paper. He had received a few strange requests for headstones in the past, but never one like this.

When the marble was chosen he set to work, taking great care. In truth, he relished the challenge and, as the massive head began to take shape, it seemed to take on a life of its own. He buffed and polished, then stood back to gaze in admiration at his finished work. He felt an enormous sense of achievement. This work surpassed any of the other angels who rested over the dead.

Grimaldi negotiated for all the cats to be bought by the Russian trainer. At first he had considered taking over the act, but every animal reminded him of her, and Mamon's empty cage broke him. It was over, there could be no going back. He arranged for the trailer to be sold and when that, too, was bought by the circus management, there was nothing left to keep him in Berlin. He made no attempt to find Rebecca, but wrote a brief note, care of the Grand Hotel, giving details of Ruda's burial. He also sent Ruda's small black tin box, feeling that perhaps the contents would mean something to her sister. But he did not want to see her. He blamed her for the end.

Luis had no thought of what he would do next, where he would go. Having had his mind occupied for the weeks after Ruda's death, he suddenly found himself at a loss. Without Ruda he didn't seem able to function in the world to which he had introduced her.

He knew just one thing. He had to wait until the headstone was ready.

The sky was clear and cloudless the day he went to say his last goodbye. Grimaldi could see him immediately, towering above the other tombstones, and his breath caught in his throat. He had done something right. Immediately after Ruda's death, when he had been inconsolable, blaming himself, the tears he had shed had broken from him in gasping sobs. Now he wept gently, tears welling up and spilling down his cheeks.

He towered above her, his wonderful head resting on his paws, his black mane, his wide black eyes. His jaw was open in warning not to touch or trespass upon the grave. Carved in gold was his name. MAMON.

RUDA GRIMALDI

Died February 1992

A Wild Animal Trainer

May she rest in fearless peace

CHAPTER 21

REBECCA HAD remained catatonic after the tragedy, and had no memory of Ruda's death. She
was kept heavily sedated until Dr Franks felt she
was mentally and physically strong enough to face the
ordeal ahead of her.

Helen Masters had returned to France, but wrote
regularly to and received detailed letters from the Baron.
He explained Rebecca's sessions, as if writing the letters
was in some way therapeutic for him. These sessions
continued every other day, and gave time for Rebecca to
accept and understand each new development. Under
deep hypnosis she was able to recall the incidents that her
adopted mother had sought to cover over. The pattern
of breakdowns linked directly to the close proximity of
Ruda. Whenever Ruda tried to contact her, be it out
of hatred or love, the communication became distorted.
Rebecca's rages, the self-abuse, even the attacks on her
family were carefully listed and dated. Louis Maréchal
worked diligently, checking each date against circus
schedules. He determined that, in each case, even though
she didn't know it, Ruda had been within a short distance
of his wife.

Rebecca's later mental breakdowns had coincided with

the arrival of Mamon in Ruda's life. Mamon's strong will, his aggression and wildness had forced Ruda to use all her willpower to train him. Reverting to the colours of the pedestals, she had reached Rebecca's subconscious. The result, when Rebecca was in close proximity, was the violent brainstorms.

Gradually the jigsaw became complete. Rebecca was taken back again to Birkenau. She gave horrifying pictures, but the descriptions were always from the eyes of a child. At times she seemed quite cheerful. She told them about all the babies, how she had wanted one as a doll. She chattered on, unconcerned, about the funny thin people, the wires, the other children. Then at one session she stunned Dr Franks by laughing.

'What is so funny?'

She described one of the young guards who used to play with the children. He used to rip up little bits of paper, put them on the end of his nose and blow them away like snowflakes. 'We called him the Snowman!' she said.

'Was this man kind to you?'

She fell silent, and Franks repeated the question. She whispered that he was not very nice, not all the time. Franks tried to find out why the 'Snowman' was not nice, but she was unsure, saying he would take them away across the wire fences, take them to the grey hot place where they baked bread. Whoever he took away never returned.

She talked for a long time about what her papa gave her, the white frilly dress, the white socks and patent leather shoes, and she said that she loved him.

She giggled a high-pitched giggle. 'I got a dolly with yellow hair. He said it was as yellow as the dirty Jews' stars.'

Often the sessions disturbed Louis. He felt a hopelessness, as if his Rebecca would never be returned to him. He had to walk out of the viewing room, but he always went back.

Six months after Ruda's death, Franks felt Rebecca was strong enough to delve more deeply, at times without hypnosis. She talked of the woman nicknamed Red Lips by Ruda. Franks surmised that the woman was the notorious SS woman Irma Griese, known for her beauty – and remembered for her cruelty to the inmates at Auschwitz. Rebecca said she always smelt of flowers.

'Ruda said she wanted to be like her when she grew up. Red Lips used to wear her whip tucked into her boots, like a lion tamer, and when she was near, we didn't smell the bread. They made bread every day, every night in the big ovens. Papa told us that was why the flames were red, the ovens had to be hot for the sweet bread.'

The next session, Franks noticed a physical change begin. The child in Rebecca had gone, she was subdued. When he asked if she was feeling unwell her voice took on a strange dullness.

'My frock is dirty.'

Franks waited but she said nothing more. He reinstigated the hypnosis and, deeply under, she sat for this session, her head remaining bowed. She didn't smile, not any more.

'Where are you, Rebecca? Where are you?'

She slowly lifted her head. Her eyes were dead, her mouth gaped open. 'Ruda's gone with the Snowman.'

'Where are you?'

She spoke in a dull, almost drugged monotone as she

began to describe the glass booth with the dark green curtain, the dentist's chair where she was lifted to sit down and face the curtain. Dr Franks could feel the child had gone; she seemed old now and wizened, yet she could have been no more than four. She described seeing what they had done to Ruda, how they would force her to look at her through the glass window.

'Papa took out her insides to show me. He said it was because I was naughty. Papa cut off her hair. Papa put something in her belly. Papa said it was a baby like me. Papa said I was a bad girl because I couldn't remember. I try, I try hard to remember! Try to feed her . . .'

After that particular session, she refused her sleeping tablets. She rang her bell, kept on ringing it. She didn't want Maja the nurse, she didn't want her husband, she wanted Franks. By the time he had been brought from his home she was hysterical, pacing up and down her room. When he let himself in, she turned on him.

'Why are you doing this to me? Why? Why are you making me remember these things? *Why?* You are killing me!'

'No, no, I'm not. I am helping you. These things happened to you, they are real events. You have to face them, go through them.'

'Why?'

'So that you can leave here, leave with your husband, to be with your children. These events happened. You have been denied the memory, and all I am doing now is opening your memory. If you wish it I can stop. It is entirely up to you.'

She went quiet and sat on the edge of the bed. 'I want to tell you something . . . about Ruda.'

Franks rested his chin on his hands, waiting. Rebecca plucked at her blanket as she explained how she had seen Ruda, seen her through the glass. Then she looked up. 'It was a mirror. I didn't see Ruda, it was a mirror.'

'I don't understand, what mirror?'

'He cheated me, he lied to me.' She twisted the blanket harder, round and round in her hands in a wringing motion. Franks quietly asked who had lied to her and she spat it out.

'Papa – lied! Don't you understand? It could not have been Ruda I saw.' Rebecca became greatly distressed, and Franks suggested that she rest. She wafted her hands. 'No, no, listen to me. You see I understand now. I mean, it wasn't logical, how could her hair have grown overnight? He didn't show me Ruda. It was me, in a mirror.'

She stood up and crossed to the window. She held the white-painted bars. 'I saw myself in the mirror. Not Ruda, but me, and then they gave me cakes, sweets, milk – and I ate everything, I saved nothing for her.'

Franks moved to her and held her shoulders. 'But you were a baby then. You cannot blame yourself, there is no guilt.'

'There is. She hates me. I ate and ate, and she went hungry.'

'Nobody hates you, and you should rest. Get some sleep before tomorrow. Rebecca?'

She sighed and turned, flopping down on to the bed. 'Rest? You open my mind all day and expect me to sleep at night? I am beginning to detest you, Dr Franks.'

591

She closed her eyes. 'They start now, even when I'm alone, without you. It's as if I cannot stop the past.'

'That's good. So, what have you remembered?'

'A soldier, the one who took me away from the camp. I remember . . . he took my hand, asked if I wanted some chocolate and I demanded another piece for Ruda because she was inside me, she needed a piece of chocolate, but . . . Please, please don't leave me alone.'

She became very upset again, and Franks assured her he would stay. He watched in silence as she stared at her own face in a small mirror, repeating over and over, 'It was a mirror . . .'

Franks stayed the entire night and was able gradually to piece together what it was she was desperately trying to release.

When the telepathy began to work beyond his first expectations, Mengele could not let Rebecca see that her sister had not been rewarded or fed as promised and instead attempted to trick her by simply placing a mirror across the booth's window. So, Rebecca did not see Ruda in the white dress, but herself . . . And the adult Rebecca was now able to realize the trickery. She was, however, consumed by guilt because she had not understood then.

Franks saw her wrestle with her conscience. 'How could I know? And Papa was very pleased with me, he kissed and cuddled me and one of the *Schutzhaftlings* took me over to the warehouse to choose a new frock. We passed the latrine cleaning group – they spat at me! One woman hurled mud at me, I remember . . . I remember the way they shouted after me. The children hit me, kicked me and I cried and cried. I said that when Ruda came back she would make them cry, too. I only wanted to show off my new dress – and they told me she'd gone with the Snowman. That she would never come back for me.'

Two days after Rebecca had been given her new frock, the camp was liberated. In the mayhem that followed the liberation, Rebecca and a number of other children from her ward ran into the main hospital wing. There she went from bed to bed, each one filled with dying children. She was trying to find Ruda, looking for Ruda, calling out for her.

Ruda was skin and bone. The lice crawled like black ants over her shaven head. Her skin was tissue thin, a deathly bluish white, and protruding from her stomach were tubes, tubes with dark congealed blood, left hanging. A filthy plaster only partially covered a jagged open wound in her distended belly. Rebecca saw the pitiful bundle of rags, and ran screaming from the sight into the arms of the young soldier. He had crushed her to him, he was crying. He carried her from the ward, not wanting her to see the corpses, the dying . . . Not knowing, unable to comprehend, that the child in his arms had lived and played among them.

The soldier carried her past the glass partition and, unwittingly, past the mirror . . . and Rebecca at last found Ruda – she was with her, in the soldier's arms. It was at this moment that Rebecca began totally and utterly to believe that Ruda and she were one being.

Franks, aware that the adult woman at last had emerged, discussed the last events of the liberation. He knew that when Mengele received news that the Russians were advancing he had determined to get rid of the evidence. He had commenced with manic energy to clear the camp of the dying; thousands lost their lives in the gas chambers only days away from liberation. Mengele himself had run, after destroying his experimental documents; they were burnt along with the corpses. As if he had wings, the Dark Angel had remained a shadowy nightmare for those who survived. Never brought to justice, never paying for his crimes against humanity, he subsequently haunted the living. The young survivors whose minds he had twisted, whose bodies he had tormented and crippled, were taken to hospitals and institutions. Many were separated, in a desperate bid to give them the medical care they needed so badly. Ruda and Rebecca were just two of the tragic children.

Rebecca was given many books from Franks's personal library, books carefully chosen by him, for her as an adult to accept and understand more fully those nightmare years. She was calm, often discussing what she had read. Then, late one afternoon, Maja sent an urgent call to Franks's home that he should return to the clinic immediately. There had been a development: Rebecca had become destructive, abusive and violent, not to herself or any of the nurses but, in a rage, she had systematically wrecked her room. As Franks hurried along the corridor, he heard her angry, hoarse screams, heard the terrible banging and thudding of furniture being hurled against the walls. He looked through the peephole in Rebecca's door, then instructed Maja to bring him a seat. He remained sitting outside the room until the banging and the screams subsided. It took another hour, and not until there was silence did he enter the room.

Rebecca stood by the barred window, her exhaustion evident as she turned to face him. She seemed utterly drained, her eyes red-rimmed from weeping, and he knew intuitively that this was not Ruda's rage – it was not Ruda rising to the surface again – but it was Rebecca's, her own unleashed blazing fury at what had been done to her. At long last it was out, and she had bravely faced it alone, she had embraced it like a primal scream, and she was cleansed.

After almost a year of treatment, Franks determined that Rebecca was now ready to be told the truth about Ruda. There was no hypnosis, they sat together in his lounge at the clinic. Even Louis was not allowed to be there, but he was waiting, as he had been throughout the entire year. Sasha had stayed with him at the hotel during her school holidays. Louis had taken care of her himself: no nanny, just father and daughter, and in the time they had spent together he had attempted to explain in simple terms her mother's illness. When Sasha asked if her mother was well again, Louis had hesitated, knowing his wife was at a critical stage. Franks had told him that being made aware of Ruda's death might mean a major setback for Rebecca, and to be prepared for it. Considering the mental anguish she had been subjected to, the impact of knowing that Ruda had been alive and now had died could possibly send her over the edge. An edge on which she had balanced precariously for years . . . Louis told Sasha only that they would know very soon.

He had been warned not to expect too much, even with the best results, that it could still be a long time before Rebecca was adjusted and able to return to Paris. He was glad his daughter was with him at the clinic, he needed her.

Franks began in a soft gentle voice, asking her first if she could recall arriving at the circus. Rebecca surprised him, looking at him with a tranquil, gentle expression on her face.

'I know. I was wondering when you would tell me, but I know. And I know her last words were to ask if I was safe . . . I remembered days ago, but I didn't want to tell you, I wanted to face it by myself. I needed time alone. She was, you see, always the stronger . . .'

'Do you blame yourself in any way?'

'Yes, of course. I endangered her, I ran into the clearing, I was stupid, but . . . I think she could have got him back in his cage, she was very calm.'

She gave Franks a strange, direct stare. 'She was also very disturbed, very confused. I wish, I wish we had found you together, but . . .'

Franks leaned forwards. 'But?'

'But we didn't. I think, throughout my entire adult life, I have somehow been searching for a mother figure. I have expected too much, loved too much – and given so much pain to those I have loved. Now at last I have found her. She lies within myself. Having mothered my sons, my daughters – albeit at times distressed them, terribly – I think I have found my first good, mothering experience . . . with you.'

She smiled at him. 'You, doctor, have given me the unconditional, loving acceptance I have always sought, the support I have always needed, the understanding I have craved. You have given me back my childhood, but most important, through my relationship with you, I have learned to accept and love myself, to give myself the kind of caring that will heal me, heal from the inside out. I am going to get stronger. I know that, because I want to live – for my children, for my husband, most of all, I want to do something with my life. My experience must be used, you must use me, reach out for others like me, Dr Franks, because I am strong now and I want to do this for me and for Ruda, who was the only mother I ever really knew.'

'But you are not Ruda.'

'No, my dear friend. I am Rebecca, just Rebecca, and I am whole – thanks to you.'

Franks couldn't help himself. He suddenly leaped from his chair and wrapped his arms around Rebecca. 'I love you, Baroness! You know what you are? A fighter. God bless you!'

Louis knew by the wonderful expression on Franks's face that they had at last broken through. Dr Franks held Sasha's hand, smiling warmly. 'You stay with me a few moments, Sasha.' He looked at Louis. 'Go and kiss your beautiful wife, Baron.'

She was leaning against the chair. Louis was unable to contain himself: he sobbed as he lifted his arms to her. There was no space, no void – he clasped her to him, as if afraid ever to let her go. They kissed, clung to each other.

'I'm coming home, Louis. I want to come home.'

Dr Franks tapped on the door, peered round, asked if another visitor could be made welcome. Opening the door wider, he ushered in Sasha. The child hung back a moment, then ran into her mother's open arms, and Rebecca swung her round and round, bent down on her knees, cupping the girl's face in her hands. 'What a wonderful surprise! Sasha! My beautiful Sasha. I am your mama, and she's coming home! Kiss your mama hello!'

Snow was falling as the Mercedes made its slow progress through the snowbound streets. Rebecca sat between Louis and Sasha; on her knees was Ruda's black treasure box. She opened it, and Sasha looked inquisitively inside.

'Do you know what this is?' Rebecca held up a small hard object. 'It's a potato!'

'But it looks like a stone, Mama.'

'When we were in the camp they were prizes worth keeping, and my sister, Ruda, kept this potato, oh, for so long, and then when we came to eat it . . . it was hard, like a small rock. It became her talisman, this funny little hard potato.'

The car drew to a halt outside the clinic, and Dr Franks hurried from the doorway, woolly hat pulled down and a big scarf wrapped around his neck. The Baron opened the door for him and, squashing himself into the back seat, Franks let Sasha sit on his knee, as the chauffeur drove away.

'Give this to your mama, Sasha.' Franks passed over a small square leather box.

Sasha gave it to her mother, and watched as Rebecca lifted the lid. It was a gold Star of David. Rebecca bent her head and kissed it, then rested against Franks's shoulder.

'Thank you,' she whispered, then gave a soft laugh. 'You know, Dr Franks, I think you have telepathic powers! This morning, before these two were even awake, you know what I did? I went to a synagogue to pray for Ruda. I have never been in one before. It felt . . .'

Dr Franks had to look away, out of the window to the snow-laden streets. He felt very emotional. 'It will feel better. Go again, go for the faith denied you, denied Ruda!'

They fell silent, a comfortable warmth between them. Only when they were within half a mile of the cemetery did Rebecca straighten. She lifted her head, still resting against Franks's shoulder, as if sensing a presence. She knew Ruda was close by.

The car stopped and Franks opened his door. Sasha bounded out, but he caught her hand, held it tightly. 'Just wait a moment, Sasha.'

The Baron took his daughter's other hand, about to offer his arm to Rebecca, but Franks gave him a small wink, an indication to let her walk alone.

'But she won't know where the grave is.'

Franks smiled. 'She will.'

Rebecca walked on ahead, at first unhurried, then quickened her pace. Hand in hand, Dr Franks, Sasha and Louis looked on as Rebecca suddenly began to run. She didn't pause, knew intuitively where she would find her. Threading her way between the big dark tombstones, across the narrow, snow-filled lanes, her feet left an impression with every step.

Grimaldi had chosen not just the headstone, but the plot where Ruda lay. It was separated from the other graves by a semi-circle of high trees. The sun broke through the grey sky, streaking brilliant shafts of light which glanced off the trees above her tomb, making a delicate white crystal cradle over the wondrous black marble head of Mamon. He roared in icy silence, protecting his beloved beneath him.

Rebecca stood staring at Mamon, then slowly she knelt

down and placed the treasured potato stone between his paws. She let her hand rest a moment, and closed her eyes. She didn't weep, but drew from the cold, hard black marble a soothing calm. 'Goodbye, Ruda, I'll come back to you every year,' she whispered.

Dr Franks followed, watching Rebecca, now hand in hand with her husband and daughter. He felt a great sense of achievement and a fatherly pride.

The snow had melted in the wintry sun, it trickled in tears from Mamon's sightless eyes. Franks knew there were tears still to be shed, lost souls to be reunited. Memories that must not be forgotten, or hidden, but kept alive so that the living will never forget. Must never forget.